LIFE AND DEATH
ARE WEARING ME OUT

Also by Mo Yan

Big Breasts & Wide Hips
The Garlic Ballads
The Republic of Wine
Shifu, You'll Do Anything for a Laugh

LIFE AND DEATH

ARE WEARING ME OUT

A NOVEL

MO YAN

**TRANSLATED FROM THE CHINESE
BY HOWARD GOLDBLATT**

**ARCADE PUBLISHING
NEW YORK**

First published in China as *Shengsi pilao* by Zuojia chubanshe

This is a work of fiction. Names, characters, places, and incidents are either the
work of the author's imagination or are used fictitously.

Arcade Publishing books may be purchased in bulk at special discounts for
sales promotion, corporate gifts, fund-raising, or educational purposes. Special
editions can also be created to specifications. For details, contact the Special Sales
Department, Arcade Publishing, 307 West 36th Street, 11th Floor, New York, NY
10018 or arcade@skyhorsepublishing.com.

Arcade Publishing® is a registered trademark of Skyhorse Publishing, Inc.®, a
Delaware corporation.

Visit our website at www.arcadepub.com.

10 9 8 7 6 5 4 3 2

Library of Congress Cataloging-in-Publication Data is available on file.

ISBN: 978-1-61145-427-7

Printed in the United States of America

The Buddha said:

Transmigration wearies owing to mundane desires
Few desires and inaction bring peace to the mind

Principal Characters

Ximen Nao
A Ximen Village landlord, executed and reincarnated as a donkey, an ox, a pig, a dog, a monkey, and the boy, Big-Headed Lan Qiansui. One of the narrators.

Lan Jiefang
Son of Lan Lian and Yingchun. Serves as Head of the County Supply and Marketing Cooperative, Deputy County Head, etc. One of the narrators.

Ximen Bai
Wife of Ximen Nao.

Yingchun
Ximen Nao's first concubine. After 1949 marries Lan Lian.

Wu Qiuxiang
Ximen Nao's second concubine. After 1949 marries Huang Tong.

Lan Lian (Blue Face)
Ximen Nao's farmhand. After 1949 becomes an independent farmer, the last holdout in all of China.

Huang Tong
Leader of the Ximen Village Militia and commander of the production brigade.

Ximen Jinlong
Son of Ximen Nao and Yingchun. After 1949, takes his stepfather's surname, Lan. During the Cultural Revolution serves as Chairman of the Ximen Village Revolutionary Committee, later becomes Head of the Pig Farm, Party Secretary of the branch Youth League, and, after the Reform Period, Secretary of the Ximen Village Branch of the Communist Party.

Ximen Baofeng
Daughter of Ximen Nao and Yingchun. Ximen Village's "Barefoot Doctor." First marries Ma Liangcai, later cohabits with Chang Tianhong.

Huang Huzhu	Daughter of Huang Tong and Wu Qiuxiang. First marries Ximen Jinlong, later cohabits with Lan Jiefang.
Huang Hezuo	Daughter of Huang Tong and Wu Qiuxiang. Lan Jiefang's wife.
Pang Hu	A hero of the Chinese Volunteer Army in Korea. One-time Manager of the Number Five Cotton Processing Plant.
Wang Leyun	Pang Hu's wife.
Pang Kangmei	Daughter of Pang Hu and Wang Leyun. One-time County Party Secretary. Chang Tianhong's wife and Ximen Jinlong's lover.
Pang Chunmiao	Daughter of Pang Hu and Wang Leyun. Lan Jiefang's lover and then second wife.
Chang Tianhong	A graduate of the provincial art academy's music department. Works as a member of the village Four Clean-ups campaign. During the Cultural Revolution is Vice Chairman of the County Revolutionary Committee. Later serves as Assistant Director of the County Cat's Meow Drama Troupe.
Ma Liangcai	Teacher and principal of the Ximen Village elementary school.

A Note on Pronunciation

Most letters in the Chinese pinyin system are pronounced roughly as in English. The main exceptions are as follows:

c (not followed by h)	*ts* as in *its*	(Ma Liang<u>c</u>ai)
he	*u* as in *huh*	(Huang H<u>e</u>zuo)
ian	*yen*	(Lan Li<u>an</u>)
le	*u* as in *luh*	(Wang L<u>e</u>yun)
qi	*ch* as in *cheese*	(Wu <u>Q</u>iuxiang)
x	*sh* as in *she*	(Wu Qiu<u>x</u>iang)
zh	*j* as in *jelly*	(Huang Hu<u>zh</u>u)

Book One

Donkey Miseries

1

Torture and Proclaimed Innocence in Yama's Hell Reincarnation Trickery for a White-Hoofed Donkey

My story begins on January 1, 1950. In the two years prior to that, I suffered cruel torture such as no man can imagine in the bowels of hell. Every time I was brought before the court, I proclaimed my innocence in solemn and moving, sad and miserable tones that penetrated every crevice of Lord Yama's Audience Hall and rebounded in layered echoes. Not a word of repentance escaped my lips though I was tortured cruelly, for which I gained the reputation of an iron man. I know I earned the unspoken respect of many of Yama's underworld attendants, but I also know that Lord Yama was sick and tired of me. So to force me to admit defeat, they subjected me to the most sinister form of torture hell had to offer: they flung me into a vat of boiling oil, in which I tumbled and turned and sizzled like a fried chicken for about an hour. Words cannot do justice to the agony I experienced until an attendant speared me with a trident and, holding me high, carried me up to the palace steps. He was joined by another attendant, one on either side, who screeched like vampire bats as scalding oil dripped from my body onto the Audience Hall steps, where it sputtered and produced puffs of yellow smoke. With care, they deposited me on a stone slab at the foot of the throne, and then bowed deeply.

"Great Lord," he announced, "he has been fried."

Having been fried to a crisp, I knew that even a light tap would turn me to charred slivers. Then, from high in the hall above me, somewhere in the brilliant candlelight in the hall above, I heard a mocking question from Lord Yama himself:

"Ximen Nao, whose name means West Gate Riot, is more rioting in your plans?"

I'll not lie to you; at that moment I wavered as my crisp body lay sprawled in a puddle of oil that was still popping and crackling. I had no illusions: I had reached my pain threshold and could not imagine what torture these venal officials would next employ if I did not yield to them now. Yet if I did, would I not have suffered their earlier brutalities in vain? I struggled to raise my head, which could easily have snapped off, and looked into the candlelight, where I saw Lord Yama, underworld judges seated beside him, oleaginous smiles on their faces. Anger churned inside me. To hell with them! I thought appropriately; let them grind me to powder under a millstone or turn me to paste in a mortar if they must, but I'll not back down.

"I am innocent!" I screamed.

Rancid drops of oil sprayed from my mouth with that scream: I am innocent! Me, Ximen Nao; in my thirty years in the land of mortals I loved manual labor and was a good and thrifty family man. I repaired bridges and repaved roads and was charitable to all. The idols in Northeast Gaomi Township temples were restored thanks to my generosity; the poor township people escaped starvation by eating my food. Every kernel of rice in my granary was wetted by the sweat of my brow, every coin in my family's coffers coated with painstaking effort. I grew rich through hard work, I elevated my family by clear thinking and wise decisions. I truly believe I was never guilty of an unconscionable act. And yet — here my voice turned shrill — a compassionate individual like me, a person of integrity, a good and decent man, was trussed up like a criminal, marched off to a bridgehead, and shot! . . . Standing no more than half a foot from me, they fired an old musket filled with half a gourd full of powder and half a bowl full of grapeshot, turning one side of my head into a bloody mess as the explosion shattered the stillness and stained the floor of the bridge and the melon-sized white stones beneath it. . . . You'll not get me to confess, I am innocent, and I ask to be sent back so I can ask those people to their face what I was guilty of.

I watched Lord Yama's unctuous face undergo many contortions throughout my rapid-fire monologue and saw how the judges around him turned their heads to avert their eyes. They knew I was innocent, that I had been falsely accused, but for reasons I could not fathom, they feigned ignorance. So I shouted, repeating myself, the same thing over and over, until one of the judges leaned over and whispered something in Lord Yama's ear. He banged his gavel to silence the hall.

"All right, Ximen Nao, we accept your claim of innocence. Many people in that world who deserve to die somehow live on while those who deserve to live die off. Those are facts about which this throne can do nothing. So I will be merciful and send you back."

Unanticipated joy fell on me like a millstone, seemingly shattering my body into shards. Lord Yama threw down his triangular vermilion symbol of office and, with what sounded like impatience, commanded:

"Ox Head and Horse Face, send him back!"

With a flick of his sleeve, Lord Yama left the hall, followed by his judges, whose swishing wide sleeves made the candles flicker. A pair of demonic attendants, dressed in black clothing cinched at the waist with wide orange sashes, walked up from opposite directions. One bent down, picked up the symbol of authority, and stuck it in his sash. The other grabbed my arm to pull me to my feet. A brittle sound, like bones breaking, drew a shriek from me. The demon holding the symbol of authority shoved the demon holding the arm and, in the tone of an old hand instructing a novice, said:

"What in damnation is your head filled with, water? Has an eagle plucked out your eyes? Can you really not see that his body is as crispy as one of those fried fritters on Tianjin's Eighteenth Street?"

The young attendant rolled his eyes as he was being admonished, not sure what to do.

"Why are you standing around?" Symbol of Authority said. "Go get some donkey blood!"

The attendant smacked his head, sudden enlightenment written on his face. He turned and ran out of the hall, quickly returning with a blood-spattered bucket. Evidently it was heavy, since he stumbled along, bent at the waist, and was barely able to keep his balance.

He set the bucket down beside me with a thud that made my body vibrate. The stench was nauseating, a hot, rank odor that seemed to carry the warmth of a real donkey. The image of a butchered donkey flashed briefly in my head, and then dissolved. Symbol of Authority reached into the bucket and took out a pig-bristle brush, which he swished around in the sticky, dark red blood, and then brushed across my scalp. I yelped from an eerie sensation that was part pain, part numbness, and part prickliness. My ears were assailed with subtle pops as the blood moistened my charred, crispy skin, calling to mind a welcome rain on drought-dry land. My mind was a tangle of disjointed thoughts and mixed emotions. The attendant wielded his brush like a house painter, and I was quickly covered with donkey blood, head to toe. He then picked up the bucket and dumped what remained over me, and I felt a surge of life swell up inside me. Strength and courage returned to my body. I no longer needed their support when I stood up.

Despite the fact that the attendants were called Ox Head and Horse Face, they bore no resemblance to the underworld figures we are used to seeing in paintings: human bodies, one with the head of an ox, the other the face of a horse. These were totally human in appearance, except, that is, for their skin, whose color was iridescent blue, as if treated with a magical dye. A noble color, one rarely seen in the world of mortals, neither on fabric nor on trees; but I'd seen flowers of that color, small marshy blossoms in Northeast Gaomi Township that bloomed in the morning and withered and died that afternoon.

With one attendant on each side of me, we walked down a seemingly endless dark tunnel. Coral lantern holders protruded from the walls every few yards; from them hung shallow platter-shaped lanterns that burned soybean oil, the aroma sometimes dense, sometimes not, which kept me clearheaded some of the time, and befogged the rest of the time. In the light of the lanterns, I saw gigantic bats hanging from the tunnel dome, eyes shining through the darkness; foul-smelling guano kept falling on my head.

Finally, we reached the end and climbed onto a high platform, where a white-haired old woman reached out with a fair, smooth-skinned arm that did not befit her age, scooped out a black, foul-smelling liquid from a filthy steel pot with a black wooden spoon, and emptied it into a red-glazed bowl. One of the attendants handed me the bowl and flashed a smile that held no trace of kindness.

"Drink it," he said. "Drink what is in this bowl, and your suffering, your worries, and your hostility will all be forgotten."

I knocked it over with a sweep of my hand.

"No, I said. "I want to hold on to my suffering, worries, and hostility. Otherwise, returning to that world is meaningless."

I climbed down off of the wooden platform, which shook with each step, and heard the attendants shout my name as they ran down from the platform.

The next thing I knew, we were walking in Northeast Gaomi Township, where I knew every mountain and stream, every tree and blade of grass. New to me were the white wooden posts stuck in the ground, on which were written names — some familiar, some not. They were even buried in the rich soil of my estate. I did not learn until later that when I was in the halls of hell proclaiming my innocence, a period of land reform had been ushered in to the world of mortals, and that the big estates had been piecemealed out to landless peasants; naturally, mine was no exception. Parceling out land has its historical precedents, I thought, so why did they have to shoot me before dividing up mine?

Seemingly worried that I would run away, the attendants held me by the arms in their icy hands, or, more precisely, claws. The sun shone brightly, the air was fresh and clean; birds flew in the sky, rabbits hopped along the ground. Snow on the shady banks of the ditches and the river reflected light that hurt my eyes. I glanced at the blue faces of my escort, suddenly aware that they looked like costumed and heavily made-up stage actors, except that earthly dyes could never, not in a million years, paint faces with hues that noble or that pure.

We passed a dozen or more villages as we walked down the riverbank road and met several people coming from the opposite direction. Among them were my friends and neighbors, but each time I tried to greet them, one of my attendants clapped his hand around my throat and turned me mute. I showed my displeasure by kicking them in the legs, but elicited no response; it was as if their limbs had no feeling. So I rammed my head into their faces, which seemed made of rubber. The hand around my neck was loosened only when we were alone again. A horse-drawn wagon with rubber wheels shot past us, raising a cloud of dust. Recognizing that horse by the smell of its sweat, I looked up and saw the driver, a fellow named Ma Wendou, sitting up front, a sheepskin coat draped over his shoulders, whip in hand, a long-handled pipe and tobacco pouch tied together and tucked into his collar to hang down his back. The pouch swayed like a public house shop sign. The wagon was mine, the horse was mine, but the man on the wagon was not one of my hired hands. I tried to run after him to find out what was going on here, but my attendants clung to me like vines. Ma Wendou had to have seen me and known who I was, and he surely heard the sounds of struggle I was making, not to mention smelled the strange unearthly odor that came from my body. But he drove past without slowing down, like a man on the run. After that we encountered a group of men on stilts who were reenacting the travels of the Tang monk Tripitaka on his way to fetch Buddhist scriptures. His disciples, Monkey and Pigsy, were both villagers I knew, and I learned from the slogans on the banners they were carrying and from what they were saying that it was the first day of 1950.

Just before we arrived at the stone bridge on the village outskirts, I grew uneasy. I was about to see the stones beneath the bridge that had been discolored by my blood and flecks of my brain. Dirty clumps of hair and strips of cloth sticking to the stones gave off a disagreeable blood stench. Three wild dogs lurked at the bridge opening, two lying down, one standing; two were black, the other brown, and all three coats shone. Their tongues were bright red, their teeth snowy white, their gleaming eyes like awls.

In his story "The Cure," Mo Yan wrote about this bridge and dogs that grew crazed on the corpses of executed people. He wrote about a filial son who cut the gallbladder, the seat of courage, out of an executed man, took it home, and made a tonic for his blind mother. We all know stories about using bear gallbladder as a curative, but no one has ever heard of the curative powers of the human gallbladder. So it was made-up nonsense from the pen of a novelist who likes to do such things, and there wasn't an ounce of truth in it.

Images of the execution floated into my head on the way from the bridge to my house. They had tied my hands behind my back and hung a condemned sign around my neck. It was the twenty-third day of the twelfth month, seven days before New Year's. Cold winds cut through us that day; red clouds blotted out the sun. The sleet was like kernels of white rice that slipped beneath my collar. My wife, from the Bai family, walked behind me, wailing loudly, but I heard nothing from my two concubines, Yingchun and Qiuxiang. Yingchun was expecting a baby any day, so I could forgive her for staying home. But the absence of Qiuxiang, who was younger and was not pregnant, bitterly disappointed me. Once I was standing on the bridge, I turned to see Huang Tong and his team of militiamen. You men, we all live in the same village and there's never been any enmity between us, not then and not now. If I have somehow offended you, tell me how. There is no need to do this, is there? Huang Tong gazed at me briefly, and then looked away. His golden yellow irises sparkled like gold stars. Huang Tong, I said, Yellow-eyed Huang, your parents named you well. That's enough out of you, he said. This is government policy! You men, I went on anyway, if I am to die, I should at least know why. What law have I broken? You'll get your answers in Lord Yama's underworld, Huang Tong said as he raised his ancient musket, the muzzle no more than half a foot from my forehead. I felt my head fly off; I saw sparks, I heard what sounded like an explosion, and I smelled gunpowder in the air . . .

Through the unlatched gate at my house I saw many people in the yard. How did they know I would be coming home? I turned to my escort.

"Thank you, brothers, for the difficulties encountered in seeing me home," I said.

Sinister smiles spread across their blue faces, but before I could figure out what those smiles meant, they grabbed my arms and propelled me forward. Everything was murky; I felt like a drowning man. Suddenly my ears filled with the happy shouts of a man somewhere:

"It's out!"

I opened my eyes to find that I was covered with a sticky liquid, lying near the birth canal of a female donkey. My god! Who'd have thought that Ximen Nao, a literate, well-educated member of the gentry class, would be reborn as a white-hoofed donkey with floppy, tender lips!

2

Ximen Nao Is Charitable to Save Blue Face
Bai Yingchun Lovingly Comforts an Orphaned Donkey

The man standing behind the donkey with a broad grin on his face was my hired hand Lan Lian. I remembered him as a frail, skinny youth, and was surprised to see that in the two years since my death, he had grown into a strapping young man.

He was an orphan I'd found in the snow in front of the God of War Temple and brought home with me. Wrapped in a burlap sack and shoeless, he was stiff from the cold; his face had turned purple and his hair was a ratty mess. My own father had just died, but my mother was alive and well. From my father I had received the bronze key to the camphor chest in which were kept the deeds to more than eighty acres of farmland and the family's gold, silver, and other valuables. I was twenty-four at the time and had just taken the second daughter of the richest man in Bai-ma, or White Horse, Town, Bai Lianyuan, as my wife. Her childhood name was Apricot, and she still had no grown-up name, so when she came into my family, she was simply known as Ximen Bai. As the daughter of a wealthy man, she was literate and well versed in propriety, had a frail constitution, breasts like sweet pears, and a well-proportioned lower body. She wasn't bad in bed either. In fact, the only flaw in an otherwise perfect mate was that she had not yet produced a child.

Back then I was on top of the world. Bumper harvests every year, and the tenant farmers eagerly paid their rent. The grain sheds overflowed. The livestock thrived, and our black mule gave birth to twins. It was like a miracle, the stuff of legend, not reality. A stream of villagers came to see the twin mules, and our ears rang with their words of flattery. We rewarded them with jasmine tea and Green Fort cigarettes. The teenager Huang Tong stole a pack of our cigarettes and was dragged up to me by his ear. The young scamp had yellow hair, yellow skin, and shifty yellow eyes, giving the impression he entertained evil thoughts. I dismissed him with a wave of the hand, even gave him a packet of tea to take home for his father. Huang Tianfa, a decent, honest man who made fine tofu, was one of my tenant farmers; he farmed five acres of excellent riverfront land, and what a shame he had such a no-account son. He brought over a basketful of tofu so dense you could hang the pieces from hooks, along with a basketful of apologies. I told my wife to give him two feet of green wool to take home and make a couple of pair of cloth shoes for the new year. Huang Tong, oh, Huang Tong, after all those good years between your father and me, you should not have shot me with that musket of yours. Oh, I know you were just following orders, but you could have shot me in the chest and left me with a decent-looking corpse. You are an ungrateful bastard!

I, Ximen Nao, a man of dignity, open-minded and magnanimous, was respected by all. I had taken over the family business during chaotic times. I had to cope with the guerrillas and the puppet soldiers, but my family property increased by the addition of a hundred acres of fine land, the number of horses and cows went from four to eight, and we acquired a large wagon with rubber tires; we went from two hired hands to four, from one maidservant to two, and added two old women to cook for us. So that's how things stood when I found Lan Lian in front of the God of War Temple, half frozen, with barely a breath left in him. I'd gotten up early that morning to collect dung. Now you may not believe me, since I was one of Northeast Gaomi Township's richest men, but I always had a commendable work ethic. In the third month I plowed the fields, in the fourth I planted seeds, in the fifth I brought in the wheat, in the sixth I planted melons, in the seventh I hoed beans, in the eighth I collected sesame, in the ninth I harvested grain, and in the tenth I turned the soil. Even in the cold twelfth month, a warm bed could not tempt me. I'd be out with my basket to collect dog dung when the sun was barely up. People joked that I rose so early one morning I mistook some rocks for dung. That's absurd. I have a good nose, I can smell dog dung from far away. No one who is indifferent to dog dung can be a good landlord.

There was so much snow that the buildings, trees, and streets were buried, nothing but white. All the dogs were hiding, so there'd be no dung that day. But I went out anyway. The air was fresh and clean, the wind was yet mild, and at that early hour there were all sorts of strange and mysterious rarities — the only way you could see them was to get up early. I walked from Front Street to Back Street and took a turn around the fortified village wall in time to see the horizon change from red to white, a fiery sunrise as the red sun rose into the sky and turned the vast snowy landscape bright red, just like the legendary Crystal Realm. I found the child in front of the God of War Temple, half buried in the snow. At first I thought he was dead and figured I'd pay for a meager coffin to bury him to keep the wild dogs away. Only a year before, a naked man had frozen to death in front of the Earth God Temple. He was red from head to toe, his pecker sticking out straight as a spear, which drew peals of laughter. That outlandish friend of yours, Mo Yan, wrote about that in his story "The Man Died, His Dick Lived On." Thanks to my generosity, the corpse of this man, the one who died by the roadside but whose dick lived on, was buried in the old graveyard west of town. Good deeds like that have wide-ranging influence and are more consequential than memorials or biographies. I set down my dung basket and nudged the boy, then felt his chest. It was still warm, so I knew he was alive. I took off my lined coat and wrapped him in it, then picked him up and carried him home. Prismlike rays of the morning sun lit up the sky and the ground ahead of me; people were outside shoveling snow, so many villagers were witness to the charity of Ximen Nao. For that alone, you people should not have shot me with your musket. And on that point, Lord Yama, you should not have sent me back as a donkey! Everyone says that saving a life is better than building a seven-story pagoda, and I, Ximen Nao, sure as hell saved a life. Me, Ximen Nao, and not just one life. During the famine one spring I sold twenty bushels of sorghum at a low price and exempted my tenant farmers from paying rent. That kept many people alive. And look at my miserable fate. Is there no justice in heaven or on earth, in the world of men or the realm of spirits? Any sense of conscience? I protest. I am mystified!

I took the youngster home and laid him down on a warm bed in the bunkhouse. I was about to light a fire to warm him when the foreman, Old Zhang, said, You can't do that, Boss. A frozen turnip must thaw out slowly. If you heat it, it will turn to mush. That made sense, so I let the boy warm up naturally on the bed and had someone in the house heat a bowl of sweet ginger water, which I poured slowly into his mouth after prying it open with chopsticks. He began to moan once some of that ginger water was in his stomach. Having brought him back from the dead, I told Old Zhang to shave off the boy's ratty hair and the fleas living in it. We gave him a bath and got him into some clean clothes. Then I took him to see my aging mother. He was a clever little one. As soon as he saw her, he fell to his knees and cried out, "Granny," which thrilled my mother, who chanted "Amita Buddha" and asked which temple the little monk came from. She asked him his age. He shook his head and said he didn't know. Where was home? He wasn't sure. When he was asked about his family, he shook his head like one of those stick-and-ball toys. So I let him stay. He was a smart little pole-shinnying monkey. He called me Foster Dad as soon as he laid eyes on me, and called Madame Bai Foster Mother. But foster son or not, I expected him to work, since even I engaged in manual labor, and I was the landlord. You work or you don't eat. Just a new way of expressing an idea that has been around for a long time. The boy had no name, but since he had a blue birthmark on the left side of his face, I told him I'd call him Lan Lian, or Blue Face, with Lan being his surname. But, he said, I want to have the same name as you, Foster Dad, so won't you call me Ximen Lanlian? I said no, that the name Ximen was not available to just anyone, but that if he worked hard for twenty years, we'd see about it. He started out by helping the foreman tend the horse and donkey — Ah, Lord Yama, how could you be so evil as to turn me into a donkey?— and gradually moved on to bigger jobs. Don't be fooled by his thin frame and frail appearance; he worked with great efficiency and possessed good judgment and a considerable bag of tricks, all of which made up for his lack of strength. Now, seeing his broad shoulders and muscular arms, I could tell he'd grown into a man to be reckoned with.

"Ha ha, the foal is out!" he shouted as he bent down, reached out his large hands, and helped me stand, causing me more shame and anger than I care to think about.

"I am not a donkey!" I roared. "I am a man! I am Ximen Nao!"

But my throat felt exactly the way it had when the two blue-faced demons had throttled me. I couldn't speak no matter how hard I tried. Despair, terror, rage. I spat out slobber, sticky tears oozed from my eyes. His hand slipped, and I thudded to the ground, right in the middle of all that gooey amniotic fluid and afterbirth, which had the consistency of jellyfish.

"Bring me a towel, and hurry!" Lan Lian shouted. A pregnant woman came out of the house, and my attention was immediately caught by the freckles on her slightly puffy face, and her big, round, sorrowful eyes. *Hee-haw, hee-haw* — She's mine, she's Ximen Nao's woman, my first concubine, Yingchun, brought into the family as a maidservant by my wife. Since we didn't know her family name, she took the name of my wife, Bai. In the spring of 1946, she became my concubine. With big eyes and a straight nose, a broad forehead, wide mouth, and square jaw, hers was a face of good fortune. Even more important, her full breasts, with their pert nipples, and a broad pelvis made her a cinch to bear children. My wife, apparently barren, sent Yingchun to my bed with a comment that was easy to understand and filled with heartfelt sincerity. She said, "Lord of the Manor [that's what she called me], I want you to accept her. Good water must not irrigate other people's fields."

She was a fertile field indeed. She got pregnant our first night together. And not just pregnant, but with twins. The following spring she gave birth to a boy and a girl, what they call a dragon and phoenix birth. So we named the boy Ximen Jinlong, or Golden Dragon, and the girl Ximen Baofeng, Precious Phoenix. The midwife said she'd never seen a woman better suited to having babies, with her broad pelvis and resilient birth canal. The babies popped out into her hands, like melons dumped from a burlap sack. Most women cry out in anguish the first time, but my Yingchun had her babies without making a sound. According to the midwife, she wore a mysterious smile from start to finish, as if having a baby was a form of entertainment. That gave the poor midwife a case of the nerves; she was afraid that monsters might come shooting out.

The birth of Jinlong and Baofeng produced great joy in the Ximen household. But so as not to frighten the babies or their mother, I had the foreman, Old Zhang, and his helper, Lan Lian, buy ten strings of firecrackers, eight hundred in all, hang them on a wall on the southern edge of the village, and light them there. The sound of all those tiny explosions made me so happy I nearly fainted. I have a quirky habit of dealing with good news by doing hard work; it's an itch I can't explain. So while the firecrackers were still popping, I rolled up my sleeves, jumped into the livestock pen, and shoveled up ten wagonloads of dung that had accumulated through the winter. Ma Zhibo, a feng shui master who was given to putting on mystical airs, came running up to the pen and said to me mystifyingly, Menshi — that's my style name — my fine young man, with a woman in childbirth in the house, you must not work on fences or dig up dirt, and absolutely must not shovel dung or dredge a well. Stirring up the Wandering God does not bode well for the newborn.

Ma Zhibo's comment nearly made my heart stop, but you can't call an arrow back once it's been fired, and any job worth starting is certainly worth finishing. I couldn't stop then, because only half the pen was done. There's an old saying: A man has ten years of good fortune when he need fear neither god nor ghost. I was an upright man, not afraid of demons. So what if I, Ximen Nao, bumped up against the Wandering God? It was, after all, only Ma Zhibo's foul comment, so I scooped a peculiar gourd-shaped object out of the dung. It had the appearance of congealed rubber or frozen meat, was murky but nearly transparent, brittle but pliable. I dumped it on the ground at the edge of the pen to examine it more closely. It couldn't be the legendary Wandering God, could it? I watched Ma's face turn ashen and his goatee begin to quiver. With his hands cupped in front of his chest as a sign of respect, he said a prayer and backed up. When he bumped into the wall, he bolted. With a sneer, I said, If this is the Wandering God, it's nothing to fear. Wandering God, Wandering God, if I say your name three times and you're still here, don't blame me if I treat you harshly. Wandering God, Wandering God, Wandering God! With my eyes tightly shut, I shouted the name three times. When I opened them, it was still there, hadn't changed, just a lump of something in the pen next to some horse shit. Whatever it was, it was dead, so I raised my hoe and chopped it in two. The inside was just like the outside, sort of rubbery or maybe frozen, not unlike the sap that oozes out of peach tree knots. I scooped it up and flung it over the wall, where it could lie with the horse shit and donkey urine, hoping that it might be good as fertilizer, so the early summer corn would grow in ears like ivory and the late summer wheat would have tassels as long as dog tails.

That Mo Yan, in a story he called "Wandering God," he wrote:

> I poured water into a wide-mouthed clear glass bottle and added some black tea and brown sugar, then placed it behind the stove for ten days. A peculiar gourd-shaped object was growing in the bottle. When the villagers heard about it, they

came running to see what it was. Ma Congming, the son of Ma Zhibo, said nervously, "This is bad, that's the Wandering God! The Wandering God that the landlord Ximen Nao dug up that year was just like this." As a modern young man, I believe in science, not ghosts and goblins, so I chased Ma Congming away and dumped whatever it was out of the bottle. I cut it open and chopped it up, then dumped it into my wok and fried it. Its strange fragrance made me drool, so I tasted it. It was delicious and nutritious . . . after eating the Wandering God, I grew four inches in three months.

What an imagination!

The firecrackers put an end to rumors that Ximen Nao was sterile. People began preparing congratulatory gifts they would bring to me in nine days. But the old rumor had no sooner been cast aside than a new one was born. Overnight, word that Ximen Nao had stirred up the Wandering God while shoveling dung in his pen spread through all the eighteen villages and towns of Northeast Gaomi Township. And not just spread, but picked up embellishments along the way. The Wandering God, it was said, was a big meaty egg with all seven of the facial orifices; it rolled around in the animal pen until I chopped it in two and a bright light shot into the sky. Stirring up the Wandering God was sure to cause a bloody calamity within a hundred days. I was well aware that the tall tree catches the wind and that wealth always causes envy. Many people could not wait for Ximen Nao to fall, and fall hard. I was troubled, but could not lose faith. If the gods wanted to punish me, why send the lovely Jinlong and Baofeng my way?

Yingchun beamed when she saw me; with difficulty she bent down, and at that moment I saw the baby she was carrying. It was a boy with a blue birthmark on his left cheek, so there was no doubt he'd come from Lan Lian's seed. How humiliating! A flame like the tongue of a poisonous viper snaked up in my heart. I had murderous urges, at minimum needed to curse someone. I could have chopped Lan Lian into pieces. Lan Lian, you're an ungrateful bastard, an unconscionable son of a bitch! You started out by calling me Foster Dad and eventually dropped the word *foster*. Well, if I'm your dad, then Yingchun, my concubine, is your stepmother, yet you've taken her as a wife and have had her carry your child. You've corrupted the system of human relations and deserve to be struck down by the God of Thunder! Then, when you arrive in hell, you deserve to have your skin flayed, be stuffed with grass, and be dried before you are reincarnated as a lowly animal! But heaven is bereft of justice, and hell has abandoned reason. Instead of you, it is I who have been sent back as a lowly animal, me, Ximen Nao, who lived his life doing good. And what about you, Yingchun, you little slut? How much sweet talk did you whisper while you were in my arms? And how many solemn pledges of love did you take? Yet my bones weren't even cold before you went to bed with my hired hand. How can a slut like you have the nerve to go on living? You should do away with yourself at once. I'll give you the white silk to do it. Damn it, no, you are not worthy of white silk! A bloody rope used on pigs, looped over a beam covered with rat shit and bat urine, to hang yourself is what's good for you! That or four ounces of arsenic! Or a one-way trip down the well outside the village where all the wild dogs have drowned! You should be paraded up and down the street on a criminal's rack! In the underworld you deserve to be thrown into a snake pit reserved for adulteresses! Then you should be reincarnated as a lowly animal, over and over and over, forever! *Hee-haw, hee-haw* — But no, the person reincarnated as a lowly animal was Ximen Nao, a man of honor, instead of my first concubine.

She knelt clumsily beside me and carefully wiped the sticky stuff from my body with a blue-checked chamois rag. It felt wonderful against my wet skin. She had a soft touch, as if wiping down her own baby. What a cute foal, you lovely little thing. Such a pretty face, and what big blue eyes! And those ears, covered with fuzz . . . the rag moved to each part of my body in turn. She was still as big-hearted as ever, and was covering me with love, that I could see. Deeply touched, I felt the evil heat inside me dissipate. My memory of walking the earth as a human grew distant and cloudy. I was nice and dry. I'd stopped shivering. My bones had hardened, my legs felt strong. An inner force and a sense of purpose combined to make me put that strength to good use. Ah, it's a little male donkey. She was drying off my genitals. How humiliating! Images of our sexual congress back when I was a human flooded my mind. A little male what? The son of a mother donkey? I looked up and saw a female donkey standing nearby, quaking. Is that my mother? A donkey? Rage and uncontrollable anxiety forced me to my feet. I stood there on four feet, like a low stool on high legs.

"It's on its feet, it's standing!" It was Lan Lian, excitedly rubbing his hands. He reached out and helped Yingchun to her feet. The gentle look in his eyes showed that he held strong feelings for her. And that reminded me of something that had occurred years before. If I remember correctly, someone had warned me to be on guard against bedroom antics by my young hired hand. Who knows, maybe they had something going way back then.

As I stood in the morning sun on that first day of the year, I kept digging in my hooves to keep from falling over. Then I took my first step as a donkey, thus beginning an unfamiliar, taxing, humiliating journey. Another step; I wobbled, and the skin on my belly tightened. I saw a great big sun, a beautiful blue sky in which white doves flew. I watched Lan Lian help Yingchun back into the house, and I saw two children, a boy and a girl, both in new jackets, with cloth tiger-head shoes on their feet and rabbit-fur caps on their heads, come running in through the gate. Stepping over the door lintel was not easy for such short legs. They looked to be three or four years old. They called Lan Lian Daddy and Yingchun Mommy. *Hee-haw, hee-haw* — I did not have to be told that they were my children, the boy named Jinlong and the girl called Baofeng. My children, you cannot know how your daddy misses you! Your daddy had high hopes for you, expecting you to honor your ancestors as a dragon and a phoenix, but now you have become someone else's children, and your daddy has been changed into a donkey. My heart was breaking, my head was spinning, it was all a blur, I couldn't keep my legs straight . . . I fell over. I don't want to be a donkey, I want my original body back, I want to be Ximen Nao again, and get even with you people! At the very moment I fell, the female donkey that had given birth to me crashed to the ground like a toppled wall.

She was dead, her legs stiff as clubs, her unseeing eyes still open, as if she had died tormented by all sorts of injustices. Maybe so, but it didn't bother me, since I was only using her body to make my entrance. It was all a plot by Lord Yama, either that or an unfortunate error. I hadn't drunk an ounce of her milk; the very sight of those teats poking out between her legs made me sick.

I grew into a mature donkey by eating sorghum porridge. Yingchun made it for me; she's the one I can thank for growing up. She fed me with a big wooden spoon, and by the time I'd grown up, it was useless from being bitten so often. I could see her bulging breasts when she fed me; they were filled with light blue milk. I knew the taste of that milk, because I'd drunk it. It was delicious, and her breasts were wonderful. She'd nursed two children, and there was more milk than they could drink. There are women whose milk is toxic enough to kill good little babies. While she fed me she said, You poor little thing, losing your mother right after you're born. I saw that her eyes were moist with tears, and could tell that she felt sorry for me. Her curious children, Jinlong and Baofeng, asked her, Mommy, why did the baby donkey's mommy die? Her time was up, she said. Lord Yama sent for her. Mommy, they said, don't let Lord Yama send for you. If he did, then we'd be motherless, just like the little donkey. So would Jiefang. She said, Mommy will always be here, because Lord Yama owes our family a favor. He wouldn't dare disturb us.

The cries of newborn Lan Jiefang emerged from the house.

Do you know who Lan Jiefang — Liberation Lan — is? This Lan Qiansui, the teller of this tale, small but endowed with an air of sophistication, three feet tall yet the most voluble person you could find, asked me out of the blue.

Of course I know. Because it's me. Lan Lian is my father, Yingchun is my mother. Well, if that's the case, then you must have been one of our donkeys.

That's right, I was one of your donkeys. I was born on the morning of the first day of 1950, while you, Lan Jiefang, were born in the evening of the first day of 1950. We are both children of a new era.

3

Hong Taiyue Rails at a Stubborn Old Man
Ximen Lu Courts Disaster and Chews on Bark

Much as I hated being an animal, I was stuck with a donkey's body. Ximen Nao's aggrieved soul was like hot lava running wild in a donkey shell. There was no subduing the flourishing of a donkey's habits and preferences, so I vacillated between the human and donkey realms. The awareness of a donkey and the memory of a human were jumbled together, and though I often strove to cleave them apart, such intentions invariably ended in an even tighter meshing. I had just suffered over my human memory and now delighted in my donkey life. *Hee-haw, hee-haw* — Lan Jiefang, son of Lan Lian, do you understand what I'm saying? What I'm saying is, when, for example, I see your father, Lan Lian, and your mother, Yingchun, in the throes of marital bliss, I, Ximen Nao, am witness to sexual congress between my own hired hand and my concubine, throwing me into such agony that I ram my head into the gate of the donkey pen, into such torment that I chew the edge of my wicker feedbag, but then some of the newly fried black bean and grass in the feedbag finds its way into my mouth and I cannot help but chew it up and swallow it down, and the chewing and swallowing imbue me with an unadulterated sense of donkey delight.

In the proverbial blink of an eye, it seems, I am halfway to becoming an adult, which will bring an end to the days when I was free to roam the confines of the Ximen estate. A halter has been put over my head and I have been tethered to a trough. At the same time, Jinlong and Baofeng, who have been given the surname Lan, have each grown two inches, and you, Lan Jiefang, born on the same day of the same month in the same year as I, are already walking. You waddle like a duck out in the yard. On a stormy day during this period, the family in the eastern addition has been blessed with the birth of twin girls. That proves that the power of the Ximen Nao estate has not weakened, since everyone seems to be having twins. The first one out was named Huzhu — Cooperation — and her sister was called Hezuo — Collaboration. They are the offspring of Huang Tong, born from a union between him and Ximen Nao's second concubine, Qiuxiang. The western rooms were turned over to my master, your father, after land reform; originally, it had been my first concubine, Yingchun's, quarters. When the eastern rooms were given over to Huang Tong, the original occupant, Qiuxiang, apparently came along with them, and wound up as his wife. The main building of the Ximen estate, five grand rooms, now served as government offices for Ximen Village. It was where daily meetings were held and official business conducted.

That day, as I was gnawing on a tall apricot tree, the coarse bark made my tender lips feel like they were on fire. But I was in no mood to stop. I wanted to see what was underneath. The village chief and Party secretary, Hong Taiyue, shouted and threw a sharp rock at me. It hit me in the leg, loud and irritating. Was that pain I felt? A hot sensation was followed by open bleeding. *Hee-haw, hee-haw* — I thought this poor, orphaned donkey was going to die. I trembled when I saw the blood, and hobbled from the eastern edge of the compound, as far away from the apricot tree as possible, all the way to the western edge. Right by the southern wall, in front of the door of the main building, a lean-to made of a reed mat over a couple of poles, open to the morning sun, had been set up to keep me out of the elements, and was a place to run to when I was frightened. But I couldn't go there now, because my master was just then sweeping up droppings from the night before. I hobbled up and he saw that my leg was bleeding; I think he'd probably also seen Hong Taiyue throw the rock. When it was on its way, it cut through the colorless air, making a sound like slicing through fine silk or satin, and struck fear into the heart of this donkey. My master was standing in front of the lean-to, a man the size of a small pagoda, washed by the sunlight, half his face blue, the other red, with his nose as the dividing line, sort of like the division between enemy territory and the liberated area. Today that figure of speech sounds quaint, but at the time it was fresh and new. "My poor little donkey!" my master cried out in obvious agony. Then his voice turned angry. "Old Hong, how dare you injure my donkey!" He leaped over me and, with the agility of a panther, got up into the face of Hong Taiyue.

Hong was the highest-ranking official in Ximen Village. Thanks to a glorious past, when all other Party cadres were turning in their weapons, he wore a pistol on his hip. Sunlight and the air of revolution reflected off his fancy brown leather holster, sending out a warning to all bad people: Don't do anything reckless, don't harbor evil thoughts, and don't think of resisting! He wore a wide-brimmed gray army hat, a button-down white jacket, cinched at the waist by a leather belt at least four inches wide, and a gray lined jacket draped over his shoulders. His pants ballooned over a pair of thick-soled canvas shoes, with no leggings. He looked like a member of an armed working team during the war. During that war, I was Ximen Nao, not a donkey. It was a time when I was the richest man in Ximen Village, a time when Ximen Nao was a member of the enlightened gentry, someone who favored resistance against the invaders and supported progressive forces. I had a wife and two concubines, two hundred acres of fine land, a stable filled with horses and donkeys. But Hong Taiyue, I say, you, Hong Taiyue, what were you then? A typical lowlife, the dregs of society, a beggar who went around banging on the hip bone of a bull ox. It was sort of yellow, rubbed shiny, with nine copper rings hanging from the edge, so all you had to do was shake it gently for it to produce a *huahua langlang* sound. Holding it by the handle, you haunted the marketplace on days ending in 5 and 0, standing on the cobblestone ground in front of the Yingbinlou Restaurant, face smeared with soot, naked from the waist up, a cloth sachet hanging from your neck, your rotund belly sticking out, feet bare, head shaved, dark eyes darting every which way as you sang tunes and did tricks. Not a soul on earth could get as many different sounds out of an ox's hip bone as you could: *Hua langlang, hua langlang, huahua langlang, hualang, huahua, langlang, hualanghualang*... it danced in your hand, its gleaming whiteness flickering, the center of attention in the marketplace. You drew crowds, quickly transforming the square into an entertainment center: the beggar Hong Taiyue banging on his ox bone and singing. It may have been more like the squawks of chickens and ducks, but the cadence had a recognizable rhythm, and it was not without a bit of charm:

> The sun emerges and lights up the western wall,
> The western edge of the eastern wall is chilly as fall.
> Flames from the oven heat the bed and the hall,
> Sleeping on the back keeps the spine in its thrall.
> Blowing on hot porridge reduces the pall,
> Shunning evil and doing good makes a man stand tall.
> If what I am saying you heed not at all,
> Go ask your mother who will respond to my call.

Then this local gem of a man's real identity was revealed, and villagers learned to their surprise that he had been an underground member of the Northeast Gaomi Township branch of the Communist Party, who had sent secret reports up to the Eighth Route Army. He'd looked me in the eye after I'd turned over all my riches and, eyes like a pair of daggers, face the color of cold iron, had announced solemnly: "Ximen Nao, during the first stage of land reform, you managed to get by with your deceptive petty favors and phony charity, but this time you're a cooked crab that can no longer sidle your way around, a turtle in a jar with no way out. You plundered the people's property, you were a master of exploitation, you ran roughshod over men and had your way with women, you oppressed all the people, you are the epitome of evil, and only your death will quell the people's anger. If we do not move you, a black rock of an obstruction, out of the road, if we do not chop you, a towering tree, down, land reform in Northeast Gaomi Township will come to a standstill and the poor and downtrodden peasants of Ximen Village will never be able to stand up on their own. The district government has approved and sent forward to the Township Government a judgment that the tyrannical landlord Ximen Nao is to be dragged up to the stone bridge on the outskirts of the village and shot!"

An explosion, a burst of light, and Ximen Nao's brains were splattered over the gourd-sized stones beneath the bridge, polluting the air around it with a disagreeable stench. These were painful thoughts. I could say nothing in my defense; they refused to let me. Struggle against landlords, smash their dog heads, cut the tall grass, pluck out the thickest hairs. If you want to accuse someone, you'll never run out of words. We'll make sure you die convinced of your crimes, is what Hong Taiyue said, but they gave me no chance to argue in my defense. Hong Taiyue, your words meant nothing, you did not make good on your promise.

He stood in the doorway, hands on his hips, face to face with Lan Lian, an intimidating presence. Even though I was able only moments before to conjure up an image of him bending over obsequiously in front of me, ox bone in hand, he instilled fear in this wounded donkey. About eight feet separated my master and Hong Taiyue. My master was born to poverty, a member of the proletariat, red as could be. But he'd once claimed a foster relationship — father and son — with me, Ximen Nao, a dubious relationship, to say the least, and though he later raised his level of class consciousness and was in the vanguard of the struggle against me, thus recapturing his good name as a poor peasant and acquiring living quarters, land, and a wife, the authorities viewed him with suspicion, owing to his special relationship with Ximen Nao.

The two men faced off for a long moment. My master was the first to speak:

"What gave you the right to injure my donkey?"

"If he gnaws on the bark of my tree again, I'll shoot him!" Hong Taiyue roundly rebuffed him, patting the holster on his hip for emphasis.

"There's no need for you to be so damned vicious with an animal!"

"As I see it, people who drink from a well without considering the source or forget where they came from when they stand tall are worse than an animal!"

"What do you mean by that?"

"Lan Lian, listen carefully to what I'm about to say." Hong took a step closer and pointed to Lan Lian's chest as if his finger were the muzzle of a gun. "After the success of land reform, I advised you not to marry Yingchun. I realize she had no choice in giving herself to Ximen Nao, and I support the government's position that it's a good thing for a widow to remarry. But as a member of the impoverished class, you should have married someone like Widow Su from West Village. Left without a room to live in or a strip of land to till after her husband died, she was forced to beg to survive. She may have a face full of pockmarks, but she's a member of the proletariat, one of us, and she could have helped you maintain your integrity as a committed revolutionary. But you ignored my advice and were set on marrying Yingchun. Since our marriage policy stresses freedom of choice, I did not stand in your way. As I predicted, over the past three years your revolutionary zeal has evaporated. You are selfish, your thinking is backward, and you want to live in a style more dissipated than even your former landlord, Ximen Nao. You have turned into a degenerate, and if you don't wake up soon, you'll find yourself wearing the label of an enemy of the people!"

My master stared blankly at Hong Taiyue, without moving. Finally, after catching his breath, he said weakly:

"Old Hong, since Widow Su has those fine attributes, why don't you marry her?"

Hong reacted to this seemingly inoffensive question as if he'd lost the power of speech. He looked hopelessly flustered before finding his voice. Without responding to the question, he said authoritatively:

"Don't get cute with me, Lan Lian. I represent the Party, the government, and the impoverished residents of Ximen Village. This is your last chance to come around. I hope you rein in your horse before you go over the cliff, that you find your way back into our camp. We're prepared to forgive your lack of resolve and your inglorious history of enslaving yourself to Ximen Nao, and we'll not alter your class standing of farm laborer just because you married Yingchun. Farm laborer is a label with a gilded edge, and you had better not let it rust or gather dust. I'm telling you to your face that I hope you will join the commune, bringing along that roguish donkey, the wheelbarrow, the plow, and the farming tools you received during land reform, as well as your wife and children, including, of course, those two landlord brats Ximen Jinlong and Ximen Baofeng. Join the commune and stop working for yourself, end your quest for independence. Stop being headstrong, an obstructionist. We have brought over thousands of people with more talent than you. Me, Hong Taiyue, I'll let a cat sleep in the crotch of my pants before I'll let you be a loner on my watch. I hope you've listened to every word I've said."

Hong Taiyue's booming voice had been conditioned by his begging days, back when he went around beating an ox hip bone. For anyone with that sort of voice and eloquence not to become an official is an affront to human nature. Even I was caught up in his monologue as I watched him berate my master; he seemed taller than Lan Lian, though he was actually half a head shorter. The mention of Ximen Jinlong and Ximen Baofeng gave me the scare of my life, for the Ximen Nao who lived in my donkey body was on tenterhooks regarding the children he'd sired and then left stranded in the midst of a turbulent world. He fretted over their future, for although Lan Lian could be their protector, he could also be an agent of doom. Just then, my mistress, Yingchun — I tried desperately to put the image of her sharing my bed and accepting the seed that produced the two children out of my mind — emerged from the western rooms. Before stepping out, she had looked into the broken remnant of a mirror hanging on the wall to check her appearance, of that I'm sure. She was wearing an indigo blue jacket over loose black pants; a blue apron with white flowers was tied around her waist, and a blue and white kerchief, matching the pattern of the apron, covered her head. It was a nicely coordinated outfit. Her haggard face was lit up in the sunlight; her cheeks, her eyes, her mouth, and her ears all combined to dredge up a host of memories. Quite a woman she was, a treasure I'd have loved to kill. Lan Lian, you bastard, you've got a good eye. If you'd married the pockmarked Widow Su from West Village, even being transformed into the Supreme Daoist Jade Emperor would not have been worth it. She walked up to Hong Taiyue, bowed deeply, and said:

"Brother Hong, you're too important to worry about the problems of small fry like us. You mustn't bring yourself down to the level of this coarse laborer."

I saw the tautness in Hong Taiyue's face fall away. Like a man climbing off his donkey to walk downhill, in other words, using her arrival as a way forward, he said:

"Yingchun, I don't have to rehash your family history for you. You two can act recklessly if you think your own situation is hopeless, but you have to think about your children, whose whole lives are ahead of them. Eight or ten years from now, when you look back, Lan Lian, you'll realize that everything I said to you today was for your own good, for you, your wife, and your children. It's the best advice anyone could give."

"I understand, Brother Hong," she said as she tugged at Lan Lian's arm. "Tell Brother Hong you're sorry. We'll go home and talk about joining the commune."

"What's there to talk about?" Lan Lian said. "Even brothers are dividing up family property, so what good is putting strangers together to eat out of the same pot?"

"You really are stubborn," Hong Taiyue said indignantly. "All right, Lan Lian, go ahead, be out there all by yourself. We'll see who's more powerful, you or the commune. Today I'm all but pleading with you to join the commune, but one day, Lan Lian, you'll get down on your knees and beg me to let you in, and that day is not far off, take my word for it!"

"I won't join! And I'll never get down on my knees in front of you!" His eyes were lowered as he continued. "Your Party regulations state, 'Joining a commune is voluntary, leaving it is permissible.' You cannot force me to join!"

"You're a stinking dog turd!" Hong Taiyue said in a furious outburst.

"Brother Hong, please don't . . ."

"You can stop that Brother this and Brother that," Hong said scornfully. "I'm the Party secretary," he said to Yingchun with a look of disgust. "And I'm the village chief, not to mention a member of the village security force!"

"Party secretary, village chief, security officer," Yingchun echoed timidly, "we'll go home and talk this over . . ." She shoved Lan Lian and sobbed, "You stubborn ass, your head is made of stone, come home with me right now . . ."

"I'm not going anywhere until I'm finished with what I have to say. Village chief, you injured my donkey, so you have to pay to fix his leg."

"I'll pay, all right, with a bullet!" Hong Taiyue patted his holster and laughed. "Lan Lian, oh my, Lan Lian, you're really something." Then, raising his voice, he exclaimed, "Tell me who this apricot tree belongs to."

"It belongs to me." Huang Tong, commander of the local militia, had been standing in his doorway, watching the argument develop. He ran up to Hong Taiyue and said, "Party secretary, village chief, security officer, this tree was given to me during land reform, but it hasn't produced a single apricot, and I've been thinking of taking it down one day. Like Ximen Nao, it has a score to settle with us poor peasants."

"That's a bunch of crap!" Hong Taiyue said coldly. "You don't know what you're talking about. If you want to be on my good side, then don't make up stories. This tree produces no fruit because you haven't taken care of it. It's got nothing to do with Ximen Nao. The tree may belong to you now, but sooner or later it's going to be the property of the commune. The road to collectivization requires the complete elimination of private ownership. Stamping out exploitation is a universal trend. And that is why you'd better start taking care of this tree. If you let that donkey gnaw at its bark one more time, I'll flay the skin off your back!"

Huang Tong nodded and forced a smile onto his face. Flashes of gold emerged from his squinty eyes. His mouth was open just enough to reveal his yellow teeth and purple gums. Huang Tong's wife, Qiuxiang, Ximen Nao's second concubine, appeared then, a carrying pole over her shoulder, with her twins, Huzhu and Hezuo, seated in a basket on each end. She had brushed her swept-back hair with osmanthus oil and powdered her face; she wore a dress with floral piping and green satin shoes embroidered with purple flowers. An audacious woman, she was dressed just as she had been when she'd been my concubine, with rouged cheeks and smiling eyes. She cut a lovely figure, with curves in all the right places, nothing like a laboring woman. I knew the woman well. She did not have a good heart. She had a sharp tongue and a devious mind, a woman whose only virtue was in bed, not someone to get close to or confide in. She had high aspirations, and if I hadn't kept her down, my wife and my first concubine would have died at her hand. Even before I became a dirty dog, this wench saw the writing on the wall and turned on me, saying I'd raped her, that I ran roughshod over her, that Ximen Bai mistreated her on a daily basis; she even opened her blouse in front of a crowd of men at the great account-settling meeting and pointed out scars on her breasts, wailing and sputtering loudly, This is where the landlord's wife burned me with the red-hot bowl of a pipe, these are where that tyrant Ximen Nao poked me with an awl. As someone who'd studied to be a stage actress, she knew exactly how to worm her way into people's hearts. I, Ximen Nao, brought her into my house out of kindness. She was at the time a teenager whose hair was still in braids as she followed her blind father from place to place and sang for money. Unfortunately, her father died on the street one day, and she had to sell herself in order to bury him. I took her in as a maidservant. You ungrateful bitch, if Ximen Nao hadn't come to your rescue, you'd have died from the elements or been forced into a life of prostitution. The whore made tearful accusations, spouting lies that sounded so truthful that the women at the foot of the stage were sobbing openly, wetting their glistening sleeves with a torrent of tears. The slogans took over, rage swept over the crowd, and that sealed my doom. I'd known that in the end I'd die at this whore's hand. She wept, she howled, but before long, she stole a glance at me out of those long, narrow eyes. If not for the two militiamen who had me by the arms, I'd have rushed up, not giving a damn what happened to me afterward, and slapped her hard — once, twice, three times. I'm not afraid to tell the truth: at home, because of all the lies she told, I did that, I slapped her three times, and she fell to her knees, wrapped her arms around my legs, tears clouding her eyes, and I saw that look, so enchanting, so pitiful, so full of affection, that my heart softened and my maleness hardened; what can you do with a woman who can't stop telling lies, who's lazy and spoiled? But three hard slaps, and they crawl into bed with you as if drunk. A flirtatious woman like that, I tell you, was my punishment. Old Master, Old Master, dear Elder Brother, go ahead, kill me, put me to death, cut me to pieces, but my soul will still wrap itself around you . . . she pulled a pair of scissors out of her bodice and tried to stab me, but was stopped by the militiamen and dragged down off the stage. Up till that moment I'd clung to the idea that she was putting on an act to protect herself; I couldn't believe that any woman could have such deep-seated loathing for someone she'd cuddled with in bed . . .

She picked up Huzhu and Hezuo in their baskets, apparently heading to market, and gave Hong Taiyue a come-hither look. Her dark little face was like a black peony.

"Huang Tong," Hong said, "keep an eye on her, she's in need of remolding. Make sure she stops acting like a landlord's mistress. Send her out to work in the fields and stop her from going from one market-place to another."

"Are you listening?" Huang Tong placed himself in front of Qiuxiang. "The Party secretary is talking about you!"

"Me? What did I do? If I can't go to market, why not shut it down? If you're afraid I'm too attractive to men, go get some sulfuric acid and ruin my face." All this chatter from her tiny mouth was a terrible embarrassment to Hong Taiyue.

"You slut, you're just itching to be smacked around!" Huang Tong growled.

"Says who, you? If you so much as touch me the wrong way, I'll fight you till both our chests are bloody!"

Huang Tong slapped her before anyone could react. Everyone stood there dumbstruck, and I was waiting for Qiuxiang to make a frightful scene, to roll around on the ground, to threaten suicide, the sorts of things she always did. But I waited in vain. She didn't resist at all. She just threw down her carrying pole, covered her face, and bawled, throwing a fright into Huzhu and Hezuo, who also started bawling. From a distance, their glistening, fuzzy little tops looked like monkey heads.

Hong Taiyue, who started the war, turned into peacemaker, trying to smooth things over between Huang Tong and his wife. Then, without a sideward glance, he walked into what had been the main house of the Ximen estate; now a badly printed wooden sign hanging on the brick wall proclaimed, "Ximen Village Party Committee."

My master wrapped his arms around my head and massaged my ears with his rough hands, while his wife, Yingchun, cleaned my injured leg with salt water and wrapped it with a piece of white cloth. At that sorrowful yet warm moment, I was no Ximen Nao, I was a donkey, one about to become an adult and accompany his master through thick and thin. Like it says in the song that Mo Yan wrote for his new play, *The Black Donkey*:

> A man's soul in a black donkey's body
> Events of the past floating off like clouds
> All beings reborn amid the six paths, such bitterness
> Desire is unquenchable, fond dreams persist
> How can he not recall his past life
> And pass the days as a contented donkey?

4

Gongs and Drums Pound the Heavens
as the Masses Join the Co-op
Four Hooves Plod through the Snow
as the Donkey Is Shod

The first of October, 1954, China's National Day, was also the day Northeast Gaomi Township's first agricultural cooperative was established. Mo Yan, about whom we've already spoken, was born on that day, as well.

In the early morning, Mo Yan's father ran anxiously up to the house and, when he saw my master, began wiping his tear-filled eyes with his sleeve, not saying a word. My master and his wife were eating breakfast at the moment, but they put down their bowls at the sight that greeted them and asked: What's happened, good uncle? In the midst of his sobs, Mo Yan's father managed to say: The baby, she had the baby, a boy. Are you saying that Aunty has had a baby boy? my master's wife asked. Yes, Mo Yan's father said. Then why are you crying? my master asked. You should be happy. Mo Yan's father just stared at my master. Who says I'm not? If I wasn't happy, why would I be crying? My master laughed. Yes, he said, of course, you're crying because you're happy. Why else would you cry? Break out the liquor, he said to his wife. We are going to celebrate. None for me today, Mo Yan's father begged off. I have to spread the good news to lots of people. We can celebrate another day. Yingchun, Mo Yan's father said as he bowed deeply to my master's wife. I have you and your Deer Placenta Ointment to thank for this. The boy's mother said she'll bring him to show you after her month of lying in. We'll both kowtow to you. She said you have stored up such good fortune that she wants the boy to be your nominal son, and if you say no, I'm to get down on my knees and plead. My master's wife said: You two are cutups. I'm happy to do it. There's no need for you to get down on your knees. — And so, Mo Yan isn't only your friend, nominally, he's your brother.

Your brother Mo Yan's father had no sooner left the house than things started heating up in the Ximen estate compound — or should I say the village government office compound. First, Hong Taiyue and Huang Tong pasted up a pair of couplets on the main gate. Then the musicians filed in, crouched down in the yard, and waited. These men looked familiar to me somehow. Ximen Nao's memory seemed to be returning, but fortunately my master came in with the feed and brought an end to my recollections. Thanks to the opening in my lean-to, I was able to watch the goings-on outside as I ate. At about mid-morning, a teenage boy came running into the yard carrying a little flag made of red paper.

"He's coming!" he shouted. "The village chief wants you to start!"

The musicians scrambled to their feet, and in no time, drums banged, gongs clanged, followed by blaring and tooting wind instruments welcoming the honored guest. I watched as Huang Tong ran around shouting, "Out of my way, make room, the district chief is here!"

Under the leadership of Hong Taiyue, head of the co-op, District Chief Chen and several of his armed bodyguards strode in through the gate. The lean district chief, with his deep sunken eyes, swayed as he walked; he was wearing an old army uniform. Farmers who had joined the co-op swarmed in after him, leading their livestock, all draped in red bunting, and carrying farm tools over their shoulders. Within minutes, the yard was filled with farm animals and the bobbing heads of their owners, bringing the place alive. The district chief stood on a stool beneath the apricot tree and waved to the massed crowd. His gestures were received with shouted greetings, and even the animals were caught up in the celebration: horses whinnied, donkeys brayed, cows mooed, increasing the happy clamor and adding fuel to the joyous fire. In the midst of all that noise and activity, but before the district chief had begun his speech, my master led me — or should I say, Lan Lian led his young donkey — through the crowd, under the gaze of the people and their animals, right out through the gate.

Once out of the compound, we headed south, and as we passed

the elementary school playground, by Lotus Bay, we saw all the bad elements, moving rocks and dirt under the supervision of two militiamen armed with rifles adorned with red tassels; they were building up an earthen platform north of the playground, the place where operas had been performed, where mass criticism meetings had been held, and where I, Ximen Nao, had stood when I was being struggled against. Deep in Ximen Nao's memory lay the recognition of all these men. Look there, that skinny old man whose knees are nearly buckling from the weight of the big rock he's carrying, that's Yu Wufu, who was head of security for three months. And look there, that fellow carrying two baskets of earth on a carrying pole, that's Zhang Dazhuang, who went over to the enemy, taking a rifle with him, when the Landlords' Restitution Corps launched an attack to settle scores. He was a carter for my family for five years. My wife, Ximen Bai, arranged his marriage with Bai Susu, her niece. When I was being struggled against, they said that I slept with Bai Susu the night before she was married to Zhang Dazhuang, which was a barefaced lie, a damned rumor; but when they called her up as a witness, she covered her face with her jacket, wailed tearfully, and said nothing, thus turning a lie into the truth and sending Ximen Nao straight down to the Yellow Springs of Death. Look over there at the young man with the oval face and slanty eyebrows, the one who's carrying that green locust log; that's Wu Yuan, one of our rich peasants, and a dear friend of mine. He's quite a musician, plays both the two-stringed *erhu* and the *suona*. During off seasons on the farm, he played with the local band as they walked through town, not for money but for the sheer pleasure of it. And then there's that fellow with a few scraggly hairs on his chin, the one with the worn-out hoe over his shoulder who's standing on the platform dawdling and trying to look busy; it's Tian Gui, the onetime manager of a flourishing liquor business, a skinflint who kept ten hectoliters of wheat in his grain bins but made his wife and kids eat chaff and rotten vegetables. Look, look, look, that woman with the bound feet carrying half a basket of dirt but having to stop and rest every four or five steps, that's my formal wife, Ximen Bai. And look there, behind her, it's Yang Qi, the village public security head, a cigarette dangling from his lips and a willow switch in his hand. Quit loafing and get to work, Ximen Bai, he snarls. She is so alarmed she nearly falls, and the heavy basket of dirt lands on her tiny feet. She shrieks, my wife does, then cries softly from the pain, and begins to sob, like a little girl. Yang Qi raises his switch and brings it down hard — I pulled the rope out of Lan Lian's hand and ran at Yang Qi — the switch snapped in the air a mere inch from Ximen Bai's nose, didn't touch her, showing what an expert the man is. The thieving, depraved bastard — a gluttonous, hard-drinking, whoremongering, chain-smoking gambler — squandered what his father left him, made his mother's life such a misery that she hanged herself from a roof beam, and here he was, a redder-than-red poor peasant, a frontline revolutionary. I was going to drive a fist right into his face — actually, I don't have a fist, so I'd have had to kick him or bite him with my big donkey teeth. Yang Qi, you bastard, with your scraggly chin hairs and dangling cigarette and willow switch, one of these days, I, Ximen Donkey, am going to take a big bite out of you.

My master jerked me back by the rope, saving that gangster Yang Qi from a bad ending. So I raised up and kicked with my hind legs, striking something soft — Yang Qi's belly. Since becoming a donkey, I've been able to take in a lot more with my eyes than Ximen Nao ever could — I can see what goes on behind me. I watched as that bastard Yang Qi hit the ground hard, and I saw his face turn ashen. It took him a long moment to catch his breath, and when he did he called out for his mother. You bastard, your mother hanged herself because of you! Calling for her won't do you any good!

My master threw down the rope and rushed over to help Yang Qi up. Back on his feet, Yang picked up the switch to hit me over the head, but my master grabbed his wrist. "I'm the only person who can do that, Yang Qi," my master said. "Fuck you, Lan Lian!" Yang Qi roared. "You, with your cozy relationship with Ximen Nao, are a bad element who's wormed his way into the class ranks. I'll use this switch on you too!" But my master tightened his grip on the man's wrist, drawing yelps of pain from someone who had abused his body by bedding all the loose women in town; finally he let the switch fall to the ground. With a shove that sent Yang stumbling backward, my master said, "Consider yourself lucky my donkey doesn't have iron shoes yet."

My master turned and led me out through the southern gate, where yellowing bristlegrass atop the wall swayed in the wind. That was the local co-op's first day, and the day I reached adulthood. "Donkey," my master said, "today I'm going to have you shod to protect you from stones in the road and keep sharp objects from cutting

your hooves. It'll make you an adult, and I can put you to work."
Every donkey's fate, I surmised. So I raised my head and brayed, *Hee-
haw, hee-haw* — It was the first time I'd actually made the sound
aloud, so loud and crisp my startled master beamed.

The local blacksmith was a master at making shoes for horses
and donkeys. He had a black face, a red nose, and beetle brows without a hair on them; there were no lashes above his red, puffy eyes, but
three deep worry wrinkles across his forehead, repositories for coal
ash. His apprentice's face, as I could see, was pale under a mass of
lines created by runnels of sweat. There was so much sweat running
down the boy's body, I worried that he was about to dry up. As for the
blacksmith himself, his skin was so parched it looked like years of
high heat had baked all the water out of it. The boy was operating a
bellows with his left hand and wielding a pair of fire tongs with his
right. He removed steel from the forge when it was white-hot, then he
and the blacksmith hammered it into the desired shape, first with a
sledge, then a finishing hammer. The *bang-bang, clang-clang* sound
bouncing off the walls and the flying sparks had me spellbound.

The pale, handsome boy should have been on the stage, winning
over pretty girls with sweet talk and tender words of love, not hammering steel in a blacksmith shop. But I was impressed by his
strength, watching as he wielded an eighteen-pound sledge that I'd
thought only the bull-like blacksmith could manage with such ease; it
was like an extension of the boy's young body. The hot steel was like
a lump of clay waiting to be turned into whatever the blacksmith and
his apprentice desired. After hammering a pillow-sized clump of steel
into a straw cutter, a farmer's biggest hand tool, they stopped to rest.
"Master Jin," my master said to the blacksmith, "I'd like to enlist your
services to make a set of shoes for my donkey." The blacksmith took
a deep drag on his cigarette and blew the smoke out through his nose
and his ears. His apprentice was gulping water out of a large, coarse
china bowl. The water, it seemed, turned immediately to sweat, giving off a peculiar smell that was the essential odor of the handsome,
innocent, hardworking boy's being. "That's some white-hoofed donkey," the old blacksmith said with a sigh. Where I was standing, just
outside the tent, not far from the road that led to the county town, I
looked down and saw my snow-white hooves for the first time.

The boy put down his bowl. "They've got two new hundred-
horsepower East Is Red tractors over at the state-run farm, each one

as powerful as a hundred horses. They attached a steel cable to a poplar tree so big it takes two people to wrap their arms around it, hooked it to one of those tractors, and it yanked the tree right out of the ground, roots and all. Those roots were half a block long." "You know everything, don't you!" the old blacksmith scolded the boy. Then he turned to my master. "Old Lan," he said, "it may only be a donkey, but it looks like you've got a good one. Who knows, some high official might get tired of riding a fine horse one day and decide it's time to ride a donkey. When that day comes, Lan Lian, donkey luck will be yours for the asking." The boy smirked at that, then burst out laughing. He stopped laughing as abruptly as he'd started, as if the laughter and the expression that flashed onto his face and immediately vanished were private business. The old blacksmith was clearly shocked by the boy's bizarre laughter. "Jin Bian," he said after a moment, "do we have any horseshoes?" As if he'd been waiting for the question, Jin Bian replied, "We have a lot, but all for horses. We can put them into the forge, heat them up, and change them into donkey shoes." And that is what they did. In the time it takes to smoke a pipe, they had turned four horseshoes into four donkey shoes. Then the boy moved a stool outside and put it on the ground behind me, so the old blacksmith could lift up my legs and trim my hooves with a pair of sharp shears. When he was finished, he stepped back to look me over. Again he sighed, this time with deep emotion. "This really is a fine donkey," the blacksmith said. "It's the best looking one I've ever seen!" "No matter how good-looking he is, he's no match for one of those combines. The state-run farm imported a bright red one from the Soviet Union. It can harvest a row of wheat in the blink of an eye. It gobbles up the wheat stalks in front and shoots the kernels out the back. In five minutes you've got a bagful." All this the boy said with breathless admiration. The old blacksmith sighed. "Jin Bian," he said, "it sounds like I won't be able to keep you here for long. But even if you leave tomorrow, today we've got to shoe this donkey." Jin Bian came up alongside me and lifted one of my legs, hammer in hand and mouth full of nails. He fitted a shoe on my hoof with one hand and hammered it on with the other, two strokes per nail, never missing a beat. One down. All four shoes took him less than twenty minutes. When he finished, he threw down his hammer and walked back inside the tent. "Lan Lian," the blacksmith said, "walk him a bit to see if there's a limp." So my master started me walking, from the supply and marketing co-op over to the butcher shop, where they were just then butchering a black pig. White knife in, red knife out, a terrifying sight. The butcher was wearing an emerald green old-style jacket, and the contrast with the red was eye-popping. We left the butcher shop and walked to the District Government Office, where we met with District Chief Chen and his bodyguard. The opening-day ceremony for the Ximen Village Farming Co-op must have ended. The district chief's bicycle was broken; his guard was carrying it over his shoulder. One look from District Chief Chen and he couldn't keep his eyes off me. How good-looking and powerful I must have been to catch his attention like that! I knew I was an intimidating donkey among donkeys; maybe Lord Yama had given me the finest donkey legs and the cream of donkey heads out of an obligation to Ximen Nao. "That's a wonderful donkey," I heard Chief Chen say. "His hooves look like they're stepping in snow. He'd be perfect at the livestock work station as a stud." I heard his bicycle-toting guard ask my master, "Are you Lan Lian from Ximen Village?" "Yes," my master replied as he slapped me on the rump to get me moving faster. But Chief Chen stopped us and patted me on the back. I reared up. "He's got a temper," he said. "You'll have to work on that. You can't work with an animal that's easily spooked. An animal like that is hard to train." Then, in the tone of an old hand, he said, "Before I joined the revolution, I was a trader in donkeys. I've seen thousands of them, I know them like the palm of my hand, especially their temperament." He laughed long and loud; my master laughed along with him, fatuously. "Lan Lian," the chief said, "Hong Taiyue told me what happened, and I wasn't happy with him. I told him that Lan Lian is one tough donkey, and you have to rub him with the grain. Don't be impatient with him, or he might kick or bite you. I tell you, Lan Lian, you don't have to join the co-op right away. See if you can compete with it. I know you were allotted eight acres of land, so see how much grain you harvest per acre next fall. Then check to see how much the co-op brings in. If you do better, you can keep working your land on your own. But if the co-op does better, you and I will have another talk." "You said that," my master said excitedly. "Don't forget." "Yes, I said it, you've got witnesses," the district chief said, pointing to his bodyguard and the people who had gathered around us. My master led me back to the blacksmith shop, where he said, "He doesn't limp at all. Every step was perfect. I'd never have believed that someone as young as your apprentice could do such an excellent job." With a wry smile, the blacksmith shook his head, as if weighed down with concerns. Then I spotted the young blacksmith Jin Bian, a bedroll over his shoulder — the corners of a gray blanket sticking out from under a dog-skin wrapping — walking out of the shop. "Well, I'll be leaving, Master," he said. "Go ahead," the old blacksmith replied sadly. "Go seek your glorious future!"

5

Ximen Bai Stands Trial for Digging Up Treasure
The Donkey Disrupts Proceedings and Jumps a Wall

Now that I'd heard so many words of praise over my new shoes, I was in a fine mood, and my master was delighted with what the district chief had said. Master and donkey, Lan Lian and I, ran happily through the gold-washed autumn fields. Those were the best days of my donkey life. Yes, better to be a donkey everyone loves than a hopeless human. As your nominal brother Mo Yan wrote in the play *The Black Donkey*:

> Hooves felt light with four new shoes,
> Running down the road like the wind.
> Forgetting the half-baked previous life
> Ximen Donkey was happy and relaxed.
> He raised his head and shouted to the heavens,
> *Hee-haw, hee-haw —*

When we reached the village, Lan Lian picked some tender grass and yellow wildflowers from the side of the road to weave into a floral wreath, which he draped over my neck behind my ears. There we met the daughter of the stonemason Han Shan, Han Huahua, and their family's female donkey, which was carrying a pair of saddlebag baskets; one held a baby in a rabbit fur cap, the other held a white piglet. Lan Lian struck up a conversation with Huahua; I made eye contact with her donkey. The humans had their speech, we had our own ways to communicate. Ours was based on body odors, body language, and instinct. From their brief conversation, my master learned that Huahua, who had been married to someone in a distant village,

had come back for her mother's sixtieth birthday and was now returning home. The baby in the basket was her infant son; the piglet was a
gift from her parents. Back then, live animals, like piglets or lambs or
chicks, were the preferred gifts. Government awards were often
horses or cows or long-haired rabbits. My master and Huahua had a
special relationship, and I thought back to when I was still Ximen
Nao, how Lan Lian would be out with his cattle and Huahua would
be out with her sheep, and the two of them would play donkeys frolicking in the grass. Truth is, I wasn't all that interested in what they
were doing now. As a potent male donkey, my immediate concern was
the female donkey with the saddlebag baskets that was standing right
there in front of me. She was older than me, somewhere between five
and seven, by all appearances, which I determined from the depth of
the hollow in her forehead. Naturally, she could just as easily —
maybe even more easily — guess my age. Don't assume that I was
the smartest donkey ever just because I was a reincarnation of Ximen
Nao — for a time I entertained that very misconception — since she
could have been a reincarnation of someone far more important. My
coat was gray when I was born, but I was turning darker all the time.
If I hadn't been almost black at the time, my hooves wouldn't have
appeared so eye-popping white. She was a gray donkey, still quite
svelte, with delicate features, perfect teeth, and when she brought her
mouth up close to me, I got a whiff of aromatic bean cake and wheat
bran from between her lips. Sexual emanations poured from her, and
at the same time I sensed the heat of passion inside, a powerful desire
for me to mount her. It was contagious: an overpowering urge to do
just that rose in me.

"Are they caught up in co-op fever where you are?"

"With the same county chief leading the charge, there's no way
to avoid it," Huahua said wistfully.

I walked over behind the donkey, who might have been offering
her hindquarters to me. The scent of passion was getting stronger. I
breathed it in deeply, and it was like pouring strong liquor down my
throat. I bared my teeth and closed both nostrils, in order to keep any
foul odors from escaping. It was the sort of pose that pretty much
melted her heart. At the same time, my black shaft reached out heroically and nudged itself up against my belly. This was a once-in-a-life-
time opportunity, fleeting to boot; just as I was raising my front legs to
consummate the deal, my eyes fell on the baby in the saddlebag

basket, sound asleep, not to mention, of course, the squealing piglet. Now, if I were to rear up into the mounting position, my newly shod hooves could wipe out those two little lives. And if I did that, Ximen Donkey could pretty much count on spending eternity in hell, with no chance of rebirth as anything. As I pondered my dilemma, my master jerked on the reins, forcing my front hooves down onto the ground as Huahua shrieked in alarm and quickly led her donkey out of "danger."

"My father instructed me that since she's in heat, I needed to be especially watchful. I forgot. In fact, he said to be sure and watch out for the donkey belonging to the Ximen Nao family. Can you imagine, even though Ximen Nao has been dead all these years, my father still thinks you're his hired hand, and he refers to your donkey as Ximen Nao's donkey."

"That's better than thinking that it's a reincarnation of Ximen Nao," my master said with a laugh.

I tell you, that shocked me. Did he know my secret? If he knew that his donkey was actually Ximen Nao reincarnated, would that work for or against me? The red ball in the sky was about to set; time for my master and Huahua to say good-bye.

"We'll talk again next time, Brother Lan," she said. "My home's fifteen *li* from here, so I'd better get going."

"So your donkey won't make it back tonight, is that it?"

Huahua smiled and said conspiratorially:

"She's a very clever donkey. After I feed and water her, all I have to do is remove her reins, and she'll run home on her own. She does it every time."

"Why do you have to remove her reins?"

"So no one can catch and take her away with them. The reins slow her down."

"Oh," my master said as he stroked his chin. "Why don't I see you home?"

"Thanks," she said, "but they're putting on a play in the village tonight, so if you leave now you can see it." Huahua turned and started off with her donkey, but stopped after a few steps, turned back, and said, "Brother Lan, my father said you shouldn't be so stubborn, that you'd be better off throwing in your lot with everybody else."

My master shook his head but didn't respond. Then he looked me in the eye and said, "Let's go, partner. I know what's on your mind, and you nearly got me into a peck of trouble! What do you think, should I take you to the vet and get you fixed?"

My heart nearly stopped and my scrotum constricted; I'd never been so scared in my life. Don't do it, Master, I wanted to howl, but the words stuck in my throat and emerged as brays: *Hee-haw, hee-haw* —

Now that we'd arrived in the village, my new shoes sang out crisply on the cobblestone road. Although I had something else on my mind, the image of her beautiful eyes and tender pink lips and the smell of her affectionate urine in my nose nearly drove me crazy. And yet my previous life as a human had made me an uncommon donkey. Misfortunes in the human world held a great attraction for me. I watched people rushing off to somewhere, and from what they spoke of along the way, I learned that a colored, glazed pottery urn filled with riches was on display in the Ximen estate compound, now the Village Government Office, headquarters of the co-op, and, of course, the home of my master Lan Lian and Huang Tong. The urn had been dug up by workers as they prepared an outdoor stage for the play. I immediately imagined the shady looks on the people's faces when they looked upon riches being removed from the urn, and Ximen Nao's memories resurfaced to dilute the amorous feelings of Ximen Donkey. I didn't recall ever hiding any gold, silver, or jewelry in that place; we had hidden a thousand silver dollars in the animal pen as well as a trove of wealth in the walls of the house, but they had been found by the Poor Peasants Brigade in searches during the land reform movement. Poor Ximen Bai had suffered grievously over that.

At first, Huang Tong, Yang Qi, and the others had locked up Ximen Bai, Yingchun, and Qiuxiang for observation and investigation, with Hong Taiyue in command. I was kept in a separate room, out of sight of the interrogations, but well within earshot. Out with it! Where did Ximen Nao hide your family's riches? Out with it! I heard the crisp sounds of willow switches and clubs banging on tables. And I heard that slut Qiuxiang cry out: Village Chief, Group Leader, good uncles and brothers, I was born to poverty, I was fed husks and rotten vegetables in the Ximen household, they never treated me like a human being, I was raped by Ximen Nao, my legs held down by Ximen Bai and my arms by Yingchun, so Ximen Nao could fuck me! — That's a damned lie! That was Yingchun shouting. The sound of beating, someone was pulling them apart. — Everything she's saying, all lies! That was Ximen Bai weighing in. In their house I was lower than a dog, lower than a pig, uncles, elder brothers, I'm an oppressed woman, I'm just like you, I'm one of your class sisters, it's you who've rescued me from a sea of bitterness, I owe you everything, I'd love nothing more than to scoop out Ximen Nao's brains and hand them to you, nothing would make me happier than to gouge out his heart and liver for you to enjoy with your wine. . . . Just think, why would they tell me where they hid their gold and silver? You class brothers, you must understand what I'm telling you, Qiuxiang pleaded tearfully. Yingchun, on the other hand, neither cried nor made a scene. She stuck to her simple defense: All I concerned myself with was my chores and raising the children. I know nothing outside of that. She was right, those two did not know where the family wealth was hidden; that knowledge was shared only by Ximen Bai and me. A concubine is just that, not someone you can trust. Unlike a real wife. Ximen Bai kept her silence until she was forced to say something. The family is just an empty shell, she said, which people might have thought was filled with gold and silver, when in fact we couldn't make ends meet. There was a little money for household expenditures, but he wouldn't give it to me. I could picture her when she said that: She'd be staring daggers with her big, blank eyes, at Yingchun and Qiuxiang. I knew she despised Qiuxiang, but Yingchun had come with her as a maidservant, and when you break the bones, the tendons stay connected; it had been her idea for Yingchun to become my concubine so I could keep the family line going. And Yingchun had carried out her end of the bargain, producing a pair of twins, a boy and a girl. Bringing Qiuxiang into the house, on the other hand, had been a frivolous idea of mine. Success during good times can turn a man's head; when a dog is happy with the way things are going, it raises its tail; when a man is happy with the way things are going, it's his pecker that gets raised. To be sure, it was her seductive charms that got to me: she flirted with her eyes and won me over with her breasts. The temptation was simply too great for Ximen Nao, who was far from being a saint. Ximen Bai made it abundantly clear how she felt about this: You're the head of the household, she said angrily, but one of these days that witch is going to be your undoing! So, when Qiuxiang said that Ximen Bai held her legs while Ximen Nao raped her, she was lying. Did Ximen Bai ever hit her? Yes. But she also hit Yingchun. Eventually, they let Yingchun and

Qiuxiang go, and from where I was locked up, in a room with a window, I saw the two of them walk out of the main house. I wasn't fooled by Qiuxiang's disheveled hair or dirty face, because I could see the smug look in her eyes, which were rolling happily in their sockets. Clearly worried, Yingchun ran straight to the eastern rooms, where Jinlong and Baofeng were crying themselves hoarse. My darling son, my precious daughter! I whimpered silently, where did I go wrong, what heavenly principles did I violate to cause such suffering, not just to me, but to my wife and children? But then I reflected that every village had land-lords who were struggled against, whose so-called crimes were exposed and criticized, who were swept out of their homes like garbage, and whose "dog heads" were beaten bloody, thousands and thousands of them, and I wondered, Was it possible that every one of them — of us — committed such evil acts that this was the treatment we deserved? It was our inexorable fate; earth and sky were spinning dizzily, the sun and moon trading places; there was no escape, and only the protection of Ximen Nao's ancestors could keep his head on his shoulders. With the world in such a state, just staying alive was a result of sheer luck; asking for more would have been preposterous. But I couldn't help worrying about Ximen Bai. If they wore her down to the point where she told them where our riches were hidden, not only would that not lessen my crimes, it would seal my doom. Ximen Bai, my loyal wife, you are a deep thinker, a woman of ideas, and you mustn't lose sight of what's important at this critical moment! The militiaman guarding my cell, Lan Lian, blocked my view out the window with his back, though I could hear the interrogation in the main house start up again. This time they really turned up the heat. The screams were deafening as willow switches, bamboo rods, and whips smacked against a table and thudded against Ximen Bai's back. My dear wife's shrieks broke my heart and shattered my nerves. — Out with it! Where did you hide your gold and silver? — We have no gold and silver. . . . — Ah, Ximen Bai, you're so stubborn it looks like you won't open up till we start knocking you around. That sounded like Hong Taiyue, though not completely. Then silence. But only for a moment, before Ximen Bai's howls erupted, and that made my hair stand on end. What were they doing to her? What could force such frightful howls out of a woman? — Are you going to tell us or not? If you don't, you'll get more of the same! — I'll tell you . . . I'll tell you . . . My heart felt like it had been rid of a stone. Go ahead, tell them. After all, a man can only die once.

Better for me to die than for her to suffer on my account. Out with it, where did you hide it? — It's hidden, it's hidden in the Earth God Temple east of the village, in the God of War Temple north of the village, at Lotus Bay, in the belly of a cow. . . . I don't know where it's hidden, because there isn't any. During the first Land Reform campaign, we handed over everything we owned! — You've got your nerve, Ximen Bai, trying to make fools of us! — Let me go, I honestly don't know anything. . . . — Drag her outside! I heard a man in the main house threaten, someone who was probably sitting in the mahogany armchair I used to sit in. Next to that chair was an octagonal table on which I kept my writing brush, ink stick, ink slab, and paper; hanging from the wall behind the table was a longevity scroll. Behind the scroll was a hollow in which forty silver coins weighing fifty ounces, twenty gold ingots each weighing an ounce, and all of Ximen Bai's jewelry were hidden. I saw two armed militiamen drag Ximen Bai out of the house; her hair was a mess, her clothes ripped and torn, and she was soaking wet. I couldn't tell if what was dripping from her body was blood or sweat, but when I saw the shape she was in, I knew that Ximen Nao had not vainly kicked up a row in this world. I suddenly realized that the militiamen who came out with her were meant to be a firing squad. My arms had been tied behind me, so all I could do, like Su Qin carrying a sword on his back, was ram my head into the window frame and scream, Don't execute her!

You vulgar bone-rapping bastard, I said to Hong Taiyue, as far as I'm concerned, a single hair on my scrotum is worth more than you, but in letting me fall into the hands of you low-class peasants, fortune has not smiled on me. I cannot fight heaven's laws. I give up, count me as your lowly grandson.

With a laugh, Hong Taiyue said, I'm glad you see things that way. Yes, me, Hong Taiyue, I am vulgar, and if not for the Communist Party, I'd be stuck with banging on that ox bone for the rest of my life. But the tables have been turned on you, and we poor peasants have had a change of luck. We've floated to the top. By settling accounts with you people, all we're doing is retrieving the riches you accumulated. I've reasoned with you more times than I can count. You did not provide your hired hands and tenant farmers with a livelihood, Ximen Nao, you and your family lived off of our labor. Hiding your riches from us was an unforgivable crime, but if you hand them over now, we are prepared to treat you with leniency.

I alone was responsible for hiding my money and valuables. The women had nothing to do with it. I knew they were unreliable, that all you had to do was pound the table to get them to reveal all our secrets. I'm willing to turn over everything I own, wealth that will astound you, enough for you to buy an artillery cannon, but you must give me your word that you will release Ximen Bai and won't take my crimes out on Yingchun and Qiuxiang, since they know nothing.

You don't need to worry about that, Hong said. We'll do everything by the book.

All right. Untie my hands.

The militiamen eyed me suspiciously, then looked at Hong Taiyue.

Again, with a laugh, he said, They're afraid you'll fight like a cornered beast, that you'll do anything to get away.

I smiled. He personally untied my hands, even offered me a cigarette. I accepted, even though I'd lost feeling in my hands, and sat in my armchair, beaten down with dejection. Finally, I reached up and pulled down the scroll. — Break open the wall with your rifle butts, I said to the militiamen.

They were dumbstruck by the sight of the riches they retrieved from the hollow, and those looks told me everything I needed to know about what they were thinking. They all wished they could walk away with that treasure and probably were already conjuring up dreams of wealth and leisure: If this house had been handed over to me and I'd stumbled upon this hidden treasure . . .

While they were standing around dazed by the riches, I reached down, grabbed a revolver that was hidden under the armchair, and fired a shot into the tile floor; the bullet ricocheted and lodged in the wall. The militiamen hit the floor in panic. Only Hong Taiyue remained standing, the bastard, showing what he was made of. Did you hear that, Hong Taiyue? If I'd pointed this at your head, right now you'd be spread out on the floor like a dead dog. But I didn't, not at you or at any of your men, since I have no account to settle with any of you. If you hadn't come to struggle against me, someone else would have. It's the times. All rich people are doomed to meet the same fate. And that's why I haven't harmed a single hair on any of you.

You're got that right, Hong said. You're a man who knows what's what, someone who sees the big picture, and as a man, I respect you. More than that, you're a man I'd be happy to share a bottle with, even become sworn brothers with. But speaking as a member of the revolutionary masses, you and I are irreconcilable foes and I am obliged to eliminate you. This is not personal hatred, it's class hatred. As a representative of a class that is marked for elimination, you could have shot me dead, but that would have made me a revolutionary martyr. The government would have then executed you, turning you into a counterrevolutionary martyr.

I laughed, roared, in fact. I laughed so hard I cried. When I was finished, I said, Hong Taiyue, my mother was a devout Buddhist, and not once in my life have I been guilty of killing anyone or anything, carrying out my filial obligations to her. She told me that if I every killed anyone or anything after her death, she would suffer torment in the afterworld. So if it's martyrdom you're looking for, you'll have to find someone else to make that possible. As for me, I've lived long enough. It's time for me to die. But my death will be unrelated to your so-called classes. I accumulated my wealth by being smart, industrious, and lucky, and I never entertained the thought of joining any class. And I certainly won't die a martyr of any sort. As far as I'm concerned, living on like this would fill me with all kinds of meaningless grievances. There are too many things I don't understand, which makes me uncomfortable, so dying is better. I put my pistol up to my temple and said, There's an urn with a thousand silver dollars buried in the animal pen. My apologies, but you'll have to dig through animal dung to get to it, which means you'll cover your bodies with a foul stench before you hold the silver dollars in your hands.

No problem, Hong Taiyue said. For a thousand silver dollars, not only are we willing to dig through animal dung, we'd roll around in a pool of shit if we had to. But I urge you not to kill yourself. Who knows, maybe we'll let you live long enough to watch us poor peasants stand up and be counted, see us fill with pride, see us become masters of our own fate and create a fair and just society.

Sorry, but I don't feel like living. As Ximen Nao I'm used to having people nod their heads and bend low to me, not the other way around. Maybe we'll see each other in the next life. Gentlemen! I pulled the trigger. Nothing happened, a dud. And when I lowered the pistol to see what was wrong, Hong Taiyue grabbed it out of my hand. His men rushed up and tied me up again. You aren't so smart, after all, my friend Hong said as he held up the pistol. You didn't have to check it. The virtue of a revolver is how often it misfires. If you'd pulled the trigger one more time, the next bullet would have spun into the chamber and you'd be on the floor chewing on a tile like a dead dog, if it too wasn't a dud, that is. He laughed smugly and ordered the militiamen to go out and start digging. Then he turned back to me. Ximen Nao, he said, I don't believe you were trying to trick us. A man who's about to kill himself has no reason to lie. . . .

Pulling me along behind him, my master managed to force his way in through the gate as, on orders from village officials, militiamen were shoving people out. The cowards couldn't move fast enough, with rifles poking them in the backside, while some brave individuals were pushing their way in to see what was going on. You can imagine how hard it was for my master to lead a big strong donkey in through that gate. The village had planned to move the Lan and Huang families out of the compound so they could free up the entire Ximen estate for government offices. But since there were no vacant buildings in which to put them, and since my master and Huang Tong were not easy heads to shave, getting them to move would have been harder than climbing to heaven, at least for the time being. That meant that on a daily basis I, Ximen Donkey, was able to enter and leave through the same gate as the village bosses, not to mention district and county officials on their inspection tours.

As the clamor persisted, the crowd in the compound pushed and shoved, until the militiamen, in no mood to strain themselves in quelling the uproar, moved away to smoke a leisurely cigarette. From where I stood, in my lean-to, I watched as the setting sun splashed its golden rays onto the apricot tree branches. A pair of armed militiamen kept guard beneath the tree, the object at their feet blocked from view by the crowd. But I knew it was the treasure-filled urn, with a surge of humanity pressing closer and closer to it. I swore to heaven that the riches in that urn had nothing to do with Ximen Nao — with me. But then, my heart skipped a beat when I saw Ximen Nao's wife, Ximen Bai, walk out of the main building in the custody of a rifle-toting militiaman and the head of public security.

Her hair looked like a ball of tangled yarn, and she was covered with dirt, as if she'd emerged from a hole in the ground. Her arms hung limp at her sides as she swayed with each step to keep her balance. When the raucous people in the compound saw her, they fell silent and instinctively parted to open up the path leading to the main building. The gate of my estate had once faced a screen wall on which the words "Good Fortune" had been inlaid, but that had been demolished by a pair of money-grubbing militiamen on a second inspection during Land Reform. They'd shared a dream that hundreds of gold ingots were hidden inside the wall, but all they retrieved was a pair of rusty scissors.

Ximen Bai tripped on a cobblestone and fell to the ground, where she lay, facedown. Yang Qi kicked her.

"Get the hell up!" he cursed. "Quit faking!"

I felt a blue flame blaze up inside my head and pawed the ground out of anxiety and rage. I could sense the heavy hearts among the villagers in the compound as the atmosphere turned forlorn. Ximen Nao's wife was sobbing. She arched her back and tried to get up by supporting herself with her hands. She looked like a wounded frog.

As Yang Qi swung his foot back for another kick, Hong Taiyue called him to a halt from the steps:

"What are you doing, Yang Qi? After all these years since Liberation, you are smearing mud on the face of the Communist Party by the way you curse and hit people!"

The mortified Yang Qi stood there, rubbing his hands and mumbling to himself.

Hong Taiyue came down the steps and walked up to where Ximen Bai lay on the ground. He bent down and helped her up, but her legs buckled as she tried to go down on her knees.

"Village Head," she sobbed, "spare me, I honestly know nothing. Please, Village Head, spare the life of this lowly dog . . .

"No more of that talk, Ximen Bai," he said, holding her up so she could not get down on her knees. He looked so obliging, but then he abruptly turned severe. Facing the crowd, he said sternly: "Get out of here! What's the big idea? What's there to see? Go on, get out of here!"

With bowed heads, the people began leaving.

Spotting a heavyset woman with long, straight hair, Hong signaled to her.

"Yang Guixiang," he said, "come over here and help."

Yang, a onetime director of the Women's Relief Society, was now in charge of women's affairs. She was a cousin of Yang Qi. Happy to assist, she helped Ximen Bai back into the house.

"Think hard, Ximen Bai, did your husband, Ximen Nao, bury this urn? And while you're thinking about that, what else did he bury? Tell us, there's nothing to be afraid of, since you've done nothing wrong. Ximen Nao is the guilty one."

Sounds of torture emerged from the main house and assailed my ears, which were standing straight up. At this moment, Ximen Nao and the donkey were one and the same. I was Ximen Nao, Ximen Nao was now a donkey, I was Ximen Donkey.

"I honestly don't know, Village Chief. That place isn't my family's land, and if my husband wanted to bury something, he wouldn't bury it there. . . ."

"Smack!" Someone banged the table with the flat of his hand.

"Hang her up if she won't tell!"

"Squeeze her fingers!"

My wife wailed pitifully, begging for her life.

"Think hard, Ximen Bai. Ximen Nao is dead, so buried riches cannot do him any good. But if we dig them up, they can make our co-op stronger. There's nothing to be afraid of, we've all been liberated. Our policy is not to beat people, and we're certainly not about to resort to torture. All you have to do is tell us, and I promise I'll cite you for meritorious service." I knew that was Hong Taiyue talking.

My blazing heart filled with sadness, and I felt as if someone was branding me with a red-hot iron or stabbing me with a sharp knife. The sun had set by then and the moon was climbing high in the sky, its chillingly gray beams trickling down onto the ground, the trees, the militiamen's rifles, and the glittery glazed urn. That urn does not belong to the Ximen family, and besides, we'd never bury our riches in a place like that. It's where people have died and bombs have exploded, where ghosts congregate, and it would be folly for me to bury anything there. Ours was not the only wealthy family in the village, why were we the only ones you accused with no proof?

I could stand it no longer, could not bear to hear Ximen Bai cry; it brought pain and guilt feelings. If only I'd treated her better. After bringing Yingchun and Qiuxiang into the house, I never again visited my wife's bed, leaving a thirty-year-old woman to sleep alone night after night. So she recited sutras and struck the wooden fish, that hollow block of wood with which my mother had beat out a rhythm when she uttered her Buddhist devotionals: *clack, clack, clack, clack, clack, clack* . . . I reared back, but I was tied to a hitching post, so I sent a tattered basket flying with a kick by my rear hooves. I lunged to one side, I sprang to the other, white-hot brays tore from my throat. That seemed to loosen the reins. I'd freed myself. I charged through the unlocked gate on my way to the middle of the compound, where I heard Jinlong, who was relieving himself against the wall, yell, "Daddy, Mommy, our donkey got loose!"

I pranced around in the compound for a moment to test my legs and hooves; they clattered on the stones and raised sparks. Moonbeams glistened on my nicely rounded rump. Lan Lian ran out of his quarters, and militiamen emerged from the main house. Rays of candlelight pierced the open doorway and lit up part of the compound. I trotted over to the apricot tree, turned and kicked the glazed urn with my rear hooves, destroying it with a loud splintering noise, some of the pieces sailing above the tree and then landing on roof tiles with a clatter. Huang Tong ran out of the main house, Qiuxiang came out of the eastern rooms. The militiamen cocked their rifles, but I wasn't afraid; I knew they wouldn't hesitate to shoot a person, but would never shoot a donkey. As barnyard animals, donkeys lack human understanding of things, and anyone who kills one will himself become a barnyard animal. Huang Tong stepped down on my loose reins, but all I had to do was rear up to put him on his backside. Then by swinging my head, the reins whipped through the air and struck Qiuxiang in the face. Hearing her wail was music to my ears. You black-hearted slut, I'd like to mount you right here! I leaped over her; people ran up to restrain me. But nothing was going to stop me from running into the main house. It's me, Ximen Nao, I've come home! I want to sit in my own chair, smoke my own pipe, pick up my little liquor decanter and down four ounces of good strong liquor, and then enjoy a nice braised chicken. All of a sudden, the room seemed awfully small, and my footsteps resounded on the tile floor. Pots and pans were smashed, furniture was on its back or its side. I saw the big, flat, golden-yellow face of Yang Guixiang, who, thanks to me, had been forced up against a wall. Her shrieks hit me like darts. Then my eyes fell on Ximen Bai, my virtuous wife, who was sprawled weakly on the tile floor, and that threw my mind into turmoil. I forgot that I now had a donkey's body and a donkey's face. I wanted to reach down and pick her up, only to discover that she was lying unconscious between my legs. I felt like kissing her, but then I saw that her head was bleeding. Love is forbidden between humans and donkeys.

Good-bye, virtuous wife. Just as I had lifted my head and turned to exit the room, a dark figure stepped out from behind the door and wrapped his arms around my neck. With hands like steel talons, he grabbed my ears and my reins. My head sagged from the pain. But as soon as I could see what was going on, the village chief, Hong Taiyue, was lying across my head like a vampire bat. My bitter rival. As a human being, I, Ximen Nao, never fought you, but I'll not suffer at your hands as a donkey. I was seeing red. Bearing up under the pain, I threw back my head and broke for the door. The doorframe scraped the parasite from my body — Hong Taiyue remained inside the room.

With a loud cry, I burst into the compound, but several people clumsily managed to close the gate before I could get to it. My heart had suddenly outgrown the compound; it was too small to hold me, and I ran around madly, sending people scurrying. I heard Yang Guixiang scream,

"The donkey bit Ximen Bai's head, it's bleeding, and he broke the village chief's arm!"

"Shoot it, kill it!" someone else shouted. I heard the militiamen cock their rifles, and I saw Lan Lian and Yingchun running toward me. Moving at the fastest speed I could manage and summoning up all the strength I had, I headed for a breach in the wall caused by heavy summer rains. I leaped, reached into the air with all four hooves, stretched to my fullest length, and sailed over the wall.

The legend of Lan Lian's flying donkey is still told by old-time residents of Ximen Village. Naturally, it's told most vividly in stories written by Mo Yan.

6

Tenderness and Deep Affection
Create a Perfect Couple
Wisdom and Courage Are Pitted
against Vicious Wolves

I headed south at top speed after flying over a toppled wall. I nearly broke a leg when my front hooves landed in mud, and I was seized with terror. I tried to free my legs from the mud, but only succeeded in sinking in deeper. So I stopped, settled down, and planted my rear legs on solid ground. Then I lay down and rolled to the side, managing to pull my front legs free. After that I climbed out of the ditch, giving proof to the words that Mo Yan once wrote: A goat can scale a tree, a donkey is a good climber.

I followed the road southwest at a gallop.

You probably recall my mention of the female donkey belonging to the stonemason, the one carrying Han Huahua's son and the piglet on her way home to her in-laws. Well, she — the donkey — ought to have been out of her halter and on her way back by this time. When we parted to go our own ways, we agreed that tonight would be ours to enjoy. Words once spoken by humans cannot be taken back, not even by a team of horses; for donkeys, it's a matter of a promise is a promise, and we would wait for one another, no longer how long it took.

Chasing the emotional message she left in the air around her at dusk, I raced down the road she'd taken, raising a clatter with my hooves that traveled far on the night air; it was almost as though I was following the sound of my own hoofbeats, or that the sound was chasing me. Roadside reeds were withered and yellow on that late autumn evening, dew had become frost, and fireflies flitting amid the grass created a spotty illumination of the ground with their blinking green lights. My nose was assailed by a stench hanging in the air, which I knew came from an old corpse whose flesh had long since rotted away, but whose bones continued to reek.

Han Huahua's in-laws lived in Old Man Zheng Village, whose richest resident, Zheng Zhongliang, had been one of Ximen Nao's friends, though they were of different generations. I thought back to the time when we were chatting over fine spirits and he had patted me on the shoulder and said, My young friend, amassing wealth creates enemies, dispensing it brings good fortune. Enjoy life while you can, take your pleasure where you can, and when your wealth is gone, fortune will smile on you. Do not take the wrong path. . . . Ximen Nao, you goddamned Ximen Nao, stay out of my business. I am now a donkey with the fires of lust burning inside me. When Ximen Nao enters the picture, even if it's only his recollections, the result is a recapitulation of a bloody, corrupt history. A river ran across the open fields between the Ximen and Old Man Zheng villages. A dozen sandy ridges meandered along both sides of the stream like writhing dragons, all covered with tamarisk bushes in such profusion I couldn't see beyond them. A major battle had been fought there, with airplanes and tanks, and the victims of that battle still lay where they died. Stretchers had filled the streets of Old Man Zheng Village, loaded with wounded soldiers, their moans and groans accompanying the chilling caws of crows in the air. But enough talk about wartime, since that is when donkeys are used to transport machine guns and ammunition in the thick of battle, and a handsome black donkey like me would not have been able to avoid conscription.

Long live peace! In peacetime, a donkey can freely tryst with the female of his choice. We'd agreed to meet on the river's edge; light from the moon and stars was reflected off the shallow water, like slithering silver snakes. Accompanied by the low chirping of autumn insects and cooled by night breezes, I left the road, climbed over the sandy bank, and stepped into the river, which swallowed up my feet. The smell of the water reminded me how dry my throat was and gave rise to a desire to drink. Which is what I did, though I made sure not to drink too much of the sweet, cold river water, since I needed to run a bit more and didn't want a lot of water sloshing around in my stomach. My thirst slaked, I climbed the opposite bank and began walking down a twisting path, moving in and out of the tamarisk bushes until

I was standing atop a high sandy ridge, where her smell swept over me, thick and powerful. My heart was beating wildly against my ribs, my blood heated up, my excitement was so great I lost the ability to bray and was reduced to emitting choppy whinnies. My darling donkey, my treasure, my most adorable, my dearest, my sweetheart! Oh, how I want to embrace you, to wrap my legs around you, to nibble your ears, to kiss your eyes and lashes and pink nose and lips like flower petals. My darling, my cherished, I fear only that my breath will melt you, that by mounting you I'll break you. My tiny-footed little donkey, I know you are near. My tiny-footed little donkey, you do not know how much I love you.

I raced toward the smell, but halfway down the ridge, I saw a sight that tested my courage. My donkey was running wild amid the tamarisk, spinning around and kicking out with her hooves, braying loudly, as she tried to sound intimidating. In front and in back, to one side or the other, she was the intended victim of a pair of gray wolves; unhurriedly, biding their time, sometimes moving as a team, sometimes as individuals, they probed, they moved in and out, they feigned an attack. A treacherous, lethal pair of predators, they were patiently wearing her down; when, her strength and will gone, she lay down on the ground, they would go straight for the throat. Then, after they'd drunk their fill of her blood, they would tear open her abdomen and eat her now useless vital organs. Only death awaited any donkey meeting up with a pair of wolves working in tandem at night on a sandy ridge. My little donkey, if I hadn't shown up, your unhappy fate would have been sealed. Love has saved you. Is there anything else that could erase the innate fears of a donkey and send him to rescue you from certain death? No. That is the only one. With a call to arms, I, Ximen Donkey, charged down the ridge and headed straight for the wolf that was tailing my beloved. My hooves kicked up sand and dust as I raced down from my commanding position; no wolf, not even a tiger, could have avoided the spearhead aimed at it. It saw me too late to move out of the way, and I thudded into it, sending it head over heels. Then I turned and said to my donkey, Do not fear, my dear, I am here! She moved close to me; I sensed the violence with which her chest was rising and falling and could feel the sweat covering her body. I nibbled her neck to comfort and encourage her. Don't be afraid, I'm here. There's nothing to fear from these wolves. Stay here while I smash their heads with my hooves of steel!

The wolves' eyes were green as, shoulder to shoulder, they held their ground, boiling with anger at my sudden appearance, as if I'd fallen out of the sky. If not for me, they'd already be feasting on donkey meat. I knew they would not take defeat lying down, that having come down from the mountains, they would not and could not pass up this opportunity. Their strategy had been to drive the poor donkey onto the sandy ridge, with its tamarisk bushes, expecting her to get bogged down in the loose sand. For us to win the fight, we had to get away from the sandy soil, and fast. After starting her down the ridge, I turned and followed, walking backward. The wolves matched our progress, at first following behind me, but then splitting up and running ahead to launch a frontal attack. My dear, I said, see that river at the foot of this ridge? The ground is rocky there, good and hard, and the shallow water is clear enough to see the bottom. All we have to do is make a mad dash for the river. Once we're in the water, the wolves will have lost their advantage, and victory will be ours. Call up all the courage you have, my dear, to run down this slope. We have size and inertia going for us. We'll also be kicking sand in their eyes. So let's make that mad dash, and we're safe. Ready to do as I said, she moved up next to me, and we took off, leaping across tamarisk bushes, the pliant branches scraping our bellies on the way. It was like riding a wave, and we were soon like two tidal waves racing toward the shore. Through my peripheral vision, I saw the wolves stumbling and tumbling and looking pathetic in the chase. They did not reach the riverbank, coats covered with sand, until we were safely in the water and catching our breath. I told her to drink. Drink it slowly, my dear, don't choke and don't drink too much or you'll be cold. Her eyes brimmed with tears as she nipped me on the rump. I love you, my good little brother, she said. If you hadn't shown up to rescue me, I'd be in the wolves' stomachs by now. By saving you, my darling, I saved myself. I've been in a deep depression ever since I was reborn as a donkey. But since meeting you, I've come to realize that even something as lowly as a donkey can know supreme happiness when love exists. I was a man in my former life, a man with a wife and two concubines, but for me there was only sex, no love. I mistakenly thought I was a happy man, but now I see how pitiable I was. A donkey seared by the flames of love is happier than any man. And a male that has the good fortune to rescue his beloved from the mouths of wolves, who can demonstrate his courage and wisdom in front of his beloved, is given a chance to satisfy his masculine vanity. Because of you, my dearest, I've become an honorable donkey and the happiest animal on the face of the earth. We nibbled away each other's itches, we rubbed each other's hides, we were a perfect couple, our shared emotions deepening with words of tenderness, to the point where I nearly forgot the wolves on the riverbank.

They were hungry wolves, salivating at the thought of our tasty flesh. There was no quit in that pair, and much as I longed to consummate our relationship, I knew that would only put us both in our graves. They were just waiting for something like that to occur. At first, they stood on rocks and lapped up water like dogs. Then they sat on their haunches, raised their heads to the sky, and howled at the forbiddingly cold half moon.

Several times I lost sight of reason and reared up on my hind legs to mount my beloved. The wolves moved toward us before my front legs touched her body. My abrupt stop sent them scurrying back to the bank. They clearly had an abundance of patience, and I knew I needed to go into attack mode, but only with my donkey love's cooperation. Together we rushed the wolves' position on the riverbank. They leaped to safety and then made their way slowly up the sandy ridge. We weren't going to fall into that trap. Instead we crossed the river and galloped off in the direction of Ximen Village. The wolves charged into the water, which came up to their bellies and slowed them down. Let's go after them, my beloved, I said, let's put these savages out of their misery. Having already mapped out a strategy, we virtually flew back to the river, where we jumped and splashed water into their eyes to confuse them before attacking with our hooves. The wolves struggled to get away, but their coats were weighted down by the water. I reared up and aimed my hooves at one of them, but it darted out of the way, so I spun around and landed on the back of the second wolf, driving it under the water, where I held it as bubbles rose to the surface. Meanwhile, the first wolf leaped onto the neck of my beloved. Seeing the danger she was in, I abandoned the drowning wolf and kicked out with my rear hooves, hitting the attacker square in the head. I felt the crack of bone and watched as it crumpled and lay flat in the water; movements in its tail showed it was still alive. Meanwhile its half-drowned partner had crawled up onto the bank, its fur sticking to its body, now revealed as gaunt, bony, and very ugly. My beloved rushed up onto the bank, cut off its escape route, and began pounding it with her hooves. Spinning and twisting to avoid the deluge of falling hooves, it slid and rolled back into the water, where I reared up again and came down hard on its head. The green lights in their eyes slowly dimmed. To make sure they were both dead, we took turns smashing our hooves into their bodies until they were pinned among the rocks in the riverbed; mud and wolf blood dirtied the water all around.

Together we walked upriver, not stopping until the water was clear again and we could no longer smell wolf blood. She turned to look at me and nibbled my hide affectionately with a twittering sound. Then she spun around and offered me the ideal position. I want you, my dear, mount up. Me, a pure and innocent donkey with a beautiful body and superior genes, in order to continue a superior lineage, I will give them to you, along with my virginity, my lovely Huahua donkey, only to you. I then rose up like a mountain, held her body with my front legs, and thrust forward. Feelings of great joy erupted, surging over me, and over her. My god!

7

Fearing Trouble Huahua Makes a Solemn Vow
Naonao Shows His Prowess by Biting a Hunter

We coupled six times that night, seemingly a physiological impossibility for donkeys. But I swear to the Jade Emperor in Heaven that I am not lying, I take a vow before the moon's reflection in the river that I am telling the truth. I was no ordinary donkey, nor was she. In a former life she'd been a woman who died for love; when she released passion that had been pent up for decades, she could not stop. Exhaustion finally set in when the red morning sun first appeared on the horizon. It was an empty, transparent exhaustion. Our spirits seemed raised to a state of sublimation by our profoundly soulful love, made beautiful beyond imagining. We combed one another's manes, thrown into disarray, and cleaned each other's mud-streaked tails, all with our lips and teeth. The tender light of devotion flowed unchecked from her eyes. Humans are overweening creatures, believing themselves to have raised amorous feelings to the greatest heights, while in fact, nothing can stir up a man's passions like a female donkey. Here, of course, I refer to my donkey, Han Donkey, the one belonging to Han Huahua. After standing in the middle of the river to drink the clear water, we sauntered up to the bank to dine on reeds that had already turned yellow, but retained enough moisture for us, and juicy red berries. We frightened birds away as we ate, and spotted a fat snake slithering out from a clump of grass. It must have been looking for a place to sleep through the winter, so it didn't pester us. After we had told one another everything there was to tell, it was time to choose pet names. She called me Naonao, I called her Huahua.

Naonao and Huahua. We'll stay together forever. Heaven and earth cannot tear us apart. How does that sound, Naonao? It sounds wonderful, Huahua. Let's become wild donkeys and live amid the meandering ridges of sand, among the lush tamarisk bushes, alongside the clear water of this worry-free river. We'll eat nice green grass when we're hungry, we'll drink from the river when we're thirsty, and we'll lie down to sleep together, coupling often, loving and caring for one another always. I'll swear to you that I'll never look at another female donkey, and you'll swear to me that you'll never let another male mount you. I swear it, my dear Naonao. Darling Huahua, I swear it too. You must not only ignore other female donkeys, but mustn't even look at a mare, Naonao, Huahua said as she nipped my hide. Humans are shameless the way they mate male donkeys with female horses to produce strange animals they call mules. Don't worry, Huahua. Even if they blindfolded me, I'd never mount a horse. But you need to promise me you'll never let one mount you, because male horses and female donkeys also produce mules. Don't worry, Naonao. Even if they tied me to a stake, I'd keep my tail tucked tightly between my legs. What I have belongs only to you. . . .

We lay in our love nest, neck to neck, like a pair of swans frolicking on the water. Words cannot chronicle our mutual affection; our tender feelings were indescribable. We stood shoulder to shoulder at the edge of the river, gazing at our reflection. Lights flashed in our eyes, our lips swelled, our beauty came from love; we were a match made in heaven.

As we stood there lost in love in the bosom of nature, a clamor rose behind us. Jerking our heads up out of our reveries, we saw a group of twenty or so people fanning in on us.

Run, Huahua! — Don't be afraid, Naonao. Look, it's people we know.

Huahua's attitude turned my heart cold. Of course I knew who they were, I could see that right off. The crowd included my master, Lan Lian, his wife, Yingchun, and two of Lan Lian's village friends, the brothers Fang Tianbao and Fang Tianyou (martial arts masters in a story by Mo Yan). My cast-off halter was cinched around Lan Lian's waist; he was holding a long pole with a noose on the end, while Yingchun was carrying a lantern whose red paper shade was so badly singed the metal frame beneath it was exposed. One of the Fang brothers was carrying a rope in his hand, the other was dragging a club behind him. Others in the crowd included Han, the humpbacked stone mason, his half-brother, Han Qun, plus some men I'd seen before but whose names I didn't know. They looked tired and dirty, which meant they'd been out looking all night.

Run, Huahua! — I can't, Naonao. — Then grab hold of my tail with your teeth, and I'll pull you along. — Where can we run to, Naonao? They'll catch up to us sooner or later, Huahua said meekly. Besides, they'll probably go back for their rifles, and no matter how fast we run, we can't outrun a bullet. Huahua, I replied, disappointed, you haven't forgotten our vows already, have you? You swore to stay with me for all eternity, swore that we would be wild donkeys, to live in freedom, with no constraints, loving one another in nature's bosom. She hung her head as tears welled up in her eyes. Naonao, she said, you're a male donkey. You were relaxed after you pulled yourself out of me, not a care in the world. But now I'm carrying your offspring. I'm probably carrying twins, and my belly will soon be getting big. I'm going to need all the nutrition I can get; I want to be eating fried black beans, freshly milled bran, and crushed sorghum, all finely mashed and run three times through a sieve to make sure there are no stones or chicken feathers or sand. It's already October, and the weather is turning cold. How am I going to eat as I drag my big belly around when the ground hardens, snow falls, the river freezes over, and the grass is covered with a blanket of snow? Or, for that matter, find water to drink? Then, when the babies are born, where will I sleep? Even if I force myself to stay with you on a sandy ridge, how will our babies stand the bitter cold? If they freeze to death in the snow and ice, their bodies lying out in the cold like logs or rocks, won't you, their father, be heartbroken? Donkey fathers might be able to callously abandon their offspring, Naonao, but not their mothers. Or maybe some mothers can, but not your Huahua. Women can abandon their sons and daughter for their beliefs, but not donkeys. I ask you, Naonao, can you understand what a pregnant donkey feels?

Under the assault of Huahua's barrage of questions, I, Naonao, a male donkey, had no adequate comeback. Huahua, I said feebly, are you sure you're pregnant?

What a foolish question, Huahua said angrily. Six times in one night, Naonao, filling me with your seed. I'd be pregnant if I were a sawhorse, or a stone, or a log!

Ahhh, I muttered, crestfallen, as I watched her obediently walk over to meet her mistress.

Tears fell from my eyes, only to dry in the white heat of a nameless anger. I wanted to run, to bound away; I could not tolerate this sort of betrayal, however justified, and could not continue to live the humiliating life of a donkey in the Ximen estate. I turned and ran to the glittering surface of the river, my objective the tall sandy ridge, where the tamarisk grew in misty profusion, the pliant red branches serving as cover for red foxes, striped badgers, and sand grouses. So long, Huahua, go enjoy your life of splendor, I'll not miss the warmth of my donkey lean-to, I must answer the call of the wild and seek my freedom. But I'd not even made it to the riverbank when I discovered that there were people lying in wait in the tamarisk, their heads camouflaged with leaves and twigs, their bodies cloaked in rush capes the color of dry grass; they were armed with muskets like the one that splattered the brains of Ximen Nao. Terror-stricken, I turned and headed east along the bank toward the early morning sun. The hair on my hide was painted flame-red; I was a galloping ball of fire, a donkey whose head was like a burning torch. Death did not scare me; I had faced ferocious wolves without a trace of fear, but the black holes of those muskets pointing at me terrified me, not the weapons themselves, but the horrible image of splattered brains they created. My master must have anticipated my path of escape, since he crossed the river up ahead, not even taking off his shoes and socks beforehand. Water flew in all directions as he lumbered through the river toward me. I changed direction, but not quickly enough to avoid the pole he swung, and the noose fell around my neck. But there was no quit in me, no easy defeat. Calling on all my strength, I raised my head and thrust out my chest, tightening the noose and making me fight for every breath. My master pulled on the pole with all his might and leaned backward until he was nearly parallel with the water. He dug in his heels; I dragged him along, his feet digging ruts in the sandbar like plows.

In the end, as my strength waned and I could hardly breathe, I stopped running and was quickly surrounded, although the people held back, not daring to approach me. It was then that I was reminded of my reputation as a donkey prone to biting people. In the village, where life was peaceful and quiet, a donkey made news by causing injury with its teeth, and that news spread through the village like wildfire. But who among those men and women knew why I'd done that? Who could have guessed that the hole taken out of Ximen Bai's head had resulted from a kiss by her reincarnated husband, who had forgotten he was now a donkey, not a man?

Yingchun, displaying considerable courage, walked up to me with a handful of fresh green grass.

"Little Blackie," she muttered, "don't be afraid. I won't hurt you. Come home with me. . . ."

When she was standing next to me, she rested her left hand on my neck and put the grass in her right hand up to my mouth, stroking me gently as she shielded my eyes with her bosom. The sensation of her soft, warm breasts was all the stimulation Ximen Nao's memories needed to flood into my head, and tears spurted from my eyes. She whispered in my ear, and the hot breath of this hot-blooded woman made me lightheaded. My legs shook; I fell to my knees.

"Little black donkey," I heard her say, "my little black donkey, I know you've grown up and that you're looking for a mate. A man thinks of marriage, a woman wants a mate, a donkey wants to sire its young. I don't blame you for that, it's perfectly normal. Well, you found your mate and you've planted your seed, so now you can come home with me. . . ."

The other people quickly put my halter on and affixed the reins, adding a rusty-smelling chain, which they put in my mouth. Someone pulled the chain tight around my lower lip. The pain was so intense I had to flare my nostrils and gasp for air. But Yingchun reached out and hit the hand that was tightening the bit,

"Let that go," she said. "Can't you see he's injured?"

They tried to get me to stand. That's exactly what I wanted. Cows and sheep and pigs and dogs can lie down, but not donkeys, not unless they're dying. I struggled to get to my feet, but my body weighed me down. Was I going to die at the tender age of three? For a donkey, that was not good news under any circumstances, but the idea of dying like this really got to me. There in front of me was a broad road, divided into many little paths, each leading to a scene worth viewing. Swept away by intense curiosity, I had to go on living. As I rose up on shaky legs, Lan Lian told the Fang brothers to stick their long club under my belly, one on each side, while he went around behind me to hold up my tail. With Yingchun holding me around the neck, the Fang brothers gripped their ends of the pole and shouted, "Lift!" With their help, I stood up, still wobbly, my head drooping heavily. But I struggled to stay upright; I mustn't fall down again. I did it, I was standing straight.

The people walked around me, amazed and puzzled by the

bloody injuries on my rear legs and my chest. How could the act of mating produce injuries like that? they wondered. I also heard members of the Han family discussing similar injuries on their female donkey. Is it possible, I heard the older Fang brother ask, that the two animals spent the whole night fighting one another? His brother shook his head. Impossible. A man who'd come to help the Han family retrieve his donkey downriver, pointed to something in the river, and yelled:

"Come over here and tell me what this is!"

One of the dead wolves was rolling slowly in the water; the other was pinned underwater by a rock.

The crowd rushed over to see what he was pointing at, and I knew that it was wolf fur on top of the water and blood on the rocks — wolf blood and donkey blood — still filling the air around the spot with its stench. The signs of a fierce battle were obvious from prints on the rocks from wolf claws and donkey hooves and from the blood-streaked injuries to my and Huahua's bodies.

Two men rolled up their pant legs, took off their shoes and socks, and waded into the water to bring the two wolf carcasses up onto the bank. I sensed people turning to me with looks of respect, and I knew that Huahua was being honored by the same looks. Yingchun threw both arms around me and lovingly stroked my face; I felt moist pearls fall from her eyes onto my ears.

"Damn you all!" Lan Lian said proudly. "The next person who says anything bad about my donkey will answer to me! Everyone says that donkeys are cowards, that they turn tail and run if they see a wolf. But not my donkey. He killed two ferocious wolves all by himself!"

"Not by himself," stonemason Han corrected him indignantly. "Our donkey deserves credit too."

"Yes, you're right," Lan Lian said with a smile. "She does. And she's my donkey's wife."

"With such severe injuries, I doubt that this marriage was ever consummated," someone volunteered lightheartedly.

Fang Tianbao bent down to examine my genitals, then ran over to check underneath the Han family's female. He lifted up her tail and took a good look.

"Yes, it was," he announced authoritatively. "Take my word for it. You Hans are going to have a new donkey."

"Old Han, you'd better send a couple of pecks of black beans over to help our black donkey regain his strength," Lan Lian said somberly.

"Like hell!" was Han's curt reply.

By this time, the musket-armed men who had been hiding in the tamarisk bushes joined the others. Light on their feet, they moved furtively. Clearly, they were not farmers. Their leader was a squat man with piercing eyes. He walked up to the dead wolves and bent over to turn the head of one with the barrel of his weapon, after which he did the same to the abdomen of the other wolf. In a voice that betrayed surprise mixed with regret, he said:

"This is the destructive pair we've been looking for!"

One of his men, also armed with a musket, turned to the crowd and announced loudly:

"That does it. We can go back and report to our superiors now."

"I doubt that you people have seen these two," one of the men said to Lan Lian and the others. "They're not a pair of wild dogs, they're gray wolves, the kind you seldom see out on the plains. They fled from Inner Mongolia and left a bloody trail. They were both tricky and vicious. In just over a month they killed a dozen or more head of livestock, including horses, cows, even a camel. We think people were next on their menu. If word had gotten out, the people would have panicked, so we organized six hunting teams in secret, searching and lying in wait for these two day and night. Now it's over." Another one, a man with an obvious sense of his own importance, kicked one of the carcasses: "You never thought this day would come, you bastard!" he cursed.

The team leader took aim at the head of one of the wolves and fired. Flames from the barrel of his musket and the smoke that followed swallowed the animal up, its head now shattered, just like Ximen Nao's, the rocks splattered with grays and reds.

Another hunter took the hint and, with a smile, shot the other wolf in the abdomen. A fist-sized hole opened up in its belly, out of which a dirty mess of guts poured.

Dumbfounded by what they'd just seen, Lan Lian and the others could only gape at one another. Once the smell of gunpowder had dissipated, the melodious sound of flowing water beguiled their ears; a flock of sparrows numbering in the hundreds came on the air, rising and falling like a dark cloud. They settled with a loud fluttering sound on tamarisk bushes, bending the pliant branches like fruit-laden trees.

Waves of bird-talk enlivened the sandy ridges. To that was added the gossamer voice of Yingchun:

"What was that for? Why shoot dead wolves?"

"Is that your damned attempt to take credit for this?" Lan Lian thundered. "You didn't kill those wolves, my donkey did."

The leader of the hunting team took two brand-new notes and tucked one under my reins, the other under Huahua's.

"Do you really think you can shut me up with money?" Lan Lian said, spitting mad. "That's not going to happen!"

"Take back your money," Han the stonemason said. "Our donkeys killed those wolves, and we're taking them with us."

The hunter smirked.

"Good brothers," he said, "with one eye open and the other shut, everyone wins. You could plead your case until your lips were chapped, and no one would believe that your donkeys were capable of doing that. Especially now that one's head has been blown open and the other's belly has a gaping bullet hole."

"Our donkeys were clawed and bitten bloody by those wolves," Lan Lian shouted.

"I agree, they have wounds all over their bodies, and no one could say they weren't caused by wolves. And so . . ." The man smirked again. "Here's what that proves: Two attacked your donkeys, causing bloody injuries, but at the moment of greatest danger, the three members of the Number Six hunting team arrived on the scene and, with no thoughts for their own safety, engaged the wolves in a life-or-death battle. The team leader, Qiao Feipeng, stood face-to-face with the male wolf, took aim, and fired, shattering its head. A second member of the team, Liu Yong, took aim at the second wolf and pulled the trigger. The gun misfired. After he'd spent a whole night hiding amid tamarisk bushes, his powder was wet. The wolf opened her mouth, which seemed to spread all the way to her ears, bared her gleaming white fangs, let loose a hideous, spine-tingling roar, and went straight for Liu Yong, who rolled out of the way of her first charge. But his heel caught between two rocks, and he lay faceup on the sandy ground. With a leap, her tail stretched out behind her, she charged again like a yellow blur. At that desperate moment, in less time than it takes to tell, Lü Xiaopo, the youngest member of the hunting team, took aim and fired at the animal's head. But since it was a moving target, the shot hit her in the abdomen. When she fell, she rolled on the ground, spilling her guts all over the place, a terrifying sight. Though she was a vile predator, it was too terrible to see. By this time, Liu Yong had reloaded his musket and fired at the wolf, which was still rolling in agony. But because of the distance between them, the buckshot sprayed the area and peppered the dying animal in many spots. She stretched out her legs and died."

While Qiao was weaving his story, Liu Yong stepped backward, aimed, and fired buckshot into the wolf's carcass, creating holes with burned edges.

"So, what do you think?" Qiao asked, smiling proudly. "Whose story do you think people will believe, yours or mine?" He put more gunpowder into the barrel of his musket and said, "You outnumber us, but don't even think of taking the wolves back with you. We hunters have an unwritten rule: Whenever there's a dispute over a kill, the hunter with the most buckshot in it keeps it. And there's another rule. A hunter is within his rights to shoot anyone who walks off with his kill. It's a matter of retaining his self-esteem."

"You're fucking thugs!" Lan Lian said. "You're going to be visited by nightmares after this. You'll pay for taking what doesn't belong to you."

The hunter just laughed. "Reincarnation and retribution are nonsense people use to trick old ladies. I don't believe them for a minute. But maybe there's something we can do together. If you'll help us carry these carcasses to town on the backs of your donkeys, the county chief will reward you handsomely and I'll give you each a bottle of the finest liquor."

I couldn't take any more of that. Opening my mouth to bare my front teeth, I took aim at that flat head of his. But he was too fast for me. He moved his head away just in time, but I got him by the shoulder. Now you'll see what a donkey can do, you thug! You people think that only felines or canines, with their sharp claws and teeth, know how to be predators, and that we donkeys, with our hooves, only know how to eat grass and husks of grain. You are all formalists, dogmatists, book worshippers, and empiricists. Well, today, I'm going to teach you that when he's irritated, a donkey will bite!

After gripping the hunter's shoulder in my teeth, I raised my head and shook it back and forth. I tasted something sour, unpleasant, and very sticky. As for the crafty, smooth-talking fellow, well, he was on the ground, bleeding from his shoulder, and unconscious.

He could always tell the county chief that one of the wolves had bitten him on the shoulder during the fight. Or he could say that when the wolf buried its fangs in his shoulder, he reacted by biting the animal on the back of its head. As to how he'd managed to finish off the wolf, well, he could say what he wanted.

Our people, meanwhile, saw that things had turned ugly, so they quickly got us on the road home, leaving the wolf carcasses and the wolf hunters on the sandbar.

8

Ouch, Ximen Donkey Loses a Gonad
A Colossal Hero Arrives at the Estate

January 24, 1955, was the first day of the first month of the Yiwei Lunar Year. Mo Yan settled on that day as his birthday. During the 1980s, officials who hoped to hold positions for several more years or who wanted to climb the bureaucratic ladder even higher would change their age down and their schooling up, but who would have thought that Mo Yan, certainly no official, would join the fad? It was a fine morning, with flocks of pigeons circling in the early morning sky, their melodic cooing coming first from one direction, then the other. My master stopped working to look up into the sky, the blue half of his face making for a pretty sight.

Over the previous year, the eight acres of Lan family land had produced 2,800 catties of grain, an average of 350 per acre. In addition, they had brought in twenty-eight pumpkins planted on the ridges between crops and twenty catties of high-quality hemp. He refused to believe the co-op's announced harvest of 400 catties per acre, and I heard him say to Yingchun more than once, "Do you think they could grow 400 catties the way they go about it? Who do they think they're fooling?" Her smile could not hide the worries she felt deep down. "You're the man of the house, but why must you always sing a different tune than the others? They've got numbers, we're all by ourselves. Remember, a powerful tiger is no match for a pack of wolves." Lan Lian glared at her. "What are you afraid of? We have the support of District Chief Chen."

My master, wearing a brown felt cap and a brand-new padded coat cinched at the waist by a green cloth sash, was brushing my coat, which was very comforting physically; his praise did the same for my spirit.

"Old Blackie," he said, "my friend, you worked hard last year. Half the credit for the good harvest goes to you. Let's do even better this year. It'll be like kicking that damned co-op in the nuts!"

I warmed up as the sunlight kept getting brighter. The pigeons were still up in the sky, the ground was covered by shredded red-and-white paper, firecracker debris. The night before, the sky had lit up and explosions had rocked the earth, creating clouds of gunpowder smoke; the compound looked and smelled like a war zone, to which was added the lingering odor of meaty dumplings, year-end cakes of sticky rice, and all kinds of sweets. The master's wife had placed a bowl of dumplings in water to cool them off, then dumped them into my food trough with my regular feed, patted me on the head, and said:

"Little Blackie, it's New Year's, have some dumplings."

I'm the first to admit that dumplings at New Year's is an exceptional courtesy to extend to a donkey. They were nearly treating me as one of their own, a human just like them. I'd earned the respect of my master after killing those two wolves and now had the finest reputation of any donkey in the eighteen villages and hamlets within a radius of a hundred *li*. So what if those three damned hunters got away with the carcasses? The people here knew what really happened. No one denied that the Han family donkey had played a role in that battle, but they knew I'd pretty much carried the day and she'd been a bit player, one whose life I'd saved, by the way. I'd already reached the gelding age, and my master had put the fear of the knife in me. But he didn't mention it again after my battlefield heroics. The previous fall I'd gone out to work in the fields with my master, followed by Xu Bao, the local veterinarian, pack over his back and a brass bell in his hand, a man who specialized in castrating so-called beasts of burden. His shifty eyes kept returning to a spot between my rear legs. His body reeked of cruelty, and I knew what he had in mind. He was one of those bastards who enjoyed swallowing a donkey or bull gonad with a cup of strong liquor. He was definitely not fated to die in bed. Well, anyway, I watched him carefully and never let my guard down. The minute he walked up behind me, I'd greet him with a pair of flying hooves right in his crotch. I wanted that cruel son of a bitch to know what it felt like to leave the field without his family jewels. And if he

approached me from the front, I'd bite him in the head. That's what I did best. He was real sneaky, turning up suddenly here and there, but always staying a safe distance away and not giving me a chance to go into action. When people on the road saw stubborn Lan Lian walking ahead of his now famous donkey, followed by that castrating son of a bitch, they asked questions like:

"Say, Lan Lian, time to turn your donkey into a eunuch?"

or:

"Xu Bao, did you find something to go with your liquor again?"

"Don't do it, Lan Lian," someone shouted. "That donkey had the balls to take on those wolves. Each nut supplies some of an animal's courage, so he must have as many as a sack of potatoes."

Some boys on their way to school fell in behind Xu Bao to sing a ditty about him:

> Xu Bao Xu Bao, sees an egg and takes a bite!
> Without an egg to bite, he sweats all night.
> Xu Bao Xu Bao, a donkey dick of a sight.
> A scoundrel who won't stand up and fly right . . .

Xu Bao stopped and glared at the little brats, reached into his pack, pulled out a gleaming little knife, and shouted threateningly:

"You'd better shut up, you little bastards! Master Xu here will cut the balls off the next one of you who makes up something like that!"

The boys huddled together and responded with goofy laughs. So Xu Bao took several steps forward, and the boys matched him, going backward. Then Xu Bao charged, and the boys scattered in all directions. Xu Bao turned back to me, gelding on his mind. The boys came back, formed up, and followed him, repeating their ditty:

> Xu Bao Xu Bao, sees an egg and takes a bite!

This time, Xu Bao had no time for those little pests. Taking a wide berth, he ran up in front of Lan Lian and started walking backward.

"Lan Lian," he said, "I know this donkey's bitten people. Every time he does that, you have to come up with medical expenses and lots of apologies. I say geld him. He'll be back in three days, completely recovered, the most obedient donkey you could ask for, guaranteed."

Lan Lian ignored him; my heart was pounding. My temper was something Lan Lian knew all too well. So he grabbed hold of the bit in my mouth and kept me from going after the man.

Xu Bao scuffled along, raising dust as he walked backward, the bastard, probably something he did a lot. He had a shriveled little face adorned with baggy triangular eyes and front teeth with a big space between them, from which spittle sprayed whenever he talked.

"Take my advice, Lan Lian," he said, "you need to geld him; gelding is good, it'll save you trouble. I usually charge five yuan, but for you I'll do it for nothing."

Lan Lian stopped, smirked, and said:

"Xu Bao, why don't you go home and geld your old man?"

"What kind of talk is that?" Xu Bao squeaked.

"If that bothers you, then let's see what my donkey has to say." He let go of my reins and said, "Sic him, Blackie!"

With a loud bray, I reared up, the way I'd mounted Huahua, aiming to come down on Xu Bao's scrawny head. People out on the street screeched in horror; the little brats swallowed their shouts. Now I'm going to feel and hear my hooves landing on Xu Bao's cranium, I was thinking. But that didn't happen. I didn't see the contorted look of shock I'd expected and didn't hear the howls of fright I'd hoped for; what I did see, out of the corner of my eye, was a slippery figure darting under my exposed belly, and I had a premonition of bad things to come. Unfortunately, my reactions were too slow; a sudden chill struck my genitals, followed by a sharp, intense pain. I felt an immediate sense of loss and knew I'd been tricked. Twisting my body to look behind me, the first thing I saw was blood on my rear legs. The next things I saw was Xu Bao, standing by the roadside, a bloody gray gonad in the palm of his hand; he was grinning from ear to ear and showing off his prize to a bunch of gawkers, who shouted their approval.

"Xu Bao, you bastard, you've ruined my donkey," my master cried out in agony. But before he could leave my side and tear into the evil veterinarian, Xu Bao dropped the gonad into his bag and flashed his knife in a threatening manner. My master fell back weakly.

"I did nothing wrong, Lan Lian," Xu Bao said as he pointed to the gawkers. "It was obvious to everyone, including our young friends here, that you let your donkey attack people, and it was my right to protect myself. It's a good thing I was on my toes, or my head would be a squashed gourd by now. So I'm the good guy here, Lan Lian."

"But you've ruined my donkey. . . ."

"That was my plan, and I'm the one who could have done just that. But I felt sorry for a fellow villager and held back. That donkey has three gonads, and I only took one. That'll calm him down a bit, but he'll still be a spirited animal. You should damn well be thanking me. It's not too late, you know."

Lan Lian bent over to examine my privates, where he discovered that Xu Bao was telling the truth. That helped, but not enough to thank the man. No matter how you looked at it, the sneaky bastard had taken one of my gonads without prior consent.

"Xu Bao, take heed," Lan Lian said. "If anything happens to my donkey because of this, you'll pay, and pay dearly."

"The only way this donkey won't live to be a hundred is if you mix arsenic into his feed. I advise you not to work him in the field today. Take him home, feed him nutritious food, and rub on some salt water. The wound will heal in a couple of days."

Lan Lian took Xu Bao's advice without any public acknowledgment. That eased my suffering a little, but it was still with me, and still strong. I glared at the bastard who would soon swallow my gonad, and was already planning my revenge. But the honest truth was, this unforeseen incident, sudden and effective, instilled in me a degree of grudging respect toward the unimpressive, bowlegged little man. That there were people like that in the world, someone who made a living castrating animals and was good at his job — relentless, accurate, fast — was something you'd have to see to believe. *Hee-haw, hee-haw* — My gonad, tonight you'll accompany a mouthful of strong liquor down into Xu Bao's guts, only to wind up in the privy tomorrow, my gonad, gonad.

We'd only walked a short distance when we heard Xu Bao call out from behind:

"Lan Lian, know what I call that gambit I just employed?"

"Fuck you and your ancestors!" Lan Lian fired back.

This was greeted with raucous laughter from the gawkers.

"Listen carefully," Xu Bao said smugly. "You and your donkey both. I call it 'Stealing peaches under the leaves.' "

"Xu Bao Xu Bao, stealing peaches under the leaves! Lan Lian Lan Lian, embarrassment teaches . . ." The young geniuses made up new lines, which they sang as they walked behind us all the way to the Ximen estate compound.

Lots of people created a lively atmosphere in the compound. The five children from the east and west rooms, all dressed in New Year's finery, were running and hopping all over the place. Lan Jinlong and Lan Baofeng had reached school age, but hadn't yet started school. Jinlong was a melancholy boy, seemingly weighted down with concerns; Baofeng was an innocent little girl, and a real beauty. Though they were the offspring of Ximen Nao, there were no bonds between them and Ximen Donkey. The true bonds had been between Ximen Donkey and the two offspring delivered to the donkey belonging to Han Huahua, but tragically, they and their mother had all died when the youngsters were barely six months old. The death of Huahua was a terrible emotional blow to Ximen Donkey. She had been poisoned; the two babies, the fruits of my loins, died from drinking their mother's milk. The birth of twin donkeys had been a joyous event in the village, and their deaths, along with their mother, had saddened the villagers. Stonemason Han had nearly cried himself sick, but someone unknown was very happy; that someone was the person who had mixed poison into Huahua's feed. District headquarters, thrown into turmoil over the incident, sent a special investigator, Liu Changfa — Long-haired Liu — to solve the case. A crude and inept individual, Liu summoned the residents in groups to the village government offices and interrogated them by asking the sorts of questions you might hear on a phonograph record. The results? No results. After the incident, in his story "The Black Donkey," Mo Yan fixed the blame for poisoning the Han family's donkey on Huang Tong, and although he made what appeared to be an air-tight case, who believes anything a novelist says?

Now I want to tell you, Lan Jiefang, born on the same day of the same month in the same year as I, I mean you, you know who you are, but I'll refer to you as He, well, He was five years old, plus a little, and as He grew older, the birthmark on his face got bluer and bluer. Granted, He was an ugly child, but a cheerful one, lively and so full of energy He couldn't stand still. And talk? That mouth of his never stopped, not for a second. He dressed like his half brother Jinlong, but since He was shorter, the clothes always looked too big and baggy.

With his cuffs and shirtsleeves rolled up, He looked like a miniature gangster. But I knew He was a good-hearted boy who found it hard to get people to like him, and my guess is He could thank his nonstop talking and his blue birthmark for that.

Now that we've gotten him out of the way, let's talk about the two girls of the Huang family, Huang Huzhu and Huang Hezuo. They wore lined jackets with the same floral pattern, cinched at the waist by sashes with butterfly knots. Their skin was fair, their eyes narrow and lovely. The Lan and Huang families were neither especially close nor particularly distant, altogether a complicated relationship. For the adults, getting together was awkward and uncomfortable, since Yingchun and Qiuxiang had both shared a bed with Ximen Nao, making them simultaneously rivals and sisters; now they were both remarried, but they still shared the same compound, living with different men in different times. By comparison, the children got along fine, a perfectly innocent and simple relationship. Given his natural melancholy, Lan Jinlong remained more or less aloof. Lan Jiefang and the Huang twins were best friends, with the girls always calling the boy Elder Brother Jiefang; as for him, a boy who loved to eat, he was always willing to save some of his sweets for the girls.

"Mother, Jiefang gave his candy to Huzhu and Hezuo," Baofeng told their mother on the sly.

"It's his candy, he can give it to anyone he wants," Yingchun said to her daughter with a pat on the head.

But the children's stories haven't really begun yet. Their dramas won't take center stage for another ten years or more. So for the time being, they'll have to stay with their minor roles.

Now is the time for a very important character to come on stage. His name is Pang Hu, which, interestingly, means Colossal Tiger. He has a face like a date and eyes like the brightest stars. He's wearing a padded army cap and a crudely stitched jacket on which a pair of medals is pinned. He keeps a pen in his shirt pocket, a silvery watch on his wrist. He walks on crutches; his right leg is perfectly normal, but his left one ends at the knee, his khaki pant leg knotted just below the stump. He wears a new leather shoe, with the nap on the outside, on his good leg. The moment he came through the gate, everyone in the compound — adults, children, even me — was awestruck. During those days, men like that could only have been heroic members of China's volunteer army who had returned from the fighting in Korea.

The battlefield hero walked up to Lan Lian, his crutches thudding against the brick path, his good leg landing heavily at each step, as if putting down root, the empty cuff on the other leg swaying back and forth.

"If I'm not mistaken," he said, "you must be Lan Lian."

Lan Lian's face twitched in response.

"Hello, there, volunteer soldier," Lan Jiefang, the chatterbox, ran up to greet the stranger, oozing reverence. "Long live the volunteer soldiers!" he said. "You're a war hero, I just know it. What do you want with my father? He's not much of a talker. I'm his spokesman."

"Shut up, Jiefang!" Lan Lian barked. "This is adult business, stay out of it."

"No harm done," the war hero said with a kindly smile. "You're Lan Lian's son, Lan Jiefang, am I right?"

"Do you know how to tell fortunes?" Jiefang sputtered, unable to conceal his surprise.

"No," the war hero said with a crafty smile, "but I know how to read faces." That said, he turned serious once more, tucking one crutch under his arm and offering his hand to Lan Lian. "Glad to meet you, my friend. I'm Pang Hu, new director of the district Supply and Marketing Co-op. Wang Leyun, who sells farming implements in the sales department of the production unit, is my wife."

Lan Lian, at a momentary loss, shook hands with the war hero, who saw in his perplexed look that he was in a bit of a fog. Turning around, the man shouted:

"Gather round, all of you!"

Just then a short, rotund woman in a blue uniform, a pretty little girl in her arms, strode in the gate. The white-framed eyeglasses she wore told everyone that she was not a farmer. Her baby had big round eyes and rosy cheeks like autumn apples. Beaming from ear to ear, she was the perfect example of a happy child.

"Ah," Lan Lian exclaimed happily, "so this is the comrade you're talking about." He turned toward the western rooms and called to his wife. "Come out here, we have honored guests."

I recognized her too. The memory of something that had happened the previous winter was still clear. Lan Lian had taken me to the county town to get some salt, and on the way back we'd met up with this Wang Leyun. She was sitting by the side of the road, heavily pregnant and moaning. She was wearing a blue uniform then too, but the bottom three buttons were undone to accommodate her swollen belly. Her white-framed eyeglasses and fair skin marked her immediately as a government worker. Her savior had arrived, as she saw it. Please, brother, help me, she said with considerable difficulty. — Where are you from? What's happened? — My name is Wang Leyun. I work at the district Supply and Marketing Co-op. I was on my way to a meeting, since I didn't think it was time, but . . . but . . . Seeing a bicycle lying nearby in the bushes, we knew at once the predicament she was in. Lan Lian walked around in circles, rubbing his hands anxiously. What can I do? he asked. How can I help you? — Take me to the county hospital, hurry. My master unloaded the bags of salt I was carrying, took off his padded coat and tied it across my back, and helped the woman get on. Hold on, Comrade, he said. She grabbed my mane and moaned some more as my master took my reins in one hand and held on to the woman with the other. — Okay, Blackie, let's go. I took off, for I was a very excited donkey. I'd carried plenty of things on my back — salt, cotton, crops, fabric — but never a woman, and I danced a little jig, toppling the woman onto my master's shoulder. Steady, Blackie! my master ordered. I got the idea. Blackie got the idea. So I started trotting, taking care to keep my gait smooth and steady, like flowing water or drifting clouds, something a donkey does best. A horse can only be smooth and steady when it gallops, but if a donkey gallops instead of trots, it makes for a bumpy ride. I sensed that this was a solemn, even sacred, mission. It was also stimulating, and at that time I felt myself existing somewhere between the realms of man and beast. I felt a warm liquid soaking into the jacket under her and onto my back, also felt sweat from the woman's hair dripping onto my neck. We were only a couple of miles from the county town, on the road leading straight to it. Weeds on both sides of us were knee-high; a panicky rabbit ran out of the weeds and right into my leg. Well, we made it into town and went straight to the People's Hospital. Back in those days, hospital personnel were caring people. My master stood in the hospital entrance and shouted: Somebody, come help this woman! I brayed to help out. A bunch of men and women in white smocks came running out and carried the woman inside, but not before I heard *waa-waa* sounds emerge from between her legs as she was taken off my back. On our way back home, my master was in obvious low spirits, grumbling over the sight of his wet, dirty padded coat. I knew he was superstitious and believed that the excretions of a woman in labor were not only dirty, they were unlucky. So when we reached the spot where we'd encountered the woman, he frowned, his face darkened, and he said, What does all this mean, Blackie? This was a new coat. What am I going to tell my wife?

Hee-haw, hee-haw — I gloated, happy to see him facing a dilemma. — Is that a smile, Blackie? He untied the rope and, with three fingers, lifted the coat off of my back. It was . . . well, you know. He cocked his head, held his breath, and flung the water-soaked and very heavy jacket as if it were made of dog skin, watching it sail into the weeds like a big, strange bird. The rope also had bloodstains, but since he needed it to tie down the sacks of salt, he couldn't throw it away, so he dropped it on the ground and rolled it around in the dirt with his foot until it changed color. Now all he was wearing was a thin jacket with several missing buttons; his chest turned purple from the cold, and with his blue face, he looked like one of Lord Yama's little attendants. He bent down, scooped up two handfuls of dirt, and rubbed it on my back, then brushed it off with some weeds he plucked from the side of the road. Blackie, he said, you and I performed an act of charity, didn't we? *Hee-haw, hee-haw* — He stacked the sacks of salt on my back and tied them down. Then he looked over at the bicycle in the weeds. Blackie, he said, as I see it, this bicycle ought to belong to me now. It cost me a coat and a lot of time. But if I covet something like this, I'll give up the credits I earned from that act of charity, won't I? *Hee-haw, hee-haw* — All right, then, let's take this good deed as far as it'll go, like seeing a guest all the way home. So he pushed the bicycle and drove me — actually, there was no need to do that — all the way back to the country town and up to the hospital entrance, where he stopped and shouted, You in there, the woman in labor, I'm leaving your bicycle here at the entrance! *Hee-haw, hee-haw* — More people ran out. — Okay, Blackie, let's get out of here. He smacked me on the rump with my reins. Let's go, Blackie . . .

Yingchun's hands were coated with flour when she came out. Her eyes lit up when she saw the beautiful little girl in the arms of Wang Leyun. She reached over.

"Pretty baby," she mumbled. "Pretty baby, so cute, so pudgy . . ."

Wang Leyun handed the baby to Yingchun, who cradled it in her arms, lowered her head, and smelled and kissed her face.

"She smells wonderful," she said, "just wonderful . . ."

Waa-waa. The baby wasn't used to all that fuss.

"Hand her back to the comrade," Lan Lian demanded. "Just look at you, more wolf than human. What baby wouldn't be scared to death?"

"That's all right, no harm done," Wang Leyun said as she took the baby back and got her to stop crying.

Yingchun tried to rub the flour off her hands.

"I'm terribly sorry," she apologized. "Look how I dirtied her clothes."

"We're all farmers," Pang Hu said. "No need to worry. We came today especially to thank you. I hate to think what might have happened if not for you."

"You not only took me to the hospital, you even made a second trip to return my bicycle," Wang Leyun said emotionally. "The doctors and nurses all said you couldn't find a more honest man than Lan Lian if you went searching with a lantern."

"I've got a good donkey," Lan Lian said to hide his embarrassment. "He's fast and steady."

"Yes, you're right, he is a good donkey," Pang Hu said with a little laugh. "And famous to boot. A famous donkey!"

Hee-haw, hee-haw —

"Say, he understands us," Wang Leyun said.

"Old Lan," Pang Hu said as he reached into a bag he was carrying, "if I were to try to reward you, that would demean you and spoil a budding friendship." He took out a cigarette lighter and lit it. "I took this from one of the American devils. I'd like you to have it as a little memento." Then he took out a little brass bell. "This I asked someone to get for me at a secondhand market. It's for your donkey."

The war hero walked up to me and draped the bell over my neck.

"You're a hero, too," he said as he patted me on the head. "This is your medal."

I shook my head, so moved I felt like crying. *Hee-haw, hee-haw —* The bell rang out crisply.

Wang Leyun took out a bag of candy and parceled it out among the children, including the Huang twins. "Are you in school?" Pang Hu asked Jinlong. Jiefang jumped in before Jinlong could reply. "No." "You need to go to school, that's something you have to do.

Young people are the future red leaders in our new society, our new nation, and they mustn't be illiterate." "Our family hasn't joined the co-op, we're independent farmers. My father won't let us go to school." "What? An independent farmer? How can an enlightened man like you be independent? Is this true? Lan Lian, is it?"

"It's true!" The resounding answer came from the gateway. We turned to see who it was — Hong Taiyue, the village chief, Party secretary, and head of the local co-op. Dressed the same as always, he seemed more gaunt than ever, and more alert. He strode into the compound, all skin and bones, offered his hand to the war hero, and said, "Director Pang, Comrade Wang, happy New Year!"

"Yes, happy New Year!" The crowd surged in, spreading New Year's greetings, but none of the old forms. No, they were new phrases to fit all the great changes; here I give only that one example.

"Director Pang, we're here to talk about setting up an advanced co-op, combining the smaller co-ops in neighboring villages into one big one," Hong Taiyue said. "You're a war hero, how about a talk?"

"I haven't prepared anything," Pang said. "I came specifically to thank Comrade Lan for saving the lives of my wife and child."

"You don't need to prepare anything, just speak to us. Tell us about your acts of heroism, we'd love to hear that." Hong Taiyue began clapping his hands, and in no time applause was sweeping over the compound.

"All right," Pang said as he was carried by the crowd over beneath the apricot tree, where someone placed a chair. "Just an informal chat." Choosing not to sit, he stood before the crowd and spoke in a loud voice: "Ximen Village comrades, happy New Year! This year's New Year's is a good one, next year's will be even better, and that is because, under the leadership of the Communist Party and Comrade Mao Zedong, our liberated peasants have taken the path of agricultural co-ops. It is a great golden highway, broadening with each step!"

"But there are some people who stubbornly tread the path of individual farming and prefer to compete with our co-ops," Hong Taiyue interjected, "and who refuse even to admit defeat!"

Everyone's eyes were on my master, who looked down at the ground and fiddled with the cigarette lighter the war hero had given him. *Click* — flame — *click* — flame — *click* — flame — His wife nudged him to stop. He glared at her. "Go in the house!"

"Lan Lian is an enlightened comrade," Pang Hu said, raising his voice. "He led his donkey in courageously taking on the wolves and he led it again in coming to the rescue of my wife and child. His refusal to join the co-op results from a momentary lack of understanding, and you people must not coerce him into joining. I fully believe that Comrade Lan Lian will one day join the co-op and travel with us down the great golden highway."

"Lan Lian," Hong Taiyue said, "if you still refuse to join the advanced co-op, I'll get down on my knees to you!"

My master untied my reins and led me over to the gate, the bell around my neck, the gift from the war hero, ringing crisply.

"Lan Lian, are you going to join or aren't you?" Hong shouted from behind.

My master stopped just outside the gate. "Not even if you get down on your knees!" His voice was muffled.

9

Ximen Donkey Meets Ximen Bai in a Dream
Following Orders, Militiamen Arrest Lan Lian

My friend, I shall now relate events of 1958 for you. Mo Yan did that in many of his stories, but he was spinning nonsense, not to be believed. What I am going to reveal is my own personal experience, a valuable window on history. At the time, the five children, including you, in the Ximen estate were all second-graders in the Northeast Gaomi Township Communist Elementary School. I shall omit any discussion of the great smelting campaign and the backyard furnaces; nothing of interest there. Nor will I touch upon the communal kitchens or the great movements of farmers throughout the county. Why prattle on about things in which you were involved? As for abolishing villages and amalgamating production brigades, creating a county-wide People's Commune overnight, well, you know more about that than I. What I'd like to relate are some experiences I, a donkey raised by an independent farmer, had in 1958, a special year; they are the stuff of legend. That is, I assume, what you'd like to hear. I'll do what I can to avoid political issues, but forgive me if they find their way into my tale.

It was a moonlit night in May. Warm breezes from the fields carried delightful aromas: mature wheat, riverside reeds, tamarisk bushes growing on sandbars, felled trees... These aromas greatly pleased me, but not enough to bolt from the home of that stubborn independent farmer of yours. If you want to know the truth, what had the appeal to get me to bite through my halter and run away, whatever the consequences, was the smell of a female donkey, a normal reaction by a healthy adult male. Nothing to be ashamed of there. Ever since losing a gonad to that bastard Xu Bao, I couldn't help feeling that I'd lost some prowess in you-know-what. Sure, I still had two of the things left, but I didn't have much faith in them to do the job. Until that night, that is, when they awoke from their dormancy; they heated up, they expanded, and they made that organ of mine stand up like a steel rod, emerging time and time again to cool off. The image of a female donkey left no room in my mind for affairs that were capturing the hearts and souls of people at the time: she had a perfect body, with nice long legs; her eyes were clear and limpid; and her hide was smooth and glossy. I wanted to meet and mate with her; that was all that counted. Everything else was nothing but dog shit.

The gate at the Ximen compound had been taken down and removed, apparently to be used as fuel for a smelting furnace. That meant that merely biting through my halter was an act of liberation. But don't forget, years earlier I had jumped the wall, so gate or no gate, there was nothing to hold me back.

Out on the street, I raced after that infatuating odor. I had no time to take in the sights along the way, all of which were related to politics. I ran out of the village, heading for the state-run farm, where the light of fires turned half the sky red. That, of course, was the largest furnace site in Northeast Gaomi Township Later events would prove that only what was produced in those furnaces could lay claim to the title of usable steel. Credit for that went to the congregation of veteran steel engineers who had studied abroad, only to return to their homeland as rightists undergoing reform through labor.

These engineers stood by the furnaces supervising the work of temporary workers taken from their farms to produce steel. The great fire inside turned their faces red. A dozen or more furnaces lined the wide river on which crops were transported. To the west of the river stood Ximen Village; to the east, the state-run farm. Both of Northeast Gaomi Township's rivers fed this larger river, and where they converged was a marshy, reedy spot with a sandbar and miles of tamarisk bushes. At first, the villagers kept their distance from the people at the state-run farm, but this was a time of unity, when the great Army Corps was doing battle. Oxcarts, horse-drawn wagons, even two-wheeled carts pulled by people, crowded the highway carrying a brown ore they said was taken from iron mines. The backs of donkeys and mules were laden with what they said was iron ore; old folks, women, even children, carried what they said was iron ore in baskets, all in a constant stream, like a colony of ants, taking their loads to the giant furnaces at the state-run farm. In later years people would say that the great smelting campaign produced nothing but smelting waste; that isn't so. The Gaomi County officials showed how clever they were by putting the rightist engineers to work, resulting in the production of usable steel.

In the mighty torrent of collectivization, the residents of the People's Commune forgot all about Lan Lian, the independent farmer, leaving him free to function outside the authorized system for several months. Then when the co-op's harvest was left to rot while people smelted steel, he comfortably brought in a bumper crop of grain from his eight acres of land. He also cut down several thousand catties of reeds at places attended by no one, with which he planned to weave reed mats to sell in the winter, when there was no farmwork to do. Having forgotten all about him, people naturally had no thoughts for his donkey either. So at a time when even rail-thin camels were brought out to carry iron ore, I, a husky male donkey, was left to freely chase after a smell that stirred my passions.

As I ran down the road, I passed many people and their animals, including a dozen or more donkeys — but not a trace of the female whose tantalizing aroma drew me to her. The farther I traveled, the weaker the scent, disappearing at times, then reappearing, as if to lead me far off into the distance. I was relying not only on my sense of smell but on intuition as well, and it told me I was not heading in the wrong direction, that the one I was following was either carrying or pulling a load of iron ore. There was no other possibility. At a time like this, with tight organization and ironclad demands, was it remotely possible that a second carefree donkey was hiding somewhere, broadcasting the fact that she was in heat? Prior to the creation of the People's Commune, Hong Taiyue flung curses at my master: Lan Lian, you're the only fucking independent farmer in all of Gaomi County. That makes you a black model. Wait till we've gotten through this busy spell, and you'll see how I deal with you! Like a dead pig that's beyond a fear of scalding water, my master struck a nonchalant pose. "I'll be waiting."

I crossed the bridge over the transport river that had been bombed out years earlier and only recently rebuilt. I skirted the area where furnaces were blazing, without seeing a female donkey. My appearance invigorated the furnace workers, who were dead on their feet, like a bunch of drunks. They moved to surround me, holding steel hooks and spades, hoping to capture me. Impossible. They were already swaying from exhaustion, and there was no chance they could summon up the energy to catch me if I ran; if they somehow managed that, they'd be too weak to hold me. They shouted, they yelled, all a bluff. The roaring fires made me seem even more impressive than usual, since they made my black hide glisten like satin, and I was pretty sure that these men could not dredge up a memory of ever having seen such a sight as filled their eyes at this moment, the first truly noble and dignified donkey they'd ever encountered. *Hee-haw* — I charged them as they were attempting to encircle me, sending them scattering. Some stumbled and fell, others ran away, dragging their tools behind them, like a defeated army beating a retreat. All but one, a short fellow in a hat made of willow twigs. He poked me in the rump with his steel hook. *Hee-haw* — That son of a bitch's hook was still hot, and I smelled something burning. Damned if he hadn't branded me! I kicked out with my rear hooves and ran out of the fiery surroundings into a dark area where there was plenty of mud and from there into the reeds.

The moist mud and watery mist gradually calmed me down and lessened the pain on my rump; but it still hurt, worse than the bite the wolf had taken out of me. Continuing along the muddy bank, I stopped to drink some river water, which had the unpleasant taste of toad piss. I swallowed some little objects that I knew were tadpoles. Nauseating, to be sure, but what was I to do? Maybe they had a curative effect, so it would be like taking a dose of medicine. I lost all my senses, didn't know what to do, when that lost odor suddenly reappeared, like a red silk thread in the wind. Afraid of losing it yet again, I took up the chase anew, this time confident that it would lead me to that female donkey. Now that I'd put some distance between me and the furnace fires, the moon seemed brighter. Frogs croaked up and down the river, and from somewhere far off I detected human shouts and the beating of drums and gongs. I didn't have to be told that I was hearing the hysterical shouts of fabricated victory by fanatical people.

And so I followed the red thread of aroma for a very long time, leaving the smelting furnaces of the state-run farm far behind. After passing through a bleak village from which no sound emerged, I stepped onto a narrow path bordered on the left by wheat fields and on the right by a grove of white poplars. Ready to harvest, the wheat field gave off a dry, scorched odor under the chilled beams of moonlight. Critters moving through the field made rustling noises as they broke tassels off the wheat stalks and sent grains raining to the ground. Light bouncing off the poplar leaves turned them into silver coins. But who had time to take in the lovely scenery? I'm just trying to give you an idea of what it was like. Suddenly —

The aroma flooded the air, like fine liquor, like honey, like husks straight from the frying pan. The red thread in my imagination became a thick red rope. After traveling half the night and encountering countless hardships, like finding a melon at the end of a vine, I was finally about to meet my true love. I bolted forward but abruptly slowed down after only a few steps, for there in the light of the moon a woman all in white sat cross-legged in the middle of the path. No trace of a donkey, female or otherwise. And yet the smell of a donkey in heat hung in the air around us. Was this a trap? Was it possible that a woman could emit a smell that could drive a male donkey crazy? Slowly, cautiously, I approached the woman. The closer I got, the more brightly Ximen Nao's memory lit up in my mind, like a series of sparks creating a wildfire, pushing my donkey consciousness into darkness and reasserting my human emotions. I didn't have to see her face to know who she was. Outside of Ximen Bai, no other woman exuded the smell of bitter almonds. My wife, you poor, poor woman!

Why do I refer to her that way? Because of the three women in my life, she suffered the bitterest fate. Yingchun and Qiuxiang both remarried peasants who had gained stature in the new society. She alone, as a member of the landlord class, had been forced to live in the Ximen ancestral caretaker's hut and suffer through unbearable reform through labor. The squat, confining hut, with its rammed earth walls and a thatched roof, was so dilapidated it could not withstand the onslaught of wind and rain, and was in danger of toppling; when that happened it would bury her forever. The bad elements had all joined the People's Commune, under the supervision of the poor and lower-middle peasants, reforming themselves through labor; in accordance with common practice, she too should have been spending her days as a member of the iron ore transport teams or breaking up large chunks of ore under the supervision of Yang Qi and his ilk, her hair in disarray, her face covered with dirt and grime, clothes torn and tattered, more ghost than human; so why was she sitting in this lovely setting, dressed in white and giving off a compelling fragrance?

"I knew you'd come, husband, I knew you'd be here. I was sure that after all these years of suffering, after seeing so much betrayal and shameless behavior, that you would recall my loyalty." She seemed to be both talking to herself and pouring out her grief to me. Her voice carried the tone of sweetness and desolation. "I knew that my husband had been turned into a donkey, but you are still my husband, the man I lean on. Only after you were turned into a donkey did I feel that we were true kindred spirits. Do you recall how we met on grave-sweeping day in the year you were born? You passed by the hut where I live on your way to pick greens with Yingchun. I saw you that day while I was secretly adding fresh dirt to your and your parents' graves, and you ran up to me, nibbling at the hem of my jacket with your soft pink lips. I looked up and saw you, such a lovely little donkey. I rubbed your nose and your ears; you licked my hand. My heart ached yet grew hot, I felt both sorrow and warmth, and tears flowed from my eyes. Through the mist I saw that your eyes were also moist, and in them I saw my own reflection. The look was one I knew well. I know you suffered injustice, my husband. I covered your grave with the dirt in my hand and then sprawled atop it, sobbing quietly with my face pressed to the fresh yellow earth. You gently touched my backside with your hoof, so I turned my head and once again saw that look in your eyes. My husband, I believe with all my heart that you have been reborn as a donkey. How unkind Lord Yama has been to turn my cherished husband into a donkey. But then, I thought, maybe that was your choice, that in your abiding concern for me, you would rather come back as a donkey to be my companion. Maybe Lord Yama planned to let you be reborn into a rich and powerful family, but you chose the life of a donkey instead, my dear, dear husband. . . . The grief welled up inside me and I could not keep myself from wailing piteously. But in the midst of my wails, the sound of distant bugles, brass drums, and cymbals came on the air. Yingchun, who was standing behind me, said softly, Don't cry, people are coming. She was still a woman of conscience. A packet of spirit money was hidden under the wild greens in her basket, and I guessed that she had brought it to burn at your grave. I forced myself to stop crying and watched as you and Yingchun rushed off into the grove of black pines. At every third step you stopped and turned to look, at every fifth you hesitated, and I knew the depth of your feelings for me. The contingent of people drew near, drums and gongs signaling their approach, red flags the color of blood, floral wreaths the color of snow. Teachers and students from the elementary school were coming to sweep the graves of martyrs. A light rain was falling, swallows were flying low in the sky. Peach flowers were like a sunset in the martyrs' cemetery, visitors' songs filled the air, but your wife did not dare cry over your grave, my husband. That night you went wild in the village office compound and bit me, and everyone thought you'd gone crazy, but I knew you were calling attention to my unfair treatment. They had already dug up the family treasure. Did they really think there was more buried at Lotus Bay? I treated that bite as a kiss from my husband. It may have been more violent than most, but that was the only way I could print it indelibly on my heart. Thank you for that kiss, my husband, for it was my salvation. When they saw the blood, they were so afraid I might die they carried me back into my home. My home, the run-down little hut by your gravesite. I lay down on the damp, dirt-covered sleeping platform, hoping for an early death, so that I too could be reborn a donkey, and we would be reunited again, a loving donkey couple . . ."

Xing'er, Bai Xing'er, my wife, my very own . . . I shouted, but all that came out were donkey sounds. The throat of a donkey thwarted my attempts at human speech. I hated my donkey body. I struggled to say something to you, but reality is cruel, and no matter what words of love I formed in my heart, all that came out was *Hee-haw, hee-haw* — So all I could do was kiss you, caress you with my hooves, and let my tears fall onto your face. A donkey's tears are as big as the biggest raindrops. I washed your face with my tears as you lay on your back looking up at me, tears filling your eyes as well as you murmured, Husband, my husband . . . I tore off your clothes with my teeth and covered you with kisses, suddenly reminded of our wedding night. You were so shy, panting so alluringly, and I could tell that you were a daughter from a refined family, a girl who could embroider a double lotus and recite the "Thousand Poets' Verses" . . .

A crowd of people, hooting and hollering, surged into the Ximen compound and snapped me out of my dream. There would be no good times for me, no conjugal bliss. They brought me back from my half human–half donkey existence. I was once again a donkey from head to tail. The people all wore scowls of arrogance as they barged into the western rooms and emerged with Lan Lian in custody; they stuck a white paper flag in his collar behind his neck. Though he tried to resist, it took little effort to subdue him. And when he tried to complain, they said, We've been ordered to inform you that you can farm your own land if that's what you want, but smelting steel and building a reservoir are national projects requiring the participation of all citizens. We overlooked you when we built the reservoir, but you're not getting out of work this time. Two men dragged him bodily out of the compound and another came to lead me out of my lean-to, a fellow with considerable experience in dealing with domestic animals: sidling up next to me, he grabbed hold of the bit and jerked it up into my mouth at the slightest sign of resistance, causing unbearable pain and making it hard for me to breathe.

My master's wife ran out in an attempt to stop him from leading me away.

"You can take my husband out to work, that's fine by me," she said, "and I'll smash rocks and smelt steel if you want. But you cannot take my donkey with you."

With a display of anger and impatience, the man said:

"What do you take us for, madam citizen, puppet soldiers out to confiscate people's livestock? We're core members of the People's Commune Militia, and we're following orders, just doing our job. We're taking your donkey on loan. You'll get him back when we're finished with him."

"I'll go in his place!" Yingchun said.

"Sorry, but those aren't our orders and we're not authorized to improvise."

Lan Lian broke loose from the men holding him.

"There's no call for you to treat me like this," he said. "Building a reservoir and smelting steel are national projects, so of course I'll go without complaint. Tell me what to do, and I'll do it. But I have one request. Let my donkey go with me."

"That's something we're not authorized to permit. Take up your request with our superiors."

So the man led me out cautiously, ready for anything, whereas Lan Lian was escorted out of the compound and the village as if he were an army deserter, past the onetime district offices and all the way over to the People's Commune, which, as it turned out, was where the red-nosed blacksmith and his apprentice had fitted me with my first set of iron shoes at their furnace. As we were passing the Ximen ancestral cemetery, some middle-school students under the supervision of their teachers were digging up graves and removing headstones; a woman in white mourning attire came flying out of the caretaker's hut and ran straight for the students, throwing herself onto the back of one of them, her hands around his neck. But a brick flew over and hit her in the back of the head. Her face was ghostly white, as if covered with quicklime. Her earsplitting shrieks angered me. Flames brighter than molten steel licked up out of my heart, and I heard human speech tear from my throat:

"Stop! I, Ximen Nao, demand that you stop digging up my ancestral graves! And don't you dare strike my wife!"

I reared up, ignoring the lip-splitting pain from the bit, lifting the man beside me up into the air and then flinging him into the mud alongside the road. As a donkey, I could have treated what I was seeing with indifference. But as a man, I could not allow anyone to dig up my ancestral graves or strike my wife. I charged into the crowd of students and bit one of their teachers on the head, then knocked down a student who was bent over to scoop out dirt. The students fled, their teachers lay on the ground. I watched Ximen Bai roll around, and cast one last glance at the open graves before turning and racing into the dark confines of a pine forest.

10

Favored with a Glorious Task, I Carry a County Chief
Meeting Up with a Tragic Mishap, I Break
a Front Hoof

My anger slowly subsided after two days of running wild across Northeast Gaomi Township territory, hunger forcing me to subsist on wild grass and the bark of trees. This coarse diet brought home the hardships of living the life of a donkey. A longing for the fragrant feed I'd gotten used to led me back to the life of a common domestic animal, and I began the trek back to my village, drawing close to human habitation.

At noontime that day, I reached the outskirts of Tao Family Village, where I saw a horse carriage at rest beneath a towering ginkgo tree. The heavy aroma of bean cakes mixed with rice straw filled my nostrils. Two mules that had been pulling the carriage were standing beside a basket hanging from a triangular trestle feasting on the fragrant feed.

I had always looked down on mules, bastard animals that were neither horse nor donkey, and wanted nothing more than the opportunity to bite them into oblivion. But on this day, fighting was the furthest thing from my mind. What I wanted was to edge up to the basket and get my share of some good food to replenish the strength I'd used up during two days of rushing headlong from one end of the territory to the other.

Holding my breath, I approached them gingerly, striving to keep the bell around my neck from announcing my arrival. Though that bell, placed there by the crippled war hero, enhanced my stature, there were times when it worked against me. When I ran like the wind, it signaled the passage of a mighty hero; at the same time, it kept me from ever breaking free of pursuit by humans.

The bell tinkled. The heads of the two mules, both much bigger than I, shot up. Knowing at once what I was after, they pawed the ground and snorted menacingly, warning me not to set hoof in their territory. But with all that good food in front of my eyes, how could I simply turn and walk away? I surveyed the scene: The black, long-necked mule was yoked in the wagon shafts, so he didn't worry me. The second animal, a young black mule that was tethered and fet-tered, would also have trouble dealing with me. All I had to do to get to the food was stay clear of their teeth.

They tried to intimidate me with irritatingly loud brays. Don't be so stingy, you bastards, there's enough there for all of us. Why hog it all? We have entered the age of communism, when mine is yours and yours is mine. Seeing an opening. I ran up to the basket and took a huge mouthful. They bit me, sending the bits clanging. Bastards, if it's biting you want, I'm the master. I swallowed the mouthful of feed, opened wide, and bit the yoked mule on the ear, chomping down and sending half its ear fluttering to the ground. The next bite landed on the neck of the other mule and left me with a mouthful of mane. Chaos ensued. Grabbing the basket in my teeth, I backed up quickly. The tethered mule charged. I spun around, showing him my backside before kicking out with both legs. One hoof hit nothing but air, the other landed smack on his nose. Pain drove him headfirst to the ground. Then, eyes closed, he got up and ran in circles until his legs got all entangled with the rope. I ate like there was no tomorrow. But tomorrow came anyway, as the carter, a blue bundle tied around his waist and a whip in his hand, ran out of a nearby yard, screaming at me. I sped up the eating process. He ran at me, whip writhing in the air like a snake and making popping sounds. He was upper-body strong and bowlegged, exactly what an experienced carter should look like. The whip was like an extension of his arm, and that was worri-some. Clubs didn't scare me, they're easy to dodge. But a whip is unpredictable. Someone who knows how to handle one can bring down a powerful horse with it. I'd seen it done and didn't want it to be done to me. Uh-oh, here it comes! I had to move out of danger, which I did, though now I could only gaze at the feed basket. The driver chased after me. I ran off a ways. He stopped, keeping one eye on the feed basket. Then he looked over at his wounded mules and cursed a blue streak.

He said that if he had a rifle, one bullet is all it would take. That made me laugh. *Hee-haw, hee-haw* — By that I meant, If you didn't have that whip in your hand, I'd run up and bite you in the head. He caught my meaning, obviously realizing that I was that notorious donkey that went around biting people. He neither dared to put down his whip nor press me too hard. He glanced around, obviously looking for help, and I knew that he both feared and wanted to get me in his clutches.

I picked up the scent of an approaching band of men. It was the militiamen who'd been after me a few days earlier. I'd only had time to eat about half of what I'd wanted, but one mouthful of such high-quality feed was the equivalent of ten mouthfuls of what I'd been eating. My energy was restored, my fighting will revitalized. You're not going to hem me in, you two-legged dullards.

Just then a square, grass-green, and very strange object sped my way, bouncing from side to side and trailing dust. I know now that it was a Soviet Jeep-like vehicle; actually, these days I know a lot more than that: I can point out an Audi, a Mercedes, a BMW, and a Toyota; I also know all about U.S. space shuttles and Soviet aircraft carriers. But at the time, I was a donkey, a 1958 donkey. This strange object, with its four rubber wheels, was clearly faster than me, at least on level ground. But it would be no match for me on rugged terrain. Allow me to repeat Mo Yan's comment: A goat can scale a tree, a donkey is a good climber.

For the convenience of my story, let's just say I knew what a Soviet Jeep was. It struck fear in me, but also piqued my curiosity, and I hesitated just long enough for the militiamen to catch up and surround me. The Soviet Jeep blocked my escape route when it stopped less than a hundred yards from me and disgorged three men. One of them I recognized right off: the former district, now county, chief. He hadn't changed much in the years since I'd last seen him; even the clothes on his back looked like the same ones he'd worn in the past.

I had no bone to pick with County Chief Chen. In fact, the praise he'd showered on me years before continued to warm my heart. He'd also been a donkey trader, and that I liked. In a word, he was a county chief with emotional ties to donkeys, and I not only trusted him, I was actually glad to see him.

With a wave of his hand, he signaled his men not to approach any closer. Then with another wave he signaled the militiamen behind me, who wanted either to capture or kill me to bring credit to themselves, to stop where they were. He alone, raising his hand to his mouth to give out a whistle that was music to my ears, walked up to me. When he was four or five yards away, I spotted the toasted bean cake in his hand and drank in its heavenly fragrance. He treated me to a familiar little whistled melody, which brought feelings of mild sadness. My tensions dissolved, my taut muscles relaxed, and I wished for nothing more than to place myself in this man's caressing hands. And then he was standing next to me, draping his right arm over my neck and holding the bean cake up to my mouth with the other. When the cake was gone, he rubbed the bridge of my nose and muttered:

"Snow Stand, Snow Stand, you are a fine donkey. Too bad people who have no understanding of donkeys turned you wild and unruly. It's all right now, you can come with me, I'll teach you how to become a first-rate, obedient, and courageous donkey that everyone will love."

He first ordered the militiamen away and told his driver to return to town. Then he climbed aboard, bareback, like a pro, straddling me right at the spot where I was most comfortable. He was a practiced rider who knew his way around a donkey. With a pat on my neck, he said:

"Let's go, my friend."

From that day forward I was County Chief Chen's mount, carrying a lean Party official with an abundance of energy all over the vast spaces of Gaomi County. Up till that time, my movements had been restricted to Northeast Gaomi Township, but after I became the county chief's companion, my traces were found north to the sandbars of the Bohai, south to the iron mines of the Wulian Mountain Range, west to the billowing waters of Sow River, and east to Red Rock Beach, where the fishy smells of the Yellow Sea permeated the air.

This was the most glorious period of my entire donkey life. During those days, I forgot about Ximen Nao, forgot about all the people and events that had colored his life, even forgot about Lan Lian, with whom I'd had such close emotional ties. As I recall those days now, the basis of my contentment was most likely linked to a subconscious appreciation of "official" status. A donkey, of course, respects and fears an official. The deep affection that Chen, the head of an entire county, held for me is something I'll remember to the end of my days. He personally prepared my feed and would let no one else brush my coat. He draped a ribbon around my neck, decorated with five red velvet balls, and added a red silk tassel to the bell.

When he rode me on an inspection tour, I was invariably accorded the most courteous reception. Villagers supplied me with the finest feed, gave me clean spring water to drink, and groomed my coat with bone combs. Then I was led to a spot on which fine white sand had been spread, where I could roll around comfortably and take my rest. Everyone knew that taking special care of the county chief's donkey made him very happy. Patting my rump was equivalent to patting the county chief's behind with flattery. He was a good man who preferred a donkey over a vehicle. It saved gasoline and was superior to walking on his inspection trips to mine sites in the mountains. I knew, of course, that at bottom, he treated me the way he did because of the deep affection he'd developed for my kind during his years as a donkey trader. The eyes of some men light up when they see a pretty woman; the county chief rubbed his hands when he saw a handsome donkey. It was perfectly natural that he would feel good about a donkey with hooves as white as snow and intelligence the equal of any man.

After I became the county chief's mount, my halter served no further purpose. A surly donkey with a reputation for biting people had, in short order, thanks to the county chief, become a docile and obedient, bright and clever young donkey — nothing less than a miracle. The county chief's secretary, a fellow named Fan, once took a picture of the county chief sitting on my back during an inspection tour of the iron mines; he sent it with a short essay to the provincial newspaper, where it was prominently published.

I met Lan Lian once during my stint as the county chief's mount. He was carrying two baskets of iron ore down a narrow mountain path while I was on my way up the mountain with the county chief on my back. When he saw me, he dropped his carrying pole, spilling the iron ore, which rolled down the mountain. The county chief was irate:

"What was that all about? Iron ore is too valuable to lose, even a single rock. Go down and bring that back up."

I could tell that Lan Lian hadn't hear a word the county chief said. His eyes flashed as he ran up, threw his arms around my neck, and said:

"Blackie, old Blackie, at last I found you . . ."

Recognizing that he was my former owner, Chen turned to Secretary Fan, who followed us everywhere on an emaciated horse, and signaled for him to come deal with the matter. Fan, always alert to what his boss wanted, jumped off his horse and pulled Lan Lian off to one side.

"What do you think you're doing? This is the county chief's donkey."

"No, it isn't, it's mine, my Blackie. He lost his mother at birth and only survived because my wife fed him millet porridge from his first days. We relied upon him for our livelihood."

"Even if what you say is true," Secretary Fan said, "if the county chief hadn't come along when he did, a group of militiamen would have made donkey meat out of him. He now has a very important job, taking the county chief into villages and saving the nation the expense of a Jeep. The county chief cannot do without him, and you should rejoice in knowing that your donkey is playing such an important role."

"I don't care about that," Lan Lian replied stubbornly. "All I know is, he's my donkey, and I'm taking him with me."

"Lan Lian, old friend," the county chief said. "These are extraordinary times, and this donkey has been an enormous help to me in negotiating these mountain paths. So let's just say I've got your donkey on temporary loan, and as soon as the steel smelting project has ended, you can have him back. I'll see that the government gives you a stipend for the duration of the loan period."

Lan Lian wasn't finished, but an official from the co-op walked up, dragged him back to the side of the road, and said sternly:

"Like a goddamn dog who doesn't know how lucky he is to be carried in a sedan chair, you should be thanking your ancestors for accumulating good luck, which is why the county chief has chosen your donkey to ride."

Raising his hand for the man to stop the harangue, the county chief said:

"How's this, Lan Lian? You're a man of strong character, for which I admire you. But I can't help feeling sorry for you, and as chief official of this county, I hope you'll soon be leading your donkey into the co-op and stop resisting the tides of history."

The co-op official held Lan Lian to the side of the road so the county chief — so that I — could pass, and when I saw the look in Lan Lian's eyes, I felt pangs of guilt and wondered to myself: Could this be considered an act of betrayal to my master on my way up to a higher limb? The county chief must have intuited my feelings, for he patted me on the head and said consolingly:

"Let's go, Snow Stand. Carrying the county representative is making a greater contribution than tagging along behind Lan Lian. Sooner or later, he'll join the People's Commune, and when he does, you'll become public property. Wouldn't it be perfectly normal for the county chief to ride on a People's Commune donkey?"

As you'll see, this was a case of: Extreme joy begets sorrow; when things reach their extreme, they turn and head in the opposite direction. At dusk on the fifth day after the encounter with my former master, I was carrying the county chief home from a visit to the iron mine at Reclining Ox Mountain when a rabbit hopped across the path in front of me. Spooked, I reared up and caught my right front hoof between some rocks when I landed. I fell, and so did the county chief, who hit his head on a sharp rock, which knocked him out and opened a gash in his head. His secretary immediately told some men to carry the unconscious county chief down the mountain. Meanwhile, some farmers tried to free my hoof, but it was stuck tight and deep. Nothing worked. They pushed, they pulled, and then I heard a *crack* rise up from the rocks and felt a pain so severe I too passed out. When I came to, I discovered that my right front hoof and the bones that connected it to my leg were still stuck in the rocks, and that my blood had stained a large section of the roadway. I was overcome by grief. My usefulness as a donkey was over, that I knew. The county chief would have no further use for me. Even my master would have no interest in feeding a donkey that could no longer work. All I had to look forward to was the butcher's knife. They'd slit my throat, and once I'd spilled all the blood in my body, they'd skin me and slice my flesh into morsels of tasty meat that would wind up in people's stomachs . . . Better that I take my own life. I glanced over at the cliff and could see the misty village below. With one loud *hee-haw* — I rolled across the roadway toward the dropoff. What stopped me was a loud cry from Lan Lian.

He had run up the mountain. He was all sweaty, and his knees were spotted with blood. He'd obviously stumbled and fallen on his way up. In a voice distorted by flowing tears, he shouted:

"Blackie, my old Blackie . . ."

He wrapped his arms around my neck as some farmers lifted up my tail and moved my rear legs to help me stand up. Excruciating pain shot up my injured leg when it touched the ground and sweat gushed from my body. Like a dilapidated wall, I toppled to the ground a second time.

I heard one of the farmers say in what passed for sympathy:

"He's a useless cripple, that's the bad news. The good news is he's got plenty of meat on his bones. We ought to be able to sell him for a decent sum to the butchers."

"Shut the fuck up!" Lan Lian swore angrily. "Would you take your father to the butchers if he broke his leg?"

That stunned everyone within earshot. But the silence was quickly broken by the same farmer.

"Watch your mouth! This donkey, is he your father?" He rolled up his sleeves, itching for a fight, but was held back by the men around him.

"Let it go," they said. "Just let it go. The last thing you want is to piss off this madman. He's the only independent farmer in the whole county. They know all about him up at the county chief's office."

The crowd broke up, leaving just the two of us. A crescent moon hung in the sky; the sight and the situation made me sad beyond words. After venting against the county chief and that bunch of farmers, my master took off his jacket and tore it into strips to bind my injured leg. *Hee-haw, hee-haw* — That really hurt. He wrapped his arms around my head, his tears falling onto my ears. "Blackie, old Blackie, what can I say to make this better? How could you believe anything the officials said? At the first sign of trouble, all they care about is saving their precious official. They don't give a damn about you. If they'd sent for a stonemason to break up the rocks that pinned your hoof, it might have been saved." The words were no sooner out of his mouth than he let go of my head and ran over to the rocky spot in the road, where he reached down and tried to retrieve my separated hoof. He cried, he swore, he panted from sheer exhaustion, and he eventually managed to retrieve it. Standing there holding it in his hand, he wailed, and when I saw the iron shoe, worn shiny after all that time, I broke down and cried too.

With the encouragement of my master, I managed to stand up

again; the thick bindings made it possible — barely — for me to rest my injured leg on the ground, but my balance, sadly, was lost. Fleet-footed Ximen Donkey was no more, replaced by a cripple who lowered his head and listed to the side with every step. I entertained the thought of flinging myself off the mountain and putting an end to this tragic life; my master's love was all that kept me from doing just that.

The distance from the iron mine at Reclining Ox Mountain to Ximen Village in Northeast Gaomi Township was about twenty miles. If all four of my legs were in good shape, that little distance would not have been worth mentioning. But now one of them was useless, making the going unbelievably hard; I left traces of flesh and blood along the way, marked by wrenching painful cries from my throat. The pain made my skin twitch like ripples on a pond.

My stump was beginning to stink by the time we reached Northeast Gaomi Township, drawing hordes of flies whose buzzing filled our ears. My master broke some branches from a tree and twisted them together to make a switch to keep the flies away. My tail hung limply, too weak to swish; thanks to an attack of diarrhea, the rear half of my body was covered with filth. Each swing of my master's switch killed many flies, but even greater numbers swarmed up to take their place. So he took off his pants and tore them into strips to replace the first bindings. Now he was wearing only shorts and a pair of heavy, thick-soled leather boots. He was a strange and comical apparition.

Along the way we dined on the wind and slept in the dew. I ate some dry grass, he subsisted on some half-rotten yams from a nearby field. Shunning roads, we walked down narrow paths to avoid encountering people, like wounded soldiers deserting the scene of battle. We entered Huangpu Village on a day when the village dining hall was open, the delightful smells wafting our way. I heard my master's stomach rumble. He looked at me with tears in his reddened eyes, which he dried with his dirty hands.

"Goddamn it, Blackie," he blurted out, "what are we doing? Why are we hiding from everyone? We've done nothing to be ashamed of. You were injured while working for the people, so the people owe you, and by taking care of you like this, I'm doing the people's work too! Come on, we're going in."

Like a man leading an army of flies, he walked with me into the open-air dining hall. Steamers heaping with lamb dumplings were brought out of the kitchen and placed on a table. They were gone almost immediately. Lucky diners skewed the hot dumplings with thin tree branches and gnawed at them from the side; others tossed them from hand to hand, slurping hungrily.

Everyone saw us come in, cutting a sorry figure, ugly and filthy, and smelling as bad as we looked. Tired and hungry, we gave them a terrific fright, and probably disgusted them in the bargain, costing them their appetite. My master swatted my rump with his switch, sending a cloud of flies into the air, where they regrouped and landed on all those steaming dumplings and on the dining hall kitchen utensils. The diners hooted unappreciatively.

A fat woman in white work clothes, by all appearances the person in charge, waddled up to us, held her nose, and, in a low, muffled voice, said:

"What do you think you're doing? Go on, get out of here!"

Someone in the crowd recognized my master.

"Aren't you Lan Lian, from Ximen Village? Is it really you? What happened to you?"

My master just looked at the man without replying, then led me out into the yard, where everyone stayed as far away from us as possible.

"That's Gaomi County's one and only independent farmer," the man shouted after us. "They know about him all the way to Changwei Prefecture! That donkey of his is almost supernatural. It killed a pair of wolves and has bitten a dozen or more people. What happened to its leg?"

The fat woman ran up.

"We don't serve independent farmers, so get out of here!"

My master stopped walking and, in a voice filled both with dejection and passion, replied:

"You fat sow, I am an independent farmer, and I'd rather die than be served by the likes of you. But this donkey of mine is the county chief's personal mount. He was carrying the chief down the mountain when his hoof got caught in some rocks and broke off. That's a work-related injury, and you have an obligation to serve him."

I'd never heard my master berate anyone so passionately before. His birthmark was nearly black. By then he was so skeletal he looked like a plucked rooster, and a very smelly one, as he advanced on the fat woman, who kept backing up until, covering her face with her hands, she burst into tears and bolted.

A man in a well-worn uniform, hair parted in the middle, looking very much like a local official, walked up to us, picking his teeth.

"What do you want?"

"I want you to feed my donkey, I want you to heat a tub of water and give him a bath, and I want you to get a doctor over here to bandage his injured leg."

The official shouted in the direction of the kitchen, drawing a dozen people out into the yard.

"Do as he says, and make it quick."

So they washed me from head to tail with hot water, and they summoned a doctor, who treated my injured leg with iodine, put a medicinal salve on the stump, and wrapped it with heavy gauze. Finally, they brought me some barley and alfalfa.

While I was eating, someone carried out a bowl of steaming dumplings and placed it in front of my master. A man who looked like a mess cook said softly:

"Eat up, elder brother, don't be stubborn. Eat what you have here and don't give a thought to your next meal. Get through today without worrying about tomorrow. In these fucked-up times you suffer for a few days, then you die, the lamp goes out. What's that, you don't want these?"

My master was sitting on a couple of chipped bricks tied together, bent over like a hunchback and staring at my useless stump; I don't think he heard a word the mess cook said. His stomach was rumbling again, and I could guess how tempting those plump, white dumplings must have been. Several times he stuck out a black, grimy hand to pick one of them up, only to quickly pull it back.

11

With a War Hero's Help, an Artificial Hoof
Starving Citizens Dismember and Eat a Donkey

My stump healed and I was out of danger, but I'd lost the ability to work and was just a crippled donkey. The slaughterhouse team came by several times with an offer to buy me and improve the lives of Party cadres with my meat. My master sent them away with loud curses.

In a story called "The Black Donkey," Mo Yan wrote:

> The mistress of the house Yingchun found a beat-up leather shoe somewhere, brought it home, and cleaned it; she filled the inside with cotton, sewed a strap onto the top, and tied it to the crippled donkey's injured leg, which helped to stabilize him. And so, in the spring of 1959, a strange scene appeared on village roads: the independent farmer Lan Lian pushing a cart with wooden wheels, piled high with fertilizer, his arms bare, his face defiant. The donkey pulling the cart wore a beat-up leather shoe on one leg as he hobbled along, his head drooping low. The cart moved slowly, the wheels creaked loudly. Lan Lian, bending deeply at the waist, pushed with all his might. The crippled donkey pulled with all his might to make his master's job a little easier. At first, people stopped and stared at this strange team, and a few even covered their mouths to stifle a laugh. But eventually the laughter died out. During the early days of their co-op labor, elementary schoolchildren would fall in behind them; one or two of the bad kids would throw stones at the donkey, but they were invariably punished at home.

In the spring, the earth takes on the quality of leavened dough;

in addition to the wheels of our heavily laden cart, my hooves also sank deeply into the ground, making it almost impossible to keep moving. The fertilizer had to be taken out into the fields, so hard work was called for; I pulled with all my might to make the job easier on him. But I hadn't gone more than a dozen steps when I left the shoe my mistress had made stuck in the dirt. When the exposed stump hit the ground like a club, the terrible pain pushed my sweat glands to the limit. *Hee-haw, hee-haw* — It's killing me! I'm worse than useless, Master. Out of the corner of my eye I saw the blue side of his face and his bulging eyes, and I was determined to help him pull the cart into the field, even if I had to crawl, in part to repay his kindness, in part as payback for all the smug looks, and in part to create a model for all those little bastards. Owing to the loss of balance, I had to bend over until my knee touched the ground. Ah, that hurt a lot less than touching it with the stump and made it easier to pull. So I went down on both knees, in full kneel, and, pulling with all my might, managed to get the cart moving again. The shaft pressed so hard against my throat, I had trouble breathing. I knew how awkward I must have looked, certainly worthy of ridicule. But let them laugh, all of them, so long as I could help my master move the cart to where he wanted it to go. That would spell victory, and glory!

After he'd unloaded the fertilizer, my master came up and wrapped his arms around my head. He was sobbing so hard he could barely get the words out:

"Blackie . . . such a good donkey . . ."

After taking out his pipe and filling it, he lit up and took a deep drag. Then he held the stem up to my mouth.

"Take a puff, Blackie," he said. "You won't feel quite so exhausted."

After following him for so many years, I'd gotten hooked on tobacco. I took a deep drag and blew streams of smoke out of my nostrils.

That winter, after learning that the Supply and Marketing Co-op director, Pang Hu, had been fitted with a prosthetic leg, my master decided that I deserved to be fitted with a prosthetic hoof. To that end, he and his wife, drawing on a friendship forged years before, went to see Pang Hu's wife, Wang Leyun, and told her what they had in mind. Happy to oblige, she let my master and mistress study Pang Hu's new leg from all angles. It had been made in a factory dedicated to producing prosthetics for crippled heroes of the revolution, a service obviously denied to me, a donkey. Even if the factory had been willing to undertake the task, my master would not have been able to afford the cost. So they decided to make a prosthetic hoof on their own. Three whole months it took them, through trial and error, until they finally managed to produce a false hoof that looked pretty much like the real thing. All that remained was to strap it on.

They walked me around the yard; the new hoof felt much better than the beat-up shoe, and while my gait was somewhat stiff, my limp was less pronounced. So my master led me out onto the street, head high, chest out, as if proudly showing off. I tried my best to match his attitude and give him the face he deserved. Village children fell in behind us to share in the excitement. Seeing the looks on people's faces and listening to what they were saying, I could tell that they held him in high regard. Then when we met up with gaunt, sallow Hong Taiyue, he remarked:

"Lan Lian, are you putting on a show for the People's Commune?"

"I wouldn't dare," my master replied. "The People's Commune and I are like well water and river water — they don't mix."

"Yes, but you're walking on a People's Commune street." Hong pointed first to the street, then to the skies above. "And you're breathing the air above the People's Commune and soaking up rays of the sun shining down on the People's Commune."

"This street was here before the People's Commune was created, and so were the air and the sun. They were given to all people and animals by the powers of heaven, and you and your People's Commune have no right to monopolize them!" He breathed in deeply, stomped his foot on the ground, and raised his face to the sun. "Wonderful air, terrific sunlight!" Then he patted me on the shoulder and said, "Blackie, take a deep breath, stomp down on the ground, and let the sun's rays warm you."

"You talk like that now, Lan Lian, but you'll soften up one day," Hong said.

"Old Hong, roll up the street, blot out the sun, and stuff up my nose if you can."

"Just you wait," Hong said indignantly.

∗   ∗   ∗

I'd intended to put my new hoof to use by working several more years for my master. But then the famine came, turning the people into wild animals, cruel and unfeeling. After eating all the bark from trees and the edible grass, a gang of them charged into the Ximen estate compound like a pack of starving wolves. My master tried to protect me by threatening them with a club, but he lost his nerve under the menacing green light that blazed in their eyes. He threw down his club and ran away. I trembled in fear in the presence of that gang, knowing my day of reckoning had come, that my life as a donkey had come full circle. All that had happened over the ten years since I'd been reborn on this spot on earth flashed before me. I closed my eyes and waited.

"Take it!" I heard someone in the yard yell. "Take the independent farmer's grain stores! Kill! Kill the independent farmer's crippled donkey!"

I heard sorrowful shouts from my mistress and the children and the sounds of pillaging and fighting among the starving people. A heavy blow on the head stunned me and drove my soul right out of my body to hover in the air above and watch the people cut and slice the carcass of a donkey into pieces of meat.

Book Two

The Strength of an Ox

12

Big-head Reveals the Secret of Transmigration
Ximen Ox Takes Up Residence in Lan Lian's Home

"Unless I'm mistaken," I ventured under the wild, piercing gaze of the big-headed child, Lan Qiansui, "you were a donkey that was hit over the head by a starving villager. You crashed to the ground, where your body was cut up and eaten by a gang of starving villagers. I witnessed it with my own eyes. My guess is, your spirit hovered about the scene in the Ximen estate compound for a while before heading back to the underworld, where, after many twists and turns, you were born into the world once more, this time as an ox."

"Exactly right." I detected a slightly melancholy tone in his voice. "By describing for you my life as a donkey, I have related about half of what happened later. During my years as an ox, I stuck to you like a shadow, and you are well versed in the things that happened to me, so there's no point in my repeating them, is there?"

I studied his head, which was so much larger than either his age or his body seemed to warrant; studied his enormous mouth, with which he talked on and on; studied all his myriad expressions, appearing one minute and vanishing the next — a donkey's natural, unrestrained dissipation, an ox's innocence and strength, a pig's gluttony and violence, a dog's loyalty and fawning nature, a monkey's alertness and mischievous qualities — and studied the world-weary and disconsolate composite expression, which incorporated all of the above. My memories involving the ox came thick and fast, like waves crashing on the shore; or moths drawn to a flame; or iron filings sucked toward a magnet; or odors surging toward your nostrils; or colors seeping outward on fine paper; or my longing for that woman born with the world's loveliest face, interminable, eternally present . . .

Father took me to market to buy an ox. It was the first day of October, 1964. The sky was clear, the air fresh, the sunlight radiant; birds were flying in the sky, locusts were sticking their soft abdomens into the hard earth to lay their eggs. I picked them up off the ground and strung them on a blade of grass so I could take them home to roast and eat.

The marketplace was bustling, now that the hard times were behind us. The harvests that autumn were unusually large, which accounted for all the happy faces. Taking me by the hand, Father led me over to the livestock market. Lan Lian was my father; they called me Lan Lian Junior. When people saw the two of us together, they often sighed: father and son, both branded with birthmarks on their faces, seemingly afraid that people wouldn't know they were related.

Mules, horses, and donkeys were available at the livestock market. On that day there were only two donkeys, one a gray female with floppy ears and a downcast, disheartened look. Her eyes were dull, with gummy yellow mucus in the corners. We didn't have to look in her mouth to know that she was an old mare. The other donkey, a black gelded male that was almost as big as a mule, had an off-putting white face. White face: no offspring. Like a villain on the Peking opera stage, he had a venomous look about him. Who'd want an animal like that? That one needed to be sent to the knackers without delay. "Dragon meat in heaven, donkey meat on earth." The commune's Party cadres were ardent fans of cooked donkey, especially the newly arrived Party secretary, who had previously served as County Chief Chen's secretary. His name was Fan Tong, which sounded just like the words for "rice bucket." He had an astonishing capacity for food.

County Chief Chen had deep emotional ties with donkeys; Secretary Fan was in love with donkey meat. When Father saw the two old and ugly animals, his face darkened and tears wetted his eyes. I knew he was thinking about the black donkey we'd owned, the "snow stander" that had been written up in the newspaper, the one that had accomplished something no other donkey in the world could match. He wasn't alone in missing that donkey; I missed him too. When I thought back to my elementary school days, I recalled how much pride that donkey brought us three children. And not just us: even Huang Huzhu and Huang Hezuo, the twin girls, got their share as well. Though Father and Huang Tong, and Mother and Qiuxiang, barely spoke and seldom even greeted one another, I always felt a special closeness to the Huang twins. If you want to know the truth, I felt closer to them than I did to my half sister Lan Baofeng.

The two donkey traders apparently knew Lan Lian, since they nodded and smiled meaningfully. Father immediately dragged me over to the oxen market, almost as if he was running away from something, or he'd received a sign from heaven. We could never buy a donkey, since no donkey in the world could compare with the one we'd once owned.

The donkey market had been nearly deserted; the oxen market was just the opposite, with all sizes, shapes, and colors of animals available. How come there are so many oxen, Dad? I thought they'd been killed off during the three years of famine we just got through. It looks like these animals popped up through cracks in the earth or something. There were Southern Shandong oxen, Shaanxi oxen, Mongol oxen, Western Henan oxen, and a bunch of mixed breeds. We entered and, without a second glance, headed straight for a young bull that had just recently been haltered. Looking to be about a year old, it had a chestnut-colored coat, a satiny hide, and big, bright eyes that signaled both intelligence and a mischievous nature. We could tell he was fast and powerful by looking at his strong legs. Young as he was, he already had the frame of a fully grown adult ox, like a young man with fuzz above his lip. His mother, a long-bodied Mongol, had a tail that dragged along the ground and forward-jutting horns. These oxen take great strides, are impatient by nature, can withstand extreme cold and rough treatment, survive easily in the wild, are excellent in front of a plow, and are well suited to pulling a cart. The animal's owner was a middle-aged man with a sallow complexion and thin lips that did not cover his teeth; a pen was hooked in the pocket of his black uniform, which had missing buttons. He looked like an accountant or storekeeper. A cross-eyed boy with shaggy hair stood behind the owner; he was about my age and, like me, a school dropout. We sized each other up; there was a spark of recognition.

"In the market for an ox?" the boy called out to me. He added conspiratorially, "This one's a half-breed. Sire's a Swiss Simmental, mother's a Mongol. They mated on the farm. Artificial insemination. The Simmental bull weighed in at eight hundred kilos, like a small mountain. If you're in the market, this is the one you want to buy. Stay away from the female."

"Shut up, you little brat!" the sallow-faced man scolded. "If I hear another word out of you I'll sew your mouth shut!"

With a giggle, the boy stuck out his tongue and ran over behind the man. Then he secretly pointed to the mother with the crooked tail, to make sure I noticed.

Father bent down and reached out to the young ox, like a member of the gentry class inviting a bejeweled, well-dressed young lady to dance in a brightly lit dancehall. Many years later, I saw that very gesture in foreign movies, and invariably thought of my father and that young ox. Father's eyes flashed, a radiance I think you only see in the eyes of a loved one from whom you've been cruelly separated for so long. What really amazed me was that the ox actually walked up, wagged his tail, and licked Father's hand, once, then a second time. Father stroked his neck.

"I'll take this one."

"You can't buy just the one," the trader said in a tone that ruled out any bargaining. "I can't take him from his mother."

"I only have a hundred yuan," Father insisted, "and I only want that young one." He took the money out of an inner pocket and held it out to the ox trader.

"You can have them both for five hundred," the man replied. "I'm not going to repeat myself. Either buy them or be on your way. I don't have time to argue."

"I said I only have a hundred." Father laid the money at the trader's feet. "I want that young one."

"Pick your money up!"

Father was on his haunches in front of the young ox, intense emotion suffusing his face. He stroked the animal. Obviously, he hadn't heard the trader's remark.

"Go on, Uncle, sell it to him . . . ," the boy said.

"Keep your opinions to yourself!" the man said as he handed the mother ox's tether to the boy. "Take her!" He walked up and pushed Father away from the young ox so he could lead it over to its mother. "I've never seen anybody like you," he said. "Don't get any ideas about taking it without my approval."

Father was sitting on the ground, looking dazed.

"I don't care," he said, as if possessed. "This is the ox I want."

Now, of course, I understand why he was so insistent on buying that particular animal, but at the time I didn't know that the ox was the latest incarnation of Ximen Nao — Ximen Donkey. What I thought was, Father was under such pressure owing to his perverse insistence on remaining an independent farmer that he wasn't himself mentally or emotionally. Now I'm convinced there was a spiritual bond between him and that ox.

In the end we bought the ox. It was inevitable, all previously arranged in the underworld. When nothing had yet been settled between Father and the ox trader, the Party branch secretary of the Ximen Village Production Brigade, Hong Taiyue, the brigade commander, Huang Tong, and some other people entered the market. They saw the mother ox and, of course, the young animal. Hong deftly opened the mother's mouth.

"The teeth are all worn down. This one belongs at the knackers."

"Elder brother," the ox trader said with a sneer, "nobody says you have to buy my animals, but you can't talk about them like that. How can you call these teeth worn down? I tell you, if the brigade wasn't so short of money, I wouldn't sell her for any amount. I'd take her home to mate and have another calf next spring."

Hong stretched his hand out of his wide sleeve to negotiate price in the tried and tested tradition of livestock markets. But the man waved him off.

"None of that. Here's the deal. Both for five hundred, the one and only price."

Father wrapped his arms around the young ox and said angrily:

"This is the ox I want, I'll pay a hundred yuan."

"Lan Lian," Hong Taiyue mocked him. "Save yourself the trouble. Go home, get your wife and kids, and join the commune. If you're so fond of animals, we'll assign you the job of tending them." Hong cast a glance at Brigade Commander Huang. "What do you say to that, Huang Tong?"

"Lan Lian," Huang Tong said, "your stubbornness has won us over. Now it's time for you to join the commune, both for the sake of your family and to enhance the reputation of the Ximen Village Production Brigade. Every time there's a meeting, the question invariably arises: Is that Ximen Village farmer still working as an independent?"

Father ignored them. Starving members of the People's Commune had killed our black donkey and eaten him, and they'd stolen all the grain we'd stored up. I might be able to understand that sort of abominable behavior, but the wounds on Father's heart would not be easily healed. He often said that he and that donkey were not linked by the traditional master-livestock relationship but were almost like brothers, joined at the heart. Despite the fact that he could not possibly have known that the black donkey was the reincarnation of the man for whom he had worked, he unquestionably sensed that he and the donkey were fated to be together. To him the comments of Hong Taiyue and the others were nothing but platitudes. Father couldn't even muster the interest to respond. He just held on to the ox's neck and said:

"This is the ox I want."

"So you're the independent farmer," the surprised ox trader said to Lan Lian. "Brother, you're something special." He studied Father's face, then mine. "Lan Lian, blue face. He really does have a blue face," he blurted out. "It's a deal. A hundred yuan. The young ox is yours!" He bent down, picked the money up off the ground, counted it, and stuffed it in his pocket. "Since you're from the same village," he said to Hong Taiyue, "you can benefit from your association with this blue-faced brother. I'll sell you this female for three hundred eighty, a discount of twenty yuan."

Father untied the rope around his waist and put it around the ox's neck. Hong Taiyue and his entourage put a new halter on the female and returned the old one to the trader. Livestock deals never include the halters.

"Better come with us, Lan Lian," Hong Taiyue said to Father. "I doubt you'll be able to drag your young ox away from its mother."

Father shook his head and walked off, the young ox obediently falling in behind him. There was no struggle, even though the mother ox bellowed her grief, and even though her son did look back and call out to her. At the time I thought he'd probably reached the age where he didn't need her as much as he once had. Now I realize that you, Ximen Ox, were Ximen Donkey, and before that, a man, one whose fate was still tied to my father. That's why there was instant recognition between them and notable emotion, and why separation was not an option.

I was about to walk off with Father when the trader's boy ran up and said furtively:

"You should know that that female is a 'hot turtle.' "

"Hot turtles" were what we called animals that slobbered and began panting as soon as they started working in the summer. I didn't know what the term meant at the time, but I could tell from the way the boy said it that a "hot turtle" was not a good ox. To this day I don't know why he thought it was important that I know that, nor do I know what it was about him that made me feel I knew him somehow.

Father said nothing on the road home. I felt like saying something a few times, but one glance at his face, caught up in his own mysterious thoughts, and I decided not to intrude. No matter how you look at it, buying that ox, one I liked at first sight, was a good thing. It made Father happy, it made me happy too.

Father stopped on the outskirts of the village to smoke his pipe and get a good look at you. Without warning, he burst out laughing.

Father did not laugh often, and I'd never heard him laugh like that. It kind of scared me. Hoping he wasn't suddenly possessed, I asked him:

"What are you laughing at, Father?"

"Jiefang," he said, staring not at me, but at the ox's eyes, "look at this animal's eyes. Who do they remind you of?"

That was not what I expected to hear, and I assumed that something was wrong with him. But I did as I was told. The young ox's moist, limpid eyes were blue-black and so clear I could see my reflection in them. He seemed to be looking at me as he chewed his cud; his pale blue mouth moved slowly as he chewed, then swallowed a clump of grass that skittered all the way down to his other stomach like a mouse. A new clump then rose to take its place.

"What do you mean, Dad?"

"You can't see it?" he said. "His eyes are an exact replica of our donkey's eyes."

With Father's help, I tried conjuring up a picture of our donkey, but all I could manage were the sheen of his coat, his mouth, which was normally open in front of big white teeth, and the way he stretched out his neck when he brayed. But try as I might, I couldn't recall what his eyes looked like.

Instead of pushing me to try harder, Father told me some tales involving the wheel of transmigration. He told me about a man who dreamed that his deceased father said to him, Son, I'm coming back as an ox. I'll be reborn tomorrow. The next day, as promised, the family ox delivered a male calf. Well, the man took special care of that young ox, his "father." He didn't put a nose ring or halter on him.

"Let's go, Father," he'd say when they went out into the field. After working hard, he'd say, "Time to rest, Father." So the ox rested. At that point in his tale, Father stopped, to my chagrin. So what happened? After hesitating for a moment, Father said, I'm not sure this is the sort of thing I should be telling a child, but I'll go ahead. That ox did a pecker pull — later on I learned that "pecker pull" meant masturbation — and was seen by the woman of the house. "Father," she said, "How could you do something like that? You should be ashamed of yourself." The ox turned and rammed its head into the wall and died on the spot. Ahhh — Father released a long sigh.

13

A Stream of Guests Urge Participation
in the Commune
Independent Farming Gains a
Distinguished Advocate

"Qiansui, I can't let you keep calling me 'Grandpa.'" Timidly, I patted him on the shoulder. "Just because I'm in my fifties and you're a five-year-old boy, if we go back forty years, that is, the year 1965, during that turbulent spring, our relationship was one of a fifteen-year-old youth and a young ox." He nodded solemnly. "It's as if it was yesterday." I gazed into the ox's eyes and saw a look of mischief, of naïveté, and of unruliness. . . .

I'm sure you remember the intense pressure our family was under that spring. Eliminating the last remaining independent farmer was one of the most important tasks confronting the Ximen Village Production Brigade as well as the Milky Way People's Commune. Hong Taiyue enlisted the help of villagers who enjoyed high prestige and commanded universal respect — Great Uncle Mao Shunshan, Old Uncle Qu Shuiyuan, and Fourth Elder Qin Buting; persuasive women — Aunty Yang Guixiang, Third Sister-in-Law Su Erman, Sister Chang Suhua, and Great Aunt Wu Qiuxiang; and clever, glib students — Mo Yan, Li Jinzhu, and Niu Shunwa. These ten people were the only ones I could recall; there were, in fact, many more, and they all made it to our door, like eager matchmakers or people wanting to display their wisdom and eloquence. The men surrounded my father, the women my mother; the students went after my brother and my sister, but did not spare me either. Smoke from the men's pipes nearly suffocated the geckoes on our walls; the women's hindquarters wore out the mats on our sleeping platform, the *kang*; and the students tore our clothes in the chase. Join the commune, please join the commune, wake up, don't be foolish. If not for yourselves, do it for your children. I think that during those days just about everything your ox eyes saw and your ox ears heard had to do with joining the commune. When my father was cleaning out your pen, those old-timers barricaded the gate like a troop of loyal soldiers and said:

"Old Lan, good nephew, join up. If you don't, your family will be unhappy, and so will your animals."

Unhappy? I was anything but. How could they know that I was in reality Ximen Nao, that I was Ximen Donkey, an executed landlord, a dismembered donkey, so why would I want to throw in my lot with my personal enemies? Why was I so reluctant to be away from your father? Because I knew that was the only way I could be engaged in independent farming.

Women sat cross-legged on our sleeping platform like nosy relatives from some distant village. With slobber building up in the corners of their mouths, they were like the tape recorders in roadside shops that play the same damned stuff over and over. Finally, my anger won out:

"Big-tits Yang and Fat-ass Su, get the hell out of our house. You make me sick!"

Angry? Not a bit. With silly grins, they said:

"Join the commune and we'll be on our way. Refuse, and our rear ends will take root here on your *kang*. Our bodies will sprout, grow leaves, and flower; we'll become trees and knock the roof right off your house!"

Of all the women, the one I hated most was Wu Qiuxiang. Maybe because she had once shared a man with my mother, she treated her with special enmity:

"Yingchun, there's a difference between you and me. I was a maidservant who was raped by Ximen Nao, but you were his precious concubine who gave him two children. Not labeling you a member of the landlord class and sending you out to be reformed through labor is better than you deserve. That's my doing, since you treated me decently. I had to beg Huang Tong to let you off the hook! But you must keep in mind the difference between dying embers and a blazing fire."

The school ruffians, with Mo Yan leading the way, loved to hear themselves talk and had an overabundance of energy, so with village support and encouragement from school, they took full advantage of this opportunity to raise hell. They were as excited as drunken monkeys, and just as sprightly. Some climbed our tree, some jumped up onto the wall and shouted through megaphones, as if our house was a counterrevolutionary bastion and they were signaling the charge.

Stubborn old Lan Lian is not our friend; independent farming is a true dead end. A single mouse dropping ruins a vat of vinegar. Jinlong, Baofeng, Lan Jiefang, put your hands over your hearts and think hard. Stay with your dad and you're as good as dead; you'll keep falling behind and can't get ahead. Mo Yan made up all those limericks; it was a talent he'd had since early childhood. Oh, was I angry! I hated that damned Mo Yan! He was my mother's "dry" son, my "dry" brother. Every New Year's Eve Mother had me take a bowl of dumplings to you! "Dry" son! "Dry" brother! Shit! The word *family* means nothing to you. So I decided to fight fire with fire. I hid in the corner, took out my slingshot, and fired a pellet at the shiny head of Mo Yan, who was sitting in the crotch of the tree in the yard shouting through his tin megaphone. With a loud shriek, Mo Yan fell out of the tree. But damned if he wasn't back up there in the time it takes to smoke a pipe, a blood blister on his forehead. He recommenced the shouting:

Lan Jiefang, you little toad, follow your dad down a crooked road.

If you dare come after me again, I'll haul you down to the station house! I raised my slingshot and took aim at his head again. This time he threw down his megaphone and shinnied down the tree.

Jinlong and Baofeng had no stomach for it. They tried to talk Father around.

"Why don't we go ahead and join, Dad?" Jinlong said. "They treat us like dirt at school."

"When we're out walking," Baofeng said, "people behind us yell, Look there, it's the independent farmer's kids."

"Dad," Jinlong continued, "I see the production brigade people out working, and they're always laughing and having a good time, like they're real happy. Then look at you and Mom, how much alone you are. What good are a few hundred extra catties of grain, anyway? Rich or poor, everyone shares equally."

Dad said nothing, but Mom, who normally went along with whatever Dad said, took the bold step of making her opinion known:

"The children are making sense," she said. "Maybe we ought to join."

Dad was smoking his pipe. He looked up and said, "I might consider it if they weren't applying so much pressure. But the way they're stewing me like I was a bird of prey, I'm not going to give them the satisfaction." He looked at Jinlong and Baofeng. "You two will soon be graduating from middle school, and under ordinary circumstances, I should be paying your way to high school and college, and then study abroad. But I don't have the money. The little bit I put aside over the years, well, they stole it all. And even if I found the means to pay your way, they wouldn't let you go, and not just because I'm an independent farmer. Do you understand what I'm saying?"

Jinlong nodded.

"We understand, Dad. We never spent a day as landlord brats, and we can't tell you if Ximen Nao was black or white, but his blood runs through our veins and he hovers over us like a demonic shadow. We are youth born in the era of Mao Zedong, and though we had no choice in who we were born as, we do have a choice in which path to take. We don't want to be independent farmers with you, we want to join the commune. Whether you and Mom join or not, Baofeng and I are going to."

"Thank you, Dad, for seventeen years of nurturing," Baofeng said with a bow. "Please forgive us for our disobedience. With a biological father like that, if we don't pursue progressive trends, we'll never make anything of ourselves."

"Well spoken, both of you," Dad said. "I've been thinking hard about this lately, and I know I can't have you following me down the dark path. You—" He pointed to us all. "You join the commune. I'll farm on my own. I vowed to stick to independent farming, and I can't turn around and slap my own face now."

"If any of us join," Mom said, with tears in her eyes, "then let's do it as a family. What's the point in working alone?"

"I've said it before. The only way I'll join the commune is if Mao Zedong orders me to. But here's what he said: 'Joining a commune is voluntary, leaving a commune is a matter of individual choice.' What right do they have to bully me into joining? Do our local officials have more say than Mao Zedong? I refuse to give in to them. I'm going to test the credibility of Mao Zedong's own words by my actions."

"Dad," Jinlong said, a trace of sarcasm slipping into his voice, "please don't keep referring to him as Mao Zedong. That's not a name we should use. To us he's Chairman Mao!"

"You're right," Dad said. "I should refer to him as Chairman Mao. As an independent farmer, I am still one of Chairman Mao's subjects. This land and this house were given to us by the Communist Party, led by Chairman Mao. A couple of days ago, Hong Taiyue sent someone to tell me that if I didn't join the commune, they'd have to resort to force. If a cow won't drink, do you force its head into the water? No. I'll appeal. I'll take my case to the county, to the province, even to Beijing, if necessary." He turned to Mother. "After I leave, you and the children join the commune. We have eight acres of land and five people. One point six acres per person. You take six point four acres with you and leave the rest for me. We have a plow that we were given during land reform. You take that with you. But the young ox stays. There's no way we can divide up this three-room house. The children are grown, and this place is too small for them. After you join the commune, ask the production brigade for a plot of land to build a house. When it's ready, you can move in and I'll stay here. As long as the place is standing, this is where you'll find me. If it collapses one day, I'll throw up a tent, but I won't go anywhere."

"Why do you have to do this, Dad?" Jinlong said. "By going against the tide of socialism, aren't you just looking in a mirror to see how ugly you are? I may be young, but I have the feeling there's a class war coming. For people like us, with no red roots to fall back on, going with the tide may be the only way to avoid disaster. Going against the tide is like throwing an egg at a rock!"

"That's why I want you to join the commune. I'm a hired hand, what do I have to be afraid of? I'm forty years old, a man who never did much of anything. So what happens? I make a name for myself by being an independent farmer. *Ha ha, ha ha ha ha.*" He laughed so hard, tears ran down his blue face. He turned to Mother. "Put some dry rations together for me," he said. "I'm going to appeal my case."

By this time, Mother was crying. "I've stayed with you all these years," she said. "I can't leave you now. Let the children join the commune. I'll stay and work with you."

"No," he said. "With your bad background, joining the commune is your only protection. If you stay with me, they have all the reason they'll need to dredge up your background, and that'll just mean more trouble for me."

"Dad," I blurted out, "I want to farm with you!"

"Nonsense! You're a child, what do you know?"

"I know, I know a lot. I hate Hong Taiyue, Huang Tong, and that bunch as much as you do. And Wu Qiuxiang disgusts me. Who does she think she is, with her bitchy dog's eyes and a mouth that looks like an asshole? What gives her the right to come to our house and pretend she's some kind of progressive?" Mother glared at me. "What kind of talk is that from a child?" "I'm going to farm with you, Dad," I said. "When you take out the fertilizer, I'll drive the oxcart. With its wooden wheels, it lets everyone know it's coming — *creak creak* — I love the sound. We'll be independents, individual heroes. I envy you, Dad, and I'm going to stay with you. I don't need to go to school. I never was much of a student. As soon as class starts, I doze off. Dad, half your face is blue, and I'm half a blue face. Two blue faces, how can you separate that? People laugh at me because of my birthmark. Well, let them laugh, they can laugh themselves to death, for all I care. Two blue-faced independent farmers, the only ones in the county, the only ones in the province. That makes me proud. Dad, you have to say okay!"

He did. I wanted to go with him to appeal his case, but he told me to stay home and take care of the young ox. Mother took some pieces of jewelry out of a hole in the wall and gave them to me. Obviously, there were gaps in the land reform campaign, and she had managed to hold on to some valuables. Dad sold the jewelry for traveling money, then he went to see County Chief Chen, the man who had indirectly destroyed our donkey, and asked for the right to remain an independent farmer. Father argued his case forcefully. In terms of policy, Chen said, you're free to farm independently. But I hope you choose not to. County Chief, Dad said, in the name of that black donkey of ours, I'd like you to issue me a guarantee that gives me the authority to farm on my own. Once I post that on my wall, no one will dare attack me. Ah, that black donkey . . . a good animal, the chief remarked emotionally. I owe you for what happened. I can't give you the kind of pass you want, but I can give you a letter that explains your situation to the Farming Village Labor Bureau of the Provincial Party Committee. So Dad took the letter to the provincial capital, where he was received by the Labor Bureau head, who also tried to convince him to join the commune. Father refused. If Chairman Mao issues an order outlawing independent farming, I'll join. If not, I won't. Moved by Father's intransigence, the Labor Bureau head wrote two lines at the bottom of the county chief's letter: While it is our wish that all farmers join the People's Communes and walk the path of collectivization, anyone who refuses to join is within his right to do so. Low-level organizations may not use coercive measures, especially illegal means, to force anyone to join a commune.

Father placed this letter, which was like an imperial edict, in a glass frame and hung it on his wall. He had returned from the provincial capital in high spirits. Now that Mother and Jinlong and Baofeng had joined the commune, only three-point-two acres of the original eight, which were completely surrounded by land belonging to the collective, remained for us to farm, a narrow strip of land like a levee trying to hold back an ocean. In accord with his wish to be independent, Father built a new room, walled it off from the other three, and opened a new door. He added a stove and a *kang*, and that's where he and I lived. Beyond this room and the ox shed against the southern wall, we owned three-point-two acres of land, a young ox, a cart with wooden wheels, a wooden plow, a hoe, an iron shovel, two scythes, a little spade, a pitchfork with two tines, a wok, four rice bowls, two ceramic plates, a chamber pot, a cleaver, a spatula, a kerosene lamp, and a flint.

Admittedly, there were many things we lacked, but we'd slowly add whatever we needed. Dad patted me on the head.

"Son, why in the world do you want to farm with me like this?"

Without a second thought, I replied:

"Looks like fun!"

14

Ximen Ox Angrily Confronts Wu Qiuxiang
Hong Taiyue Happily Praises Lan Jinlong

During the months of April and May 1965, while my father was making an appeal in the provincial capital, Jinlong and Baofeng joined the People's Commune with my mother. On that day, a solemn ceremony was held in the Ximen estate compound. Hong Taiyue spoke from the steps of the main house. The chests of my mother, Jinlong, and Baofeng were decorated with large red paper flowers; a red cloth was tied to our iron plow. My brother, Jinlong, delivered an impassioned speech expressing his determination to hew to the path of socialism. He was normally not much of a talker, so everyone was taken by surprise. To be honest, it turned me off. I hid out in the ox shed, with my arms around your neck out of a fear that they'd come and take you away with them. Before setting out, Father had said to me: Son, be sure to take good care of our ox. We needn't worry as long as we have him, because then we'll be able to hold out as independent farmers. I gave him my word, you heard me. Remember? I said, Dad, go now and come back as soon as you can. If I'm here, the ox will be here. He rubbed the horns that had just started growing on your head and said: Ox, you do as he says. We won't be able to harvest the wheat for another six weeks, so there won't be enough for you to eat. Let him take you out where there's wild grass, which will tide you over till we bring in the wheat. I saw tears in Mother's eyes as she glanced our way from time to time. This wasn't the path she'd wanted to take, but she had no choice. As for Jinlong, though he was only seventeen, he already had definite views of things, and the force of his words seemed to frighten Mother, at least a little. I could tell that her feelings for Father weren't as strong as those she'd held for Ximen Nao. She married him because she had to. And her feelings for me weren't as strong as those she held for Jinlong and Baofeng. Two different men's seed. But I was still her son, and she worried about me, even if she didn't want to. Mo Yan led a bunch of schoolboys in shouting slogans outside the ox shed:

> A headstrong man, a headstrong boy, choosing to farm apart.
> Pulling an ox the size of an insect, pushing a wood-wheeled cart.
> Sooner or later you'll have to join, and sooner is better than later to
>   start . . .

Faced with that sort of harassment, my courage began to falter, but not my excitement. The scene before me was like a play in which I was cast as the number-two character. Yes, a negative character, but more important than the positive characters out there. I felt it was time to make an appearance. I needed to go onstage, for the sake of my father's character and self-respect, but also to bear witness to my courage and, of course, for the sake of your ox-glory. So I led you out of the shed in plain view of everyone. I thought you might have stage fright, but you surprised me by your total absence of fear. Your halter was actually nothing more than a thin rope tied loosely around your neck. One tug, and you could have snapped it. If you hadn't wanted to follow me, I couldn't have done a thing about it. But you did, willingly, even happily. All eyes were on us, so I raised my head and stuck out my chest to make myself look like someone they'd have to deal with. I couldn't see what I looked like, but their laughter told me what a comical figure I must have cut, a little clown. Then you picked the wrong time to act up and bellow, the antic and the soft sound proving you were still a youngster. Then you got it into your head to charge the village leaders lined up in the doorway of the main house.

Who was there? Well, Hong Taiyue was there; so were Huang Tong and Yang Qi. Wu Qiuxiang was there too. She'd replaced Yang Guixiang as head of the Women's Association. I pulled on the rope to keep you from charging. All I'd wanted to do was take you into the yard to show you off, to let them see how handsome and spirited an independent farmer's ox can be. I wanted them to see that before long, you'd be the best-looking ox in Ximen Village. But you chose that moment to show how perverse you can be and, with hardly any effort, dragged me behind you like a monkey on a string. When you pulled a little harder, the rope parted. Standing there holding half a length of rope in my hand, I watched as you headed straight for the leading figures. I thought Hong Taiyue would be your primary target, either him or Huang Tong, so I was surprised to see you heading straight for Wu Qiuxiang. At the time that made no sense to me, but I understand now. She was wearing a purple jacket and blue pants; her hair was oiled, with a plastic hair clasp, a sort of come-hither butterfly effect. The crowd looked on slack-jawed as this startling scenario began to play out, and by the time anyone reacted, you'd already butted Wu Qiuxiang to the ground; not content with that, you kept butting her, wrenching shrieks of horror from her as she rolled on the ground. She clambered to her feet to get away, but you made sure that didn't happen by ramming your head into her large hip as she waddled along, tilting from side to side; with a loud croak, she tumbled forward and landed at the feet of Huang Tong, who turned and ran, with you in hot pursuit. Jinlong sprang into action. He jumped onto your back — that's how long his legs were — wrapped his arms around your neck, and held on for all he was worth. You kicked, you reared, you twisted, but you couldn't throw him off. So then you ran madly around the yard, sending people fleeing for their lives, their panicky screams hanging in the air. Jinlong grabbed your ears and pinched your nose till he brought you under control. Then people rushed up and pinned you to the ground.

"Put a ring in his nose," someone shouted, "then geld him, and hurry!"

I hit out with the rope in my hand, not caring who it landed on.

"Let my ox go!" I screamed. "You thugs, let him go!"

My brother Jinlong — brother, my eye!—was still on you, his face ashen, a dazed look in his eyes, his fingers stuck up your nostrils. I laid into him with my rope.

"You traitor!" I roared. "Take your hand away, take it away!"

My sister Baofeng ran up to stop me from beating her brother. Her face was bright red, and she was sobbing. I couldn't tell whose side she was on.

My mother stood there like a block of wood and muttered:

"My sons, ah . . . stop it, you two, what do you think you're doing?"

Hong Taiyue's voice was heard over the crowd:

"Go get me a rope, and hurry!"

Huang Tong's daughter, Huzhu, ran home and came back dragging a rope behind her. She flung it down in front of the ox, turned, and ran off. Her sister, Hezuo, was crouching under the big apricot tree rubbing Qiuxiang's chest and weeping:

"Mom, oh, Mom, are you okay . . ."

Hong Taiyue tied the ox's front legs together, then reached up and lifted Jinlong off the animal's back. My brother's legs were shaking; he couldn't straighten them out. His face was nearly bloodless, and his arms were stiff. The crowd quickly moved away, leaving me alone there with the young ox, my ox, my brave independent ox, who might have been killed by a traitorous member of the independent farming family! I patted his rump and sang a dirge for it. Ximen Jinlong, if you've killed my ox, this world isn't big enough for the two of us. I was shouting and, without a second's hesitation, had called Lan Jinlong Ximen Jinlong. It was not a casual mistake. First of all, it drew a line between me — Lan Jiefang — and him. Second, it was a reminder to people not to overlook his origins, the son of a landlord, a boy in whose veins flowed the blood of Ximen Nao, the person with whom the Communist Party stood in mortal enmity.

I saw Ximen Jinlong's face turned as white as paper, and he began to rock, as if hit with a club. At the same time, the young ox suddenly struggled to stand. At the time, of course, I didn't know you were the reincarnation of Ximen Nao, and was clueless about the complexity of feelings you were experiencing in the presence of Yingchun, Qiuxiang, Jinlong, and Baofeng. A tangled mess, I suppose. When Jinlong hit you, it was a son striking his father, wasn't it? And when I yelled at him, I was cursing your son, isn't that so? Your heart must be full of conflicting emotions. A mess, a real mess, your mind all twisted out of shape, and only you can make any sense of it.

— I sure can't!

You tried standing, obviously still lightheaded, your legs sore. You still felt like acting up, but not with your legs tied. You wobbled a bit, nearly fell down, but finally you were on your feet. Your red eyes signaled the rage inside you, the labored breathing indicated the depth of your anger. Dark blood oozed from your pastel blue nostrils. From one of your ears as well, bright red, where a chunk was missing, probably bitten off by Jinlong. I looked around, but couldn't find the missing chunk; maybe Jinlong had swallowed it. King Wen of the Zhou was forced to eat the flesh of his own son. He spit out several lumps of meat, which turned into rabbits that ran away. By swallowing a piece of your ear, Jinlong was eating his own father's flesh, but he'll never spit it out, and it will turn into waste that he'll expel. What will it become after that?

You stood in the middle of the yard, or should I say, we stood in the middle of the yard, not sure if we were victors or victims, which meant I couldn't say if we suffered from humiliation or reveled in glory.

Hong Taiyue patted Jinlong on the shoulder.

"Good going, young man. Your first day as a commune member, and you've already rendered outstanding service. You're a quick-witted, brave boy who isn't afraid to look danger in the face. Just the sort of fresh blood the commune needs!"

Jinlong's cheeks reddened; Hong Taiyue's praise obviously excited him. My mother walked up to rub his shoulder and squeeze his arm. The look on her face showed the depth of her concern for him, but it went unnoticed by Jinlong, who avoided her and edged up close to Hong Taiyue.

I wiped your bloody nose and announced to the crowd:

"You bunch of thugs, look what you did to my ox! You have to pay!"

"Jiefang," Hong Taiyue said sternly. "Your father isn't here, so what I have to say I'll say to you. Your ox knocked down Wu Qiuxiang, and her medical expenses are your responsibility. As soon as your father returns, you tell him he has to fit the ox with a nose ring, and if he injures another member of the commune, he'll be killed."

"Who are you trying to scare?" I said. "I've gotten this big by eating grains, not by being scared by anybody. Do you think I don't know national policy? An ox is a big livestock, a tool of production. Killing one is against the law."

"Jiefang!" Mother cried out sternly. "How dare you talk to Uncle that way!"

"*Ha ha, ha ha.*" Hong Taiyue laughed out loud. "Will you listen to that, everybody? He sure talks big. He actually knows that an ox is a tool of production. Well, you listen to me. The commune oxen are tools of production, but an ox belonging to an independent farmer is a tool of reactionary production. You're right, if an ox belonging to the People's Commune butted someone, we wouldn't dare kill it, but if an ox belonging to an independent farmer butts someone, I'll pronounce the death sentence without delay!"

Hong struck a pose like holding a sword, with which he could cut my ox in half. I was, after all, still young, and Father wasn't around. I was over my head and spouting nonsense. I was totally deflated, and a horrifying scene popped into my head: Hong Taiyue raises a blue sword and cuts my ox in two, but another head comes out of its chest. Each decapitation produces another head. Hong throws away the sword and flees, and I laugh, *Ha ha . . .*

"That kid must have lost his mind!" The people were buzzing, wondering why I was laughing at a time like that.

"See the father and damned if you won't know the son!" Huang Tong said

Now that she'd gotten her breath back, Wu Qiuxiang railed at her husband: "You damned turtle, always tucking your head back in. You coward, instead of coming to my rescue when the ox butted me, you pushed me right into it. If not for Jinlong, I'd have been dead meat on that animal's horns . . ."

Once again, all eyes were on my brother. Brother? What kind of brother was he? But, after all, he and I had the same mother, and that isn't a relationship you can forget about. Wu Qiuxiang's gaze at my brother was different from the others. And that of her daughter, Huang Huzhu, simply dripped with emotion. Now, of course, I realize that my brother's manner had already begun to take on the outline of Ximen Nao, and Qiuxiang could see her first man in him. She insisted that she'd been taken into the household as a maidservant, and then raped by the master, leading to a life of bitterness and taste for vengeance. But that's not what happened. Men like Ximen Nao are masters at taming women, and I knew that in Qiuxiang's heart, her second man, Huang Tong, was little more than a reeking pile of dog shit. And the emotion Huzhu felt for my brother? It was the budding flower of love.

Look here, Lan Qiansui — calling you by that name isn't easy for me — you've used Ximen Nao's cock to complicate what should be a very simple world.

15

Ox-herding Brothers Fight on a Sandbar
Unbroken Lines of Fate Make an Awkward Dilemma

In the same way the donkey wreaked havoc in the village government office and drew the widespread notice of the villagers, you, the bastard offspring of a Simmental ox and a Mongol ox, gained fame by disrupting the commune's welcoming ceremony for Mother, Jinlong, and Baofeng. Someone else gained face that day — my half brother, Jinlong. People saw how his fearless heroics subdued you. According to Huang Hezuo, who later became my wife, her sister, Huzhu, fell in love with him when he jumped on your back.

Father still hadn't returned from the provincial capital, and there was no more feed for you, so, recalling what he had said to me before he left, I took you out to the sandbar on the Grain Barge River to graze. Since it was one of your old haunts when you were a donkey, you knew the place well. Spring came late that year, so ice on the river hadn't melted, even though it was already April. The brittle reeds on the sandbar rustled in the wind when wild geese perched on them, which was often, and which usually frightened fat rabbits hidden among them. I occasionally saw a lustrous fox when it appeared suddenly among the reeds.

We were not alone in suffering a shortage of animal feed: the production brigade also had to take its twenty-four oxen, four donkeys, and two horses out into the wild to graze, tended by the herder Hu Bin and Jinlong. My half sister, Baofeng, had been sent to train at the county health department; she would return as our first formally educated midwife. Both she and her brother were given important tasks as soon as they joined the commune. Now you might assume that midwifery was an important task, while tending livestock was not. But

Jinlong was given the added responsibility of recording work points. Every evening he went to a small office, where he calculated the daily work activities of each commune member in a ledger. If that isn't an important task, I don't know what is. Seeing her children given such important tasks kept a smile on Mother's face, but when she saw me take my ox out to graze all by myself, she heaved a long sigh. I was, after all, her son too.

Well, that's enough meaningless chatter for now. Let's talk about Hu Bin, a small man with an accent that marked him as an outsider. Onetime head of the commune's post office, he'd been engaged in an illicit relationship with the fiancée of a soldier and was sentenced to a period of hard labor. When his sentence was up, he settled in our village. His wife, Bai Lian, a village switchboard operator with a big, round, plump face, red lips, nice white teeth, and a cheerful voice, had a cozy relationship with many of the commune cadres. Eighteen telephone wires on a China fir pole all fed into the window of her home and were connected to a unit that resembled a dressing table. When I was in elementary school, I could hear her singsong voice drift into the classroom: Hello. What number please? Please hold — Zheng Village on the line. We kids used to sprawl outside her window and look through tears in the window paper to watch as she nursed her baby with one arm and, with her free hand, effortlessly plugged the pegs into or pulled them out of the switchboard. To us, this was both a mystery and a wonder, and not a day passed that we didn't hang around there, until a village cadre shooed us away. But we'd be right back as soon as he left. We not only watched Bai Lian at work, but were also treated to plenty of scenes that were unsuitable for children. We saw her and the village's commune representative carry on flirtatiously, even get physical, and we saw Bai Lian scold Hu Bin in that singsong voice of hers. And we learned why none of Bai Lian's children looked alike. Eventually, the paper in her window was replaced by glass and a curtain, and there were no more shows. All we could do was listen to what went on inside. Even later, the wires were buried underground after being electrified. Mo Yan got zapped by a hot wire outside her window one day and peed his pants as he screamed pathetically. When I tried to pull him away, I got zapped too, but I didn't pee my pants. After this episode, we stopped hanging around outside her window.

Sending Hu Bin, who wore a felt cap with earflaps, miner's

goggles, a tattered uniform under a grimy army greatcoat, with a pocket watch in one pocket and a code book in the other, to tend live-stock was an insult. But someone should have told him to keep his pants zipped. My brother told him to round up the strays, but he'd just sit on the riverbank in the sunlight to flip through his code book and read aloud, until tears fell and he'd begin to sob. Then he'd raise his voice to the heavens:

"What did I do to deserve this? One time, that's all, not even three minutes, and now I have nothing to look forward to!"

The brigade's oxen spread out across the riverbank, all so under-fed you could count their ribs. Even though their coats were peeling, this taste of freedom injected life into their eyes; they looked pleased with their lot. I held on to your halter so you wouldn't mix with the others and tried to lead you over to where the grass was more nutri-tious and tastier. But you balked and dragged me back to the river-bank, where the reeds had grown tall the year before, with white-tipped leaves like knives, a spot where the brigade oxen walked in and out of view. You were so strong, I was helpless in trying to lead you, even with the halter. You just dragged me wherever you wanted to go. By then, you were a fully grown ox, horns sprouting from your forehead like new bamboo, glossy as fine jade. The childish inno-cence in your eyes had been replaced by a shifty, somewhat gloomy, look. You dragged me over to the reeds, getting closer and closer to the brigade oxen, which were pushing the reeds back and forth as they nibbled on dead leaves. They raised their heads to chew, crunching so loud it sounded like chewing on iron, giving them the appearance not of oxen but of giraffes. I saw the Mongol ox, with her twisted tail, your mother. Your eyes met. She called out to you, but you didn't reply; you just stared at her as if she were a stranger or, even worse, a bitter foe. My brother snapped his whip to vent his frustration. We hadn't spo-ken since he joined the commune, and I wasn't about to start now; if he tried to start a conversation, I'd ignore him. The fountain pen in his pocket sparkled, and I experienced a feeling that was hard to describe. Staying with my father as an independent farmer had not been a choice I'd made after careful consideration. It was actually something I'd decided in the heat of the moment, sort of like watching a play in which one of the roles is missing and deciding to go up onstage as a stand-in. A performance requires a stage and an audience; I had nei-ther. I was lonely. I stole a look at my brother, who had his back to me as he sent the tips of reeds flying every which way with his whip, like a sword. The ice on the river had begun to melt, cracks revealing the blue water below and reflecting blinding rays of light. The land on the other side of the river belonged to the state-run farm. Rows of modern buildings with red roofs created a stark contrast with the rammed-earth, thatch-roofed farmhouses in the village. A deafening roar came our way from across the river, and I knew that the spring plowing was about to get under way; the farm equipment teams were testing and repairing the machinery. I could even see the ruins of primitive ovens they'd used to smelt steel some years earlier; they looked like untended graves. My brother stopped snapping reed tips with his whip, stood up straight, and said coldly:

"You shouldn't be doing his dirty work!"

"You shouldn't be so proud of yourself!" I had to give him tit for tat.

"Starting today, I'm going to hit you every day until you bring your ox into the commune." He still had his back to me.

"Hit me?" He was so much bigger and stronger than me that I had to hide my fear with bluster. "Hah, try it! I'll beat you so badly there won't be enough of you left to bury."

He turned and faced me.

"Fine," he said with a laugh. "Now's your chance."

He reached out with the butt of his whip, picked my hat off my head, and laid it gently on a clump of weeds.

"I don't want to make Mother angry by dirtying your hat."

Then he rapped me on the head with the butt.

It didn't hurt much; in school, I banged my head on the door frame a lot and the other kids frequently hit me with chips of brick and tile, and all that hurt much more. But nothing made me as mad. Explosions of thunder in my head merged with the roar of machines on the far side of the river, and I saw stars. Without a second thought, I threw down the halter and rushed him. He jumped out of the way and kicked me in the pants on my way by. I wound up spread-eagled in the weeds, where a snakeskin almost wound up in my mouth.

Snakeskin, also known as snake slough, has medicinal properties. One year, a boil the size of a small saucer on his leg had Jinlong screeching in pain. Mother was told to fry some snake slough with eggs, so she sent me out to look for some. When I couldn't find any, Mother said I was worse than useless. So Father took me back out, where we found a six-foot-long black snake with a fresh layer of skin, which meant it had recently molted. The snake's black forked tongue licked out at us from very close. Mother fried the slough with seven eggs, a golden plateful that smelled wonderful and made me salivate. I tried to keep from looking at it, but my eyes slanted that way on their own. What a good brother you were then. Come on, you said, let's share. I said, No, none for me, you need this to get better. I saw tears in your eyes . . . now you're beating me. I picked the skin up with my teeth and imagined myself to be a poisonous snake as I rushed him again.

This time he didn't manage to get out of the way; I wrapped my arms around him and stuck my head up under his chin to push him over. But he adroitly slipped his leg between mine, grabbed me by the shoulders, and hopped on one leg to keep from falling. My eyes accidentally fell on you, the bastard offspring of a Simmental ox and Mongol ox, standing off to the side, just standing there quietly, looking despondent and sort of helpless, and I have to admit I was disappointed in you. I was fighting someone who'd bit off part of your ear and bloodied your nose; why didn't you come help me? To knock him over, all you had to do was give him a gentle nudge in the small of his back. Put a little more into it, and he'd sail through the air, and when he landed, I'd pin him to the ground. I win, he loses. But you didn't move. Now, of course, I understand why — he was your son, while I was your best friend. I brushed your coat, I chased away the gadflies, I cried for you. It was hard for you to choose one over the other, and I believe that what you wanted was for us both to stop, separate, shake hands, and go back to being loving brothers. His legs kept getting tangled up in the weeds, nearly causing him to fall, but as long as he could hop he could keep his balance. My strength was ebbing fast and I was panting like an ox; the pressure on my chest was becoming unbearable. All of a sudden, sharp pains struck both my ears; he'd taken his hands from my shoulders and was pulling on my ears. Hu Bin's shrill voice rose beside us:

"Good! Great! Fight! Fight!"

He was clapping his hands. With the pain killing me, Hu Bin's shouts distracting me, and your refusal to come to my aid disappointing me, I felt his leg wrap around mine; he flipped me onto my back and piled on, digging his knee into my belly. That hurt so much I think I peed my pants. Still holding my ears, he pressed my head into the ground. I saw white clouds and a bright sun in the blue sky above, and then I saw Ximen Jinlong's long, skinny, angular face, with a downy mustache above his hard, thin lips, a high nose bridge, and eyes that held a menacing glow. There's no way he had pure Han Chinese blood; maybe, like my ox, he had a mixed racial background, and by looking at his face I could imagine his likeness to Ximen Nao, a man I'd never met, but whose appearance had become the stuff of legend. I felt like cursing, but he was pulling my ears tightly, stretching the skin around my cheeks and mouth so taut that even I couldn't make sense of what came out of my mouth. He lifted up my head and slammed it into the ground, once for each word:

"Are — you — going — to — join — or — aren't — you?"

"No . . . never join . . ." My words emerged bathed in spittle.

"As I said, starting today, I'm going to beat you every day until you agree to join the commune. Not only that, each day will be worse than the one before!"

"I'll tell Mother!"

"She's the one who told me to do this!"

"I'll see what Dad says," I said in a more accommodating tone.

"No, you have to join before he returns. And not only you, the ox comes with you."

"He was always good to you. Is this how you repay him?"

"I'm bringing you into the commune to repay him."

Hu Bin was circling us the whole time. In near ecstasy, he was pulling at his own ears, rubbing his cheeks, clapping his hands, and chattering nonstop. Hovering around us, the black-hearted cuckold in his green hat who thought so highly of himself, and loathed everyone, though he didn't dare actually oppose anyone, took great pleasure in seeing two brothers fight; in fact, he took pleasure from anyone else's misery and pain. And at this point, you showed what you were made of.

The ox lowered his head and drove it into Hu Bin's backside, sending him sailing through the air like a cast-off coat, six feet off the ground, before gravity worked its magic and drove him into the reeds at a fateful slant, where he announced his landing with a screech that was as crooked as the tail of the Mongol ox. Clambering to his feet, Hu Bin careened off tall reeds that bent low with a loud rustle. The ox charged again, and Hu Bin was once again in flight.

Ximen Jinlong immediately let go of me, jumped up, raised his whip, and brought it down on the ox. I got to my feet, wrapped my arms around him, and flipped him to the ground, landing on top of him. How dare you hit my ox! You're a landlord's kid with no sense of friendship, someone who repays kindness with hatred. A dog has eaten your conscience! The landlord's kid arched upward and flung me off his back. Then he got to his feet, hit me with his whip, and ran over to rescue the whining Hu Bin, who was flailing and stumbling as he tried to escape from his reedy surroundings, like a beaten dog. It was a sight to behold! The evil man had gotten what he deserved, at last; justice had been served. It would have been perfect if you'd punished Ximen Jinlong before dishing out retribution to Hu Bin. But of course now I realize that you were being true to the notion that a mighty tiger will not eat one of its own, so that was understandable. Your son Ximen Jinlong went in pursuit with his whip. Hu Bin was running away — no, I shouldn't say running. Buttons on his tattered army greatcoat, the emblem of his glorious history, were popping off as his coat flapped in the wind like the broken wings of a dead bird. His hat had fallen off and was trampled into the mud by the ox's hooves. Help . . . ! Save me . . . ! Actually, that wasn't what I heard, but I knew that the sounds that emerged from his mouth contained a plea for someone to come to his rescue. My ox, brave, embodying human traits, was in hot pursuit. He kept his head low as he ran; red rays spurting from his eyes and penetrating the span of history appeared before me. His hooves kicked up white alkaline soil that sliced into the reeds like shrapnel, that peppered my and Ximen Jinlong's bodies, and, farther off, that pelted the liberated water in the river like hailstones. The smell of clean water filled my nostrils, that and the odor of melting ice and the aroma of once frozen mud, plus the stink of female ox piss. The smell of an animal in heat signaled the arrival of spring, the rebirth of countless beings; the season for mating was nearly upon us. Snakes and frogs and toads and all manner of insects that had slept through the long winter were awakening. Infinite varieties of grasses and edible greens were jolted out of their slumber; vapors imprisoned in the soil were released into the air. Spring was coming. That day the ox chased after Hu Bin, Ximen Jinlong chased after the ox, and I chased after Ximen Jinlong. We were bringing with us the spring of 1965.

Hu Bin thudded to the ground like a dog going after a pile of turds. The ox butted him over and over, calling to mind the scene of a blacksmith hammering on his anvil. Each butt produced a weak complaint from Hu Bin, whose body seemed thinner and longer and wider, like a cow patty. Ximen Jinlong arrived on the scene and cracked his whip on your rump, over and over, each snap leaving a red mark. But you didn't turn on him, you offered no resistance, though at the time I wished that you'd turned and butted him all the way into the river, where he'd crack through the ice and be half drowned or half frozen to death — two half deaths would have meant one complete one — though I didn't really want him to die, since that would have crushed Mother, who, I knew, cherished him more than she cherished me. So I broke off some thick reeds, and while he was lashing you on the rump, I lashed him on the head and neck. Perturbed by my lashing, he turned and used his whip on me. Ow! Dear Mother! That not only hurt, it tore open my padded coat. Blood trickled from a cut on my cheek. Then you turned around.

Oh, how I wanted you to butt him. But you didn't. Still, he warily backed off. You made a low, grumbling sound. Your eyes were so sad. The sound you made was, after all, a call to your son, something he didn't understand. You came toward him; what you wanted was to stroke him, but he didn't understand that either. He thought you were coming after him, so he raised his whip and brought it down on you. It was a brutal hit, and right on target — it hit you in the eye. Your knees buckled into a kneel; tears gushed from your eyes and dripped noisily to the ground.

"Ximen Jinlong," I screamed, horrified, "you thug, you've blinded my ox!"

He hit you again on the head, even harder, opening a gash on your face; this time it was blood that dripped to the ground. My ox! I ran up and covered your head. My tears dripped onto your juvenile horns. I protected you with my slender body. Go ahead, Ximen Jinlong, use your whip, rip my coat to shreds, slice my flesh like mud and spread it over the dead grass, but I won't let you hit my ox anymore. I felt your head throbbing against my chest; I scooped up some of the alkaline soil and rubbed it into your wounds, and I tore padding from my coat to dry your tears. I was heartsick that he might have blinded you. But as the saying goes, You cannot cripple a dog and you cannot blind an ox: your eyesight was spared.

Over the month that followed, the same scene played out every day: Ximen Jinlong pressuring me into joining the commune before

Father returned. I said no, he beat me, and my ox took it out on Hu Bin. And each time Hu Bin was the target, he hid behind my brother. The two of them — my brother and my ox — squared off against one another, neither giving ground for several minutes, until they both backed off and the day passed without further incident. At first, a fight to the death seemed inevitable, but as time passed, it turned into a game. What made me proud in all this was the fear my ox instilled in Hu Bin, and how that cruel, evil mouth of his lost its insolence. The minute the jabbering began, my ox would lower his head and bellow, his eyes would turn red, and he'd tense before charging. All the panicky Hu Bin could do was hide behind my half brother, who never again raised his whip against my ox. Maybe he had an inkling of something. You two were, after all, father and son, and there must have been some sort of connection. As for his beatings of me, they too became more symbolic than real. That was in reaction to the bayonet I wore in my belt and the helmet I had begun wearing after that first violent struggle. I'd stolen the two additions from a scrap pile during the steel smelting campaign years before. After keeping them hidden in the ox shed for so long, it was time to put them to use.

16

A Young Woman's Heart Is Moved as
She Dreams of Spring
Ximen Ox Displays His Might as He Plows a Field

Ah, Ximen Ox! The spring planting season were happy days for us. The letter Dad brought back from the provincial capital served its purpose well. You'd grown into an adult ox by then, and had pretty much grown out of the cramped quarters our tiny ox shed provided. The young oxen belonging to the production brigade had already been castrated, and people were urging my dad to put a nose ring on you for purposes of work, but he ignored them all. I agreed, since our relationship had gone beyond that of farmer and farm animal; not only were we kindred spirits, intimate friends, we were also comrades-in-arms walking hand in hand, standing shoulder to shoulder, united in our commitment to independent farming and our firm opposition to collectivization.

Our three-point-two acres of farmland were surrounded by land belonging to the commune. Given the proximity to the Grain Barge River, our thick, rich topsoil was ideal for plowing. With these three-point-two acres and a strong ox, my son, you and I can look forward to eating well, Dad said. He'd returned from the provincial capital with a severe case of insomnia, and I often awoke from a deep sleep to find him sitting fully dressed on the edge of the *kang*, leaning against the wall and puffing on his pipe. To me, the thick tobacco smoke was slightly nauseating.

"Why aren't you sleeping, Dad?" I'd ask.

"I will," he'd say, "soon. You go back to sleep. I'll go give the ox a bit more hay."

I'd get up to pee — you should know all about my bed-wetting.

When you went out to graze as a donkey, I'm sure you spotted my bedding drying in the sun. Whenever Wu Qiuxiang saw my mother taking it out to dry, she'd call out for her daughters: Hey, Huzhu, Hezuo, come out here and take a look at the world map Jiefang drew on his bedding. The girls would come running with a stick to point at the stains on my bedding. This is Asia, this is Africa, here's Latin America, this is the Atlantic Ocean, the Indian Ocean . . . humiliation made me want to crawl into a hole and never come out, and it sparked a desire to set fire to that bedding. If Hong Taiyue had witnessed that, he'd have said, Master Jiefang, you could throw that bedding over your head and charge an enemy pillbox. No bullet could penetrate it and a hand grenade would bounce right off it! — But what was the use in dredging past humiliations? The good news was, once I'd joined Dad as an independent farmer, my bed-wetting problem cured itself, and that was one of the more important reasons I stood up for independent farming and in opposition to collectivization. The moonlight, limpid as water, turned our little room silvery; even mice scrounging for scraps of food became silver rodents. I heard Mother's sighs on the other side of the wall, and I knew she too suffered from sleeplessness. She couldn't stop worrying about me, and she wished Dad would take me into the commune, so we could be a happy family again. But he was too stubborn to do that just because she wanted him to. The beauty of the moonlight drove away all thoughts of sleep, and I wanted to see how the ox spent his nights in the shed. Did he stay awake all night or did he sleep, just like people? Did he sleep lying down or standing up? Eyes open or eyes shut? I threw my coat over my shoulders and slipped out into the yard. The ground was cold against my bare feet, but I didn't feel a chill. The moonlight was even denser out in the yard, turning the apricot tree into a silvery tower that cast a dark arboreal shadow on the ground. Dad was out there tossing feed in a sifter, seeming bigger than he was in the daylight, as a broad moonbeam lit up the sifter and his two large hands. The sound — *shush shush* — emerged rhythmically from the sifter, which seemed to hang in the air; Dad's hands looked like appendages to it. The feed was dumped into the trough, after which came the slurping sound of a bovine tongue licking it up. I saw the ox's shining eyes, I smelled its hot bovine odor. Blackie, I heard Dad say, tomorrow we start the plowing, so eat up. You'll need your strength. We'll do ourselves proud, Blackie, and give those socialists an eyeful. Lan Lian is the world's greatest farmer, and

Lan Lian's ox is the world's greatest ox! The ox shook his large head in response. They want me to put a nose ring on you, Dad continued. Bullshit! My ox is like my son, more human than animal. I treat you like a man, not an ox. Do people put nose rings on men? And they want me to geld you. Double bullshit! I told them to go home and geld their sons! What do you think of that, Blackie? Before you came, Blackie, I had a donkey, the best donkey in the world. A hard worker, like you, more human than animal, and prone to violence. He'd still be alive today if they hadn't killed him during the steel-smelting campaign. But on second thought, if that donkey hadn't passed on, I wouldn't have you. I knew you were the one I wanted the minute I laid eyes on you at the livestock market.

Blackie, I can't help feeling that you're the reincarnation of that donkey, that fate has brought us together!

I couldn't see my dad's face in the shadows, only his hands resting on the feed trough, but I could see the ox's aquamarine eyes. The ox's coat, chestnut colored when we first brought him home, had darkened until it was nearly black, which is why Dad called him Blackie. I sneezed, startling Dad. Flustered, he slinked out of the shed.

"Oh, it's you, son. What are you doing standing here? Go back inside and get some sleep."

"How about you, Dad?"

He looked up at the stars.

"All right," he said, "I'll go with you."

As I lay there half asleep, I could sense Dad crawling quietly out of bed, and I wondered why. So as soon as he was out the door, I got up, and once I was out in the yard, the moonlight seemed brighter, almost like undulating sheets of silk above me — immaculately white, glossy, and so cool I felt I could tear them out of the sky and fold them around me or roll them into balls and put them in my mouth. I looked over at the ox shed, which had grown bigger and brighter, obliterating all the darkness; the ox dung looked like white steamed buns. But, to my amazement, neither Dad nor the ox was in the shed. I knew I'd been right behind him and had watched him enter the shed, so how could he have simply vanished? And not only him, but the ox as well. They couldn't have been transmuted into moonbeams, could they? I walked over to the gate and looked around. Then I understood. Dad and the ox had gone out. But what were they doing out there in the middle of the night?

There were no sounds on the street. The trees, the walls, the ground, all silver; even the propaganda slogans on the walls were dazzling white: "Ferret Out Those in Power within the Party Who Are Taking the Capitalist Road," "Pursue the Four Clean-ups Campaign to its Conclusion!" Ximen Jinlong had written that one. What a genius! I'd never before seen him write a slogan, but he'd walked up that day carrying a bucket filled with black ink and an ink-saturated brush made of twisted hemp fibers, and written that one on our wall. Every stroke was vigorous, every line straight and even, every hook powerful. At least as big as a pregnant goat, each character drew gasps of admiration from anyone who saw them. My brother was the best-educated and most highly respected youngster in the village. Even the college students who made up the Four Clean-ups Brigade and other brigade workers not only liked him, they were his friends. He was already a member of the Communist Youth League and, or so I heard, had submitted his application to join the Party. An active participant in Party activities, he drew as close as possible to Party members in order to help his case. Chang Tianhong, a talented member of the Four Clean-ups Brigade, and a former voice student at the provincial art academy, taught my brother elements of Western styles of singing. There were days during that winter when the two of them sang revolutionary songs, dragging the notes out longer than a braying donkey; their duets became a standard opening before meetings of the brigade members. My brother's friend, whom we called Little Chang, was often seen entering and leaving our compound. He had naturally curly hair, a small, pale face with big bright eyes, a wide mouth, stubble that looked blue, and a prominent Adam's apple. A big young man, and tall, he stood out from all the other young villagers. Many of the envious young fellows gave him a nickname: "Braying Jackass," and since my brother studied singing with him, his nickname was "Junior Jackass." The two "jackasses" were like brothers, so close their only regret was that they couldn't both fit into the same pair of pants.

The village Four Clean-ups campaign created torment in the lives of every cadre: Huang Tong, the militia company commander and brigade commander, was removed from his positions over the misappropriation of money; Hong Taiyue, the village Party secretary, was removed from his position for roasting and eating a black goat that was being raised in the brigade goat nursery. But they were back at their posts in short order; not so fortunate was the brigade accountant, who stole horse feed from the production brigade. His dismissal was permanent. Political campaigns, like stage plays, are spectacles, events incorporating clamorous gongs and drums, wind-blown banners, slogans on walls, with commune members working during the day and attending meetings at night. I was a minor independent farmer, but noise and excitement appealed to me too. Those were days when I desperately wanted to join the commune, so I could follow behind the "two jackasses" and see the sights. The cultured behavior of the "two jackasses" did not go unnoticed by the young women; love was in the air. Watching with cool detachment, I could see that my sister, Ximen Baofeng, had fallen for Little Chang, while the twins, Huang Huzhu and Huang Hezuo, had fallen for my brother. No one fell for me. Maybe in their eyes I was just a dumb little boy. How could they know that love burned in my heart? I was secretly in love with Huang Tong's elder daughter, Huzhu.

Well, enough of that. So I went out into the street, and still found no trace of my dad and the black ox. Could they have flown to the moon! I conjured up an image of Dad on the back of the ox, hooves pounding the clouds, tail moving back and forth like a rudder as they levitate, higher and higher. It had to be an illusion, because Dad wouldn't fly to the moon and leave me behind. So I knew I had to keep my feet planted on earth and look for them in the same realm. I stood still, concentrating all my energy. First, I sniffed the air, nostrils wide open. It worked. They hadn't gone far; they were southeast of where I was standing, in the vicinity of the decrepit village wall, at one of the dead-infant sites, a spot where villagers used to discard children who had died in infancy. Later on, fresh dirt was brought in to level the ground and turn it into the brigade threshing floor. Perfectly flat, it was surrounded by a waist-high wall, alongside which some stone rollers and stone mills had been left. It was a favorite place for children to play. They chased each other around, dressed only in red stomachers, their bare bottoms fully exposed. I knew they were actually the ghosts of dead children who came out to play when the moon was full. So cute, those spirit-children, as they lined up and jumped from the stone rollers to the stone mills and from the stone mills back to the stone rollers. Their leader was a little boy with a vertical pigtail who had a shiny whistle in his mouth, which he blew rhythmically. The other children echoed his whistle each time they jumped, in perfect cadence, a treat for the eyes. I was so mesmerized I nearly felt like joining their number. When they tired of jumping from the stone rollers to the stone mills, they climbed the wall and sat in a straight line, legs hanging down as they pounded the wall with their heels and sang a ditty that moved me so much I stuck my hand in my pocket and took out a handful of fried black beans. When they reached out, I placed five beans in each hand, on which I saw fine yellow hairs. They were captivating children, with bright eyes and lovely white teeth. From the top of the wall rose the crunching of beans and an alluring scorched aroma. Dad and the ox were performing drills out on the threshing floor as more red children than I could count appeared on the top of the wall. I put my hand over my pocket. What would I do if they all wanted black beans? Dad was wearing skin-tight clothes with a green lotus-shaped piece of cloth on each shoulder and a tall horn-shaped piece of tin plate on his head. He had painted the right side of his face with red grease paint, creating a stunning contrast with the blue birthmark on the left side. He was barking unintelligible commands as he drilled; to me they sounded like curses, but I was sure the red children on the wall understood every word, because they clapped rhythmically and thumped their heels against the wall and whistled; a few even took little horns out from under their stomachers and tooted along, while others brought drums up from the other side of the wall, placed them between their knees, and pounded away. At the same time, our family ox, sporting red satin cloth on his horns and a big red satin flower on his forehead, which made him look like a jubilant bridegroom, was running around the outer edge of the threshing floor. His body glistened, his eyes were bright as crystal, his hooves like lit lanterns that carried him in a graceful, smooth, and easy gait. Each time he passed by the red children, they pounded their drums and shouted their approval, producing waves of cheers. In all, he circled the floor ten times or more before joining Dad in the center, where Dad rewarded him with a chunk of bean cake. Then Dad rubbed his head and patted him on the rump.

"Watch the miracle!" he sang out in a more resonant voice even than Braying Jackass.

Big-head Lan Qiansui gave me a puzzled look, and I knew he was having trouble believing my narration. You've forgotten after all these years; or, maybe what I saw that night was a fanciful dream. But dream or no dream, you played a role; or maybe I should say that, without you, there'd have been no such dream.

As Dad's shout died out, he cracked his whip on the ground, producing a crisp little explosion that sounded as if he'd hit a plate of glass. The ox reared up until he was nearly vertical, supported solely by his hind legs. That is not a difficult maneuver for an ox, since it replicates the mating posture of a bull. What was not so easy was how he kept his front legs and body up straight with nothing to help him keep his balance but his hind legs; then he began to walk, one awkward step at a time, but remarkable enough to cause stupefied gapes from anyone who saw him. That a massive ox could actually stand up and walk on his hind legs, and not just four or five steps, or even nine or ten steps, but all the way around the outer edge of the threshing floor, was something I'd never imagined, let alone seen with my own eyes. He dragged his tail along the ground, his front legs curled in front of his chest, like a pair of stunted arms. His belly was completely exposed, his papaya-sized gonads swung back and forth, and it was almost as if the sole function of the spectacle was to show off his maleness. The red children on the wall, normally eager to make noise, were silent. They forgot to toot their horns and beat their drums, they just sat there slack-jawed, looks of disbelief on their little faces. Not until the ox had made a complete revolution and once again had all four hooves on the ground did the red children regain their composure and once again hoot and holler, clap their hands, beat their drums, blow their horns, and whistle.

What followed was even more miraculous. The ox lowered his head until it was touching the ground, then, straining hard, he lifted his hind legs off the ground, very much like a human headstand, but infinitely harder to manage. It didn't seem possible that an animal weighing 800 or more catties could support all that weight on his neck alone. But our family ox did just that. — Allow me to once again describe those papaya-sized gonads: stuck up all alone against the skin of his belly, they appeared somehow redundant . . .

You went out to work the next morning for the first time — plowing the field. Our plow was made of wood, its blades, which had been forged by a blacksmith in Anhui, shiny as a mirror. Wooden plows like ours were no longer being used by the production brigade; they had been replaced by Great Harvest brand steel plows. Deciding to stick to tradition, we shunned those industrial tools, which reeked of paint. Since we had chosen to remain independent, Dad said, it was important to keep a distance from the collective in every respect. And since Great Harvest brand plows were tools of the collective, they weren't for us. Our clothes were made of local fabric, we made our own tools, and we used kerosene lamps and flints for fire. That morning, the production brigade sent nine plows out, to compete with us, it seemed. On the east bank of the river, the state-run farm's tractors were also out in the fields, their bright red paint making them look like a pair of red devils. Blue smoke billowed from their smokestacks as they set up a deafening roar. Each of the production brigade's nine plows was pulled by a pair of oxen working in a flying geese formation. They were being driven by highly experienced plowmen, all driving their teams with hard-set faces, as if participating in a solemn ceremony, not plowing fields for crops.

Hong Taiyue, in a brand-new black uniform, arrived at the edge of the field, looking much older, his hair turned gray, his cheek muscles slack, the corners of his mouth sagging. Jinlong followed behind him, carrying a clipboard in his left hand and a fountain pen in his right, sort of like a reporter. For the life of me, I couldn't figure out what he was going to record — not every word uttered by Hong Taiyue, I hoped. After all, even with his revolutionary history, Hong was merely the Party secretary of a small village, and since grassroots cadres of those days were all the same, he shouldn't have postured so much. Besides, he'd cooked and eaten a goat belonging to the collective and had nearly been cashiered during the Four Clean-ups campaign, which meant that his political consciousness was less than ideal.

With unhurried efficiency, Dad lined up the plow and checked the harness on the ox, leaving nothing for me to do but look on excitedly, and what stuck in my mind were the stunts I'd watched him and his ox perform on the threshing floor the night before. The sight of the powerful figure of our ox reminded me what a difficult maneuver it had been. I didn't ask Dad about it, wanting it to be something that had actually happened and not something I'd dreamed.

Hong Taiyue, hands on his hips, was giving instructions to his subordinates, citing everything from Quemoy and Matsu to the Korean War, from land reform to class struggle. Then he said that agri-

cultural production was the first battle to be fought against imperial-
ism, capitalism, and independent farmers taking the capitalist road.
He brought the experience he'd cultivated during his days of beating
his ox hip bone into play, and even though his speech was peppered
with mistakes, his voice was strong, his words hung together, and the
plowmen were so intimidated they stood frozen in place. So did the
oxen. I saw our ox's mother among them — the Mongol — immediately identifiable by her long, crooked tail. She seemed to be casting
glances our way, and I knew she was looking at her son. Hey, at this
point I can't help but feel embarrassed for you. Last spring, when I
was fighting with my brother on the sandbar after I'd taken you out to
graze, I saw you try to mount her. That's incest, a crime. Naturally,
that doesn't count for much with oxen, but you're no ordinary ox —
you were a man in your previous life! There is, of course, the possibility that in her previous life she was your lover, but she's the one who
gave birth to you — the more I ponder the mysteries of this wheel of
life, the more confused I get.

"Put those thoughts out of your mind, right now!" Big-head said
impatiently.

All right, they're out. I thought back to when my brother Jinlong
was down on one knee with his clipboard on his other knee writing at
a frantic pace. Then Hong Taiyue gave the order: Start plowing! The
plowmen took their whips off their shoulders, snapped them in the air,
and shouted as one: "*Ha lei-lei-lei—*" It was a command readily understood by the oxen. The production brigade plows moved forward,
creating waves of mud to both sides. With mounting anxiety, I said
softly: Dad, let's get started. He smiled and said to the ox:

"All right, Blackie, let's get to work!"

Without recourse to a whip, Dad spoke softly to our ox, who
lurched forward. The plow dug deep and jerked him back.

"Not so hard," Dad said. "Pull slowly."

But the overeager ox was set on taking big strides. His muscles
bulged, the plow shuddered, and great wedges of mud, shimmering in
the sunlight, arced to the sides. Dad adjusted the plow as they went
along to keep it from getting stuck. As a onetime farmhand, he knew
what he was doing. What surprised me was that our ox, tilling a field
for the first time, moved in a straight line, even though his movements
were somewhat awkward and his breathing was, from time to time,

irregular. Dad didn't have to guide or control him. Our plow was being pulled by a single ox, the production brigade's plows by teams of two, yet we quickly overtook their lead plow. I was so proud I couldn't contain my excitement. As I ran back and forth, our ox and plow created the image of a sailing vessel turning the mud into whitecaps. I saw the production-brigade plowmen look over at us. Hong Taiyue and my brother walked up, stood off to one side, and watched with hostility in their eyes. After our plow had reached the end of our land and turned back, Hong walked up in front of our ox and shouted:

"Stop right there, Lan Lian!"

With fire in its eyes, the ox kept coming, forcing Hong to jump out of the way in fright. He knew our animal's temper as well as anybody. He had no choice but to fall in behind our plow and say to Dad:

"I'm warning you, Lan Lian, don't you dare so much as touch land belonging to the collective with your plow."

Dad replied, neither haughtily nor humbly:

"As long as your oxen don't step on my land, mine won't step on yours."

I knew that Hong was trying to make things difficult, because our three-point-two acres were a wedge in the production brigade's land. Since our plot was a hundred yards long and only twenty-one yards wide, it was hard not to touch theirs when the plow reached the end or went along the edges. But when they plowed the edges of their land, it was just as hard to avoid touching ours. Dad had nothing to fear.

"We'd rather sacrifice a few feet of plowed land than step foot on your three-point-two acres!" Hong said.

Hong could make that boastful statement since the production brigade had so much land. But what about us? With the few acres we worked, we couldn't sacrifice any. But Dad had a plan. "I'm not going to sacrifice even an inch of my land," he said. "And you still won't find a single one of our hoofprints on collective soil!"

"Those are your words, remember them," Hong said.

"That's right, those are my words."

"I want you to keep an eye on them, Jinlong," Hong said. "If that ox of theirs so much as steps on our land—" He paused. "Lan Lian, if your ox steps on our land, what should your punishment be?"

"You can chop off my ox's leg," Dad said defiantly.

What a shock that gave me! There was no clear boundary

between our land and that belonging to the collective, nothing but a rock in the ground every fifty yards, and keeping a straight line by walking was no sure thing, let alone an ox pulling a plow.

Since Dad was employing the cleft method of plowing — starting from the middle and working his way outward — the risk of stepping on their land was minimal for a while. So Hong Taiyue said to my brother:

"Jinlong, go back to the village and prepare the bulletin board. You can come back and keep watch on them this afternoon."

When we went home for lunch, a crowd had gathered around the bulletin board on our wall. Two yards wide and three yards long, it served as the village's center for public opinion. In the space of a few hours my talented brother had made it a feast for the eyes with red, yellow, and green chalk. On the edges he had drawn tractors, sunflowers and greenery, commune members behind steel plows, their faces beaming, and oxen pulling the plows, their faces beaming as well. Then in the lower right-hand corner, in blue and white he'd drawn a skinny ox and two skinny people, one adult and one child — obviously, me, my dad, and our ox. In the middle he'd written in ancient block letters: SPRING PLOWING: PEOPLE ARE HAPPY, OXEN ARE LOWING. Below that in regular script he'd added: "A clear-cut comparison between the bustling activity of the People's Commune and State-Run Farm as, bursting with energy, they engage in spring plowing, and the village's obstinate independent farmer Lan Lian and his family, who tills his land with a single ox and plow, the ox with its head lowered, the farmer looking crestfallen, a solitary figure looking like a plucked chicken, his ox like a stray dog, miserable and anxious, having come to a dead end."

"Dad," I said, "look at the way he's made us look!"

With our plow over his shoulder and leading the ox behind him, he wore a smile as cold and brilliant as ice.

"He can write what he wants," he said. "That boy has talent. Whatever he draws looks real."

The onlookers' gazes snapped around and fell on us, followed by knowing smiles. Facts spoke louder than words. We had a mighty ox and our blue faces glowed, for, thanks to a good morning's work, we were in high spirits and very proud of ourselves.

Jinlong was standing off a ways observing his masterpiece and its spectators. Huang Huzhu was leaning against her door frame holding the tip of her braid in her mouth, her eyes fixed on Jinlong, the dazed look in her eyes proof that the stirrings of love had grown strong. My half sister, Baofeng, came up the street toward us from the west, a leather medical satchel with a red cross painted on it slung over her back. Now that she had learned midwife skills and how to give injections, she was the village health worker. Huang Hezuo rode up unsteadily from the east, apparently having just learned how to ride a bike, and finding it hard to steer. When she spotted Jinlong leaning against the wall, she shouted, Oh, no, watch out! as she careened toward Jinlong, who stepped out of the way and grabbed the wheel with one hand and the handlebars with the other; Huang Hezuo nearly landed in his lap.

I looked over at Huang Huzhu, who jerked her head around so hard her braid flew; red in the face, she spun on her heel and stormed into the house. I was sick at heart, feeling nothing but sympathy for Huzhu and loathing for Hezuo, who had cut her hair short and combed it with a boy's part, a style that was a current fad among middle-school students in the commune. The barber Ma Liangcai, an expert Ping-Pong player who was also pretty good on the harmonica, was responsible for all those haircuts. He went around dressed in a blue uniform that had been laundered nearly white, had a thick head of hair, deep black eyes, and a case of acne, and always smelled like hand soap. He had a thing for my sister. He often brought his air gun into our village to shoot birds, and was always successful. At first sight of him and his air gun, the village sparrows flew to spots unknown. The village health clinic was located in a room just east of the Ximen estate main house. What that means is, any time that fellow showed up at the local clinic, reeking of hand soap, he was lucky if he could escape the gazes of members of our family, and if he somehow managed that, he'd fall under the scrutiny of members of the Huang family. The fellow never passed up a chance to get close to my sister, who would frown and try not to make her feelings of disgust obvious as she reluctantly chatted with him. I knew that my sister was in love with Braying Jackass, but he had left with the Four Clean-ups team and vanished like a weasel in the woods. Since my mother could see that this marriage was anything but assured, outside of sighing in frustration, all she could do was try to reason with my sister.

"Baofeng, I know what you're feeling, but are you being realistic? He grew up in the provincial capital, where he went to college. He's talented and good looking, and has a bright future. How could someone like that fall for you? Listen to your mother and give up such thoughts. Lower your sights a bit. Little Ma is a teacher on the public payroll. He's not bad looking, he's literate, he plays the harmonica, and he's a crack shot. He's one in a hundred, if you ask me, and since he has his eye on you, why the hesitation? Go on, say yes to him. Take a good look at the eyes of the Huang sisters. The meat is right in front of you, and if you don't eat it, someone else will. . . ."

Everything Mother said made sense. To me, Ma Liangcai and my sister were well suited for one another. Sure, he couldn't sing like Braying Jackass, but he could make his harmonica sound like birds singing and could rid the village of its sparrows with his air gun, both virtues Braying Jackass lacked. But my sister had a stubborn streak, just like her father; Mother could talk till her lips were cracked, and her reply was always:

"Mother, I'll decide whom I marry!"

We returned to the field that afternoon. Jinlong, a metal hoe over his shoulder, followed us step for step. The glinting blade of his tool was so sharp he could sever an ox's hoof with one swing if he felt like it. His attitude of forsaking friends and family disgusted me, and I took every opportunity to let him know how I felt. I called him Hong Taiyue's running dog and an ungrateful swine. He ignored me, but each time I blocked his way, he threw dirt in my face. When I tried to retaliate, Dad stopped me with an angry curse. He seemed to have eyes in the back of his head and invariably knew what I was up to. I reached down and picked up a dirt clod.

"Jiefang, what do you think you're doing?" he roared.

"I want to teach this swine a lesson!" I said angrily.

"Shut up!" he railed. "If you don't, I'll tan your hide. He's your older brother and he's acting in an official capacity, so don't get in his way."

After two rounds of tilling, the production brigade oxen were panting from exhaustion, especially the female Mongol. Even from far away, we could hear what sounded like a confused hen trying to imitate a crowing rooster emerge from deep down in her throat, and I recalled what the youngster had whispered to me back when we were buying the young ox. He had called its mother a "hot turtle" that was ill equipped for hard work and useless during the hot summer months. Now I knew he was telling the truth. Not only was she gasping for breath, she was foaming at the mouth; it was not a pretty sight. Eventually, she collapsed and lay on the ground, her eyes rolling back into her head, like a dead cow. All the other oxen stopped working, and the plowmen ran up to her. Opinions flew back and forth. The term "hot turtle" had been the brainchild of an old farmer. One of the men recommended going for the veterinarian, but that suggestion was met with cold disdain. The comment, She's beyond help, was heard.

When Dad reached the end of our plot, he stopped and said to my brother:

"Jinlong, there's no need for you to follow behind me. I said we won't leave a single hoofprint on public land, so you're just tiring yourself out for nothing."

Jinlong responded with a snort, and that's all.

"My ox will not step on public land," he repeated. "But the agreement was that your oxen and people would not step on my land either. By following me, you're walking on my land. You're standing on it right now, as a matter of fact."

That stopped Jinlong in his tracks. Like a frightened kangaroo, he jumped off our land all the way to the riverbank road.

"I ought to lop off those hooves of yours!" I shouted.

His face bright red, he was too embarrassed to say a word.

"Jinlong," Dad said, "how about you and me, father and son, tolerating each other's position? Your heart is set on being progressive, and I'm not going to stand in your way. In fact, you have my full support. Your biological father was a landlord, but he was also my benefactor. Criticizing and attacking him was what the situation demanded, something I did for the benefit of others. But I'll always be grateful to him. As for you, well, I've always treated you like my own flesh and blood, and I won't try to stop you from going your own way. My only hope is that there'll always be a spot of warmth in your heart and that you won't let it become cold and hard like a chunk of iron."

"I stepped on your land, that I can't deny," Jinlong said grimly, "and you have every right to chop off my leg!" He flung his hoe toward us; it stuck in the ground between Dad and me. "If you don't want to do it, that's your problem. But if your ox, or either one of you, so much as steps foot on commune land, whether you mean to or not, don't expect any favors from me!"

The expression on his face and the green flames that seemed to be shooting from his eyes sent chills down my spine and raised goose-flesh on my arms. My half brother was no ordinary young man; if he said he'd do something, he'd do it. If one of our feet or our ox's hooves crossed that line, he'd come at us with his hoe without blinking an eye. What a shame for a man like him to be born during peacetime. If he'd been born only a few decades earlier, he'd have worn the mantle of hero, no matter whom he fought for, and if banditry had been his calling, he'd have been a king of slaughter. But this was, after all, peacetime, and there was little call for such ruthlessness, such daring and tenacity, and such incorruptibility.

Dad, too, seemed shaken by what he heard. He quickly looked away and fixed his gaze on the hoe stuck in the ground at his feet.

"Jinlong," he said, "forget what I said. I'll ease your concerns and, at the same time, carry out my pledge by tilling my land right next to yours. You can watch, and if you think it's necessary to put your hoe to use, then go ahead. That way I won't waste any more of your time."

He walked up to our ox, rubbed its ears, and patted it on the forehead.

"Ox," he whispered in its ear, "ah, my ox! It's all been said. Keep your eye on the boundary marker and walk straight ahead. Don't veer an inch!"

After adjusting the plow and sizing up the boundary, he gave a low command, and the ox started walking. My brother picked up his hoe and stared with bulging eyes at the ox's hooves. The animal appeared unconcerned about the danger lurking behind him; he walked at a normal pace, his body limber, his back so smooth and steady he could have carried a full bowl of water without spilling a drop. Dad walked behind, stepping squarely in the new furrow. The work was totally reliant on the ox; given that his eyes were on either side of his head, how he managed to move in a perfectly straight line was beyond me. I simply watched as the new furrow neatly separated our land from theirs, with the boundary markers standing between the two. The ox slowed down each time he neared one of the stone markers to let Dad lift the plow over it. Every one of his hoof prints remained on our side, all the way to the end; there was nothing Jinlong could do. Dad exhaled loudly and said to Jinlong:

"You can head back home now, worry free, can't you?"

So Jinlong left us, but not before casting one last reluctant glance at the ox's perfect, bright hooves, and I knew how disappointed he was at not being able to chop one off. The hoe, slung over his shoulder as he walked off, glinted silvery in the sunlight, and that sight was burned into my memory.

17

Wild Geese Fall, People Die, an Ox Goes Berserk
Ravings and Wild Talk Turn into an Essay

As for what happened next, should I continuing telling or do you want to take over? I asked Big-head. He squinted, as if he were looking at me, But I knew that his thoughts were elsewhere. He took a cigarette out of my pack, held it up to his nose to smell it, and curled his lip without saying anything, as if contemplating something very important. That's a bad habit somebody your age should avoid. If you started smoking at the age of five, you'd have to smoke gunpowder when you reach the age of fifty, right? He ignored me and cocked his head; his outer ear twitched, as if he were straining to listen to something. I won't say any more, I said. There isn't much to say, anyway, since it's all things we experienced. No, he said, you started, so you ought to finish. I said I didn't know where to begin. He rolled his eyes.

Begin with the marketplace, focus on the fun part.

I saw plenty of people paraded through the marketplace, something that never failed to excite me, excite and delight.

I saw County Chief Chen, the man who had been friendly to Dad, paraded publicly through the marketplace. His head was shaved, the skin showing black — afterward, in his memoirs, he said he'd shaved his head so the Red Guards couldn't pull him by the hair — and a papier-mâché donkey had been tied around his waist. As the air filled with drumbeats and the clang of gongs, he ran around to the beat, dancing with a goofy smile on his face. He looked like one of the local entertainers at New Year's. Because he'd ridden our family's donkey on inspection trips during the iron- and steel-smelting campaign, people had saddled him with the nickname Donkey Chief. Then when the Cultural Revolution broke out, the Red Guards wanted to enhance the pleasure, the visual appeal, and the ability to draw a crowd when they were parading capitalist-roaders, so they made him wear that papier-mâché donkey. Plenty of cadres later wrote their memoirs, and when they related what had occurred during the Cultural Revolution, it was a tale of blood and tears, describing the period as hell on earth, more terrifying than Hitler's concentration camps. But this official wrote about his experiences in the early days of the Cultural Revolution in a lively, humorous style. He wrote that he rode his paper donkey through eighteen marketplace parades, and in the process grew strong and healthy. No more high blood pressure and no more insomnia. He said the sound of drums and gongs energized him; his legs quaked, and, like a donkey spotting its mother, he stamped his feet and snorted through his nose. When I linked his memoirs and my recollection of him wearing the papier-mâché donkey, I understood why that goofy smile had adorned his face. He said that when he followed the beat of the drums and gongs and started dancing in his papier-mâché donkey, he felt himself slowly changing into a donkey, specifically the black donkey that belonged to the independent farmer Lan Lian, and his mind began to wander, free and relaxed, as if he were living somewhere between the real world and a wonderful illusion. To him it felt as if his legs had become a set of four hooves, that he had grown a tail, and that he and the papier-mâché donkey around his waist had fused into one body, much like the centaur of Greek mythology. As a result, he gained a firsthand perception of what it felt like to be a donkey, the joys and the suffering. Marketplaces offered few items for sale during the Cultural Revolution, and most of the hustle and bustle derived from people who had gathered to witness a variety of spectacles. Winter had recently arrived, so the people were bundled up, except for youngsters who preferred the look of thin clothing. Everyone wore red armbands, which were especially prominent on the arms of youngsters in thin khaki or blue military jackets. On the older residents' black, tattered padded coats, shiny with grime, the armbands were incongruous adornments. An old chicken peddler stood in the entrance to the Supply and Marketing Cooperative holding a chicken in her hand; she too wore a red armband. Have you joined the Red Guards too, Aunty? someone asked her. She pursed her lips and said, Red is all the rage, so why wouldn't I join? Which unit? Jinggang Mountain or Golden Monkey? Go to hell, she said, and don't waste my time with that nonsense. If you're here to buy a chicken, then buy one. If not, get the fuck off!

The propaganda team drove up in a Soviet truck left over from the Korean War. Its original green paint had faded after years of being buffeted by the elements, and a frame with four high-powered loudspeakers had been welded to the top of the cab. A gas-driven generator was mounted in the truck bed, the two sides of which were lined with Red Guards in imitation army uniforms, each gripping the side with one hand and holding up a *Little Red Book* in the other. Their faces were crimson, either from the cold or from revolutionary passion. One of them, a slightly cross-eyed girl, was grinning from ear to ear. The loudspeakers blared so loud a farmer's wife had a miscarriage, a pig ran headlong into a wall and knocked itself out, a whole roost of laying hens took to the air, and local dogs barked themselves hoarse. The first sounds after the playing of "The East Is Red" were the roar of the generator and static from the loudspeaker. They were followed by a melodious woman's voice. I climbed a tree so I could see inside the bed of the truck, where there were two chairs and a table on which rested some sort of machine and a microphone wrapped in red cloth. One of the chairs was occupied by a girl with little braids, the other by a boy who wore a part in his hair. I'd never seen her before, but he was Little Chang, who'd come to our village during the Four Clean-ups campaign, the one they called Braying Jackass. I later learned that he had been assigned to the county opera troupe and, as a rebel, the commander of the Golden Monkey Red Guard faction. I shouted down to him from my perch up in the tree: Little Chang! Little Chang! Jackass! But my shouts were swallowed up by the loudspeaker.

The girl shouted into the microphone, and the loudspeaker carried her voice like thunderclaps. Here is what everyone in Northeast Gaomi Township heard: Capitalist-roader Chen Guangdi, a donkey trader who wormed his way into the Party, opposed the Great Leap Forward, opposed the Three Red Banners, is a sworn brother to Lan Lian, Northeast Gaomi Township's independent farmer who stubbornly hews to the Capitalist Road, and acts as the independent farmer's protective umbrella. Chen Guangdi is not only an ideological reactionary, he is also immoral. He had sexual relations with a donkey and made her pregnant. She gave birth to a monster: a donkey with a human head!

Yes! The crowd roared its approval. The Red Guards on the

truck followed Jackass's lead in shouting slogans: Down with County Chief Donkey-head Chen Guangdi! Down with County Chief Donkey-head Chen Guangdi! Down with the donkey rapist Chen Guangdi! Down with the donkey molester Chen Guangdi! Jackass's voice, magnified by the loudspeaker, became a vocal calamity, as a flock of wild geese flying overhead dropped out of the sky like stones. Now, the meat of these birds is a delicacy, and nutritious to boot, a rarity for the people below. For them to fall out of the sky at a time when the people's nutritional lives were so impoverished seemed to be a blessing from heaven, when in fact it was anything but. The people went crazy, pushing and shoving and shouting and screeching, worse than a pack of starving dogs. The first person to get his hands on a fallen bird must have been wild with joy, until, that is, everyone around him tried to snatch it away. Feathers fluttered to the ground, fine down floated in the air; it was like tearing apart a down pillow. The bird's wings were torn off, its legs wound up in someone else's hands, its head and neck were torn from its body and held high in the air, dripping blood. People in the rear pushed down on the heads and shoulders of those in front to leap like hunting dogs. People were knocked to the ground, squashed where they stood, trampled where they lay. Shrill cries of Mother! . . . Mother! . . . Help, save me . . . emerged from dozens of black knots of humanity that seethed and churned. Screams and shouts — Ow, my poor head!—merged with the howl of the loudspeaker. Chaos turned to tangled fighting and from there to violent battles. The final tally: seventeen people were trampled to death, an unknown number suffered injury.

Some of the dead were taken away by kin, others were dragged to the doorway of the Butcher Section to await identification and removal. Some of the injured were taken to the clinic or taken home by relatives, some walked or crawled away on their own; some limped away to wherever they wanted to go, some just lay on the ground and wept or wailed. These were Northeast Gaomi Township's first reported deaths in the Cultural Revolution. In the months to follow, while there were pitched battles, with bricks and tiles flying in the air and an assortment of weapons, from knives to guns to clubs, the number of casualties paled in comparison with this incident.

I was perfectly safe up in the tree, where I saw the whole incident unfold in all its detail. I saw the birds fall from the sky and watched as they were torn apart by people. I saw the whole range of expressions — greed, madness, astonishment, suffering, ferocity — during the incident; I heard everything from cries of torment to those of wild joy; I smelled blood and other noxious odors; and I felt both chilled currents and overheated waves in the air. All this reminded me of tales of wartime, and even though the county annals of the Cultural Revolution recorded the wild geese incident as a case of bird flu, I believed then, and I believe now, that they were knocked out of the sky by the high-volume shrillness of the loudspeaker.

After things quieted down, the parades started up again, although the incident had a cautionary effect on the observing crowds. A gray path opened up in the market where heads once bobbed; it was now dotted with bloodstains and squashed bird carcasses. Breezes carrying a heavy stink blew feathers here and there. The woman who had been selling chickens was hobbling up and down the street, wiping her nose and drying her eyes with her red armband and moaning: My chickens, oh, my chickens . . . give me back my chickens you bastards, you ought to be shot. . . .

The truck was parked between the livestock and lumber markets. By now most of the Red Guards had climbed off the truck and were sitting lethargically on a log that smelled of pine tar. Chef Song, the pockmarked cook from the commune kitchen, came out with two buckets of mung-bean soup to welcome the Red Guard little generals from the county seat; fragrant steam wafted from the full buckets.

Pockmarked Song carried a bowl of the soup over to the truck, where he offered it up with both hands to Braying Jackass and the female Red Guard who was in charge of broadcasting. Ignoring the offering, the commander shouted into the microphone: Drag out the ox-demons and snake-spirits!

At that signal, the ox-demons and snake-spirits, led by County Chief Donkey Chen Guangdi, charged out of the compound with boundless joy. As we have already seen, Donkey Chief Chen's body had fused with the papier-mâché donkey, and as he came on the scene now, he had a human head. But that changed with a scant few motions. In one of those scenes you see in the movies or on TV, his ears got longer and stood straight up, like fat leaves growing out of a tropical stem or large gray butterflies emerging from cocoons, looking like satin glistening with an elegant gray luster, covered by a layer of long downy hairs, without doubt soft to the touch. Then his face elongated; his eyes grew bigger and moved to the sides of his widening nose, white in color and covered with short, downy hairs, without doubt soft to the touch. His mouth sagged and split into a pair of thick fleshy lips, also without doubt soft to the touch. Two rows of big white teeth were covered at first by donkey lips, but the moment he laid eyes on the female Red Guard, with her red armband, his lips flared back and the big teeth made an appearance. We'd owned a donkey before, so I was well acquainted with donkey ways, and I knew that when one of them flares back his lips, sexual excitement is on its way, and he will display his enormous organ, up till then safely sheathed. Happily, County Chief Chen retained enough of his human instincts that the donkey transformation remained incomplete, and though he flared his lips, he kept his organ hidden from view. Fan Tong, former commune Party secretary, was next to appear — that's right, County Chief Chen's onetime secretary, the one who absolutely loved donkey meat, especially the male organ — so the Red Guards fashioned one for him out of a big white turnip, Northeast Gaomi Township's most abundant crop. Actually, there wasn't much fashioning involved: a few swipes with a knife on the head and some black ink was all it took. There are few things richer than the people's imagination. No one needed to be told what the black-dyed turnip represented. This Fan fellow, his face twisted in a frown, moved slowly owing to the fat he carried on his body; he could not keep up with the rhythm of the drums and gongs, and that threw the entire column of ox-demons and snake-spirits into mass confusion. A Red Guard tried to remedy the situation by smacking him on the rump, which only succeeded in making him jump and cry out in pain. The smacks then moved to his head, which he tried to ward off with the fake donkey dick in his hand. But it snapped in two, exposing its true nature as a turnip: white, crunchy, high water content. The crowd laughed uproariously, including even the Red Guards. Fan Tong was handed over to two female Red Guards, who forced him to eat the two halves of the fake donkey dick in front of everyone. The black dye, he said, was toxic, and he refused to eat. The female Red Guards' faces reddened, as if they'd been humiliated. You hoodlum, you stinking hoodlum! A beating is too good for you, what you need is to be kicked! They stepped back and began kicking Fan Tong, who rolled around on the ground, crying piteously, Little generals, little generals, don't kick me, I'll eat it, I'll eat . . . He scooped up the turnip and bit off a chunk. Faster, eat faster! He bit off another chunk. His cheeks bulged so much he couldn't even chew, so he tried to force it down his throat and ended up choking himself until his eyes rolled back in his head. A dozen or more ox-demons and snake-spirits followed County Chief Donkey out, each with a unique trick and display, an entertainment extravaganza for the lookers-on. The drums, gongs, and cymbals were handled with high professional standards, since the musicians were members of the county opera percussion division. Their repertoire consisted of dozens of cadences, and the local musicians were not in their league. In comparison with them, our Ximen Village percussion team was like a bunch of kids banging on pieces of scrap metal trying to scare off sparrows.

The Ximen Village parade made its way up from east of the marketplace. Sun Long — Dragon Sun — carried a drum on his back; Sun Hu — Tiger Sun — beat it from behind. The gong was struck by Sun Bao, Panther Sun; the cymbals clanged by Sun Biao, Tiger Cub Sun. The four Sun brothers were from a poor peasant family, and it made sense for the loud percussion instruments to be in their hands. They were preceded by the village ox-demons and snake-spirits, and the capitalist-roaders. Hong Taiyue had managed to slip by during the Four Clean-ups, but not the Cultural Revolution. A paper dunce cap rested on his head; a big-character poster in forceful ancient script was pasted on his back. One look told me it was more of Ximen Jinlong's handiwork. Hong was carrying the hip bone of an ox with brass rings on the edges, a reminder of his glorious history. The ill-fitting dunce cap kept tipping to the side, forcing him to reach up and hold it steady with his hand. If he was slow in doing so, a bushy-browed young man behind him kicked him in the rear. Who was he? None other than my half brother, Ximen Jinlong. Publicly he was known as Lan Jinlong. He was smart enough to know not to change his surname, because that would make him the offspring of a tyrannical landlord, a subhuman. My dad was an independent farmer, but his status as a farmhand did not change. The farmhand designation was like gold that glittered brightly during those times. It was priceless.

My brother was wearing a real army tunic, which he'd gotten from his friend Little Chang. Beneath the tunic, he was wearing blue flannel trousers and plastic white-soled khaki shoes. A wide leather belt with a brass buckle circled his waist; it was the type worn by Eighth Route or New Fourth Army soldiers. Now he was wearing one. He had rolled up his sleeves; the Red Guard armband hung loosely from his upper arm. All the villagers' red armbands had been stitched together with red fabric, the words added in yellow with a stencil. My brother's was made of silk, the words embroidered in gold-colored thread. Throughout the county there were only ten of those, all embroidered overnight by the finest seamstress in the county handi- craft factory; she spit up blood and died when she was halfway through the tenth one, which, owing to the bloodstains, spoke of the tragedy. That was the one my brother wore; embroidered only with the word *Red*, and stained with the maker's blood. My sister, Ximen Baofeng, had embroidered the word *Guard* for him. He came into pos- session of this treasured item when he went to the headquarters of the Golden Monkey Red Guard faction to call on his friend Braying Jackass. The two "jackasses," excited to see one another again after so long, shook hands, embraced, and shared a revolutionary salute, after which they exchanged news of what had happened since they were last together and talked about the revolutionary situation in the vil- lage. Now I wasn't there at the time, but I'm positive that Braying Jackass asked after my sister, since she was surely on his mind.

My brother had gone to the county seat to "fetch scriptures." Trouble was brewing in the village when the Cultural Revolution broke out, but no one knew just how to nip it in the bud. He had a knack for getting to the root of a problem, so all Braying Jackass had to say was: Struggle against the Party cadres the same way we did against the tyrannical landlord! Obviously, no quarter was to be given to the landlords, rich peasants, and counterrevolutionaries already beaten down by the Communist Party either.

My brother understood exactly what to do as hot blood raced through his veins. As he was leaving, Braying Jackass handed him the unfinished red armband and a spool of gold-colored silk thread. Your sister is a clever girl, he said, she can finish it for you. My brother reached into his knapsack and took out a gift for him from my sister: a pair of insoles embroidered in multicolored threads. For girls from our area to give anyone insoles was a virtual pledge to marry. The pattern was of a pair of mandarin ducks frolicking in the water. The reds and greens, the exquisitely fine stitches, and the poignant pattern all bespoke deep affection. The two "jackasses" blushed. As he accepted the gift, Braying Jackass said: Please tell Comrade Lan Baofeng that mandarin ducks and butterflies all represent sentiments belonging to the landlords and capitalist-roaders. Proletarian aesthetics are found in green pine trees, the red sun, the vast oceans, high mountains, torches, scythes, and axes. If she wants to do embroidery, she should concentrate on those. My brother nodded solemnly, promising to pass on the comment. The commander then took off his army tunic and said in a somber tone: An instructor friend of mine in the army gave this to me. See, four pockets, an authentic officer's tunic. The guy who runs the county hardware company brought in a brand-new Golden Stag bicycle, and I wouldn't swap this with him!

As soon as he returned to the village, my brother organized a Ximen Village branch of the Golden Monkey Red Guard faction. When the flag was raised, the village rose up in response. Most of the young villagers held my brother in awe, and now they had their opportunity to get behind him. They occupied the brigade headquarters, sold off a donkey and two oxen for 1,500 yuan, and bought red material, with which they made armbands, red flags, and red tassels for spears, plus a loudspeaker and ten buckets of red paint, which they used to paint the headquarters doors, windows, and walls. They even painted the apricot tree in the yard bright red. When my dad showed his disapproval, Tiger Sun slapped red paint on Dad's face, making it half red and half blue. Jinlong stood off to the side watching with cold detachment when my dad cursed the youngsters. Throwing caution to the wind, he confronted Jinlong. Has there been another dynastic change, young master? he asked. Jinlong just stood there with his hands on his hips, chest out, and said curtly: That's right, there has been. Does that mean that Mao Zedong is no longer chairman? Dad asked politely. Caught unprepared, Jinlong paused before responding angrily: Paint the blue half of his face red! The Sun brothers — Dragon, Tiger, Panther, and Tiger Cub — rushed up; two held Dad's arms, one grabbed him by the hair, and the last one picked up the brush and covered his face with a thick coat of red paint. When Dad reacted by cursing angrily, the paint ran into his mouth and coated his teeth red. He was a fright, with two black eye holes into which paint from his eyebrows could drip at any moment. Mother ran out of the house, crying and screaming: Jinlong, he's your dad. How can you treat him like that? Jinlong replied icily: The whole nation is red, leaving no spot untouched. The Cultural Revolution is going to seal the doom of the capitalist-roaders, landlords, rich peasants, and counterrevolutionaries. No independent farmer is going to slip through the cracks. If he refuses to abandon his independent activities and continues down the path of capitalism, we'll drown him in a bucket of red paint! Dad wiped the red paint from his face to keep it from running into his eyes, that was his greatest fear, but all he managed to do, the poor man, was to rub it into his eyes. Blinded by the sting of the paint, he jumped around in agony and screamed pitifully. Soon exhausted by all that jumping, he rolled around on the ground, where he was soiled from head to toe with chicken droppings. Mom's and Wu Qiuxiang's chickens, thrown into a panic by all the red paint and the red-faced man, were afraid to stay in their roosts; they flew up onto the wall, onto branches of the apricot tree, even up onto the eaves of the house, and everywhere they landed they left red imprints of their claws. Jiefang, my son, Mother cried out in great sorrow, go get your sister, bring her back to save your dad from going blind! Armed with a red-tasseled spear I ripped out of a Red Guard's hand, and boiling with anger, I was determined to poke holes in Jinlong and see what flowed out of the body of this brother who had turned his back on his own family. My feelings were, his blood must be black. Mother's anguished cries and Dad's agonizing wails made it necessary for me to hold off on my desire to poke holes in Jinlong, at least for the moment. Saving my dad's eyesight took priority over everything. I ran out onto the street, dragging my spear behind me. Have you seen my sister? I asked a white-haired old woman. She shook her head as she dried her tears; I'm not sure she even understood me. Have you seen my sister? I asked a bald, stoop-shouldered old man. He smiled foolishly and pointed to his ear. Ah, he's deaf, he can't hear me. Have you seen my sister? I asked a fellow pushing a cart, grabbing him by the shoulder. His cart tipped over, spilling a load of shiny stones, which clicked against one another as they rolled along the street. He shook his head, a sad smile on his face. He had every right to be angry, but he wasn't. He was Wu Yuan, one of our rich peasants, a man who could tease the saddest notes out of a flute, which he played with refined elegance. He belonged to the ancients, a man who, as you say, had befriended the tyrannical landlord Ximen Nao. I ran off, leaving Wu Yuan to load the stones back onto his cart. They were to be delivered to the Ximen compound on orders from the Ximen Village branch of the Golden Monkey Red Guard faction commander, Ximen Jinlong. I ran smack into Huang Huzhu. Most of the village girls had cut their hair short, with a part, like the boys, exposing the skin on their scalp and neck. She alone stubbornly clung to her braid, which she tied off at the end with a red ribbon: feudal, conservative, diehard, an attitude that easily rivaled that of my dad, who stubbornly refused to abandon independent farming. Before long, however, that braid served her well, for when the revolutionary model opera *Red Lantern* was staged, she was a natural for the role of Li Tiemei, who wore a braid just like that. Even actresses in the county opera troupe who were assigned the role of Li Tiemei had to wear fake braids. Our Li Tiemei had the real thing, every strand of hair firmly attached to her scalp. I later learned why Huang Huzhu was so dead set on keeping her braid. That was because of all the fine capillaries in her hair; if she'd cut her hair they'd have oozed blood. Her hair was thick and lush, a quality rarely seen. Hu Zhu, I said when I bumped into her, have you seen my sister? She opened her mouth, as if she wanted to say something, but immediately shut it again. She was cold, scornful, absolutely off-putting. I couldn't let her expression bother me. I asked you, I said in a very loud voice, have you seen my sister? Pretending she didn't know, she asked me: And just who is your sister? You fucking Huang Huzhu, are you telling me you don't know who my sister is? If you don't know that, then you must not even know who your own mother is. My sister, Lan Baofeng, health worker, a barefoot doctor. Oh, her, she said with a slight and very contemptuous twist of her mouth. Outwardly proper, but dripping with jealousy, she said. She's at school, entangled with Ma Liangcai. Go now, or you'll miss it, two dogs, a mutt and a bitch, one more aroused than the other, they'll be coupled any minute! That threw me. I never expected coarse language like that from someone as old-fashioned as Huzhu —

Another accomplishment of the Great Cultural Revolution! Big-head Lan Qiansui said coldly. His fingers were bleeding profusely. I handed him the medicine I'd prepared beforehand. He rubbed it on his fingers, stopping the bleeding at once.

— Her face reddened and her chest swelled, and I knew exactly what that was all about. While she may not have been secretly in love with Ma Liangcai, seeing him cozy up to my sister upset her. I'm not going to worry about you now, I said. I'll take care of you later, you tramp. Falling for my brother — No, he's no longer my brother, hasn't been for a long time, he's just Ximen Nao's bad seed. So's your sister, she said. That stopped me. My throat felt like it was clogged by a hot sticky pastry. They're different, I said finally. She's decent and gentle, good-hearted, red-blooded, humane. She's my sister. — She has almost no humanity left. She smells like a dog. She's the bastard off-spring of Ximen Nao and a mongrel bitch, and you can smell it on her every time it rains, Huzhu said, clenching her teeth. I turned my spear around. During the revolutionary period, the people had the power to execute individuals. The Jia Mountain People's Commune passed the execution authority down to the village level, and Mawan Village had killed thirty-three people in a single day, the oldest eighty-eight, the youngest thirteen. Some were clubbed to death, and some were sliced in half with hay cutters. I aimed my spear at her chest. She threw out her chest to meet the tip. Go ahead, kill me if you've got the guts! I've lived long enough already. Tears sprang from her lovely eyes. Something strange there, something I couldn't figure out. Huzhu and I had grown up together. We'd played together on the riverbank, naked as the day we were born, and she developed such a special interest in my little pecker that she ran home in tears, telling her mother, Wu Qiuxiang, that she wanted one. How come Jiefang has one and I don't? Wu Qiuxiang stood under the apricot tree and really chewed me out: Jiefang, you little thug, if you take ever advantage of Huzhu again, I'll cut your pecker off when you're not looking. It seemed like only yesterday, but now, suddenly, Huzhu had become as enigmatic as a river turtle. I turned and ran. A woman's tears always rattle me. As soon as a woman starts to cry, I get nose-aching sad. I get lightheaded. I've suffered over that sign of weakness my whole life. Ximen Jinlong dumped red paint in my dad's eyes, I shouted back, and I have to find my sister to save his eyesight . . . Serves him right. Your family, dog eat dog . . . Her hateful comment chased me down. I guess you could say I'd broken free from Huzhu at that moment, though my growing hatred for her was tempered by the same amount of lingering fondness. I knew she had no feelings for me, but at least she'd told me where my sister was.

The elementary school was located at the west end, near the village wall. It had a large yard encircled by a wall made of bricks from gravesites, which ensured that there would always be spirits of the dead hanging around, coming out at night to wander. A large grove of pine trees beyond the wall was home to owls whose chilling screeches struck fear into anyone who heard them. It was a miracle those trees hadn't been cut down as fuel during the iron- and steel-smelting campaign, something that can be attributed to a single old cypress tree that actually bled when they tried to chop it down. Who'd ever seen blood from a tree before? It was like Huzhu's hair, which bled if it was cut. By all appearances, the only things that were pre-served were the unusual ones.

I found my sister in the school office. There was no romanticiz-ing with Ma Liangcai; she was treating a wound on him. Someone had hit him, opening a gash in his head, and my sister was wrapping a bandage around it, leaving exposed only one eye so he could see where he was going, his nostrils so he could breathe, and his mouth so he could eat and drink. To me he resembled the Nationalist soldiers we'd seen in movies after they'd been beaten bloody by Communist forces. She looked like a nurse, but totally devoid of expression, as if carved out of cold, polished marble. All the windows had been smashed, and all the shards of broken glass had been scooped up by children who had taken them home to their mothers, mostly for use in peeling potatoes. People had put the larger pieces in papered-up window frames so they could see outside and get some sunlight. Late August evening winds blew in from the pine grove, carrying the smell of pine tar, blowing papers off the office desktop onto the floor. My sister took a little vial from her reddish brown leather medical satchel, poured out a few tablets, and wrapped them in a piece of paper she picked up off the floor. Two at a time, three times a day, she told him. After meals. He forced a smile. Don't waste them, he said. There's no before or after meals, I'm not going to eat. I'm going on a hunger strike as a show of resistance against the savagery of those Fascists. I come from three generations of poor peasants, red to our roots, so why did they beat me? My sister gave him a sympathetic look and said softly: Teacher Ma, don't get upset, it'll make your injury worse. . . . He thrust out his hands and grabbed hold of my sister's hand. Baofeng, he said almost hysterically, Baofeng, I want you to like me, I want you to be mine. . . . All these years, I think of you when I'm eat-ing, when I'm sleeping, when I'm out walking, I don't know what to do with myself, I'm in a daze. I don't know how many times I've walked into a wall or a tree, and people assume I'm thinking about my studies, but I'm really thinking about you. . . . I found all that lovesick claptrap emerging from a little hole in the bandages preposterous; his

eyes were strangely bright, like wet lumps of coal. My sister struggled
to free her hands; she drew her head back and shook it from side to
side to get away from the hole in the bandages that was his mouth.
Don't fight me, he said, do it my way. . . . Ma Liangcai was beginning
to rant. The guy was unscrupulous. Sister! I shouted as I kicked open
the door and ran into the room armed with my spear. Ma Liangcai
abruptly let go of my sister's hands and stumbled backward, knocking
over the basin stand and spilling water all over the brick floor. Kill! I
shouted as I jammed my spear into the wall. Ma Liangcai lost his balance and sat down hard on the pulpy wet newspaper, obviously scared
witless. I pulled the tip of the spear out of the wall and said to Lan
Baofeng, Sister, Jinlong had people brush red paint into Dad's eyes.
When I left he was rolling on the floor in agony. Mother sent me to get
you. I've been looking for you everywhere. Come with me and keep
Dad from going blind. She picked up her medical satchel, cast a fleeting glance at Ma Liangcai shaking in a corner, and ran out with me, so
fast I couldn't keep up. Her satchel swung back and forth, banging
noisily against her backside as she ran. The stars were out; in the western sky Venus shone brightly alongside a crescent moon.

My dad was still rolling around in the yard, and no one could hold
him down. He kept rubbing his eyes and crying out in pain, sending
cold shivers down people's spines. All my brother's toadies had
slipped away, leaving only him and his protectors, the four Sun brothers. My mother and Huang Tong were each holding one of my dad's
arms to try to keep him from rubbing his eyes. But he was too strong
for them, and his arms kept slipping out of their grasp, like slippery
catfish. My mother, gasping from exertion, kept cursing: Jinlong, you
unconscionable beast, he may not be your biological father, but he
raised you from childhood. How could you be so savage?

My sister charged into the compound like a savior from the heavens. Lan Lian, Mother said, stop struggling, Baofeng's here. Baofeng,
help your father, don't let him go blind. He may be stubborn, but he's
a good man, and he was especially good to you and your brother. . . .
Night had not fallen completely, but the red throughout the compound and on Dad's face had turned dark green. The smell of paint
hung in the air. Bring me some water, and hurry! My sister was still out
of breath. Mother ran into the house and came out with a dipper full
of water. That's not enough! I need lots of water, the more the better!
She took the dipper, took aim at Dad's face, and said: Close your eyes,

Dad! Actually, they'd been closed all along, since he couldn't open
them. She splashed the dipper full of water into his face. Water! she
screamed hoarsely. Water! Water! I was shocked to hear a sound like
that from my gentle sister. Mother came out of the house with a bucket of water, stumbling toward us. Astonishingly, Huang Tong's wife,
Wu Qiuxiang, a woman whose only fear was that things would go
smoothly, who wished terrible afflictions on absolutely everyone,
came out of her house also carrying a bucket of water. Darkness had
fallen. From the shadows my sister cried out: Throw it all into his
face! One dipper full of water after another splashed into Dad's face,
creating the sound of crashing waves. Bring me a lantern! she
demanded. My mother ran into the house and came back with a small
kerosene lantern, walking cautiously and shielding the flickering
flame with her hand. A breeze blew by and put it out. Mother lost her
footing and lay sprawled on the ground. The lantern must have sailed
a long way away; I detected the smell of kerosene wafting from a distant corner of the wall. I heard Jinlong say to one of his toadies in a
low voice: Go light the gas lamp.

Outside of the sun, the brightest source of light in Ximen Village
at the time was a gas lamp. Though only seventeen, Tiger Cub Sun
was the village expert on that lamp. He could light it off in ten minutes, whereas it took others half an hour. They invariably broke the
wicker filament; he never did. He'd stare at the filament, so white it
hurt the eyes, and listen to the hiss of the gas, mesmerized. The compound was black as ink, but a light was beginning to glow inside the
house, as if a fire were spreading. Surprised looks appeared on people's faces as Tiger Cub Sun emerged from the Ximen Village Red
Guard headquarters with a gas lamp on a pole, like bringing out the
sun to invest the red wall and red tree with radiance, fiery, blindingly
red. Every face in the crowd was immediately visible: Huang Huzhu,
standing in the doorway of her house, fingering the tip of her braid
like the spoiled daughter of a feudal family; Huang Hezuo, standing
under the apricot tree, casting looks all over the place, her boyish haircut starting to grow out, bubbles oozing from between her teeth; Wu
Qiuxiang running around, as if there were so many things she wanted
to say, but no one to talk to; Ximen Jinlong, hands on his hips in the
middle of the yard, a somber look in his eyes, his brows furrowed as if
he were pondering weighty questions; three of the Sun brothers
fanned out around Ximen Jinlong like a pack of running dogs; and

finally, Huang Tong, who was busy splashing water into my dad's face. The water: some of it splashed back into the radiant light and some of it dripped down my father's face; by then he was sitting up, hands on his stretched-out legs, his face raised to receive the water bath. He was calm: no more violent thrashing, no more cries of anguish; most likely my sister's arrival had eased his mind. My mother was crawling on the ground and mumbling, My lantern, where's my lantern? Covered in mud, she looked terrible, especially in the glaring light of the gas lamp, which showed her hair to be silvery white. She looked much older than her age of not quite fifty, and my heart ached for her. It appeared as if the paint on Dad's face had thinned out a bit, but it was still bright red, and beads of water rolled off it like raindrops from a lotus leaf. Gawkers had gathered outside the compound, until the gateway was black with people. My sister stood there as calmly as a battlefield general. Bring the lamp over, she said. Tiger Cub Sun carried it up, taking very small steps. The second Sun brother — Tiger — came flying out of the headquarters with a bench, probably acting on orders from my brother, and set it down a couple of yards from my dad so his brother would have something to set the lantern on. My sister opened her satchel and removed some cotton and a pair of tweezers. Picking up a piece of cotton with the tweezers, she soaked it in water and cleaned the area around Dad's eyes; after that, she cleaned his eyelids. She worked with great care and speed. When that was done, she filled a syringe with water and told my dad to open his eyes. He couldn't do it. Who'll come over and pry his eyes open? my sister asked. Mother crawled up, bringing all that mud with her. Jiefang, my sister said, come pry Dad's eyes open. I shrank back. Dad's red face was terrifying to me. Hurry up! she said. So I stuck my spear in the ground and went up to her, tiptoeing like a chicken in the snow. I looked at her, looked at the syringe in her hand, and tried to pry one of Dad's eyes open. His agonizing shriek cut into me like a knife, and I jumped way back from sheer fright. What is it with you? my sister asked angrily. It's okay with you if your dad goes blind, is that it? Huang Huzhu, who had been standing in her doorway, walked nimbly up to us. She was wearing a red-checked coat over a gaily patterned blouse, with both collars turned up. Her braid rolled back and forth along her spine. I can still see it after all these years. The distance from her doorway to our ox shed was about thirty paces. In the bright light of the gas lamp, those thirty paces were a wonderful show of their own, projecting shadows of a beautiful woman. All eyes were on her, but none more intensely than mine. After all the terrible things she had said about my sister, here she was, boldly walking up to be her assistant. I'll do it! she said in a loud voice that arrived on the air like a robin redbreast. The mud didn't deter her; so what if her pretty white-soled shoes were badly soiled? Everyone knew what a clever, deft young woman she was. The insoles my sister embroidered were lovely, but not as lovely as Huzhu's. When the apricot tree was in bloom, she'd stand under it, eyes on the flowers, fingers flying as she transferred the flowers to the insole, making them more beautiful and fragile than those on the tree. She kept those insoles in little piles under her pillow, and I wondered who she was going to give them to. Braying Jackass? Ma Liangcai? Jinlong? How about me?

Her eyes shone in the extraordinary glare of the gas lamp, as did her teeth. She was, undeniably, a beauty, with a nicely rounded bottom and pert bosom, and I, in my single-minded dedication to follow my dad in independent farming, had completely overlooked the beauty right beside me. In that brief moment, the time it took to walk from her doorway to our ox shed, I fell hopelessly in love with her. She bent over, extended her long delicate fingers, and pried open one of my dad's eyes. He cried out in agony, but I heard a little popping sound when the eyelid was unstuck, like bubbles released by fish from the bottom. The eye socket looked like an open wound from which bloody fluids flowed. My sister took aim with her syringe and squirted a slow silvery stream of water, controlling the force so the irrigation would be effective without damaging the eye. Once in the eye, the water turned to blood and then streamed down his face. Dad groaned in agony. With the same degree of accuracy and the same speed, my sister and Huzhu, mortal enemies who had reached a silent agreement to work together, irrigated my dad's other eye. They then washed them clean — left, right, left, right — over and over. Finally, my sister put eye drops in both eyes and covered them with a bandage. Jiefang, she said, take Dad in the house. I ran over and lifted him up by his armpits. Getting him to stand was like pulling a turnip out of muddy ground.

At that moment a strange sound — somewhere between a cry, a laugh, and a sigh — emerged from the ox shed. It was our ox. Tell me, were you crying or laughing or sighing?

Go on with your story, Big-head Lan Qiansui said icily. Don't ask me that.

— The startled crowd of gawkers turned to look at the shed, suffused with light. The ox's eyes were like lamps giving off a blue light; golden emanations radiated from his body. Dad struggled to go into the shed. Ox! he cried. My ox! You're all I have, my whole family! The note of despair in those cries chilled the heart of everyone who heard them. Jinlong may have betrayed you, but my sister, Mother, and I love you. How can you say that the ox is your whole family? His body may have been an ox, but his heart and soul were Ximen Nao, so all those people in the yard — his son, his daughter, his first and second concubines, as well as his farmhand and me, his farmhand's son — produced feelings in him that were all jumbled up: love, hate, enmity, and gratitude —

It may not have been as involved as you make it out to be, Big-head Lan Qiansui said. Maybe I made that strange sound because I had a clump of grass caught in my throat. But you've taken a simple matter and turned it inside out, deliberately complicating it in your jumbled narration.

— It was a jumbled world back then, which makes it hard to speak with clarity. But let me pick up where I left off: The Ximen Village parade came over from the eastern head of the marketplace, accompanied by gongs and drums and red banners snapping in the wind. Brigade Commander Huang Tong was being paraded through the streets by Jinlong and his Red Guards, in addition to the former Party secretary Hong Taiyue, along with the onetime security head, Yu Wufu, the rich peasant Wu Yuan, Zhang Dazhuang the traitor, and Ximen Bai, wife of the landlord Ximen Nao, all old-line bad elements. My dad, Lan Lian, was also under escort. Hong Taiyue was clenching his teeth and staring straight ahead. Zhang Dazhuang wore a worried frown. Wu Yuan was weeping. Ximen Bai was slovenly and dirty. The paint hadn't been cleaned off my dad's face; his eyes were blood red and tear-filled. The tears resulted from damaged corneas, not any sort of internal weakness. On the cardboard sign around Dad's neck Jinlong himself had written: "Stinking, Obstinate Independent Farmer." Dad was carrying our plow over his shoulder, the one they'd given him during land reform. He had a hempen rope around his waist, which was tied to a set of reins, which in turn were tied to a bull ox. It was a reincarnation of the tyrannical landlord Ximen Nao; in other words, you. Feel free to interrupt me anytime and pick up where I leave off. You can relate what happened after that. I see the world through human eyes, but yours is an animal universe, so you can probably tell a more interesting story. No? All right, I'll continue. You were a mighty ox, with horns like steel, broad shoulders, powerful muscles, and incandescent eyes that radiated malevolence. A pair of tattered shoes had been hooked on your horns. That was the brainchild of the Sun brother who was such an expert in the use of gas lamps. He meant only to make you look bad, not imply that you dallied with loose females, as such things symbolize. That son of a bitch Jinlong was going to include me in the public exposure parade, but I threatened him with my red-tasseled spear. I'll stick this into anyone who tries to parade me like that, I said. That gave him a shock, but he chose discretion in the face of my intransigence. I couldn't help thinking that if Dad had stood up like I did by taking down the hay cutter and brandishing it in front of the shed, threatening to use it, my brother would have backed down. But my dad was the one who backed down, letting them lead him away and hang a cardboard sign around his neck. If our ox had displayed its bullish temper, no one could have gotten away with hanging a pair of tattered shoes on its horns and parading it in the street, but it had also gone along with it obediently.

Commander of the Golden Monkey Red Guard faction, Little Chang, the Braying Jackass, and commander of the Ximen Village branch of the Golden Monkey faction, Jinlong, Junior Jackass, linked up in the middle of the marketplace, that is, the square in front of the Supply and Marketing Cooperative Restaurant, where they held hands and exchanged revolutionary greetings, red glints seeming to emanate from their eyes, their hearts bursting with revolutionary fervor; they may have been thinking about how the combined forces of China's peasants, workers, and soldiers at Jinggangshan had vowed to plant red flags all over Asia, Africa, and Latin America and free all oppressed members of the proletariat from the abyss of suffering. The two Red Guard units linked up, county and village; the two groups of capitalist-roaders linked up, with Donkey County Chief Chen Guangdi, Donkey-dick Secretary Fan Tong, an alien class enemy, Hong Taiyue, a capitalist-roader who beat his ox hip bone, and Hong's running dog, Huang Tong, who had married the concubine of a land-lord. They cast furtive glances all around, letting their facial expressions convey their reactionary thoughts. Lower your heads. Lower. Lower! The Red Guards kept pushing their heads down, lower and lower, until their hindquarters were as high in the air as they'd ever get; one more push, and they'd be on their knees. Instead, their assailants pulled them back by their hair and their collars. My dad refused to lower his head, and owing to his special relationship with Ximen Jinlong, the other Red Guards let him get away with it. Braying Jackass was the first to speak. He stood on a table that had been moved out from the dining hall; with his left hand on his hip, he waved his right in a variety of gestures: a sword slice, a bayonet stab, a fist pound, and a judo chop, each gesture matched by the oration, the tone, and the cadence. Saliva gathered in the corners of his mouth, his words bristled with ferocity, but with no substance, like red condoms blown up in the shape of wax gourds to fly around, crashing noisily into one another until they exploded with loud pops. One of the more interesting episodes in the history of Northeast Gaomi Township involved a nurse who had once blown up a condom until it burst and injured her eyes. Braying Jackass was a master speechmaker. He modeled himself after Lenin and Mao Zedong, especially the way he thrust out his right arm at a right angle, tossed his head back, chin out, and gazed far into the distance. When he shouted: "Attack, attack, and again attack the class enemies!" he sounded like Lenin reborn. The Lenin of *Lenin in 1918* had arrived in Northeast Gaomi Township. Silence fell over the crowd, as if the people's throats were squeezed shut, but only for a moment, and then shouts arose — Hooray! by the uncultured, Long Life! by their opposite numbers. The Hoorays and Long Life shouts were not intended for Braying Jackass, but, like a blown-up condom, he was so carried away he was virtually floating. There were even grumblings down below, such as: We can't treat that bastard lightly! uttered by an old-timer who had studied in a private school, could read just about everything, and who hung around the barbershop, where he said to men getting haircuts, Ask me how to write any character you want, and if I can't do it, I'll pay for your haircut. A couple of middle-school teachers asked him how to write several obscure characters they'd found in dictionaries, and even they couldn't stump him. One teacher decided to trick him by making up a character, a simple circle with a dot in the middle. The man sneered.

Think you can stump me, do you? This one is pronounced *peng*, and is the sound of a stone tossed into a well. I got you this time, the teacher said. I made it up. In the beginning, the man said, all characters were made up. The teacher was at a loss for words; the self-satisfied man beamed. Junior Jackass followed Braying Jackass onto the bench, but his speech was a pale imitation of the one by his predecessor.

Now, Ximen Ox, I should relate what you were doing on that market day. At first, you meekly followed behind my dad, matching him step for step. But your glorious image and your obedient behavior seemed odd to people, especially to me. You were a spirited animal that had displayed extraordinary behaviors in prior months and years. If, at the time, I'd been aware that the arrogant soul of Ximen Nao and the memory of a renowned donkey were hidden deep inside you, I'd have been disappointed in your behavior. You should have fought back, should have raised havoc in the marketplace, should have played the major role in that carnivalesque episode, like one of those bulls in a Spanish corrida. But you didn't. You held your head low, tattered shoes hanging from your horns, a symbol of shame, unhurriedly chewing your cud, as people could tell from the rumblings down in your stomachs. And so it went, from early morning till noon, from chilled air to warm, till the ground baked in the sun, till the fragrance of braised buns emerged from the Supply and Marketing Cooperative dining hall. A one-eyed young man with a badly worn coat thrown over his shoulders came limping out of the marketplace, dragging an impressive yellow dog behind him. He was an infamous dog-killer. Born into a poor family, and quickly orphaned, he was sent to school by the government free of charge. But, hating school with a passion, he ruined what could have been a glorious future. Preferring a life of complete freedom over one involving books and study, he made no attempt to better himself, and the Party could do nothing about it. Killing dogs and selling them for their meat, he enjoyed life to the fullest. Now at the time, private butchering was illegal, whether it was pigs or dogs. The government held a monopoly in the trade. But they left one side of the net open for this particular dog-killer. Any government, whatever its makeup, would treat someone like him with leniency. He was a dog's natural enemy. Neither very tall nor very big, he wasn't particularly quick on his feet and had poor eyesight. A dog wouldn't have trouble tearing him limb from limb. But any dog, from mild-mannered to vicious, tucked its tail between its legs, shrank in on itself, and, with naked fear in its eyes, whimpered imploringly when it saw him, accepting its fate as it let him put a rope around its neck and hang it from a tree. He'd then drag the strangled animal back to the hole beneath a stone bridge where he lived and worked to skin and clean the dog with river water, then chop it up and toss the meat into a pot. After he fired up his stove with kindling, the water would come to a boil and release dense steam from under the bridge; as it followed the currents, the fragrance of dog meat would suffuse the river all around.

An evil wind rose up, snapping the banners so ferociously that one of the poles snapped in two, sending that banner circling into the air to dance for a moment before landing on the ox's head. That's when you went wild, exactly what I'd been waiting for, me and many of the gawkers in the marketplace. This farce could only end riotously.

You began by shaking your head in an attempt to flick off the banner. I know what it's like to look at the sun by covering my head with a red flag; bright red, like a vast ocean, as if the sun were immersed in an ocean of blood, and I was struck by a feeling that the end of the world was upon me. Since I'm not an ox, I don't know how you felt with a red banner covering your head, but the violence of your movements led me to assume that you were terror-stricken. The tips of your steely horns were those of a fighting bull. If a pair of knives had been attached to them, you could have decimated the crowd and routed the survivors. Even after many shakes of your head and sweeps of your tail, the red banner stayed put, and panic set in; you ran. Now, your reins were tied to my dad's waist, so when you, a four-year-old bull weighing nearly five hundred catties, without an ounce of unwanted fat, an animal filled with the vigor of youth and unimaginable strength, took off running, you dragged him behind you as if he were a mouse on the tail of a cat. You ran straight into the crowd, drawing fearful howls and screams. My brother could have been giving the best speech ever heard at that moment, and no one would have been listening. Truth is, they all came to watch the show, and couldn't care less if you were revolutionary or counterrevolutionary. Take that red banner off his head! someone yelled. But who was willing or brave enough to do that? Taking it off would have ended a good show. In running for cover, the people subconsciously formed tight clusters. Old women were crying, children were bawling. Goddamn it, you're crushing my eggs! You're trampling on my children! You broke my bowl, you bastards! A while before, when the wild geese were falling out of the air, the people had surged to the middle of the yard; now, with the running of the ox, the people were sprinting right and left to get out of its way. Piling up on each other, some ran to the wall, where they were flattened like thin cakes; others ran into the butcher's rack, where they crashed to the ground along with the expensive raw pork, some winding up in their mouths. Before goring anyone in the ribs, the ox squashed a little piglet. The peddler, a butcher named Zhu Jiujie who was so outrageously rude he might as well have been a member of the imperial family, picked up his butcher knife and swung it at the ox's head. With a loud clang, it struck one of the horns and flew off into the air, while the severed half of the horn wound up on the ground. The red banner jumped at that opportunity to detach itself from the ox's head. The animal stopped dead in its tracks, panting loudly, belly heaving, foam gathering around its mouth, eyes bloodshot, as a liquid, flecked with blood, oozed from the stump of the severed horn. This liquid was the ox's essence, what's known as "ox-horn essence," reputed to be an exceptional aid for male virility, as much as ten times more powerful than the palm tree extract found on Hainan Island. A particularly corrupt authority figure, a former member of the provincial Party Committee who was exposed by the Red Guards, had taken a girl in her twenties as his wife when he was already turning gray. Too old to perform in bed, he asked around for something to restore his virility, and this ox-horn essence is what the people recommended. He sent some of his thugs out to force all the farmers in the county and those belonging to the province to send their uncastrated and unmated young bulls to a secret location, where their horns were cut off and the liquid extracted; then the bones were crushed and delivered to their boss, the senior official. Sure enough, his gray hair was black again, his wrinkles disappeared, and his organ stood up like a machine gun with a crooked barrel, to mow down a phalanx of women like rolling up a mat.

I need to talk about my dad here. His injury was not yet healed. At first, everything he saw was veiled in red. Then this happened, and he had no idea where he was. All he could do was stumble along after the ox, but he quickly gave that up, wrapped his arms around his head, and was dragged behind the ox like an embroidered ball. Fortunately, he was wearing a padded coat that absorbed most of the bumps and he sustained no major injuries. When the ox lost its horn and stopped running, Dad wasted no time in standing up and untying the rope around his waist. If the ox started running again, this time he wouldn't be dragged along. But then he looked down and saw the severed half of the ox's horn on the ground, and cried out in horror, nearly passing out from the shock. My dad had said that the ox was his family, his whole family, so how could he not be anxious, be pained, be enraged, when his family suffered an injury? His gaze moved to the fat, oily face of the pig butcher, Zhu Jiujie. At a time in history when no Chinese had enough oil in their diet, the officials and pig butchers like him not only ate the fattest, oiliest food, but did so with smug self-satisfaction, proudly enjoying the good life that Communism offered. As an independent farmer, my dad had no interest in the affairs of the commune. But now this People's Commune pig butcher had lopped off our ox's horn, and my dad cried out in horror, My ox! before fainting dead away. I knew that if he hadn't fainted at that moment, he'd have picked up the butcher knife and gone for the pig butcher's big, fat head. I hate to think what that would have led to. I was glad he fainted. But the ox was very much awake, and you can imagine how losing that horn hurt. With a loud bellow, he lowered his head and charged the fat butcher. What caught my attention at that instant was the cluster of long hairs sticking out from the ox's navel, like a fine, wolf-hair writing bush. It too was on the move, rising and falling, as if composing a line of seal characters. I looked away from this mystical writing brush just in time to see the ox twist his head to one side and bury his good horn in Zhu Jiujie's plump belly. His head kept moving, so the horn didn't sink in to the hilt. Then he jerked his head upward like an erupting mountain of flesh, and out from the hole in Zhu Jinjie's belly poured big yellow clumps of fat.

My dad came to after everyone else had run away, and the first thing he did was pick up the butcher knife to stand guard in front of his one-horned ox. Although he said nothing, the determined look in his eyes made an unmistakable statement to the Red Guards who were encircling him: You'll have to kill me to get to this ox. Zhu Jiujie's spilled fat reminded the Red Guards of the man's tyrannical disposition and disgusting conduct, and they could not have been happier. Holding the butcher knife in one hand and the tether in the other, Dad walked off with his ox like a man who has raided an execution ground to rescue the condemned, all the way home. The blazing sun had long since vanished and gray clouds had gathered in the sky. Light snowflakes danced in the light breezes before settling onto Northeast Gaomi Township's land.

18

A Deft Hand Mends Clothes, Huzhu
Declares Her Love
Heavy Snows Seal a Village, Jinlong Takes Command

During that long winter, when every third day saw a light snowfall and every fifth day a heavy one, the telephone lines connecting Ximen Village to the commune and the county town were downed by snow. At the time, all broadcasts from the county traveled on telephone wires, so when the wires went down, the broadcasting stations went mute. And when the roads were blocked by snowbanks, there was no newspaper delivery. Ximen Village was cut off from the outside world.

You ought to recall that winter's snows. Every morning my dad took you outside the village. If it was a nice day, the red sunbeams would drench the snow and ice with brilliance. My dad would hold your reins with his right hand and carry the knife he'd taken from the pig butcher in his left. You both exhaled pink steam from your mouths and nostrils. The hair around your mouth and my dad's beard and eyebrows were coated with frost. You headed out into the wild, into the sun, crunching the snow under your feet.

Armed with revolutionary fervor, my half brother Ximen Jinlong called upon his imagination in leading the four Sun brothers — his four warrior protectors — and a pack of bored kids — his shrimp soldiers and crab generals — as well, it goes without saying, as a bunch of adults who dearly loved a show, in taking the Great Cultural Revolution into its second year, when spring arrived on the land.

They built a platform under the apricot tree with a wooden plank, then hung hundreds of red cloth streamers from the branches of the tree to represent flowers in bloom. Every night, the fourth Sun brother — Tiger Cub — climbed up onto the platform and, puffing out his cheeks, blew his bugle to call the masses to gather round. It was a lovely little bronze bugle, adorned with a red tassel. When it first fell into his hands, Tiger Cub puffed his cheeks out and practiced on it every day, making sounds like a lowing cow. But he mastered the instrument in the days leading up to spring, and was able to produce sweet music, mostly from popular folk tunes. He was a talented youngster, a quick study, no matter what he put his hand to. My brother had people mount a rusty old cannon on top of the platform and scoop several dozen holes out of the compound wall for gun ports, then had them stack cobblestones alongside each hole. Though there were no firearms to hand out, village youngsters with red-tasseled spears stood sentry beside the holes. Every few hours, Jinlong would climb onto the platform and survey the surroundings with a pair of homemade binoculars, creating the impression of a general observing enemy activities. The air was so cold his fingers were like carrots that had been washed in ice water; his cheeks, fittingly, were as red as late-autumn apples. Dressed only in his military tunic and unlined pants, in order to preserve the desired image, he kept his sleeves rolled up high and wore only a brown imitation army cap. Pus and blood oozed from chilblains on his ears; his nose ran continuously. Physically, he was a mess, but he was bursting with energy. The fires of passion burned in his eyes.

Seeing him out there like that, my mother worked through the night to make a padded coat for him; to preserve the image of a commanding officer, Huzhu helped to give the coat a military look. They even sewed a floral pattern into the collar with white thread. My brother refused to wear it. Mother, he said somberly, don't fuss like an old woman. The enemy could attack at any minute, and my men are manning their stations in the snow and ice. Should I be the only person wearing a padded coat? My mother glanced all around and discovered that my brother's "four warrior attendants" and his running dogs were similarly dressed in imitation military uniforms they'd dyed brown, and that they too suffered from running noses, the frozen tips of which looked like hawthorn fruit. And yet, a look of sacred dignity was frozen on each little face.

My brother mounted his platform every morning, a bullhorn fashioned out of sheet metal in his hand as he held forth to his running dogs below, to villagers who came to be entertained, and to the entire snowbound village, adopting the tone of a great man, which he had learned at the feet of Braying Jackass, exhorting his little revolutionary generals and poor and lower-middle peasants to wipe the scales from their eyes and sharpen their vigilance, to hold their ground to the very last, to wait patiently for spring to arrive with its warmth and new flowers, when they would link up with the main forces under the command of Commander in Chief Chang. His oration was frequently interrupted by a spell of hacking coughs; wheezing sounds like clucking chickens emerged from his chest, hacking sounds emerged from his throat, and we knew that signified the presence of phlegm. But clearing his throat and spitting out the phlegm as he stood on the platform would not become a military commander, so he swallowed the offensive material, to the disgust of all. My brother's hacking coughs were not the only cause of interruption; shouted slogans from the foot of the platform frequently broke into his oration. The second Sun brother — Tiger Sun — took the lead in shouting slogans. He had a booming voice, was somewhat educated, and knew just when to shout to incite the crowd into reaching the apex of revolutionary fervor.

During a particularly heavy snowstorm one day, as if the sky had opened up and sent ten thousand eiderdown pillows to earth, my brother mounted the platform, raised his megaphone, and was about to harangue his audience when he rocked back and forth, dropped his megaphone, and tumbled to the ground, landing with a thud. Stunned by what they'd just seen, people screamed and ran up to him, all talking at once: What's wrong, Commander? Commander, what's wrong? My mother ran crying out of the house, with only a tattered goatskin coat thrown over her shoulders to ward off the cold, and which made her appear unusually big.

That goatskin coat had been one of a lot of tattered coats our village's former public security chief Yang Qi had bought from Inner Mongolia on the eve of the Cultural Revolution. Emitting a rank odor, it was stained by cow dung and dried sheep's milk. When he tried to peddle those coats, Yang Qi was accused of profiteering and brought under escort to the commune by Hong Taiyue, who threw him in jail. The coats were locked in the storeroom awaiting final disposition by the commune. Then the Cultural Revolution was launched, and Yang Qi was released and sent home, where he joined Jinlong's rebel faction and was the strongest voice of the people when Hong Taiyue was held up to public criticism. Yang worked hard to curry favor with my

brother, desperate to be appointed deputy commander of the Ximen
Village Red Guard detachment. My brother refused his request. The
Ximen Village Red Guard detachment, he said decisively, is under
unified leadership. There are no deputies. Deep down, he was contemptuous of Yang Qi, a repulsively ugly man with shifty eyes.
Considered one of the proletarian thugs, he possessed a belly full of
wicked thoughts and was exceedingly destructive. He could be used,
but not in a position of authority. I personally overheard my brother
say that to his trusted followers in the command headquarters. In a
foul mood over having failed in his attempt to gain favor, Yang Qi then
conspired with the locksmith Han Liu to break into the storeroom and
retrieve the coats that had been taken from him, which he decided to
sell out on the street. With winds whistling and snow falling, icicles
hanging like sawtooth fangs from the eaves, this was ideal weather for
goatskin coats. Villagers crowded round, turning the coats — stained
and dirty, patchy, covered with mouse droppings, and nauseatingly
foul smelling — over in their hands. Smooth-tongued Yang Qi spoke
of his tattered, rotting goods as if they'd once been part of the imperial wardrobe. He picked up a short, black coat, slapped the greasy,
worn-out fur — *pow pow*. Listen to that. Take a look. Feel it, try it on.
Listen, it's like a brass gong. Look, it's like silk and satin. Look again,
the fur is black as paint, and you'll start to sweat when you slip it on.
With one of these coats over your shoulders, you can crawl on ice and
lie in the snow without feeling the least bit cold! A nearly new black
goatskin coat for only nineteen yuan, about the same as finding one
lying in the street. Go ahead, Great-Uncle Zhang, try it on. Oh, oh, my
dear uncle. That coat fits like the Mongolian tailor made it just for
you. One inch more and it's too long, one inch less and it's too short.
So, what do you think, hot enough for you? It's not? Touch your forehead, you're sweating, and you say it's not hot? Eight yuan? If not for
the neighborhood connection, I wouldn't sell it for fifteen. You won't
go higher than eight? Old Uncle, what can I say? Last autumn, I
smoked a couple of your pipes, so I owe you for that. A man can't rest
till he pays off a debt. All right, then, nine yuan, and I lose money on
this sale. Nine yuan and it's yours. Take it home with you, but first get
a rag and wipe the sweat from your forehead. You don't want to catch
cold. Eight, you say? How about eight-fifty? I'll lower it a bit and you
raise it a bit. After all, you're a generation older than me. If it was anybody else I'd smack him in the ear so hard he'd roll all the way down

to the river. Eight yuan, it's like I'm giving you a transfusion of my own blood, type O, the same as Dr. Bethune. All right, eight yuan, but Old Zhang, now you're the one who owes me a favor. He counted the sticky bills: five, six, seven, eight, all right, the coat is yours. Now take it home and show the missus. Sit around in it for half an hour, and I guarantee the snow on your roof will melt. The heat you give off, even from a distance, will turn the snow in your yard into little rivers and the icicles hanging from your eaves will clatter to the ground. . . .

With my brother valiantly leading the way, his "four warrior attendants" arrayed spiritedly around him, the Red Guard forces came raucously up the street. A weapon was tucked into my brother's belt, a starter's pistol he'd taken from the elementary school PE instructor. Light glinted off the chrome barrel, which was shaped like a dog's dick. The "four warrior attendants" were also sporting belts, made from the hide of a Production Brigade cow that had recently starved to death. Not completely dry and not yet tanned, the belts stank something awful. Each of them had a revolver tucked into his belt, the ones used by the village opera troupe, all beautifully carved out of elm by the skilled carpenter Du Luban, and then painted black. They were so real-looking that if they fell into the hands of bandits, they could be used in robberies. The back part of the one in Dragon Sun's belt had been hollowed out to make room for a spring, a firing pin, and a detonating cap. When fired, it produced a louder crack than a real pistol. My brother's pistol used caps, and when he pulled the trigger, it popped twice. The underlings behind the "four warrior attendants" were all carrying red-tasseled spears over their shoulders, the metal tips polished to a shine with sandpaper and razor sharp. If you buried one in a tree, it was hard work pulling it out. My brother led his troops at a fast clip. The eye-catching red tassels against the virgin snow created a spectacular tableau. When they were about fifty yards from the spot where Yang Qi was selling his rank goods, my brother drew his pistol and fired it into the air: *Pow! Pow*! Two puffs of smoke quickly dissipated above him. Comrades! he shouted. Charge! Holding their spears as weapons, the words *Kill Kill Kill* thundered overhead as they sloshed through the snow, turning it to mud with loud crunches. As soon as they reached the spot, my brother gave them a signal, and they surrounded Yang Qi and a dozen or so of his potential goatskin coat customers.

Jinlong glared at me, and I glared right back. Truth be told, I was feeling lonesome and would have loved to join his Red Guard unit. Their mysterious yet solemn movements excited me. The pistols in the four warrior attendants' belts excited me even more. They were impressive, even if they were fake, and I was itching to have one just like them. So I asked my sister to tell Jinlong that I wanted to join his Red Guard unit. He told her: Independent farming is a target of revolution, and he does not qualify to be a Red Guard. The minute he takes his ox into the commune I'll accept him and even appoint him as a team leader. He raised his voice so I could hear every word without having my sister repeat it. But joining the commune, especially the ox, was not my decision to make. Dad hadn't uttered a word since the incident in the marketplace. He just stared straight ahead, a vacant look on his face, holding the butcher knife in his hand as a threat. After losing half a horn, the ox had the same vacant look. It looked at people out of the corner of its half-closed eyes, its abdomen rising and falling as it emitted a low growl, as if ready to bury its good horn in someone's belly. No one dared to go near the ox shed, where Dad and his ox were staying. My brother led his Red Guards into the compound every day to stir things up, with gongs and drums, attempts to fire the cannon, attacking bad elements and shouting slogans. My dad and his ox seemed not to hear any of it. But I knew that if any of them got up the nerve to enter the ox shed, blood would be spilled. Under those circumstances, if I tried to lead the ox into the commune, even if Dad said okay, the ox would never do it. So going out to watch Yang Qi peddle his goatskin coats was just an attempt to kill some time.

My brother raised his arm and aimed his starter's pistol at Yang Qi's chest. Trembling, he commanded: Arrest the profiteer! The four warrior attendants ran up and pointed their fake revolvers at Yang Qi's head from four directions. Put your hands up! they shouted in unison. All Yang Qi did was sneer. Boys, he said, who do you think you're going to scare with knots from an elm tree? Go ahead, shoot, if you've got the balls. I'm prepared to die a hero's death, to die for a cause. Dragon Sun pulled the trigger. A loud crack, a puff of yellow smoke, a broken gun barrel, and blood spilling from between his thumb and forefinger; the smell of gunpowder hung over them all. Yang Qi, frightened by the noise, paled; a moment later, his teeth were chattering. He looked down at the hole burned in the breast of his coat.

Brothers, he said, you really did it! To which my brother responded, Revolution is not a dinner party. I'm a Red Guard, too, Yang Qi said. My brother said that they were Chairman Mao's Red Guards, while he was just a ragtag Red Guard faction. Since Yang Qi was in a mood to argue, my brother told the Sun brothers to take him to the command headquarters to be criticized and denounced. Then he told the Red Guard troops to confiscate the goatskin coats Yang Qi had laid in the grass beside the road.

The public meeting to criticize and denounce Yang Qi went on all night. A bonfire was lit in the compound using wood from furniture the bad elements had been forced to break apart and bring over. That included several pieces of valuable sandalwood and rosewood furniture — all burned. Bonfires and public criticism meetings were nightly affairs. The fires melted the snow on the rooftops; black gooey mud was the runoff. My brother knew there was only so much furniture they could use as firewood, but he had an idea. Feng Jun, a pockmarked villager who had been to Northeast China, once told him that, because of the sap, even green pine trees will burn. So my brother told his Red Guards to take the bad elements out behind the elementary school and have them cut down pine trees. One after another, the downed trees were dragged over to the street outside the command headquarters by the village's pair of scrawny horses.

The denouncement of Yang Qi centered on his capitalist activities, his verbal abuse of the little generals, and his failed plan to set up a counterrevolutionary organization. After beating and kicking him mercilessly, they ran him out of the compound. The goatskin coats were passed out to Red Guards on night duty. From the time the revolutionary tide began to sweep through the land, my brother slept only in the original brigade office, now command headquarters, in his clothes, and always in the company of his four warrior attendants and a dozen or more underlings. They laid straw and blankets out on the floor and were kept warm by the addition of the newly acquired coats.

But let's return to what we were talking about earlier: My mother rushed out of the house with the goatskin coat over her shoulders, which made her appear unusually big. The coat had been allocated to my sister by my brother, since she was the Red Guard doctor first, then the village doctor. True to her filial nature, she gave the coat to my mother to ward off the cold. She ran up to where my brother lay, knelt down beside him, and lifted up his head. What's wrong, son? My brother's face was purple, his lips dry and cracked, and his ears oozed pus and blood; he looked like he'd become a martyr. Your sister, where's your sister? She went to Chen Dafu's to deliver his baby. Jiefang, my mother wailed, be a good boy and go get her. I looked down at Jinlong, then over at the now leaderless Red Guards, and my heart ached. We had the same mother, after all. Sure, he liked to throw his weight around, and that made me a little jealous. But I admired him. He was a rare talent, I knew that, and I didn't want him to die. So I raced out of the compound and down the street, headed west for a couple of hundred yards, then turned north into a lane, where Chen Dafu and his family lived in three rooms with a thatched roof and a rammed-earth wall, the nearest compound to the river about a hundred yards down the lane.

Chen's scrawny dog greeted me with ferocious barking. So I picked up a brick and threw it at him, hitting him in the leg. With a series of pained yelps, he ran into the yard on three legs, just as Chen Dafu emerged from inside carrying a very big and very intimidating club. Who hit my dog? I did! I replied with an angry glare. Seeing it was me, the towering dark man softened; his features relaxed as he flashed an ambiguous smile. Why be afraid of me? Because I had something on him. I'd seen what he and Huang Tong's wife, Wu Qiuxiang, were doing in the willow grove one day. Embarrassed to be caught in the act, she ran off, bent at the waist, abandoning her laundry basin and mallet. A checkered article of clothing floated down the river. As he was buttoning up his pants, Chen Dafu threatened me: If you tell anyone, I'll kill you! If Huang Tong doesn't kill you first, I replied. His tone softened and he tried to soft-soap me instead, saying he'd get his wife's niece to marry me. The image of a sandy-haired girl with tiny ears and snot on her lip floated into my mind. Hell! I said. Who wants that yellow-haired niece of yours? I'd rather go through life as a bachelor than marry anyone as ugly as that! Ah, my boy, you're raising your sights too high. I tell you, I'm going to see that you and that ugly girl are married one day! Then I guess you'd better get a rock and beat me to death, I said. Kid, he replied, let's you and me make a gentleman's agreement. You don't tell anyone what you saw here, and I won't try to fix you up with my wife's niece. If you break your promise, I'll have my wife take her niece to your place and set her down on your bed, then have her tell people you raped her.

How would you like that? I thought for a moment. Having that ugly, stupid girl sit on my bed and then telling people I raped her would spell big trouble. Despite the saying, "An upright person does not fear a slanted shadow, and dried excrement does not stick to walls," I thought this might be more than I could handle. So we reached an agreement. But over time, based upon the way he treated me, I realized that he was more afraid of me than I was of him. That's why I didn't have to worry, even if I crippled his dog, and why I could talk back to him like that. Where's my sister? I said. I need to find her. She's with my wife, delivering a baby. I gazed at the five snot-nosed children in his yard, each slightly taller than the one before, and mocked him: That's quite a wife you've got there, popping them out like a bitch, one litter after the other. He bared his teeth. Don't talk like that. You're too young to say hurtful things like that. You'll see why when you grow up. I haven't got time to argue with you, I said. I'm here to get my sister. I turned and faced his window. Sis! I shouted. Mother sent me here to get you. Jinlong's dying! The shrill cry of a newborn baby erupted inside the house, drawing Chen Dafu to the window as if his pants were on fire. What is it? he shouted. The woman inside responded weakly, It's got that thing between its legs. Chen covered his face with his hands and walked in tight circles in the snow beneath the window. *Wu!* he uttered at the end of each circle. *Wu!* The old man in the sky has opened his eyes, finally, and Chen Dafu now has an heir — My sister tore out of the house and asked me what was wrong. Jinlong's dying, I said. He fell off the platform and hit the ground. He won't last long.

My sister elbowed her way through the crowd and knelt at Jinlong's side. First she put her finger under his nose, then she rubbed his hand, and finally felt his forehead. Take him inside, she commanded, and hurry! The four warrior attendants picked him up and headed for the office, but my sister stopped them. Take him home and put him on the *kang*! They turned and carried him into my mother's house, where there was a heated *kang*. My sister made sideward glances to the Huang sisters, Huzhu and Hezuo, who were looking on, teary-eyed. The fair skin of their faces was dotted with chilblains like ripe cherries.

First my sister relieved my brother of the leather belt he wore day and night and tossed it, along with the starter's pistol, into a corner, where it landed on top of a curious mouse, which squeaked once

and died, blood seeping from its nose. Then she pulled down my
brother's pants to expose his discolored, louse-covered buttocks. With
a frown, she opened an ampoule with a pair of tweezers, drew some
liquid into a syringe, and jammed it haphazardly into him. In all she
gave him two injections and hooked him up to an IV drip. She deftly
found a vein on her first attempt, just as Wu Qiuxiang entered with a
bowl of ginger tea, which she planned to spoon-feed my brother. With
her eyes, my mother anxiously sought the opinion of my sister, who
simply nodded noncommittally. Wu Qiuxiang began spooning the ginger tea into my brother's mouth, her own mouth opening and closing
in concert with his, so typical of mothers, something that cannot be
faked. Wu Qiuxiang saw herself as my brother's true mother. I knew
that her feelings toward my brother and sister were complex, since
relations between our two families were messy, to say the least. Her
mouth was moving in concert with his not because of any special ties
between our families, but because she knew what was in her daughters' hearts and had witnessed my brother's exceptional talents during
the revolution. She was determined that one of her daughters would
marry him, the ideal prospective son-in-law. The thought seared my
mind, driving out my concern for my brother's survival. I'd never
cared much for Wu Qiuxiang, but seeing her run out of the willow
grove, bent at the waist, that day had actually brought us closer
together. That was because every time we met, her face reddened and
she did her best to avoid eye contact. I began to take notice of her:
thin waist and pale ears with a red mole on one lobe. There was
magnetism in her laugh, which was deep and low. I was in the shed
one night, helping Dad feed the ox, when she slipped in quietly and
handed me two warm chicken eggs. She put her arm around me and
held my head up against her breast. You're a good boy, she said softly.
You didn't see anything, did you? In the darkness, I heard the ox ram
his good horn into a post; his eyes were like burning torches. Given a
fright, she pushed me away and slipped back outside. I followed her,
a shifting silhouette in the starlight, experiencing feelings I couldn't
describe.

I'll be honest with you. When she pressed my head up against
her breast, my little pecker stiffened. That seemed terribly wrong,
and it bothered me for the longest time afterward. I was enchanted by
Huang Huzhu's long braid, and from that became enchanted by her. I
drifted into a fantasy world, wishing that Wu Qiuxiang would marry

Hezuo, the daughter with the boyish haircut, to Jinlong, and let me marry Huzhu. But it was far more likely that she'd marry Huzhu to my brother. She was no more than ten minutes older than her sister, but even one minute still made her the elder sister, and elder sisters were always expected to marry first. I was in love with Huzhu, but given the ambiguous relationship between me and her mother, who had pressed my head against her breast in the ox shed and caused my pecker to stiffen, there was no chance she'd be allowed to marry me. I hurt, I was anxious, I had guilt feelings. And if that weren't enough, I'd been exposed to all sorts of misinformation about sex by Hu Bin when we were grazing animals together. Things like: "Ten drops of sweat equal one drop of blood, and ten drops of blood equal one drop of semen." Or: "After the first ejaculation, a boy stops growing." These cockeyed concepts had me in their grip, and the future looked bleak. Looking at Jinlong's finely developed body, then at my own scrawny frame, and finally at Huzhu's voluptuous figure, all I could feel was despair. I even contemplated suicide. Wouldn't it be wonderful to be an empty-headed bull? I thought. Now, of course, I know you were anything but empty-headed, that in fact there were all kinds of thoughts running through your mind, and not limited to affairs of the mortal world, but included concerns of the netherworld, past, present, and future.

My brother was on the mend. He was pale as a ghost, but he struggled out to lead the revolution. While he lay unconscious for several days, my mother had thrown his clothes into boiling water, drowning all the fleas, but his handsome Dacron military tunic came out so badly wrinkled it looked like something a cow had chewed and spit out. His imitation army cap came out faded and wrinkled, resembling nothing so much as the scrotum of a castrated bull. The sight of his badly transformed tunic and cap put him in panic mode. He flew into a rage; dark blood spewed from his nostrils. Mother, he said, why didn't you just kill me? Stung by feelings of remorse, she didn't know what to say. As my brother's anger subsided, sadness welled up inside him and tears streamed down his face. He climbed up onto the *kang*, covered his head with the quilt, and for the next two days wouldn't eat or drink a thing and responded to nothing anyone said. Poor Mother came into the room and went back out, over and over, the cold sores at the corners of her mouth, a sign of her anxiety. *Ai*, how stupid could I be? she muttered. What a stupid old woman! Finally, my sister could stand it no longer. She pulled the bedding back to reveal a haggard, stubbly young man with sunken eyes. It's just an old tunic! she said, clearly rankled. Is that worth nearly driving Mother to suicide? He sat up, his eyes glazed, and sighed. His tears began to flow even before he spoke. You don't know what that tunic meant to me. You know the saying, "Humans need nice clothes, horses require a fine saddle." It was that tunic that made it possible for me to issue commands and intimidate the bad elements. Well, there's nothing you can do about it now, my sister said. Do you expect your tunic to recapture its original shape because you lie in bed like a dead man? My brother thought that over. All right, I'll get up. I'm hungry. Those last two words sent Mother scurrying into the kitchen, where she set to work preparing noodles and frying some eggs, the fragrance quickly saturating the compound.

Huang Huzhu walked into the house bashfully while my brother was wolfing down the food. Well, young lady, my mother commented with notable interest. We all share a single compound, but this is the first time you've been in our house in a decade. Mother looked her over with unmistakable affection. Huzhu didn't look at my brother, she didn't look at my sister, and she didn't look at my mother. She just stared at the wrinkled bundle that was my brother's tunic. Aunty, she said, you made a mess of Jinlong's tunic when you washed it, but I know something about fabric, and I know how to sew. Would you be willing to let me work on it? Like they say, "treating a dead horse as if it were alive"? Maybe I can restore it to its original shape. Young lady, my mother said, eyes bright as she took Huzhu's hands in hers, you really are quite the young lady. If you can restore Brother Jinlong's tunic to its original shape, I'll get down on my knees and kowtow three times to you!

Huzhu took only the tunic with her. She kicked the imitation army cap into the corner where the mouse hole was. Huzhu left, and hope was on its way. Mother wanted to see what sort of magic Huzhu would use on the tunic, but she got no farther than the apricot tree before her courage left her. Huang Tong was standing in his doorway chopping up elm roots with an ax. Wood chips flew like bullets. Scarier still was the enigmatic look on his tiny little face. As a class-two capitalist-roader, he had been attacked by my brother in the early days of the Cultural Revolution, and stripped of his powers and functions. He had to have a belly full of loathing for my brother, just waiting for the chance to retaliate. Still, I knew his thoughts weren't all that clear-cut. Decades of living in our society had taught him the importance of observing things carefully. He'd never have missed noting the feelings his two precious daughters had for my brother. So Mother asked my sister to go see what was happening, but she just snorted contemptuously. I wasn't sure why, but I knew from the hostile words Huzhu had said to my sister that the enmity between them was deep. So then Mother asked me to go. You're too young to be worried about losing face. In her eyes I was still a child, the sad story of my life. But since I was curious to see how Huzhu was going to restore my brother's tunic, I slinked up near her house. My legs turned wobbly when I saw Huang Tong chopping up those elm roots.

The next morning, Huzhu came over with a bundle under her arm. My brother hopped excitedly out of bed. My mother's lips trembled, but she said nothing. Huzhu looked calm, but the corners of her mouth and the tips of her eyebrows gave her sense of pride away. She laid the bundle down on the bed and opened it. There, folded neatly, lay a restored tunic and, atop it, a brand-new army cap. Though it too was made of white material dyed yellow, it was so beautifully done it could pass for authentic. The centerpiece, however, was a red star she'd embroidered on the front with knitting wool. She handed it to my brother, then shook out the tunic for him. The wrinkles were still visible, but just barely. She lowered her eyes and blushed. Aunty, you boiled it too long, she said apologetically. This is the best I could do. Oh, my, her modesty was like a hammer striking my mother and brother's hearts. Tears virtually sprayed from Mother's eyes, while my brother could not stop himself from reaching out and taking Huzhu's hands. Rather than pull them back right away, she let them fall away slowly before sitting down on the edge of the *kang*. My mother opened the cupboard and took out a chunk of hard candy, which she smashed into smaller pieces and handed to Huzhu. She chose not to eat them, so Mother literally put a piece into her mouth. As she sucked on the candy, she stared at the wall and said, Try them on, see if they fit. I can alter them if they don't. My brother took off his padded coat and put on the tunic and cap, tied his leather belt around his waist, and hung the starter's pistol from it. The commander was once again the figure of absolute authority, maybe even more so than before. She was like a true seamstress, and like a true wife as she walked around, examining my brother, straightening the hem here and tugging on the collar there. Then she stood in front of him and adjusted the cap with both hands. It seems a bit tight, she said with a sense of regret. But it's the only piece of fabric I had, so it'll have to do. In the spring I'll go into town and buy a few yards of better fabric and make you a new cap.

It was clear — I didn't stand a chance.

19

Jinlong Stages a Play to Welcome Spring
Lan Lian Would Die Before Giving Up His Vow

My brother's recalcitrance softened considerably after he and Huzhu got together. Revolutions reform societies, women remold men. Within the space of a month or so, he not only held no criticism sessions where the targets were kicked and beaten, but he actually organized ten or more Peking operas in the modern revolutionary style. Huzhu, once bashful and timid, was transformed into a bold, forceful woman with unrestrained passion. That she had a fine voice and knew the music from so many revolutionary operas took everyone by surprise — I had to admit that my fantasies surrounding Huzhu were nothing but a toad hungering over the flesh of a swan. Years later, even Mo Yan himself revealed to me that he too had entertained illusions about Huzhu. So, to my surprise, big toads and little ones both hunger over the flesh of swans — The Ximen compound came alive with strains of music from flutes and bowed instruments, with men and women joining their voices in song. The center of revolutionary activities metamorphosed into a culture salon. Daily beatings and criticisms, with howls and wails, had been exciting at first, but they grew disturbing as time passed. By abruptly changing the shape of the revolutionary format, creating new sights and sounds, Jinyang brought smiles to the people's faces

The rich peasant Wu Yuan, who played the two-stringed *huqin*, was brought into the troupe of musicians. So was Hong Taiyue, with his rich musical background as a singer. He served as conductor by banging on his glorious ox bone. Even the bad elements, whose duty was to sweep the streets clean of snow, hummed to the music emerging from the compound as they worked.

On New Year's Eve, my brother and Huzhu braved snow to travel to the county town. They left the village as roosters were greeting the dawn; they returned at dusk the following day. They went by foot but returned on an East Is Red caterpillar tractor made in the city of Luoyang. Given its high horsepower, it was intended for farm work — plowing and harvesting — but had been appropriated by Red Guards for transportation. Now nothing could stop them from traveling where they wanted to go, not storms and not muddy roads. The tractor crossed the frozen river into the village rather than try to negotiate the unstable stone bridge, then drove down the main road to our compound. It traveled worry-free in high gear and, gas pedal pushed to the floor, nearly flew down the road, its caterpillar tracks sending snow and mud flying and leaving two deep ruts in the ground. Great puffs of green smoke were expelled from its overhead exhaust pipe like brass cymbals that circled and made loud, echo-producing crashes, drawing terrified shrieks from sparrows and crows that flew off to points unknown. People watched as my brother and Huzhu jumped down out of the cab. They were followed by a young man with a thin face and melancholy look. His hair was cut short, he wore a pair of black-rimmed glasses, his cheeks twitched, and his ears were red from the bitter cold. He had on a once-blue uniform turned nearly white from many washings; displayed prominently on the breast was a large Chairman Mao badge, while low down on his sleeve hung a Red Guard armband. One look told you he was an old-line, battle-scarred Red Guard.

My brother told Tiger Cub Sun to summon everyone with his bugle. Blow the general assembly call. Actually, there was no need for the bugle, since every villager who could walk was already there and had surrounded the tractor. Just seeing this powerful giant was not enough; the chatter was coming fast and furious. One self-designated expert pointed out: Weld a turret on top of that thing and add a cannon, and you've got a tank! The sky was darkening; a sunset blazed in the west, an array of pink clouds that promised snow for tomorrow. My brother issued an emergency command to light the gas lamp and build a bonfire. He would be making an announcement regarding a happy event. Now that he'd issued his orders, he leaned over to converse with the old-line Red Guard. Huang Huzhu ran into her house to have her mother fry some eggs, one for the man talking to my brother, the other for the driver, who was still sitting in the tractor. Both men politely declined the invitation to be guests in their house and refused to go into the office to warm up. So Wu Qiuxiang, who should have known better, came out carrying bowls with steaming eggs, Huang Hezuo in tow. She glided like one of those vamps you see in movies. The Red Guard refused the offer, a look of disgust on his face. Jinlong snarled under his breath: What do you think you're doing? Take that back inside!

Something was wrong with the gas lamp, which was spewing yellow flames and black smoke, but the bonfire blazed, the sap on the green pine limbs crackling and spreading a sylvan fragrance over the compound. My brother climbed onto the platform amid the flickering firelight, excited as a panther that has pounced on a golden pheasant. He began to speak: When we reported on the village revolutionary situation, we were warmly received by Comrade Chang Tianhong, vice chairman of the County Revolutionary Committee. He was satisfied with our revolutionary work and sent the assistant director of the County Revolutionary Political Work Section, Comrade Luo Jingtao, to direct our village revolutionary activities and announce the names of the Ximen Village Revolutionary Committee members. Comrades, my brother said loudly, the Milky Way Commune has not yet set up a revolutionary committee, but we in Ximen Village have! This pioneering effort by Vice Chairman Chang has brought great glory to our village. Now I'll turn the meeting over to Director Luo, who will announce the names.

My brother hopped down from the platform to give Assistant Director Luo a boost up. But Luo declined the use of the platform and stood some five yards away from the bonfire, where half his face glowed and the other half was in shadows; he took a folded piece of paper out of his pocket, shook it open, and began to read in a low, husky voice:

I hereby declare that Lan Jinlong is chairman of the Gaomi County Milky Way Commune Ximen Village Production Brigade Revolutionary Committee, with Huang Tong and Ma Liangcai as deputy vice chairmen . . .

A cloud of thick smoke was blown into Assistant Director Luo's face, forcing him to move out of the way. Without reading any more, he handed the paper to my brother, said good-bye and shook hands, then turned on his heel and walked off. His actions had my brother at a momentary loss. His lips parted as he watched the man climb into the cab of the tractor, which started up, turned around, and headed back the way it had come, leaving a large indentation in the ground. We saw the tractor headlights light up the street like a bright alley, while the red taillights peered out like the eyes of a fox. . . .

On the third evening following the establishment of the revolutionary committee, the loudspeaker mounted in the branches of the apricot tree came to life, blaring "The East Is Red." When the anthem ended, a woman's voice broadcast news of the county. The lead item was an enthusiastic message of congratulations to the first village-level revolutionary committee in the county. The Gaomi County Milky Way Commune Ximen Village Production Brigade Revolutionary Committee was established, she announced, adding that the leading group of the Ximen Village Production Brigade Revolutionary Committee, including Lan Jinlong, Huang Tong, and Ma Liangcai, embodied the "Three-in-One" revolutionary organizational principle. The masses looked up at the source of the announcement and made no comment, although they were inwardly showering my brother with admiration: so young to be a chairman, and if that wasn't enough, he was being assisted by his future father-in-law, Huang Tong, and Ma Liangcai, who was so tight with my sister.

The next day a youngster in a green uniform came puffing his way into our compound with a stack of newspapers and letters on his back. He was the new postman, an innocent-looking fellow whose eyes shimmered with curiosity. After laying down the newspapers and letters, he took a little wooden box out of his bag and handed it, along with a notebook and pen, to my brother to sign. This is from Vice Chairman Chang, he said to Huzhu after reading the inscription. I knew he was talking about Braying Jackass, Little Chang, an exemplary rebel who, in his role as vice chairman of the County Revolutionary Committee, was in charge of propaganda and the arts, as I overheard him tell my sister, who reacted to the news with what appeared to be mixed emotions. I knew she had strong feelings for Little Chang, but his meteoric rise in stature created an obstacle. It was certainly possible for love to develop between a talented student in an arts academy and a pretty girl with a peasant background, but there was no chance that a leading county-level cadre in his twenties would ever actually marry a peasant girl, no matter how pretty or fetching she might be. Of course my brother was aware of her feelings, and I heard him urge her to lower her sights a bit. Ma Liangcai was a royalist at first. Why then was he named vice chairman? Can you really not see what he had in mind? Was he the one who appointed him? my sister asked stubbornly. My brother nodded. Does he want me to marry Ma Liangcai? Isn't it obvious? Did he tell you that in so many words? Did he have to? Is an important person supposed to put all his intentions into words? You have to figure things out for yourself. No, my sister insisted. I want to hear it from him. If he tells me to marry Ma Liangcai, I'll come home and marry him! By this time in their conversation, my sister's eyes were brimming with tears.

My brother opened the box with rusty scissors and took out some old newspaper print, two sheets of white window paper, and a layer of crumpled yellow crepe paper. Beneath it all was a piece of red satin. He unfolded it to reveal a ceramic Chairman Mao badge as big as the mouth of a teacup. He held it in the palm of his hand as tears slid down his cheeks, although he wasn't sure if he was moved more deeply by Chairman Mao's smiling countenance or by Little Chang's expression of friendship. He held it out for all to see. A sacred and solemn atmosphere prevailed. After he'd shown it all around, my sister-in-law to be, Huzhu, carefully pinned the badge onto my brother's breast. The heft alone made his tunic sag a bit.

In order to celebrate the new year, my brother and his friends decided to stage a performance of *The Red Lantern*. Huzhu, with her long braid, was a natural for Tiemei; my brother was all set to play the leading role of Li Yuhe, until he lost his voice, and Ma Liangcai was given the part. Speaking from the heart, I'd have chosen Ma over my brother anyway. Volunteers quickly claimed the remaining roles in the revolutionary model opera, and the entire village got caught up in the excitement that winter. Held in the Revolutionary Committee office in the light of the gas lamp, the rehearsals drew a crowd every night, filling the room, rafters included. Those who didn't make it into the room crowded up against the windows and the door to watch, pushing and shoving to catch a glimpse of what was going on inside. Hezuo also landed a part, that of Tiemei's neighbor, while Mo Yan pestered my brother for one of the other parts, until Jinlong told him to get lost. But Commander, Mo Yan said, blinking in disappointment, I've got unique talents. He turned and did a somersault. Honest, my brother said, there are no parts left. You can add one, Mo Yan insisted. So my brother thought for a moment. All right, he said, you can be an enemy agent. Granny Li was one of the major roles, with plenty of singing and talking, too much for the local uneducated girls to master, so in the end the role was offered to my sister, who coldly turned it down.

As the year's end approached, still no one had come forward to play Granny Li, and the performance was scheduled for New Year's day. Then Vice Chairman Chang phoned to say he might come by to direct the performance and enhance our prospects of becoming a model village for popularizing model revolutionary operas. The news both excited and worried my brother, whose mouth was quickly covered with cold sores, and whose voice was hoarser than ever. When he told my sister that Vice Chairman Chang might come to take over the direction, she broke into tears and sobbed: I'll take the role.

Soon after the Cultural Revolution was launched, I'd felt left out in the cold, thanks to my status of independent farmer. All the other villagers, including the crippled and the blind, had joined the Red Guards, but not me. Heat from their revolutionary fervor rose to the heavens, but I could only watch on with eyes hot with envy. I was sixteen that year, an age when I should have been flying high and burrowing low, roiling the waters with my youth. But no, I was forced into other frames of mind: self-loathing, shame, anxiety, jealousy, longing, fantasy, all coming together within me. I once screwed up the courage and the nerve to plead my case with Ximen Jinlong, who saw me as a mortal enemy. I bowed my head in a desire to participate in the torrent of revolutionary activities. He said no.

So I went to see my dad in the ox shed, which had become his refuge, his place of safety. Ever since the marketplace parade that occupied such a notorious page in the history of Northeast Gaomi Township, Dad had become a virtual mute. Still only in his forties, he was completely gray. Stiff to begin with, his hair, now that it was nearly white, stood up like porcupine quills. The ox stood behind the feeding trough, head bowed, its stature notably diminished by the loss of half a horn. Sunbeams framed its head and lit up its eyes like two pieces of sorrow-laden amethyst, deep purple and heartbreakingly moist. Our fierce bull ox was completely transformed. I knew such things happened when oxen were castrated, but I never imagined that the loss of a horn could have the same effect. Then it saw me enter the shed and, after a brief glance, lowered its eyes, as if that was all it needed to see what was on my mind. Dad was sitting on a pile of hay beside the feed trough, leaning up against straw-filled sacks, his hands hidden in the sleeves of his coat. He was resting with his eyes shut, sunbeams lighting up his head and face and turning his gray hair slightly red. Bits of straw in his hair made it appear that he had just crawled out of a haystack. Only a few traces of red paint remained here and there on his face. The birthmark had reappeared, now darker than ever, almost indigo blue. I reached up and touched my own birthmark; it felt like leather. My mark of ugliness. When I was young, people called me "Junior Blue Face," which brought me pride, not shame. But as I grew older, anyone who called me "Blue Face" was in for a hard time. I'd heard people say that we were independent farmers because of our blue faces, and there were even comments that my dad and I kept ourselves hidden during daylight, and only came out to work the land at night. I don't deny that there were nights we worked by moonlight, but not because of our blue birthmarks. Tying our independent streak to a biological defect was bullshit. We chose independence out of a conviction that we had the right to stand alone. I'd gone along with Dad because I'd thought it would be fun. But now I was drawn to something a lot more fun than that. Especially grating was the fact that I was an independent farmer *and* had a blue face. I'd begun to regret my decision to follow Dad, was beginning to hate him and his independent farming. I looked at his blue face with a measure of disgust; I hated him for passing that defect on to me. A man like you, Dad, should have stayed a bachelor, but if that was impossible, you should never have had a child!

"Dad!" I shouted. "Dad!"

He opened his eyes slowly and stared at me.

"Dad, I want to join the commune!"

Obviously, this came as no surprise. The look on his face didn't change. He took out his pipe, filled it, stuck it in his mouth, struck his flint to send a spark onto some sorghum stalks, then blew on the tiny flame until he could use it to light his pipe. He sucked in deeply and exhaled two streams of smoke though his nose.

"I want to join the commune. Let's take the ox and join up, all three of us. . . . Dad, I can't take it anymore—"

His eyes snapped fully open. "You little traitor!" he said, drawing out each word. "You go ahead if you want to, but not me, and not the ox!"

"Why?" I was feeling both abused and angry. "Here's where things stand. When the campaign was just getting under way, an independent farmer in Pingnan County was strung up from a tree and beaten to death by the revolutionary masses. My brother said that by parading you through the streets, he was covertly protecting you. He said that after they take care of the landlords, rich peasants, counter-revolutionaries, bad elements, and capitalist-roaders, they'll come after the independent farmers. Dad, Jinlong said the two thick limbs on the apricot tree were just waiting for you and me. Dad, are you listening?"

He knocked the bowl of the pipe against the sole of his shoe, stood up, and started preparing food for the ox. The sight of his bent back and sunburned neck reminded me of my childhood, when he'd carry me on his shoulders to market to buy persimmons for me. The thought saddened me.

"Dad," I said, starting to get worked up, "society is changing. County Chief Chen has been overthrown, and I'll bet the bureau head who gave you safe passage has too by now. It doesn't make sense for us to keep farming independently. If we join the commune while Jinlong is chairman, it'll make him and us look good. . . ."

Dad stayed bent over low as he worked the sieve, completely ignoring me. I was starting to get steamed.

"Dad," I said, "no wonder people say you're like a rock in the crapper, hard and stinky! Sorry to say it, Dad, but I can't follow you down this dead end into darkness. If you won't look out for me, I'll have to look out for myself. I'm not a child any longer. I want to join the commune, find a wife, and walk down a bright, shiny road. You can do what you want."

Dad dumped the straw into the feed trough and stroked the ox's deformed horn. Then he turned to face me, not a hint of anger on his face. "Jiefang," he said gently, "you're my son, and I want only the best for you. I know perfectly well how things stand these days. That Jinlong has a heart as hard as a rock, and the blood that flows through his veins is more lethal than a scorpion's tail. He'll do absolutely any-thing in the name of 'revolution.' " He looked up, squinting in the bright sunlight. "How," he wondered, "could the landlord, a good and decent man, sire an evil son like that?" Tears glistened in his eyes. "We've got three-point-two acres of land. You can take half of that with you into the commune. The wooden plow was given to us as one of the 'fruits of victory' during land reform. You can take that too, and you can have the one-room house. Take what you can with you, and after you join, if you want to throw in your lot with your mother and them, go ahead. If not, then go it alone. I don't want anything, nothing but this ox and this shed."

"Why, Dad? Tell me why." I was nearly crying. "What purpose is served by you hanging on to your independence?"

"None at all," he said calmly. "I just want to live a quiet life and be my own master. I don't want anyone to tell me what to do."

I went looking for Jinlong.

"Brother," I said, "I talked it over with Dad, and I want to join the commune."

Excited by the news, he doubled up his fists and banged them together in front of his chest.

"Wonderful," he said, "that's just wonderful, one more great achievement of the Cultural Revolution! The last independent farmer in the county is finally taking the socialist road. This is wonderful news. Let's go inform the County Revolutionary Committee!"

"But Dad isn't joining," I said. "Just me, with half our land, our wooden plow, and a seeder."

"What do you mean?" His face darkened. "What the hell is he trying to do?"

"He says he isn't trying to do anything. He's just gotten used to a quiet life and doesn't want to answer to anyone."

"That old son of a bitch!" He banged his fist on the table beside him, so hard an ink bottle nearly bounced off onto the floor.

"Don't get too excited, Jinlong," Huang Huzhu said.

"And how do I do that?" he said in a low growl. "I'd planned to present two gifts to Vice Chairman Chang and the County Revolutionary Committee at New Year's. One was the village production of the revolutionary opera *The Red Lantern*; the other was that we'd eliminated the last independent farmer, not only in the county or in the province, but in the whole country. I was going to do what Hong Taiyue failed to do. That would cement my authority up and down the line. Your joining without him means there's still one independent farmer. I won't have it. I'm going to talk to him. You come with me!"

Jinlong stormed angrily into the ox shed, the first time he'd stepped foot inside in years.

"Dad," he said. "I shouldn't be calling you Dad, but I will this time."

Dad waved him off. "Don't," he said. "I'm not worthy."

"Lan Lian," Jinlong continued, "I have but one thing to say to you. For the sake of Jiefang, and for yourself, it's time to join the commune. I'm in charge now, and you have my word you won't have to perform heavy labor. And if you don't even want light jobs, then you can just rest up. You're getting on in years, and you deserve to take life easy."

"That's more than I deserve," Dad said icily.

"Climb up onto the platform and look around," Jinlong said. "Take a look at Gaomi County, or at Shandong Province, or at all of China's nineteen provinces (not counting Taiwan), its metropolitan areas, and its autonomous regions. The whole country, awash in red, with only a single black dot, here in Ximen Village, and that black dot is you!"

"I'm fucking honored, the one black dot in all of China!"

"We are going to erase that black dot!" Jinlong said.

Dad stuck his hand under the feed trough and took out a rope covered in ox dung. He threw it at Jinlong's feet.

"Do you plan to hang me from the apricot tree? Well, be my guest!"

Jinlong leaped backward, as if the rope were a snake. Baring his teeth and clenching and unclenching his fists, he jammed his hands into his pants pockets and then took them out again. He took a cigarette out of his tunic pocket — he'd taken up smoking after being appointed chairman — and lit it with a gold-colored lighter. His forehead creased, obviously in deep thought. But after a moment he flipped away his cigarette, stomped it out, and turned to me.

"Go outside, Jiefang," he said.

I looked first at the rope on the ground, then at Jinlong and Dad, one scrawny, the other brawny, pondering who would win and who would lose if a fight broke out, as well as whether I'd stand by and watch or jump in and, if the latter, whose side I'd be on.

"Say what you want to say," Dad said. "Let's see what you're made of. Stay where you are, Jiefang. Keep your eyes and ears open."

"Fine with me," Jinlong said. "Do you think I won't hang you from the apricot tree?"

"Oh, you'll do it, all right, you'll do anything."

"Don't interrupt me. I'm only letting you off for the sake of Mother. I'm not going to beg you to join the commune, since the Communist Party has never begged anything from capitalist-roaders. Tomorrow we'll hold a public meeting to welcome Jiefang into the commune, along with his land, his plow, and his seeder. The ox too. We'll present him with a red flower, and do the same for the ox. At that moment, you'll be all alone in this ox shed. It will be heartbreaking for you when the clash of cymbals, the pounding of drums, and the resounding cracks of firecrackers enter this empty shed. You'll be cut off from the masses, living apart from your wife, and separated from your children, and even the ox that would not betray you will be forcibly taken from you. What will your life mean then? If I were you," Jinlong said as he kicked the rope and looked up at the overhead beam, "if I were you, I'd loop that rope over the beam and hang myself!"

He turned and walked out.

"Evil bastard—" Dad jumped up and cursed Jinlong's back before dejectedly hunkering down on the straw.

I was devastated, shocked by Jinlong's behavior. I felt so sorry for Dad at that moment, and ashamed of wanting to abandon him. I'd been helping the enemy in his evil ways. I threw myself down at Dad's feet, grabbed his hands, and said through my tears:

"I won't join, Dad. I'm going to stay with you and be an independent farmer even if it means I have to live the rest of my life as a bachelor—"

He wrapped his arms around my head and sobbed for a moment. Then he pushed me away, dried his eyes, and straightened up. "You're a man already, Jiefang, so you must stand by what you say. Go ahead, join the commune, take the plow and the seeder with you. As for the ox—" He looked over at the ox; the ox returned the look. "You can take it too!"

"Dad!" I shouted in alarm. "Are you really going to take the road he points out?"

"Don't worry, son," he said as he jumped to his feet. "I don't take roads anybody points out for me. I take my own road."

"Don't you dare hang yourself, Dad!"

"Why would I do that? Jinlong still has a bit of conscience left. He'd have no problem getting people to kill me the same way the people in Pingnan County killed their independent farmer. But his heart isn't in it. He's hoping I'll die on my own. If I do, the last black spot in the county, in the province, in all of China, will erase itself. But I'm not about to die. If they want to kill me, there's nothing I can do about it, but it's wishful thinking to expect me to die on my own. I'm going to live, and live well. China's going to have to get used to this black spot!"

20

Lan Jiefang Betrays Father and Joins the Commune
Ximen Ox Kills a Man and Dies a Righteous Death

I took my one-point-six acres of land, a wooden plow, a seeder, and the ox into the commune. When I led you out of the shed, firecrackers exploded, cymbals and drums filled the air with their noise. A group of half-grown kids wearing gray imitation army caps ran in amid the smoke and confetti to grab up all the firecrackers with their fuses intact. Mo Yan mistakenly picked up one without a fuse and, bang, his lips parted as it tore a hole in his hand. Serves you right! A firecracker nearly blew off my finger as a kid, and the memory of Dad treating it with paste flashed in my mind. I turned and looked back at Dad, and it was almost more than I could bear. He was sitting on a pile of cut straw, staring at the coiled rope in front of him.

"Dad," I called out anxiously. "Don't you dare think of . . ."

He looked over and, appearing disheartened, waved a couple of times. I walked into the sun and left Dad in the dark. Huzhu pinned a big red paper flower on my chest and smiled at me. I could smell the Sunflower brand lotion on her face. Hezuo hung a paper flower the same size on the ox's deformed horn. The ox shook his head and sent the flower to the ground.

"The ox tried to gore me!" Hezuo shrieked, exaggerating the movement.

She turned and bolted into the arms of my brother, who pushed her away with an icy look and walked up to the ox. He patted it on the head, then rubbed its horns, first the whole one, then the deformed one.

"Ox," he said, "you've set out on a bright, sunny road, and we welcome you."

I saw lights flash in the ox's eyes, but it was only tears. My dad's ox was like a tiger whose whiskers had been pulled off, no longer awesome, gentle as a kitten.

My dream had come true: I was admitted into my brother's Red Guard organization. Not only that, I was given the role of Wang Lianju in the revolutionary opera *The Red Lantern*. Every time Li Yuhe called me a traitor, I was reminded of how Dad had used the same word on me. The feeling that I had in fact betrayed Dad by joining the commune grew stronger as time passed, and I couldn't shake the worry that one day he'd take his own life. But he didn't; he neither hanged himself from a rafter nor jumped into the river. Instead, he moved out of the room and began sleeping in the ox shed, where he set up a stove in a corner and used a steel helmet as a wok. In the long days that followed, since he had no plow, he worked his land with a hoe, and since he couldn't manage a wheelbarrow by himself, he carried fertilizer into the field in baskets over his shoulder and used a gourd as a seeder. From 1967 to 1981, his one-point-six acres were a thorn in the side of the authorities, a tiny plot of land smack in the middle of the People's Commune. His existence was both absurd and sobering; it aroused pity and commanded respect. In the 1970s, Hong Taiyue, back in his role as Party secretary, came up with a variety of schemes to eliminate the last independent farmer, but my dad thwarted all of them. Each time he'd throw the length of rope at Hong's feet and say:

"Go ahead, hang me from the apricot tree!"

Jinlong had been counting on my surrender to the commune and the successful performance of a revolutionary opera to make Ximen Village a model for the county, and when that happened, as a village leader, he'd enjoy a meteoric rise through the ranks. But things did not turn out as he had hoped. First of all, despite the waiting, day and night, by him and by my sister, Little Chang never did come back on the tractor to direct the opera, and then one day word reached them that he had been removed from his post for his unsavory dealings with women. With him gone, my brother's backing crumbled.

Then, as the days grew warmer, my brother's situation worsened, since the masses rejected his plans to stage more revolutionary operas. Some old-timers from redder-than-red poor peasant backgrounds said to him one day while he was smoking a cigarette up in the apricot tree:

"Commander Jinlong, shouldn't you be organizing some farm

work? Neglecting the land for even a short time can cost a whole year. When workers make revolution, the state pays their wages, but the only way we peasants survive is by planting crops!"

While they were speaking their piece, they saw my dad walk out the gate with two baskets of manure. The smell of fresh dung in that early spring air energized them.

"Crops are to be planted in revolutionary land. Production is fine, but only when it's an integral part of the revolutionary line!" My brother spat out the butt and jumped down out of the tree, landing awkwardly and falling in a heap. The old peasants tried to help him up, but he shoved them away with a snarl. "I'm on my way to see the Commune Revolutionary Committee. You wait here, and don't do anything foolish."

After changing into high-topped galoshes, he went over to the makeshift toilet to relieve himself before heading out on the muddy road to the commune. There he met Yang Qi. They had become enemies over the affair with the goatskin coats, but that was hidden below the surface.

"Commander Ximen," Yang said with an irritating grin, "where are you off to? You look more like a Japanese MP than a Red Guard."

Shaking his penis, Jinlong snorted to show his contempt for Yang Qi, who continued to grin and said:

"You've lost your backing, buddy, and I wouldn't be surprised if you were next. If you're smart, you'll give up your position and hand it to someone who knows something about farming. Singing opera doesn't put food on the table."

With a sneer, my brother said, "The County Revolutionary Committee made me chairman, and they're the only ones who can take it away from me. The Commune Revolutionary Committee does not have that authority."

Trouble was sure to come, and when my brother spoke so angrily to Yang Qi, the big ceramic Chairman Mao badge fell off his tunic, right into the latrine pit. My brother was stunned. Yang Qi was stunned. When my brother had gotten his bearings back and was about to jump into the latrine to retrieve the badge, Yang Qi also got his bearings back. He grabbed my brother by the lapels and shouted:

"Counterrevolutionary, I've caught a counterrevolutionary!"

My brother, along with the landlords, rich peasants, counterrevolutionaries, bad elements, and capitalist-roader Hong Taiyue, was assigned to supervised labor. As for me, I was sent to the brigade feeding tent to feed the livestock, working for Old Fang Liu and Hu Bin, who had been released after serving out his sentence.

By moving my bedding to the sleeping platform in the feeding tent, I was finally able to leave the compound I loved and hated in equal measure. My departure also freed up a bit of space for Dad, who had begun sleeping in the ox shed when I told him I was joining the commune. For all its virtues, the shed was still a lean-to made to house an ox; in spite of its shortcomings, it was still a roof over his head. I urged him to move back into the room I vacated and told him not to worry, that I'd keep looking after our ox.

Although it was Yang Qi who had denounced my brother, costing him his position as chairman and pinning on him the label of active counterrevolutionary, he was not chosen to be the new chairman; the Commune Revolutionary Committee chose Huang Tong as chairman of our village committee, since he had performed well over the years as director of the Production Brigade. He would stand in the middle of the threshing ground like a commander deploying his forces when he passed out work assignments. Those from good families were given light work; those with bad backgrounds were sent out into the fields to man the plows. My brother stood with Yu Wufu, the onetime security chief, Zhang Dazhuang the turncoat, Wu Yuan, the rich peasant, Tian Gui, who had run the distillery, and Hong Taiyue, the capitalist-roader. A look of anger was stamped on my brother's face; Hong Taiyue wore a sneer. Bad elements who had been undergoing labor reform for years showed no expression. By now used to spring plowing, they already knew which ox and which plow they were assigned. So they walked into the storeroom, brought out their plows and harnesses, and went over to the oxen that were waiting for them. Those animals have rested all winter and aren't in shape, Fang Liu said, so go easy on them the first day. Let them lead. Then he picked out a black, gelded Bohai ox and a Western Shandong for Hong Taiyue, who deftly harnessed them; though he'd spent years as Party secretary, he was born a farmer and knew what he was doing. After watching the others, my brother lined up his plow, laid out the harness, and, curling his lip to show his unhappiness, said to Fang Liu:

"Which two animals do I get?"

Fang looked my brother over and said under his breath, but loud enough for my brother to hear, It's good for a young man to temper himself. He untied a female Mongol ox from the tethering pole, one my brother was very familiar with. Early one spring years before, when we were tending oxen by the river, my brother's figure had been reflected in her eyes. She stood obediently beside him chewing her cud, and a large chunk of chewed grass slid noisily down her throat. He tossed the halter over his shoulder, getting no resistance from her. Fang Liu's gaze swept over the tethering pole and fell on our ox as if he'd just that moment discovered what a good animal it was, for his eyes lit up and he made a clicking noise with his mouth.

"Jiefang," he said, "you can take the one you brought us and let it team up with its mother."

Jinlong took the reins and commanded the ox to walk over to where he could be harnessed. But the ox kept his head low, leisurely chewing his cud. So Jinlong tugged at the reins to get the animal to move; that didn't work either. Our ox had never had a ring placed through his nose, so his head was immovable. It was, as it turned out, his strength that brought about the punishment of a nose ring. Ox, that didn't have to happen, and wouldn't have if you'd displayed the same human understanding that was so evident when you were with Dad. Your obedience could well have established you as the only ox in the history of Northeast Gaomi Township to never have a nose ring. But you chose to ignore the attempts to get you to move.

"How does anyone get an ox to do what it's told without a nose ring?" Fang Liu asked. "Does Lan Lian use magic incantations to get it to do what he wants?"

Ximen Ox, my friend, they hogtied you and stuck a hot poker through the septum of your nose. Who did it? My brother Jinlong. I didn't know then that you were a reincarnation of Ximen Nao, so I couldn't appreciate what you were feeling at that moment. The person who fitted a brass ring through the burned hole in your nose was your own son. How did that make you feel?

Once the nose ring was in place, they led you out into the field, where springtime, the season of rebirth, was making itself felt everywhere. But as soon as you reached the plot of land to be plowed, you lay down on the ground. All the farmers, veterans of many spring plowings, had watched you pull a plow by yourself, seemingly with ease, spreading waves of soil as you created one straight row after the other. They were curious, even mystified, by your behavior. What's this all about? My dad was out on his narrow strip of land that day, a handheld hoe a substitute for an ox and a plow. Bent at the waist, eyes fixed on the ground at his feet, he moved slowly, one swipe of his hoe at a time. "This ox," a farmer said, "wishes it could be working with him, the way it used to."

Jinlong stepped backward, took his whip off his shoulder, and brought it down on the ox's back. It left a white welt on your hide. You were in the prime of your life then, so your hide was tough and resilient. Jinlong's lashing did no serious damage. If you'd been old and weak or young and underdeveloped, it would have split your hide.

There's no denying that Jinlong was a very talented young man. Whatever he put his hand to, he did better than anyone. There weren't more than a handful of men in the village who could handle one of those four-yard-long whips with accuracy, and he was one of them. The dull sound of the whip on your hide dispersed in the air around you, and I know Dad must have heard it. But he didn't look up or pause in his work. I knew the depth of his feelings toward you, so the punishment you were taking must have hurt him a great deal. But rather than run over to protect you, he kept working. My dad was suffering as much from the lashing as you were!

Jinlong gave you twenty lashes and only stopped from exhaustion; he was gasping for breath, his forehead was bathed in sweat. But you lay there, head on the ground, hot tears squeezed out of your tightly shut eyes and darkening your face. You didn't move and you didn't make a sound, but the spastic ripples on your hide proved that you were still alive. If not for that, no one witnessing the scene would have doubted that they were now looking at a dead ox. With a steady stream of curses on his lips, my brother walked up and kicked you in the face.

"Get up, damn you," he snarled. "Get up!"

You stayed where you were, eyes still shut. Enraged by your defiance, he kicked you in the head and the face and the belly, over and over and over, and from a distance he looked like a shaman in a dance of exorcism. You put up with the assault without moving, while the Mongol ox beside you, your mother, trembled as she watched what was happening to you; her crooked tail went stiff, like a petrified snake. Out in the field, my father sped up the pace of work, digging deeply into the earth.

The other farmers, having finished their plowing, returned, surprised to see that Jinlong's ox was still lying on the ground. As they gathered round, the good-hearted rich peasant Wu Yuan said:

"Is he sick?"

Tian Gui, who consistently played the role of a progressive, said, "Look how plump he is, how glossy his coat is. Last year he pulled Lan Lian's plow, this year he's lying on the ground pretending he's dead. This ox opposes the People's Commune!"

Hong Taiyue glanced over at my dad, who still hadn't looked up from his labors. "The kind of master you have determines the kind of ox you get," he said coldly. "Like master, like ox."

"Let's beat him!" the traitor Zhang Dazhuang said. "I don't believe he'll keep lying there if we really beat him." The others agreed.

And so, seven or eight plowmen formed a circle around the ox, took their whips off their shoulders, held the handles, and let the lashes hang down behind them. They were getting ready to start the beating when the Mongol ox crumpled to the ground like a toppled wall. But she immediately began pawing at the ground and got back to her feet. She quaked from head to tail, her eyes were glazed over, her tail was tucked between her legs. The men laughed.

"Would you look at that!" one of them said. "She's paralyzed with fear before we even begin."

My brother untied the Mongol ox and led her off to the side, where she stood as if she'd been spared from something horrible. She was still quaking, but a look of calm was in her eyes.

And still you lay there, Ximen Ox, like a sandbar, as the plowmen stood back and, one after the other, as if it were a competition, expertly swirled their whips in the air and brought them down on your hide, filling the air with a tattoo of loud cracks. The ox's back was crisscrossed with lash marks. Before long, there were traces of blood, and now that the tips of the whips were bloodied, the cracks were louder and crisper. Harder and harder they came, until your back and your belly looked like cutting boards covered with chunks of bloody flesh.

My tears started to flow as soon as they began beating you. I wailed, I begged, I wanted to throw myself on top of you to share your suffering, but my arms were pinned to my sides by the mob that had gathered to watch the spectacle. I kicked and I bit, but the pain I caused had no effect on the people, who refused to let go. How could such decent villagers, young and old, get any enjoyment out of such a bloody tragedy, as if their hearts had turned to stone?

Eventually, they tired. Rubbing their sore arms, they walked up to see if you were dead. You weren't. But your eyes were tightly shut; there were open wounds on the side of your face, staining the ground around your head with blood. You were gasping for breath, and there were violent spasms in your belly, like a female in labor.

The men who had used their whips on you were sighing over a stubborn streak the likes of which they'd never seen before. The looks on their faces were awkward, almost remorseful. They'd have felt better if you'd been a defiant animal, but you weren't, you submitted meekly to their cruelty, and that they found perplexing. So many ancient ethical standards and supernatural legends stirred in their hearts and minds. Is this an ox or some sort of god? Maybe it's a Buddha who has borne all this suffering to lead people who have gone astray to enlightenment. People are not to tyrannize other people, or oxen; they must not force other people, or oxen, to do things they do not want to do.

As feelings of compassion rose up in the whip-wielding men, they urged Jinlong to bring things to a halt. But he refused. The traits he shared with that ox burned in him like sinister flames, turning his eyes red and changing the features on his face: his twisted mouth reeked, his whole frame trembled, and he seemed to be walking on air, like a common drunk. By then he had lost his grip on reality and was under the control of a demonic being. In the same way that the ox displayed its iron will and preserved its dignity by refusing to stand up, even in the face of death, my brother Jinlong was prepared to do whatever it took, at whatever cost, to make the animal stand in order to display *his* iron will and preserve *his* dignity. There could be no better example of a meeting of mortals, a clash of unyielding personalities. My brother led the female Mongol ox up to Ximen Ox, where he tied the rope affixed to your nose ring to the shaft. My god, he's going to pull Ximen Ox by the nose with the strength of his mother. Everyone there knew that the nose is an ox's most vulnerable spot, and that it is the nose ring that ensures an ox's obedience. The mightiest ox is turned submissive as soon as its nose is controlled by humans. Stand up, Ximen Ox. You've already taken more punishment than any ox could be expected to take, and your reputation won't be tarnished if you stand now. But you did not stand — I knew you wouldn't. If you had, you wouldn't have been Ximen Ox.

My brother smacked the rump of the Mongol ox hard, and she lurched forward, still quaking. The rope grew taut, pulling the nose ring with it. Oh, no, Ximen Ox! Jinlong, you monster, let my ox go! I fought to break free, but the people holding me seemed to have turned to stone. Ximen Ox's nose was pulled out of shape, like a piece of rubber. But the Mongol Ox, the heartless beast, charged ahead with all her strength every time my brother hit her, jerking Ximen Ox's head up off the ground. Yet the rest of him stayed put. It seemed to me that his front legs bent inward, but I was just seeing things. You had no intention of getting to your feet. Sounds like a bawling infant emerged from your nostrils. It was heartbreaking. Oh, Ximen Ox, a crisp sound, a pop, marked the splitting of your nose, followed by the thud of your raised head hitting the ground again. The female ox's front legs gave out on her, but she immediately stood up again.

Ximen Jinlong, now you can stop. But he didn't. He was a madman. Howling like an injured wolf, he ran over to a furrow, scooped up a handful of cornstalks, and piled them behind you. Was that evil bastard planning to set the ox on fire? Yes, that's exactly what he had in mind. He lit the stalks, and white smoke carrying a subtle fragrance rose into the air, the unique smell of cornstalks. Everyone held their breath and stared wide-eyed, but not one of them tried to put an end to my brother's brutal behavior. Oh, no, Ximen Ox, oh, no, Ximen Ox, who would rather die than stand up and pull a plow for the People's Commune. I saw my dad throw down his hoe and sprawl on the ground, facedown, as he dug his hands deep into the soil. He was quaking like a malaria sufferer, and I knew that he was sharing the ox's agonies.

The ox's hide was burning, giving off a foul, nauseating odor. No one threw up, but everyone felt like it. Ximen Ox, your face was burrowing into the ground, your back was like a trapped snake, writhing and popping from the heat. The leather halter caught fire. Belonging to the collective, it mustn't be lost. Someone ran up, released the catch, and flung it to the ground, then stomped out the flames that were consuming the rope, releasing a stench that even drove away birds in the sky. Oh, no, Ximen Ox, the charred rear half of your body was too horrible to look at.

"Burn, damn you . . . ," Jinlong was screaming. He ran over to a pile of cornstalks, and no one made a move to stop him. They wanted to see how perversely evil he could be. Even Hong Taiyue, whose job it was to teach people to cherish property belonging to the collective, looked on dispassionately.

Jinlong came back with an armload of cornstalks, stumbling as he walked. My half brother was out of his mind. Jinlong, how would you have felt if you'd known that the ox was actually the reincarnation of your real father? And you, Ximen Ox, how did you feel knowing that it was your son who punished you so savagely? Countless forms of gratitude and resentment, of love and enmity, exist among people all over the world, but something occurred at that moment that stupefied everyone who witnessed it. Ximen Ox, you stood up on shaky legs, minus your harness, your nose ring, and your tether, a free ox, totally liberated from all human control. You began to walk, how hard that must have been, weak in the legs, swaying uncontrollably from side to side; dark blood dripped from your torn nose, slid down to your belly, and from there dripped to the ground like tar. The people gaped silently, wide-eyed and slack-jawed. Step by agonizing step, you walked toward my dad, leaving the land belonging to the People's Commune and entering the one-point-six acres of land belonging to the last independent farmer in the nation, Lan Lian; once there, you collapsed in a heap.

Ximen Ox died on my dad's land. What he did went a long way toward clearing the minds of people who had become confused and disoriented during the Cultural Revolution. Ah, Ximen Ox, you became the stuff of legend, a mythical being. After your death, there were those who wanted to butcher and eat you, but when they ran up with their knives and saw the bloody tears mixed with mud on my dad's face, they turned and went away quietly.

Dad buried you in the middle of his land, under a prominent grave mound, known today as Righteous Ox Tomb, one of Northeast Gaomi Township's noted sights.

As an ox, you will likely gain immortality.

Book Three

Pig Frolics

21

With More Cries of Injustice, a Return to Yama's Hall Deceived Again to Be Reborn as a Lowly Pig

After shedding my ox skin, my indomitable spirit hovered above Lan Lian's one-point-six acres of land. Life as an ox had been a tragic existence. After my incarnation as a donkey, Lord Yama had pronounced judgment that I'd be sent back as a human, but I wound up sliding out through the birth canal of an ox. Anxious to complain he'd made a fool of me, I nonetheless continued to hover above Lan Lian, reluctant to leave. I looked down on the bloody carcass of the ox; and the gray head of Lan Lian as he sprawled across the ox's head and wailed piteously; and the obtuse expression on the face of my grown son Jinlong; and the young lad with the blue face, born to my concubine Yingchun; and the face of the youngster's friend Mo Yan, smeared with snot and tears; and the faces of all those other people that seemed so familiar. As my spirit left the body of the ox, the ox memories began to fade, replaced by those of Ximen Nao. I was a good man who hadn't deserved to die, but had been shot anyway. Lord Yama knows a mistake was made, one that was hard to make good on.

"Yes," Lord Yama said coldly, "a mistake was made. So what do you think I should do about it? I am not authorized to send you back as Ximen Nao. Having undergone two reincarnations already, you know as well as I that Ximen Nao's time has ended. His children are grown, his corpse has rotted away in the ground, and nothing but ashes remain from his dossier. Old accounts have been settled. Why can you not put those sad recollections out of your mind and seek happiness instead?"

I knelt on the cold marble floor of Lord Yama's Hall. "Great Lord," I said, a note of agony creeping into my voice, "I want more than anything to do that, but I cannot. Those painful memories are like parasites that cling stubbornly to me. When I was reborn as a donkey, I was reminded of Ximen Nao's grievances, and when I was reborn as an ox, I was reminded of the injustice he suffered. These old memories torment me relentlessly, Great Lord."

"Do you mean to say that Granny Meng's amnesia elixir, which is a thousand times more potent than knockout drops, does not work on you?" Lord Yama asked doubtfully. "Did you go straight to Homeward Terrace without drinking it?"

"Great Lord, I tell you the truth, I did not drink the tonic when I was sent back as a donkey. But before I was reborn as an ox, your two attendants pinched my nose shut and poured a bowl of it down my throat. They even gagged me to keep me from throwing it up."

"Now that is strange." Lord Yama turned to the judge sitting beside him. "Could Madame Meng have produced a counterfeit tonic?

The judges shook their heads.

"Ximen Nao, I've had all I can take from you. If every ghost was as much trouble as you, chaos would reign in this hall. Given your charitable acts as a human and the suffering you underwent as a donkey and an ox, I will bestow a special mercy on you by sending you to be reborn in a distant, stable country whose citizens are rich, a place of natural beauty where it is springtime year-round. Your father to be is thirty-six years old, the country's youngest mayor. Your mother is a gentle and beautiful professional singer whose voice has won for her many international prizes. You will be their only son, a jewel dropped into their hands. Your father has a brilliant future ahead of him: at forty-eight he will rise to the position of governor. When she reaches middle age, your mother will give up her professional career and go into business as the owner of a famous cosmetic company. Your father drives an Audi, your mother a BMW; you will drive a Mercedes. Fame and fortune beyond your imagining will be yours, and you will be lucky in love — many times. You will be richly compensated for the suffering and injustice you have experienced on the Wheel of Life so far." Lord Yama tapped the table with his fingertip and paused briefly. He gazed up into the darkness of the hall canopy and said pointedly, "What I have just said should make you very happy."

But wouldn't you know it, Lord Yama fooled me yet again.

Prior to this rebirth, they covered my eyes with a black blindfold.

On Homeward Terrace, I was assaulted with a hellishly cold wind and a horrible stench. In a hoarse voice, the old woman cursed me bitterly for laying false accusations. She banged me over the head with a wooden spoon, then grabbed me by the ear and ladled her broth into my mouth. What a strange taste it had, like peppered guano. "I hope you drown, you stupid pig, for saying my broth was faked. I want to submerge your memories, submerge your previous lives, leaving you only with a memory of swill and dung!" The demonic attendants who had brought me there were holding my arms the whole time this evil old woman was torturing me; their gloating laughter filled my ears.

I stumbled down off the platform, still in the grip of the attendants, who ran me so fast I don't think my feet touched the ground; I felt like I was flying. Finally my feet touched something soft, almost cloudlike. Each time I wanted to ask where I was going, a hairy claw stuffed something foul-smelling in my mouth before I could speak and a sour taste filled my mouth, like the dregs of aged liquor or a fermented bean cake; it was, I knew, the smell of the Ximen Village Production Brigade feeding shed. My god, the ox memory is still with me. Am I still an ox? Was all that other stuff a dream? I put up a fight, struggling as if trying to break free of a nightmare. I squealed and scared myself. So I fixed my eyes on my surroundings, and discovered that there were a dozen or more squirming lumps of flesh all around me. Black ones, white ones, yellow ones, even some black-and-white ones. Lying on the ground in front of all those lumps of flesh was a white sow. I heard the familiar voice of a pleasantly surprised woman say:

"Number sixteen! My god! Our old sow has produced a litter of sixteen piglets!"

I blinked to clear the mucus out of my eyes. I didn't need to look at myself to know that I'd come back as a pig this time, and that all those squirming, squealing lumps of flesh were my brothers and sisters. I knew what I must look like, and I was furious over how backstabbing Lord Yama had fooled me again. How I loathed pigs, those filthy beasts. I'd have been fine with coming back as another donkey or an ox, but not a pig, condemned to roll around in the muck and mud. I'll starve myself, that's what I'll do, so I can get back down to the underworld and settle accounts with that damned Lord Yama.

It was a sweltering summer day, by my calculations — the sunflowers beyond the pigpen wall hadn't yet bloomed, though the leaves

were big and plump — sometime during the sixth lunar month. There
were flies everywhere and dragonflies circling the air high above me.
I felt my legs growing strong and my eyesight improving fast. I saw the
two people who had been standing by when the sow had her litter:
one was Huang Tong's older daughter, Huzhu, the other my son,
Ximen Jinlong. My skin tightened at the sight of my son's familiar
face, and my head began to ache; it was almost as if a huge human
form, or a crazed spirit, were confined in my tiny piglet body.
Suffocating, I'm suffocating! Misery, oh, such misery! Let me go, let
me spread out, let me slough off this filthy, abominable pig shell, to
grow and regain the manly form of Ximen Nao! But of course, none of
that was possible. I fought like mad, but still wound up in the palm of
Huang Huzhu. She tweaked my ear with her finger and said:

"Jinlong, this one seems to be having convulsions."

"Who cares? The old sow doesn't have enough teats as it is, so
let's hope a few die," he said venomously.

"No, they're all going to live." Huzhu put me down and wiped
me clean with a soft red cloth. She was so gentle. It felt wonderful.
Without meaning to, I squealed, that damned pig sound.

"Did she have her litter? How many?" That voice was outside
the pigpen, loud and very familiar. I shut my eyes in total despair. I
not only recognized Hong Taiyue's voice I could even tell he'd
regained his official post. Lord Yama, oh, Lord Yama, all those fine
words about being reborn as the pampered son of a high official in a
foreign country, when all along you meant to fling me into a Ximen
Village pigpen. You tricked me, you shameless, backbiting liar! I
fought to free myself from Huzhu's hands and landed on the ground
with a thud. A single squeal, and I passed out.

When I came to, I was lying in a bed of leaves, bright sunlight filtering down through the branches of an apricot tree. The smell of
iodine was in the air; shiny ampoules were strewn on the ground
around me. My ears were sore, so was my rump, and I knew they'd
brought me back from the verge of death. All of a sudden, a lovely face
materialized in my head, and I knew she was the one who'd given me
the shots; yes, it was her, my daughter, Ximen Baofeng. Trained as a
people doctor, she often treated sick animals as well. Dressed in a
blue-checked, short-sleeved shirt, she seemed worried about something. But she always looked like that. She tweaked my ear with her
cold finger and said to the person next to her:

"He's okay now, you can take him back to the pen to suckle."

Hong Taiyue rushed up and rubbed my silky skin with his coarse hand.

"Baofeng," he said, "don't think that treating a pig is unworthy of your talent!"

"The thought never occurred to me, Party secretary," Baofeng replied matter-of-factly as she picked up her medical kit. "As far as I'm concerned, there's no difference between animals and humans."

"I'm glad to hear that," Hong said. "Chairman Mao has called upon people to raise pigs. Raising pigs is a political act, and by doing a good job at it you're showing your loyalty to Chairman Mao. Do you understand what I'm saying, Jinlong and Huzhu?"

Huzhu said yes, but Jinlong leaned against the apricot tree, smoking a cheap cigarette.

"I asked you a question, Jinlong," Hong said, obviously displeased.

Jinlong cocked his head. "I'm listening, aren't I?" he said. "Would you like me to recite the entirety of Chairman Mao's supreme directive on raising pigs?"

"Jinlong," Hong said as he stroked my back, "I know you're upset, but keep in mind that Li Renshun of Taiping Village wrapped a fish in a newspaper with Chairman Mao's image, and was sentenced to eight years. He is undergoing labor reform as I speak. Your problem is far worse than his!"

"Mine was unintentional, and that's the difference."

"If yours had been intentional, you'd have been shot," Hong replied, his anger rising. "Do you know why I protected you?" He looked over at Huzhu. "Partly because Huzhu and your mother got down on their knees and begged me. But the main reason was that I know all about you. You come from bad stock, but grew up under the red flag and were the kind of youngster we wanted to foster in the period before the Cultural Revolution. You're an educated youngster, a middle-school graduate, just what the revolution needs. Don't think that raising pigs is unworthy of your talents. Under current circumstances, no job is more glorious or more arduous than raising pigs. By assigning you here, the Party is testing your attitude toward Chairman Mao's revolutionary line!"

Jinlong flipped his cigarette away, stood up straight, and bowed his head to receive Hong Taiyue's reprimand.

"You two are lucky — but since the proletariat frowns on luck, let's talk about circumstances." Hong raised his hand, with me in it, into the air. "Our village sow has produced a litter of sixteen piglets, a rarity anywhere in the province. The county government happens to be looking for a pig-raising model right now." He lowered his voice and said with a hint of mystery, "A model, know what I'm saying? You know the meaning of the word, don't you? The rice paddies at Dazhai are a model. The oil fields at Daqing are a model. The fruit orchards at Xiadingjia are a model. Even the dances for old ladies organized at Xujiazhai are a model. So why can't the pig farms of Ximen Village be a model? Lan Jinlong, you put on a model opera a few years back, didn't you? You brought Jiefang and your dad's ox into the commune, didn't you? Weren't you trying to create models?"

Jinlong looked up, eyes flashing. How well I knew the temperament of that son of mine, how his sharp mind turned out outstanding ideas that would amount to what today might be seen as absurd, but at the time were enthusiastically praised.

"I'm getting old," Hong said, "and now that I've been given a second chance, all I hope for is to do a decent job with village affairs and be worthy of the trust of the masses and my superiors. But the prospects for you young people are unlimited. So long as you do your best, you'll get credit for your successes, and if problems arise, I'll take the responsibility." Hong pointed at the commune members digging ditches and building walls in the apricot grove. "A month from now there'll be two hundred garden-style pigpens out there, with a goal of five pigs for every person. The more pigs we raise, the more fertilizer we'll get and the greater the harvests we'll bring in. Grain rolls in, worries fade out; ditches deep, grain stores vast. No more hegemony, only support for worldwide revolution. Every pig is a bomb flung into the midst of the imperialists, revisionists, and reactionaries. So this old sow of ours, with her litter of sixteen piglets, has presented us with sixteen bombs. The old sows are aircraft carriers that will launch all-out attacks against the world's imperialists, revisionists, and reactionaries. By now you two ought to understand the importance of assigning you to this post."

I kept my eyes on Jinlong as I listened to this grandiose speech by Hong Taiyue. Now that I'd undergone several rebirths, our father-son relationship had weakened, until it was little more than a faint memory, a few words inscribed on a family register. Hong Taiyue's speech acted on Jinlong like a powerful stimulant, setting his mind in motion and his heart pumping; he was itching to get started. Rubbing his hands excitedly, he walked up to Hong, cheeks twitching, big, thin ears quivering, and I readied myself for the familiar prolonged monologue that was forthcoming — but this time I was wrong, there was no monologue; a series of setbacks in life had obviously matured him. He took me from Hong Taiyue and held me so close I could feel his heart pound. He bent down and kissed me on the ear. That kiss would one day become a significant detail in the glorified dossier of model pig farmer Lan Jinlong: "Lan Jinlong performed mouth-to-mouth resuscitation in a life-saving attempt on a newborn piglet, snatching the piglet with the purple splotches from the jaws of death. The piglet heralded its salvation with piggish squeals. But Lan Jinlong, enervated by the effort, passed out in the pigpen after uttering resolutely:

" 'Party Secretary Hong, from this day forward, all boars are my father, and all sows are my mother!' "

"That's what I like to hear!" Hong said joyfully. "Young people who view our pigs as their mothers and fathers are exactly what we need."

22

Piglet Sixteen Monopolizes the Sow's Teats
Bai Xing'er Is Honored with the Title of Pig Feeder

Despite all the grandiose treatment bestowed upon the pigs by the fanatical people, a pig was still a pig. They could have showered me with all the love they had, but I was dead set on starving myself right out of this pig existence. I wanted another audience with Lord Yama, where I would make a scene, claiming my right to be human and demanding a rebirth I could be proud of.

By the time they returned me to the pigpen, the old sow was lying on her side, legs stretched out on a bed of hay as a row of piglets squeezed up to her exposed teats. They were sucking greedily and noisily. The unfortunate ones left out were shrieking their displeasure and trying to force their way in among their brothers and sisters. Some made it, forcing others out, while some others climbed up on top of the sow to jump up and down and raise a stink. The old sow lay there grunting, eyes closed, and all I felt were pity and loathing.

After handing me to Huzhu, Jinlong bent down and pulled one of the sucking piglets away from its teat, but not before it stretched it out like a rubber band. Another little pig filled the vacuum. So Jinlong pulled all those greedy little pigs away and put them outside the pen, where they protested ineffectually. Now only ten remained stuck to the sow's belly, exposing a pair of usable teats. Both were red, puffy, and disgusting, thanks to the previous users. Picking me up from Huzhu, Jinlong put me down by the sow's belly. I shut my eyes, which made me disgustingly conscious of the sucking sounds from my repulsive brothers and sisters. I'd have thrown up if I'd had anything in my stomach. You already know I wanted to die, so there was no way I was going to put one of those filthy teats in my mouth. I knew that the day

I started sucking nonhuman milk was the day I'd give up half my humanity and sink forever into the abyss of the animal kingdom. The minute I put my mouth around that sow's teats, I'd be seized by pigness. A pig's temperament, a pig's interests and concerns, and a pig's desires would flow with her milk and course through my veins, transforming me into a swine that retained a mere smidgeon of human memories, thus completing a filthy and shameful reincarnation.

"Go on, drink up!" Jinlong positioned me so my mouth was up against a very plump teat, and when the saliva smeared on the nipple by my siblings touched my lips, I nearly puked. I kept my mouth tightly shut and my teeth clenched to avoid temptation.

'What a stupid pig. It doesn't have the sense to open its mouth when there's a teat right in front of it." Jinlong whacked me on the rump to underscore his comment.

"Don't be so rough on him," Huzhu complained as she pushed Jinlong away and pulled me up to her, where she gently rubbed my belly. I sort of purred, it felt so good, I couldn't help it, though it was really a pig noise of contentment, but not that hard on the ears. Huzhu murmured, "You precious thing, foolish little piglet sixteen, your mother's milk is really good, just taste it. You have to eat to grow up." Thanks to her mutterings, I learned that I was the sixteenth piglet in a litter of sixteen, in other words, the last one out of the old sow's belly. In spite of my extraordinary experiences in the worlds of light and darkness, that is, life and death, my knowledge of human and animal existences, in the eyes of the people, I was a pig, that's all. A crushing tragedy; but even greater tragedies lay ahead.

Huzhu brushed the sow's teat against my lips and nose, and that tickled my nose. I sneezed. That surprised her, I felt that in the way her hand jerked. Then she laughed. "I've never heard a pig sneeze before," she said. "Sixteen, Piglet Sixteen, since you can sneeze, you ought to be able to eat." She grabbed hold of the teat and squirted a warm liquid onto my lips. I licked it tentatively. Yow! My god! I never would have believed that a sow's milk, my mother sow's milk, could be so delicious, so fragrant, like silk, like love itself, so wonderful it made me forget the humiliation of being reborn as a pig and completely changed my impression of my surroundings, so glorious I couldn't help feeling that the pig mother lying on the crushed grass supplying milk for a litter of boy and girl piglets was a noble beast, sacred and pure, solemn and beautiful. Without further hesitation, I wrapped my lips around that nipple, nearly taking Huzhu's finger along with it, and opened the flow of milk into my mouth and down to my stomach. With each minute, each second, I felt myself grow stronger, felt my love for my pig mother increase; I heard Huzhu and Jinlong clap their hands and laugh, and out of the corner of my eye, I saw their youthful faces glow like cockscomb flowers. They were holding hands, and that sent fragments of historical memory flashing through my head, all of which I wanted only to forget. I shut my eyes so I could concentrate on the joys of a baby pig at its mother's teat.

Over the days that followed, I became the most tyrannical piglet in the litter. My appetite shocked Jinlong and Huzhu; I had a natural gift for eating. I was always able to unerringly find the teat with the most milk, outmaneuvering my dull-witted brothers and sisters, who closed their eyes as soon as they wrapped their lips around a teat, while my eyes were open from start to finish as I sucked madly on the biggest nipple and covered up the ones next to it with my body. I vigilantly kept my eyes peeled, waiting for one of my pitiful siblings to come looking for a meal; I'd send him or her flying with a butt to the head. Then as soon as I'd sucked the big teat dry, I'd move to the next one.

Seven days after I was born, Jinlong and Huzhu came and moved eight of my siblings to a neighboring pen, where they fed them millet gruel. A woman was put in charge of their care, but the wall between us was too high for me to get a look at her. Her voice, her lovely voice, sounded familiar, but when I tried to dredge up a memory of who she was and what she looked like, I just got sleepy. The three marks of a good pig are: big eater, deep sleeper, fast grower. I mastered all three. Sometimes the murmuring of the woman on the other side of the wall would be my lullaby. She fed the eight little pigs six times a day, sending the fragrance of corn or millet gruel wafting over the wall, and I could hear my brothers and sisters feasting happily. "My little darlings," she'd mutter to them, "you little dears," and I could tell she was a bighearted woman who treated the little pigs like her own children.

After a month, I was more than twice the size of my siblings. My sow mother's twelve teats were pretty much mine alone. Every once in a while one of the other piglets, crazed from hunger, would attempt the death-defying act of charging one of the nipples. All I had to do was stick my snout under his belly and easily send him rolling to the wall behind our mother, who would moan weakly and say, Sixteen, oh, Sixteen, won't you let them have a little? I brought you all into this world, and I can't bear to see any of you go hungry! That sickened me, so I ignored her and sucked so hard her eyes rolled back in her head. Later on, I discovered that I could kick out with my hind legs, like a donkey, which meant I didn't even have to let loose of a nipple or use my snout to rid the area of a hungry sibling. Whenever I saw one of them approach, red-eyed and squealing, I'd simply arch my back and kick out. Even if two came up at the same time, I could drive them back by landing well-placed kicks on their heads. All they could do then was run in circles and squeal out of jealousy and hatred, cursing me as they foraged for scraps at the base of our mother's feed trough.

It didn't take Jinlong and Huzhu long to see what was happening, so they invited Hong Taiyue and Huang Tong to watch from the other side of the wall. I knew they remained silent in hopes that I wouldn't know they were there. So I pretended I didn't know and ate with such exaggerated gusto that Mother Sow lay there moaning. I intimidated my brothers and sisters with one-legged kicks and struck fear into them with the two-legged variety, until all they could do was roll around and squeal miserably.

"That's no pig, it's a goddamned baby donkey!" Hong Taiyue shouted excitedly

"You're right," Huang Tong agreed. "See how it kicks with its hind legs."

I spat out the now dry teat, stood up, and strutted around the pen. Raising my head, I looked at them and let loose with two loud oinks. That threw them.

"Get those other seven piglets out of there," Hong Taiyue said. "We're keeping this one for stud. Let him have all her milk so he'll grow big and strong."

Jinlong jumped into the pen and made a noise to call to the other piglets. The old sow raised her head and gave Jinlong a menacing look, but he was so quick he had two of them in his hands before she knew it. She jumped up and charged him; he forced her back with a kick. The two pigs hung in the air, squealing frantically. Huzhu managed to take one of them from Jinlong; Huang Tong took the other. I could tell they both wound up with their eight dull-witted siblings in the pen next to mine, where those eight little assholes took out after the two new little assholes; they'd get no sympathy from me, I was too happy. By the time Hong Taiyue had smoked a cigarette, Jinlong had removed all seven of the little morons. The pen next to mine turned into a battlefield, with the eight early arrivals fighting it out with the seven late arrivals. Me? I was alone, casually taking it in. I looked at the old sow out of the corner of my eye and saw that she was grief-stricken. But she'd also been relieved of a heavy burden. Let's face it, she was just an ordinary pig, incapable of having her emotions stirred, humanlike. Look, she's already forgotten the torment of losing her litter. She's standing at her trough gobbling up the food.

The smell of food came rushing toward me on the wind. Huzhu walked up to the gate with a bucket of feed wearing a white apron with "Ximen Village Production Brigade Apricot Garden Pig Farm" embroidered in big red letters. She also had white protective sleeves covering her arms and a soft white cap on her head. She looked like a baker. Using a metal ladle, she scooped the contents into the feed trough. Mother Sow raised up and buried her front legs right in the middle of it. The slops splashing all over her face looked like yellow shit. It had a sour, rotten smell I found disgusting. It was a product of the minds of the brigade's two most intelligent members, Lan Jinlong and Huang Huzhu, a fermented feed made of chicken droppings, cow dung, and greens. Jinlong emptied the bucket into the trough. The sow had no choice but to eat it.

"Is that all she gets?" Hong Taiyue asked.

"Up till a few days ago we added some bean cake," Huzhu said, "but yesterday Jinlong said no more bean cakes."

Hong stuck his head inside the pen to get a closer look at the sow. "We want to be sure the little porker gets what he needs, so let's prepare food for her separately."

"There isn't enough fodder in the brigade stock room as it is," Huang Tong said.

"I thought there was a storage shed filled with corn."

"That's part of our combat readiness! If you want to tap into that you have to get permission from the Commune Revolutionary Committee."

"This pig is destined to be part of combat readiness!" Hong said. "If war comes, our People's Liberation Army soldiers will need to eat meat to win the battles." Seeing that Huang Tong was still hesitant, he said firmly, "Open up the shed. I'll take the responsibility. I'll report to the commune this afternoon. Feeding pigs takes precedence over other political tasks, so I don't expect any opposition. What's most important," he said, sounding somewhat mysterious, "is to expand our pig farm and increase the numbers of animals. There'll come a day when all the grain in the county stockrooms will be ours."

Knowing smiles spread across Huang Tong and Jinlong's faces as the agreeable smell of millet gruel approached them and stopped at the next pen over.

"Ximen Bai," Hong called out, "starting tomorrow you're to feed this sow too."

"Yes, Secretary Hong."

"Dump half the bucket you're carrying into the sow's trough."

"Yes, Secretary Hong."

Ximen Bai — that had a familiar ring to it. Ximen Bai. I tried to recall what that name meant to me. Then a kindly but weary face appeared in front of my pen, and I was racked by spasms, as if I'd been given an electric shock. At the same time, the gate to my memory was flung open and the past came flooding in. "Xing'er," I shouted, "you're still alive!" But what emerged from my throat was a long, shrill pig noise. It not only scared the people outside the pen, it scared me. Tragically, I had no choice but to return to reality, to the present, no longer Ximen Nao but a little pig, the son of the white sow I shared this pen with.

I tried to calculate her age, but the fragrance of sunflowers confused me. Yet even though no number emerged, I knew she was over fifty, because the hair at her temples had turned white, there were fine wrinkles around her eyes, and her once beautiful white teeth had begun to yellow and wear out.

Slowly she scooped the millet into the trough with a wooden ladle.

"You heard what I said, didn't you?" Hong Taiyue asked harshly.

"You needn't worry, Secretary Hong," Ximen Bai said in a soft but firm voice. "I have no children of my own, so these pigs will be my sons and daughters."

"That's what I like to hear," Hong said, satisfied with her response. "What we need is more women who are willing to raise our pigs as their own sons and daughters."

23

Piglet Sixteen Is Moved to a Cozy Nest
Diao Xiaosan Mistakenly Eats an Alcohol-laced Bun

Brother, or should I say, Uncle, you seem upset. Your eyes are hooded by puffy lids, and you seem to be snoring, Big-head Lan Qiansui said harshly. If you're not interested in the lives of pigs, let me tell you about dogs.

No, no, no, I'm interested, I really am. You know, I assume, that I wasn't always at your side during those years you were a pig. At first I worked in the pig farm, but my job was not to feed you. Then, later, Huang Hezuo and I were sent to work in the cotton mill, and most of what we learned about your illustrious accomplishments came to us as hearsay. I really want to hear you talk about your experiences, down to the last detail. Don't give another thought to my puffy eyelids, because when my eyes are hooded, that means I'm concentrating.

The events that followed were varied and very complex. I can only touch on the highlights and the more spectacular incidents, Big-head Lan Qiansui said.

Even though Ximen Bai painstakingly fed my sow mother, I went on suckling like a crazed piglet — what you might call extraction — which led to the paralysis of the rear half of her body. Her hind legs were like dried-out loofahs, so she had to drag herself around the pen by her front legs. By this time I was nearly as big as she was. My hair was so glossy it looked waxed; my skin was a healthy red color with a wonderful odor. My poor mother's skin was filthy, the foul-smelling rear half covered in shit. She howled every time I took one of her teats in my mouth, and tears spilled out of her tiny eyes. She dragged herself along the ground, trying to get away from me and pleading: Son, my good son, show your mother some mercy. You're sucking the marrow out of my bones. Can't you see the miserable shape I'm in? You're a full-grown pig, so you should be eating solid food like me. I turned a deaf ear to her pleading, nudged her onto her side with my snout, and wrapped my lips around two teats at the same time. As my ears filled with her shrill cries of agony, I couldn't help feeling that the teats that had once secreted that sweet-tasting milk had turned rubbery and tasteless and produced no more than a tiny amount of rank, salty, sticky liquid that was closer to poison than milk. In disgust, I rolled her over with my snout. I could hear the pain in her voice as she cursed me: Oh, Sixteen, you are a beast with no conscience, a demon. You were sired by a wolf, not a pig. . . .

Ximen Bai was reprimanded by Hong Taiyue over my sow mother's paralysis. "Secretary," she said tearfully, "her son's willfulness caused that, not negligence on my part. If you'd seen the way he eats, like a wolf or a tiger, you'd agree that even a cow would have wound up paralyzed with him at her teat. . . ."

Hong looked into the pen; on an impulse I stood up on my hind legs, unaware that the only other pigs that could do that were trained circus performers. For me it seemed perfectly natural. With my front legs propped up on the wall, my head was right under Hong Taiyue's chin. He backed up, obviously shocked, and looked around. Seeing they were alone, he said to Ximen Bai softly:

"It wasn't your fault. I'll isolate this king of pigs and assign someone to feed him."

"That's what I suggested to Chairman Huang, but he said he wanted to wait for you to return. . . ."

"Any moron should be able to decide something as minor as this," he grumbled.

"It's the respect everyone has for you," Ximen Bai said, glancing at him before lowering her head and murmuring, "You're a veteran revolutionary who has great concern for the people and deals with them fairly—"

"That's enough of that talk," Hong said with a wave of his hand as he looked into Ximen Bai's reddening face. "Do you still live in that cemetery hut? I think you'd better move over to the feeding shed. You can move in with Huang Huzhu and them."

"No," Ximen Bai said. "My background is no good, I'm old and I'm dirty, and I don't want to displease the youngsters—"

Hong looked into Ximen Bai's face, then turned and stared at the lush sunflowers. "Ximen Bai," he said softly, "if only you hadn't been a landlord . . ."

I grunted. I had to do something to give voice to my mixed feelings. To be honest, I wasn't really jealous, but the relationship between Hong Taiyue and Ximen Bai, getting more intriguing every day, instinctively made me unhappy. There was no end in sight, and you know how tragically it ended, but I'll fill in the details anyway.

They moved me into a large, newly built, single-occupant pen in a row of them about a hundred yards from the two hundred regular pens. The canopy of an apricot tree at the rear shaded half my pen. I lived in a shed that was open in the front, where the eaves were short, and the rear, where the eaves were long, so there was nothing to keep the sunlight from streaming in. The floor was laid with bricks, and there was a hole in one wall, covered by an iron grate that made it easy for me to relieve myself without dirtying my quarters. A pile of golden wheat stalks against my bedroom wall made the room smell fresh. I strolled around my new quarters, taking in the smell of new bricks, new earth, fresh parasol wood, and fresh sorghum stalks, and I was pleased. Compared to the squat, filthy quarters I'd shared with the old sow, my new digs were a mansion. They were airy, sunny, and constructed of environmentally appropriate materials that gave off no noxious fumes. Just look at that parasol wood beam, so newly hewn that puckery sap still oozed from the white interior of the cut ends. The sorghum stalks in the wall surrounding my quarters were also fresh, the fluid secretions still wet, still fragrant, and, I bet, still tasty. But these were my living quarters, and I wasn't about to tear them down just to satisfy my appetite. That's not to say I couldn't take a bite just to see how it tasted. I could stand on my hind legs and walk like humans, but I wanted to keep that a secret as long as possible.

What thrilled me was that my new home was supplied with electricity. A lamp with a hundred-watt bulb hung from the beam. I later learned that all two hundred of the new pens had electricity, but they were lit with twenty-five-watt bulbs. The on-off pull string hung down alongside one of the walls, and all I had to do was reach up, catch the string in my cloven hoof, and tug lightly to make the light go on. That was great. The spring breeze of modernization had blown into Ximen Village along with the east wind of the Cultural Revolution. Quick, turn it off, don't let them know I know how to do that.

I moved into my new quarters in the fall, when the sunlight was more red than white, and the red sun dyed the leaves of the apricot tree red. Each evening or early morning, when the sun was sinking or rising, breakfast and dinnertime for the pig farmers, the pens were unusually quiet. That's when I stood up on my hind legs and, with my front legs curled in front of me, began eating apricot leaves right from the tree. Slightly bitter, but loaded with fiber, they helped lower my blood pressure and keep my teeth clean.

One day, when the apricot leaves were bright red, around the tenth day of the tenth lunar month — yes, that was the day, my memory's still sharp — early on the tenth, just after the sun, big and red and gentle, had climbed into the sky, Lan Jinlong, whom I hadn't seen in a very long time, returned. He was accompanied by the four Sun brothers, who attended to his every need and desire, and the brigade accountant, Zhu Hongxin, who had bought 1,057 pigs for the astonishingly low cost of 5,000 yuan, or less than 5 yuan apiece. I was performing my morning exercises when I heard the roar of motors. I looked outside in time to see three vehicles with trailers coming my way from beyond the apricot grove. They were so dusty they looked like they'd come straight from the desert, the hoods so dirty it was impossible to see what color they were. They bumped and rattled their way through the grove behind the new pigpens and into a clearing littered with broken bricks and tiles and mud-covered wheat stalks. Looking like long-tailed monsters, they took their time coming to a complete stop, after which I saw Lan Jinlong, his hair a mess and his face covered with grime, climb out of the first cab. Then Zhu Hongxin and Dragon Sun climbed out of the second vehicle, and finally, the remaining three Sun brothers and Mo Yan climbed out of the last one. All four faces in this last group were coated with dust, looking like the terracotta warriors of the First Emperor. Then I heard the *oink-oink*s of pigs in the three trailers, getting steadily louder, until it was a shrill chorus. Was I excited! I knew the day of the pigs had arrived. I couldn't see these newcomers; I could only hear them and smell the strange odor of their droppings. I was ready to bet they were an ugly lot.

Hong Taiyue rode up like the wind on his brand-new Golden Deer; bicycles were a rarity at the time, and only the branch secretaries were permitted to buy them. Hong parked his bike at the edge of the clearing, up against an apricot tree, half of whose top had been cut off. He didn't lock it, which shows how fired up he was. He greeted Jinlong with open arms, a conquering hero. Now don't think he was about to give Jinlong a hug — that's for foreigners, something Chinese didn't practice during the pig-raising era. So when Hong reached the spot where Jinlong was standing, he dropped his arms, then reached out and patted Jinlong on the shoulder.

"I see you bought them."

"One thousand fifty-seven altogether, exceeding the assigned quota!" Jinlong said as he started to sway and, before Hong could catch him, crumpled to the ground.

Almost immediately the four Sun brothers and Zhu Hongxin, who was clutching a Naugahyde briefcase, started to sway as well. Only Mo Yan was full of energy. He raised his arms and shouted:

"We fought our way back! We were victorious!"

The red sun shining down made it a somewhat solemn and tragic scene. Hong Taiyue summoned the brigade's cadres and militiamen to carry these pig buyers who had performed such meritorious service, and the three drivers, over to the buildings housing the animal keepers.

"Huzhu, Hezuo, go find some women to make noodles and eggs for these men in recognition of their services," he shouted. "Then get people to unload the trailers."

I got my first look at the ghastly animals as soon as the tailgates came down. Those aren't pigs! How could anybody call *them* pigs? Some big, some small, different colors, and every one filthy, covered with their own shit, and stinking to high heaven! I shoved a couple of apricot leaves up my nose. I thought they'd be bringing over some pretty little pigs to keep me company and supply the future king of pigs with a harem. Who came up with the idea of bringing a bunch of freakish offspring of wolves and pigs? I didn't have the heart to look any longer, but their funny accents piqued my curiosity. Old Lan, I might have the spirit of a man somewhere inside me, but I'm still a pig, and I'd advise you not to expect too much from me. If humans are curious animals, then what do you expect from a pig?

I rested my front hooves and chin in the crotch of the tree to lessen the pressure on my hind legs. The branches sagged and shook. A woodpecker on one of the limbs cocked his head and stared down at me, his beady, black eyes filled with curiosity. Not knowing bird talk, I couldn't speak to him, but I could tell I was freaking him out. I watched through the leaves of my tree as the newcomers were unloaded. They were all semiconscious, barely able to stand, a pitiful bunch. A sow with a cylindrical snout and pointy ears, apparently too old and weak to travel long distances, passed out as soon as she hit the ground. Some of the rest tilted to one side, others were sprawled on the ground, and some were scratching themselves against the bark of apricot trees — *scrape scrape.* My god, what thick hides! Yes, they had fleas and they had scabies, and I had to be sure to keep my distance. One black male caught my attention. He was scrawny, but looked to be clever and bright. Here's what he looked like: long snout, tail dragging on the ground, dense, hard bristles, broad shoulders, pointy ass, thick limbs, tiny, keen eyes, two yellow front teeth that stuck out between his lips. In short, the next thing to a wild boar. So while all the others looked wretched from the long trip, this one sauntered around taking in the sights, like a whistling hoodlum walking around with his arms crossed. A few days later, Jinlong gave this one a name: Diao Xiaosan. That was the name of a bad character in the model revolutionary opera *Shajiabang.* Yes, he was the bad guy who snatched a girl's bundle and wanted to take advantage of her. Diao Xiaosan and I would have some interesting times together, but I'll get to that later.

I watched the commune members, under Hong Taiyue's direction, herd the pigs into the two hundred pens. It was chaos. The animals, with their low IQs, were used to running wild and oblivious to the reality that once inside the pens, they could live in ease and comfort. They thought they were being rounded up for the slaughterhouse, so they squealed and bawled and ran for their lives and crashed into each other, fighting like cornered beasts. Hu Bin, who'd done all those bad things during my ox years, was put flat on his back by a crazed white pig that butted him in the belly. He struggled to sit up, ashen-faced and bathed in a cold sweat, holding his belly with his hands and moaning. This luckless bumpkin who harbored dark thoughts and had too high an opinion of himself wanted to be a part of damned near everything, and he always got the worst of things. So while he was despicable, he was also to be pitied. You probably remember how I got even with him on the sandbar by the Grain Barge River, don't you? Well, in the years since, he'd gotten old and even had trouble speaking, now that his teeth had fallen out. And here I was, a pig not even a year old, young and sprightly, enjoying life. Being reborn over and over may wear a guy out, but it has its advantages.

Another animal, an angry castrated male with half an ear missing and a ring in its nose, bit Chen Dafu on the finger. This rotten individual, who'd once had illicit dealings with Qiuxiang, screamed so loud you'd have thought the pig had taken off his whole hand. In contrast to these useless men, the slow-moving middle-aged women — Yingchun, Qiuxiang, Bai Lian, and Zhao Lan — bent at the waist, stretched out their arms, made gentle sounds with their tongues, and, with friendly smiles, got close to some of the pigs that had been forced into a corner. Despite the filth covering the animals, there were no looks of disgust on the faces of these women, just genuine smiles. The pigs oinked but didn't run away, so the women reached out, disregarding the filth on their bodies, and scratched their hides. Pigs never pass up a good scratching, and people love to be flattered. The animals' fighting will evaporated; shutting their eyes blissfully, they swayed a moment or two and then slumped to the ground. The only thing left was for the women to pick up their velvet prisoners and, still scratching them between their legs, carry them over to the pens.

Hong Taiyue praised the women and scorned the rough-and-tumble men.

Amid an earsplitting clamor, all but three of the 1,057 pigs from the Mount Yimeng area were caught and put into pens. One, a dirty yellow female, died, and so did a young black-and-white. The third one was the black boar Diao Xiaosan, who slipped under one of the vehicles and refused to come out. Wang Chen, a core member of the militia, emerged from the feeding shed with a plane tree pole and tried to poke the pig out with it. Diao Xiaosan bit it in two after a tug-of-war, and though I couldn't see Diao under the vehicle, I could picture what he looked like down there. When he bit the pole in two, the bristles on his back stood straight up and scary green lights flashed in his eyes. He was no pig, he was a wild beast, one that would teach me lots of things over the months to come. He started out as my enemy and wound up as my adviser. As I said earlier, the story of Diao Xiaosan and me will unfold in the pages to come, all dyed in bold colors.

The muscular militiaman and Diao Xiaosan were perfectly matched, and the pole had made only meager inroads. A crowd that had gathered looked on, spellbound. Hong Taiyue leaned over to look under the vehicle; other people did the same, and I tried to conjure up an image of that stubborn, stalwart scalawag. Finally, some of the gawkers decided to come help Wang Chen, but I scorned them all. A fair fight is one-on-one. A bunch of men can't take pride from ganging up on one pig! I was worried that sooner or later the pole would force him out from under the vehicle, like digging a big turnip out of the ground, but then I heard a *crack*, and the men holding the pole fell backward in a heap, bringing half the pole with them, teeth marks on the truncated end.

A roar of approval went up from the crowd. Everybody's like that: they hate the little wrongdoings and minor eccentricities, but revere the big sins and the grotesque. Diao Xiaosan's behavior hadn't reached the level of big sin or grotesque, but it had moved well beyond little wrongdoing and eccentricity. Someone brought out another pole and probed around with it. A *crack* from under the vehicle, and the man threw down his pole and ran away in fear. The ideas came fast and furious after that: some suggested shooting him, others recommended stabbing him with a spear, and some recommended smoking him out. Hong Taiyue shot down all those cruel suggestions. "Those ideas stink worse than shit!" he said sternly. "We're supposed to be 'raising' pigs, not 'braising' pigs." So then someone recommended having one of the bolder women crawl under the vehicle and start scratching him. Even the wildest boar will respect the fairer sex, won't it? Not even the meanest pig can stay wild if a woman is scratching it, can it? A good idea, but who to send was the obvious question. Huang Tong, still supposed vice chairman of the Revolutionary Committee, but wielding no real authority, supplied an answer: "When great rewards are offered, brave women will respond! Whoever crawls under the vehicle and subdues that wild boar gets a bonus of three days' work points!" With a sneer, Hong Taiyue said, "That sounds like a good job for your wife!" Wu Qiuxiang quickly moved to the back of the crowd. "You and your big mouth," she berated Huang Tong. "It gets you into trouble every time! I wouldn't go under there for three hundred work points!" Her words still hung in the air when Ximen Jinlong emerged from the pig feed preparation room of the pig-tenders dormitory, at the far end of the apricot grove, between the lovely Huang daughters. He pushed them away, but they came together and followed him, like a pair of comely bodyguards. Bringing up the rear of this procession were Ximen Baofeng, medical kit on her back, Lan Jiefang, Bai Xing'er, Mo Yan, and others. Except for Ximen Jinlong, whose face was grimy, they were all carrying buckets of pig feed. I could smell the fragrance even with apricot leaves stuffed up my nose: it was a mash made of cottonseed cake, sweet potatoes, black bean paste, and sweet potato leaves. Milky white steam rose from the sunlit wooden buckets, spreading the fragrance around. Great clouds of steam poured from the buckets. It was a motley procession, yet there was a certain solemnity about it, sort of like mess cooks taking food to front-line soldiers, and I knew that the half starved Mount Yimeng pigs would be chomping and chewing in no time; their days of ease and comfort were under way.

"Here he is," the crowd roared, "he'll save the day."

"Jinlong," Hong Taiyue said, "be careful. That's a crazed animal down there. I don't want to see it injured, and I certainly don't want you to be hurt. You're both too valuable to the Ximen Village Brigade."

Jinlong bent down and looked under the vehicle, then picked up a piece of broken tile and threw it in. In my mind's eye I could see Diao Xiaosan crunch the tile into pieces, an angry, bone-chilling glare spewing from his tiny eyes. Jinlong stood up, the hint of a smile on his cheeks. It was a look I knew well, one that meant he had a plan, and it was almost always an intriguing plan. He whispered something to Hong Taiyue, as if keeping a secret from Diao Xiaosan. There was no need for that, since, as far as I knew, no pig in the world, except me, understood human language.

Hong smiled, thumped Jinlong on the shoulder, and said:

"Only you could come up with something like that!"

After about as long as it takes to smoke half a cigarette, Ximen Baofeng came running over with a couple of snow-white steamed buns that had been soaked in liquid, the redolence of liquor heavy in the air, and I knew what Jinlong had in mind. He'd get Diao Xiaosan drunk. If I'd been Diao, I wouldn't have fallen for it. But he was, after all, a pig, and he lacked the intelligence to match his wildness. Jinlong tossed the liquor-soaked buns under the vehicle. Don't eat those, brother, I muttered to myself. You'll fall into human hands if you do. He ate them. How did I know? By the triumphant grins on Jinlong and Hong Taiyue's faces.

Jinlong crawled under the vehicle and dragged the loopy Diao Xiaosan out with ease. He dumped the grunting drunk into a new pen separated from mine by a wall. Our pens were reserved for single occupants, specifically stud animals; obviously, Diao Xiaosan would be expected to sire litters of new pigs, which seemed absurd to me. I was a husky, long-bodied animal with a nice pink hide, a short snout, and fat ears — in other words, a handsome pig. Selecting me for stud purposes made perfect sense. But you've already been informed of Diao Xiaosan's appearance and lack of grace. What kind of progeny could an inferior animal like that produce? Years later I came to realize that Jinlong and Hong Taiyue's decision had been the right one. Back in the 1970s, when everything was in short supply, pork was hard to come by, and the people longed for meat that would melt in their mouths. But now, with the standard of living so high, the jaded people had lost their taste for domesticated ones. Diao Xiaosan's offspring could be sold as game animals. But we'll come to that later.

Needless to say, as a pig with extraordinary intelligence, my first concern was self-protection. So when I saw them carrying Diao Xiaosan my way, I knew what they had in mind. I quickly and quietly sprawled atop a pile of dry grass and leaves in a corner of the wall to pretend I was asleep. I heard the racket in the pen next to mine, including Diao Xiaosan's snores and praise for me from Hong Taiyue and Jinlong. I watched them by opening my eyes just a crack. The sun was high in the sky, lighting up their faces with a golden sheen.

24

Brigade Members Light a Bonfire to Celebrate Good News
Pig King Steals Knowledge and Listens to Fine Words

Uncle, or should I say, Brother, Big-head Lan Qiansui said to me in the accent of a Beijing hoodlum, from here on let's recall together that glorious late autumn, and the most glorious day in that glorious late autumn. The leaves in the apricot grove were red as cinnabar under a cloudless sky, as, for the first and last time in the history of Gaomi County, in support of the pig-raising program, an on-site conference was held at the Ximen Village Apricot Garden Pig Farm. It was heralded as an event of great creativity, a report to which the provincial newspaper devoted considerable space. County and commune cadres associated with this on-site conference were promoted in its wake, and in the area's historical chronicles it constituted a glorious page for Ximen Village.

In planning for the on-site conference, members of the production brigade, under the leadership of Hong Taiyue, the direction of Jinlong, and the guidance of Guo Baohu, vice chairman of the Commune Revolutionary Committee, worked day and night for a week. Happily, it was a slack time in the fields, with no crops in the ground, so there was no interference with village farm work; but it wouldn't have mattered even had it occurred during the busiest time of the season, since politics came first, production second. Raising pigs was a political enterprise, and politics was everything; all else had to give way to it.

News of the impending gathering lent a holiday mood to the village. Party secretary Hong Taiyue made the announcement over the loudspeaker, the excitement in his voice bringing villagers out of their houses, even though it was after nine at night, and the "Internationale" had already been played over that same loudspeaker. Normally, at this time, commune members would be in bed, including the newlyweds of the Wang family who lived at the western edge of the village, and who would be having sex about then. But the good news fired up the villagers and introduced a change in their lives. Now why haven't you asked me how a pig living in a pen in the depths of an apricot grove would know what was going on in the village? Well, I'll admit that by then I was in the habit of jumping over the wall at night to check out the other pigpens and flirt with the young sows from Mount Yimeng, and then take a risky stroll through the village, so I was privy to all its secrets.

The commune members paraded up and down the streets with torches in their hands and smiles on their faces. Why were they so happy? Because the village would derive great benefits from becoming a model. The procession ended in the brigade compound, where the people awaited the arrival of the Party secretary and other dignitaries. Hong Taiyue, a jacket draped over his shoulders, stood in the light of the gas lantern and said: Comrade commune members, holding a countywide pig-raising on-site conference in our village demonstrates the Party's affection for us and, at the same time, is a test of our abilities. We must make every effort in planning for this gathering and take advantage of the east wind it creates to elevate our pig-raising to new heights. We now have only a thousand head, but we must increase that to five thousand, to ten thousand, and then when we reach twenty thousand pigs, we will travel to the capital to report to Chairman Mao!

The people were in no mood to leave after the Party secretary had spoken, especially young men and women, who were always looking for a way to release their bottled-up energy. They were fired up, ready to climb trees and go down in wells, to commit murder and arson, to fight the imperialists, revisionists, and reactionaries to the death; this was no night for sleeping! The four Sun brothers burst into the office without the Party secretary's permission and took the cymbals and drums from the desk, where they had gathered dust for a very long time. Mo Yan, who always wanted to be a part of everything and was a real pain most of the time, someone who was not easily shamed and could not care less, led the way by putting the drum on his back; after that the other youngsters furnished themselves with Cultural Revolution banners, and the whole bunch of them formed a loud, colorful procession that wound its way from east to west, then turned and wound its way back from west to east, throwing such a scare into perching crows that they flew off with loud caws. The procession ended in the center of the pig farm. Slightly west of my pen and north of the two hundred pens holding the Mount Yimeng pigs, on the very spot where the wild boar Diao Xiaosan had gotten drunk, Mo Yan recklessly, if boldly, lit a bonfire of limbs and branches of apricot trees left over from construction of the pens. With flames licking upward and creating a sound like gale winds, the unique aroma of burning fruit trees spread throughout the compound. Hong Taiyue was of a mind to chastise Mo Yan until he saw the excitement on the faces of youngsters who danced around the fire and sang at the top of their lungs, so he changed his mind and joined in. The people celebrated boisterously; the pigs were frightened witless. As Mo Yan fed the fire, the flames cast a blinding glow onto his face, giving him the appearance of a freshly painted temple demon. Now, though I hadn't formally been anointed Pig King, my authority among the pigs was well established. So I rushed up to the rows of pens.

"Don't be frightened," I announced at the first pen in each row. "The good times are on their way!

"A conference in conjunction with the pig-raising program will be held in our village, which means the good times for us are on their way," I shouted before returning to my pen. I didn't want people to be aware of my night roaming until I was anointed Pig King, though even if they'd known, there'd have been no way to stop me. I'd no sooner leaped over the wall than I heard a shrill cry as my hooves landed on something soft and springy. What I saw enraged me. My next-door neighbor, Diao Xiaosan, had made good use of my absence by coming into my home and sleeping on my bed. My skin began to itch and my eyes nearly popped out of my head when I looked down at that ugly, filthy body sleeping in my luxury quarters. Those poor golden wheat stalks! Those poor red and redolent apricot leaves! The bastard had soiled my bed, and I was sure it wasn't the first time. Anger boiled up in me, my strength rose to my head, and I heard the gnashing of my own teeth. And damned if he didn't look up with a smile, nod, and run over to the apricot tree to take a piss. As a cultured creature who valued hygiene, I always relieved myself out next to the southwest wall, where there was a hole. I made sure my stream went out through the hole, not leaving a drop inside my pen. The apricot tree, on the other hand, was where I did my daily exercise, since the ground there was smooth and clean, as if paved with marble. When I did my pull-up exercises, my hooves clicked on the ground when I landed. But now my beautiful spot was polluted by this bastard's piss.

Concentrating all my strength up front, like a Qigong master who breaks rocks with his head, I took aim at the bastard's rump — to be accurate, I took aim at the big pair of balls that hung just below there — and charged. I hit him and bounced backward; my hind legs crumpled and I wound up sitting on the ground. When I looked up, there he stood, rump high in the air, spilling a load of you-know-what just before he went headfirst into the wall, like a cannonball, and bounced right back. All that happened in a split second, and to me it seemed half real and half illusion. The reality part was seeing that bastard lying at the base of the wall like a dead pig, right where I had my bowel movements, just the spot for a smelly bag of shit like him to sleep in. The bastard was twitching, balling up, his back arched like a threatening cat, and all I could see of his eyes were the whites; the best comparison I can think of is the look of contempt a working man gives to a bourgeois intellectual. I felt a little dizzy, my nose hurt, and I had tears in my eyes.

The son of a bitch had to be dead, which, to be honest, was not what I wanted. I kind of liked his primitive wildness. So I tapped his belly. He twitched and he grunted. At least he wasn't dead. That was good news. I tapped him again, and again he grunted, but this time his eyes began to return to normal, though his body remained motionless.

I'd read in *Reference News* that a virgin male animal's urine had life-giving properties. The ancient physician Li Shizhen mentioned this in his classic compendium *Materia Medica*, but with few details. In the days I'm referring to, *Reference News* was the only newspaper in the country that printed a bit of the truth; only lies and hollow words found their way into the other media. For that reason I was so obsessed with *Reference News* that, if you want to know the truth, one of the reasons I went out walking at night was to sneak over to the brigade HQ to listen to Mo Yan read from *Reference News*, his favorite newspaper. At the time, his hair was dry and brittle, his ears covered with chilblains. He wore a tattered lined coat and a pair of beat-up straw sandals. When you add in his squinty eyes, you can see what an ugly sight he presented. But this strange apparition was a devoted patriot and a keen internationalist. He volunteered for the post of late-night HQ watchman in order to gain the privilege of reading *Reference News*.

I poured some of my urine into Diao Xiaosan's mouth, and when I saw his blackened teeth, I thought, You bastard, I'm cleaning your damned teeth for you. Some of the urine splashed into his eyes, though I tried to control my aim. You bastard, I'm giving you eye-drops. He swallowed what for him was top-quality medicine and began to grunt. His eyes opened all the way; my magical tonic had brought him back from the dead. Shortly after I finished pissing, he stood up, took a few tentative steps; his hindquarters wobbled a bit, like the tail of a fish struggling in shallow water. He leaned up against the wall, shook his head, and came to, like waking from a dream.

"Ximen Pig," he cursed, "fuck you!"

The bastard knew who I was! That was a surprise. After several rebirths, I don't mind admitting that I'd pretty much stopped linking myself with that poor bastard Ximen Nao of many years before. And one thing's for certain, not a single villager knew a thing about my past. So you can imagine how puzzled I was that this Mount Yimeng bastard had called me Ximen Pig. But one of my greatest attributes was the ability to put anything that stumped me out of my mind. Ximen Pig was Ximen Pig, the victor, and you, Diao Xiaosan, the loser.

"Diao Xiaosan," I said, "I opened your eyes today. There's no reason to feel humiliated by drinking my urine. In fact, you should be grateful. Without it, you wouldn't be breathing now, and if you weren't breathing, you'd miss tomorrow's festivities. And if you missed tomorrow's festivities, you'd have lived a pig's life for nothing."

"You and I aren't finished," Diao said through clenched teeth. "One of these days you'll feel the might of a Mount Yimeng pig. I'll teach you that a tiger does not survive by eating corn cakes, and that the Earth God's pecker is made of stone."

I laughed off his threats and told him I accepted his challenge, that I'd be waiting: There can only be one tiger on a mountain, and two donkeys cannot be tethered to the same trough. The Earth God's pecker may be made of stone, but his female counterpart does not have a clay receptacle. A pig farm can have but one pig king, and the day will come when you and I will fight to the death. Today's run-in doesn't count. It was just one louse pitted against another, pig against pig. But the next time it'll be out in the open. In the interest of fairness and transparency, just so there'll be no doubt as to the outcome, we can select several fair-minded, ethical old pigs who are familiar with the rules of competition and widely knowledgeable as judges. Now I ask only that the gentleman leave my quarters. I raised a front leg and saluted him, my hoof looking as if it were carved from fine jade in the light of the bonfire.

I'd expected the wild bastard to leave in spectacular fashion, but he disappointed me. He merely made himself as thin as possible and squeezed through the metal slats of the gate. His head was the hardest to get through, and required lots of bumping and clanging, but once that was through, the rest of his body followed easily. I didn't have to see to know that was how he'd reenter his own pen. Crawling through openings to get into something is the way dogs and cats do it; no proper pig would ever lower himself to that sort of behavior. If you're going to be a pig, then your schedule should be: eat and sleep, sleep and eat; fatten up for your owner, get good and meaty for your owner, then be taken by your owner to the slaughterhouse. Otherwise, be like me: Have a good time doing something that shocks them when they finally see it. And so, after seeing that mangy dog of a pig, Diao Xiaosan, slink his way through the slats of my gate, his stock plummeted in my eyes.

25

A High Official Speaks Grandly at an
On-site conference
An Outlandish Pig Puts on a Show beneath
an Apricot Tree

Sorry I'm only now getting around to talking about the glories surrounding the pig-raising local on-site conference. The entire commune was caught up in preparations for the gathering for a whole
week, and I devoted an entire chapter to it.

Let me begin with the pig farm walls, which were newly whitewashed — to sterilize them, we were told — then covered with slogans in red, all pig-related, but also tied to world revolution. Who
wrote them? Who else but Ximen Jinlong! The two most talented
youngsters in Ximen Village were Ximen Jinlong and Mo Yan. Here's
how Hong Taiyue evaluated the two of them: Ximen Jinlong had
upright talents, Mo Yan had deviant talents. Mo Yan was seven years
younger than Jinlong, and when Jinlong was in the spotlight, Mo Yan
was building up strength, like a fat bamboo shoot still in the ground.
At the time, no one paid the kid any attention. He was almost unbelievably ugly and carried on in the most peculiar ways. Given to saying crazy things that had people scratching their heads, he was to some
an annoyance and to others a pariah. Even members of his family
called him a moron. "Mom," his sister often asked their mother, "is he
really your son? Couldn't Father have found him abandoned in a mulberry grove when he was out collecting dung?" Mo Yan's elder brothers and sisters were tall and good looking, easily the equals of Jinlong,
Baofeng, Huzhu, and Hezuo. Mother would sigh and say, "The night
he was born, your father dreamed that an imp dragging a big writing

brush behind him came into our house, and when your father asked him where he'd come from, he said the Halls of Hell, where he'd been Lord Yama's personal secretary. Your father was puzzling over the dream when he heard the loud wails of a baby in the next room, after which the midwife came out and announced: "Congratulations, sir, your wife has given you a son." I suspect that Mo Yan's mother made up most of this tale to give her son some respectability in the village, since stories like that have been a part of China's popular tradition for a long time. If you go to Ximen Village today — the village has been turned into the Phoenix Open Economic Region, and the farmlands of those days have been supplanted by towering structures that look neither Chinese nor Western — people still talk — more than ever, actually — about Mo Yan, Lord Yama's personal secretary.

The 1970s were Ximen Jinlong's era; Mo Yan would have to wait a decade for his talents to be on display. For now, what I saw was Ximen Jinlong about to plaster slogans over all the walls in preparation for the pig-raising on-site conference. Wearing blue sleeve covers and white gloves, he was assisted by Huang Huzhu, who held a bucket of red paint, and Hezuo, who had yellow paint. The smell of paint was heavy in the air. Before that day, the slogans had all been written in chalk. The funds allocated for the gathering made it possible to buy paint. With his customary mastery of the written word, Jinlong painted the headings in red with a big brush, then outlined them in yellow with a small one. The effect was astonishingly eye-catching, like a woman made beautiful with red lipstick and blue eyeliner. The crowd watching him work was loud in its praise. The sixth wife of old Ma, who was a bigger flirt even than Wu Qiuxiang, said with all the charm she could manage:

"Brother Jinlong, if I were twenty years younger, I'd be your wife no matter how many women I had to fight off. And if not your wife, then your mistress!"

"You'd be last in line for anybody choosing a mistress!" someone commented.

Ma's sixth wife batted her eyes at Huzhu and Hezuo.

"You're right," she said. "If these two fairies were in that line, I'd be last for sure. Shouldn't you be plucking these two flowers, young man? You'd better move fast before somebody else tastes their freshness first!"

The Huang sisters blushed bright red; Jinlong was noticeably embarrassed too. "Shut up, you slut," he said, raising his brush threateningly, "or I'll paint your mouth shut!"

I know how the mere mention of the Huang sisters affects you, Jiefang, but I can't omit them when I'm turning back the pages of history. Besides, even if I left them out of my narration, Mo Yan would be bound to write about them sooner or later. Every resident of Ximen Village will find himself in one of Mo Yan's notorious books. So, as I was saying, the slogans were written and the trunks of apricot trees whose bark hadn't been scraped clean were lime-washed; school kids, who climbed like monkeys, had decorated the limbs and branches with strips of colored paper.

Any campaign that lacks the participation of students lacks life. Add students, and things start to happen. Even if your stomach is grumbling, there's a festive holiday spirit. Under the leadership of Ma Liangcai and the young teacher who wore her hair in a braid and spoke Mandarin, more than a hundred of Ximen Village's elementary students scurried in all directions amid the trees, like an assembly of squirrels. About fifty yards due south of my pigpen there were two apricot trees roughly five yards apart at the base but whose canopies seemed to have grown together. Several excited, raucous boys took off their tattered coats and went naked from the waist, wearing only tattered pants, with moldy cotton leaking out of the crotches, like the dirty tails of Tibetan yaks, swinging from tough but pliable limbs like a bunch of monkeys until they were moving fast and far enough to let go and sail from one tree to the other.

Now, then, let's continue with the gathering. The trees, as we've seen, had been decorated to look like old witches, and red banners had been planted every five yards on both sides of the north-south path down the middle of the pig farm. A platform had been raised in the clearing, with rush mats, covered by red cloth, on each side. A banner had been hung horizontally in the center, with writing on it, of course. The words? Given the occasion, any Chinese knows the answer to that, so there's no need for me to go into it here.

What I want to relate is that in honor of the gathering Huang Tong drove a double-axle donkey cart to the sundries section of the commune supply and marketing co-op and returned with two large Boshan vats, three hundred Tangshan ceramic bowls, ten metal ladles, ten *jin* of brown sugar, and ten *jin* of refined sugar. What for? So people could help themselves to a free bowlful of sugar water any time they wanted while the on-site conference was in progress. I knew that Huang had pocketed some of the money he'd been given to make these purchases. How did I know that? By the way he fidgeted when he handed the receipts to the accountant and the person in charge of brigade finances. I'm also sure he sampled the sugar on the way over, though he blamed the shortage on the people at the co-op. The way he hid behind an apricot tree to puke proved that a lot of the sugar had found its way into his stomach.

Next I want to talk about one of Ximen Jinlong's bold ideas. Since this was a gathering on raising pigs, the pigs played the leading role. In other words, the meeting would succeed or fail based upon the appearance of the pigs. Here's the way Jinlong put it to Hong Taiyue: You can say that the Apricot Garden Pig Farm is as pretty as a fresh flower if you want to, but if the pigs are ugly, you won't fool the masses. And since the high point of the on-site conference will be reached when the masses and visiting VIPs tour the pens, if the pigs they see there are unattractive, the on-site conference will be a failure, and the dream of Ximen Village to become a model for the county, the province, even the whole country, will go up in smoke. Upon his return to service, Hong Taiyue was clearly grooming Jinlong as his successor, and after Jinlong's successful purchase of the pigs from Mount Yimeng, his words gained weight. Secretary Hong gave Jinlong his full support.

His recommendation? Wash the pigs three times in salt water, then remove their bristles with barber's shears. This time Huang Tong was sent to the co-op in the company of the man in charge of finances to purchase five big cook pots, two hundred *jin* of table salt, fifty barber kits, and a hundred bars of the most expensive and most fragrant toilet soap. But carrying out the plan proved to be more difficult than Jinlong had imagined. About the only way they could have bathed and trimmed a bunch of crafty pigs from Mount Yimeng was to stab them to death first. The plan was put into effect three days before the meeting began, but by noon on the first day they still hadn't cleaned up a single pig, and the man in charge had had a bite taken out of his rear end by one of the animals.

It pained Jinlong to see his plan failing. Then, two days before the meeting opened, he smacked himself on the forehead, like a man who'd snapped out of a dream. "How could I have been so stupid?" he said. Reminded of the liquor-soaked bun he'd used to trick Diao

Xiaosan not long before, he immediately went to report to Hong Taiyue, who also saw the light. Back to the co-op, this time to buy liquor. Seeing no need to buy good stuff just to get pigs drunk, they settled on potato liquor that sold for half a yuan per *jin*. Everyone was sent home to steam the buns, but that order was quickly countermanded. Pigs, after all, will eat rocks if you let them, so why waste the flour? Hard corn bread would work just as well. For that matter, who needs corn? They could simply soak the pigs' bran meal with the liquor in the trough. So they placed a big vat of liquor beside the stove, poured three ladles' full into each bucket of bran, mixed it, and cooked it; then you, Jiefang, and the others carried the mixture over to the pigpens and dumped it into their troughs. The smell of alcohol lay so heavy over the pens that pigs with the smallest capacity for liquor got drunk just by breathing in the air.

Now I was a stud pig who would soon take up a special job assignment, one that required a body in perfect condition. The head of the farm, Ximen Jinlong, knew this better than anyone, and he made sure I was well fed, meat included, and no cottonseed filler, from the very beginning. Cottonseed filler had something in it that could kill male sperm cells. My feed contained bean cake, dried yams, and a small amount of fine leaves. It had a wonderful fragrance, was highly nutritious, and was good enough for people to eat, let alone pigs. As time passed and concepts changed, people began to recognize the fact that what I was given was true health food. Its nutritional value and safety were a considerable improvement over the poultry, fish, and meat humans normally eat.

Well, they put a ladle full of alcohol into my feed as well. In all fairness, I had a respectable capacity for alcohol, not unlimited, but a stiff drink or two had no effect on my thinking, my awareness, or my movements. I was nothing like my neighbor, that clown Diao Xiaosan, who'd fallen into a drunken stupor after eating a couple of liquor-soaked buns. But a ladleful of the stuff in my feed hit me hard within minutes.

Shit! I was dizzy, my legs were like cotton, and I felt like I was floating on a cloud. My home started to spin, the apricot tree began to sway, and the unpleasant squeals and grunts of the Mount Yimeng pigs suddenly filled my ears like lovely folk songs. It was the alcohol, I knew it. When Diao Xiaosan got drunk, his eyes rolled back into his head and he was out like a light, snoring and farting loudly. But I was different: I wanted to dance and sing. As the king of pigs, I retained my poise and graceful demeanor even when drunk. Except that I forgot to keep my special skills secret. All eyes were on me as I leaped into the air, like an earthling jumping to the moon, all the way up into the apricot tree, where I landed perfectly on two adjacent limbs. If it had been a poplar or willow, I'd have broken the limbs for sure, but apricot limbs have lots of give, and for me it was like riding a wave. I saw Lan Jiefang and the others as they crisscrossed Apricot Garden with food for the pigs; I saw pink smoke rising from the makeshift stove the pens; and finally I saw my neighbor Diao Xiaosan lying on his back, feet in the air, so drunk you could have slit his belly open and he wouldn't have murmured a complaint. Then I saw the lovely Huang twins and Mo Yan's elder sister in their clean white work smocks with red "Apricot Garden Pig Farm" lettering on the breast, watching Master Lin, the barber sent over from the commune HQ, as he showed them how to use the scissors in their hands. Master Lin, whose hair was as coarse as pig bristles, had a thin, gaunt face and big, bony knuckles. He had such a heavy southern accent the girls could hardly understand a word he said. I watched the pigtailed Mandarin-speaking teacher patiently teach the youngsters how to dance and sing. We quickly learned that the skit was called "The Little Pig Red Girl Goes to Beijing," a popular skit that borrowed music from the folk tradition. Playing the part of Red Girl was the prettiest girl in the village; the other parts were for boys, all of them wearing pig masks with foolish expressions. As I watched the children dance and listened to them sing, my artistic cells got the itch, and I started to move, which made the limbs I was standing on creak. I opened my mouth to sing, and surprised — no, frightened — myself by the loud oinks that emerged. All along I'd thought I'd be able to sing like humans, but what did I get? Oinks! How depressing! But I reminded myself that mynah birds can imitate human speech, and I have heard that dogs and cats can too, and by thinking hard, I recalled how, both as a donkey and an ox, at critical moments, I was able to squeeze human sounds out of my coarse throat that could rouse the deaf and awaken the unhearing.

My "speech" drew the attention of the girls who were learning how to give pig haircuts. Mo Yan's sister was the first to react: "Look, there's a pig in the tree!" Mo Yan, who'd tried everything to be assigned a job at the pig farm, only to be denied the opportunity by

Hong Taiyue, squinted and shouted: "If the Americans can make it to the moon, why get excited about a pig in a tree?" His words, unfortunately, were drowned out by the girls' screams; no one heard him. Then he said, "There's a wild boar in the South American rain forest that builds its nest in the crotch of a tree. They're mammals that have feathers and lay eggs that hatch in seven days!" Once again his words were drowned out by the girls' screams, and no one heard him. All of a sudden I found myself wanting to become friends with this guy. "Pal," I wanted to say, "as long as you understand me, when I have the time one day, I'll treat you to a few drinks." But that was drowned out by the girls' screams too.

The thoroughly delighted girls came running toward me, led by Ximen Jinlong. I waved with my left hoof. "How do you do?" I said. They didn't understand me, of course, but they knew it was a friendly gesture. But then they doubled up laughing. "What's so funny? Behave yourselves!" I know, I know, those giggling girls still didn't understand me. Crinkling his brow, Jinlong said, "This one's got a trick or two up his sleeve. I hope he'll climb that tree again at tomorrow's gathering." He opened the gate to my pen and said to the girls behind him, "Come on, girls, we'll start with this one." He walked up to the tree and scratched my belly with an experienced hand. It felt so good I could have died right then and there. "Pig Sixteen," he said, "we're going to give you a bath and a haircut. When we're finished, you'll be the handsomest pig in the world. I hope you'll cooperate and set a good example for the rest of them." He turned and gave the high-sign to four militiamen behind him who ran up and — you guessed it — each grabbed one of my legs. They were strong and, since they were used to treating people roughly, hurt me as they pulled me down out of the tree. "You pricks!" I cursed angrily. "Instead of lighting incense in the temple, you're destroying the idol!" My curses went in one ear and out the other as they dragged me on my back up to the cook pot filled with salt water and tossed me in! Some deep-seated fear gave me strength I didn't know I had, and the liquor I'd consumed turned to cold sweat. A thought hit me like a hammer: I recalled that before the new butcher law took effect, pork was eaten with the skin still on, and pigs scheduled for slaughter were tossed into just this sort of pot to soften up their bristles, which were shaved away before their heads and feet were cut off, their bellies slit open, and they were hung on a rack to be sold. The second my feet hit the bottom of the pot, I jumped out so fast I scared them all. Just my bad luck to jump out of one pot and into another, and this time the warm water swallowed me right up. I can't tell you how good that felt. It broke my will. I didn't have the strength to jump out this time. The girls surrounded the pot and started scrubbing me with coarse brushes under Ximen Jinlong's direction. I moaned, my eyelids drooped, and I just about fell asleep. When they were finished, the militiamen lifted me out of the pot, and when the cool air hit my body, I was sluggish and light as a feather. So the girls started in with their scissors, trimming the hair on my head and then brushing the bristles on my back. Ximen Jinlong thought it would be nice to cut the hair on both sides in the shape of plum blossoms, but they wound up shaving it all off. There was nothing Jinlong could do about that except add slogans with red paint: "Mate for the revolution" on the left side, "Bring benefits to the people" on the right. Then he dressed up the slogans by adding plum blossoms and sunflowers with red and yellow paint, turning me into a sort of bulletin board. When he was finished, he stepped back to admire his handiwork, wearing a mischievous smile that couldn't cover up the look of self-satisfaction. Everyone was shouting and calling me a great-looking pig.

If they could have beautified all the pigs on the farm the way they did me, then every one of them would have been a work of art. That would have been hard. Merely bathing them in salt water was out of the question, especially since the day of the on-site conference was rapidly approaching. Absent any obvious solution, Jinlong had to adjust his plans. What he came up with was to draw some simple but artistic samples of facial makeup, which he gave to twenty clever and skillful young men and women, along with a bucket of paint and two brushes, with instructions to paint the pigs' faces while they were still under the influence: red paint for the white pigs, white for the blacks, and yellow for all the others. For a while, the youngsters threw themselves into their work, but slapdash results soon became the norm. Even though the late-autumn skies were clear and the air was fresh, a horrible stink hung over the pigpens, not the sort of atmosphere that fostered a good work ethic. The young women dedicated themselves to the task at hand from the start and refused to do sloppy work no matter how unhappy they might be. The young men would have none of that. They just slapped paint on the pigs' bodies. White pigs wound up with red spots all over, as if they'd been hit by a shotgun blast with red pellets; black pigs were given white faces that made them look like sly old scoundrels or treacherous court officials. One of the youths, Mo Yan, to be precise, painted large-framed white spectacles on four black animals and red legs on four white sows.

Finally, the pig-raising convention got under way, and since I'd already given away my tree-climbing secret trick, there was no reason to hold back. In an attempt to keep the pigs from acting up and to impress the visiting VIPs, the quality of feed was raised and the quantity of liquor doubled. The pigs were blind drunk by the time the gathering was called to order. The smell of alcohol in the air was unmistakable, but Jinlong brazenly announced that what they smelled was a newly perfected fermented feed. He told everyone that the new feed required very little high-quality ingredients, but the nutritional value was surprisingly high and kept the animals from acting up or running around. They ate, they slept, and they put on weight. In recent years a lack of nutritional food, which had adversely influenced the birth rate of pigs, had become a matter of great concern. The creation of this new fermented feed solved that problem and paved the way for the commune to actively develop its pig-raising enterprise.

"Esteemed leaders, comrades, I am pleased to announce that our new fermented feed is an international breakthrough. We make it out of leaves, grass, and grain stalks. In other words, we've turned cast-off items into high-quality pork, which in turn produces a more nutritious food for our citizens and digs a grave for the imperialists, revisionists, and reactionaries."

A cool breeze brushed my belly as I lay cradled up in the apricot tree. A cluster of audacious sparrows that had landed on my head were pecking away at crumbs from the corners of my mouth all the way back to my ears. Their pointy beaks had a numbing, even slightly painful effect on my ultrasensitive ears, with their tight web of capillaries and nerves, sort of like an acupuncture treatment. Such contentment, I could barely keep my eyes open. I knew Jinlong would have liked nothing more than for me to be fast asleep up there. That way he could put that oily mouth of his to use — he could talk a dead pig back to life — saying anything he wanted. But I didn't want to sleep. In the long history of humankind, this was surely the first such meeting focused on pigs, and who could say if there would ever be a second? If I slept through such a momentous meeting, the remorse would last for three thousand years! Since I was a pampered pig, I could sleep pretty much whenever I wanted. Now was not one of those moments. I flapped my ears as a means of slapping my cheeks and letting everyone know I had standard ears, not the kind that adorned the heads of the Yimeng pigs, which stood straight up like dog ears. I realize, of course, that these days there are lots of urban dogs whose ears hang down like worn-out socks. Modern people have too much time on their hands, so they bring all sorts of unrelated animals together to mate and produce bizarre offspring, a true blasphemy to God, who will punish them one day. After flapping my ears vigorously to shoo some sparrows away, I picked a blood-red leaf from the apricot tree, put it in my mouth, and began to chew, its bitter, puckery taste working like tobacco to keep me wide awake. So then, from my commanding position, I began observing the goings-on around me to get a thorough grasp of what transpired at the pig-raising convention, taking comprehensive mental notes in a way that surpassed the most technologically advanced machines of today, since they are limited to recording sounds and images, while I could include overall flavors and my feelings.

Don't argue with me. Pang Hu's daughter messed up your mind so much that even though you're only in your early fifties, your eyes are glazed over and your reactions are dulled, both warning signs of dementia. So I advise you not to stick stubbornly to your opinions or think you can debate me. I can confidently tell you that when the pig-raising convention was held in Ximen Village, the village was not equipped with electricity. That's right, you yourself said it, people were burying concrete poles in the fields just outside the village at the time, but those were for high-voltage wires for the state-run farm, which belonged to the Jinan Military District and was designated an independent production and construction corps. Its leading cadres were military men on active duty, its laboring force made up of rusticated high-school graduates from Qingdao and Jinan. It goes without saying that an operation like that required electricity; we would have to wait a decade for electrification to reach Ximen Village. What that meant at the time was when night fell during the convention, except for the pig farm, blackness settled over the entire Ximen Village Production Brigade.

That's right, my pen was lit up by a hundred-watt bulb, which I taught myself how to turn on and off. The electricity was supplied by the Apricot Garden Pig Farm. In those days we called it "self-generated power." A twelve-horsepower diesel motor generated the power. It was Jinlong's idea. Go ask Mo Yan if you don't believe me. He came up with a wild idea that ended up very badly. I'll get to that in a minute.

A pair of loudspeakers hanging from the sides of the stage amplified the words of Ximen Jinlong a good five hundred times, and I figured all of Northeast Gaomi Township was within range of his boastful speech. Six tables taken from the elementary school were lined up at the rear of the stage and covered with red cloth. County government and commune VIPs, in their blue or gray uniforms, were seated on six benches, also taken from the school. Fifth from the left, a man whose army uniform was nearly white from many launderings was a recently retired regimental commander who'd taken charge of the production division of the County Revolutionary Committee. Ximen Village Brigade Party Secretary Hong Taiyue sat to his right. He was freshly shaved and had just had his hair trimmed; the bald spot on top was covered by a gray army-style cap. His ruddy face looked like an oilpaper lantern shining through the darkness of night. My guess was that he was dreaming of moving up the promotional ladder. If the State Council established a "Pig-Raising" Command Post, he might possibly be tapped as commander. There were fat officials and thin ones, and they all faced the east, looked into the Red Sun, so their faces were always ruddy, their eyes in a perpetual squint. One of them, a dark, fat man, was wearing a pair of sunglasses, something rarely seen in those times. With a cigarette dangling from his mouth, he looked like the leader of a gang of thieves. Jinlong was sitting at a desk also draped with red cloth in front of the stage, speaking into a microphone wrapped in red satin. In those days, that was awesome hightech equipment. Mo Yan, as always filled with curiosity, had sneaked up to the microphone and tested it out with a couple of dog barks. The magnified barking of dogs rocked the apricot grove and traveled out into the fields with astonishing effect. Mo Yan later wrote about this incident in an essay. This all goes to show that the power for the amplified microphone at the pig-raising convention was not supplied by high-voltage wires strung by the government, but by our own Apricot Garden Pig Farm diesel motor. A five-yard-long, twenty-centimeter-wide leather belt linked the turbine to a generator; when the motor was running, so was the generator, and electric power was the result, something that seemed nearly miraculous. It wasn't only the more dull-witted residents of Ximen Village who were virtually dumbstruck by what they were witnessing; even I, a very smart pig, had no explanation for what was right in front of my eyes. That's right, what in the world is this invisible thing called electricity? Where does it come from, and where does it disappear to? After a bonfire burns out, ashes are left behind; digested food becomes feces. But electricity? What does it turn into? This leads me back to when Ximen Jinlong set up the machinery in the two red-brick rooms close to a tall apricot tree in the southeastern corner of the Apricot Garden Pig Farm. After working all day, he did extra duty at night with the aid of a lantern, work that was so mysterious it attracted hordes of curious villagers, including just about all the people I mentioned earlier, with that disgusting Mo Yan elbowing his way all the way up front. Not content to just watch, he talked nonstop, to Jinlong's great annoyance. Several times Huang Tong grabbed Mo Yan by the ear and dragged him outside, only to have him reappear up front in less than half an hour, leaning up so close his slobber nearly fell on the back of Jinlong's greasy hands.

I didn't dare press up to get a look, and I couldn't climb that particular apricot tree, since the goddamned trunk was too slippery and the lower branches were too high. It looked like one of those white poplars up north, where the branches are all up high, giving it the shape of a torch. But heaven smiled down on me. Behind the rooms where this was all going on was a large grave mound where a dog that had died saving a child was buried. The dog, a black male, had jumped into the roiling waters of Grain Barge River to save the life of a girl who'd fallen in, but the effort had been too much for it, and it had died.

By standing on the grave mound, I could look in through a hole in the wall where a window was supposed to go, and see everything that went on inside. The gas lantern lit the place up like daytime, while outside the sky was pitch-black. It was like they said about class warfare: The enemy is in the light, we're in the dark. We see what we want to see; we can see them, but they can't see us. I watched as Jinlong turned the pages of the grimy handbook and wrote things between the lines of a newspaper. Hong Taiyue took out a cigarette, lit it, and took a deep drag, then stuck it in Jinlong's mouth. Revering intelligence and talent, Hong was one of the rare enlightened cadres of the time. Then there were the Huang twins, who kept Jinlong's brow dry with their handkerchiefs. I saw you were unmoved when

Huang Hezuo dried his sweaty brow, but noticed the look of jealousy on your face when Huang Huzhu did the same thing. You overrate your own appeal, and later events proved that the blue birthmark on your face not only did not keep you from attracting women, it actually was what drew them to you.

I bring this up not to make fun of you. I respect you too much to do that. You must be the only deputy county chief in the country who's willing to leave his lover without saying good-bye and make a living by the sweat of his brow.

But enough small talk. After the motor was set up, they tested it and found it did in fact produce electric power. And Jinlong became the second most powerful person in Ximen Village. Now I know all about your prejudice against your stepbrother, but you benefited from that relationship. If not for him, would you have been put in charge of the livestock unit? Or would you have been fortunate enough to be assigned as a contract worker at the cotton processing plant in the fall of the second year? And without that experience, would you still have made it into the ranks of officials? You have only yourself to blame for the mess you've gotten yourself in now. It's your fault you couldn't be master of your own pecker. Ah, what good does all this talk do? Let Mo Yan write about this stuff in his stories.

The meeting went forward without a hitch. After Jinlong outlined their advanced experience, he turned the microphone over to the uniformed production official to sum up. The man strode purposefully up to the table, where he spoke without a prepared speech, with eloquence and authority, although no one could hear him. A man who looked like his secretary ran up to the table at a crouch and bent the microphone straight up, but still not high enough to reach the official's mouth. The secretary knew what to do intuitively: he placed the bench on top of the table and set the microphone on top of that. A decade later this quick-witted individual would be given the post of county revolutionary committee office manager, in part on the basis of this one incident. The immediate effect was to blare the powerful voice of the onetime regimental commander far and wide.

"Every pig born is a cannon shell fired into the stronghold of the imperialists, revisionists, and reactionaries. . . ." He waved his fist as he shouted his incendiary message to the crowd. That shout and gesture reminded this wise and experienced pig of a movie scene and had me wondering whether being shot from a cannon would be a dizzying and shuddering experience. And what would happen if a fat pig suddenly fell into the stronghold of the imperialists, revisionists, and reactionaries? They'd probably die of sheer joy.

It was, by this time, ten in the morning, and there was no sign that the speech would end anytime soon. I looked over at a pair of green Jeeps at the edge of the clearing, where the white-gloved drivers were leaning against the cabs, one having a leisurely smoke, the other, clearly bored, checking his wristwatch every few seconds. Back then, a Jeep commanded greater respect than a Mercedes or BMW does today, and a watch was far more estimable than a diamond ring now. That watch sparkled in the bright sunlight and caught the eye of several youngsters. Hundreds of bicycles stood in neat rows behind the Jeeps, the means of transportation for all the grassroots attendees from the county, the commune, and the village. A dozen or so armed militiamen formed a protective semicircle around all this material wealth, a clear symbol of the status of the owners.

"We must ride the mighty east wind of the Cultural Revolution to carry out the pig-raising program outlined in the supreme directive of our great leader Chairman Mao, to study the advanced experience of the Ximen Village Production Brigade, and to elevate the raising of pigs to the level of politics. . . ." The official spoke fervently, accentuating his speech with forceful gestures. Shiny saliva bubbles gathered at the corners of his mouth, like a crab trussed up with rice straw.

"What's going on?" Diao Xiaosan asked as he stood up in his urine-soaked quarters. He had a vacant look in his bloodshot eyes, showing the effects of the alcohol he'd drunk. I had no desire to engage the moron in conversation, but he rose up and rested his chin on the top of his wall to see what was happening outside. He was so hung over he couldn't keep his balance, and he'd barely gotten his front legs off the ground when his hind legs gave out and deposited him in his own filthy leavings. The almost ridiculously unhygienic pig had piss and shit piled in every corner of his living quarters; just my bad luck to live next door to someone like that. There was white paint on his face and his protruding front teeth were yellow, like a couple of gold inlays favored by rich upstarts.

I saw a dark figure slip out of the audience — the meeting was well attended, anywhere from three to five thousand — and head for the big ceramic vat beneath the apricot tree, where the person bent over and looked inside. I knew what he wanted — sugar water. That was long gone. The people ahead of him had drunk deeply, not because they were thirsty, but for the sugar, one of the sparest commodities of the day, something you got only with a ration card. A mouthful of sugar back then was probably more satisfying than sex is today. For the sake of image, countywide, the leaders of the Ximen Village Production Brigade had called a meeting of commune members to go over all aspects of the on-site conference. One of the items was to forbid any commune member, adult or child, to help himself to sugar water; anyone who had the audacity to disobey would lose a hundred work points. The ugly looks on the faces of people from outlying villages as they fought over the drink was shameful, and I was proud of the Ximen villagers for their high degree of consciousness, or, should I say, their degree of self-control. I noticed the perplexed looks in their eyes as they watched the outsiders drink the sugar water, and though I knew those looks represented complex feelings, I admired the people nonetheless. Holding back like could not have been easy.

But there was one person for whom holding back was simply too difficult. I don't have to name names for you to know who that person was. He leaned into the vat like a horse drinking water, trying to lick up the last few drops at the bottom. But his neck was too short, the vat too deep, so he found a ladle, strained to tip the vat over, then dipped the ladle into the pooled water. When he let go of his hand, the vat tipped back straight, and I could tell by how carefully he held the ladle that his effort had not been in vain. He either brought the ladle up to his mouth or brought his mouth down to the ladle, I'm not sure which. From the look on his face, I knew he was enjoying a brief taste of the good life. He scraped the last bit of sweetness from the vat with the ladle, making a sound that set my teeth on edge. It was worse than the blaring of loudspeakers and made me tense and uncomfortable. I wished someone would stop him from embarrassing all of Ximen Village; I was afraid I'd fall out of my tree if he kept it up much longer, and I could hear the other pigs stirring. "Stop that scraping," they shouted through an inebriated haze. "You're killing us!" Well, he tipped over both vats and crawled into one, probably to lick the bottom. It's a true marvel to have such a greedy mouth. He reemerged after a while, his clothes shiny; he reeked of something sweet. If it had been springtime, he'd have been swarmed over by bees or butterflies,

but it was wintertime — no bees, no butterflies. There were, however, ten or fifteen big, fat flies buzzing around him, two of which
landed on his filthy, kinky hair.

". . . and we must employ ten times the passion and put forth a
hundred times the effort to expand Ximen Village's advanced experience. Every member of the commune and production brigade must
personally take charge. The workers, youth, women, and mass organizations must strive to work together. We must draw tight the class
struggle bowstring and reinforce the control and surveillance of
all landlords, rich peasants, counterrevolutionaries, bad elements,
and rightists, and be on guard against sabotage by concealed class
enemies . . ."

Mo Yan, smiling happily and whistling, caught my attention by
strutting over to the generator room, so I followed him with my eyes,
watching him go inside, where the diesel motor was humming along.

"The storekeepers of each brigade must rigorously protect
against the theft of pesticides and their introduction into pig feed by
class enemies . . ."

Jiao Er, the duty watchman for the generator, was leaning up
against the wall, sound asleep in the warmth of the sun, which gave
Mo Yan the opportunity to work his mischief. He undid his belt,
dropped his pants, grabbed his pecker with both hands — up till this
moment I had no idea what he was planning to do — and took aim at
the fan belt, wetting it with a clear stream of piss. A strange sound preceded the slippage of the belt, which hit the ground like a dead boa.
The loudspeaker went silent as the generator squealed, its motor
spinning uselessly. The clearing and the thousands of people in it
were, it seemed, submerged underwater, for the speaker's voice was
suddenly weak and drab, like the dull pops of fish bubbles as they
reached the surface. The desired atmosphere was in a shambles. I saw
Hong Taiyue stand up, followed by Ximen Jinlong, who got to his feet
and strode toward the generator room. At that moment I knew that
Mo Yan had done something terrible and that bitter fruit awaited him.

Too dumb to know what trouble he was in, Mo Yan stood in front
of the slipped fan belt looking puzzled, wondering how the little bit
of water he'd made had caused the belt to come off like that. The first
thing Ximen Jinlong did when he burst into the room was slap Mo Yan
on the head. The second thing he did was kick Mo Yan in the ass, and
the third thing he did was bend down, pick up the fan belt, and

replace it on the turbine. But as soon as he let go, off it came again. He tried again, this time using a metal pole, and managed to make it stay. He then coated the belt with a layer of wax, and it held.

"Who told you to do this?" he yelled at Mo Yan.

"Nobody . . ."

"Then why'd you do it?"

"To cool the belt off."

The interruption caused by the loudspeaker failure had dealt such a blow to the production HQ VIP that he brought an abrupt end to his speech. After a brief flurry of confusion, the pretty elementary teacher Jin Meili mounted the stage to announce the program. In not-terribly-standard-but-pleasant-sounding Mandarin, she announced to the masses in the clearing and, more important, to the officials who had by then taken seats on both sides of the stage: "The Ximen Village Elementary School Mao Zedong Thought Propaganda Team theatrical performance will now begin!" By this time the electricity had been restored to the loudspeakers, from which shrill screeches blasted into the air like darts aimed at birds overhead. Teacher Jin had cut off her braid for the performance and combed her hair in a style made fashionable by Ke Xiang, heroine of the Cultural Revolution drama *The Red Lantern*; that made her more valiant-looking and, at the same time, prettier and more competent than ever. I was watching people seated on the sides of the stage; all eyes were on her. Some of the men were gazing at her face, others were staring at her waist; the eyes of the first secretary of the Milky Way Commune, Cheng Zhengnan, were glued to her nicely rounded bottom. Ten years later, after a decade of hard times, Jin Meili wound up married to Cheng, now Party secretary of the County Politics and Law Committee. There was a twenty-six-year difference in their ages, which didn't sit well with people then. Nowadays, who'd even notice?

When she'd finished, Teacher Jin moved off to the side, where an accordion had been placed on a chair, its enamel buttons glittering in the sunlight. Ma Liangcai stood beside her with a bamboo flute, looking somber. After strapping on the accordion, Teacher Jin sat down and began playing beautifully; she was quickly joined by Ma, who produced a sound that could pierce clouds and shatter rocks. As they played a little introductory tune, a group of pudgy revolutionary piglet boys wearing red stomachers with the word *loyalty* embroidered on their breasts set their stumpy legs in motion and rolled and climbed their way onto the stage. They were such empty-headed, noisy, unthinking little pigs they needed a leader, which came in the person of a young female in red shoes, Little Red, who somersaulted onto the stage. Her mother was a rusticated, artistic woman from Qingdao, so she was blessed with good genes and a remarkable capacity for learning. Little Red's entrance drew enthusiastic applause, whereas that of the little boy pigs drew only snickers. But they made me happy. Never in the history of the world had a pig performed on a stage for humans; it was a breakthrough that made us real pigs extremely proud. From where I sat in my tree, I raised a hoof and sent a revolutionary salute to Jin Meili, the teacher who had choreographed the performance. I wanted also to salute Ma Liangcai, who'd played the flute fairly well, and to Little Red's mother, who deserved my respect for her ability as the wife of a peasant to produce such fine progeny. Passing on a talent for dance was worthy of respect, but even more worthy of respect was the way she remained backstage and provided the singing for her daughter's dance. She had a strong yet mellow alto voice — in one of his later stories, Mo Yan would write that she had a low voice, which earned him derision from people who knew a thing or two about music — and when the notes emerged from her throat, they danced in the air like strips of satin. "We are revolutionary red pigs who have come to Tiananmen from Gaomi"—those lyrics would not be appropriate today, but they were right for their time, and history cannot be changed on a whim — the little boy pigs were walking on their hands, their red shoes lifted into the air and clapping. The applause was loud, long, and celebratory. . . .

When the dance ended — successfully, I might add — it was my turn. Since being reborn as a pig, honesty compels me to say that Jinlong treated me well, and since we'd once enjoyed a special father-son relationship, I wanted to put on a show for the VIPs and make him look good in their eyes.

I tried limbering up, but I was still dizzy, my vision was blurred, and there was a ringing in my ears. Some ten years or so later, I invited a bunch of my canine friends — hounds and bitches — to a party where we drank Sichuan Wuliangye liquor, Maotai from Guizhou, French brandy, and Scotch whisky, and it finally dawned on me why, that day at the pig-raising on-site conference, my head ached, my eyes were dazed, and my ears rang. It wasn't my capacity for alcohol, but the rotgut sweet-potato liquor I drank. Of course here I must admit that while public morality was a sometime thing back then, at least people weren't so immoral as to substitute industrial alcohol for fermented liquor. Some time later, when I was reborn as a dog, a friend of mine, an experienced, knowledgeable, and wise German shepherd assigned to guard a city government guesthouse, concluded: People in the 1950s were innocent, in the 1960s they were fanatics, in the 1970s they were afraid of their own shadows, in the 1980s they carefully weighed people's words and actions, and in the 1990s they were simply evil. I'm sorry, I keep getting ahead of myself. It's a trick Mo Yan uses all the time, and I foolishly let it affect the way I talk.

Knowing he'd done something terrible, Mo Yan remained in the generator room meekly waiting for Jinlong to come punish him. When Jiao Er returned after his nap and found Mo Yan standing there, he lambasted him: "What are you standing here for, you little prick? Planning more bad tricks?" "Brother Jinlong told me to stand here!" Mo Yan replied, as if that were all that was needed. "So what!" Jiao Er said pompously. "Your 'Brother Jinlong' isn't worth what's hanging between my legs!" "Okay," Mo Yan said as he started to walk off, "I'll just go tell him." "Stay right where you are!" Jiao Er said, grabbing Mo Yan's collar and pulling him back, in the process sending the last three buttons of Mo Yan's worn jacket flying; the jacket opened up to reveal his belly. "You tell him what I said and you're a dead man!" He held his fist under Mo Yan's nose. "You'll have to kill me to stop me from talking," Mo Yan replied, refusing to back down.

Jiao Er and Mo Yan were two of Ximen Village's worst citizens, so let's forget about them. They can do what they want there in the generator room. Meanwhile, Jinlong led the throngs of attendees up to my pen, where I won over the crowd without a word of introduction. They'd seen plenty of pigs sprawled in the mud, but never one up a tree; they'd also seen lots of slogans painted in red on walls, but never on the sides of a pig. The county and commune VIPs laughed until it hurt; the production brigade officials laughed like little fools. The uniformed head of the production command stood there staring at me.

"Did he climb up there by himself?" he asked Jinlong.

"Yes, he did."

"Can he show us?" the commander asked. "What I mean is, can you have him come down from there and then get him to climb up again?"

"I'll try, but it won't be easy," Jinlong said. "He's smarter than other pigs, and has powerful legs. But he can be stubborn and he likes to do things his own way. He doesn't take orders well."

So Jinlong tapped me on the head with a switch and said in a voice that seemed to beg cooperation and promise lenience.

"Wake up, Pig Sixteen, come down and relieve yourself."

Anyone could see he wanted me to perform for the VIPs. Relieve myself, what a joke! That made me unhappy, though I understood why he was doing it. I wouldn't disappoint him, but I wouldn't be docile in the process either; I wasn't about to do what he wanted just because he wanted me to. If I did, instead of being a pig with an attitude, I'd be a lapdog performing tricks to please my master. I smacked my lips, yawned, rolled my eyes, and stretched. That was met with laughter and an interesting comment: "That's no pig, it can do anything a man can do." The idiots thought I didn't understand what they were saying. For their information, I understood people from Gaomi, Mount Yimeng, and Qingdao. Not only that, I picked up a dozen Spanish phrases from a rusticated youngster from Qingdao who dreamed of studying abroad one day. So I shouted something in Spanish, and those morons froze on the spot. Then they burst out laughing. Go ahead, laugh, laugh yourself into your graves and save the country some rice! You want me to take a leak, is that it? Well, I don't need to climb down for that. Stand tall, pee far. Just so I could have some fun with them, I let fly from where I was, alternating between fast and slow, spurting and dribbling. The morons couldn't stop laughing. I glared at them. "What are you laughing at?" I said. I meant business. "Have you forgotten that I'm a cannon shell fired into the stronghold of the imperialists, revisionists, and reactionaries? If a cannon shell takes a leak, that means the powder got wet, so what are you laughing at?" The morons must have understood me, because they laughed until snot ran from their noses. The hint of a smile even appeared on the permanent scowl of an official who always wore an old army coat, as if his face were suddenly covered by a layer of golden bran flakes. He pointed to me.

"What a wonderful pig!" he said. "He deserves a gold medal!"

Now I was someone who had little interest in fame and fortune, but hearing such praise from the mouth of a high official turned my head. I wanted to learn how to walk on my hands from Little Red. Doing that up in a tree would be especially hard, but when I eventually mastered the technique, everyone would sit up and take notice.

So I planted my front hooves in the crotch of the tree and raised my hind legs, head down until it was resting in a space between branches. But I'd eaten too much that morning, and my strength was affected by my heavy gut. I pressed down on the branch with all my might, causing it to shake and sway. Yes! I said. Okay, I can see the ground. All my weight was now on my front legs, and the blood rushed to my head. My eyes were getting sore, ready to pop out of their sockets. Hold on, hold on for ten seconds and you've done it! I heard applause. I'd done it. Unfortunately, my left front hoof slipped, I lost my balance, everything went dark, and I felt my head bang into something hard. Thud! I passed out.

Damn it! That rotgut liquor really messed me up.

26

A Jealous Diao Xiaosan Destroys a Pigpen
Lan Jinlong Cleverly Gets Through a Bitter Winter

The winter of 1972 was a test of survival for the Apricot Garden pigs. In the wake of the pig-raising on-site conference, the county government rewarded the Ximen Village Production Brigade with 20,000 *jin* of pig feed, but that was just a number. The actual delivery of the feed was entrusted to a man named Jin, a granary official whose nickname — Golden Rat — spoke to his fondness for rat meat. Well, this granary rat actually sent us some moldy dry-yam-and-sorghum mix that had lain in a corner for years, and far less than 20,000 *jin* of it. There was probably a ton of rat shit mixed in with the feed, which was why a peculiar cloud of rank air hung over the farm all winter. Yes, around the time of the pig-raising on-site conference, we were given tasty food and strong drinks, enjoying the decadent life of the landlord class. But after the conference, the brigade granary was critically low and cold weather was on its way, and it looked as if the snow, despite its romantic image, would bring us bone-chilling days. Hunger and cold were to be our constant companions.

The snowfalls that year were abnormally heavy, and that's no exaggeration. You can check the records of the county weather bureau, the county gazetteer, even Mo Yan's story "Tales of Pig-Raising."

Mo Yan, always ready to deceive people with heresy, is in the habit of mixing fact and fantasy in his stories; you can't reject the contents out of hand, but you mustn't fall into the trap of believing everything he writes. The times and places in "Tales of Pig-Raising" are accurate, as are the parts dealing with the winter weather; but the head count of pigs and their origins have been altered. Everyone knows they were from Mount Yimeng, but in the story they're from Mount Wulian. And there were 1,057 of them, though he gives the number at something over 900. But since we're talking about fiction here, the details should not concern us.

Now even though I was contemptuous of that gang of Mount Yimeng pigs, being a pig myself was a source of shame; when all was said and done, we belonged to the same species. "When the rabbit dies, the fox grieves, for his turn will come." The Mount Yimeng pigs were dying off in twos and threes, and a tragic pall hung above Apricot Garden Pig Farm. To keep up my strength and lessen the dissipation of body heat, I cut back on the number of night rounds. I pushed the shredded leaves and powdered grass I'd used for such a long time into a corner of the wall, leaving a line of hoofprints that looked like a designed pattern. I lay down on this bed of leaves and grass, holding my head in my hands to gaze at the snowy landscape and smell the cold, fresh air that is so common to snowfalls. I was overcome by melancholy. To tell the truth, I wasn't a pig normally given to sadness or emotionalism. Most of the time I was euphoric, either that or defiant. You'd be hard put to associate me with the petty bourgeois affinity for sentimentality.

Wind from the north whistled, river ice splintered with ear-shattering *crack crack crack crack*, as if Fate had come rapping on a door in the middle of the night. A snow drift in front of the pen seemed to merge with sagging, snow-laden apricot branches. Throughout the grove, explosions of sound announced the snapping of branches unable to bear up under the weight of wet snow, while dull thuds gave voice to accumulations of snow falling to the ground. On that dark night, all I could see was an expanse of white. The generator, thanks to a scarcity of diesel fuel, had long since stopped producing electricity. A dark night like that, covered by a blanket of white, ought to have created the ideal atmosphere for fairy tales, should have been a source of dreams, but cold and hunger shattered both fairy tales and dreams. I have to be honest with you and tell you that when the quantity of pig feed had dwindled to a dangerous low and the Mount Yimeng pigs were reduced to eating moldy leaves and cast-off seedpods from the cotton processing plant to survive, Ximen Jinlong continued to ensure that a fourth of what I was given to eat was nutritious food. While it was only dried moldy yams, it was certainly better than bean-plant leaves and cotton seedpods.

So I lay there suffering through the long night, alternating between dream-filled sleep and wakeful reality. Stars peeked out through the darkness from time to time, sparkling like a diamond pendant on a woman's bosom. The restless sounds of pigs struggling to stay alive made peaceful sleep impossible, and a palpable sense of bleakness settled around me. Tears filled my eyes as I revisited the past, and when they spilled out onto my hairy cheeks, they froze into ice crystals. My neighbor, Diao Xiaosan, was in torment, and was now eating his own bitter — and unhygienic — fruit. There wasn't a dry spot in his pen, which was littered with frozen turds and iced urine. My ears were assailed by wolfish howls that echoed those in the wild, as he ran around cursing the unfairness of life in this world. At mealtimes he railed at everyone in sight: Hong Taiyue, Ximen Jinlong, Lan Jiefang, even Bai Xing'er, the widow of the long-dead Ximen Nao, whose job it was to deliver his food. She came each day with two buckets of feed on a carrying pole, slowly making her way through the snow on tiny, once-bound feet, her tattered coat shifting back and forth as she walked. She wore a kerchief tied around her head; I could see her breath and the frost that had formed on her brows and her hair. Her hands were rough and cracked, the fingers like wood that has survived a fire. As she made her way through the farm, she kept from falling by using her long-handled ladle as a crutch. Little steam rose from the buckets, but the odor was strong enough to identify the quality of the food inside. The contents of the bucket in front were for me; those of the bucket in back were for Diao Xiaosan. After putting down her load, she scraped the thick layer of snow off the wall, then reached over to clean out my trough with her ladle. Finally she lifted up the bucket and dumped in the black contents. Even before she'd finished, I'd be in such a hurry to get to the food that some of the sticky stuff would fall on my head and in my ears; she'd clean it off with her ladle. What I was given was pretty disagreeable, and not meant for slow chewing, since that kept the unpleasant taste in my mouth longer than it needed to be there. I gobbled it up so noisily she invariably said with an emotional sigh:

"Pig Sixteen, you're such a good little pig, you eat whatever I give you."

Bai Xing'er always fed me before Diao Xiaosan; watching me eat seemed to make her happy. If he hadn't raised such a stink, I believe she might have forgotten all about him. I'll never forget the look of tenderness in her eyes as she bent down to watch me, and I'm certainly aware of how well she treated me. But I don't want to dwell on that, since it was years ago and we went our separate ways — one human, the other animal.

I heard Diao Xiaosan clamp his teeth around the wooden ladle and looked up to see his hideous face as he stood with his feet on the top of the wall — sharp, uneven teeth and, oh, those bloodshot eyes. Bai Xing'er rapped him on the snout with her ladle. Then, after dumping his food into the trough, she said:

"You filthy pig, eating and relieving yourself in the same spot. I don't know why you haven't frozen to death yet!"

Diao Xiaosan had barely taken a mouthful of food before he cursed her back:

"You old witch, I know you like him better than me. You give Sixteen all the good food and save the rotten leaves for me! Well, fuck you and the whore that brought you into this world!"

The curses quickly turned to self-pitying sobs, but Bai Xing'er ignored him and his foul language. She picked up her buckets, hung the ladle from one of them, and walked off, swaying from side to side.

Once she was gone, Diao turned to me and started in with the complaints, spraying my pen with his foul spittle. I pretended I didn't see the hatred in his eyes and went back to my food.

"Pig Sixteen," he said, "what kind of world are we living in? We're both pigs, so how come people don't treat us the same? Because I'm dark and you're light? Or because you're local and I'm not? Or is it because you're good looking and I'm ugly? Which isn't to say that you're all that good looking."

What could I say to a moron like that? The world has never been fair. Just because an officer rides a horse doesn't mean his soldiers ought to as well, does it? A generalissimo in the Soviet Red Army rode a horse, and so did his troops. But his mount was a magnificent steed, theirs were nags. Differential treatment.

"I'll sink my teeth into all of them one of these days, then I'll rip open their bellies and pull their guts out . . ." With his front feet resting on the wall between our pens, he ground his teeth and said, "Where there's oppression there's resistance. Do you believe that? You don't have to if you don't want to, but I do."

"You're right," I said. No need to offend him. "I believe you've got guts and certain abilities," I added, "and I'm waiting for the day when you do something spectacular."

"Well, then," he said, starting to drool, "how about sharing some of that food she gave you?"

I had a low opinion of him to begin with, but that fell even lower when I saw the greedy look in his eyes and the filth around his mouth. I was reluctant to let that disgusting mouth pollute my feed trough. Considering his petty request, I knew it would be hard to turn it down out of hand, so I stammered:

"Old Diao, I tell you the truth, there's no real difference between what you and I got. . . . You're being childish, assuming that somebody else's cake is bigger than yours."

"How fucking stupid do you think I am?" he said angrily. "My eyes might fall for that, but not my nose! Hell, my eyes won't fall for that either." He bent down, scooped some feed out of his trough, and flung it down in front of mine. Anyone could see the difference. "Look at that and tell me what you're eating and then what I'm eating. Shit, we're both boars, so how come we get different treatment? You're going to 'serve the revolution by mating,' well, am I serving the counterrevolution then? If people divide themselves into revolutionary and counterrevolutionary, does that mean there are classes of pigs too? It's all because of favoritism and crazy thoughts. I saw the way Bai Xing'er was looking at you. That was the look a woman gives her husband! Maybe she wants to mate with you, what do you think? If you do, then next spring, she'll have a litter of piglets with human heads, or monsters with pig heads. Won't they be beautiful?" he said hatefully, then flashed an evil grin, showing that his slanderous outburst had driven the gloom from his mind.

I scooped up the clump of feed he'd tossed over and flung it far over the wall. "I was seriously considering doing you a favor," I said contemptuously, "but after what you just said, sorry, brother Diao, but I'll dump the rest of the food on a pile of shit before I'll give it to you." I reached down, scooped up what was left in my trough, and tossed it on the ground, where I relieved myself. Then I went back and lay down on my straw bed. "If you're still hungry, sir," I said, "be my guest."

Diao Xiaosan's eyes flashed green; his teeth ground noisily. "Pig Sixteen," he said, "the old saying goes, 'You don't know your legs are

muddy till you step out of the water.' The river flows east for thirty
years and west for thirty years! The sun's rays are on the move. They
won't always shine down on your nest!" Now that he'd had his say, his
hideous face disappeared from view. But I could hear him pacing anxiously on the other side of the wall and, from time to time, banging his
head against the gate or scraping the wall with his hooves. That went
on for a while until I heard a strange noise from his side. It took a number of guesses before I figured out that he had stood up on his hind
legs and, partly for warmth and partly to vent his spleen, had begun
tearing sorghum stalks out of the canopy over his pen. Unfortunately,
some came from my side.

I rose up on my hind legs and stuck my head over the wall. "Stop
that," I protested.

With a stalk of sorghum clenched between his teeth, he tugged
and tugged until he brought it down, then chewed it into pieces.
"Shit," he said, "who gives a damn! If I'm going to die, then I'm taking others with me! The ways of the world aren't fair, so the little
demons will tear down the temple." He rose up on his hind legs, a
sorghum stalk in his mouth, and came down as hard as he could, the
concussion sending one of the red tiles crashing to the ground and
opening a hole in the canopy, through which snow fell in on his head.
With a shake of that big head, the green lights in his eyes crashed into
the wall and shattered like glass. Obviously, the guy was nuts. I nervously looked up at the canopy above me and started pacing, on the
verge of jumping over the wall to stop that nonsense. But taking on a
madman only ensures that both sides will suffer, and in my anxiety I
let out a shriek that sounded like an air-raid warning. I've tried to imitate the revolutionary style of singing, pinching my vocal cords, but it
never worked. Now, in my high state of anxiety, my howl was actually
closer to an air-raid warning than anything. That came as a memory of
my youth, when there were countywide air-raid drills to put us on
guard against attacks by imperialists, reactionaries, and counterrevolutionaries. In every village and hamlet in the county, loudspeakers first
blared a low, rumbling sound. That's what enemy bombers sound like,
a baby's voice announced. That was followed by an ear-splitting
shriek. That's what enemy planes sound like when they come in for
strafing attacks. . . . Finally, demonic howls emerged. All county
revolutionary cadres and all poor and lower-middle peasants, listen
carefully to the differences. These are international air-raid warnings,

and when you hear one of them, drop what you're doing and take refuge in an air-raid shelter. If there isn't one nearby, cover your head with both arms and hunker down. . . . I was like a student of opera who finally finds his voice and is overjoyed. I paced the confines of my pen and howled, and in order to send my warning as far as possible, I shot up an apricot tree. Snow on the branches, like flour or cotton wadding, fell to the ground, drizzling here and fluttering there, spongy in some places and heavy in others, and everywhere purple twigs peeked out from the white snow, glossy and brittle, like legendary ocean coral. From one limb to the next I climbed all the way to the top of the tree, where I could see not only all of Apricot Garden Pig Farm, but the whole village. I saw chimney smoke lazing into the sky, I saw thousands of trees whose canopies were like giant steamed buns, and I saw crowds of people running out of buildings that seemed about to collapse from the weight of rooftop snow. The snow was white, the people black. Traveling through knee-high drifts was closer to staggering than walking. It was my air-raid alert that had brought them out of their houses, and the first to emerge — from their heated five-room compound — were Jinlong and Jiefang. They walked around a bit and then looked into the sky — I knew they were searching for imperialist, revisionist, or counterrevolutionary bombers — and finally fell to the ground, where they wrapped their arms around their heads, as a flock of loudly cawing crows flew right over them. The birds had built their nests in a grove of trees east of the Grain Barge River, but with so much snow on the ground, finding food was especially hard, so they came every day to the Apricot Garden Pig Farm to forage. After a while Jinlong and Jiefang stood up and looked into the sky — which had cleared up after the snowstorm — again; following that, they looked down and eventually discovered the source of the air-raid warning.

Lan Jiefang, now I have to talk about you. You raised your bamboo whip and charged me bravely, although you slipped and fell twice because of the ice-covered bits of pig food on the path through the trees: once you fell forward and sprawled on the ground like a dog fighting over shit; the other time you fell backward and landed like a turtle sunning its underbelly. The gentle sun's rays and the snowy landscape made for a beautiful setting; the crows' wings seemed gilded. The blue half of your face glowed. You were never considered one of the major personalities in Ximen Village; in fact, except for

Mo Yan, who you often chewed the fat with, just about everybody ignored you; even me, a pig at the time, never gave you much thought, even though you were a so-called feed boss. But at this moment, with that whip trailing you as you came at me, I discovered to my surprise that you'd grown into a slender young man. Sometime later I counted on my hooves and discovered that you were already twenty-two. Yes, you'd grown up.

With my arms wrapped around a limb and sunbeams filtering through the red clouds, I opened my mouth and released a swirling air-raid alert. People who had gathered at the base of the tree were steaming, the embarrassed looks on their faces somewhere between laughter and crying. An old man named Wang intoned sadly:

"A demon emerges, the nation submerges!"

But Jinlong cut him off:

"Watch your tongue, Gramps Wang!"

Knowing he'd said something he shouldn't have, Gramps Wang slapped himself. "Who told you to rant like that?" he cursed himself. "Secretary Lan, a great man overlooks a small man's mistakes. Forgive this old man's crime!"

At the time Jinlong was a newly minted member of the Party and was already a member of the Branch Party Committee, as well as Party secretary of the Ximen Village Communist Youth League. He was more than proud, he was haughty. With a wave of his hand to the old man, he said:

"I know you've read heretical books like *Warring Kingdoms* and that they've found their way into your heart, so you like to show off. If not for that, that one sentence alone would be enough to label you a counterrevolutionary."

Jinlong's comment had a chilling effect on the atmosphere, and that gave him the opportunity to deliver a sermon; he remarked that inclement weather presents an opportunity for imperialists, revisionists, and counterrevolutionaries to attack; it also creates ideal conditions for hidden class enemies in the village to carry out sabotage. He then turned his attention to me, declaring me to be an enlightened pig. "He may be a pig, but he's achieved a higher degree of awareness than many people."

Dizzy with pride, I forgot why I was sounding air-raid warnings in the first place. Like a pop singer responding to an admiring audience with a rousing encore, I cleared my throat for another burst of sound, but before it left my throat, I saw Lan Jiefang twirl his whip at the base of the tree, and before I saw it coming, the tip flicked against my ear. Boy, did that hurt! But the worst thing was, my head suddenly felt heavier than the rest of my body, and I fell out of the tree into the snow.

When I managed to get to my feet, I saw blood on the snow — my blood. The whip had opened up an inch-long gash in my right ear, one that would accompany me through the second, and most glorious, half of my life. It was also the reason I bore a grudge against you from then on, though I later understood why you resorted to such cruelty. I forgave you in theory, but could never quite let it go emotionally.

Although I was on the receiving end of a whip that day and scarred for life, my neighbor Diao Xiaosan suffered a much crueler fate. There was a certain charm to my climbing a tree and sounding air-raid alerts, but there was no redeeming feature in his foul-mouthed attacks on society and the destruction of property. Some people criticized Lan Jiefang for using his whip on me, but when he whipped Diao Xiaosan bloody, he was universally praised. Shouts of "Beat him, beat the bastard to death!" were on everyone's lips. At first, Diao hopped around so violently he broke two steel rods in the gate to his pen. But his strength gradually gave out, and people rushed in, grabbed his hind legs, and dragged him out into the snow. Jiefang's hatred hadn't abated; he stood with his legs bent like wickets, each snap of his whip opening a new gash on Diao's body. His gaunt blue face was twitching; knots protruded on his cheeks from clenching his teeth. "You scumbag, you whore!" he shouted with each lashing of his whip, switching back and forth as each hand tired. That, of course, was no mean feat. At first, Diao Xiaosan rolled around on the ground, but after a few dozen lashes, he laid out flat, like a hunk of dead meat. Jiefang still wasn't satisfied. Everyone knew he was taking out his frustrations on the pig, but no one tried to stop him, even though they could see that the pig might well not survive the beating. Finally Jinlong stepped up and grabbed Jiefang's arm. "Enough," he said coldly. Diao Xiaosan's blood stained the snowy ground. My blood was red, his was black. Mine was sacred, his was foul. In order to punish him for his wrongs, the people pierced his nose and put in a pair of rings. They also chained his front legs. In the days that followed, that chain rattled as he paced his pen, and every time the famous aria by Li Yuhe from the model revolutionary opera *The Red Lantern*—"These

chains may shackle my hands and feet, but they cannot keep my aspirations and ideals from soaring into the heavens!"—blasted from the
loudspeaker, for some reason I felt a tinge of respect for this mortal
enemy, almost as if he'd become a hero, and I was the one who had
sold him out.

Yes, as Mo Yan wrote in his story "Revenge," the Apricot Garden
Pig Farm entered a period of crisis as the Lunar New Year approached.
The pig food had all been eaten, so had the piles of rotten beans and
leaves. There was nothing left but moldy cottonseed mixed with
snow. Desperate times. A time, as it turned out, when Hong Taiyue
fell gravely ill; his heavy responsibilities now rested on the shoulders
of Jinlong, just when he was experiencing emotional torment. The
person he loved ought to have been Huang Huzhu, a relationship that
began when she repaired a uniform for him. Their bonds had early on
been consummated, when Huang Hezuo made her move, and they
sported among the clouds and rain. As they all grew older, the Huang
twins both clamored to marry Jinlong. Who knew these secrets? In
addition to me, a pig that pretty much knew everything, only Lan
Jiefang. I remained above it all, but you, whose love for Huang Huzhu
was not reciprocated, were tormented and horribly jealous. That was
one of the reasons you knocked me out of my tree with your whip and
why you dealt so cruelly with Diao Xiaosan. Now that we can look
back, don't you think the feelings that tormented you at the time were
pretty insignificant compared to what happened later? Besides, the
world is unpredictable, and conjugal bliss is dictated by heaven. The
person you are to marry has already been determined. Isn't that so,
since Huang Huzhu eventually shared your bed?

During that winter, pigs that had frozen to death were dragged out of
their pens every day, and every night I was awakened by the wails of
grief-stricken Yimeng pigs whose pen-mates had died from the cold.
Every morning I looked out through the metal slats of my gate and
saw Lan Jiefang or somebody else dragging a pig carcass in the direction of the five-room building. The dead animals were skin and bones,
their legs stiff as boards. Hot-tempered Howling Wolf died, so did the
slutty Rape Flower. At first they died at the rate of three or four a day,
but by the latter days of the twelfth month, as many as six or seven
were dying each day. On the twenty-third of that month, sixteen dead
pigs were dragged out of their pens. I did a quick calculation and came

up with the figure of more than two hundred pigs that had departed for the Western Heaven by the end of the year. I had no way of knowing if their souls had gone down to hell or up to heaven, but their earthly remains were piled up in dark corners at the rear of the building, where they were cooked and eaten by Ximen Jinlong and the other humans. That is a memory that sticks with me even now.

People sitting under lamplight around a blazing stove watching the meat of butchered pigs cooking is something Mo Yan wrote about in great detail in his "Tales of Pig-Raising." He described the fragrance of the burning apricot branches, he described the stench of the meat cooking in the pot, he even described how the starving people bit off big chunks of it, a scene that would disgust people nowadays.

I can add one thing to Mo Yan's descriptions, and that is: As the day approached when all the pigs in the Apricot Garden Pig Farm would die of starvation, on the last day of the year, when firecrackers were noisily seeing out the old and welcoming in the new, Jinlong abruptly smacked himself on the forehead and announced:

"That's it! I know how to save the farm."

It wouldn't be hard to eat pork from dead pigs like that once, but the smell would make me puke the second time. Jinlong ordered people to convert the dead pigs into food for living pigs. At first I noticed that my feed tasted different somehow, so late at night I sneaked out of my pen to see what was going on in the building where our food was prepared, and that's when I learned their secret. I have to admit that for animals as stupid as pigs, cannibalism is not a significant taboo, nothing to get excited about. But to an extraordinary soul like me, it gives rise to a whole bunch of painful associations. Yet the will to live is more powerful than spiritual torment. Actually, I was worrying myself needlessly. If I was a man, eating pork was perfectly natural. And if I were a pig, as long as the other pigs were okay with eating their dead brothers and sisters, who was I to complain? Go ahead, eat. Close your eyes and eat it. After I'd learned how to sound air-raid warnings, I got the same food the other pigs got. I knew they weren't doing this to punish us, but because it was the only thing they had for us to eat. The fat started falling off my body, I was constipated, and my urine was reddish yellow. I was a little better off than the others, only because I could get out and walk around at night, picking up rotten vegetables here and there, however infrequently. What I'm saying is, if we hadn't eaten the unique feed Jinlong prepared for us, none of us would have survived the winter and been greeted by the warmth of spring.

Jinlong mixed the meat from dead animals with some horse and cow dung, and chopped up sweet potato vines to make his unique pig feed. It saved the lives of a lot of pigs, and that included me and Diao Xiaosan.

A new batch of traditional pig feed was sent down to us in the spring of 1973, bringing new life to the Apricot Garden Pig Farm. But before this occurred, more than six hundred pigs from Mount Yimeng had been converted into protein, vitamins, and plenty of other things needed to sustain life, thereby extending the lives of some four hundred others. So we howled for three full minutes to salute these self-sacrificing heroes, and as we howled, apricot flowers bloomed, the moon bathed the farm in its watery beams, and a floral perfume tickled our noses. The curtain was lifted on the year's romantic season.

27

A Sea of Jealousy Rages as Brothers Go Crazy
Fast-talking, Glib Mo Yan Encounters Envy

The moon that night rose eagerly into the sky even before the sun had set. In the rosy sunset, the atmosphere in the Apricot Garden Pig Farm was warm and congenial. I had a premonition that something important was going to happen that night. I stood up and rested my front hooves on the apricot tree, whose blossoms sent out a wonderful aroma. I looked up and, through the gaps in the tree, saw the moon — big, round, and silvery, as if cut out of a piece of tin — rise into the sky. At first I could hardly believe it was really the moon, but the brilliant beams that showered down soon convinced me.

At the time I was still an immature, impressionable pig who became excited over anything new and strange and wanted to share it with the other pigs. Mo Yan was a lot like that. In an essay entitled "Brilliant Apricot Blossoms" he wrote about how he discovered Ximen Jinlong and Huang Huzhu one day at noon; they had climbed an apricot tree filled with blossoms and were moving so hot and heavy they sent flower petals falling to the ground like snow. Eager to share his discovery with as many people as possible, Mo Yan ran over to the feed preparation shed and shook the sleeping Lan Jiefang awake. He wrote:

> Lan Jiefang sat up abruptly, rubbed his bloodshot eyes, and asked: "What's up?" The grass mat on the *kang* had created patterns on his face. "Come with me," I said mysteriously. I led him around the two individual pens reserved for the boars and deep into the apricot grove. Typical lazy weather for late spring, and the pigs were all sound asleep in their pens, including the boar who was always acting strange.

Hordes of bees were buzzing tirelessly around the flowers for their nectar; bright, pretty thrushes flitted around in the trees' high branches, frequently signaling their presence with crisp, mournful cries. "Damn," Lan Jiefang cursed unhappily. "What is it you want to show me?" I put my finger to my lips to shush him. "Squat down and follow me," I said softly as we squatted down and inched forward. A pair of ocher rabbits were chasing each other among the trees; a beautiful, bright-colored pheasant clucked as it dragged its tail feathers along the ground and flapped its wings, quickly flying off into the brush behind a deserted graveyard. After skirting the two buildings that had once housed the generator, we reached a dense grove with dozens of apricot trees so big around it took two people to circle it with their arms. The canopies formed a virtually seamless cover high above us. There were red flowers, pink ones, and white ones, and from a distance they took on the appearance of clouds. Owing to the complex root systems of these enormous trees and the villagers' reverence for big trees, this grove had been spared during the 1958 iron-smelting campaign and the pig-raising disaster of 1972. I'd personally seen Ximen Jinlong and Huang Huzhu choose an old tree whose trunk leaned slightly to one side and climb it like a couple of squirrels. But now there was no sign of them. A breeze rose up and set the upper branches in motion. The petals of fragile flowers rained down on the ground like snowflakes, forming a layer of what looked like fine jade. "I asked you what you want to show me," Lan Jiefang repeated, this time much louder, as he balled up his fists. In Ximen Village, in fact, throughout Northeast Gaomi Township, the blue-faced father and son were famed for their stubbornness and bad temper, so I had to be careful not to provoke this youngster. "With my own eyes I saw them climb the tree—" "Saw who?" "Jinlong and Huzhu!" Jiefang thrust out his neck, the way he might if an invisible fist had landed on his chest, right above the heart. Then his ears twitched and the sun's rays danced on the blue half of his face, lighting it up like jade. He seemed hesitant for some reason, struggling to make up his mind, but in the end a devilish force propelled him in the direction of the tree . . . he looked up . . . half his face like blue jade . . . he let loose with a loud wail and threw himself down on the ground . . . flower petals rained down as if to bury him. . . . Ximen Village apricot blossoms are renowned far and wide; in the 1990s city folk arrived by car every spring, children in tow, just to admire the apricot blossoms.

At the end of the essay, Mo Yan wrote:

> I never imagined this incident would cause Lan Jiefang such anguish. People came out to pick him up and carry him back to his *kang*. They pried open his teeth with a chopstick and poured some ginger water into his mouth to revive him. What in the world did he see up there in the tree, they asked me, that could put a spell on him like this? I said that the boar had taken the little sow called Butterfly Lover up the tree with romance on his mind. . . . That can't be, they said doubtfully. When Lan Jiefang came to, he rolled around on the *kang* like a young donkey. His wails sounded like the boar imitating an air-raid alarm. He pounded his chest, pulled his hair, clawed at his eyes, and scratched his cheeks. . . . Some kind-hearted people had no choice but to tie his arms to keep him from doing serious injury to himself.

I couldn't wait to tell people all about the celestial beauty of the sun and the moon, as they vied to outshine each other, but was stopped from doing so by Lan Jiefang, who, having lost his mind, threw the pig farm into sheer chaos. Party Secretary Hong, who had just gotten out of a sickbed, came as soon as he heard. He walked with a cane, his pallor, sunken eyes, and chin stubble showing the effects of an illness serious enough to turn a hard-as-nails member of the Communist Party into an old man. He stood at the head of the *kang* and banged on the floor with his cane, as if hoping to strike water. The harsh light made him look even more sickly and turned the face of Lan Jiefang, who was lying on the *kang* wailing, piteously hideous.

"Where's Jinlong?" Hong asked, the tone showing his frustration.

The people in the room exchanged glances, apparently unaware of what had happened to him. Finally it was left to Mo Yan to answer timorously:

"Probably in the generator room."

The comment reminded everyone that this was the first time they'd had electricity since the generator had been shut down the previous winter, and they were puzzled over what Jinlong was up to.

"Go get him."

Mo Yan slipped out of the room like a slippery mouse.

At about that time I heard the sad sounds of a woman crying out on the street. My heart nearly stopped, and my brain froze. What happened next came like a raging torrent. I squatted down in front of a tall pile of apricot leaves, roots, and branches in the feed preparation room to think about the past, veiled in mist, and examine the present. Bones of the Mount Yimeng pigs that had died the year before had been placed in large baskets outside the room, where they showed up white in the moonlight, with specks of green glittering here and there. They gave off an unpleasant odor. I gazed out to see what appeared to be a dancing figure walking toward the moon, which by now looked like a ball of quicksilver, and turn on to the path to the Apricot Garden Pig Farm. She looked up, and I saw her face, which looked like a used water ladle, a sort of burnished yellow; owing to the fact that she was wailing, her open mouth was like a black mouse hole. She held her arms close to her chest, her legs were so bowed a dog could have run between them, and her feet pointed outward as she walked. The range of her rocking from side to side appeared almost greater than her movement forward. That's how bad she looked as she "ran" along. She had changed drastically since my days as an ox, but I knew who she was as soon as I laid eyes on her. I tried to recall how old Yingchun would be, but my pig consciousness overwhelmed my human consciousness, and as they merged they created mixed feelings: excitement and sorrow.

"Oh, my son, what's happened?" By looking through the gaps in the window, I saw her throw herself on the *kang*, weeping as she nudged Lan Jiefang.

The way his upper body was trussed up, he could hardly move, so he kept kicking the wall, which, not all that sturdy to begin with, seemed in danger of coming down; gray peelings like noodle dough floated to the ground. Chaos reigned in the room, until Hong Taiyue commanded:

"Get a rope and tie his legs!"

An old man named Lü Biantou, who also worked on the pig farm, dragged a length of rope up and climbed clumsily onto the *kang*. Lan Jiefang's legs were kicking out like the hooves of a wild horse, making it impossible for Lü to get the job done.

"I said tie them!" Hong bellowed.

So Lü pressed Jiefang's legs down with his body, but Yingchun immediately began tearing at his clothes and wailing, Let go of my son — Get up there, somebody, and help him! Hong shouted. You sons of bitches! Jiefang cried out. You're a bunch of pig sons of bitches — Pass the rope underneath! The third son of the Sun family burst into the room. Get up on that *kang* and give him a hand! The rope was wrapped around Jiefang's legs, but also around Lü Biantou's arms, and then tightened. Loosen the rope, and let me get my arms back! Jiefang kicked the rope loose; it twisted like a crazed snake. Ow, Mother . . . Lü Biantou reeled backward and banged into Hong on his way to the floor. The Sun boy, with the strength of youth, sat down on Jiefang's belly and, ignoring Yingchun's clawing and cursing, quickly tightened the rope and eliminated the possibility of Jiefang mounting any resistance. On the floor, Lü Biantou was holding his nose, dark blood oozing out between his fingers.

Son, I know you don't want to acknowledge any of this, but every word of what I've said is the unvarnished truth. When people are driven nearly mad, they are imbued with superhuman strength and are capable of almost supernatural deeds. That old apricot tree still has several egg-sized scars from injuries it sustained when you banged your head against it in a fit of rage. Under normal conditions, in any battle between a tree and a human head, the tree will win. But when they go a bit crazy, people's heads get harder. So when your head and the tree met, it wobbled and sent snowflakes fluttering to the ground. You, meanwhile, recoiled backward and landed on your backside. A knot swelled up on your forehead, but the poor tree lost a chunk of bark, exposing the whiteness underneath.

Bound hand and foot, you writhed and twisted in a mighty attempt to get free. So Baofeng gave you a sedative and you slowly relaxed, your eyes open but unfocused, sounds of sleep leaving your mouth and nose. The tension in the room dissolved. I breathed a sigh of relief. Now, Lan Jiefang, you're not my son, so whether you lived or died, whether you were crazy or just stupid, should have meant nothing to me. But I really did, I breathed a sigh of relief. After all, I concluded, you'd emerged from Yingchun's womb, and in a previous life, that womb had been my — that is, Ximen Nao's — property. The one I should have been concerned about was Ximen Jinlong, who was my son. With this thought in my head, I rushed over to the generator room, light blue moonlight on my shoulders. Apricot petals drifted to the ground like moonbeams. The whole grove of apricot trees trembled from the frenzied roar of the diesel motor. I heard the revitalized Yimeng pigs: some were talking in their sleep, others were whispering back and forth.

In the blindingly bright light of the naked two-hundred-watt bulb that lit up the generator I saw Ximen Jinlong on the brick floor, leaning against the wall with his legs stretched out in front of him, his feet pointing upward, drops of oil from the generator spraying onto his toenails and the backs of his feet, looking like sticky dog's blood. His shirt was open to expose a purple vest. His hair was uncombed, his eyes bloodshot, like a madman, yet sort of cool. He probably wanted to drink himself to death, because I saw an empty liquor bottle lying next to his leg and a half-empty bottle in his hand . . . and if the youngster didn't drink himself to death he'd surely drink himself stupid.

Mo Yan was standing beside him, squinting. "You've had enough, brother Jinlong," he said. "Secretary Hong is waiting to give you hell."

"Secretary Hong?" Jinlong looked up out of the corner of his eye. "Secretary Hong's a prick! I'll give *him* hell!"

"Brother," Mo Yan said wickedly, "Jiefang saw what you and Huzhu were doing up in the apricot tree and went nuts. A dozen strong young men tried but failed to restrain him. He actually bit through a thick steel rod. You should go see him. After all, he's your blood brother."

"My blood brother? Who are you talking about? You're the one who's his blood brother!"

"Whether you go see him or not is your business, Jinlong," Mo Yan said. "I've done my job by telling you."

But Mo Yan seemed in no hurry to leave. He kicked the bottle on the ground, then bent down and picked it up. He squinted and looked inside; seeing some green contents, he tipped his head back and drained it, then licked his lips noisily. "Good stuff," he said, "worthy of its name."

Jinlong raised the bottle in his hand and drank deeply. The room filled with the aroma of strong liquor as he flung the bottle at Mo Yan, who raised his bottle. When bottle met bottle, shards of exploding glass rained down to the ground. Now the aroma was stronger than ever. "Get lost!" Jinlong bellowed. "Get the hell out of here!" As Mo Yan backed up, Jinlong picked up a shoe, a screwdriver, and some other stuff, and threw them at him, one after the other. "You goddamn spy, you little prick, get out of my sight!" "You're crazy!" Mo Yan muttered as he dodged the missiles. "You've gone nuts before he even comes out of it!"

Jinlong stood up shakily and wobbled back and forth, like one of those tip-over dolls. The moment Mo Yan stepped out the door, the moonlight lit up his shaved head and turned it into a honeydew melon. I was watching the two weirdoes from my hiding place behind the tree, worried sick that Jinlong might fall onto the generator belt and be crushed. Fortunately, that didn't happen. Instead, he stepped over it, then stepped back. "Crazy!" he screamed. "Crazy! Everybody's gone goddamned crazy—" He picked up a broom from the corner and threw it out, then followed that with a tin bucket used for diesel oil, the smell of which spread beneath the moonlight and merged with the aroma of apricot blossoms. Jinlong stumbled over to the generator and bent down as if to engage the turbine in a conversation. Be careful, son! I shouted inwardly as my muscles tightened and I prepared to run over and rescue him if necessary. He was bent so low his nose was nearly touching the belt. Be careful, son! Another inch and you'll have no nose. But that tragedy didn't happen either. He put his hand on the throttle and pressed it all the way down. The generator screeched like a man when you squeeze his balls. The machine shuddered and sent oil flying in all directions. Black smoke poured out of the exhaust, while the bolts securing the generator to its wooden base began to shudder and seemed in danger of pulling loose altogether. At the same time, the needle on the power gauge shot past the danger mark and the high-wattage bulb above them lit up before it popped and sent slivers of glass flying into the wall and up to the rafters. I didn't know till later that when the bulb in the generator room blew, so did all the lights in the pig farm. The next thing I heard was the loud slap the belt made when it hit the wall, followed by Jinlong's terrified screams. My heart sank. That's it, I figured; my son, Ximen Jinlong was probably a goner.

Slowly the darkness gave way to the light of the moon and I saw Mo Yan, down on his hands and knees, rear end sticking up in the air, just like an ostrich; scared stiff, he slowly got to his feet. Curious but cowardly, virtually useless yet pigheaded, stupid and cunning at the same time, he was incapable of doing anything worthwhile and unwilling to do anything spectacularly bad; in other words, someone who was always causing trouble and forever complaining about his lot. I knew about all the scandals he'd been involved in and could pretty much read his mind. He slipped cautiously back into the moonlit generator room, where Ximen Jinlong was sprawled on the floor, striped by moonlight filtering in through the slats in the window. One of the moonbeams fell on his head, including his hair, of course, from which threads of blue-tinted blood seeped down across his face, like a millipede. Mo Yan bent down, mouth agape, and touched the wet, sticky blood with two fingers that were black as a pig's tail. First he examined it with his eyes, then with his nose, and finally with his mouth. What the hell was he doing? Whatever it was, it was strange, to say the least, so bizarre that even an intelligent pig like me couldn't figure it out. He couldn't tell if Ximen Jinlong was dead or alive just by looking at, smelling, or tasting his blood, could he? Or maybe this was his involved way of determining whether the blood on his fingers was real or fake. So there I was, trying to decipher his strange behavior, when, like someone who's just emerged from a nightmare, he screeched, then jumped high in the air and ran out of the generator room.

"Come over here, everybody! Ximen Jinlong's dead!" he shouted in a voice that sounded joyful.

Maybe he saw me hiding behind an apricot tree, maybe not. The moonlit trees and mottled leaves had a dizzying effect on people's eyes. The sudden death of Jinlong was probably the first and most noteworthy news he'd ever had the opportunity to spread. He had no interest in talking to the apricot trees as he ran, shouting at the top of his lungs. I started following him after he'd tripped on a pile of pig shit and fallen headfirst to the ground.

People emerged from the buildings, their faces taking on a pale hue in the moonlight. The absence of screams inside the room proved that the sedatives had taken effect on Jiefang. Baofeng was holding an alcohol-soaked pad of cotton to her cheek, which had been cut by flying glass when the lightbulb exploded. A faint scar would be left after the wound healed, living testimony to the unbelievable chaos of that night.

People came running, some stumbling along, some nearly falling, and all of them horribly flustered. In a word, a disorderly crowd ran toward the generator room, following Mo Yan, who kept turning sideways to describe with showy exaggeration what he'd seen. I had the feeling that whoever it was, whether Ximen Jinlong's kin or those with no familial ties to him, felt disgust toward the gabby youngster. Shut your filthy mouth! I took several quick steps and hid behind a tree, where I picked a piece of tile up out of the mud with my mouth — it was bigger than I wanted, so I bit it in two — grasped it in the cleft of my right front hoof, stood up humanlike on my hind legs, took aim at Mo Yan's shiny scalp, and flung the tile as I landed on my front legs. I miscalculated the distance, and instead of hitting Mo Yan, the missile struck Yingchun in the forehead. The loud crack froze my heart and awoke slumbering memories. Oh, Yingchun, my virtuous wife, tonight you are the unluckiest person on earth! Two sons, one of them mad, the other dead, a daughter with an injured face, and now I've nearly killed you!

Heartbroken, I let out a long *oink* and buried my snout in the ground, remorse driving me to chew the remaining half of the tile into powder. Like a scene from one of those high-speed movie cameras, I saw Yingchun's mouth open to release a scream like a silver snake dancing in the moonlight as she fell backward like a figurine. Don't think for a minute that just because I'm a pig I don't know what a high-speed camera is. Hell, these days anyone can be a film director! All you need is a light-filtering lens and a high-speed camera that you use to get a full shot or a closeup. The tile broke into pieces when it hit Yingchun's forehead and flew in all directions, followed immediately by drops of blood. Onlookers looked on in jaw-dropping astonishment. . . . Yingchun lay on the ground. Mom! Ximen Baofeng was shouting. She kneeled by her mother and laid her medical kit on the ground. With her right arm around Yingchun's neck, she studied the wound on her forehead. What happened, Mom? . . . Who did this? Hong Taiyue bellowed as he ran over to the spot where the tile had been launched. I didn't even try to hide, knowing I could disappear any time I wanted to. I had really messed up this time, no matter how good my intentions were, and I deserved to be punished. Hong Taiyue was the first to go looking for the rotten individual who had injured one of the villagers with a piece of tile, but he wasn't the one who discovered me standing behind the apricot tree. Getting on in years, he wasn't as sprightly as he'd once been. No, the first to come around the tree and find me was Mo Yan, whose stealthy movements perfectly matched his almost pathological curiosity. Here's who did it!

he gleefully announced to the swarm of people behind him. I sat there stiffly, a low guttural sound in my throat declaring my remorse and my readiness to receive the punishment I deserved. The puzzled looks on the people's faces showed up clear in the moonlight. He's the one, I guarantee it! Mo Yan said to the crowd. With my own eyes I once saw him write on the ground with a twig. Hong Taiyue thumped him on the shoulder.

"Old man," he mocked Mo Yan, "have you also seen him take a knife in his hoof and carve a seal for your dad, using the plum-blossom style of calligraphy?"

As someone who didn't know what was good for him, Mo Yan continued shooting off his mouth, so the third brother of the Sun family ran up and, like the bully he was, grabbed Mo Yan by the ear and kneed him in the rear end.

"Buddy," he said as he dragged him away from the scene, "keep that beak of yours shut!"

"Who let this boar out of its pen?" Hong Taiyue asked angrily. "Who's responsible for taking care of the pigs? Somebody has a terrible work ethic and ought to be docked some work points!"

Moving as fast as possible on her tiny, bound feet, Ximen Bai tottered up from the roadway, which was paved in moonlight, scattering apricot blossoms that looked like snowflakes as she came. Memories that had lain deep in the sediment of my mind were once again stirred up, like mud on a riverbed, and began squeezing my heart.

"Get that pig back in his pen!" Hong Taiyue growled. "This is ridiculous! Totally ridiculous!" With a phlegmatic cough he walked over to the generator room.

I think it must have been concern for her son that made it possible for Yingchun to come around so quickly; she struggled to stand. "Mom . . . ," Baofeng cried out as she put her arm under Yingchun's neck and opened her medical kit. Huang Huzhu, a look of detachment on her face, knew what to do: she picked up an alcohol-soaked cotton ball with a pair of tweezers and handed it to Baofeng. "My Jinlong . . ." Yingchun pushed Baofeng's arm away and propped herself up. Her movements were jerky, her balance precarious; clearly she was still lightheaded. But she stood and, with an agonizing cry on her lips, staggered off toward the generator room.

She was not the first to enter the room, nor was Hong Taiyue. Huang Huzhu beat them both. Next in was neither Yingchun nor

Hong; it was Mo Yan, who had already been badly treated by Sun Three and mocked by Hong Taiyue. None of that appeared to bother him, for after breaking free from Sun's grip, he slipped back into the generator room, no more than a step behind Huang Huzhu, who threw herself on Jinlong's body, like a mother protecting her offspring, the moment she spotted him lying there, bathed in moonlight, his forehead bloodied. Powerful feelings and sadness at what had befallen him drove all thoughts of modesty and decorum out of her mind.

At about the same time, Ximen Bai staggered up to me. As I looked into her sweaty face, I heard her gasp:

"Pig Sixteen, how did you get out of your pen?"

She patted me on the head. "Be good now and come back with me. Secretary Hong blamed me for letting you loose. You know I was a landlord's wife, not a good thing to be these days, and Secretary Hong has done me a favor by letting me tend to you. You mustn't act up, that will only bring me trouble!"

What a tangle of thoughts ran through my mind as tears welled up in my eyes and dripped to the ground.

"Are you crying, Pig Sixteen?" Surprised? Yes, she was. But also saddened. Stroking my ears, she looked up at the moon. "My husband," she said, "with Jinlong dead, the Ximen family has truly come to its end . . ."

Jinlong, of course, was not dead. If he'd died, the curtain would have fallen on this drama. Baofeng's medical skills brought him back from certain death, only to have him rant and rave, leaping and jumping, eyes bloodshot, wanting nothing to do with friends or family. "I don't want to live!" he shouted. "No more for me. . . ." He clutched his chest. "I feel terrible, I can't stand it, I want to die, Mother. . . ." Hong Taiyue stepped up, grabbed him by the shoulders and shook him. "Jinlong!" he roared. "What do you think you're doing? You call yourself a member of the Communist Party? The branch secretary of the Youth League? You disappoint me. You embarrass me!" Yingchun rushed up and pulled Hong's arms away, then stood between them. "I won't let you treat my son like that!" she threatened. Then she turned and threw her arms around Jinlong, who was a head taller than she, rubbed his face, and murmured, "Good boy, don't be afraid, Mother's here, she won't let them hurt you. . . ."

Jinlong pushed her away and forced the others, who tried to block his way, to back off; lowering his shoulder, he ran out. The moonlight settled on his arms like a blue curtain of gauze that gently laid him down on the ground, where he rolled around like an over-worked donkey. "Mother, I can't stand it, I want to die. Bring me two more bottles of liquor, two more bottles, two more . . ." "Is he crazy or is he drunk?" Hong asked Baofeng sternly. Her mouth twitched. "Drunk, I expect," she said with a sneer. With a look at Yingchun, Huang Tong, Qiuxiang, Hezuo, and Huzhu, Hong Taiyue could only shake his head, like a powerless father. He sighed. "You people have really let me down." He turned and walked off, swaying slightly, but instead of heading toward the village, he went into the apricot grove, leaving light blue footprints in the carpet of apricot petals.

Meanwhile, Jinlong was still donkey-rolling on the ground. "Go get some vinegar, Hezuo," Qiuxiang chirped, "and pour it down his throat. Do you hear me, Hezuo? Go home and get it." But Hezuo had her arms wrapped around an apricot tree and her face pressed up against the bark, until she nearly looked like an outgrowth of the tree itself. "Huzhu, you go then." But the girl's silhouette had blended with the distant moonbeams. Once Hong Taiyue had left, the crowd began to disperse. Even Baofeng, medical kit over her back, walked off. "Baofeng!" Yingchun cried out to her, "give your brother an injec-tion of something. All that alcohol will rot his insides . . ."

"Here's the vinegar," Mo Yan called out, holding a bottle in his hand. "I've got it." He was fast, really fast, and an eager helper. He was one of those youngsters who feels the rain as soon as he hears the wind. "I got the snack shop to open," he announced proudly, "and when the clerk asked me for money I said this was Secretary Hong's vinegar, so put it on his bill. He gave it to me without a word of protest."

It took some doing, but Sun Three finally managed to pin donkey-rolling Jinlong to the ground, though not without a struggle — teeth, feet, everything. Qiuxiang put the vinegar bottle up to his lips and began to pour. A peculiar sound tore from his throat, sort of like a roos-ter that has carelessly swallowed a poisonous bug. His eyes had rolled back in his head — unmistakably all white in the moonlight. "You heartless brat, you've killed my son!" Yingchun cried out as Huang Tong thumped Jinlong on the back, driving streams of sour, rank liquid out of his mouth and nose . . .

28

Hezuo Marries Jiefang against Her Will
Huzhu Is Happily Mated to Jinlong

Two months passed, and neither of the brothers, Lan Jiefang and Ximen Jinlong, was on the road to recovery. Something was wrong with the mental state of the Huang sisters as well. If Mo Yan's story is to be believed, Lan Jiefang's madness was real, Ximen Jinlong's was feigned. Feigning madness is like a red veil that masks shame; when worn, it effectively covers up all scandals. Once madness appears, what else is there to say? By then, the Ximen Village pig farm enjoyed a far-flung reputation. Taking advantage of the short break before the harvest began, the county administration organized another round of activities to observe and learn from the Ximen Village pig-raising experience. Residents from other counties would also be participating. At this critical moment in local history, Jinlong and Jiefang's madness effectively cut off both of Hong Taiyue's arms at the shoulder.

A telephone call from the Commune Revolutionary Committee informed him that a delegation from the Military District Logistics Department, accompanied by local and county officials, was on its way to observe and study. So Hong Taiyue called together the best minds of the village to devise ways of dealing with the situation. In Mo Yan's story, Hong suffered from fever blisters around the mouth and had eyes that were bloodshot day and night. He also wrote that you, Lan Jiefang, lay on your *kang* staring into space like a crocodile with severed nerves and frequently weeping, muddy tears falling like condensation from the rim of a pig-feed wok. Meanwhile, Jinlong sat in the next room, looking transfixed, like a chicken that's barely survived poisoning. He looked up each time someone entered the room and giggled like an idiot.

According to Mo Yan, as the leaders of the Ximen Village Production Brigade were bemoaning their anticipated fate, feeling utterly helpless, he entered the scene with a plan. But it would be a mistake to take him at his word, since his stories are filled with foggy details and speculation, and should be used for reference only.

Mo Yan wrote that when he walked into the room where the meeting was being held, Huang Tong tried to bum-rush him back outside. But rather than leave, he jumped into the air and landed on the edge of the conference table in a seated position, his stumpy legs swinging back and forth like loofah gourds on a trellis. Panther Sun, who by then had been promoted to captain of the local militia and head of security, jumped to his feet and grabbed Mo Yan by the ear. Hong Taiyue waved Sun off.

"Have you gone mad too, young man?" Hong mocked Mo Yan. "I wonder what kind of feng shui this village has to produce a great citizen like you."

"I am not crazy," Mo Yan wrote in his infamous "Tales of Pig-Raising." "My nerves are as thick and tough as gourd vines, which won't break even when supporting a dozen gourds that swing back and forth in the wind. The rest of the world can go mad, and I'll keep my sanity." He added humorously: "But your two esteemed members have lost their sanity, and I know that's what's got you all scratching your heads, like a bunch of monkeys trapped in a well."

"That's exactly what has us concerned," Mo Yan wrote. "Hong Taiyue said, 'We're worse off even than monkeys. We're like a bunch of donkeys stuck in the mud. What can you do to help us, Mr. Mo Yan?' " Mo Yan's story continued:

> With his hands clasped in front of his chest, Hong Taiyue bowed like an enlightened lord showing respect to a smart man, though his intention was to ridicule me, to mock me. The best way to deal with ridicule and mockery is to feign ignorance and turn the so-called wit into a matter of playing a zither to an ox or singing to a pig. So I pointed a finger at the bulging pocket in the tunic Hong had worn for at least five winters and six summers without coming in contact with soap and water. "What?" Hong asked as he looked down at his pocket. "Cigarettes," I said. "You've got a pack of cigarettes in your pocket. Amber brand." In those days Amber cigarettes cost as much as the renowned Front Gates, thirty-nine cents a

pack, and even a commune Party secretary smoked them sparingly. Thanks to me, Secretary Hong was forced to pass them around. "Don't tell me you have X-ray vision, young fellow. Your talents are undervalued here in Ximen Village." I smoked one of his cigarettes, just like a longtime smoker, blowing three smoke rings and linking them with a smoke pillar. "I know you all think I'm beneath contempt," he said, "seeing me as no smarter than a dog fart. Well, I'm eighteen years old, an adult, and while I'm small and have a baby face, no one in Ximen Village is as smart as me."

"Is that so?" Hong said with a smile as he glanced around the table. "I didn't know you had reached the age of eighteen, and certainly didn't know of your superior intelligence." That was met by laughter all around.

Mo Yan continued:

So I kept smoking and said, with impeccable logic, that Jinlong and Jiefang's unbalanced state came as a result of emotional disturbances. No medicine can cure that. Only ancient exorcisms will work. You must arrange marriages between Jinlong and Huzhu and Jiefang and Hezuo, what people call a 'health and happiness' wedding, but more accurately a 'health through happiness' wedding to drive away evil spirits.

I see no need to debate whether or not it was Mo Yan who made the weddings between you brothers and the Huang sisters possible, but there's no disputing that they occurred on the same day, and I personally witnessed them both from start to finish. Sure, they were hastily arranged, but Hong Taiyue assumed the responsibility of seeing that everything ran smoothly, and that what was normally considered a private affair became public. By mobilizing the talents of the village women, he ensured that it would be both a festive and a solemn event.

The weddings took place on the sixteenth day of the fourth lunar month that year, under a full moon that was unusually bright and hung low in the sky, seemingly reluctant to leave the apricot grove, almost as if it had shown up in honor of the weddings.

When the moon was at its height it looked down on me with cool detachment. I blew it a kiss and hightailed it to the row of eighteen buildings on the northern edge of the pig farm, near the main village road. That was where the pig tenders lived and where the animal feed was mixed, cooked, and stored; the buildings also housed the farm offices and the farm honor room. The three westernmost rooms were reserved for the two sets of newlyweds, the middle room to be used jointly, the outer rooms for their private use. In his short story Mo Yan wrote:

"Wash basins filled with cucumbers with oil fritters and oil fritters with radishes had been placed on the ten tables set up in the spacious room. A lantern hanging from a rafter lit the room up bright as snow. . . ."

More trumped-up nonsense. The room was no more than twelve by fifteen, so how could they have fit ten tables in it? Nowhere in Northeast Gaomi Township, let alone Ximen Village, was there a hall that could accommodate ten tables set for a hundred dinner guests.

The truth is, the wedding dinner was held in the narrow strip of open land in front of that row of buildings. Rotting limbs and branches and moldy grass and weeds were piled up at the far end of the strip of land, where weasels and hedgehogs had set up housekeeping. The reception required one table, the rosewood table with carved edges that normally sat in the brigade office; that's where the wind-up telephone rested, along with two bottles of dried-up ink and a kerosene lamp with its glass shade. Later on, the table was taken over by Ximen Jinlong during his heyday — something that Hong Taiyue characterized as the tyrannical act of a landlord's son to settle old scores with the lower and middle poor peasants — and wound up in his bright office to become a family heirloom. Hey! That son of mine, I don't know if I ought to pat him on the back or kick him in the pants — Okay, okay, I'll leave that for later.

They carried out twenty black-topped double-student tables with yellow legs from the elementary school. The tabletops were covered with red and blue ink stains and dirty words cut in with knives. Also moved out of the school building were forty benches painted red. The tables were laid out in two rows, the benches in four, turning the strip of land into what looked like a site for an outdoor classroom. There were no gas lanterns or electric lights, just a single tinplate hurricane lantern in the center of Ximen Nao's rosewood desk, which put out a murky yellow light, attracting hordes of moths that threw themselves noisily into the shade. Truth is, there was no need for the lantern, since the moon was so close to earth that night, its light bright enough for women to do embroidery.

Roughly a hundred people — men, women, old, and young — sat on opposite sides in four rows of tables weighted down with good food and fine liquor, the looks on their faces a mixture of excitement and anxiety. They couldn't eat, not yet, because Hong Taiyue was holding forth from behind the tables. Some of the younger — and hungrier — children sneaked bits of oil fritters when no one was looking.

"Comrade Commune Members, tonight we are celebrating the marriages of Lan Jinlong and Huang Huzhu and Lan Jiefang and Huang Hezuo, outstanding youth of the Ximen Village Production Brigade who made great contributions to the construction of our pig farm. They are model revolutionary workers and models for our program of late marriages, so let's congratulate them with a round of applause. . . ."

I was hiding behind the pile of rotting wood, quietly watching the ceremony. Jinlong and Huzhu sat on benches to the left of the tables, Jiefang and Hezuo to the right. Huang Tong and Qiuxiang sat at the end closest to me, so all I could see were their backs. The place of honor, at the far end, was where Hong Taiyue, the speaker, stood. Yingchun sat with her head down, making it impossible to tell if she was happy or sad. Seeing her with mixed emotions at this moment struck me as perfectly reasonable, and that was when it dawned on me that one very important individual was missing at the head table. Who? Why, Northeast Gaomi Township's celebrated independent farmer, of course, Lan Lian. He was, after all, your biological father, Jiefang, and Jinlong's nominal father. Jinlong's formal surname was Lan, after your father. How could a father not be present when both his sons are to be married?

During my days as a donkey and an ox, I was in almost daily contact with Lan Lian. But after I returned as a pig, my old friend and I were estranged. Thoughts of the past flooded my mind, and the desire to see Lan Lian again began to sprout. As Hong Taiyue was nearing the end of his speech, three riders rode up to the banquet on their bicycles, preceded by the ringing of bells. Who were these people? One had once been in charge of the Supply and Marketing Co-op, but was now director and Party secretary of Cotton Processing Plant Number Five, Pang Hu. Accompanying him was his wife, Wang

Leyun, someone I hadn't seen in years. She had gotten so fat, all the curves had disappeared. Her face was ruddy, the skin glossy, testimony to the good life. The third rider, a young tall, svelte young woman, I recognized immediately as Pang Kangmei, a character in one of Mo Yan's stories, the girl who nearly came into the world in some roadside weeds. Wearing her hair in two short braids, she had on a red-checked shirt on which was pinned a white badge with "Farm Academy" in red letters. Pang Kangmei was a student specializing in animal husbandry at the "Farm Academy" attached to the Workers, Peasants, and Soldiers University. Standing straight as a poplar tree, she was half a head taller than her father and a whole head taller than her mother. She wore a reserved smile. She had every reason to look reserved: any young woman born into a family of such envious social status was as unattainable as the Lady in the Moon. As Mo Yan's dream girl, she appeared in much of his fiction, a long-legged beauty whose name changed from story to story. All three members of the family had made a special trip to attend your wedding.

"Congratulations! Congratulations!" Pang Hu and Wang Leyun said with broad smiles, offering their best wishes to all.

"Oh, my, oh, my." Hong Taiyue interrupted his speech and jumped down off of the bench he was standing on. He ran up and enthusiastically shook Pang Hu's hand. "Director Pang," he blurted out emotionally, "no, what I mean is, Secretary Pang, Manager Pang, you honor us with your presence! We heard you'd assumed factory leadership and we didn't wish to disturb you."

"Old Hong, I thought we were friends," Pang Hu said with a laugh. "Holding a momentous wedding in the village without letting us know. You weren't afraid I'd come and drink up all the wedding liquor, were you?"

"Not at all. We were afraid that such an honored guest wouldn't come even if we sent an eight-man sedan chair to bring you here. For Ximen Village, your presence here today—"

"Your gracious presence lends glitter to our humble surroundings," Mo Yan proclaimed loudly from his seat at the end of the first row, a comment that not only caught the attention of Pang Hu, but of his daughter, Kangmei, as well. Raising her eyebrows in surprise, she fixed Mo Yan with a piercing stare at the same time as the other guests turned to look at him. He grinned complacently, revealing a row of golden yellow teeth. That's the best I can do to describe the strange sight he presented as he jumped at yet another opportunity to show off.

Pang Hu removed his hand from Hong Taiyue's grip and, along with the other hand, reached out to Yingchun. The hardened hands of this grenade-throwing war hero had softened over years of a more genteel life, and Yingchun, flustered and moved, but clearly grateful for the gesture, just stood there, her lips quivering, unable to speak. Pang Hu took her hands, shook them warmly, and said, "How happy you must be!"

"Happy, happy, everybody's happy . . . ," Yingchun managed to mutter through her tears.

"Happy together, happy together!" Mo Yan interjected.

"Why isn't Lan Lian here, ma'am?" Pang Hu's gaze swept past the two rows of tables.

The question tied Yingchun's tongue in knots and thoroughly embarrassed Hong Taiyue. An ideal opportunity for Mo Yan to speak up again.

"He's probably taking advantage of the bright moonlight to till his one-point-six acres of land."

Panther Sun, who was sitting next to Mo Yan, must have stepped on Mo Yan's foot. "Why'd you do that?" he screamed with patent excess.

"Shut that stinking mouth of yours. No one would mistake you for a mute," Sun said menacingly, keeping his voice down. He reached down and pinched Mo Yan on the thigh, drawing a loud screech and turning his face white.

"Okay, enough of that," Pang Hu said to break the awkwardness. He then gave his best wishes to the four newlyweds. Jinlong wore a silly smile, Jiefang seemed to be about to cry, Huzhu and Hezuo displayed indifferent looks. Pang Hu turned to his wife and daughter: "Bring the wedding gifts."

"I can't believe this, Secretary Pang," Hong Taiyue said. "You've already lent glitter to our humble surroundings by your gracious presence, and there was no need to go to any additional expense."

Pang Kangmei held a framed mirror with the dedication in red "Congratulations to Lan Jinlong and Huang Huzhu in becoming a revolutionary couple" in one corner. The mirror was decorated with a drawing of Chairman Mao in a long gown, bundle in hand, as he encouraged miners to rebel in the city of Anyuan. Wang Leyun held up a similar framed mirror with the same dedication, with "Lan Jiefang and Huang Hezuo" replacing the other names, in red in the corner. The inlaid photograph was of Chairman Mao in a woolen overcoat standing on the beach at the resort city of Beidaihe. Jinlong or Jiefang ought to have stood up to receive the gifts, but they sat there as if glued to their seats, making it necessary for Hong Taiyue to urge Huzhu and Hezuo to go up in their stead, since they appeared to be reasonably alert. After taking the mirror, Huang Huzhu bowed deeply to Wang Leyun, and when she looked up there were tears in her eyes. She was wearing a red top over red pants, her thick black braid falling all the way to her knees, bound at the end with a red bow. Wang Leyun reached out and touched the braid with tender affection. "You must hate the idea of cutting it off, I guess," she said.

At last the opportunity presented itself for Wu Qiuxiang to speak up. "It's not that, ma'am. My daughter's hair is different from other girls'. If she cut it, blood would seep from it."

"How strange," Wang said. "But now I know why it felt sort of fleshy when I touched it. There must be capillaries running through it."

Hezuo refrained from bowing when she took the mirror from Pang Kangmei. She merely thanked her modestly. Kangmei offered her hand in friendship. "I wish you every happiness," she said as Hezuo took the hand, turned her head, and said through her tears, "Thank you."

In my view, her fashionable hairstyle, her slim waist, and her dark skin made Hezuo prettier than Huzhu, and with her you got better than you deserved, Jiefang. She's the one who ought to feel cheated, not you. With that blue birthmark, you could be the best person in the world and you'd still scare the hell out of anyone who saw you. Where you belong is down in the bowels of hell as one of Lord Yama's attendants, not here on earth as an official. But you made it, you became an official, and you felt that Hezuo was beneath you. Everything about this world befuddles me, I'll tell you that.

Once that was behind them, Hong Taiyue made room at the table for Pang Hu and his family. "You," he said sternly, pointing to where Mo Yan was sitting, "scoot over and free up some space for our guests." A bit of chaos ensued, punctuated with complaints from the dislodged guests.

Once the new arrivals were seated, the wedding guests, eager to start eating, jumped to their feet and noisily raised their glasses in a toast. Then they sat down, some quicker than others, picked up their chopsticks, and took aim on the morsels of food they'd had their eyes on all along. Compared to cucumbers and turnips, the oil sticks were considered gourmet food, which led inevitably to momentous clashes of chopsticks above the tables. Mo Yan's greedy mouth had a well-deserved reputation, but his behavior that night was uncharacteristically subdued and genteel. Why? We needn't look beyond Pang Kangmei. Though he'd been banished to the far end of the table, his heart remained stuck on the head table. He kept looking that way, now that the college student Pang Kangmei had snared his soul, as he wrote in one of his stupid essays:

> From the moment I laid eyes on Pang Kangmei my heart grew. The ones I'd always thought were fairylike beauties — Huzhu, Hezuo, and Baofeng — in that instant became unimaginably common. Only by leaving Northeast Gaomi Township was it possible to find girls like Pang Kangmei, tall and slender, with beautiful features, nice white teeth, lovely voices, and bodies that gave off a subtle perfume. . . .

Well, Mo Yan wound up getting drunk — one glass did it — so Panther Sun picked him up by the scruff of the neck and deposited him in the pile of grass and weeds, not far from where the pig bones had been dumped. Back at the head table, Jinlong guzzled half a glassful, and life returned to his eyes. Out of motherly concern, Yingchun muttered, "You shouldn't drink so much, son." And then there was Hong Taiyue, who, having thought things out carefully, said, "Jinlong, it's time to put a period to all that's happened in the past. Your new life begins today, and I expect you to sing well for me in all the shows to come." To which Jinlong replied, "Over the past two months, I've experienced mental blockage that has blurred my thinking. But I've come to my senses, and the blockage has disappeared." He offered his glass in a toast to Pang Hu and his wife: "Secretary Pang, Aunty Wang, thank you for coming to my wedding and for a gift we'll treasure." Then he turned to Pang Kangmei. "Comrade Kangmei, you are a college student, an advanced intellectual. We welcome your views of our work here on the pig farm. Please don't hold anything back. As someone who studies animal husbandry, if you don't know something, no one on earth does." Jinlong's feigned madness and crazy actions had run their course. The same would be true of Jiefang's madness in short order. Now that Jinlong had recovered the ability to control events, he went around toasting all the people he ought to have toasted, thanked all those who deserved it, and, finally and perhaps unnecessarily, held out his glass to Hezuo and Jiefang, wishing them happiness and a long life together. Hezuo thrust the mirror with the inlaid drawing of Chairman Mao into Jiefang's lap, stood up, and held out her glass with both hands. The moon abruptly rose high in the sky, shrinking in size as it cast quicksilver beams that put everything below in stark relief. Weasels' heads emerged from the weeds as they marveled over the unusual light; bold hedgehogs scurried among the legs under the tables in their search for food. What occurred next happened in less time than it takes to tell about it. Hezuo flung the contents of her glass into Jinlong's face and then threw the empty glass down on the table. Shock registered on everyone's face over this unforeseen turn of events. The moon jumped even higher in the sky, blanketing the ground with quicksilver beams. Hezuo covered her face and burst into tears.

Huang Tong: "That girl . . . ?"

Qiuxiang: "Hezuo, what was that all about?"

Yingchun: "Oh, you foolish youngsters."

Hong Taiyue: "Secretary Pang, to your health." He raised his glass. "A little disagreement, that's all. I hear you're looking for contract workers at the processing plant. I can speak up for Hezuo and Jiefang. A change of scenery would do them good. They're both outstanding youngsters who deserve the chance to toughen up a bit—"

Huzhu picked up the glass in front of her and flung the contents at her sister. "What did you think you were doing?"

I'd never seen Huang Huzhu so angry, had never even imagined she knew how to be angry. She took out a handkerchief to dry Jinlong's face. He pushed her hand away, but she brought it up to him again. I tell you, I was a smart pig, but the girls of Ximen Village turned my brain to mush that day. Meanwhile, Mo Yan had crawled out of the weeds and, like a boy with springs tied to the soles of his feet, bounced unsteadily up to the table, where he picked up a glass, held it high over his head, and, like a poet — maybe Li Bai and maybe Qu Yuan — shouted crisply:

"Moon, Moon, I salute you!"

Mo Yan splashed the liquor in his glass in the direction of the moon; it spread out in the air like a green curtain and the moon abruptly dropped low in the sky, then floated gently upward to its normal height, where, like a silver plate, it cast indifferent rays down on the world.

Down below, now that the festivities had ended, the people began drifting away. There was still plenty to do that night; no time to waste. Me? I felt like going to see my old friend Lan Lian, who, I knew, was in the habit of working his land on moonlit nights. I thought back to my days as an ox and what he once said to me: Ox, the sun is theirs, the moon is ours, and I can find my land from the surrounding commune land with my eyes closed. The one-point-six acres of land are a reef, a strip of private land that will never sink in the vast ocean. Lan Lian had gained a provincewide reputation as a negative model, and I felt honored to have served him as a donkey and an ox, glory to the reactionary. "Only claiming the land as one's own allows us to be masters of the land."

Before going out to see Lan Lian, I passed stealthily by my pen, making no noise at all. A pair of militiamen were sitting under an apricot tree smoking and eating apricots, and to avoid them I hopped from one patch of shade to another, feeling light as a swallow, and exited the grove after only about a dozen hops, where my way was blocked by an irrigation ditch roughly five yards across and filled with clear water, the surface as smooth as glass. I was being observed by the moon's reflection. Now I'd never tried to swim, not since the day I was born, but instinct told me that I knew how. But not wanting to frighten the moon, I decided to leap across the ditch. I stepped back ten yards or so, took several deep breaths to fill my lungs, and took off running, heading at full speed toward a ridge that showed up white, an ideal launching pad. The moment my front hooves touched the hard-packed earth, I sprang forward with my rear legs and lifted off, as if shot out of a cannon. My belly was cooled by a breeze that hugged the surface of the water; the moon winked as I passed overhead, just before landing on the opposite bank.

I saw him. He was wearing a jacket made of local fabric with a button-down front, a white cloth sash around his waist, and a conical hat woven of sorghum stalks that hid most of his face from view, but not the luminous blue half or the intensely sad yet unyielding light in his eyes. He was waving a long bamboo pole with a piece of red cloth tied to the end, like the swishing tail of an ox, driving the egg-laying tussock moths away from his wheat stalks and onto the cotton plants or cornstalks belonging to the production brigade. Reduced to using this clumsy primitive method to protect his crops, it appeared as if he was doing battle with destructive insects, when in fact the real foe was the People's Commune. Old friend, back when I was a donkey and then when I was an ox, I shared your comforts and your hardships; but now I'm a People's Commune stud boar, and I can't help you. I thought about relieving myself in your field to supply you with some organic fertilizer, but what if you stepped in it? Wouldn't that turn a good deed into a bad one? I could bite through the People's Commune cornstalks or uproot all their cotton plants, but that won't do you any good, since they aren't your enemy either. Old friend, keep at it, don't waver. You are China's sole independent farmer, so don't forget, perseverance is victory. I looked up at the moon; the moon nodded at me and then leaped into the western sky. It was getting late, time for me to head back. But I'd no sooner started out through the wheat field than I spotted Yingchun hurrying my way with a rattan basket. The wheat tassels rustled when they brushed her hips as she passed by. The look on her face was that of a wife who is late delivering food to her husband as he labors in the field. Though they lived apart, they hadn't divorced. And though they hadn't divorced, the joys of the bedroom were denied them. Deep down I felt good about that. As a pig, I shouldn't have given a damn one way or the other where human sex was concerned, but after all, I'd been her husband when I walked the earth as Ximen Nao. The distinct aroma of liquor emanating from her hung in the chilled farmland air. She stopped when she was no more than a couple of yards from Lan Lian to look at his slightly hunched back as, with great agility, he fanned away the moths with his bamboo pole. Back and forth it waved, whistling in the wind. Their wings weighted down by dew, their bellies heavy with eggs, the moths flew awkwardly. I'm sure he knew he was being watched, and probably guessed it was Yingchun, but instead of stopping, he merely slowed down the pace of his waving.

"Children's father . . ." Finally she spoke.

The pole stopped in midair after a couple more swings. Like a scarecrow, he just stood there without moving.

"The children are married. We needn't worry any longer," Ying-chun said. Then she sighed. "I've brought you a bottle of liquor. Whatever else he may be, he's still your son."

Lan Lian made a grunting sound and swung the pole back and forth twice.

"Director Pang brought his wife and daughter to the banquet and presented both couples with framed mirrors inlaid with images of Chairman Mao." Raising her voice slightly, she said emotionally, "Director Pang has been promoted to head of a cotton processing plant, and he's agreed to give jobs to Jiefang and Hezuo. It was Secretary Hong's idea. Jinlong, Baofeng, and Jiefang have been treated well by Secretary Hong, who is a good man. Don't you think we should comply with his wishes?"

The pole waved violently in the air, snagging some flying moths in the red cloth; with loud chirps they crashed to the ground.

"Okay, I shouldn't have said anything. Don't be angry. Do as you wish. By now everyone's used to what you're doing. This is, after all, our sons' wedding day, and I've come out here in the middle of the night so you can drink some of the wedding liquor. I'll leave after that."

Yingchun took a bottle out of her basket; it sparkled in the moonlight. After removing the cork, she walked up and handed it to him from behind.

The pole stopped again. He stood frozen to the spot. I saw tears glisten in his eyes as he rested the pole on his shoulder and tipped back his hat to gaze at the moon, which, naturally, looked down sadly at him. He took the bottle, but didn't turn his head.

"Maybe you're right, all of you, maybe I'm the only one who's wrong. But I made a vow, and if I'm wrong, then that's how I'll end up."

"After Baofeng is married," Yingchun said, "I'll leave the commune and stay with you."

"No, independent farming means doing it alone. I don't need anybody else. I have nothing against the Communist Party and I definitely have nothing against Chairman Mao. I'm not opposed to the People's Commune or to collectivization. I just want to be left alone to work for myself. Crows everywhere in the world are black. Why can't there be at least one white one? That's me, a white crow!" He splashed some of the liquor up toward the moon and, in a voice as rousing, as stirring, and as desolate as I've ever heard, cried out, "Moon, you've accompanied me in my labors all these years, you're a lantern sent to me by the Old Man in the Sky. I've tilled the soil by your light, I've sown seeds by your light, and I've brought in harvests by your light. . . . You say nothing, you are never angry or resentful, and I'm forever in your debt. So tonight permit me to drink to you as an expression of my gratitude. Moon, I've troubled you for so long!"

The colorless liquor dispersed in the air like pearls tinged with blue. The moon trembled slightly and winked at Lan Lian. I can't remember being so moved by anything. In an age when throngs of people sang the praises of the sun, it was unheard of for someone to hold such deep feelings for the moon. Lan Lian poured the last few drops of the liquor into his mouth, then held the bottle up over his shoulder.

"Okay," he said, "you can go now."

With a wave of his pole, he started walking. Yingchun got down on her knees, brought her hands together, and raised them to the moon, which shone down gently on her dancing tears, her graying hair, and her quivering lips . . .

In the face of this mutual love, I stood up in total disregard of the possible consequences, for I believed they would know in their hearts who I was and would not take me as some sort of monster. Supporting my front hooves on the springy tops of wheat stalks, I walked up to them along one of the field ridges. Clasping my hooves together, I bowed to them and made a pig noise to greet them. They gaped at me, blank looks that held shock and puzzlement. I am Ximen Nao, I said. I distinctly heard human sounds emerge from my throat, but there was no reaction from them. After what seemed like a long time, Yingchun shrieked, while Lan Lian pointed his pole at me and said:

"Pig demon, kill me if that's what you want, but I beg you, please don't trample my crops."

Crippling sadness suddenly filled my heart. Humans and beasts walk down separate roads that virtually never intersect. Lowering myself down on all fours, I fled through the wheat field, crestfallen. But my mood improved the closer I came to Apricot Garden. All creatures on earth follow their own nature. Birth, old age, sickness, and death; joys and sorrows, partings and reunions, are dictated by irreversible objective laws. I was a boar at the time, so I had to carry out my boar responsibilities. Lan Lian stuck by his obstinacy to remain apart from the masses, so it was necessary for me, Pig Sixteen, to use my great intelligence, extreme courage, and extraordinary physical abilities to accomplish something that would stun the world, and crowd my piggish way into human history.

After entering Apricot Garden, I pretty much put Lan Lian and Yingchun out of my mind. Why? Because I saw that Diao Xiaosan had already seduced Butterfly Lover and had her hot to trot. Of the other twenty-nine sows, fourteen had already escaped from their pens, while the remaining fifteen were either banging their heads against the gates or crying to the moon. A grand prologue to mating was slowly opening. Before the major player had made his appearance, his understudy was already onstage. Damn him! I wouldn't allow it.

29

Pig Sixteen Battles Diao Xiaosan
The Straw Hat Song Accompanies a Loyalty Dance

Diao Xiaosan sat with his back against the renowned apricot tree, holding an upturned straw hat filled with yellow apricots. One after another, he picked them up with his right hoof and tossed them into his mouth, smacking his lips as he ate the fruit and then spit out the pits, which landed several yards away. Resting under a skinny apricot tree separated some four or five yards from Diao Xiaosan, Butterfly Lover held a broken plastic comb in one hand and a hand mirror in the other, putting on flirtatious, coquettish airs. Ah, dear sow, your weakness is coveting petty gains. A tiny mirror and a broken comb, and you would take any boar to bed. Every so often Diao threw one of his apricots over to where the dozen or so sows that had escaped from their pens were glancing longingly in his direction and oinking suggestively. They fought over every one. Little Brother, don't hanker only after Butterfly Lover, we love you too and we'd be happy to help you carry on your line. The sows teased him with the most suggestive language they knew. The thought of obtaining a wife and a harem made him deliriously happy, as if floating on air. After shaking his legs, he began to hum a little tune and, hat in hand, danced a jig. The sows joined in, some twirling in place and others rolling on the ground. The wretched quality of their dancing aroused feelings of contempt in me. Butterfly Lover laid her mirror and comb down at the base of the tree and began wiggling her bottom, setting her tail in motion as she sidled over to Diao Xiaosan. As soon as she was near enough, she dropped her head and raised her hindquarters. With that in sight, I leaped into the air like an antelope out on the Serengeti and landed in the space between Butterfly Lover and Diao Xiaosan. Now they could only dream about the joy they nearly made a reality.

My appearance on the scene threw cold water on Butterfly Lover's burning desire. She turned and retreated back to the skinny apricot tree, where she put her purple tongue to work picking up wormy red apricot leaves that had fallen to the ground and curling them into her mouth. She chewed the fruit with gusto. Fickleness and a tendency to change their mind whenever they saw something new was part of the sows' nature, so they could hardly be blamed for doing what came naturally. That in itself guaranteed that supplying sperm with the finest genes to merge with their eggs in the womb was the way to produce superior offspring. That logic is so simple even pigs understand it, so how could a boar with the intelligence of Diao Xiaosan not? He flung his straw hat at me along with the remaining apricots.

"You spoiled my fun, you son of a bitch!" he cursed angrily.

I jumped out of the way and, with a good eye and quick hoof, snatched up the hat by its brim, and reared back until I was standing up straight. Holding my free hoof up in the air, I spun around and, with the gathered momentum, flung the hat and its apricot contents like a discus thrower. The golden yellow hat curved in a beautiful arc on its way to the moon. Suddenly, the strains of a moving straw hat song filled the air above us: *La-la-la — La-ya la-la-ya-la — Mama's straw hat is flying la — Mama's straw hat is flying to the moon — La-ya la-la-ya-la —* The sows under the tree were joined in song by hundreds of pigs in the farm; some jumped out of their pens, while those that lacked the ability stood up with their hooves on the walls, and all of them gazed up at the moon. I settled back down on all fours and said calmly, yet decisively:

"Old Diao, I did what I did to ensure that the generations of pigs to come are produced by the finest genes, not to spoil your fun."

Once again I raised up on my hind legs and charged him; he reacted by charging me, and we crashed into each other — snout to snout — five or six feet above the ground. I not only got a firsthand sensation of how hard his snout was, but also got a whiff of the sickly sweet odor in his mouth. My snout ached and a song was echoing in my ears as I hit the ground. I was on my feet after a quick somersault. I rubbed my nose with a hoof, which came away stained with drops of blue blood.

"You motherfucker!" I cursed under my breath.

Diao Xiaosan also somersaulted himself back onto his feet and rubbed his nose. His hoof also came away stained with drops of blue blood. "You motherfucker!" he cursed under his breath.

La-la-la — La-ya la-la-ya-la — I've lost the straw hat Mama gave me — The straw-hat song swirled in the air, the moon rolled back toward me and stopped directly overhead, where it rose and fell like a flying boat being tossed about by wind currents. The straw hat circled it gracefully, like a satellite to the moon. *La-ya-la — La-ya la-la-ya-la — Mama's straw hat is lost —* Some of the pigs smacked their front hooves together, some stomped their rear hooves on the ground, rhythmically, as they sang the straw hat song.

I picked up an apricot leaf, chewed it, then spit it out into my hoof and stuffed it up my bloody nose. Now I was ready for the next assault. I saw that Diao was bleeding from both nostrils, blue blood that dripped to the ground, where each drop shone like a will-o'-the-wisp. Deep down I was happy. The first round had produced no victor and no vanquished, although I knew I held the advantage, since only one of my nostrils was bleeding, not both. Diao's eyes rolled furtively, almost as if he were searching for an apricot leaf. I guess you'd like to stuff leaves up your nose, too, pal, is that it? Well, I'm not giving you the chance. With a loud battle oink, I flashed him a piercing glare and flexed every muscle in my body, concentrating all my power into one mighty leap.

This time, instead of leaping into the air, the sly devil slithered along the ground, and I just sailed through the air, all the way to the canopy of the crooked apricot tree. I immediately heard a series of loud cracks, just before I crashed to the ground, headfirst, carrying a thick forked limb down with me. A quick somersault and I was back on my feet again, but dizzy as can be and my mouth full of mud. *La-la-la — La-ya la-la-ya-la —* The sows clapped their hooves and sang. They were not my fans. Too easily swayed, they were ready to raise their bottoms to accept whoever came out on top. Conquest makes you the king. Diao Xiaosan, extremely pleased with himself, stood up on his hind legs and bowed in the direction of the huddled sows. He blew them a kiss. Despite the fact that dirty blood was still dripping from his nose and despite the fact that the blood had badly soiled his chest, the sows raised a chorus of cheers. That made him even more pleased with himself. Taking large, confident strides, he walked up next to me, grabbed the broken, fruit-laden limb with his teeth, and pulled it out from under my hindquarters. The insolent bastard! But I was still dizzy. *La-la-la — La-ya la-la-ya-la —* I just let my eyes follow him as he dragged the fruit-laden limb out from under me and backed away. He rested a few seconds before continuing on his way. The limb made a scraping noise as it scratched the surface of the ground. *La-la-la — La-ya la-la-ya-la — Little Brother, aren't you something!—* I was furious and itched to charge him again, but I was still too dizzy to do anything. Diao Xiaosan dragged the limb up to Butterfly Lover and stood up on his hind legs. He then took a step backward with his right leg, bent over at the waist, and held out his right front hoof, like a white-gloved gentleman. With a half-circle sweep of the hoof, he said, For you, young lady . . . *La-ya la-la-ya-la —* Turning to the dozen sows and the castrated boars farther off, he waved them over. With a chorus of joyful oinks, they converged on the limb, quickly tearing it apart. A couple of the bolder males made an attempt to sidle up to the apricot tree, and so I stood up. I saw a sow strutting proudly away with a heavily laden branch she'd managed to get away with, her big, floppy ears slapping her cheeks. Diao Xiaosan walked around blowing kisses until a sinister-looking castrato stuck his front hooves in his mouth and sent a loud whistle knifing through the air. The pigs all quieted down.

I fought to compose myself, knowing that in a contest of raw courage I'd suffer a humiliating defeat. That I could live with, somehow, but not the loss of a wife and harem to Diao Xiaosan, because in another five months, the farm would be increased by several hundred new pigs — long-nosed, pointy-eared little monsters. I made my tail twitch and shook out my limbs; I spit out the mud in my mouth and, while I was at it, scooped up some apricots that blanketed the ground, nearly all of which had fallen to the ground when I hit the tree — ripe, sweet, honeyed. *La-ya-la — La-ya la-la-yala — Mama's straw hat is flying around the moon, changing from a golden color to a silvery one —* Chewing and swallowing several apricots calmed me down and soothed my mouth and throat. And so, seeing no need for anxiety, I slowly ate my fill. I watched as Diao picked up an apricot with his hoof and put it up next to Butterfly Lover's mouth. With little-girl coyness, she refused to eat it. My mother told me I wasn't supposed to eat just anything from a boar, she said with sweet affection. Your mother doesn't know what she's talking about, Diao said as he shoved the apricot into her mouth, enough of a distraction for him to plant a noisy kiss on her ear. Kiss! the pigs all called out. Kiss! *La-ya-la — La-ya la-la-yala —* They'd forgotten all about me, I figured. They must have thought the outcome was clear, and I had no choice but to admit defeat. Most had come from Mount Yimeng with Diao Xiaosan, and they favored him. God-fucking-dammit! The time had come. I mustered all my strength and charged Diao Xiaosan again, soaring in the air and inspiring Diao to repeat his previous tactic of slipping under me as I passed overhead. Well, my friend, that's exactly what I wanted you to do. I landed solidly at the foot of the skinny apricot tree, right beside Butterfly Lover. In other words, Diao and I changed places. And the first thing I did was lift a front hoof and slap Butterfly Lover across the face, then I pushed her to the ground, drawing a shriek from her. There was no doubt in my mind that Diao would turn around and come at me, and at that moment, my two enormous balls, the most vulnerable and treasured part of my body, were hanging out there in his line of sight. If he butted his head into them or took a bite out of them, that'd be the end of that. It was a dangerous game of chess, like cutting off all avenues of escape. So I looked behind me out of the corner of both eyes, knowing I had to seize the moment, and saw the blood that was spurting from the savage beast's wide-open mouth and the ominous glare in his eyes. *La-ya-la — La-ya la-la-ya-la —* My life was hanging by a thread, so I rested my front hooves on Butterfly Lover's body and raised my rear legs, a sort of handstand, if you will, and when Diao came at me like a shot, he slipped under my belly, and all I had to do was settle back and I was astride him. He was totally defenseless. I stuck my hooves in his eyes — no more glare. *La-ya-la — La-ya la-la-ya-la — Mama's straw hat has flown up to the moon — Taking my loves and my ideals with it —* Sure, the tactic was on the cruel side, but this was such an important moment that I couldn't concern myself with sermons of hypocrisy.

Diao Xiaosan careened around frantically until he finally managed to throw me from his back. Blue-tinged blood oozed from his eye sockets. Covering his eyes with his hooves, he cried out in agony as he rolled on the ground:

"I can't see . . . I'm blind . . ."

La-ya-la — La-ya-la — All the pigs were quiet, looking very solemn. The moon flew high up into the sky, the straw hat fell to earth, bringing an end to the straw hat song; now the only sounds swirling around the air of Apricot Garden were the agonizing shrieks of Diao Xiaosan. The castrated boars headed back to their pens, their tails between their legs, whereas the sows, under Butterfly Lover's leadership, circled me and turned their heads outward, offering up their backsides to me. Master, they muttered, beloved master, we are yours, all of us, for you are the king, and we are lowly concubines fully prepared to become the mothers of your offspring . . . *La-ya-la — La-ya la-la-ya-la —* The straw hat that had fallen out of the sky was crushed beneath Diao Xiaosan's body as he rolled on the ground. My mind was a blank, except for soft strains of the straw hat song, and those soft strains were, in the end, like pearls sinking to the bottom of a lake. Everything had returned to normal; the watery rays of the moon were chilled, causing me to shiver and raising goose bumps on my skin. Is this how territory was won? Is this how you gained dominance? I couldn't possibly handle all that many sows, could I? To be perfectly honest, by then I'd lost interest in mating with any of them. But all those nice rear ends raised in my direction were like an indestructible wall penning me in, with no way out. How I wished I could escape on the wind, but a voice from on high made my position clear: King of Pigs, you have no right to escape, just as Diao Xiaosan has no right to mate with them. Mating with them is your sacred obligation! *La-ya-la — La-ya la-la-ya-la —* The straw hat song rose slowly to the surface like pearls. Yes, a monarch has no domestic affairs; politics rest on a monarch's sex organ. It was necessary for me to faithfully discharge my duties by mating with those sows. I absolutely had to fulfill my obligation to deposit my seed in their wombs. It made no difference whether they were pretty or ugly, whether they were white or black, whether they were virgins or had already mated with other boars. The real problem that presented itself was selection. They were all equally demanding, equally passionate, so who was I to choose? Or, to put it differently, who was going to be honored by an imperial visit? With all my heart, I wished I could be aided in my selection by one of the castrated boars, but there was no time for that now. The moon, close to fulfilling its nightly obligation, had retreated to the western edge of the sky, until only half of its red face was still visible above the treetops. A shark's-belly silver-gray sky had already appeared on the eastern horizon; dawn was breaking, the morning stars sparkled. I nudged Butterfly Lover's rear end with my hard snout as notice that I had selected her for the first imperial visit. She moaned coquettishly. Ah, Great King, your slave's body has long awaited this moment. . . .

For the moment, I put aside all thoughts of past lives and gave no thought to what would follow my present life. I was a pig, through and through, so I rose up and mounted Butterfly Lover . . . *La-ya-la — La-ya la-la-ya-la —* The straw hat song rose triumphantly. As the background music swelled, a sonorous tenor voice rose into the sky: *Mama's straw hat has flown up to the moon — Taking my loves and ideals with it —* All the other sows, free of jealousy, took the tail of the pigs in front in their mouths and began a circle dance around Butterfly Lover and me to the rhythms of the straw hat song. With Apricot Garden birds singing and a morning glow lighting up the sky, my first mating went off without a hitch.

As I lowered myself from Butterfly Lover's back, I spotted Ximen Bai walking unsteadily, aided by a homemade cane, baskets of food over her shoulder. Calling upon what energy remained, I leaped over the wall and into my pen to await Ximen Bai's food delivery. The scent of black beans and bran made me drool. I was famished. Ximen Bai's face, burnished red by the morning glow, appeared above the wall of my pen. There were tears in her eyes. Nearly overcome by emotion, she said:

"Sixteen, Jinlong and Jiefang are now married, and so are you. You are all grown-ups. . . ."

30

Miraculous Hair Brings Xiaosan Back to Life
The Red Death Wipes Out the Swine Horde

The weather during the eighth month of that year was sweltering, with so much rain it was as if the heavens had sprung a leak. The canal running alongside the pig farm swelled with floodwaters, the saturated ground rising like dough in the oven. Several pathetic old apricot trees, unable to withstand the watery onslaught, shed their leaves and waited for death to claim them. Branches of poplars and willows that served as roof beams above the pigpens sprouted fresh appendages, while fences made of sorghum stalks were covered with gray spots of mildew. Pig waste that had begun to leaven filled the air with a moldy smell. Frogs that ought to have gone dormant instead began mating, interrupting the nightly stillness with croaks that kept the pigs from their sleep. And then a powerful earthquake struck the city of Tangshan, its shock waves collapsing more than a dozen pens with weak foundations and causing my roof beams to creak and sway. That was followed by a meteorite shower, with meteors streaking across the sky, accompanied by great explosive rumblings and blinding lights in the black curtain of night; the earth shook. All this occurred as my harem of twenty or more pregnant pigs awaited the impending birth of their litters, teats swelling with milk.

Diao Xiaosan was still my neighbor. Our violent struggles left him with one totally blind eye and one with seriously impeded vision. That constituted his great misfortune and my deep remorse. During that spring, two of the sows failed to get pregnant even after several couplings, and I thought about inviting him to try his luck with them as an expression of my regret over what had happened. Imagine my surprise when he responded somberly:

"Pig Sixteen, I say, Pig Sixteen, you can kill a warrior but you mustn't humiliate him. You beat me, Diao Xiaosan, fair and square, and all I ask is a measure of dignity. Do not disgrace me with such an offer."

Deeply moved, I was forced to view this onetime bitter foe with renewed respect. I tell you, in the wake of our fight, Diao Xiaosan became a very somber pig, one whose gluttony and talkativeness ended abruptly. But, as they say, calamities never come alone: a far greater tragedy was about to befall him. Seen from one angle, what happened involved me; seen from another angle, it did not. Pig farm personnel wanted Diao to mate with the two sows I was unable to impregnate, but he merely sat behind them, quietly, not aroused, like a cold stone carving, which led those people to assume that he had become impotent. In an attempt to improve the quality of meat of retired boars, castration was called for, a shameful human invention. Diao Xiaosan was fated to suffer that cruelty. For an immature male pig, castration is a simple procedure accomplished in a few minutes. But for a grown pig like Diao Xiaosan, who must have enjoyed hot, passionate romance back in Mount Yimeng, it was the sort of operation that could leave his life hanging by a thread. A squad of ten or more militiamen held him down beneath the crooked apricot tree and encountered resistance the likes of which they hadn't seen before. At least three of the men suffered disfiguring bites on their hands. In the end, one man grabbed each of his legs and flipped him onto his back, while two others pressed his neck down with a stick, and one of the others crammed a stone into his mouth, one too large either to spit out or swallow. The man wielding the knife was an old-timer with a shiny bald head surrounded on the sides and back with a few scraggly gray hairs. I harbored a natural loathing for that man; the mere mention of his name — Xu Bao — called to mind a previous life, when he'd been my mortal enemy. He'd gotten very old and had a severe case of asthma that had him gasping for air from the slightest exertion. He stood off to the side looking as the others immobilized Diao Xiaosan. Once that was accomplished, he walked up, the light of occupational excitement flashing in his eyes. The old reprobate, who had lived longer than he had any right to, nimbly sliced off Diao Xiaosan's scrotum, scooped a handful of lime out of a sack at his hip, and spread it over the wound before walking off with his prize — a pair of large purple ovals.

"Uncle Bao," I heard Jinlong call out, "should we sew this up?"

"What the fuck for?" was the wheezy reply.

With a shout, the men jumped back away from Diao Xiaosan, who slowly got to his feet and spit out the stone, quaking from excruciating waves of pain. The spiky hairs on his back stood up straight, and blood flowed freely from the open wound between his legs. Not a single moan escaped from Diao's mouth, no tears fell from his eyes. He just clenched his jaw and ground his teeth with a loud scraping sound. Xu Bao stood beneath the apricot tree holding Diao Xiaosan's testicles in the palm of his bloody hand and looking them over, unconcealed glee oozing from the deep wrinkles in his face. I knew how much the cruel old man liked to eat animals' testicles, as I recalled the day he sneakily removed one of my three donkey balls and ate it with hot peppers. How many times I felt like leaping across the wall of my pen and biting off that bastard's testicles to avenge Diao Xiaosan, to wreak some vengeance of my own, and to gain retribution for all the stallions, male donkeys, bulls, and boars who had suffered at his hand. I never knew what it meant to be afraid of a human being, but I must admit in all honesty that that son of a bitch — a malignancy in the lives of all male animals — scared the hell out of me. What his body gave off was neither an odor nor heat, but a bloodcurdling message.

Poor old Diao Xiaosan walked laboriously over to the apricot tree and, with one side of his belly up against the trunk, lay down wearily. Blood was now spurting from the wound, staining his legs and the ground behind them. He was shivering despite the heat. He'd lost his vision, so his eyes gave away nothing of what he was feeling. *La-ya-la* — *La-ya-la-la-ya-la* — Notes from the straw hat song rose slowly in the air, but the lyrics had undergone a major change: *Mama — My testicles are gone — The testicles you gave me are gone —* Tears welled up in my eyes and, for the first time in my life, I understood the torment implicit in the saying "all beings grieve for their own kind." I also regretted the underhanded tactics I'd used in my fight with him. I heard Jinlong curse Xu Bao:

"What the hell have you done, Xu? You must have severed one of his arteries."

"There's no need for you to seem so shocked, pal," Xu replied coldly. "All boars like him are that way."

"I want you to take care of him. He'll die if he keeps bleeding like that," Jinlong said with mounting anxiety.

"Die, you say? Isn't that a good thing?" Xu Bao said with a false smile. "This one's got plenty of fat on him, a couple of hundred *jin* at least. The meat from a boar might be on the tough side, but it's a far sight better than bean curd."

Diao Xiaosan did not die, though I'm sure there were moments when he wished he had. Any boar who has that punishment inflicted on him suffers not only physically but, to a far greater extent, psychologically. There is no greater humiliation. Diao Xiaosan bled and bled and bled, at least enough to fill two basins, and all the blood was absorbed by the tree; the fruit produced by that tree the following year was yellow with streaks of red blood. He grew withered, sort of dried up, from the loss of all that blood. I jumped the wall between our two pens and stood by him hoping, but failing, to find words to comfort and console him. So I picked a plump pumpkin from the roof of the abandoned generator room and laid it on the ground in front of him.

"Eat something, old Diao, it'll make you feel better."

Raising his head off the ground, he looked up at me out of his good eye and managed to say through clenched teeth: "Pig Sixteen, what I am today is what you'll become tomorrow . . . it's the fate of all boars. . . ."

His head dropped back to the ground, and all his bones seemed to come unglued.

"You can't die, old Diao," I cried out, "you can't! Old Diao . . ."

This time he didn't respond, and tears finally came to my eyes, tears of remorse. As I pondered what had just happened, I could see that while it may have seemed that Diao Xiaosan's death came at the hands of Xu Bao, in fact I was the cause of his death. *La-ya-la — La-ya-la-la la-ya-la —* Old Diao, my good brother, go in peace. I hope your soul will soon find its way to the underworld, where Lord Yama will arrange a good rebirth for you, maybe even as a human being, at least I hope so. You can leave this world worry-free. I'll avenge you by giving Xu Bao a taste of his own medicine. . . .

As these thoughts raced through my mind, Baofeng came running up behind Huzhu, her medicine bag over her shoulder. By that time, Jinlong might well have been sitting in the rickety old armchair at Xu Bao's house sharing a bottle with Xu Bao as they enjoyed Xu's favorite dish — boar's eggs. In the end, women are more kindhearted than men. Just look there at Huzhu, sweat beading her forehead, tears clouding her vision, as if Diao Xiaosan were her blood relative, not a scary-looking boar. By then it was the sixth lunar month, nearly two months after your wedding. You and Huang Hezuo had already been working in Pang Hu's cotton processing plant for a month. The cotton was just then blooming; in three months it would be on the market.

During those days, I — Lan Jiefang — along with the head of the cotton inspection office and a bunch of girls, was sent over from a number of villages and the county town to weed the enormous compound and prepare the surface for the cotton sale. The Cotton Processing Plant Number Five occupied a thousand acres of land and was ringed by a brick wall. The bricks had been taken from the graveyard as a cost-cutting measure initiated by Pang Hu himself. New bricks sold for ten fen; old bricks from the graves cost only three. For the longest time, none of the other workers knew that Huang Hezuo and I were man and wife, since I stayed in the men's dorm and she stayed in the women's. A place like the cotton processing plant, where employees worked on a seasonal basis, could not afford to supply married housing. But even if there had been quarters for us to share, we wouldn't have wanted to, since our marriage was like a child's game; at least it felt that way to me. It was a sham, almost like being told upon awakening: From today on this is your wife. You are now her husband. How could anyone accept something that absurd? I had feelings for Huzhu, not for Hezuo, and this was the root of a lifetime of agony. On my first morning at the cotton processing plant I laid eyes on Pang Chunmiao, a lovely six-year-old girl with pretty white teeth and red lips, eyes like stars and lustrous skin, a crystalline beauty. She was practicing handstands in the plant doorway. Her hair was tied with a piece of red satin, she was wearing a navy blue skirt, a white short-sleeved shirt, white socks, and red plastic sandals. Urged on by the people around her, she bent over, put both hands on the ground, and lifted her feet up in the air, until her body was arced at the right angle to begin walking on her hands to shouts and applause. But her mother, Wang Leyun, ran up and turned her right side up. Don't be silly, my angel, she said. But I can keep doing it, her daughter said reluctantly.

I can see this as if it had happened yesterday, not nearly thirty years ago. Even great seers like Zhuge Liang and Liu Bowen could not predict that many years into the future. I gave up everything for love. By running off with that little girl, I created a huge scandal throughout Northeast Gaomi Township. But I was confident that what began as a scandal would one day be seen as a true love story. At least that's what my good friend Mo Yan predicted when we were at the end of our rope. . . .

— Hey! Big-head Lan Qiansui pounded the table like a judge with his gavel and snapped me back to reality. Don't start woolgathering, listen to me. You'll have plenty of time to daydream about and ponder, even complain about that ridiculous affair of yours, but for now I want you to listen and listen carefully to my glorious history as a pig. So where was I? Oh, right, your sister, Baofeng, and your sister-in-law — there's no other way to describe her — Huzhu rushed up to Diao Xiaosan, who was barely alive after a botched operation, as he lay beneath the crooked apricot tree bleeding to death. There was a time when the mere mention of that crooked romantic tree would have had you foaming at the mouth until you passed out. But now, we could put you on the ground right under it and you, like a battle-scarred veteran, would sigh emotionally on a visit to an ancient — for you — battle-ground. In the face of life's great healer, time, no matter how deep the torment, all wounds will one day heal. Hell, I was a damned pig then, so what's with the somber attitude?

Anyway, as I was saying, Baofeng and Huzhu arrived on the scene to come to Diao Xiaosan's aid. I stood off to the side, crying my eyes out like a dear old friend. At first, like me, they thought he had died, then they found that he had a heartbeat, but just barely. Baofeng took over immediately, taking a syringe out of her medical kit and giving Diao three consecutive injections: a stimulant, a blood thickener, and glucose, all intended for use on humans. But what I want to call your attention to is how she stitched up his open wound. Lacking both surgical needle and thread, she turned to Huzhu, who cleverly took a pin from her blouse — you know how married women carry pins on their clothing or in their hair. But what would they use for thread? As her face reddened, Huzhu said:

"How about a strand of my hair, would that work?"

"Your hair?" Baofeng asked, slightly incredulous.

"Yes. My hair has capillaries in it."

"Sister-in-law," Baofeng said with undisguised emotion, "your hair ought to be reserved for the likes of Golden Boy and Jade Girl, not a pig."

"Listen to you, sister," Huzhu said with growing agitation. "My hair is worth no more than that of an ox or a horse. If not for my peculiarity, I'd have cut it all off long ago. But while it can't be cut, it can be pulled out."

"Are you sure, sister-in-law?"

Baofeng had her doubts, but Huzhu went ahead and pulled out two strands of the most mysterious and most valuable hair anywhere in the world, each roughly five feet in length, a dark golden color — at the time, hair that color was considered especially ugly, whereas now it's considered by some a sign of elegant beauty — and so much coarser than normal hair that it appeared to the naked eye to have considerable heft. Huzhu threaded one of the strands and handed the needle to Baofeng, who cleansed the wound with iodine, held the needle with a pair of tweezers, and stitched up Diao Xiaosan's wound with Huzhu's miraculous hair.

When that was done, both Huzhu and Baofeng spotted me, with my tear-streaked face, and were deeply moved by my deep concern and loyalty. Since only one of the strands was used to stitch up Diao's wound, Huzhu threw the second strand away. Baofeng retrieved it, wrapped it in gauze, and placed it in her medical kit. The women waited; whether Diao would live or die was now up to him. We've done our best, they said as they walked off together.

I couldn't say if it was a result of the injections or if it was Huzhu's hair, but Diao's wound stopped bleeding and his heartbeat regained its strength and rhythm. Ximen Bai brought over a basin half filled with rice gruel and placed it in front of him. He got up on his knees and slowly lapped it up. It was a miracle he didn't die that time. Huzhu told Jinlong that Baofeng's skills deserved all the credit, but I couldn't help feeling that Huzhu's miraculous hair played a major role in the pig's recovery.

Postoperative Diao Xiaosan disappointed those who hoped he'd do little but eat and drink and gain lots of weight in a hurry. Fattening up after castration leads straight to the slaughterhouse. Knowing that, he ate in moderation; not only that, as I became aware, he did pushups every night in his pen, not stopping until every bristle on his body was wet with sweat. My respect for him increased daily, as did my sense of dread. Just what this victim of the ultimate humiliation, who had been brought back to life from certain death and who appeared to meditate during the daytime and work out at night, was up to escaped me. One thing was certain, however: he was a hero who was only temporarily lodged in a pigsty. At first he'd been an embryonic hero only. But after Xu Bao wielded that knife, a flash of understanding had sped up the process. I knew he'd be incapable of seeking a life of ease, content to grow old in a pigpen. A grand plan was surely taking form in his breast, with escape from the pig farm at its core. . . . But what could a nearly blind castrated boar do once he'd gotten free? I guess that's a question for another time. Let's continue the tale of events from August of that year.

Shortly before the sows I impregnated were about to come to term, that is, on or about the twentieth of August 1967, following several unusual occurrences, a devastating epidemic struck the pig farm.

The first signs occurred when a castrated boar named Butting Crazy developed a chronic cough, accompanied by a high fever and a loss of appetite. The disease spread to four of his sty mates in short order. All this went unnoticed, since Butting Crazy and his friends were thorns in the side of farm personnel, a bunch of pigs who refused to grow. From a distance, they looked like normal little piglets of three to five months, but up close they shocked the observer with their scraggly bristles, coarse skin, and hideous faces. They'd experienced pretty much everything the world had thrown at them, and showed it. Back at Mount Yimeng, they'd been sold off every couple of months, since their voracious appetites had no effect on weight gain. They were menacing eating machines, seemingly lacking normal small intestines. Whatever they ate, regardless of quality, it went from their throats to their stomachs and straight to their large intestines, where, in less than an hour, it emerged in horribly foul form. They squealed when they were hungry, which was all the time, and if they weren't fed, their eyes turned red and they ran headfirst into a wall or a gate, more crazed by the minute, until they foamed at the mouth and passed out. But as soon as they regained consciousness, it was back to the head butting. Anyone who bought them and raised them for a month or so could see they hadn't gained an ounce, so it was back to the marketplace, where they were sold for whatever their owners could get. People sometimes asked the obvious question: Why not just kill and eat them? Well, you've seen them, so I don't need to tell you, but if the people who asked that question took one look at Butting Crazy, you wouldn't hear any more talk about killing and eating those pigs, whose meat was more disgusting than that of toads in a latrine. And that was how those little pigs got to enjoy considerable longevity. After being sold and resold on Mount Yimeng, they were bought for almost nothing and brought over by Jinlong. And you couldn't say that Butting Crazy wasn't a pig. He and his friends contributed to the pig population.

Who would pay any attention to pigs like that just because they were coughing, ran a fever, and had lost their appetite? The person responsible for feeding them and cleaning out their pen was someone who has appeared and reappeared up to now and will continue to do so down the line, our old friend Mr. Mo Yan. By kissing up to any and everybody at the farm, he eventually realized his goal of becoming a pig tender. His "Tales of Pig-Raising" had gained him quite a reputation, since it was a work that was clearly related to his experience and position at Apricot Garden Pig Farm. There was talk that the renowned film director Ingmar Bergman thought about bringing "Tales of Pig-Raising" to the silver screen, but where was he going to find that many pigs? I've seen plenty of today's pigs. Like chickens and ducks these days, they're nothing but empty-headed animals, thanks to chemical feed and all sorts of additives, which have made them feebleminded. You won't find any pigs as classy as we were these days. Some of us had strong, healthy legs, some had extraordinary intelligence, some were crafty old scoundrels, and others had the gift of gab. In a word, we were good-looking animals with strong personalities, the sort you won't find again on this earth. Nowadays, you get moronic porkers that weigh three hundred *jin* at five months and couldn't qualify as extras in any film. And that is why, to my way of thinking, Bergman's planned filming will never take place. Yes, yes, yes, you don't have to tell me, I know Hollywood, and I know all about digital special effects. But those are expensive and tricky. But most of all, I'll never believe that any digital pig could come close to matching the style and substance of Pig Sixteen. Or for that matter, Diao Xiaosan, Butterfly Lover, even Butting Crazy.

Now Mo Yan was never much of a farmer. His body may have been on the farm, but his mind was in the city. Lowborn, he dreamed of becoming rich and famous; ugly as sin, he sought the company of pretty girls; generally ill-informed, he passed himself off as a knowledgeable academic. And with all that, he managed to establish himself as a writer, someone who dined on tasty pot stickers in Beijing every day, while I, the classy Ximen Pig . . . ah, the ways of the world are so incomprehensible it does no good to talk about them. Mo Yan wasn't much of a pig raiser either, and it was my good luck that he was not assigned to take care of me. Fortunately, that assignment was given to Ximen Bai. I don't care how fine a pig you have, let Mo Yan look after it for a month or so, and you'll wind up with a crazed animal; so, as I saw it, it was a good thing Butting Crazy and the others had survived a sea of troubles in their lives, or they never would have survived being looked after by Mo Yan.

To be sure, seen from a different angle, Mo Yan's motive for join- ing the pig-raising enterprise was a good one. He was curious by nature and given to daydreaming. At first, he wasn't terribly put off by Butting Crazy and his friends, believing that they were incapable of putting on weight no matter how much they ate because the ingested food spent so little time in their intestines, and all that was needed was for that passage to be slowed down enough for the nutrients to be absorbed into their bodies. This idea went to the heart of the matter, so he began to experiment. His rudimentary solution was to install a valve in the pigs' anus, to be opened and closed by farm personnel. Obviously, this proved to be impractical, so he next turned his atten- tion to food additives. Both Chinese and Western antidiarrhea reme- dies were available, but they were too expensive and hard to obtain if you didn't know someone. So he tried mixing grass and tree ash into the feed, which drew a chorus of curses from the crazy pigs, not to mention a frenzy of head butting. But Mo Yan refused to relent, and eventually the crazies had no choice but to eat what was put in front of them. I recall hearing him pound on the feed bucket and say to Butting Crazy and his friends, Come on, eat up. Ash is good for your eyes and your heart and will make your intestines healthier than they've ever been. But when ash proved ineffective, Mo Yan tried adding dry cement to the feed. Now this did the trick, but nearly killed Butting Crazy and his friends in the process. They rolled around on the ground in agony and only escaped death when they were able to pass what looked like a bellyful of pebbles.

Butting Crazy and his friends carried loathing for Mo Yan in their bones. He felt nothing but disgust for the incorrigible animals. At the time, you and Hezuo were off working in the cotton processing plant, so he was feeling somewhat out of sorts. He dumped feed into the pigs' trough and said to the hacking, feverish, whining Butting Crazy and his friends, What's up with you little devils? Is this a hunger strike? Mass suicide? Fine with me, go ahead and kill yourselves. You're not pigs anyway. You're unworthy of the name. You're nothing but a bunch of counterrevolutionaries who are wasting the commune's valuable food.

The "Butting Crazies" lay dead the next day, their skin dotted with purple splotches the size of bronze coins, their eyes open, as if they'd died with unresolved grievances. As we've seen, it was a rainy month, hot and humid, ideal weather for swarms of flies and mosquitoes, so by the time the commune veterinarian had rafted across the rain-swollen river to the Apricot Garden Pig Farm, the pigs' carcasses were bloated and foul-smelling. The old veterinarian wore a rain slicker and rubber rain boots. With a gauze mask over his nose and mouth as he stood outside the pen, he looked over the wall and said, "They died of what we call the Red Death. Cremate and bury them immediately!"

The pig farm personnel — including, of course, Mo Yan — dragged the five contaminated carcasses out of the pen, under the veterinarian's supervision, all the way to the southeast corner of the farm, where they dug a hole. They hadn't gone down more than a couple of feet before water began gurgling to the surface. So they flung the pigs in, doused them with kerosene, and tossed in a match. Since there were strong southeast winds, foul-smelling smoke was carried to the pig farm and beyond, to the village itself — the stupid bastards couldn't have chosen a worse location for the cremation — and I was forced to bury my nose in the dirt to blot out what must be the worst stench in the world. I later learned that Diao Xiaosan had escaped from the farm the night before the carcasses were burned; he swam across the canal and headed east into the wilds, which meant that the noxious air of latent death had no effect on his health.

You weren't witness to what happened after that, though I'm sure you heard all about it. An epidemic spread quickly through the farm and infected more than eight hundred pigs, including the twenty-eight pregnant sows. I was a rare survivor, thanks to my highly developed immune system and to the quantity of garlic Ximen Bai added to my feed. Sixteen, she said repeatedly, it's peppery, but go ahead and eat it. Garlic protects against all kinds of poisons. Now I knew this was no common sickness, and eating some garlic was a cheap price to pay to avoid it. During those days it would have been more accurate to say I survived on garlic than on pig feed. Each peppery meal was accompanied by tears and sweat, and raised hell with my mouth and stomach. But the garlic did the trick — I survived.

After the Red Death decimated the pig population, several more veterinarians crossed the river to our farm. One of them was a brawny, hardy woman with a bad case of acne whom everyone called Station Chief Yu. She had a firm hand and dealt with things decisively. When she placed a phone call to the county from the farm office, you could hear her a mile away. Under her supervision, the veterinarians gave the sows shots and drew blood from them. I heard that around sunset, a motorboat came up the river with badly needed medicines. But none of that kept the majority of pigs alive, and that spelled the doom for the Apricot Garden Pig Farm. Carcasses were piled so high there was no way they could be cremated, so a burial ditch was dug; but once again, water rose to the surface a couple of feet down, so that was out. Driven to desperation, farm personnel had no choice but to wait until the veterinarians left and, in the fading light of dusk, load the carcasses onto a flatbed wagon and haul them down to the river, where they were tossed into the water to float downstream — out of sight and out of mind.

The disposal of pig carcasses wasn't wrapped up until the early days of September, following a series of heavy rainfalls that eroded the shabbily constructed hog house foundations. Most of the buildings collapsed in a single night. I heard the loud laments of Jinlong in the northern row of buildings. Obsessively ambitious, he had hoped to move up the promotion ladder by displaying his talents during activities scheduled for the delegation from the Military Region Logistics Command, whose arrival had been delayed by the rainstorms. But now that would never happen. The pigs were dead, the farm was in ruins, and I was heartsick as I reflected on the glorious days now a thing of the past.

31

A Fawning Mo Yan Rides on
Commander Chang's Coattails
A Resentful Lan Lian Weeps for Chairman Mao

On the ninth day of September, an event occurred that was as cata-
clysmic as a mountain collapsing or the earth opening up. Despite all
attempts to save him, your Chairman Mao passed away. I could, of
course, have said *our* Chairman Mao, but I was a pig at the time, and
that would have sounded disrespectful. The river behind the village
had overflowed its banks and sent floodwaters that toppled a utility
pole and snapped the phone line, turning the village phone into a
mere decoration and muting the loudspeaker. So word of Chairman
Mao's passing came to us from Jinlong, who'd heard the news on the
radio. That radio had been a gift from his good friend Chang
Tianhong, who'd been taken into custody by the Military Control
Commission for the crime of hooliganism, only to be released owing
to a lack of evidence. He was in and out of trouble until finally being
appointed assistant troupe leader of the county Cat's Meow Drama
Troupe. As a music academy graduate, he was an ideal choice for the
position. He plunged enthusiastically into the work: not only did he
adapt the eight model revolutionary operas for the Cat's Meow stage,
but he followed current trends by writing and directing a production
of *Tales of Pig-Raising* based upon events at our Apricot Garden Pig
Farm — in a postscript to his story "Tales of Pig-Raising" Mo Yan
referred to this development, even claiming that he had been a coauthor, but I'm pretty sure that's a bunch of bull. It's true that Chang
Tianhong came to our pig farm to get a feel for life here, and it's true
that Mo Yan tagged along behind him like a parasite. But coauthor?
No way. Chang let his imagination soar for this contemporary Cat's

Meow production, giving the pigs speaking parts and separating them into two cliques, one of which advocated extreme eating and shitting to get fat in the name of revolution; the remaining pigs were hidden class enemies, represented by Diao Xiaosan, with Butting Crazy and his friends, who ate without putting on weight, as accomplices. On the farm it wasn't just humans pitted against humans; pigs were also pitted against pigs, and these swine struggles comprised the production's central conflict, with humans as the supporting cast. Chang had studied Western music in college, with a concentration on Western opera. His contributions to the Cat's Meow production were not limited to innovations in content; he also introduced drastic changes to traditional Cat's Meow melodies, including an aria for the major positive male role of Whitey, a truly wonderful movement. I always assumed that Whitey was a dramatic version of me, but in "Tales of Pig-Raising" Mo Yan wrote that Whitey symbolized a vital and upward-moving, healthy and progressive, freedom-and-happiness-seeking force. Man, could he stretch the truth, what nerve! I knew how much effort Chang put into creating this production, integrating local and Western traditions, brilliantly merging romanticism and realism, creating a model of serious ideological contents and moving artistic form that brought out the best in each. If Chairman Mao had died a few years later, there might well have been a ninth model opera: the Gaomi Cat's Meow version of *Tales of Pig-Raising.*

I recall one moonlit night when Chang Tianhong stood beneath the crooked apricot tree holding a libretto of *Tales of Pig-Raising,* with its squiggly musical notations, as he sang Whitey's aria for the benefit of the youthful Jinlong, Huzhu, Baofeng, and Ma Liangcai (who was then principal of the Ximen Village Elementary School). Mo Yan was there too, with a water bottle in a holder of woven red and green plastic threads. Steeping in the bottle were a pair of medicinal fruit seeds, and Mo Yan was ready to hand the bottle to Chang if and when he needed it. In his other hand he held a black oilpaper fan with which he was fanning Chang's back — I found his fawning behavior thoroughly disgusting. But that's how he participated in the creation of the Cat's Meow version of *Tales of Pig-Raising.*

Everyone recalls how the villagers had once given Chang Tianhong the insulting nickname of Braying Jackass. Well, after the passage of more than ten years, the villagers' outlook had gradually broadened, and a new understanding of Chang's singing artistry had emerged. The Chang Tianhong who returned this time to get a feel for life in the village and create a new drama was a changed man. The superficiality and haughtiness people had found so off-putting was gone. There was a sense of melancholy in his eyes, his face had an ashen quality, stubble decorated his chin, and his temples had turned gray; he looked a lot like one of those Russian Decembrists. The people viewed him with reverence as they waited for him to sing, and with one front hoof on the quivering apricot branch and my chin resting on the other hoof, I settled in to enjoy an enchanting evening performance by the lovely youth. Laying her left hand on Huzhu's left shoulder and resting her chin on her sister-in-law's right shoulder, Baofeng gazed at Chang's thin, moonlit face and naturally curly hair. Although her face was in the shadows, the moonlight revealed the sad helplessness in that look. On the farm even we pigs knew that Chang and Pang Hu's daughter, Pang Kangmei, who'd been assigned out of college to the county production headquarters, were romantically involved and, we heard, to be married on October 1, National Day. She'd come to see him twice while he was on the farm. Endowed with a lovely figure and bright eyes, and refusing to put on airs as an urban intellectual, she made a fine impression on both the people and us pigs. Each time she came she inspected our production station — after all, she worked with livestock at the production headquarters — and looked in on all the farm animals, mules, horses, donkeys, oxen. I was pretty sure Baofeng knew that Kangmei was slated to marry Chang, whom she had fallen for, and Kangmei seemed aware of Baofeng's feelings. Around dusk one day, I saw them talking under the crooked apricot tree, and watched as Baofeng laid her head on Kangmei's shoulder and wept. Kangmei, who also had tears in her eyes, stroked Baofeng's head consolingly.

None of this, of course, has anything to do with the story I'm telling. What I really want to talk about is that radio, a Red Lantern transistor radio made in Qingdao, which Chang Tianhong had given to Jinlong. No one said it was a wedding present, but that's what it was. And while Chang gave him the gift, originally, Pang Kangmei had brought it back with her when she was sent on temporary assignment to Qingdao; and though Jinlong was the recipient, in fact Pang Kangmei personally gave it to Huang Huzhu and told her how to install batteries, how to turn it on and off, and how to find radio stations. Given my penchant for roaming, I saw it on the night of Jinlong's wedding. For the wedding banquet, Jinlong had placed it on a table with a lit lantern. It was tuned to the loudest and clearest station he could find. Farm personnel — boys and girls, men and women — gathered round to listen excitedly. Everyone felt like touching the obviously expensive object, but no one could get up the nerve to do it. What if they broke it? After Jinlong wiped the sides with a piece of red satin, the people crowded round to listen to a thin-voiced woman sing. What she sang did not concern them. They were too busy trying to figure out how she'd gotten into that little box. I wasn't *that* stupid, since I was somewhat familiar with electronics. I not only knew that there were many radios in use in the world, but that there was something even more advanced — television. I also knew that an American had landed on the moon, that the Soviet Union had launched spaceships, and that the first animal to go into space was a pig. By "they" I was referring to the regular pig farm personnel. That did not include Mo Yan, who had learned many things by reading *Reference News*. There was, of course, another "them," the critters that hid in or behind our haystacks. They too were mesmerized by the sounds emerging from the strange box.

Here's a rough summary of what happened at two o'clock that afternoon: We'll start with the sky, which was, for the most part, clear, though there were some dark clouds. Gale-force winds blew from the southeast and served as a key to open up the sky, as northern peasants all know. As the clouds were blown across the sky, moving shadows skittered past Apricot Garden. Then there was the steaming ground, over which large toads were crawling. Finally, there were the people. A dozen or so farm personnel were spraying liquid lime over the still standing pigpens. Hardly any pigs were left alive, and the scene of desolation had thrown the people into a deep depression. They scrubbed the top of my wall with the liquid lime and did the same to the low-hanging apricot branches over my quarters. Was that going to kill off agents of the Red Death? Hell no! What a joke. From their conversation I discovered that, including me, only seventy pigs or so had survived. I'd pretty much stayed put while the epidemic was raging, so I was curious to learn as much as possible about the seventy other pigs that survived. What type were they, and were any of them my siblings? Were there any wild boars like Diao Xiaosan? Well, just as I was exercising my brain over such thoughts; and just as the farm

personnel were trying to figure out what the future held; and just as
the abdomen of a pig that had been buried burst under the blazing
sun; and just as a bird with a brightly colored tail, one that even I, with
all my knowledge and experience, had never seen before, flew in low
and landed on the crooked, waterlogged apricot tree, which had lost
all its leaves; and just as Ximen Bai spotted the bird, whose colorful
tail hung down nearly to the ground, and shouted excitedly, her lips
quivering, "Phoenix!" Jinlong stumbled out of his wedding chamber,
clutching the radio to his chest. His face had lost its color and he
looked like someone whose soul had left him. Staring wide-eyed, he
announced hoarsely:

"Chairman Mao is dead!"

Chairman Mao is dead. Are you joking? Spreading a rumor?
Launching a vicious attack? Saying that Chairman Mao is dead is like
signing your own death warrant! How could Chairman Mao be dead?
Doesn't everyone say that he could live at least 158 years? Doubts
and questions swirled in the people's minds when the news broke.
Even me, a pig, was puzzled beyond measure, finding it hard to
believe. But the tears in Jinlong's eyes and the solemn look on
his face told us that the news was true. The mellow voice from Central People's Broadcasting Station had a slightly nasal quality as it
solemnly informed the Party, the military, and people of all ethnic
groups in the country of the death of Chairman Mao. I looked up at
the sky, where dark clouds were roiling, and then at the trees, with
their bare branches, and finally at the clutter of collapsed pigpens, and
I listened to the incongruous croaking of frogs out in the fields and the
occasional explosion of another ruptured pig's belly from a shallow
grave; my nostrils filled with a variety of foul smells as I saw images of
all the strange things that had happened over the course of several
months, including the sudden disappearance of Diao Xiaosan and all
the mysterious things he'd said, and I knew conclusively that
Chairman Mao was dead.

What followed was this: Holding the radio in his hands like a filial son carrying his father's ashes, Jinlong walked solemnly toward the
village. Pig farm personnel dropped what they were doing and fell in
behind him, somber, respectful looks on their faces. The death of
Chairman Mao was a loss not only for humans but for us pigs as well.
With no Chairman Mao there could be no New China, and with no
New China there could be no Ximen Village Production Brigade

Apricot Garden Pig Farm, and with no Ximen Village Production Brigade Apricot Garden Pig Farm there could be no Pig Sixteen! That is why I followed Jinlong and the others out onto the street.

Radio stations throughout China were of one voice those days, aided by the finest equipment, so naturally, Jinlong turned the volume on his radio all the way up, and whenever he met someone along the way he announced in a manner and style we'd gotten used to, "Chairman Mao is dead!" This announcement was invariably met with stupefied looks. The faces of some contorted in agony; other people merely shook their heads, and others beat their chests and stomped their feet. All fell meekly in line behind Jinlong, and by the time we reached the village a long line stretched out behind me.

Hong Taiyue emerged from brigade headquarters, but before he could ask what was going on, Jinlong announced, "Chairman Mao is dead!" Hong reacted by doubling up his fist to punch Jinlong in the face. But his fist stopped in mid flight when he realized that virtually the entire village had turned out and saw how the radio in Jinlong's hands was so loud it vibrated. He pulled his fist back and pounded his own chest, as a shriek of desolation tore from his throat: "Ah, Chairman Mao . . . you have left us . . . how will we get through the days to come?"

A dirge began to play over the radio, and the slow, solemn strains had Huang Tong's wife, Wu Qiuxiang, and all the village women wailing piteously. Overcome by grief, they sat down in the mud, many of them pounding the ground with their fists and sending water splashing in all directions. Some covered their mouths with hankies and gazed heavenward, others covered their eyes and released grief-stricken cries. As the wails mounted, words followed:

"We are the earth, Chairman Mao the sky — Now Chairman Mao has died, the sky has fallen—"

As for the men, lamentations came from some, silent tears from others. When they heard the news, even the landlords, rich peasants, and counterrevolutionaries came running to stand off a short distance and weep silently.

As a member of the beastly kingdom, who was nonetheless influenced by my surroundings, I was saddened by the news, but maintained my emotional equilibrium. I walked among the crowd, watching and thinking. The death of no other man in recent Chinese history had the effect on people that the passing of Mao Zedong did.

Those who didn't shed a tear even when their own mothers died wept over Mao Zedong until their eyes were red. As always, there were exceptions. Among the thousand or more residents of Ximen Village, when even landlords and rich peasants, who should have held a grudge against Chairman Mao, wept openly over his death, and all who heard the news laid down their work, two individuals neither wailed nor wept silently but kept right on with what they were doing. One was Xu Bao, the other was Lan Lian.

Xu Bao mixed stealthily among the crowd, following behind me. At first I wasn't aware of his presence, but it didn't take long to spot that greedy, malignant look of his, and as soon as I realized that his eyes were fixed on my substantial testicles, I felt greater shock and anger than I'd ever known before. At a time like this, all Xu Bao had on his mind was getting his hands on my testicles. Obviously, he was not saddened by Chairman Mao's death, and if I could have found a way to inform the people what he was thinking, he might well have died at the hands of the mourners. Too bad I was still incapable of human speech, and too bad the people were so caught up in their grief they paid no attention to Xu Bao. Fine, then, I thought. I admit I was once afraid of you, Xu Bao, and I'm still leery of that quick hand of yours. But since even a man like Chairman Mao cannot live forever, I might as well not worry about whether I live or die. I'm here waiting for you, Xu Bao, you bastard. Tonight the fish dies or the net breaks.

The other person who shed no tears for Mao Zedong was Lan Lian. While everyone else was at the Ximen family compound keening over Chairman Mao, he sat alone on the doorstep of his room to the west, honing his rusty scythe with a whetstone. The scraping sound set people's teeth on edge and chilled their hearts. It certainly didn't suit the occasion, and it hinted at something dark. Jinlong, unable to stand it a moment longer, handed the radio to his wife and, with the entire village looking on, ran up to Lan Lian, bent down, grabbed the whetstone out of his hand, and flung it to the ground. It broke in two.

"Are you human or aren't you?" Jinlong cursed between his teeth.

Lan Lian narrowed his eyes to size up Jinlong, who was shaking in anger. He stood up slowly, still holding his scythe.

"He's dead," he said, "but I have to keep on living. There's millet that needs harvesting."

Jinlong picked up a metal bucket with a rusted bottom next to the ox pen and threw it at Lan Lian, who let it hit him in the chest without even trying to get out of the way. It fell at his feet.

Jinlong's eyes were red. Picking up a carrying pole, he raised it high and was about to hit Lan Lian in the head when, fortunately, Hong Taiyue stopped him.

"What kind of a man are you, old Lan?" Hong said unhappily.

Tears began to flow from Lan Lian's eyes as he got down on his knees.

"I loved Chairman Mao more than any of you imposters," he said indignantly.

Everyone just stared terrified, at a loss for words.

Lan Lian pounded the ground with his fists and keened:

"Chairman Mao — I'm one of your people too — I received my plot of land from you — you gave me the right to be an independent farmer—"

Yingchun, still weeping, walked over and bent down to help him up. But his knees seemed to have taken root. Yingchun fell to her knees in front of him.

A yellow butterfly flitted down from the apricot tree and settled like a dead leaf on a white chrysanthemum she wore in her hair.

Wearing a white chrysanthemum in the hair to mourn a loved one was a village custom. Other women rushed over to Yingchun's door to pick white mums, hoping that the butterfly would flit over to their heads; but after landing on Yingchun's head, it tucked in its wings and stayed put.

32

Old Xu Bao's Greed Costs Him His Life
Pig Sixteen Chases the Moon and Becomes King

I quietly walked away from the compound, left the perplexed crowd around Lan Lian. I saw the evil eyes of Xu Bao half hidden amid the crowd and guessed that the old thief didn't dare make his move quite yet, leaving me time to ready myself to fight him head-on.

Not a single person remained at the farm, and as night began to fall — mealtime for us seventy or so survivors — the sounds of hunger rose. I'd have opened the pens and freed all the pigs, if not for the possibility that they'd pepper me with questions. Go ahead, pals, make as big a scene as you want. I don't have time to worry about you, since I see the slippery figure of Xu Bao behind the crooked apricot tree. Actually, it's more a case of sensing the murderous aura emanating from that cruel man's body. My mind was spinning as I worked on strategies from my hiding spot in the pen. I backed into a corner, figuring that was the best way to keep my jewels out of harm's way. I hunkered down, feigning ignorance; but I had a plan: observe, wait, and employ passive resistance. Come on, Xu Bao. You think you're going to get your hands on my jewels to go with your liquor. Well, I'll bite yours off and avenge all the animals you mutilated.

The evening sky darkened, and steam rose from the wet ground. The pigs were so hungry they stopped clamoring. The only sounds were the croaks of frogs. The murderous aura seemed to be drawing nearer, and I knew he was about to strike. His dry little face appeared, like a greasy walnut. No eyebrows, no eyelashes, no chin stubble. The guy actually smiled, and I nearly wet myself. But, goddamn it, I don't care how much you smile! He opened the gate and stood in the opening, where he waved to me and uttered a greeting: "Soo-ee." He wanted to trick me into leaving my pen, I saw that immediately. He'd leap into action as I walked out the gate and make off with my jewels. Well, you little bastard, nice try, but old Pig Sixteen isn't about to fall for your tricks today. The pen could collapse but I won't budge, and you can give me gourmet food but I won't eat. Xu Bao tossed a corn cake into my pen. Pick it up and eat it yourself, you little bastard. Xu Bao played every trick he knew, but I stayed hunkered down in my corner.

"That's one demonic damned pig!" he cursed angrily.

If Xu Bao had quit at that moment, would I have had the guts to run up and take him on? Hard to say. The son of a bitch was so addicted to eating animals' testicles that he didn't leave; he was so attracted by those objects hanging between my hind legs that he got down on his hands and knees in the mud and crawled into my pen.

A mixture of anger and fear, like blue and yellow flames, flared up in my mind. The hour for revenge had arrived. Clenching my teeth and keeping still, I forced myself to stay calm. Okay, here I am. Come closer, a little closer. Wait till the enemy is in your house before you strike. Close combat, night combat, I'm ready. He wavered when he was a yard or so away and made faces to tempt me to come out to meet him. Forget that, you little bastard. Come on, here I am, just a dumb pig, no danger to you. Probably thinking he'd overestimated my intelligence, Xu Bao let his guard down and approached slowly, with hopes of scaring me into moving. He bent down a yard in front of me, and I felt my muscles tense, like a bow pulled taut. The arrow was on the string. I knew if I attacked then, he could hop like a flea and still not get away.

It was no longer a case of will commanding body; it attacked on its own, driving itself right into Xu Bao's belly and lifting him off the ground. His head hit the wall, and he thudded to the ground right where I normally relieved myself. His scream hung in the air well after he landed. His fighting capacity was gone. He lay in my refuse like a cadaver. I decided to carry out my complete plan in order to avenge my mutilated friends. I'd use the man's own strategy against him. I was feeling slightly disgusted and hesitant, but since I'd put my idea into play, I had to see it through to the end. I bit down between his legs. I came up empty! Nothing but pants material. I pulled back and ripped the material off his crotch, and what I saw terrified me. Xu Bao, it turned out, was a natural-born eunuch. I was stupefied, but now I knew what he was all about, I understood why he had such loathing for testes in other males, why he'd honed his special skill, and why he'd developed such a taste for that delicacy. Come to think of it, he was a luckless creature. Maybe he believed in the idea that you are what you eat, which is on the order of believing you can get blood out of a turnip or that a dead tree can sprout new leaves. In the heavy darkness I saw two lines of green blood snake out of his nostrils. How could he be so fragile that one head butt did him in? I stuck a hoof under his nose. I could feel no air coming out. Damn, the little bastard really was dead. I'd overheard someone from the country hospital tell villagers about CPR, and I'd personally seen Baofeng bring a drowning victim back to life. So I laid the guy out straight and pressed down on his chest with both hooves. Once, twice ... Pushing with all my might, I could hear his rib cage creak, and I saw more blood come out of his mouth and nose. . . .

As I stood in the gateway of my pen I made the most important decision of my life: Chairman Mao had died, which meant great changes were unavoidable in the human world. As for me, I'd become a homicidal pig, and if I stuck around, all I could look forward to was the butcher's knife and a pot of boiling water. At that moment I thought I heard a voice summoning me from the distance:

"Rebel, brothers!"

Before fleeing into the wild, I opened the gates on the pens of the pigs who had survived the Red Death and let them out.

"Brothers," I said to them from a high spot of ground, "rebel!"

They just stared at me blankly, having no idea what I was saying, all but one skinny immature sow — an unspoiled body with a black-and-white belly — who emerged from the crowd and said, "I'll follow you, my king." The rest of them just rooted around in their pens looking for something to eat. A few walked back inside to lie down lazily and wait to be fed by the humans.

So with the little sow behind me, I headed southeast on ground so soft our legs sank in up to the knees. We left a clear trail. When we reached the bank of the deep, water-filled canal, I asked her:

"What's your name?"

"They call me Little Flower, my king."

"Why do they call you that?"

"Because there are two little floral patterns on my belly, my king."

"Did you come here from Mount Yimeng, Little Flower?"

"No, my king."

"Then where did you come from?"

"I don't know, my king."

"You're the only one who came with me. Why?"

"I worship you, my king."

As I looked this simple little animal over, naïve Little Flower, I was both moved and saddened. I nudged her belly with my snout as a sign of friendship.

"All right, Little Flower," I said, "humans no longer have any control over us, just like our ancestors. We're free. But starting today, we'll dine on the wind and drink the dew. It will be a hard life, and it's not too late for you to change your mind."

"I'm not going to change my mind, my king," she said decisively.

"That's wonderful news, Little Flower. Can you swim?"

"Yes, my king, I can."

"Great!" I patted her on the rump and jumped into the water.

The water was warm and gentle, and it felt wonderful to be immersed in it. I'd originally planned to swim to the opposite bank and walk from there, but I changed my mind. At first the surface of the water looked frozen in place, but once we were in it I realized that it flowed northward, toward the great canal once used by the Manchu government to transport grain, at a speed of at least five yards a minute. The speed of flow and our buoyancy would make our passage an effortless one. By barely kicking with my front legs, I sailed through the water like a shark, and when I turned to look, there was Little Flower, right behind me, all four legs churning in the water, head high, eyes flashing; she was breathing through her nose.

"How're you doing, Little Flower?"

"I'm doing fine, my king." But with that brief bit of conversation her nose dipped beneath the surface, which led to snorts and a spurt of frantic leg kicks.

I lifted her up until she was nearly out of the water. "You'll be fine," I said. "We pigs are born swimmers. The key is not to panic. I've decided to stay off the roads and travel by water. That way we won't leave a trail for those disgusting humans. Can you hold out?"

"Yes . . ." She was gasping slightly.

"Good. Here, why don't you climb onto my back?" She refused, preferring to tough it out. So I dove underwater, and when I floated up to the surface I had her perched on my back. "Hold tight," I said. "Don't let go no matter what."

With Little Flower on my back, I floated down the canal past the Apricot Garden Pig Farm and on to the grand canal, heading east amid billowing waves. A fiery sunset put on a beautiful show in the western sky, with mutating cloud formations — a green dragon, a white tiger, a lion, a wild dog — with rays of sunlight filling the gaps between clouds and lighting up the surface of the water.

Waves chased us; we chased waves; waves chased one another. Great canal, where did you get such power? You carry with you mud, corn, sorghum, potato vines, even uprooted trees, on your eastward journey. You also deposit dead pigs in your tree-lined shallows, where they swell up, rot, and give off foul odors. When I saw them I was more convinced than ever that by drifting downstream with Little Flower I'd transcended the life of pigs, transcended the Red Death, even transcended the now-ended Mao Zedong era.

I know that in his "Tales of Pig-Raising," Mo Yan had this to say about the pig carcasses that had been thrown into the river: "A thousand dead pigs from the Apricot Garden Pig Farm formed a corps of floating dead. Their carcasses swelled up, began to rot, exploded, were eaten by maggots, were torn apart by fish, all the while drifting downstream until they disappeared into the roiling waters of the Eastern Sea, where what was left of them was swallowed up, dismembered, and turned into all sorts of materials to join the transforming cycle of material objects." I'm not going to say the guy can't write, only that he missed a wonderful opportunity, for if he'd seen me, Pig Sixteen, with Little Flower on my back, riding waves in the golden waters of the river, instead of writing about death, he'd have praised life, praised us, praised me! I am the power of life, I am passion, freedom, and love, the most beautiful spectacle the world has to offer.

We drifted with the flow toward that moon of the lunar eighth month, sixteenth day, a much different moon than the one under which you were married. The moon that night had fallen from the sky, but this night it rose out of the river, just as big and round as the other one, red at first, like an innocent child sent to earth from some hidden spot in the universe, bawling and bleeding and turning the water red. Your moon, sweet and melancholic, came down for your wedding. My moon, solemn and bleak, rose up for Mao Zedong. We saw him sitting on the moon — his bulk pressing down and altering its shape into an oval. He wore a red flag like a cape, held a cigarette in his fingers, and raised his heavy head slightly. A pensive look was frozen on his face.

With Little Flower on my back, I drifted eastward, chasing the moon and chasing Mao Zedong. We wanted to get closer to the moon so we could see Mao Zedong's face with even greater clarity. But the moon moved with us, the distance remaining constant no matter how hard I paddled, even as I moved through the water like a torpedo. Little Flower dug her hooves into my ribs and shouted "Faster! Faster!" as if I were her horse.

Where Northeast Gaomi Township and Pingdu County met, a sandbar called the Wu Family Sandy Mouth divided the river, sending one stream northeast, the other southeast; the two streams merging again near Two County Hamlet. Now picture this scene. A fast-moving river suddenly divides into two, and at this juncture, schools of red carp, white eels, black-capped soft-shelled turtles, fly up to the moon, an expression of romanticism; but before they reach their goal, the pull of gravity brings them back in a bright and lovely, but ultimately tragic arc, for when most of them land on the surface of the water, scales fly, fins snap off, and gills shatter, turning the returned water creatures into meals for waiting foxes and wild boars. A small number manage to return to the safety of the water by virtue of their strength or by pure luck, and continue swimming to the southeast or the northeast.

Now, given my body weight and the fact that I was carrying Little Flower on my back, although I too went skyward at that juncture, I started falling back before I was ten feet out of the water, and it was only the springy nature of the scrub brush that kept either of us from injury. We were, of course, too large for the foxes to consider eating; and to the wild boars, with their well-developed front halves and tapered rear ends, we had to be considered relatives; they would never eat their own kin. We landed safely on the sandbar.

Food came easily to those foxes and wild boars, good, nutritious food, and they were all much rounder than they should have been. All foxes eat fish, that's a rule of nature. But when we saw a dozen or so wild boars dining on fish, we could hardly believe our eyes. They'd grown so picky, their mouths so pampered, that they ate only the brains and the roe; the fat, rich meat held no attraction for them.

Astounded to find us there, the wild boars slowly gathered round, mean looks in their eyes, moonlight glinting off their terrifying white fangs. Little Flower wrapped her legs around me even tighter, and I could feel that she was quaking. I started backing up, backing up, not giving these brutes the chance to fan out and surround us. I counted them, there were nine altogether, male and female, all weighing at least two hundred *jin*. They had long, hard, stupid-looking snouts, pointed wolflike ears, and spiky bristles; their oily black skin showed how well-fed they all were, and the smell they emitted spoke to their raw, wild power. At the time I weighed five hundred *jin* and was as big as a rowboat. Having come from and through the human, donkey, and ox realms, I was both smart and strong, and none of them would have been a match for me, one-on-one. But in a fight with nine at the same time, I stood no chance. All I could think at the moment was back up, keep backing up, all the way to the water's edge, where I could let Little Flower swim safely away. Then I'd turn and fight with all the wit and courage I possessed. After dining on an exclusive diet of fish brains and roe, these animals' intelligence was nearly on a par with foxes, so they were probably not going to be fooled by my strategy. I spotted two of the boars move around behind me so they could surround me before I reached the water. I realized that retreat was a dead-end street, that it was time to go on the offensive, to feint to the east and attack to the west in order to break through the encirclement and flee to the expansive center of the river sandbar. I needed to adapt Mao Zedong's guerrilla tactic of forcing changes in their formation and attack their weaknesses. I signaled Little Flower to let her know what I was planning.

"My king," she said softly, "go on, don't worry about me."

"I can't do that," I said. "We're in this together, like brother and sister. Where I am is where you'll be."

I charged the male that was launching a frontal attack. He wobbled and started to back up, but I abruptly changed directly and headed toward a nearby female. When our heads hit, it sounded like the crash of broken pottery, and I was treated to the view of her body tumbling backward at least ten feet. Now the circle had been rent, but I could hear the snorts from their noses behind me. With a swinish yell, I ran like the wind toward the southeast. But when I realized that Little Flower was not behind me, I put on the brakes and spun around to wait for her to catch up. But poor Little Flower, dear Little Flower, the only one willing to escape with me, loyal Little Flower, had been bitten on the rump by a savage male wild boar; her screams of pain and terror blanched the moon. "Let her go!" I roared as I charged the offending boar.

"My king," she yelled, "go on, don't worry about me."

You've listened to me this far, and I'd be surprised if you weren't deeply moved or if you didn't see our actions — pigs or not — as noble. Well, that boar held on and continued his savage attack. Her cries nearly drove me crazy. Nearly? Hell, I *was* crazy. But a pair of males ran up and blocked my way, keeping me from rescuing Little Flower. Abandoning all battle strategies and tactics, I charged one of them, who didn't get out of the way fast enough to avoid getting bitten in the neck. I felt my teeth bite through his thick skin and sink all the way down to bone. He rolled over and got away, leaving me with a mouth filled with rank-tasting blood and spiky bristles. Meanwhile, the second boar ran up and bit my hind leg. I kicked out like a mule — a trick I'd learned as a donkey — and connected on his cheek. Then I spun around and went at him. He ran off screeching. My leg hurt like crazy; it was gushing blood, but I had no time to worry about that, with Little Flower being ravaged by that other bastard. I jumped up with a loud war whoop and charged. When I hit the bastard I felt his innards rip and tear, and he was dead before he hit the ground. Little Flower was still alive, but barely. As I picked her up, her innards tumbled out of the wound in her belly. I didn't know what to do about all that steamy, slippery, foul-smelling stuff. I was helpless, helpless and heartbroken.

"Little Flower, my darling Little Flower, I failed you . . ."

She struggled to open her eyes. A blue and white, and very bleak, gaze emerged.

"My king," she managed to say as saliva and blood seeped from her mouth, "would it be all right . . . if I call you Big Brother instead?"

"Yes, of course," I replied through my tears. "My little sister, the closest person in the world to me . . ."

"I'm so lucky . . . Big Brother . . . so very lucky . . ." She stopped breathing and her legs stiffened, like four little clubs.

"Little Sister!" I was weeping as I stood up and walked straight toward the remaining boars, determined to fight them to the death — my death.

They formed up and, fearful but disciplined, began backing off. When I charged, they spread out to surround me. Abandoning tactics altogether, I butted here, bit there, and fought like a mad pig, wounding them all and getting my share of wounds in the process. When the shifting battle lines brought us to the middle of the river sandbar, to the edge of a row of abandoned military structures, with roof tiles and crumbling walls, I saw a familiar figure seated beside a stone feeding trough half buried in mud.

"Old Diao, is that you?" I shouted in amazement.

"I knew you'd come one day, my brother," Diao Xiaosan said before turning to the approaching wild boars. "I cannot be your king. This is your true king!"

After a momentary hesitation, they fell to their knees and, with their snouts in the dirt, announced in unison:

"Long live the great king!"

I was about to say something, but with this latest development, what could I say? So, in a state of utter bewilderment, I became king of the sandbar wild boars and received their fealty. As for the human king, the one sitting on the moon, he had already flown off millions of miles from earth, and the gargantuan moon had shrunk down to the size of a silver platter, so small and far away that I could no longer have seen the human king, even with a high-powered telescope.

33

Pig Sixteen Has Thoughts of Home
A Drunk Hong Taiyue Raises Hell in a Public House

"Time flies." Before I knew it, I was entering my fifth year as king of the boars on this desolate and virtually uninhabited sandbar.

At first, I'd planned to implement a system of monogamous relationships, as practiced in civilized human society, and had assumed that this reform measure would be greeted with cheers of approval. Imagine my surprise when, instead, it was met with strong opposition, not only by the females but also by the males, who grumbled their dissatisfaction, even though they would have been the primary beneficiaries. Not knowing how to resolve the issue, I took my problem to Diao Xiaosan, who was sprawled in the straw shed we'd provided to protect him from the elements.

"You can abdicate if you want," he said coldly. "But if you plan to stay on as king, you'll have to respect local customs."

My hooves were tied. I had no choice but to let stand this cruel jungle practice. So I shut my eyes and fantasized images of Little Flower, of Butterfly Lover, and, less clearly, of a female donkey, even the hazy outline of some women, as I mated almost recklessly with all those female wild boars. I avoided it whenever possible and cut corners when avoidance was out of the question, but as the years passed, the sandbar population was increased by dozens of wildly colorful little bastards. Some had golden yellow bristles, others had black, and some were spotted like those dalmatians you see in TV ads. Most of them retained their wild boar physical characteristics, but they were clearly smarter than their mothers

In 1981, during the fourth lunar month, when the apricot trees were blooming and the female wild boars were in heat, I swam over to the south bank of the river. The water was warm on the surface, but icy cold below, and at the point where the warm and cold water met, I encountered schools of fish swimming upstream against the current. I was deeply moved by their indomitable desire to return to their spawning grounds, whatever the difficulty, however great the sacrifice. Moving over to shallow water, I became lost in my own thoughts as I stood and watched them struggling heroically ahead, their fins flapping.

Suddenly I was struck by an outlandish thought — actually it was more like an urgent internal desire, to travel back to Ximen Village, as if I had an appointment made years before, one virtually impossible to reschedule.

It had already been four years since I'd paired up with Little Flower and fled from the pig farm, but I could have found the way back there blindfolded, in part because the fragrance of apricot blossoms came to me on winds from the west but mainly because it was my home. So I struck out, walking along the narrow but comfortably smooth bank of the river, heading west. Uncultivated fields stretched out south of me, nothing but scrubland to the north.

When I reached the one-point-six-acre plot belonging to Lan Lian, I planted my hooves in the ground, having chased the moon westward to my destination. I looked off to the south, where Ximen Village Production Brigade land surrounding Lan Lian's tiny strip was blanketed with mulberry trees, under whose lush foliage women were picking mulberries in the moonlight, and the sight stirred my emotions. I could see there were changes in farming villages following the death of Mao Zedong. Lan Lian was still planting an old variety of wheat, but the mulberry trees all around him were sapping the soil of nutrients, having an obvious effect on at least four rows of his cultivated land, with anemic stalks and tassels as tiny as houseflies. Maybe this was another scheme Hong Taiyue had dreamed up to punish Lan Lian: Let's see how an independent farmer deals with this. By the light of the moon I saw the bare back of someone digging a ditch beside the mulberry trees, waging a battle against the People's Commune. He was digging a deep, narrow ditch on the land between his and the mulberry plots belonging to the production brigade and chopping off the yellow mulberry roots that crossed that line with his hoe. That could have been a problem; on your own land you could dig as you wanted. But cutting the roots of brigade trees was considered destruction of property belonging to the collective. My mind was a blank as I gazed at old Lan Lian, bent over like a black bear clumsily digging away. Once the mulberries on both sides were tall, mature trees, the independent farmer would be the owner of a tract of barren land. But I soon learned how wrong I was. By this time, the production brigade had broken up and the People's Commune existed in name only. Agricultural reform had entered the land-parceling phase, and the land surrounding Lan Lian's plot had been distributed to individual farmers, who could decide on their own whether to plant mulberries or wheat.

My legs carried me to the Apricot Garden Pig Farm. The apricot tree was still there, but the pigpens weren't. The spot where I had once sprawled lazily to daydream was now planted with peanuts. I rose up on my hind legs and rested my front hooves on branches of the tree I'd practiced on every day as a young pig. It was immediately clear that I was a lot heavier and clumsier than I'd been back then, and I was obviously out of practice where standing upright was concerned. In sum, as I roamed the ground of the onetime pig farm, I couldn't help feeling nostalgic, which in itself was a sure sign that I was well ensconced in middle age. Yes, I'd experienced a great deal of what the world had to offer a pig.

I discovered that the two rows of buildings that had served as dormitories and workplaces for personnel who prepared our food had been converted to the task of raising silkworms. The sight of all those bright lights told me that Ximen Village had been added to the national electricity grid. And there, in front of a wide array of silkworm racks, stood Ximen Bai, her hair white as snow. She was bent over, the willow basket in her hands nearly filled with mulberry leaves, which she was spreading over the white silkworm beds. Crunching noises rose into the air. Your wedding suite, I noted, had also been converted to silkworm raising, which meant that you'd been given new quarters.

I stepped onto the road that ran through the center of the village; only now it was paved and probably twice as wide as before. The squat rammed-earth walls on either side had been taken down and had given way to rows of identical buildings with red-tile roofs. North of the road stood a two-story building fronted by an open square in which a hundred or more people — mostly old women and children — were watching an episode of a TV drama on a twenty-one-inch Matsushita Japanese television set.

I observed the crowd of TV watchers for about ten minutes before continuing on, heading west. You know where I was going. But now I needed to stay off the road. Causing the death of Xu Bao had made me a household name throughout Northeast Gaomi Township, and there'd be hell to pay if they spotted me. I wasn't worried that I couldn't hold my own if it came to that, but I wanted to avoid anything that might involve innocent bystanders. In other words, I was afraid, not of them, but of causing trouble. By staying in the shadows of the buildings south of the road, I was able to make it unobserved to the Ximen family compound.

The gate was open; the old apricot stood there as always, its branches covered with fresh blossoms that filled the air with their fragrance. I stayed in the shadows and gazed in at eight tables with plastic tablecloths. A light that had been strung outside and hung from a branch of the apricot tree lit the compound up like daytime. I knew the people who were sitting at the tables. A bad lot, all of them. The onetime puppet security chief Yu Wufu, the turncoat Zhang Dazhuang, Tian Gui the landlord, and the rich peasant Wu Yuan were seated at one table. Seated at one of the other tables were the onetime chief of security Yang Qi and two of the Sun brothers, Dragon and Tiger. The tables were littered with the leavings of a banquet; the guests were already good and drunk. I later learned that Yang Qi was in the business of selling bamboo poles — he'd never been much of a farmer — which he purchased in Jinggangshan and transported to Gaomi by train and from there to Ximen Village by truck. He sold his entire first load to Ma Liangcai, who used the poles to build a new school. Almost overnight Yang Qi became a wealthy man. Sitting there as the village's richest man, he was dressed in a gray suit with a bright red tie. By rolling up his sleeves, he was able to show off his digital wristwatch. He took out a pack of American cigarettes and tossed one to Dragon Sun, who was gnawing on a braised pig's foot, and another to Tiger Sun, who was wiping his mouth with a napkin. He crumpled the empty pack, turned, and shouted toward the east-side room:

"Boss lady!"

The boss lady came running outside. What do you know, it was her, Wu Qiuxiang! Would you believe it, Boss Lady? That was when I noticed that the wall just east of the compound gate had been whitewashed to accommodate a sign in red: Qiuxiang Tavern. Wu Qiuxiang, the proprietress of Qiuxiang Tavern, ran up to where Yang Qi was sitting. Her smiling face was heavily powdered; she had a towel over one shoulder and a blue apron around her waist — obviously a shrewd, competent, enthusiastic, professional innkeeper. This was a different world — reforms and openings to the outside world had brought profound changes to Ximen Village. Qiuxiang was all smiles as she asked Yang Qi:

"What can I do for you, Boss Yang?"

"Don't call me that," Yang said with a glare. "I'm just a peddler of bamboo poles, not the boss of anything."

"Don't be modest, Boss Yang. At ten yuan apiece, the sale of ten thousand makes you a wealthy man. If you're not a boss, then there can't be a soul in Northeast Gaomi Township worthy of the title." Matching her exaggerated compliment with a touch on Yang's shoulder, Qiuxiang continued. "Just look at how you're dressed. What you're wearing had to cost at least a thousand."

"You women, open your bloody mouths and out comes the flattery. At this rate, you'll won't be happy until I explode like one of those bloated dead pigs back on the pig farm."

"Okay, Boss Yang, you're not worth a thing, a pauper, does that sound better to you? You close the door on me before I have a chance to ask for a loan. Now then," Qiuxiang said with a pout, "what can I get for you?"

"Huh? Are you mad at me? Don't pout like that, it gives me a hard-on."

"To hell with you!" Qiuxiang fired back, slapping Yang Qi on the head with her greasy towel. "Now tell me, what do you want?"

"A pack of cigarettes. Good Friends."

"That's all? What about liquor?" With a quick glance at the red faces of Tiger and Dragon Sun, she said, "These brothers look to be in dire need of a drink."

"Boss Yang is buying today," thick-tongued Dragon said, "so we ought to drink less."

"Is that an insult directed my way?" Yang Qi exclaimed as he banged his fist on the table. "I may not be rich," he said with feigned anger, "but I won't go broke buying a few drinks for you two." He reached out and pinched Qiuxiang on the rear and said, "Okay, two bottles of Black Vat."

"Black Vat? Too low-class. For friends like this, the least you can do is treat them to some Little Tiger."

"Damn, Qiuxiang, you sure know how to take a hint and run with it," Yang Qi said with a note of resignation. "All right, make it Little Tiger."

Lan Jiefang, I'm painting a detailed picture of what was going on in the Ximen family compound, describing what I heard and saw as a pig at the gate, in order to bring the conversation around to a very important individual, Hong Taiyue. After a new office building was built for the production brigade, the original headquarters — the five rooms belonging to Ximen Nao — were taken over by Jinlong and Huzhu as their living quarters. And there's more. Immediately after announcing the rehabilitation of the bad elements in the village, Jinlong announced that he was changing his name from Lan to Ximen. All this held considerable meaning, and the loyal old revolutionary Hong Taiyue was greatly puzzled.

Following his retirement, Hong began acting more and more like Lan Lian, cooped up at home during the day, and out the door as soon as the moon climbed into the sky. Lan Lian worked his land under moonlight; Hong roamed the village like an old-time night watchman, up and down all the streets and byways. Jinlong said: The old branch secretary's level of consciousness is high as always — he's out there every night protecting us. That, of course, wasn't what Hong intended. He had a heavy heart over the changes that had occurred in the village and didn't know what to do about it. So he walked and he drank out of a canteen people said had belonged to the Eighth Route Army. He wore an old army jacket over his shoulders, a wide leather belt around his waist, and straw sandals on his feet, topped by army leggings. The only thing that kept him from total resemblance to an Eighth Route soldier was the absence of a repeater rifle slung over his back. He'd take a couple of steps, then a swig from his canteen, and finally utter a loud curse. By the time the canteen was empty, the moon would be low in the western sky and he'd be falling-down drunk. On some nights he made it back to his bed to sleep it off; on other nights he'd simply bed down by a haystack or on an abandoned millstone and sleep till sunrise. He was spotted sleeping by a haystack by early-morning market goers, his brows and beard coated with frost, his face nice and ruddy, with no sign of feeling the cold. He'd be snoring away so peacefully no one wanted to wake him from whatever he was dreaming. Sometimes he'd head out to the fields on a whim and start a conversation with Lan Lian, but not by stepping on Lan Lian's plot of land. No, he'd stand on somebody else's property and engage the independent farm in a verbal battle. But since Lan Lian was busy working, he had little time for idle chatter, so he just let the old man talk, which he was only too happy to do. When Lan Lian did open his mouth, though, a pointed comment as hard as a rock or as sharp as a knife emerged and shut the old man up on the spot, so enraging him he could hardly stand. During the "Contract Responsibility System" phase, for instance, Hong Taiyue said to Lan Lian:

"Isn't this the same as bringing back capitalism? Wouldn't you say it was a system of material incentives?"

In a low, muffled voice, Lan Lian replied: "The best is yet to come, just you wait and see!"

Then when that led to the phase of a system of "household responsibility for production," Hong stood alongside Lan Lian's plot of land and jumped up and down, cursing:

"Shit, are they really giving up on the People's Commune, ownership at the three levels of commune, brigade, and production team levels, with the production team as the base, from each according to his ability and to each according to his needs, all that?"

"Sooner or later, we'll all be independent farmers," Lan Lian said coldly.

"Dream on," Hong said.

"You just wait and see."

Then when the subsistence system went into effect, Hong got roaring drunk and came up to Lan Lian's land, wailing and cursing angrily, as if Lan Lian himself were the person responsible for all the earth-shaking reforms:

"Lan Lian, you motherfucker, it's just like you said, you bastard. This subsistence system is nothing but independent farming, isn't it? After thirty hard, demanding years, we're right back to the days before Liberation. Well, not for me. I'm going to Beijing, right up to Tiananmen Square, and I'll go to Chairman Mao's Memorial Hall and weep to his spirit. I'll tell Chairman Mao I'm going to file a complaint against all of you. Our land, the land we fought for and turned red, and now they want a new color. . . ."

Grief and anger drove Hong out of his mind, and as he rolled on the ground, he lost sight of boundaries. He rolled onto Lan Lian's land just as Lan was cutting down beans. Hong Taiyue, rolling on the ground like a donkey, rolled into the bean lattice, crushing the pods and sending beans popping and flying all over the place. Lan pressed Hong to the ground with his sickle and said unsparingly:

"You're on my land! We struck a deal many years ago, and now it is my right to sever your Achilles tendon. But I'm in a good mood today, so I'm going to let you off."

Hong rolled right off of Lan Lian's land and, by holding on to a scrawny mulberry tree, got to his feet.

"I refuse to accept it. Old Lan, after thirty years of struggle, you still wind up the victor, while those of us of unquestionable loyalty and hard, bitter work spend thirty years of blood and sweat, only to wind up the losers. You're right and we're wrong. . . ."

"In the land distribution, you got yours, didn't you?" Lan asked in a less confrontational tone. "I'll bet you got every inch you had coming. They wouldn't dare shortchange you. And you still receive your six-hundred-yuan cadre-level pension, don't you? And will they take away your monthly army supplement of thirty yuan? Not hardly. You have nothing to complain about. The Communist Party is paying you for everything you did, good or bad, every month like clockwork."

"These are two different matters," Hong replied, "and what I won't accept is that you, Lan Lian, are one of history's obstacles, a man who was left behind, and here you are, part of the vanguard. You must be proud of yourself. All Northeast Gaomi Township, all Gaomi County, is praising you as a man of foresight!"

"I'm not the sage. That would be Mao Zedong, or Deng Xiaoping," Lan Lian said, suddenly agitated. "A sage can change heaven and earth. What can I do? I just stick to one firm principle, and that is, even brothers will divide up a family's wealth. So how will it work to throw a bunch of people with different names together? Well, as it turns out, to my surprise, my principle stood the test of time. Old Hong," Lan Lian said tearfully, "you sank your teeth in me like a mad dog for half my life, but you can't do that anymore. Like an old toad used to hold up a table, I struggled to bear the weight for thirty years, but now, at last, I can stand up straight. Give me that canteen of yours."

"What, you're going to take a drink?"

Lan Lian stepped over the boundary of his land, took the liquor-filled canteen out of Hong Taiyue's hand, tipped his head back, and drank every last drop. Then he flung away the canteen, got down on his knees, and said with a mixture of sadness and joy:

"You can see, my friend, I held out long enough, and now I can work my land in the light of day. . . ."

I didn't personally see any of this, so it has to be considered hearsay. But since a novelist by the name of Mo Yan came from there, fact and fiction have gotten so jumbled up, figuring out what's true and what's not is just about impossible. I should be telling you only stuff from my personal experience or things I saw or heard, but, I'm sorry to say, Mo Yan's fiction has a way of wriggling in through the cracks and taking my tale to places it shouldn't go.

So, as I was saying, I hid in the shadows outside the gate of the Ximen family compound and watched as Yang Qi, who by then was pretty drunk, picked up his glass and, wobbling back and forth and swaying from side to side, made his way over to the table where the bad people from earlier days were sitting. Since they had gathered for a special occasion, everyone at the table was in an agitated mood as they recalled the wretched times they had survived, approaching a point where they could easily be intoxicated without the aid of alcohol. So they were shocked to see Yang Qi, the onetime head of public security, who, as representative of the dictatorship of the proletariat, had used a switch on them, shocked and angry, as he braced himself with a hand on the table and raised his glass with the other.

"Worthy brothers," he said, his thick tongue blurring the words a bit, "gentlemen, I, Yang Qi, offended all of you in the past, and today I come to offer my apologies."

He tipped his head back and poured the contents in the direction of his mouth, most making it only as far as his neck, where it soaked his necktie. He reached up to loosen his tie, but wound up making it tighter, and tighter, until his face began turning dark. It was almost as if the only way he could rid himself of the torment he was experiencing was to commit suicide this way and expatiate his guilt.

The onetime turncoat Zhang Dazhuang, at heart a good man, stood up to rescue Yang by removing his tie and hanging it from a branch of the tree. Yang's neck was red, his eyes bulging.

"Gentlemen," he said, "the West German chancellor got down on his knees in the snow before a memorial to the murdered Jews and asked forgiveness for the deeds of Hitler. Now I, Yang Qi, the onetime head of public security, kneel before you to ask your forgiveness."

The bright light from the lantern lit up his face, which had grown pale, as he knelt on the ground beneath the necktie that hung over his head like a bloody sword. How symbolic. I was deeply moved by the scene, even if it was slightly comical. This coarse, disagreeable man, Yang Qi, not only knew that the West German chancellor had gone down on his knees to ask forgiveness, but his conscience had told him he had to apologize to men he had mistreated in the past. I couldn't help looking at him with new eyes, giving him a bit of grudging respect. Vaguely I recalled hearing Mo Yan say something about the West German chancellor, another piece of information he'd gleaned from *Reference News.*

The leader of this band of onetime bad characters, Wu Yuan, ran over to help Yang Qi to his feet, but Yang wrapped his arms around a table leg and refused to stand.

"I'm guilty of terrible things," he wailed. "Lord Yama has sent his attendants to flay me with their lashes . . . ow . . . that hurts . . . it's killing me . . ."

"Old Yang," Wu Yuan said, "that's all in the past. Why hold on to those memories when we've already forgotten? Besides, society forced you to do what you did, and if you hadn't beaten us, somebody else would've. So get up, get up now. We've come through it and have been rehabilitated. And you? You've gotten rich. And if your conscience still bothers you, donate the money you made to the cause of rebuilding a temple."

Racked by sobs, Yang roared: "I won't donate money I worked so hard to put aside. How dare you even suggest that! . . . What I want is for you to come beat me the way I beat you years ago. I don't owe any of you a thing. You owe me. . . ."

Just then I saw Hong Taiyue walk up on unsteady legs. He passed right by me, reeking of alcohol. In all the years I'd been on the run, this was the first time I'd been able to closely observe the onetime supreme leader of the Ximen Village Production Brigade. His hair, which had turned white, still stuck up in the air like spikes. His face was puffy and he was missing several teeth, which gave him a somewhat dull-witted look. The moment he stepped through the gate, the clamor stopped abruptly, surefire evidence that the men in the compound had not lost their fear of the man who had ruled Ximen Village for many years.

Wu Qiuxiang rushed up to greet him, and the onetime bad individuals jumped to their feet as a sort of conditioned reflex. "Ah, Party secretary!" she called out with enthusiasm and familiarity as she took Hong Taiyue by the arm, something he was not at all accustomed to. He jerked his arm free, nearly falling over in the process. Qiuxiang reached out and steadied him; this time he let her hold his arm as she led him to a clean table, where he sat down. Since it was a bench, Hong was in constant danger of falling backward; sharp-eyed Huzhu reacted by quickly moving over a chair for him. Resting one arm on the table, he turned sideways to stare at the people under the tree, his eyes bleary and unfocused. After wiping the table in front of Hong in a practiced move, Qiuxiang asked genially:

"What can I get for the Party secretary?"

"Let's see, what'll I have . . ." He blinked, his heavy eyelids moving slowly up and down. Then he banged his fist on the table, sending the dented old revolutionary canteen bouncing into the air. "What can you get?" he shouted in anger. "Liquor, that's what! That and two ounces of gunpowder!"

"Party Secretary," Qiuxiang said with a smile, "I think you've had enough for one day. For now, I'll have Huzhu make you a bowl of fish broth. Drink it hot and then go home and get some sleep. What do you say?"

"Fish broth? Are you implying I'm drunk?" He glared at her, crusted material in the corners of his puffy eyes. "I'm not drunk!" he bellowed unhappily. "My bones and my flesh might be affected by alcohol, but my mind is as clear and bright as the moon or a shiny mirror. Don't think you can put something over on me, no ma'am! Liquor, where's the liquor? You small-time capitalists, you petty entrepreneurs, are like winter leeks. The roots may be withered and the outer skin dry, but the spark of life persists until the weather turns good and you start sprouting buds. Money is the only language you people speak. Well, I've got money, so bring me some liquor!"

Qiuxiang winked at Huzhu, who carried a white bowl over to Hong.

"Party Secretary, try this first."

Hong Taiyue took a sip and spit it out. He wiped his mouth with his sleeve and said in a loud voice that sounded both dreary and tragic:

"I never thought you'd gang up on me, too, Huzhu. I ask you for liquor, and you give me vinegar. My heart has been steeping in vinegar for so long that my spit is sour, and you give me vinegar. Where's

Jinlong? Call him over here so I can ask him if Ximen Village is still part of the Communist Party realm."

From the moment Hong walked into the compound, he was the focus of attention. All the while he was entertaining the crowd with witty remarks, everyone — including Yang Qi, who was kneeling on the ground — was enthralled, watching him with open mouths, not to snap out of it until Hong was drinking again.

"All of you, come over here and beat me, give me back everything I gave you . . . ," Yang Qi implored. "If you don't, you have no right to call yourselves human, and if you aren't human, then you must be the offspring of horses, mule spawn, sprung from the eggs of chickens, little bastards covered with fuzz . . ."

"Yang Qi," Wu Yuan, leader of the onetime bad elements, said, unable to hold back any longer, "Elder Yang, we give up, how's that? When you were beating us you did so as a representative of the government to teach us a lesson. If you hadn't done that, how could we ever have reformed ourselves? It was your rattan switch that made it possible for us to cast off our old selves and be transformed into new people, so get up, please get up." Wu Yuan called the others over. "Come, let's drink a toast to Yang Qi to thank him for educating us." The onetime bad elements raised their glasses and offered a toast to Yang; he refused to accept it. "Stop that!" he insisted as he wiped the beer foam from his face. "That's not going to work. I'm not getting up until you do as I ask. Murder demands the death penalty, and borrowed money has to be repaid. You owe me."

Wu Yuan looked around and, seeing no way out, said, "Elder Yang, since you're going to be stubborn, it looks like hitting you is the only way this will be settled. So on behalf of all bad elements, I'll slap you across the face and the account will be settled."

"No way will one slap settle accounts. I gave you people no fewer than three thousand lashes, so you owe me three thousand slaps, not one less."

"Yang Qi, you son of a bitch," Wu Yuan said as he walked up close to Yang, "you're going to drive me out of my mind. A bunch of us who suffered for decades are here to enjoy ourselves, but you've made that impossible. You call this an apology? This is just another way for you to bully us. . . . Well, I'm not going to take it any longer. I'm slapping you today, no matter who you are." And that's exactly what he did, right across Yang Qi's pear-shaped face.

With the sound reverberating in the air, Yang wobbled on his knees, but managed to stay upright. "More!" he cried out fiercely. "That was one. You've just started. You're not men if you don't give me 2,999 more."

His shout hadn't even died out when Hong Taiyue slammed his canteen down on the table and got to his feet, however unsteadily. He pointed to the table where the onetime bad elements were sitting, his right index finger straight as the cannon on a sailing ship being tossed on the waves.

"You're rebellingYou bunch of landlords, rich peasants, traitors, spies, and historical counterrevolutionaries, enemies of the proletariat, every one of you, how dare you sit there like normal people drinking and enjoying yourselves! Stand up!"

Hong had been relieved of his position of authority for years, but he was still a man to be listened to. He was used to ordering people around, and had the voice for it. The recently rehabilitated bad elements jumped up as if they were shot out of their seats, sweat dripping from their faces.

"And you —" Hong pointed at Yang Qi, ratcheting up his anger a notch or two. "You damned turncoat, you lily-livered scumbag who kneels before class enemies, you stand up too!"

Yang tried, but when his head bumped up against the wet necktie hanging from a low branch, his legs buckled and he sat down hard, his back resting against the apricot tree.

"You, you . . . you people—" Like a man standing on the deck of a wave-tossed boat, he tried but failed to point steadily at any of the men standing at their open-air tables. "You people," he said, launching into a tirade, "think you're home free. Well, look around and you'll see that this spot under the sky —" He pointed skyward and nearly fell over. "This spot still belongs to the Communist Party, even though there are dark clouds in the sky. I'm telling you, here and now, that your dunce caps have only been removed temporarily, and before long there'll be new ones for you to wear, this time made of iron or steel or brass. We'll weld them to your scalps, and you'll wear them to your death, into your coffin. That is the answer you get from this proud member of the Communist Party!" He pointed to Yang Qi, who was snoring away under the apricot tree. "You're not only a turncoat who kneels before class enemies, you're a profiteer who has dug holes at the base of the wall that is our collective economy." He then turned to Wu Qiuxiang. "And you, Wu Qiuxiang, I took pity on you and spared you from having to put on a dunce cap. But it's in your blood to exploit the masses, and you were just biding your time till the weather turned so you could sink roots and began to flower. Listen to me, all of you. Our Communist Party, we members of Mao Zedong's party who have survived countless intraparty struggles over the proper line, we tempered Communists who have weathered the storms of class struggle, we Bolsheviks, will not knuckle under, we will never surrender! Land distribution? I'll tell you what that is. It's a scheme to make the broad masses of middle and lower poor peasants suffer a second time, be beaten down all over again." Raising his fists in the air, Hong shouted, "We will keep the struggle alive, we will bring Lan Lian to his knees, we'll lop the top off this black flag! That is the mission of enlightened Communists of the Ximen Village Production Brigade and all middle and lower poor peasants! The cold, dark night will come to an end —"

The sound of an engine and a pair of blinding lights coming from the east brought Hong's tirade to an end. I flattened up against the wall to keep from being discovered. The engine was shut down, the lights turned off, and out from the cab of the ancient Jeep emerged Jinlong, Panther Sun, and others. Vehicles like that are considered trash these days, but for a rural village in the early 1980s, it had a domineering presence. Obviously, Jinlong, a village branch secretary of the Communist Party, was somebody to reckon with. This signaled the beginnings of his progress up the ladder.

Jinlong strode confidently in through the gate, followed by his companions. All eyes were on the current top leader of Ximen Village. Hong Taiyue pointed to Jinlong and cursed:

"Ximen Jinlong, I must be blind. I thought you were born and grew up under the red flag, that you were one of us. I had no idea that the polluted blood of the tyrannical landlord Ximen Nao ran in your veins. Ximen Jinlong, you're been a fraud for the last thirty years, and I fell for it. . . ."

Jinlong signaled Panther Sun and the others with his eyes. They ran up and grabbed Hong Taiyue by the arms. He fought, he cursed:

"You're a bunch of loyal sons and grandsons of counterrevolutionaries and members of the landlord class, running dogs and spitting cats, and I'll never knuckle under to you!"

"That's enough, Uncle Hong. This play is finished." Jinlong

hung the battered canteen around Hong Taiyue's neck. "Go home and get some sleep," he said. "I've spoken to Aunt Bai. We'll pick a good date for the wedding. That way you can wallow in the muck with the landlord class."

Jinlong's companions spirited Hong away, his feet dragging along the ground like a couple of gourds. He turned his head, refusing to yield.

"Don't think I'm giving up. Chairman Mao came to me in a dream and said there are revisionists in Party Central."

Jinlong turned to the crowd and said with a smile, "You folks should go home now."

"Party Secretary Jinlong, we bad elements would like to drink a toast to you."

"Jinlong, you must be tired," Qiuxiang said affectionately to her son-in-law. "I'll have Huzhu make you a bowl of thin noodles."

Huzhu was standing in her doorway, head down, her miraculous hair stacked up high, her hairstyle and facial expression reminiscent of a neglected palace girl.

Jinlong frowned. "I want you to close down this restaurant and put the compound back the way it was. And everybody has to move out."

"We can't do that, Jinlong," Qiuxiang said anxiously. "Business is too good."

"How good can it be in a little village like ours? If you're looking for good business, open up in the township or the county town."

Just then, Yingchun, a child in her arms, came out of the northern rooms. Who was that child? It was Lan Kaifang, the son born to you and Hezuo. You say you had no feelings for Hezuo. Then where did that child come from? Don't tell me that they had test-tube babies back then. You're such a hypocrite!

Yingchun turned to Qiuxiang. "Please keep your door shut. Arguing late at night, smoking and drinking, I don't know how your grandson ever gets any sleep."

All the players had shown up, including Lan Lian, who walked in the gate with a bundle of mulberry roots. Without so much as a glance at anyone else, he walked straight up to Wu Qiuxiang and said:

"Roots of the mulberry trees on your land crept into mine. I chopped them off. Here they are."

"I've never seen a more stubborn man in my life," Yingchun said. "What else are you incapable of doing?"

Huang Tong, who had been sleeping in a reclining chair, got up, yawned, and walked over.

"If you're not afraid of tiring yourself out, go dig up all those trees. These days only the dumb pigs make a living off the land!"

"Everybody out!" Jinlong shouted with a frown before turning and walking into the main building of the Ximen family home.

The people left the compound in silence.

The Ximen compound gate closed with a thud. The village was shrouded in silence. Only the moon, with no place to go, accompanied me as I strolled around the area. The moon's rays seemed to be made up of cold grains of sand falling on my body.

34

Hong Taiyue Loses His Male Organ in Anger
Torn Ear Turns Chaos into the King's Throne

In "Tales of Pig-Raising," Mo Yan wrote in detail about how I bit off Hong Taiyue's testicles and turned him into a cripple. He wrote that I waited until Hong was squatting beneath the crooked apricot tree doing his business and attacked him from behind. He made a great show of reporting truthfully by describing the moonlight, the fragrance of the apricot tree, the honeybees buzzing around the apricot blossoms as they gathered nectar, and ended it all with what appeared to be a sentence of great beauty: "Bathed in moonbeams, the road curved like a stream for washing water buffalo." I came off looking like an abnormal pig strangely addicted to eating human testicles. Me, Pig Sixteen, a true hero for half my life, since when would I launch a sneak attack on someone taking a shit? His mind was in the gutter when he wrote that, and I was disgusted when I read it. He also wrote that during that spring I ran around Northeast Gaomi Township doing despicable things and that I bit to death sixteen head of cattle belonging to a peasant. He said I waited till they were doing their business and then ran up, sank my teeth into their anuses, and pulled out their twisted gray-white intestines. "The frenzied animals ran in excruciating pain, dragging their guts in the mud behind them until they fell dead." The rat drew upon his evil imagination to make me look like some kind of monster. You know who really butchered those animals? A demented old wolf that came down from Mount Changbai, that's who. He was so sneaky he left no tracks, so everybody pinned it on me. Later on that wolf slipped back to Wu Family Sandy Mouth and my savage sons and grandsons, without my even having to show my face, stomped him flat and tore him to pieces.

Here's what really happened: I spent that night in the company of the lonesome moon wandering the streets and lanes of Ximen Village. When we made our back to Apricot Garden, I spotted Hong Taiyue under the crooked apricot tree taking a piss. His flattened canteen hung around his neck, resting on his chest. He reeked of alcohol. A man once known for his capacity for liquor, by now he was a drunk, plain and simple. As he was buttoning up his pants, he cursed:

"Let me go, you bunch of mongrels . . . you think you can keep me down by tying my hands and feet and putting a gag in my mouth. Not a chance! You can chop me up into little pieces, but you'll never still the heart of a true Communist. Believe me, you little bastards. Who cares. All that counts is that I believe. . . ."

The moon and I, attracted by his rants, fell in behind him, moving from one apricot tree to another, and whenever one of the trees bumped into him, he raised his fist and glared at it:

"I'll be damned, even you come after me. Well, here's a taste of a Communist's steel fist. . . ."

He wandered over to the silkworm shed, where he pounded on the door with his fist. The door was opened from the inside, lamplight spilling out into the night to merge with the moonbeams. I saw Ximen Bai's bright face; she had opened the door while holding a basket of mulberry leaves. The crisp fragrance of the leaves and the sound of silkworms chewing their leaves, like the pitter-patter of an autumn rainfall, spilled out through the door with the light. I could see in her eyes that she was taken by surprise.

"Party Secretary . . . what are you doing here?"

"Who did you think it was?" Hong was obviously having trouble keeping his balance, his shoulders bumping into the racks of silkworm cocoons. "I heard you shed your landlord dunce cap," he said in a strange voice, "and I'm here to congratulate you."

"I have you to thank for that," Ximen Bai replied as she set down her basket and wiped her eyes with her sleeve. "If not for your support all those years, they'd have beaten me to death long ago. . . ."

"Nonsense!" He was clearly angry. "We Communists have never ceased treating you with revolutionary humanitarianism!"

"I understand, Secretary Hong, in my heart I understand everything." Somewhat incoherently, she continued, "I thought about talking to you back then, but the dunce cap was still on my head, and I didn't dare approach you, but now, no more dunce cap, I'm a co-op member. . . ."

"What is it you want to say?"

"Jinlong sent someone to tell me I should look after you. . . ." She blushed. "I said if Secretary Hong has no objections, I'd be happy to look after him from now on. . . ."

"Bai Xing, oh, Bai Xing, why were you a landlord?" Hong muttered softly.

"I no longer wear that cap," she said. "I'm a citizen now, a member of the co-op. There are no more classes. . . ."

"Nonsense!" Hong was now agitated. He walked up closer to her. "No cap doesn't mean you're not a landlord, it's in your blood, poison running through your veins!"

Bai Xing backed up, all the way to the silkworm rack. The hurtful words emerging from Hong's mouth belied the depth of feeling apparent in his eyes. "You will always be our enemy," he roared. But a liquid light flashed in his eyes as he reached out and grabbed hold of Bai Xing's breast.

With a defiant moan, she said, "Secretary Hong, don't let the poison in my veins contaminate you—"

"You're still the target of the dictatorship. I tell you, just because you've shed your cap, you're still a landlord!" He wrapped his arms around her waist and pressed his reeking, stubble-covered mouth against her face; the two bodies crashed into the sorghum-woven silkworm racks and knocked them over. Bai Xing's silkworms wriggled and squirmed beneath the bodies; those that weren't squashed flat just kept chewing their mulberry leaves.

Suddenly a cloud floated in front of the moon, and in the haze all sorts of reminiscences of the Ximen Nao era — sweet, sour, bitter, hot — surged into my head. As a pig, my mind was clear, but as a human, there was only confusion. Yes, I knew that no matter how I'd died all those years ago, justly or not, fairly or not, Ximen Bai had every right to be intimate with another man, but I could not endure seeing Hong Taiyue do it to her while he was cursing her. What an insult, both to Ximen Bai and to Ximen Nao. To me it felt like dozens of fireflies were flitting around in my head. Then they came together to form a ball of fire that burned its way into my eyes and caused everything I saw to resemble a will-o'-the-wisp. The silkworms were a phosphorescent green; so were the people. I charged, initially intending only to knock him off her body. But his testes came in contact with my mouth, and I honestly could find no reason not to bite them off. . . .

Yeah, a moment of rage had incalculable consequences. Ximen Bai hanged herself from a beam in the silkworm shed that night; Hong Taiyue was sent to the county medical center, hanging on to life by a thread. He lived, but as some sort of freak with a monstrous temper. Me, I was labeled a fearful murderer with the savagery of a tiger, the cruelty of a wolf, the craftiness of a fox, and the wildness of a boar.

Mo Yan wrote that after biting Hong Taiyue, I went on a rampage in Northeast Gaomi Township, wreaking destruction on the peasants' field oxen, and even wrote that for the longest time the locals were afraid to relieve themselves out in the woods, afraid of having their guts pulled out through their anuses. As I indicated before, that's bullshit! Here's what really happened. After I had, in a moment of confusion, taken that mortal bite out of Hong Taiyue, I rushed back to Wu Family Sandy Mouth. A bunch of sows sashayed up next to me, but I shoved them away. I knew this was far from over, so I went looking for Diao Xiaosan to come up with a strategy to deal with the situation.

I gave him a quick rundown on what had happened. He sighed and said:

"Brother Sixteen, as I see it, love's a hard thing to forget. I knew right off that you and Ximen Bai had something special. Now, what's done is done, and there's no use in trying to figure out what's right and what's wrong. Let us go raise some hell, what do you say?"

Mo Yan's accuracy improved with events that followed. Diao Xiaosan got me to call all the young studs together on the sandbar, where, like a well-tested commander, he intoned the glorious history of their ancestors in struggles against humans and predatory animals. Then he related the strategies those ancestors had conceived:

"Tell these youngsters, Great King, how to cover themselves with pine tar, then go roll in the dirt, and repeat this procedure over and over. . . ."

A month later, our bodies were covered with a natural golden armor no knife could penetrate and sounded like a rock or tree hit it when you bumped into it. At first, it slowed us down, but we quickly got used to lugging it around with us. Diao also taught us some battle techniques: how to set an ambush, how to launch a surprise attack, how to lay siege, how to retreat, etc. He spoke with the authority of someone with battle experience. We sighed with admiration. We told Old Diao he must have been a military man in his previous incarnation. He released an enigmatic snigger. Then that iniquitous old wolf foolishly swam over to the shoal. At first he probably thought we were no match for him, but after trying to take a bite out of our virtually impenetrable hide, which kept us safe from injury, his savagery left him. My sons and grandsons, as I said earlier, stomped him flat and tore him to pieces.

August was the rainy season, which raised the water level in the river to flood stage. On moonlit nights, great numbers of fish, drawn to the surface by the moon's reflection, wound up beached on the shoal. This was the season when we fattened up on watery delicacies. More and more wild animals congregated on the shoal, which led to more violent fights over food. A fierce territorial battle erupted between the pigs and the foxes and ended when the armored cadre drove the foxes off the shoal's golden hunting grounds and monopolized the triangular protuberance in the middle of the river. But not without a cost: many of my descendants received serious, even crippling, injuries in the battle with the foxes. Why? Because it was impossible to protect our eyes and ears with the armor that covered our bodies, leaving them vulnerable to attacks by the foxes, whose last-ditch tactic was to release noxious gases from their anuses. They proved lethal when they entered the eyes and nose. The stronger pigs managed to survive the attacks; the others slumped to the ground and were immediately set upon by foxes who bit down on their ears and gouged out their eyes with their claws. Afterward, under Diao Xiaosan's command, we split up into two groups, one to launch an attack, the other to lay in wait. When the foxes released their gases, courageous warriors with mugwort stuck up their noses counterattacked. Our commander, Diao Xiaosan, knew that the foxes could not sustain the level of toxicity, that while the first gassing was lethal, those that followed were only mildly noxious. On top of that, pigs that had survived the first poisonous cloud fought courageously, wanting to latch on to their enemies, even if that meant their eyes might be gouged out and their ears bitten off. One assault followed another until at least half the foxes lay dead or injured; their corpses and broken bodies lay strewn across the shoal; bushy fox tails hung from the tips of red willows here and there. Sated flies darkened the willow branches and weighted them down, like heavy fruit, until they nearly touched the ground. The battle with the foxes turned the pig troops into a veteran fighting force. Serving as a training exercise for the pigs, it was a prelude for a war with humans.

Old Diao and I were prepared for an attack by hunters from Northeast Gaomi Township; but two weeks after the Mid-Autumn Festival, we were still waiting, so Old Diao sent a few of the cleverest pigs across the river as scouts. They never came back, and I figured they had fallen into some sort of trap, to be skinned, gutted, and chopped into filling for human consumption. By that time, the human's standard of living was on the rise, and people, having grown weary of eating domestic fare, were on the lookout for wild, edible game. As autumn deepened, that development ushered in a campaign to "eradicate the wild boar scourge," while in fact the goal was to put wild meat on the people's tables.

Like so many major events in their infancy, the six-month-long pig hunt began in an atmosphere of fun. It all started on the first afternoon of the National Day holiday, a sunshiny early winter day when the shoal was bathed in the fragrance of wild chrysanthemums mixed with the aroma of pine tar and the pleasant medicinal odor of mugwort. Naturally, there were less pleasant smells as well. The prolonged period of peace had taken the edge off our tension.

So on one lovely day, when a dozen or more boats sailed up the river, red flags at the mast and a steel drum on the lead boat loudly announcing their arrival, none of us believed that a pig slaughter was about to commence. We thought it was just members of a delegation of Communist Youth Leaguers on an autumn outing.

Diao Xiaosan and I stood on a rise watching the boats draw up our shoal and seeing the passengers come ashore. In a soft voice I reported to Old Diao what I was seeing. He cocked his head and pricked up his ears to hear exactly what was going on. There must be a hundred of them, I said. Tourists, it appears. A series of whistles has them forming up on the shore, I said, as if someone has called a meeting. The whistles and bits of conversation came to us on the wind. Someone is having them line up, he said to me, repeating what he heard. Close together, like a net, and don't fire your guns. We'll drive them into the water. What? They're got guns? I said, shocked by the news. They're coming for us, Old Diao said. Give the signal. Muster the troops. Diao Xiaosan took three deep breaths, raised his head, and, with his mouth half open, released a shrill sound from deep in his throat, like an air-raid alarm. Tree branches shook, wild grass waved, as wild boars — big, little, young, and old — appeared beside us on the rise from all directions. Foxes were startled, so were badgers and wild hares; some fled in fright, some hid in burrows, and some just ran in circles.

Our pine-tar, yellow-sand armor made us look as if we were all dressed in brown uniforms. Heads raised, mouths open, fangs bared, and eyes blazing, those two hundred pigs were my army — most of them my relatives. They were biding their time, they were excited, they were jittery, and they were ready to go, grinding their teeth and stomping their feet.

"My children," I said to them, "the war has come to us. They're armed with guns, so our strategy will be to exploit our advantage by being evasive. Do not let them drive you to the east. Circle around behind them if you can."

One of the more excitable young males jumped up and shouted:

"I oppose that strategy! We need to close up ranks and attack them straight on. Drive them into the river!"

This particular boar, whose real name was unknown, was called Split Ear. Weighing in at about 350 *jin*, he had a large head that was covered in pine tar armor and an ear that was nearly chewed off in his heroic confrontation with a fox. My most powerful warrior, he was one of the few animals who was not related to me. This leader of shoal forces was too young to have fought me way back then, but now he was all grown up, and though I'd made it clear that King of the Pigs was not a role I had sought, I was reluctant to pass it on to this particularly cruel specimen.

"Do what the king tells you to do!" Diao Xiaosan said to underscore my authority.

"So if the king says surrender, that's what we do?" Split Ear grumbled.

His grumblings were echoed by several of his boar brethren, a development that was particularly troubling; I could see that this force would not be easy to lead, and I needed to overpower Split Ear or it could split into two factions. But with the enemy massing in front of us, there was no time to deal with internal squabbles.

"Carry out my orders!" I commanded. "Break ranks!"

As ordered, most of the boars immediately took positions amid the trees and in clumps of grass. But forty or more, Split Ear's loyalists, went out to meet the humans under his leadership.

The human force formed a straight line from east to west and began their advance. Some wore straw hats, others had on canvas caps; others wore sunglasses, others had on reading glasses; some were in jackets, others were wearing suits; some had on leather shoes, others were in sneakers; some were beating gongs, others had firecrackers stuffed in their pockets; some were beating down the tall grass with clubs, others were armed with rifles and shouted as they moved forward. Not all were young and full of vigor; some were gray-haired, sharp-eyed, stoop-shouldered old-timers. A dozen or so young women filled out the mostly male ranks, a sort of rear eschelon.

Pow — pow! Double-kick firecrackers created clouds of yellow smoke when they exploded. *Bong!* A cracked gong rang out.

"Come out, come out now, or we'll open fire!" someone carrying a club cried out.

This ragged force looked nothing like a team of hunters; instead they were reenacting the 1958 campaign against sparrows, wanting to shock us into submission. I saw there were workers from the Cotton Processing Plant Number Five among the advancing force. Know how? Because I spotted you, Lan Jiefang. By that time you were a full-time employee of the plant, in charge of quality control. Your wife, Huang Hezuo, was also kept on full-time as kitchen help. With your sleeves rolled up, I could see you were wearing a shiny wristwatch. Your wife was there that day too, probably planning on transporting some pork back to the plant to upgrade the workers' standard of living. Besides you, there were people from the commune, from the co-op, and from every village in Northeast Gaomi Township. The man in charge wore a whistle around his neck. Who was he? Ximen Jinlong. A case could be made for saying he was my son, which meant that this looming battle would be pitting father against son.

Birds nesting in the willows were frightened off by the shouts from the invaders; foxes driven out of their dens scampered into the tall grass. The cocky invaders advanced a thousand yards, closing the distance. Someone cried "Pig King!" The scattered troops closed up ranks, until no more than fifty yards separated them from the suicide squad, lined up like an old-time battle formation. Split Ear crouched at the head of his two dozen savage warriors. Ximen Jinlong stood before his human troops, a shotgun in one hand, a gray-green field glass that hung from his neck beside the whistle in the other. I knew that Split Ear's hideous face, captured in the lens of his field glass, threw a shock into him. "Beat the gong!" I heard him shout. "Call to battle!" He planned to use the swallow tactic to frighten his enemy and send them fleeing, so he could drive them into the river.

The gong sounded, shouts rose into the air, but it was all bluster. No one dared attack. No humans, that is. With a battle cry, Split Ear led the charge against the humans. Jinlong was the only man who fired his weapon; the buckshot hit one of the willow trees, destroying a bird nest and wounding a pitiful bird inside. Not a single pellet struck a boar. All the others human invaders turned tail and ran. Huang Hezuo's screams were shriller than all the others as she tripped and fell; Split Ear took a bite out of her rear end, turning her into a half-assed cripple for the rest of her life. The boars were on the offensive, and though they did not escape being struck by an assortment of weapons, nothing could penetrate their armor-protected hides. You showed your mettle by taking Hezuo out of harm's way, earning you a reputation for bravery and a measure of my esteem.

The maverick Split Ear and his troops had to be considered the victors of this battle, to which the scattered shoes, hats, and abandoned weapons on the field of battle bore clear witness. They became the spoils of war, and that made him more arrogant than ever.

"Now what, Old Diao," I asked him one moonlit night after sneaking into his cave following the battle. "Should I abdicate and let Split Ear be the new king?"

With his chin resting on his front hooves, faint light emanating from his blind eyes, he was sprawled in the cave, the sounds of running water and rustling trees coming from outside.

"What do you think, Old Diao? I'll do whatever you say."

He exhaled loudly, the faint light in his eyes now gone. I nudged him. His body was soft; there was no reaction. "Old Diao!" I shouted out of a sense of alarm. "Are you okay? You can't die on me!"

But he did. Tears sprang from my eyes. I was grief-stricken.

I emerged from the cave and was met by a line of glinting green eyes. A savage glare shot from the eyes of Split Ear, who was crouched in front of the others. I wasn't afraid. I actually felt totally at ease. With a look of indifference in my eyes, I walked up to him.

"My dear friend Diao Xiaosan is dead," I said. "I feel just terrible, and I'm willing to abdicate as king."

That was probably the last thing Split Ear expected to hear, since he had backed up, thinking I was coming for him.

"Of course if you will only be happy by fighting me for it, I'll happily oblige," I said.

He just stared at me, trying to figure out what he should do. I weighed over five hundred *jin* and had a hard head and fearsome teeth. From his point of view, the outcome of a fight with me was anything but certain.

"We'll do it your way," he said finally. "But you must leave the shoal immediately and never return."

I nodded in agreement, waved my hoof at the crowd behind him, turned, and walked off. When I reached the southern edge of the shoal, I stepped into the water, knowing that fifty or more pairs of pig eyes were watching my departure, eyes filled with tears. But I didn't look back. I started to swim, closing my eyes to let the river wash away my own tears.

35

Flamethrowers Take the Life of Split Ear
Soaring onto a Boat, Pig Sixteen Wreaks Vengeance

About half a month later, the boars living on the shoal were massacred. Mo Yan wrote about the incident in detail in "Tales of Pig-Raising":

> On the third day of January, 1982, a squad of ten men under the command of Zhao Yonggang, an ex-soldier who had distinguished himself in the War with Vietnam, and the highly experienced hunter Qiao Feipeng as an adviser, sailed to the shoal in motorboats. Most hunters stalk their prey by moving stealthily in order to take them by surprise. But not this group; they marched in with clear intentions armed with automatic rifles and armor-piercing bullets that could easily penetrate the hide of a wild boar, armored or not. But the most powerful weapons in their arsenal were three flame throwers, which looked like converted pesticide sprayers once used by farmers on commune fields. They were operated by three battle-tested ex-soldiers in asbestos suits.

Mo Yan continued:

> The landing by this squad of hunters was immediately noted by boar scouts. The eyes of Split Ear, newly crowned king, who was eager to go to war with humans to establish his authority, turned red when the report reached him. He immediately called his troops together, two hundred and more of them.

Mo Yan continued with a grisly account of the battle, which was almost more than I, a pig myself, could bear to read:

... The battle progressed much like the early encounter, with Split Ear crouching at the head of his force, an echelon of a hundred boars lined up behind him; two additional groups of fifty boars raced to the two flanks to complete the encirclement, with the river as the fourth side. Victory was assured. And yet the humans seemed not to sense the danger they faced. Three of them stood in front, facing east, directly opposite the boar forces and their king, Split Ear. Two men stood to the side, facing south; two more stood on the other side, facing north, opposite the flanking forces. The three men with flamethrowers stood behind the front row, sweeping the area with their eyes, showing no signs of concern. With light-hearted banter they began moving eastward as the boars closed their encirclement. When the humans drew to within fifty yards of Split Ear, Zhao Yonggang ordered his troops to open fire. Assault rifles began shooting at the enemy on three sides. The automatic fire was the sort of military might the boars could never have imagined. At least 140 bullets left seven rifle muzzles within five seconds, felling thirty or more boar warriors, most from head shots, where there was no armor. Split Ear ducked when the first shots were fired, but not in time to keep his good ear from taking a direct hit. Screaming in agony, he charged the hunters straight on, just as the experienced fighters with flamethrowers took three steps forward, sprawled on the ground, and fired, releasing red hot flames and a noise like a hundred geese shitting at the same time. The sticky tips of the flames wrapped around Split Ear and shot ten feet into the air. The king disappeared. The boars to the north and south suffered the same end, thanks in part to the flammability of the thick layer of pine tar in their armor. Most of the inflamed boars took off running, screaming in agony. Only a few of the smarter ones immediately rolled on the ground instead of running. The remaining boar warriors, those that had escaped both bullets and flames, were paralyzed by fear. Like a swarm of headless flies, they banged and bumped into each other, allowing the hunters to take aim and pick them off one at a time, sending them all down to meet Lord Yama ...

Then Mo Yan wrote:

Viewed from the perspective of environmental protection, the slaughter was excessive. The cruelty with which the

boars were dispatched cannot be condoned. In 2005, I traveled
to Korea and was taken to the Demilitarized Zone, where I
saw wild boars frolicking, birds nesting, and egrets soaring
above the treetops. I thought back to the massacre at the shoal
and experienced deep remorse, even though the boars had
been guilty of all sorts of evil. The use of flamethrowers
started a fire that consumed all the pine and willow trees on
the shoal, not to mention the ground cover. As for the other
creatures on the shoal, those with wings flew away, while those
confined to the ground escaped either by crawling into burrows or jumping into the river; most, however, burned along
with the trees. . . .

I was there among the red willows on the southern bank of the
Grain Barge River that day. I heard the pops of rifle fire and the terrifying screams of the wild boars, and, of course, smelled the suffocating fumes that came on winds from the northwest. I knew that if I
hadn't abdicated as king I'd have suffered the same fate as all the
other boars, but, strange as it may seem, I was not in a mood to rejoice
over my good fortune. I'd rather have died with the boars than live an
ignoble life.

After the massacre had ended, I swam back to the shoal, a scene
of burned-out trees, incinerated boars, and, along the banks of the
river, the bloated carcasses of various critters. My mood vacillated
between outrage and grief, with the two emotions gradually coming
together, like a two-headed snake attacking my heart from two sides.

I had no thoughts of revenge as overwhelming grief burned
inside me, making me as restless as a mentally disturbed soldier on
the eve of battle. I swam parallel to the riverbank, following a scent of
diesel fuel and the burned hides of wild boars, with the occasional
pungent odors of tobacco smoke and cheap liquor mixed in. After a
day of tracking the scents, the image of a boat drenched with evil took
shape in my head, like a scene emerging from dense fog.

The boat was a dozen yards in length and constructed of steel
plates crudely welded together. It was a ponderous, ugly steel monster
that was carrying the remnants of a team of ten hunters upriver. The
six ex-soldiers who had jobs to return to, having accomplished what
they'd come for, had taken a bus back to town. That left the leader,
Zhao Yonggang, and the hunters Qiao Feipeng, Liu Yong, and Lü
Xiaopo. Thanks to such factors as a population explosion, land

scarcity, deforestation, and industrial pollution, small game animals had virtually disappeared, and most professional hunters had taken up new trades. These three were the exceptions. They enjoyed an excellent reputation, thanks to their appropriation of the two wolves actually killed by the donkey. The wild boar massacre would add to their prestige and turn them into media darlings. With Diao Xiaosan's carcass as a trophy, they were steaming upriver to the county town, some hundred or more *li* away; given the speed of their motorized craft, they could be there that evening. But they chose instead to turn the trip into a victory tour, stopping at every village along the way to give the locals a chance to lay eyes on the body of the Pig King, which they would carry ashore and lay out on the ground for villagers to see. Families of means, those that owned cameras, would invite friends and relatives to have their pictures taken with the dead boar. The tour was followed by print and television journalists sent out from the county town.

On the last night of the tour, with a chill in the air, pale light from the nearly full moon settled on the stagnating river; ice that was forming on the shallow water near the banks gave off a fearsome glint. I was crouching in a grove of red willows, observing the activity around the simple, log-built pier through the naked branches of the trees. I watched as the steel hull of the boat drew up to the pier. The town, the largest in Gaomi County, was called Donkey Inn, since it had served as a gathering place for donkey merchants a hundred years earlier. The modest three-story government building was brightly lit; deep red tiles had been fastened onto the outside of the walls, looking almost as if they had been painted with pigs' blood. A gala reception for the hunter heroes was underway in one the spacious reception inside; the clink of glasses as toasts were given seeped out through the windows. The square in front of the building — Ximen Village had one of those, so how could a county town be without one?—was also brightly lit, and was the scene of a loud commotion. I knew without looking that the citizenry was oohing and ahing over Diao Xiaosan's carcass and that constables with police batons were standing guard over it. The people had heard that toothbrushes made from boar bristles could turn black teeth white, and young folks whose teeth were black were salivating over the prospect of getting hold of bristles from the Pig King.

At around eleven o'clock that night, my patience paid off. First, a dozen or so strapping young men put Diao Xiaosan's body onto a wooden door and walked with it toward the pier, chanting as they walked, led by a pair of pretty young women in red who were lighting the way with a red lantern. A white-haired old man bringing up the rear of the procession called out a monotonous cadence in a funereal voice:

"Oh, Pig King — to the boat — Oh, Pig King — to the boat —"

Diao Xiaosan's body had begun to stink and was stiff as the door it lay on; the freezing air was all that kept it from decomposing altogether. When they laid his body on the deck, the boat settled more deeply in the water. I was thinking that among the three of us — me, Pig Sixteen, Split Ear, and Diao Xiaosan — Old Diao was the true king. Even lying on the boat's deck he had a commanding presence, which was further enhanced by the pale moonlight. It almost seemed that he could, whenever he wanted, get up and jump into the river or leap onto the bank.

Finally the four hunters emerged, so drunk they had to be supported by local officials, and staggered toward the pier. They too were led by young women in red carrying a red lantern. By that time I had stealthily made my way to a spot no more than ten yards from the pier, where the liquor-and-tobacco stench from the hunters' mouths fouled the air. I was actually quite calm, calm as could be, as if totally divorced from the scene in front of me. I watched them board the boat.

Now safely aboard, they thanked their hosts with mouthfuls of hypocrisy, and received the same in return from the people seeing them off. Once they were seated, Liu Yong pulled the rope ignition to start the diesel motor, but it appeared to have frozen up in the icy air. He decided to warm it up with a torch he made by soaking some cotton in the diesel oil. The yellow flames drove the moonbeams away and lit up Qiao Feipeng's sallow face and sunken mouth; they lit up Lü Xiaopo's puffy face and bulbous red nose; and they lit up Zhao Yonggang's face, stamped with a sneer. When it lit up Diao Xiaosan's mouth, with its missing fangs, I grew even calmer, like an old monk standing before a sacred idol.

In the end, the motor took hold, and its horrible sound on the river assaulted the night air and the moon. The boat moved slowly out into the river. By stepping on the ice at the river's edge with a swagger, I made my way to the pier, looking like a domestic pig that had stepped out from the crowd of people seeing the hunters off. The red lanterns waved back and forth like balls of fire, creating just the right atmosphere for my leap through the air.

I wasn't thinking anything, I just acted, just moved.

The boat lurched to one side and Diao Xiaosan seemed about to stand up. Liu Yong, who was bent over starting the motor, went flying into the river, raising blue-white shards of water into the air. The motor sputtered, emitting black smoke and weak complaints. My ears seemed waterlogged. Lü Xiaopo teetered, his open mouth reeking of alcohol, as he fell backward, his body half in the boat and half in the water for a moment, his waist fulcrumed on the steel plate railing, until he tipped headfirst into the river, he too raising blue-white, silent shards of water into the air. I started jumping up and down, five hundred *jin* of pig making the boat lurch from side to side. Qiao Feipeng, the hunters' adviser, who years before had had dealings with me, fell weakly to his knees and kowtowed. How funny was that! Without a thought running through my head, I picked him up and threw him out of the boat. More silent shards of water. That left only Zhao Yonggang, the only one who looked like a worthy opponent. He swung a club and hit me in the head. The sound of it breaking in two went from my skull to my ears; one half of the club flew into the water, the other half was still in his hand. I didn't have time to consider the pain in my head. My eyes were fixed on what remained of his club as it came straight toward my mouth; I grabbed it in my teeth and held on. He put all his considerable strength in trying to pull it out until his face turned as red as a lantern trying to outshine the moon. I let go, and he flew backward into the water; you might think I planned it like that, but I really didn't. At that moment all sound, all color, all smells rushed toward me.

I jumped into the river, sending a column of water several yards into the air. The water was cold and felt sticky, like liquor that had aged for years. I saw all four of them floating on the surface. Liu Yong and Lü Xiaopo were so drunk they could neither function nor think clearly, so there was no need for me to hasten their departure from the world. Zhao Yonggang was the only real man among them, and if he could make it to dry land, then I'd let him live. Qiao Feipeng was the nearest to me; he struggled to keep his purple nose above water.

Disgusted by the way he was gasping for air, I conked him on the head with my hoof. He didn't move after that, except for his rear end, which floated to the surface.

I let the current take me downriver. Water and moonbeams formed a silvery liquid, like donkey milk about to freeze. Behind me, the boat's motor was making crazy noises, while from the riverbank came a chorus of shouts. The only one I could distinguish was:

"Shoot him! Shoot!"

The six ex-soldiers had taken the assault rifles with them back to town. Since it was peacetime, the planners of the massacre were punished for using such advanced weapons to hunt wild animals.

I dove to the bottom, leaving all sound above and behind me, just like a certain first-rate novelist.

36

Thoughts Throng the Mind as the Past Is Recalled
Disregarding Personal Safety, Pig Saves a Child

Three months later, I was dead.

It all happened one afternoon when the sun was hidden. A bunch of kids were playing on the gray ice covering the river behind Ximen Village. They ranged in age from three and four up to seven and eight. Some were sledding across the ice, others were playing with tops, and I was watching this next generation of Ximen Village residents from the woods. I heard the welcoming call from the other side of the river:

"Kaifeng Geming Fenghuang Huanhuan — all you kids, come home."

I saw the weathered face of the woman, the blue kerchief over her head waving in the wind, and I recognized her. It was Yingchun. I would be dead an hour later, but for now I was so caught up in turbulent memories of the past ten years or so I forgot all about my pig body. I knew that Kaifeng was the son of Lan Jiefang and Huang Hezuo, that Geming was the son of Ximen Baofeng and Ma Liangcai, that Huanhuan was the adopted son of Ximen Jinlong and Huang Huzhu. Fenghuang was the daughter of Pang Kangmei and Chang Tianhong, and I knew that her biological father was Ximen Jinlong, conceived beneath the renowned lover's tree in Apricot Garden.

The children were having too much fun to climb up the bank, so Yingchun walked gingerly down the slope, just as the ice broke and the children fell into the icy water.

At the moment I was a human, not a pig; by no stretch of the imagination was I a born hero, but I was basically good and willing to do anything for a just cause. I jumped into the water while Yingchun scrambled back up the bank and shouted for help from the village. Thank you, Yingchun, my beloved. To me the water felt warm, not cold, and as the blood coursed through my veins I swam like a champion. I was not intent on saving the three children who were carrying on my line; I just swam for the nearest ones. I bit down on the pants of one of the boys and flung him back onto the ice. One after the other I tossed the children back onto the ice. They quickly crawled to safety. I took the foot of the fattest of the children in my mouth and brought him up out of the water; icy bubbles shot from his mouth as he hit the surface, just like a fish. The boy landed on the ice, which cracked under the weight, so this time I rammed my snout into his soft belly, moved all four of my legs as fast as I could — even with four legs treading water, I was still human — and flung him far off onto the ice. This time it held, thank goodness. The inertia from the effort drove me under the surface; water rushed up my nose, and I choked. When I made it back to the surface I coughed and gasped for air. I saw a crowd of people racing down the slope. Stay where you are, you stupid people! I put my head back under the water and dragged another child, a chubby little boy whose face was coated with ice, like syrup, when he broke the surface. The other kids I'd saved were still crawling along the ice, some of them crying, proof they were still alive. Go on, cry, all of you. In my mind's eye I could see a bunch of girls, one after the other, crawling along the ground in the Ximen family compound and then climbing up the big apricot tree. The first girl in line passed gas. That was met by laughter. They all slid back down to the ground and dissolved into giggles. I saw their laughing faces. Baofeng's laughing face, Huzhu's laughing face, Hezuo's laughing face. Back underwater I went, this time swimming after a boy who had been carried downriver. I caught him and raced for the surface, where the ice was thick and hard. I was running out of air; my chest felt as though it was about to explode. I rammed my head into the ice. Nothing. I did it a second time. Still nothing. So I turned and swam against the current. When I finally surfaced I saw red. Was it the setting sun? I flung the nearly drowned boy onto the ice. Through the red haze I saw Jinlong, Huzhu, Hezuo, Lan Lian, and many more . . . they all seemed made of blood, so red, poles and ropes and hoes in their hands as they crawled out onto the ice to rescue the children . . . how smart and how good they were. I had nothing but good feelings for all of them, was grateful even to the ones who had made my life as

a pig so difficult. My thoughts were of a mysterious play being performed on a stage seemingly thrown up at the edge of a cloud as I hid
among a copse of rare trees with golden limbs and jadeite leaves;
music curled into the air above the stage, a song sung by a female
opera performer dressed in a costume made of lotus petals. I was
deeply moved, though I couldn't say why. I felt hot all over; the water
around me was getting warmer. It felt so good as I sank slowly to the
bottom, where I was met by a pair of smiling blue-faced demons who
looked very familiar.

"Well, old pal, you're back!"

Book Four

Dog Spirit

37

An Aggrieved Soul Returns as a Dog
A Pampered Child Goes to Town with His Mother

The two underworld attendants grabbed my arms and dragged me out of the water. "Take me to see Lord Yama, you rotten bastards!" I raged. "I'm going to settle scores with the damned old dog!"

"Heh heh," Attendant One giggled. "After all these years, you're still a hothead."

"As they say, You can't keep a cat from chasing mice or a dog from eating shit," Attendant Two mocked.

"Let me go!" I railed. "Do you think I can't find the damned old dog on my own?"

"Calm down," Attendant One said, "just calm down. We're old friends by now. After all these years, we've actually missed you."

"We'll take you to see the damned old dog," Attendant Two said.

So they raced down the main street of Ximen Village, dragging me along with them. A cool wind hit me in the face, along with feather-light snowflakes. We left dead leaves fluttering on the road behind us. They stopped when we reached the Ximen family compound, where Attendant One grabbed my left arm and leg, Attendant Two took my right arm and leg, and they lifted me off the ground. After swinging me back and forth like a battering ram slamming into a bell, they let go and I went flying.

"Go on, go see that damned old dog!" they cried out together.

Wham! My head really did feel as if I'd rammed it into a bell, and I blacked out. When I came to, well, you know without my saying so, I was a dog, after landing in the kennel belonging to your mother, Yingchun.

In order to keep me from causing a scene in his hall, that is the underhanded tactic rotten Lord Yama had stooped to: shortening the reincarnation process by sending me straight into the womb of a bitch, where I followed three other puppies out through the birth canal.

The kennel I landed in was unbelievably crude: two rows of brick remnants under the house eaves for walls, wooden planks topped by tarred felt as a roof. It was my mother's home — what was I supposed to do? I had to call her Mother, since I popped out of her body. My childhood home too. Our bedding? A winnowing basket full of chicken feathers and leaves.

The ground was quickly covered by a heavy snowfall, but the kennel was nice and bright, thanks to an electric light hanging from the eaves. Snowflakes slipping in through cracks in the felt turned the kennel bone-chillingly cold. Along with my brothers and sister I kept from shivering by nuzzling up against our mother's warm belly. A series of rebirths had taught me one simple truth; when you come to a new place, learn the local customs and follow them. If you land in a pigpen, suck a sow's teat or starve, and if you're born into a dog kennel, nuzzle up to a bitch's belly or freeze to death. Our mother was a big white dog with black tips on her front paws and tail.

She was a mongrel, no doubt about that. But our father was a purebred, a mean German shepherd owned by the Sun brothers. I saw him once: a big animal with a black back and tail and a brown underbelly and paws. He — our father — was kept on a chain in the Suns' yard. He had blood-streaked yellow eyes, pointy ears, and a perpetual scowl.

Dad was a purebred, Mom a mongrel, which made us mongrels. No matter how different we might look when we were grown, you could hardly tell the difference between any of us when we were first born. Yingchun was probably the only person who knew which of us came when.

When your mother brought out some steaming broth with a soup bone for our mother, snowflakes circled her head like white moths. My eyesight hadn't sharpened to the point where I could see her face clearly, but I had no trouble picking up her unique odor, that of toon tree leaves rubbed together. Not even the smell of the pork bone could overwhelm it. My mother cautiously lapped up the broth while your mother swept the snow off our roof. That let in plenty of daylight and plenty of cold air. Wanting to do something good for us, she'd actually managed to do just the opposite. Having come from peasant stock, how could she not know that snow is a blanket that keeps wheat sprouts warm? She had rich experience in raising children, but was woefully ignorant about nature. But then when she saw that we were nearly frozen to death, she carried us into the house and laid us down on the heated *kang*.

"You poor little darlings," she said.

She even brought our mother inside, where Lan Lian was feeding kindling into the *kang* opening. His skin was bronze, and golden lights shone off his white hair. Wearing a thickly padded jacket, he was smoking a pipe like a very contented head of household. Now that peasants had been given land, everyone was an independent farmer, just like the old days. So your father and mother once again were eating together and sleeping together.

The *kang* was so warm it quickly drove the chill from our nearly frozen bodies, and as we started moving around, I could tell by looking at my canine brothers and sister what I must have looked like. The same thing had happened back when I'd been reborn as a pig. We were clumsy, covered with fuzz, and cute as hell — I guess. There were four children on the *kang* with us, all about three years old. A boy and three girls. We were three males and a female.

"Would you look at that!" your mother exclaimed in happy surprise. "The exact opposite of the children!"

Lan Lian snorted noncommittally as he took the charred remains of a mantis egg capsule from the *kang* opening. He cracked it open; inside were two steaming mantis eggs that smelled bad. "Who wet the bed?" he asked. "Whoever did it has to eat these."

"I did!" Two of the boys and the girl answered in unison.

That left one boy who said nothing. He had fleshy ears, big eyes, and a tiny little mouth that made him seem to be pouting. You already know that he was the adopted son of Ximen Jinlong and Huang Huzhu. Word had it that he was the biological son of a pair of high-school students. Jinlong was rich enough to get anything he wanted, and powerful enough to back his wishes up. So a few months before the deal was made, Huzhu began wearing padding around her middle to fake a pregnancy. But the villagers knew. The boy was named Ximen Huan — they called him Huanhuan — and he was the pearl in their palm.

"The guilty party keeps his mouth shut, his innocent brothers and sister can't confess fast enough!" Yingchun said as she passed the hot mantis eggs from one hand to the other while blowing on them. Finally, she held them out to Ximen Huan. "Here, Huanhuan, eat them."

Ximen Huan took them from his grandmother and, without even looking at them, flung them to the floor. They landed in front of our mother, who gobbled them down without a second thought.

"That child, I don't know what to say!" Yingchun said to Lan Lian.

Lan Lian shook his head. "You can always tell where a child comes from."

All four children looked curiously at us puppies and reached out to touch us.

"One apiece, just right," Yingchun said.

Four months later, when buds began to appear on the old apricot tree in the front yard, Yingchun said to the four couples — Ximen Jinlong and Huang Huzhu, Ximen Baofeng and Ma Liangcai, Chang Tianhong and Pang Kangmei, and Lan Jiefang and Huang Hezuo:

"It's time for you to take your children home with you. That's why I asked you here. First, since we don't know how to read or write, I'm afraid that keeping them here will slow their development. Second, we're getting old. Our hair is white, our eyesight dimmed, and our teeth are loose. Life has been hard on us for many years, and I think we deserve a little time for ourselves. Comrades Chang and Pang, it's been our good fortune to have your child with us, but Uncle Lan and I've talked it over, and we feel that Fenghuang ought to start kindergarten in town."

The moment had arrived with all the solemnity of a formal handover ceremony: four little children were lined up on the eastern edge of the *kang*; four little puppies on the western edge. Yingchun picked up Ximen Huan, kissed him on the cheek, and handed him to Huzhu, who cradled him. Then Yingchun picked up the oldest puppy, rubbed his head, and put him in the arms of Huanhuan. "This is yours, Huanhuan," she said.

She then picked up Ma Gaige, planted a kiss on his cheek, and handed him to Baofeng, who cradled him. She picked up the second puppy and put him in Ma Gaige's arms. "Gaige," she said, "this is yours."

Yingchun then picked up Pang Fenghuang and lovingly gazed at her pink little face; with tears in her eyes, she kissed her on both cheeks, then turned and reluctantly handed her to Pang Kangmei.

"Three bald little boys aren't the equal of one fairy maiden."

Yingchun picked up the third puppy, patted her on the head, rubbed her mouth, stroked her tail, and put her in Fenghuang's arms.

"Fenghuang," she said, "this is yours."

Finally Yingchun picked up Lan Kaifeng, half of whose face was covered by a blue birthmark, which she rubbed. With a sigh, her face now streaked with tears, she said, "You poor thing . . . how come you're also . . ."

She handed Kaifeng to Hezuo, who held her son close. Because a wild boar had taken a chunk out of her rear end, she now had a hard time keeping her balance and often leaned to one side. You, Lan Jiefang, reached out to take the third generation of blue-faced boy from her, but she refused.

Yingchun picked me, the runt of the litter, up from the *kang* and put me into Lan Kaifang's arms.

"Kaifang," she said, "this one's yours. He's the smartest."

All the while this was happening, Lan Lian rested on his haunches beside the dog kennel, where he covered the bitch's eyes with a piece of black cloth and rubbed her head to keep her calm.

38

Jinlong Raves about Lofty Ideals
Hezuo Silently Recalls Old Enmities

I just about jumped out of the wicker chair, but managed to hold back. I lit a cigarette and slowly puffed on it to calm down. I stole a glance at the eerie blue eyes of Big-head Lan, and in them I saw the cold, hostile look of the dog that accompanied my former wife and my son for fifteen years. But then I discovered it was similar to the look of my deceased son, Lan Kaifang: just as cold, just as hostile, just as unforgiving toward me.

I'd been assigned as head of the Political Section at the County Supply and Marketing Cooperative, and no matter how you look at it, I was one of those people who amused himself by writing florid little essays for the provincial newspaper.

By that time, Mo Yan had already been sent to help out at the Reports Section of the County Committee Propaganda Department, and even though he held a peasant household registration, his almost fanatical ambition was known throughout the county. He wrote day and night, never combing his hair; his clothes, which reeked of cigarette smoke, were only washed when it rained and he could hang them outside in time. My former wife, Huang Hezuo, was so fond of this slob she never failed to lay out tea and cigarettes when he dropped by, while my dog and my son seemed hostile to him.

Anyway, soon after I was transferred over to the County Supply and Marketing Cooperative, Hezuo was assigned to the restaurant at the co-op's bus station, where her job was to fry oil fritters. I never said she was a bad woman, and I'd never go public with any of her shortcomings. She cried when I told her I wanted a divorce and asked me: What is it you don't like about me? And my son asked: Papa, what did

Mama ever do to you? My parents were less generous: You're no big shot, son, so what makes you think you're too good for her? My in-laws were the bluntest of all: Lan Jiefang, you bastard son of Lan Lian, take a piss and look at yourself in the puddle. Finally, my superior assumed a somber tone when he heard the news: Comrade Jiefang, you could use a little self-awareness! Yes, I admit it, Huang Hezuo did nothing wrong, and she was easily my equal, or better. But I, well, I simply didn't love her.

The day that Mother returned the children to their parents and handed out the puppies, Pang Kangmei, then deputy head of the County Committee Organization Department, had her driver take a group photo of the four couples, four children, and four puppies under the apricot tree in the family compound. To look at the photo, you'd think we were one happy family, whereas in fact dark schemes rested in all our hearts. Copies of the photo hung in six homes, but probably none of them has survived.

After the picture was taken, Chang Tianhong and Pang Kangmei offered to take us home in their car. While I was trying to make up my mind, Hezuo thanked them but said she wanted to spend the night at Mother's house. Then, as soon as the car drove off, she picked up our son and the puppy and said she wanted to go; nothing anyone said could change her mind. Just then the puppies' mother broke free of Father's grip and ran outside, the blindfold having slipped down around her neck and looking like a black necklace. She went straight for my wife before I could stop her and sank her teeth into Hezuo, who shrieked and was only able to keep from falling by sheer force of will. She insisted we leave immediately, but Baofeng ran inside for her medical kit and tended to Hezuo's injured buttock. Jinlong took me aside, gave me a cigarette, and lit one for himself. Little clouds of smoke veiled our faces. In a tone of voice that was somewhere between sympathy and ridicule, he said:

"Can't take it anymore, is that it?"

"No," I replied coldly. "Everything's fine."

"That's good," he said. "It's all a comedy of errors anyway, but you're a man of standing. And women? Well, they are what they are." He rubbed his thumb against two fingers, then drew an imaginary official's cap, and added, "As long as you've got those, they'll come when you call them."

Hezuo walked toward me, with Baofeng's help. Our son, who

was holding his puppy in one hand and his mother's shirttail with the other, was looking up at her. Baofeng handed me some anti-rabies medicine and said:

"Put this in the refrigerator as soon as you get home. The instructions are on the box. Follow them exactly, in case . . ."

"Thank you, Baofeng," Hezuo said as she gave me an icy glare. "Even dogs can't stand me."

Wu Qiuxiang, stick in hand, had taken out after the dog, who ran straight to the kennel, where she snarled at Qiuxiang, her eyes green.

Huang Tong, whose back by then was badly bent, was standing beneath the apricot tree; he railed at my parents:

"You Lan people have so little feelings for family, even your dog bites its own! Strangle the damn thing, or someday I'll burn down that kennel with her in it."

My father poked his nearly bald broom in the kennel. The yelps of pain from inside the kennel brought my mother hobbling out the door.

"Kaifang's mother," she said apologetically to Hezuo, "don't be angry. That old dog was just trying to protect her pups, and that's the only way she knows how."

No matter how insistently Mother, Baofeng, and Huzhu tried to get her to stay, Hezuo was determined to leave. Jinlong looked at his watch and said:

"It's too late for the first bus, and the second one won't leave for a couple of hours. If you don't think my car is too run-down for you, I'll drive you home."

With a sideways glance at him, she took our son by the hand and, without saying good-bye to anyone, limped off in the direction of the village. Still holding the puppy in his arms, Kaifang kept turning to look back.

My father came up beside me. The years had softened the blue birthmark on his face, and the fading sunlight made him look older than ever. With a quick look at my wife and son up ahead, I stopped and said:

"Go on back, Dad."

He sighed and, obviously crestfallen, said, "If I'd known I'd pass this birthmark on to my descendants I'd have remained a bachelor."

"Don't talk like that," I said. "I don't consider it a blemish, and if it bothers Kaifang he can get a skin graft when he grows up. There have been lots of medical advances lately."

"Jinlong and Baofeng belong to somebody else now, so your family is the only real worry I've got."

"We'll be fine. Just look after yourself."

"These past three years have been the best of my life," he said. "We have more than three thousand *jin* of wheat stored up and several hundred more of other grains. Your mother and I will have food to eat even if we don't harvest a thing over the next three years."

Jinlong's Jeep drove up on the bumpy road. "Dad," I said, "you go on back. I'll come see you when I get some free time."

"Jiefang," he said sadly, his eyes fixed on the ground in front of him, "your mother says that two people are fated to be together. . . ." He paused. "She wants me to tell you to be faithful to your vows. She says that people in official circles can ruin their future by divorcing their wives. Hers is the voice of experience, so keep that in mind."

"I understand, Dad." As I looked into his homely, somber face, my heart was gripped by sadness. "Go back and tell Mom not to worry."

Jinlong pulled up and stopped next to us. I opened the passenger door and got in.

"Thanks, your eminence," I said. He turned his head and spit the cigarette in his mouth out the window.

"Eminence be fucked!" he replied, and I laughed with a loud sputter. "Watch what you say when you're around my son, okay?" He grunted. "Actually, what difference does it make? Males should start thinking about sex when they're fifteen. If they did, they wouldn't always complain about women."

"Then why not begin with Ximen Huan?" I replied. "Maybe you can coach him into becoming a big shot someday."

"Coaching alone isn't enough," he said. "It all depends on what he's made of."

We caught up with Hezuo and Kaifang. Jinlong stuck his head out the window.

"Sister-in-law, let me give you and my worthy nephew a ride."

Limping badly as she walked hand-in-hand with Kaifang, who was holding the puppy in his other arm, she walked right past us, head held high.

"How stubborn can you get!" Jinlong exclaimed as he banged his fist against the steering wheel, producing an urgent honk. He kept his eyes on the road ahead.. "Don't underestimate that woman," he said. "She's a handful."

We caught up with her a second time, and Jinlong stuck his head out the window again, beeping his horn to get her attention.

"You're not ignoring me because my car's so run-down, are you, sister-in-law?"

Hezuo kept walking, head high, eyes fixed relentlessly on the road ahead. She was wearing gray pants; the right pant leg was rounded, the left sort of caved in, and there was a blood or an iodine stain on the seat. She had my sympathy, no doubt about that, but I still found her repulsive. Bobbed hair that revealed the pale skin of her neck, emaciated ears with virtually no lobes, a wart on her cheek with two black hairs — one long and one short — and the greasy smell of oil fritters that never washed off, I found them all repulsive.

Jinlong drove up ahead and stopped in the middle of the road, where he opened the door and climbed out. Standing beside the Jeep with his hands on his hips, legs apart, he wore a defiant look. I hesitated for a moment before joining him outside.

The stalemate was set, and I was thinking that if Hezuo had the legendary powers of superheroes, she'd step on me, step on Jinlong, and flatten the Jeep, neither stopping nor walking around us. The late-afternoon sunlight on her face highlighted her dark, bushy eyebrows, which nearly met in the center of her forehead, her thin lips, and a pair of smallish eyes, which were now filled with tears. How could I not sympathize with someone like that? Still, I found her repellent.

The look of displeasure on Jinlong's face gave way to a mischievous smile.

"Young sister-in-law, I know what a come-down it is for you to ride in a run-down car like this, and I know you've always looked down on me, a simple peasant. I also know that you'd walk all the way to the county town before you'd get into my car. Sure, you can keep walking, but Kaifang can't. So won't you help me out of this awkward situation, for the sake of my worthy nephew, if nothing else?"

Jinlong walked up to her, bent down, and picked up Kaifang and the puppy. Hezuo put up feeble resistance, but he had already opened the car door and deposited Kaifang and the puppy on the backseat.

Kaifang cried out "Mama," his voice cracking. Puppy Four added a couple of weak barks. I opened the door on the other side, glared at her, and said mockingly:

"Your chariot, your Highness!"

She didn't move.

"Huanhuan's aunt," Jinlong said, smiling broadly, "if your husband weren't here, I'd pick you up and put you in the car."

Hezuo blushed. The look in her eyes as she stared at Jinlong was a complex one. I knew what she was thinking at that moment. I'm being truthful when I say that my feelings of repulsion toward her had nothing to do with what had happened between her and Jinlong, just as I wouldn't be repelled by intimacies between a woman I loved and her husband. To my surprise, she got into the car, but from Jinlong's side, not mine. I slammed my door shut; Jinlong shut his door.

As we started off down the bumpy road, I glanced into the rearview mirror to see that she had her arms wrapped tightly around her son, whose arms were in turn wrapped tightly around the puppy. That really upset me.

"You're going too far this time," I muttered, just as we were negotiating a small, narrow stone bridge. She abruptly opened the door and would have jumped out if not for Jinlong, who kept his left hand on the steering wheel, reached back with his right, and grabbed her by the hair; I spun around and held her by the arm. The boy started crying, the dog started barking. When we reached the far end, Jinlong drove his fist into my chest.

"Stupid bastard!" he growled.

He stopped the car and climbed out; wiping his sweaty forehead with his sleeve, he kicked the door and cursed:

"You're a stupid bastard too!" he growled at Hezuo "You can die, he can die, and so can I. But what about Kaifang? A three-year-old boy, what's he done to deserve that?"

Kaifang was still bawling; Puppy Four was yelping like crazy.

With his hands in his pockets, Jinlong turned, walked in circles, and puffed loudly. Then he opened the door, reached in, and wiped Kaifang's face dry of tears and snot. "Okay, little one, no more tears. The next time you come, your uncle here will pick you up in a fancy VW sedan." Then he patted Puppy Four on the head.

"What are you yelping about, you little son of a bitch?"

We flew down the road after that, leaving everyone else —

horse- and donkey-drawn wagons, tractors of the four- and three-wheeled varieties, and people on bikes and on foot — in our dust. Bouncing around and rattling noisily, we rode along as Jinlong kept his foot on the gas and his fist on the horn. I held on for dear life.

"Is everything bolted down tight on this thing?"

"Don't worry. I'm a world-class race-car driver." We began to slow as we passed the donkey market and the road followed the contours of the river. The water sparkled like gold in the sunlight; a little blue-and-white motorboat sped past.

"Worthy nephew Kaifang," Jinlong said, "your uncle is an ambitious man who plans to turn Northeast Gaomi Township into a land of great joy and make Ximen Village a riverside pearl. That run-down county town you live in will one day be a Ximen Village suburb. What do you think of that?"

There was no response from Kaifang, so I turned around and said, "Your uncle asked you a question!" He was fast asleep, drooling onto the head of Puppy Four, whose eyes were barely open. Probably carsick. Hezuo was looking out the window at the river, showing me the side of her face with the mole. Her lips were pursed in what could only be a scowl.

We spotted Hong Taiyue just before we reached town. He was riding an old bicycle — from our pig-raising days — and straining to keep moving. The back of his shirt was sweat-stained and spotted with mud.

"It's Hong Taiyue," I called out.

"I saw him," Jinlong replied. "He's probably on his way to the County Committee with another complaint."

"Against who?"

"Whoever he can." Jinlong paused, then said with a laugh, "He and my old man are like two sides of the same coin." He honked as we shot past the bicycle. "Even with all their disputes, Hong Taiyue and Lan Lian are two of a kind!"

I turned in time to see Hong's bicycle wobble a time or two, but he stayed upright and quickly faded into the distance, but not before his curses reached us on the air:

"Fuck you, Ximen Jinlong! You're the bastard offspring of a tyrannical landlord!"

"I've already committed his curses to memory," Jinlong laughed. "Actually, I kind of like the old guy."

We pulled up to our door and stopped. But Jinlong kept the engine running.

"Jiefang, Hezuo, we're looking back at thirty or forty years, and we must have learned one thing to survive till now, which is, we don't have to get along with others, but we have to get along with ourselves."

"That's the truth," I said.

"Actually, it's crap!" he said. "I met a pretty girl last month in Shenzhen, who said to me, 'You can't change me!' What did I say to that? Then I'll change myself!'"

"What does that mean?" I asked.

"If you have to ask, you'll never understand." He made a spectacular U-turn, stuck his arm out the window, and made a couple of strange, childish gestures with his white-gloved hand before speeding off.

As we stood in the yard, Hezuo said to the boy and the dog:

"This is our home."

I took the box of anti-rabies ampoules out of my bag and handed it to her.

"Put this in the refrigerator," I said coldly. "One injection every three days. Don't forget."

"Did your sister say that rabies is always fatal?" she asked.

I nodded.

"Wouldn't that solve all your problems?" She snatched the ampoules from me and walked into the kitchen to put them in the refrigerator.

39

Lan Kaifang Happily Explores His New Home
Puppy Four Misses His Old Kennel

I received the best treatment anyone could ask for my first night in your home. Though I was a dog, I slept indoors. When your son was taken back to Ximen Village to be raised by your mother, he was only a year old, and he hadn't been back since. Like me, he was curious about this new place. I followed him inside and immediately began running around to familiarize myself with the layout.

It was quite a home, a palace compared to the kennel under the eaves of Lan Lian's place in Ximen Village. The living room floor was made of marble from Laiyang, so highly waxed I could slide across it, and when your son stepped inside the first time, he was enthralled by its mirrorlike quality. He looked down at his reflection, and so did I. Then he skated across the floor as if it were an ice rink. The walls, with their fine-grained wood baseboards, were painted white, and so was the ceiling, from which hung a light blue chandelier with lights like flower buds. An enlarged photograph of a pair of swans on a pond of green, tulip-bordered water in a wooded area hung on the wall opposite the front door. To the east a long, narrow study with a book-case that covered one wall but held only a few dozen books. There was a bed in one corner; next to it a desk and a chair. A hallway off to the west of the living room led to one room directly ahead and another to the right, each furnished with a bed and had oak floors. The kitchen was at the rear. That house was all the evidence anyone needed to see that you'd done well for yourself, Lan Jiefang. You weren't that high up the official ladder, but your talents had made you a man to reckon with.

Now, since I was a dog, I had a canine responsibility to carry out.

Which was? I had to mark my new home with my personal scent, in part as a sort of beacon in case I got lost away from home.

I left my first dribble to the right of the front door, the second on the living room baseboard, and the third on Lan Jiefang's bookcase. The last one earned me a kick from you, which sent the remaining liquid back up inside. Thoughts of that kick stayed with me over the next decade and more. You may have been the head of the household, but I never considered you my master. In fact, I wound up considering you my enemy. My first master — mistress, actually — was that woman with a chunk of her rear end missing. My second master was the boy with the big blue birthmark. You? Shit, in my mind you were nothing!

Your wife placed a basket in the hallway, filled with newspapers. Your son added a little ball, and that was where I was to sleep. It looked okay to me. Since it even came with a toy, I figured I had it made. But the good times didn't last. In the middle of the first night, you moved my bed out to the coal shed. Why? Because I kept thinking about my kennel back in Ximen Village, or the warm bosom of my mother, or the smell of that kindly old woman, and couldn't stop whimpering. Even your son, who slept in the arms of your wife, woke up in the middle of the night crying for his grandma. Boy and dog were the same. Your son was three years old, I was three months old and wasn't permitted to miss my mother. Besides, I didn't just miss my canine mother, I missed your mother too. But none of that was worth mentioning, since you flung open the door, picked up my basket, and exiled me to the coal shed, where you left me with an angry curse: "Any more noise from you, you little mongrel bastard, and I'll throttle you!"

You hadn't even been in bed. No, you were hiding in the study, chain-smoking until the room was yellow with smoke, just so you wouldn't have to sleep with your wife.

My coal shed was pitch-black, but there was enough light for a dog to distinguish one thing from another. The smell of coal was thick in the air — large, glistening chunks of good coal. Most families couldn't burn coal that good back then. I jumped out of my bed basket and ran into the yard, where I was drawn to the smell of fresh well water and the aroma of parasol blossoms. I left my mark on four separate parasol trees and at the gate, and everywhere else that was called for. The place was becoming mine. I'd left the bosom of my mother and come to a strange new place; from now on I had no one to rely upon but myself.

I took a turn around the yard to learn the layout. I walked past the front door and, owing to a temporary weakness, rushed up and clawed at it, accompanied by some agonizing yelps. But I quickly got my feelings under control and returned to my basket bed, feeling that I'd grown up in that short time. I looked up at the bright red face of the half moon, like a shy farm girl. Stars filled the sky as far as I could see, and the light purple flowers on the four parasol trees looked like living butterflies in the murky moonlight, about to flit away. In the very early hours of the morning I heard strange, mysterious sounds coming from town and detected a complex mixture of smells. All in all, I felt like I'd wound up in a vast, new world; I was eagerly looking forward to tomorrow.

40

Pang Chunmiao Sheds Pearl-like Tears
Lan Jiefang Enjoys a Taste of Cherry Lips

Over a period of six years, I virtually flew up the official ladder: from director of the County Supply and Marketing Cooperative Political Section to deputy Party secretary of the cooperative, and from there to concurrent head and Party secretary of the cooperative, and then from there to deputy county chief in charge of culture, education, and hygiene. There was plenty of talk regarding my meteoric rise, but my conscience was clear. I had no one to thank but myself: my hard work, my talents, contacts among colleagues that I established, and a support base among the masses that I'd organized. In a higher-sounding vein, let me add that, of course, I was nurtured by the organization and received help from comrades, and I didn't try to curry favor with Pang Kangmei. She certainly didn't seem to care much for me, for not long after I'd assumed office, we met by accident in the County Party Committee compound, and when she saw there was no one around to hear her, she said:

"I voted against you, you ugly shit, but you got the promotion anyway."

That hit me like a fist in the gut, and I couldn't speak for a moment. I was a balding forty-year-old man with a potbelly. She was the same age, but had a girlish figure and a radiant young face; time seemed not to have left its mark on her. I watched her walk away, my mind a blank. Then the image of her tailored brown skirt, brown medium-height heels, tight calves, and thin waist left my mind in a hopeless tangle.

If not for my affair with Pang Chunmiao, I might well have

climbed higher up the official ladder, either as a county chief some-where, or a Party secretary. At the very least I'd have made it to the National People's Congress or the People's Political Consultative Conference and been assigned as someone's deputy, enjoying life to its fullest into my late years. I wouldn't have wound up as I did, with a sullied reputation, badly scarred, and trying to get by in this tiny spot I call home. But I have no regrets.

"Looked at from one angle," Big-head said, "just knowing you have no regrets earns my respect as a man." He laughed, almost a giggle. The expression of that dog of mine began to emerge on his face, as if developed from the negative of a photograph.

Not until the day Mo Yan brought her to my office did the full meaning of "time flies" hit me. I'd always thought I was close to the Pang family and that I saw them often. But as I thought back, the impression of her that I'd come away with was of a girl doing a hand-stand in the entrance to the Cotton Processing Plant Number Five.

"You . . . you're all grown up," I said as I looked her over, like an old uncle. "That day, your legs . . . straight up in the air . . ."

The fair skin of her face reddened; a drop of sweat dotted the tip of her nose. That was Sunday, the first of July 1990. It was a hot day, so I'd left the window of my third-floor office open. Cicadas in the lush canopy of the French parasol tree outside my window were chirp-ing like falling rain. She was wearing a red dress with a modestly plunging neckline and lacy piping. She had a thin neck above promi-nent collarbones, highlighted by a tiny green piece of jewelry, maybe jade, attached to a red string. She had big eyes and a small mouth with full lips; she wore no makeup. Her front teeth, ivory white, seemed slightly pressed together. Like an old-fashioned girl, she wore her hair in a braid, which caused a stirring in my heart.

"Please, have a seat," I said as I poured tea. "Time really does fly, Chunmiao. You've grown into a lovely young woman."

"Please don't bother, Uncle Lan. I ran into Mr. Mo Yan on the street, and he treated me to a soft drink." She sat demurely on the edge of the sofa.

"Don't call him uncle," Mo Yan said. "Chief Lan and your elder sister were born in the same year. And his mother was your sister's nominal mother."

"Nonsense!" I tossed a pack of China brand cigarettes on the table in front of Mo Yan. "Nominal mother, normal mother, those vulgar views of relationships never played a role in our family." I placed a cup of Dragon Well tea in front of her. "Call me whatever you like. Don't listen to this guy. I understand you work in the New China Bookstore."

"County Chief Lan, always the bureaucrat," Mo Yan said as he put the pack of cigarettes in his pocket and took a cigarette out of the box on my desk. "Miss Pang is a clerk in the children's section of the bookstore, but in her spare time she's an artist. She plays the accordion, she performs the peacock dance beautifully, she can sing sentimental songs, and her essays have been published in the county newspaper literary supplement."

"Is that so!" I remarked. "I'd say your talents are wasted in that bookstore."

"You said it!" Mo Yan remarked. " 'Let's go see County Chief Lan,' I said to her. 'He can get you a job in a TV station.' "

Her face was redder than ever now. "That's not what I meant, Mr. Mo."

"By my calculation, you're twenty," I said. "So why don't you take the college entrance exam? You could be an art major."

"I don't have that kind of talent. . . ." She hung her head. "I just do those things for fun. Besides, I wouldn't pass the entrance exam. I get flustered the minute I enter an exam hall. I actually faint. . . ."

"Who needs college?" Mo Yan said. "True artists don't come out of higher education. Take me, for example."

"You're shameless, and getting worse," I said. "Braggarts like you never amount to anything."

"All right, enough about me," Mo Yan said. "And since there are no outsiders here, I'll call you Big Brother Lan and urge you to do what you can for our young sister here."

"Of course," I said. "But what can I do that Party Secretary Pang can't do better?"

"That's what makes young Chunmiao so special," Mo Yan said. "She's never asked a favor of her sister."

"Okay, tell us, writer of the future, what have you been working on lately?"

At that point Mo Yan began telling us about the novel he was writing, and though I tried to look as though I was listening, I was actually recalling all my dealings with the Pang family. I swear I didn't think of her as a woman that day or for a long time afterward. It felt good just looking at her.

But two months later, everything changed. Also on a Sunday afternoon.

I'd spoken to her about working in television. I could have made it happen if that's what she'd wanted. One well-placed comment was all it would have taken. Not because my word carried much weight, but because she was Pang Kangmei's sister. She rushed to defend herself. "Don't listen to Mo Yan. That really isn't what I had in mind." She said she didn't want to go anywhere, that she was content selling children's books.

She'd come to see me six times over those two months. This was her seventh visit. The first few times she'd sat in the same place on the sofa as on the day we'd met. She'd also worn the same red dress and sat as demurely as ever, all very proper. At first, Mo Yan had accompanied her, but then she'd started coming alone. When Mo Yan was present, he never shut up. Now he wasn't, and an awkward silence hung in the air. To break the ice on one of the previous occasions, I'd taken a book from my bookcase and said she could borrow it. After flipping through it she said she'd already read it. I handed her another. She'd read that one too. So I told her she could look for one she hadn't read. She pulled out a book entitled *How to Treat a Sick Domestic Animal*. It was one she hadn't read. I couldn't keep from laughing. "Girl," I said, "you're a riot! Okay, if that's the one you want, read on." I picked up a stack of documents and started reading, occasionally glancing at her out of the corner of my eye. She sat back in the sofa, legs together, resting the book on her knees, absorbed in what she was reading, softly mouthing the words.

But the seventh time she came, her face was ghostly white; she sat with a bewildered look. "What's the matter?" I asked. She looked at me, her lips quivered, and — *Wah!*—she burst out crying. Since someone was working overtime in the building that day, I ran over and opened the door. The sounds of her crying soared up and down the corridor like birds on the wing. I ran back over and shut the door. For me, this was a new, and extremely troubling, experience. Wringing my hands nervously, I paced the room, like a monkey that's been thrown into a cage, and said over and over, "Chunmiao Chunmiao Chunmiao, don't cry don't cry don't cry . . ." It did no good — she cried with abandon, louder and louder. I thought about opening the door again, but quickly realized that was a bad idea. So I sat down beside her and grabbed her ice-cold hand with my sweaty one and put my other arm around her; I patted her shoulder. "Don't cry," I said, "please don't cry. Tell me what's wrong. I want to know who had the nerve to make our little Chunmiao so sad. Tell me who it was, and I'll go twist his head till he's looking behind him. . . ." But she kept crying, eyes shut, mouth open, like a little girl, pearl-like teardrops streaming down her cheeks. I jumped to my feet, but sat back down. A young woman crying in the office of a deputy county chief on a Sunday afternoon was nothing to joke about. If only, I thought, I could be like one of those kidnappers you read about, I'd have wadded up a sock and stuffed it in her mouth to keep her quiet. What I actually did might be seen by some as the epitome of foolishness and by others as the height of intelligence. I held one of her hands, pulled her close by the shoulders, and covered her mouth with mine.

She had a very small mouth; I had a very big one. Mine covered hers completely. Her cries rattled around inside my mouth and produced a loud hum in my inner ears. Soon the cries turned to sobs, and then the crying stopped. At that moment I was overcome by a strange, powerful, unprecedented emotion.

Now I was a married man with a child of his own, and you might think I'm lying when I tell you that in fourteen years of marriage we'd had sex (that's the only way to describe contact in which love played no role) a total of nineteen times. Kiss? Once, and that wasn't a real one. It was after we'd seen a foreign movie, and I was affected by the passionate love scenes. I wrapped my arms around her and puckered up. She turned her face this way and that to avoid contact, but eventually our mouths touched, barely, and all I felt was teeth; not only that, her breath smelled like spoiled meat. It made my head swim. I let her go and never again entertained a similar thought. On each of those rare sexual encounters I put as much distance between me and her mouth as possible. I tried to get her to have her teeth looked at, but she gave me an icy stare and said, "Why should I? My teeth are fine." When I told her I thought she might have halitosis, she replied angrily, "Your mouth is full of shit."

Later on I told Mo Yan that that afternoon's kiss was a first for me, and it rocked my soul. All I wanted to do was suck on her full lips, almost as if I wanted to swallow her whole. Now I knew why Mo Yan

was forever using that particular phrase when he had his male characters falling head-over-heels in love in his novels. The moment my
mouth was on hers, she stiffened and her skin turned cold. But just for
a moment; when she relaxed, her body seemed to grow and to soften;
then came the heat, like an oven. At first my eyes were open, but not
for long. Her lips swelled, and the smell of fresh scallops filled my
mouth. I began to explore with my tongue, something I'd never done
before, and as soon as our tongues met, they frolicked together. I
could feel her heart beating against my chest as she wrapped her arms
around my neck. My mind was wiped clean of everything but her lips,
her tongue, her smell, her warmth, and her soft moans. I don't know
how long we stayed like that, until a ringing telephone intruded into
our world. We separated as I went to answer the phone, but I immediately fell to my knees. I felt light as a feather, all because of a single
kiss. I didn't answer the phone, after all. I pulled the plug and stopped
the ringing. She was lying on the sofa, faceup, so pale and her lips so
red and swollen a person might have thought she'd died there.
Naturally, I knew she hadn't, and not just because tears were rolling
down her cheeks. I dried them with a tissue. She opened her eyes and
wrapped her arms around my neck. "I feel dizzy," she murmured. I
stood up and brought her up with me. She rested her head on my
shoulder, tickling my ear with her hair, as the voice of the office clerk
suddenly filled the corridor, and I quickly came to my senses. I gently
pushed her away, opened the door a crack, and, rather hypocritically, I
think, said, "Forgive me, Chunmiao, I don't know what came over
me." Still teary-eyed, she said, "Does that mean you don't like me?"
"Oh, no," I sputtered, "I like you very much. . . ." She came up to me
again, but I took her hand and said, "Dear Chunmiao, the janitor will
be coming in to clean in a minute. You go now. I have so much to say
to you, but it will have to wait a few days." She walked out of my
office, and I collapsed in my leather swivel chair, listening to her footsteps until they died out at the end of the hallway.

41

Lan Jiefang Feigns Affection for His Wife
Dog Four Watches over a Student

If you want to know the truth, when you came home that evening you had a new smell, one that could make man and dog happy. It was nothing like the one you brought home after shaking a woman's hand or sharing a meal or dancing with a woman. It wasn't even the way you smelled after sex. Nothing got past that nose of mine. Big-head Lan Qiansui's eyes lit up when he said this.

His expression and the look in his eyes made me realize that at that moment it wasn't Pang Fenghuang's exceptional child, with whom I had such an unbelievably complicated relationship, talking to me; no, it was my long-dead dog. Nothing got past that nose of mine, he'd said.

That fresh, new smell merged with your personal odor and changed the way you smelled altogether. That told me that a deep and abiding love had developed between you and that woman. It seeped into your blood and your bones, and no power on earth could separate the two of you after that.

The show you put on that night was, in truth, wasted effort. After dinner you went into the kitchen and washed the dishes, then you asked your son what he'd learned in school that day — both things you almost never did. Your wife was so touched she went in and made you a cup of tea. You had sex that night. By your count it was the twentieth time; it would also be the last time. From the strength of the odor I could tell that the sex wasn't bad, even though it held no real meaning. In the midst of your sense of moral obligation, guilt feelings temporarily overwhelmed the physical revulsion you normally felt for your wife. Meanwhile, the smell of that other woman was beginning to germinate, like a seed in the ground, and when its buds burst to the surface, no power in the world could drag you back into the arms of your wife. My nose told me that you'd experienced a rebirth, one that portended the death of this family.

Seven years had passed from the day I arrived at your house up to the day of your and Pang Chunmiao's first kiss, during which time I'd grown from a little puppy into a large, powerful dog. Your son had grown from a little baby into a fourth-grade student. Everything that happened over that period was enough to fill a novel, or it could be written off with a single stroke of the pen.

Now I think it's time to talk about your son.

He was a filial boy, no doubt about that. When he started school, your wife took him there and picked him up on her bicycle. But the school schedule interfered with her work schedule, which put a strain on her. And whenever something put a strain on your wife, she started to complain; and when she started to complain, curses flew at you; and whenever curses flew at you, your son frowned. So you see, he really did love you. "Ma," he said, "you don't have to take me to school or pick me up. I can go by myself." She'd have none of it. "What if you got hit by a car or were bitten by a dog or got picked on by bullies or got taken off by a slap-lady or were kidnapped for ransom?" Five ugly scenarios in a row, without taking a breath. Public safety was a big problem in the early 1990s. People knew there were some women from the south — known on the street as slap-ladies — who traded in children. Pretending to be selling flowers or candy or shuttlecocks made with colorful chicken feathers, they hid a spell-binding drug in their clothes, and when they saw a good-looking child, they slapped him or her on the head, and the child walked off with them. Well, your son slapped his own face, right on the birthmark, and said, "Slap-ladies only deal in good-looking children. If someone looking like me volunteered to walk off with them, they'd shoo me away. And what could you, a woman, do if someone tried to kidnap me? You can't run away—" He looked at your injured hip, which made your wife so sad her eyes reddened and she began to sob. "Son," she said, "you're not ugly, your mother's the ugly one, with half her buttocks missing. . . ." Well, he threw his arms around her waist. "You're not ugly, Mother, you're the most beautiful mother anywhere. Really, you don't have to take me to school. I'll take Little Four with me." They turned to look at me, and I rewarded them with a couple of authoritative barks as a way of saying: I'll do it. No problem, leave everything to me!

"Little Four," your son said as he wrapped his arms around my neck, "you'll take me to school, won't you?"

Arf! Arf! Arf! I barked so loud, the leaves on the parasol tree rustled and scared the wits out of a pair of ostriches our neighbor was raising. My meaning was clear: No–prob–lem!

Your wife rubbed my head. I wagged my tail for her.

"Everybody's afraid of our Little Four, isn't that right, son?"

"Yes, Mama."

"Little Four, Kaifang will be your responsibility. You're both from Ximen Village and grew up together, so you're like brothers. Isn't that right?" *Arf arf!* That's right. She rubbed my head again, looking sort of melancholy, before removing my chain-link collar and signaling for me to follow her. When we reached the front gate, she stopped and said, "Little Four, listen carefully. I have to be at work early in the morning to fry oil fritters. I'll have your breakfast ready for you. At six thirty get Kaifang up. At seven thirty, after you've had breakfast, start out for school. Don't take shortcuts. Stay to the main streets. It's okay if it's a bit farther, since safety is the most important. Walk on the right side of the streets, look both ways before you cross the street and then to the left when you're halfway across, looking out for motorbikes, and especially, motorcycles with riders in black leather jackets, since they're all members of gangs and act like they can't tell the difference between red and green lights. After you've left Kaifang at the school gate, head east, cross the street, then go north straight to the bus station restaurant. You'll find me out front frying oil fritters. Come up and bark twice, and I'll know everything's fine. Then go back home. This time you can take a shortcut. The door will be locked, so you'll have to wait at the gate till I get there. If it's a hot day, you can cross the lane and lie beneath the pagoda pine on the other side of the wall. You can doze off in the shade, but don't fall asleep. With all the thieves around, you need to keep an eye on our place. They carry master keys, and if they find an empty house — they first knock at the door as if they were normal visitors — they walk in and take what they want. You know all our relatives by sight, so if you see a stranger going into our house, don't hesitate, run over and bite them. I'll be home by eleven thirty, so you can come in and have some water before taking the shortcut back to school to bring Kaifang home for lunch. Then back you go in the afternoon, but this time, after you've reported to me, run home to make sure everything's okay, then run to school, since there are only two classes in the afternoon. Come back home with him and watch while he does his homework. Don't let him play till he's finished. Do you understand all that, Little Four?"

Arf arf arf, Un–der–stand.

Before your wife went to work in the morning, she always put the alarm clock on the windowsill and smiled at me. A mistress's smile — a pretty thing. I'd watch her walk out the door. *Arf arf*, Bye-bye, *arf arf*, Don't worry. Then I'd make my rounds in the yard, feeling like the master of the house. When the alarm sounded, I'd run into the boy's room, where the smell of youth was strong. Not wanting to startle him awake by barking, I'd go over and lick him on the face, feeling the tickle of his peach fuzz. He'd open his eyes and ask, "Time to get up, Little Four?" *Bow-wow*, I'd answer him softly, It's time. Then he'd get dressed, give his teeth a quick brushing, wash his face like a kitten, and sit down for breakfast. Most of the time it was soybean milk and oil fritters, or regular milk and oil fritters. Sometimes I ate with him, sometimes I didn't.

The first day we followed your wife's instructions to the letter, partly because her smell followed us most of the way; she was watching us. Perfectly understandable — she was a mother, after all. I walked a yard or so behind your son, keeping my ears and eyes open, especially when crossing the street. A car was coming our way, driving normally, still two hundred yards away, plenty of time to cross. Your son wanted to, but I grabbed his shirt with my teeth and wouldn't let him. "What's wrong with you, Little Four?" your son said. "Don't be chicken." But I wouldn't let go. It was my job to keep my mistress from worrying. Once the car had passed, I let go of him, but remained on my guard, prepared to protect your son with my life, if necessary, as we crossed the street. I could tell by the smell that your wife's mind was at ease. She followed us all the way to school. I watched her ride off on her bike and then trotted after her, keeping a distance of a hundred yards or so between us. I waited till she put her bike away, changed into her work clothes, and started her day before running up and barking softly to let her know everything was all right. A look of gratification came over her, and the smell of love was strong.

We started taking shortcuts on the third day, after letting your son sleep till seven o'clock. We could make it to the school gate in twenty-five minutes if we took our time and fifteen if we ran. After you were kicked out of the house you often stood at your office window with Russian binoculars to watch us as we passed down a nearby lane.

In the afternoons we were in no hurry to get home. "Little Four, where's Mama now?" he'd ask me. I'd sniff the air to pick up her scent. I'd only need a minute to fix her location. If she was at work, I'd face north and bark; if she was home, I'd face south and bark. When she was home, that's where we headed, no matter what. But if she was at work, we could have a little fun.

Your son was a good boy. He never followed the example of those unruly kids who left school with their backpacks and went to one roadside stall or department store after another. The only thing he liked to do was go to the New China Bookstore and borrow children's books for a fee. Once in a while he'd buy one, but most of the time he just paid to borrow them. The person in charge of selling and lending children's books? Your lover, that's who. But she wasn't your lover then. She was nice to your son; I could smell the good feelings, and not just because we were regular customers. I didn't pay much attention to how she looked, since her scent was intoxicating enough. I could distinguish a couple of hundred thousand scents floating around in the city by then, from plants to animals, from mining ores to chemicals, and from food to cosmetics. But none of them pleased me like Pang Chunmiao's scent. To be perfectly honest, there were in the neighborhood of forty local beauties who emitted a lovely scent. But they all had impurities. All but Chunmiao. Hers was like a mountain spring or the wind in a forest of pine trees, fresh, uncomplicated, and never-changing. How I yearned for her touch — not the sort of yearning associated with family pets, but . . . damn it, even a great dog can experience a momentary weakness. As a rule, dogs weren't allowed inside the bookstore, but Pang Chunmiao made an exception for me. You couldn't find another shop in town that was as deserted as the New China Bookstore, which employed three female clerks, two middle-aged women, and Pang Chunmiao. The other two women did their best to butter up Chunmiao, for obvious reasons. Mo Yan, who was one of the bookstore's rare customers, once saw Lan Kaifang sitting in a corner absorbed in a book, so he went over and tugged on the boy's ear. Then he introduced him to Pang Chunmiao, telling her he was the son of Director Lan of the County Supply and Marketing

Cooperative. She said that's who she thought he was. Just then I barked to remind Kaifang that his mother had gotten off work and that her scent had traveled to the hardware store, and if we didn't leave now, we wouldn't get home before she did. "Lan Kaifang," Chunmiao said, "you'd better be getting home now. Listen to your dog." Then she said to Mo Yan, "That's a very intelligent dog. Sometimes Kaifang gets so wrapped up in a book he forgets everything. When that happens, the dog runs in from outside, grabs his clothes in his teeth, and drags the boy out of the shop."

42

Lan Jiefang Makes Love in His Office
Huang Hezuo Winnows Beans at Home

After that first kiss, I wanted to back off, wanted to run away. Sure, I was happy, but I was also afraid and, of course, suffering from guilt feelings. That twentieth and last time I had sex with my wife had been a product of the internal conflict I was feeling that night. I tried my best to be a decent lover, but I finished much too soon.

Over the six days that followed, off in the countryside or at a meeting, cutting a ribbon at an opening ceremony or as a guest at a banquet, in the car or on a stool, standing or walking, awake or asleep, Pang Chunmiao was constantly on my mind, and I was trapped in intoxicating feelings from which I simply could not extricate myself in spite of the inner voice that kept saying: Stop here, go no further. It was a reminder that grew progressively weaker.

At noon on the following Sunday I was a guest at a luncheon for a visiting official from the provincial government. I ran into Pang Kangmei at the county guesthouse. She was wearing a dark blue dress and a string of pearls. Her face was lightly powdered. The guest of honor was a man I'd come to know during a three-month course at a Party school, and though the banquet was hosted by the organization department, he asked that I be invited. I sat through the meal as if needles were poking up out of my chair. The way I sputtered and stammered, I must have sounded like an idiot. As hostess, Pang Kangmei toasted the guest and invited him to eat and drink, witty remarks falling like pearls until he was tongue-tied and enchanted. During the meal, she cast three chilled looks my way, each boring right through me. When the meal was over, she saw our official to his room, smiling all the way and making small talk with all the other luncheon guests. Since her car was the first to arrive, we shook hands to say good-bye. The mere touch of her skin was repulsive, but she said in a tone that sounded filled with concern, "You don't look well, Deputy Chief Lan. If you're sick, you should go see a doctor."

As I rode off I pondered Kangmei's comment and shuddered. Over and over I warned myself: Lan Jiefang, if you don't want to wind up broken physically and saddled with a ruined reputation, you must keep from plunging over the cliff. But when I stood at my office window and looked down at the weather-beaten New China Bookstore signboard, my fears and worries dried up and flew away, leaving only thoughts of her behind, thoughts etched deeply in my mind. In forty years on this earth I'd never felt anything like that. After adjusting the pair of Soviet Red Army binoculars a friend had brought back from Manzhouli, I focused my gaze on the bookstore entrance. The double doors, with their rusty metal handles, were unlocked; from time to time someone walked out, and my heart raced. Each time I was hoping to see her slender figure emerge, then gracefully cross the street and walk elegantly up to me. But it was never her, always book buyers, young or old, male or female. When their faces were pulled into the lenses of my binoculars, their expressions were very much alike — mysterious and bleak. I'd start thinking crazy thoughts. Had something bad happened in the store? Had something happened to her? More than once I entertained the thought of going to see for myself, pretending to be a customer, but with what little reason remained, I managed to hold back. I gazed up at the clock; it was only one thirty, still an hour and a half to go before the time we'd agreed upon to meet. I thought about taking a nap on the army cot I kept behind the screen, but I was too worked up to sleep. I brushed my teeth and washed my face. I shaved and trimmed my nose hairs. Then I studied my reflection in the mirror, half red, half blue — truly ugly. I gently tapped the blue side and cursed: Ugly shit! My self-confidence was on the verge of crumbling. Several times I heard light footsteps coming my way, and I rushed to open the door to greet her. But the hall was always empty. So I sat where she always sat and waited impatiently, flipping through the book I'd handed to her; I could almost see her sitting there reading. Her smell was on that book, her fingerprints were all over it. . . .

Finally, I heard a knock at the door and felt cold all over. I was shivering, my teeth were chattering. I rushed over and opened the door. The smile on her face found its way into my soul. I forgot everything, the words I'd planned to say to her, Pang Kangmei's veiled warning, all my fears. I took her in my arms and kissed her; she kissed me back.

Between kisses we looked into each other's eyes. There were tears on her cheeks; I licked them dry — salty and fresh. "Why, dearest Chumiao? Is this a dream? Why?" "Dearest Lan, everything I have is yours, you want me, don't you. . . ." I struggled. We kissed again, desperately, and what followed was inevitable.

We lay on the cot in each other's arms; somehow it didn't seem so narrow now. "Dearest Chunmiao, I'm twenty years older than you, I'm ugly as sin, and I'm so afraid I'll bring calamities down on you. I don't deserve to live. . . ." I was nearly incoherent. She stroked my chin and my face. With her mouth pressed against my ear, she said, "I love you."

"Why?"

"I don't know."

"I'll be responsible for what happens."

"I don't want you to be responsible. I'm a willing partner. I won't leave you until we've been together a hundred times."

I was like a starving cow that has suddenly spotted a patch of fresh new grass.

A hundred times came and went in a hurry, but we still found it impossible to part.

On the hundredth time, we wished it would never end. She touched my face and said tearfully, "Take a good look at me. Don't forget me."

"Chunmiao, I want to marry you."

"No."

"I've made up my mind," I said. "What awaits us is probably an abyss. But I have no choice."

"Then we'll jump in together," she said.

That night I went home to lay my cards on the table. My wife was in the side room, winnowing mung beans — a tricky job, but one she was good at. As her hands moved up and down and sideways, the beans fairly flew and the husks soared out.

"What's up?" I asked for lack of anything better to say.

"His granddad sent over some mung beans." She reached down and picked out some gravel. "They came from his garden. I don't care if other things go bad, but not these. I'll have some bean sprouts for Kaifang."

She went back to work.

"Hezuo"—I hardened my heart—"I want a divorce."

Her hands stopped in midair and she stared blankly at me, as if she didn't comprehend what I was saying.

"I'm sorry, Hezuo, but I think that's best."

The winnowing basket tipped slowly forward, sending a few, then a dozen or so, then a hundred or more beans spilling out onto the cement floor, like a green waterfall.

The basket fell out of her hand and she began listing to the side, losing her sense of balance. I thought about reaching out to steady her, but she leaned up against a chopping board on which some onions and dry oil fritters lay. She covered her mouth with her hand and began to sob. Tears gushed from her eyes.

"I really am sorry, but please do this for me."

She flung her hand away from her mouth and wiped the tears from her eyes with her fingers. Clenching her jaw, she said:

"Over my dead body."

43

Angered, Huang Hezuo Bakes Flat Bread
Drunk, Dog Four Displays Melancholy

While you were laying your cards on the table with your wife, still covered with the heavy scent of passionate lovemaking with Pang Chunlai, I was outside crouching under the eaves, gazing at the moon, deep in thought. There was a deranged quality to the wonderful moonbeams. Since it was a full moon, all the dogs in the county were scheduled to meet in Tianhua Square. The first item on the agenda was a memorial for the Tibetan mastiff who could not adapt to life below sea level, causing his internal organs to fail, which led to internal bleeding and death. Next was to arrange a celebration for my third sister, who had married the Norwegian husky belonging to the county Political Consultative Conference chairman four months earlier, and had just had a litter of three white-faced, yellow-eyed bastard pups a month ago.

Lan Jiefang, you rushed out of the house and gave me a meaningful glance as you passed by. I saw you off with a series of barks: Old friend, I think the happy times are coming to an end for you. I felt mildly hostile toward you; the smell of Pang Chunmiao you carried with you worked to diminish the hostility I'd otherwise have felt.

My nose told me you headed north, on foot, the same route I used when taking your son to school. A lot of noise from your wife came from inside the house, thanks to the open door, through which I saw her raise her cleaver and, with loud thuds, shred the onions and oil fritters on the chopping board. The pungent smell of chopped onions and rancid odor of oil fritters spread vigorously through the room. By now your scent placed you at the Tianhua Bridge, where it merged with the putrid smell of foul water running below. With each blow from her cleaver, her left leg wobbled a bit, accompanied by a single clipped word: "Hate! Hate!"

Your son came running out of the main house to see what was going on in the side room. "Mama!" he shouted in alarm. "What are you doing?" Two more violent chops finally vented the hatred she was feeling; she put down her cleaver, turned her back to him to dry her tears, and said, "Why aren't you in bed? Don't you have school tomorrow?" He walked up in front of her. "You're crying, Mama!" he cried out shrilly. "What do you mean, crying? What's there to cry about? It's the onions." "Why are you chopping onions in the middle of the night?" "Go to bed. If you're late for school tomorrow, I'll show you what it means to cry." The anger in her voice was unmistakable. She picked up the cleaver, throwing a fright into your son, who backed up and started muttering to himself. "Come back here!" she said, rubbing his head with one hand and gripping the cleaver in her other. "I want you to study hard and bring credit to yourself. I'll make some onion-stuffed flat bread for you." "I don't want any, Mama," he said. "You're tired, you work so hard. . . ." But she pushed him out the door. "I'm not tired. Now be a good boy and go to bed." He took a few steps, then stopped and turned back. "Papa came home, didn't he?" She didn't say anything for a moment. Then: "Yes, but he left, he had to work overtime tonight." "How come he always has to work overtime?"

I found the whole episode depressing. Among dogs I could be totally unfeeling. But in a family of humans, emotions came at me from all directions.

As promised, your wife set to work making onion-stuffed flat bread. She kneaded the dough, so much that she wound up with a pile half the size of a pillow. What was she thinking, that she'd treat your son's whole class to freshly baked flat breads? Her bony shoulders rose and fell as she worked, sweat darkened the back of her jacket. Intermittent spells of crying spoke to her anger, to her sorrow, and to so many of her memories. Some of the tears fell on her jacket front, some fell on the backs of her hands, and some fell into the dough, which was getting softer and softer and producing a slightly sweet aroma. Adding some flour, she continued to knead the dough. She sobbed from time to time, but quickly stopped and dried her tears with her sleeves. Soon her face was dotted with white flour, a comical yet pitiful appearance. She occasionally stopped working, let her hands fall to her sides, and walked around the room, as if looking for something. On one of those occasions, she slipped on some scattered mung beans and fell to the floor, where she sat for a moment, looking straight ahead, as if staring at a gecko on the wall. Then she banged her hands against the floor and wailed, but just for a moment, before getting to her feet and going back to work.

Once the dough was ready, she set her pan on top of the stove, turned on the gas, and lit a fire. After carefully pouring in a bit of oil, she laid in the first prepared flat bread, which sizzled and sent bursts of fragrance into the kitchen air and from there to the yard outside and the street beyond; once it had spread through town I was able to relax a bit, after being so fidgety. I looked up into the western sky, where the moon now hung, and listened to what was happening at Tianhua Bridge. The scent told me that our regular meeting was ready to begin, and that they were all waiting for me.

The hundreds of mongrels seated around the central fountain stood up when I made my entrance at Tianhua Square and welcomed me boisterously.

Deputy chairmen Ma and Lü escorted me to the chairman's podium, a marble foundation on which a replica of the Venus de Milo had stood before someone walked off with it. As I rested there to catch my breath, from a distance I must have looked like a memorial to a brave canine. My apologies, but I'm not a statue. I'm a living, breathing, powerful dog who carries the genes of the local big white dog and a German shepherd, in short, Gaomi County's dog king. I gathered my thoughts for a couple of seconds before beginning my address. In that first second my sense of smell was still focused on your wife; the heavy aroma of onions coming from your home told me that everything was normal. In the final second I switched to you, sprawled at the window in your smoky office, gazing dreamily at the moon. That too was perfectly normal. I looked out into the flashing eyes and shiny fur of all those animals arrayed before me and announced in a loud voice:

"Brothers, sisters, I call this eighteenth full-moon meeting to order!"

A roar rose from the crowd.

I raised my right paw to quiet them down.

"During this past month our brother the Tibetan mastiff passed away, so let's send his soul off to the plateau with three loud cheers!"

The chorus of cheers from several hundred dogs rocked the town. My eyes were moist: sadness over the passing of our brother and gratitude over the expressions of friendship.

I then invited the dogs to sing and dance and chat and eat and drink in celebration of the one-month birthday of my third elder sister's litter of three.

Whoops and hollers.

She passed her male pup up to me. I kissed him on the cheek and raised him over my head for all to see. The crowd roared. I passed him down, and she passed up a female. I kissed her and raised her over my head, and the crowd roared again. Then she handed up the third pup, another female. I brushed her cheek with my lips, raised her over my head, the crowd roared for the third time, and I passed her down. The crowd roared.

I jumped down off the platform. My sister came up to me and said to her pups, "Say, Hello, Uncle. He's your mother's brother."

Hello Uncle, Hello Uncle, Hello Uncle.

"I hear they've all been sold, is that right?" I asked her icily.

"You heard right," she said proudly. "They'd barely been born before people were beating down our door. My mistress sold them to Party Secretary Ke from Donkey County, Industry and Commerce Department Chief Hu, and Health Department Chief Tu. They paid eighty thousand."

"Are you sure it wasn't a hundred thousand?" I asked, again icily.

"They brought a hundred, but our master would only accept eighty. My master isn't a money-grubber."

"Shit," I said, "that's not selling dogs, it's selling—"

She cut me off with a shrill rebuke: "Uncle!"

"Okay, I won't say it," I promised in a soft voice. Then I announced to the crowd, "Come on, dance! Sing! Start drinking!"

A pointy-eared, slender German dachshund with a hairless tail came up to me with two bottles of beer. When he popped them open with his teeth, foam spilled over the sides and released the delightful aroma.

"Have one, Mr. Chairman." So I took one of the bottles and clinked it against the one he held for himself.

"Bottoms up!" I said. So did he.

With two paws on the bottles, we tipped them up and slugged

down the contents. More and more dogs came up to drink with me, and I didn't send any of them away. A pile of empties formed behind me. A little white Pekinese, her hair in pigtails and a ribbon tied around her neck, came rolling up to me like a little ball, with some locally produced sausage in her mouth. She was wearing Chanel No. 5 perfume, and her coat glistened like silver.

"Chairman . . . Mr. Chairman . . ." She stammered a little. "This sausage is for you."

She undid the wrapping with her tiny teeth and with two paws carried the sausage up to my mouth. I accepted her gift and took a small bite, then chewed it slowly as a sign of respect. Vice chairman Ma walked up with a bottle of beer then, and clinked it against mine.

"How was the sausage?"

"Not bad."

"Damn it. I told them to bring over one case, but they brought twenty cases of the stuff. Old Wei, over at the warehouse, is going to be in deep shit tomorrow." There was a noticeable degree of pride in his voice.

I spotted a mongrel crouching off to the side with three bottles of beer lined up in front of him, along with three chunks of sausage and some cloves of garlic. He took a swig of beer, then a bite of sausage, and flipped a clove of garlic into his mouth. He smacked his lips as he chewed, as if he was the only dog around. He was enjoying himself immensely. The other local mutts were drunk by then. Some were howling at the moon, others were belching loudly, and some were spouting incomprehensible rubbish. I wasn't happy about that, of course, but I didn't do anything about it.

I looked up at the moon and could see that the night was coming to an end. During the summer months, the days are long, the nights are short, and in an hour, no more, birds would be chirping; people would be out airing their caged birds and others would practice tai chi with their swords. I tapped Vice Chairman Ma on the shoulder.

"Adjourn the meeting," I said.

Ma threw down the beer bottle he was holding, stretched out his neck, and released a shrill cry toward the moon. All the canine participants tossed away their beer bottles and, drunk and sober alike, gave me their undivided attention. I jumped up onto the platform.

"Tonight's meeting is hereby adjourned. All of you must vacate the square within the next three minutes. The date of our next meeting will be announced later. Adjourn!"

He released another shrill cry, and the dogs began heading home as fast as their bloated bellies would allow. Those who had drunk too much reeled from side to side, frequently losing their footing in their haste to clear the square. My third sister and her Norwegian husky husband piled their three pups into a fancy Japanese import stroller and left quickly, one pushing, the other pulling. The pups stood up with their paws on the outer edge and yelped excitedly. Three minutes later the clamorous square was deserted, littered with empty beer bottles and odorous chunks of leftover sausage, and befouled by countless puddles of dog piss. I nodded with a sense of satisfaction, slapped paws with Vice Chairman Ma, and left.

After quietly making it back home, I looked into the eastern side room, where your wife was still making flat breads, labor that seemed to bring her peace and happiness. An enigmatic smile graced her face. A sparrow on the plane tree chirped, and within ten or fifteen minutes the whole town was blanketed by birdcalls. The moonlight weakened as dawn was about to break.

44

Jinlong Plans to Build a Resort Village
Jiefang Sends Emotions Through Binoculars

I thought I was reading a document submitted by Jinlong, who wanted to turn Ximen Village into a resort with a Cultural Revolution theme. In his feasibility report, he wrote dialectically: While the Cultural Revolution was destroying culture, it also created a new culture. He wanted to paint new slogans on walls where they had been removed, reinstall loudspeakers, build another lookout perch in the apricot tree, and erect a new Apricot Garden Pig Farm on the site where the old one had been ruined in a rainstorm. Beyond that, he wanted to build a golf course on five thousand acres of land east of the village. As for the farmers who would lose their cropland, he proposed that they act out the village tasks they'd had during the Cultural Revolution, such as: organizing criticism sessions, parading capitalist-roaders in the streets, performing in Revolutionary Model Operas and loyalty dances. He wrote that Cultural Revolution artifacts could be turned out in large quantities: armbands, spears, Chairman Mao badges, handbills, big character posters. . . . Tourists would be permitted to participate in Recalling Bitterness meetings, watch Recalling Bitterness plays, eat Recalling Bitterness meals, and listen to elderly poor peasants relate tales of the old society. . . . And he wrote: The Ximen family compound will be converted into an Independent Farming Museum, with wax statues of Lan Lian, his donkey with the prosthetic foot, and his ox with the missing horn. He wrote that the piece of land farmed by the independent farmer Lan Lian would be covered by an enormous clear plastic canopy to protect a sculpture garden that included pieces of statuary showing the independent farm at each historical juncture, employing the tools he'd used to plant and harvest crops. All these postmodern activities, Jinlong said, would greatly appeal to urbanites and foreigners, which would lead them to generously open their pocketbooks. They'd spend, we'd earn. Once they'd toured our Cultural Revolution village, he wrote, they'd be taken to a glitzy modern-day adult entertainment complex. With obsessive ambition, he planned to gobble up all the land from Ximen Village east to the Wu Family Sandy Mouth and turn it into the finest golf course anywhere in the world, plus a massive amusement park that left nothing to be desired. Then on the sandbar at Wu Family Sandspit he wanted to build a public bath fashioned after ancient Rome's bathhouses, a gambling casino to rival Las Vegas, and yet another sculpture garden, the theme of this one being the stirring battle between men and pigs that had occurred on this spot more than a decade earlier. The theme park would be primarily intended to get people thinking about environmental protection and underscore the concept that all sentient beings are endowed with a form of intelligence. The incident in which a pig sacrificed himself by diving into icy water to save a child was one that needed to be played up. Also included in the document was the author's intent to build a convention center in which annual international meetings of family pets would be convened, bringing both foreign visitors and foreign exchange to the nation. . . .

As I read the feasibility report he'd sent to all pertinent county offices, plus the approving comments by big shots on the Party committee and in the county government, I could only shake my head and sigh. In essence I'm a man who is most comfortable with the old ways. I love the land and the smell of manure; I'd be content to live the life of a farmer; and I have enormous respect for old-school peasants like my father, who live for the land. But someone like that is too far behind the times to survive in today's society. I actually went and fell so madly in love with a woman that I asked my wife for a divorce, and it doesn't get much more old-school than that; again, out of step with the times. There was no way I could state my personal views in regard to the report, so I merely drew a circle, signifying approval, near my name. But something was bothering me. Who had actually been responsible for drafting such an outlandish report? Just then, Mo Yan's head, a wicked smile on his face, appeared at my window. Now how in the world was that possible, since my third-floor window was maybe fifteen yards from the ground?

Suddenly some noise erupted out in the hallway, so I opened the door to see what it was. It was Huang Hezuo, a cleaver in one hand and a long rope in the other. Her hair was a fright and there was blood at the corners of her mouth. She was limping toward me, a vacant stare in her eyes. My son, schoolbag on his back, was right behind her, carrying a handful of steaming, greasy oil fritters, no discernible expression on his face. Behind him came that brute of a dog, my son's cartoon-decorated plastic water bottle hanging around his neck and, since it was so long, banging into his knees as it swung back and forth with each step.

I screamed, and woke myself up. I'd fallen asleep in my clothes on the sofa. My forehead was covered with cold sweat, my heart was racing. My head felt numbed, thanks to the sleeping pill I'd taken, and the sunlight streaming in the window stung my eyes. I managed somehow to get up and splash water on my face. The clock on the wall said 6:30. The phone rang. I picked it up. Silence. I didn't dare say anything. I just stood there waiting. "It's me," she said, her voice cracking. "I didn't sleep all night. . . ." "Don't worry, I'm fine." "I'll bring you something to eat." "No, don't come over," I said. "It's not that I'm afraid, I'd be willing to stand on a rooftop and announce to the world that I love you, but I shudder to think what it might lead to. . . ." "I understand." "I think we should see a bit less of one another for a while. I don't want to give her an opportunity to—" "I understand. I've done a terrible thing to her. . . ." "Don't ever think that. If it's anyone's fault, it's mine. Besides, didn't Engels say that a loveless marriage is a sin against morality? Truth is, we've done nothing wrong." "I'll go buy some stuffed buns and leave them for you in the receptionist's office—" "No," I said, "I don't want you to come, Chief. Don't worry, if an earthworm won't starve neither will I. I can't say how things will be later on, but for now I'm still a deputy county head, so I'll go get something to eat at the guesthouse, where there's plenty of food." "I miss you—" "Me too. When you go to work, stand in the bookstore entrance and look toward my window. That way I'll be able to see you." "But I won't be able to see you—" "You'll know I'm up here. Okay, my dear. . . ."

But I didn't go to the guesthouse to get something to eat. Since the day we first touched, I felt like a frog in love, no appetite, nothing but unbridled passion. But appetite or not, I had to eat, so I forced myself to eat some snacks she'd brought me, though I tasted none of them. Still, they provided life-giving calories and nutrition.

I leaned against the window with my binoculars, prepared for my daily ritual. The clock in my head was remarkably accurate. Since in those days the town had no tall buildings, nothing blocked my view. If I'd wanted to I could have brought the faces of the old folks doing their morning exercises in Tianhua Square right into my eyes. First I aimed my binoculars at the entrance to Tianhua Lane. One Tianhua Lane was my house. The gate was closed. My son's enemies had drawn a picture and written slogans in chalk on the gate: a fanged little boy, half of whose face was filled in with chalk, the other not. He was holding his sticklike hands in the air, a sign of surrender. Down between his sticklike legs hung an enormous penis from which a single line ran all the way down to the bottom of the gate.

I lowered my binoculars, which spat out Tianhua Square and Tianhua Lane. My heart skipped a beat. There was Huang Hezuo, straining to walk her bicycle down the three steps outside the gate. She spotted the graffiti when she turned to lock the gate, so she parked her bike, looked around, and crossed the street, where she broke off a branch of the pine tree there and used it to wipe off as much of the chalk as possible. I couldn't see her face, but I knew she'd be grumbling. After the chalk was smeared beyond recognition, she got on her bike and headed north for a dozen yards or so before disappearing behind a row of houses. How had she managed to get through the night? Had she lain awake or had she slept like a baby? No way to know. Though there'd never been a time during all these years that I'd actually loved her, she was, after all, the mother of my son, and our lives had been closely bound up together. She reappeared on the road leading to the square in front of the station. Even when she was riding a bicycle she wobbled, and now more than ever, since she looked to be in a tearing hurry. Now I could see her face, which seemed covered by a smoky veil. She was wearing a black top with a yellow phoenix design. I knew she had plenty of clothes; on a business trip once, probably driven by deep-seated guilt feelings, I'd bought her a dozen skirts, all of which she'd immediately put away at the bottom of a trunk and never wore. I thought she might glance over at my window when she passed by the government office building, but she didn't. She looked straight ahead, and I heaved a sigh. I knew that this woman was not about to give me my freedom, not without a fight. But since the battle had begun, it would have to be a fight to the finish.

Once again I trained my binoculars on the door of my house on Tianhua Lane, which was actually a wide boulevard, the preferred route by parents taking their children to the Phoenix Elementary School in the southern district. It was teeming with parents and children at this early morning hour.

My son and his dog walked out the gate, dog first, followed by the boy, who opened one side a crack and slipped through. Clever boy. If he'd opened both sides, he'd have had to turn around and close them both, a waste of time and energy. After locking up, he jumped from the top step to the sidewalk and headed north. I saw him wave to a boy riding by on a bike; the dog barked at the boy. They walked past the Tianhua Barbershop, which was directly opposite a shop that made home aquariums and sold tropical fish. The south-facing door showed up bright in the morning sunlight. The shopkeeper, a retired bookkeeper who'd worked at a cotton storage and transportation station, was a dignified old man who displayed his fish in aquariums out on the sidewalk. My son and his dog stopped to watch the ungraceful movements of big-bellied goldfish. The shopkeeper appeared to say something to my son, whose head was too low for me to see his mouth. He might have answered, he might not have.

They were back on the road, heading north, and when they reached the Tianhua Bridge, my son appeared to want to go down to the water, but the dog grabbed his clothes in his teeth to stop him. A good, loyal companion. My son struggled to get free, but was no match for the dog. Finally, he picked up a piece of brick and threw it into the water; it landed with a splash. A yellow dog greeted our dog with a bark and a wagging tail. The green plastic awning over the farmer's market sparkled in the bright sunlight. My son stopped at just about every shop along the way, but the dog invariably grabbed his clothes or nudged him behind the knee to keep him going. When they reached Tianhua Lane, they sped up; that was when my binoculars began sweeping the area in front of the New China Bookstore, which was on Tianhua Lane.

My son took a slingshot out of his pocket and aimed at a bird in the pear tree in front of the home of my colleague, another deputy county head by the name of Chen. Pang Chunmiao appeared in front of the bookstore as if she'd fallen out of the sky. Son, dog, I've got no more time for you today.

Dressed in a spotless white dress, she was a vision of loveliness. Her freshly washed face was free of makeup, and I could almost smell the sandalwood fragrance of her facial soap and the natural fragrance of her body, which intoxicated and nearly transported me into another world. She was smiling. Her eyes sparkled; morning light reflected off what I could see of her teeth. She was looking up at me and knew that I was looking down at her. It was rush hour; the street was clogged with cars; the pedestrian lanes were alive with motorbikes spewing black smoke; bicycles weaved in and out of cars and motorbikes coming at them, inviting a chorus of honking from exasperated drivers. On any other day I'd have found this all quite repellent, but today it was a glorious sight.

She stood out there until her coworker opened the door for her; just before she walked inside, she put her fingers to her lips and tossed me a kiss. Like a butterfly, that kiss flew across the street, hovered briefly in the air just beyond my window, and then landed on my mouth. What a wonderful girl. I'd have died for her without hesitation.

My secretary came in to tell me I was to attend a meeting that afternoon in the County Committee conference room to discuss the Ximen Village Resort development plans. Attendees would include the county Party secretary, his deputy, the county chief, the Party Committee, all county government department heads, and leading bankers. Jinlong, I knew, was going for broke this time, and down the line what awaited him, as well as me, would not be garlands of flowers and smooth sailing. I had a hunch that a cruel fate was in store for my brother and me. But we would both forge ahead, and in this regard, we were truly brothers, for good or ill.

Before clearing my desk to leave for the meeting, I picked up my binoculars and took my customary position at the window, where I spotted my son's dog leading my wife across the street and up to the door of the New China Bookstore. I've read several of Mo Yan's stories in which he writes about dogs; they always seem more clever than humans, and that always gave me a laugh — such nonsense, I thought. But now, all of a sudden, I became a believer.

45

Dog Four Follows a Scent to Chunmiao
Huang Hezuo Writes a Message in Blood

A silver Crown Victoria pulled up and parked in front of the school gate when I dropped your son off. A nicely dressed girl stepped out of the car, and your son waved to her, like any American boy might, and said, "Hi, Fenghuang!" She waved back. "Hi, Jiefang!" They walked in through the gate together.

I crossed the street, turned east, then headed north, walking slowly toward the train station. Your wife had tossed me four onion rolls that morning and, so as not to appear ungrateful, I ate them all. Now they lay heavily in my stomach. When the Hungarian wolfhound who lived behind a restaurant smelled me out, he barked a friendly greeting. I didn't feel like responding. I wasn't a happy dog that morning. I had a hunch that before the day was over, bad things would happen to man and dog alike. Sure enough, I met your wife on the way before reaching her work site. I greeted her with dog sounds to let her know her son was safely in school. She jumped down off her bicycle and said:

"Little Four, you saw it with your own eyes, he doesn't want us anymore."

With a sympathetic look, I walked up to her and wagged my tail to try to make her feel better. Just because I didn't care for the greasy odor that clung to her body didn't alter the fact that she was my mistress. She walked her bike over to the curb and signaled for me to come to her, which I did. The roadside was littered with white blossoms from roadside Chinese scholar trees. A foul smell from a nearby panda-shaped trash can hung in the air. Farm tractors pulling trailers with vegetables and spurting black smoke from their exhaust pipes rumbled down the street until they were stopped by a traffic cop in the intersection. A couple of dogs had met their end the day before thanks to chaotic traffic conditions. Your wife touched my nose.

"He's got another woman, Little Four," she said. "I could smell it on him. You have a better nose than I do, so you must have known too." She lifted her black leather purse, parts of which had turned white from use, out of her bicycle rack, took out a sheet of paper, and unfolded it. In it were two long strands of hair. She held it up to my nose. "This is her," she said. "They were on his clothes. I want you to help me find her." Her eyes were moist, but I saw flames in them.

I didn't hesitate. This was my job. Truth is, I didn't have to sniff at those strands of hair to know who I should go looking for. Well, I trotted along seeking out a smell like mung-bean noodles, your wife following me on her bike. Because of her injury, she kept her balance better riding fast than riding slow.

I did hesitate when we reached the New China Bookstore, since the scent from Pang Chunmiao's body gave me a good feeling. But when I looked back and saw your wife limping toward me, I made up my mind to go through with it. I was, after all, a dog, and dogs are supposed to be loyal to their masters. I barked twice at the entrance, and your wife pushed open the door to let me go in first. I barked twice at Pang Chunmiao, who was wiping down a counter with a damp cloth, then I lowered my head. I simply couldn't look Pang Chunmiao in the eye.

"How could it be her?" your wife said. Keeping my head down, I whined. Your wife looked up into Pang Chunmiao's red face. "How could it be you?" she said uncertainly, her voice betraying feelings of agony and forlornness. "Why is it you?"

The two middle-aged clerks gave the newcomer and her dog suspicious looks. The red-faced one, whose breath reeked of pickled tofu and leeks, shouted angrily:

"Whose dog is that? Get him out of here!"

The other clerk, whose rear end smelled of hemorrhoid ointment, said softly:

"Isn't that County Chief Lan's dog? Then that must be his wife. . . ."

Your wife turned and glared hatefully at them. They lowered their heads. Then in a loud voice your wife confronted Pang Chunmiao.

"Come outside," she said. "My son's class monitor sent me to talk to you."

After your wife opened the door to let me out, she went through the door sideways and, without looking behind her, walked over to her bicycle, unlocked it, and pushed it down the street, heading east. I was right behind her. I heard the door of the New China Bookstore open and close, and I didn't need to look to know that Pang Chunmiao had come outside. Her smell was stronger than ever, a case of nerves.

In front of a chili sauce shop your wife stopped and grasped a French plane tree with both hands; her legs were trembling. Chunmiao walked up with obvious hesitation and stopped three yards before she reached us. Your wife was staring straight ahead at the tree trunk. I kept an eye on each of the two women.

"You were only six years old when we started at the cotton processing plant," your wife said. "We're twenty years older than you, different generations.

"He must have tricked you," she continued. "He's a married man, you're a young maiden. That's completely irresponsible of him, he's a brute and he's hurt you." Your wife turned around, rested her back against the tree, and glared at Pang Chunmiao. "With that blue birthmark he looks three parts human, seven parts demon. For you to be with him is like planting a fresh flower on a pile of cow shit!"

A pair of speeding squad cars, sirens blaring, drew curious looks from people out on the street.

"I've already told him the only way he'll get his freedom is over my dead body," your wife said emotionally. "You know what's what. Your father, your mother, and your sister are all public figures. If word of your affair were to get out, the shame they'd feel would be overwhelming; they'd have no place to hide their faces. As for me, what do I care? Half my bottom is missing, and I have no reputation worth saving, so I have nothing to lose."

Children from the kindergarten were just then crossing the street, with one nanny in front, another at the rear, and two more running up and down to keep the children in line, shouting the whole time. Cars in both directions were stopped at the crosswalk.

"I advise you to leave him and find someone else to fall in love with. Get married, have a child, and you've got my word I'll never tell anyone about this. Huang Hezuo may be ugly and someone to be pitied, but she means what she says." Then your wife wiped her eyes with the back of her hand before sticking the first finger of her right hand in her mouth. I saw her jaw muscles tense. She pulled her finger out of her mouth, and I smelled blood. The tip of her finger was bleeding, and I watched as she wrote two words in blood on the glossy trunk of the French plane tree:

LEAVE HIM

With a moan, Pang Chunmiao covered her mouth with her hand, spun around, and stumbled off down the street, running a few steps, then walking, running and walking, running and walking, the way we dogs move. She kept her hand over her mouth the whole time. The sight saddened me. Instead of going back to New China, she turned and disappeared down a lane. I looked over at your wife's ashen face and felt chilled. It was clear that Pang Chunmiao, a silly little girl, was no match for your wife, the victim in all this; her tears refused to leave the safety of her eyes. It was time, I thought, for her to take me home; but she didn't. Her finger was still bleeding, too much to waste, so she filled in missing strokes and reapplied the fuzzy parts. There was still blood, so she added an exclamation mark to the words. Then another, and another . . .

LEAVE HIM!!!

A perfectly good slogan, though she seemed to want to write more. But why gild the lily? So she shook her finger and stuck it in her mouth, then reached under her collar with her left hand and pulled a medicinal plaster off her shoulder to wrap her injured finger. She'd put it on just that morning.

After stepping back to admire the slogan, written in blood to goad Chunmiao into action and as a warning to her, she smiled contentedly before pushing her bike down the street, with me some three or four yards behind her. She stopped to look back at the tree a time or two, as if afraid someone would come along and rub the words out.

At an intersection we waited for the green light, though we crossed with our hearts in our throats, thanks to all the black-jacketed motorcyclists for whom a red light was a mere suggestion and the drivers of cars who paid little attention to traffic lights. In recent days a bunch of teenagers had formed what they called a "Honda Speed Demons Gang," whose purpose was to run their Honda motorcycles over as many dogs as possible. Whenever they hit one, they ran over it over and over, until its guts were spread all over the street. Then with a loud whistle it was off to the next one. Just why they hated dogs so much was something I never could figure out.

46

Huang Hezuo Vows to Shock Her Foolish Husband
Hong Taiyue Organizes a Government Protest

The meeting to discuss Jinlong's idiotic proposal went on till noon.
The elderly Party secretary, Jin Bian — the onetime blacksmith who
had fitted my dad's donkey for shoes — had been promoted to vice
chairman of the Municipal People's Congress, and it was a foregone
conclusion that Pang Kangmei was next in line for the Party position.
She was the daughter of a national hero and a college graduate with
rich experience at the grassroots level. Barely forty years old and still
attractive, she had the enthusiastic backing of her superiors and the
support of those beneath her. In other words, she had everything she
needed for success. The meeting was highly contentious, with neither
side willing to back off its position. So Pang Kangmei simply pounded
her gavel and announced: "We'll do it! For the initial phase we'll need
300 million yuan. We'll leave it up to the banks to come up with that
amount. We'll form a Merchants Investment Group to attract investment capital from both domestic and overseas sources."

I was distracted throughout the discussion, using visits to the toilet as an excuse to make phone calls to the New China Bookstore.
Pang Kangmei's gaze followed me like a laser. I could only smile
apologetically and point to my stomach.

I phoned the bookstore three times. Finally, on the third try, the
clerk with the husky voice said heatedly:

"You again. Stop calling. She was led outside by the crippled
wife of Deputy County Chief Lan, and she still hasn't returned."

I called home. No answer.

My seat felt like a heated grill, and I know how bad I must have
looked as I sat through the meeting, one scary image after another

racing through my mind. The most tragic image was of my wife murdering Chunmiao in an out-of-the-way village or remote spot, then killing herself. A crowd of rubberneckers had gathered around the bodies and police cars, sirens blaring, were speeding to the scene. I sneaked a look at Kangmei, who was volubly describing aspects of Jinlong's blueprints with a pointer, and all my benumbed brain could think about was how, in the next minute, the next second, anytime now, this huge scandal would land in the midst of this meeting like a suicide bomb, sending fragments of steel and flesh flying. . . .

The meeting was adjourned amid applause that carried complex implications. I rushed out of the conference room, followed by a malicious comment by one of the attendees: "County Chief must have a crotch-full by now."

I ran to the car, catching my driver by surprise. But before he could scamper around to open the door for me, I'd already climbed into the backseat.

"Let's go!" I said impatiently.

"We can't," he said helplessly.

He was right, we couldn't. The administrative section had lined up the cars by seniority. Pang Kangmei's silver Crown Victoria sedan was at the head of the line in front of the building. Next in line was the county chief's Nissan, then the People's Consultative Conference chairman's black Audi, the National People's Congress municipal director's white Audi . . . My VW Santana was twentieth. They were all idling. Like me, some of the attendees were already in their cars, while others were standing near the gate, engaged in hushed conversations. Everyone was waiting for Pang Kangmei, whose laughter preceded her out of the building. She was wearing a high-collared sapphire blue business suit with a glittering pin on her lapel. She told everyone that she owned only costume jewelry, which, according to her sister, could fill a bucket. Chunmiao, where are you, my love? I was on the verge of climbing out of my car and running out onto the street when Kangmei finally got into her car and drove off, followed by a procession of automobiles leaving the compound. Sentries stood at attention on both sides of the gate, right arms raised in salutes. The cars all turned right.

"Where is everybody going, Little Hu?" I asked anxiously.

"To Ximen Jinlong's banquet." He handed me a large red, gilded invitation.

I had a vague recollection of someone whispering during the meeting, "Why all this discussion? The celebration banquet's there waiting for us."

"Turn the car around," I said anxiously.

"Where are we going?"

"Back to the office."

He was not happy about that. I knew that not only were the drivers treated to some good food at these events, but they were also given gifts. Not only that, Chairman of the Board Ximen Jinlong had a reputation of being especially generous in this regard. To try to console Little Hu, and to cover myself for my behavior, I said:

"You should be aware of my relationship with Ximen Jinlong."

Without responding, he made a U-turn and headed back toward my office building. Just my luck to run up against market day at Nanguan. Hordes of people on bicycles and tractors, in donkey wagons and on foot, crowded into People's Avenue. Despite a liberal use of his horn, Little Hu was forced to go slowly with the flow of traffic.

"The goddamn traffic cops are all off drinking someplace!" he grumbled.

I ignored him. What did I care if the cops were off drinking? Finally, we made it to the office, where my car was immediately surrounded by a crowd of people that seemed to have risen out of the ground.

Some old women in rags sat down in front of my car, slapping their hands on the ground and filling the air with tearless wails. Like magicians on a stage, several middle-aged men unfurled banners with slogans: "Give us back our land," "Down with corrupt officials," things like that. A dozen men were kneeling behind the wailing old women and holding up sheets of white cloth with writing on them. Then there were people behind the car passing out handbills in the practiced manner of Red Guards during the Cultural Revolution or professional mourners scattering spirit money during rural funerals. People swarmed around us, penning us in with no way out. Fellow villagers, you've surrounded the person who least deserves it. I spotted Hong Taiyue's white hair; supported by a couple of young men, he was walking toward me from the pagoda pine east of the main gate. He stopped just in front of the farmers and behind the seated old women, a space that had obviously been saved for him. This was an organized, disciplined crowd of petitioners, led, of course, by Hong

Taiyue. He desperately missed the collective spirit of the people's commune and the stubborn perseverance of Lan Lian, the independent farmer. The two eccentrics of Northeast Gaomi Township had been like a pair of oversize lightbulbs, spreading their light in all directions, like two flying banners, one red, the other black. He reached behind him and took out his ox hip bone, now yellowed with age, but retaining all nine copper coins around the edge; he raised it in the air, then lowered it, over and over, faster and faster, creating a *hua-la-la hua-la-la* rhythmic sound. That bone was an important memento from his glorious history, like the sword used by a warrior against his enemy. Shaking it was Hong's special skill. So was clapper talk:

> *Hua-lang-lang, hua-lang-lang,* the hip bone sings and I begin
>   my theme.
> What is my story today? Ximen Jinlong's restoration scheme.

More people crowded up, filling the compound with noise, but quieting down almost at once.

> Now there's a Ximen Village in Northeast Gaomi Township,
>   scenic as a dream,
> Where once was a famous Apricot Garden where pigs were raised,
>   each to a team.
> Grain grew high, animals thrived, Chairman Mao's revolutionary
>   line was like the sun!

At this point, Hong flung the bone into the air, spun around, and, so all could see, caught it before it hit the ground. While it was in the air, it sang out its unique sound, almost like a living being. Amazing! The crowd roared. Scattered applause. The expression on Hong's face underwent a dramatic change. He continued:

> The village's tyrannical landlord, Ximen Nao, left behind
>   a bastard white-eyed wolf.
> The fellow's name is Jinlong, from childhood a smooth-talking
>   phony do-gooder
> Who wormed his way into the Youth League and
>   the Communist Party.

By usurping authority he became Party secretary to settle
old scores likea madman.
He parceled out land for independent farming and stole People's
Commune property.
He restored landlords, rehabilitated the bad, making
ox-demons and snake-spirits happy.

My heart breaks when I say these things, tears and snivel run down my face . . .

He flung the bone into the air and caught it with his right hand as he dried his eyes with his left. The next time he caught it with his left hand and dried his eyes with his right. That bone was like a white weasel jumping from one hand to the other. The applause was deafening, almost but not quite drowning out the sound of police sirens.

With increased passion, Hong continued:

Then in 1991, the little rogue came up with another evil plot,
He wants to drive us out of the village and turn it into
a tourist resort.
To destroy good farmland for a golf course, a gambling casino,
a brothel, a public bath, and turn socialist Ximen Village
into an imperialist pleasure dome.
Comrades, villagers, beat your chests and think, is it time for
class struggle?
Should Ximen Jinlong be killed? Even with his money,
his prestige, his support; even if his brother, Jiefang, is deputy
county chief. United we are strong. Let us sweep away the
reactionaries, sweep them away, sweep them all away . . .

The crowd responded with a roar. People cursed and swore, they laughed, they stomped their feet, and they jumped in anger. Chaos reigned at the gate. I was just looking for an opportunity to climb out of the car and, as a fellow villager, get them to leave. But Hong Taiyue's clapper talk had by then implied that I was Jinlong's backer, and I shuddered to think what might happen if I confronted this fired-up crowd. All I could do was put on my shades to hide my face and lean back in the seat until the police came and broke up the demonstration.

I watched as a dozen cops standing on the perimeter of the

demonstration brandished their clubs — no, now they're in the midst of the surging crowd, surrounded.

I adjusted my shades, put on a blue cap, did my best to cover my blue birthmark, and opened the car door.

"Don't go out there, Chief," my driver said, clearly alarmed.

But I did, and I forged ahead at a crouch, until I tripped over an extended leg and found myself sprawled on the ground. The earpiece of my glasses had broken off, my cap had flown off my head, and my face was lying on the noon-baked concrete. My nose and my lips hurt. Suddenly I was in the grip of incapacitating despair; dying there would have been the easy way out. I might even have been given a hero's funeral. But then I thought of Pang Chunmiao; I couldn't die without seeing her one more time, even if my last glimpse of her was in her coffin. Just as I managed to get back on my feet, a chorus of shouts thundered all around me:

"It's Lan Jiefang, it's Blue Face! He's Ximen Jinlong's backer!"

"Grab him, don't let him get away!"

Everything went black, then a blinding light, and the faces around me were all twisted, like horseshoes dunked in water after emerging from the forge, emitting steel blue rays of light. My arms were twisted roughly behind my back. My nose was hot and itchy, and it felt as if a pair of worms had wriggled onto my upper lip. Someone kneed me in the buttocks, someone else kicked me in the calf, and someone else slugged me in the back. I saw my blood drip onto the concrete, where it immediately turned to black steam.

"Is that you, Jiefang?" The familiar voice came from somewhere up ahead, and I quickly composed myself, forced the cobwebs out of my head so I could think, and focused my eyes as best I could. There in front of me was Hong Taiyue's face, the picture of suffering and hatred. For some strange reason, my nose began to ache, my eyes seemed hot, and tears spilled out, the very thing that happens if you spot a friend when you're in danger. "Good uncle," I sobbed, "tell them to let me go. . . ."

"Let him go, all of you, let him go. . . ." I heard his shouts and saw him wave his ox bone like a conductor's baton. "No violence, this is a peaceful demonstration!"

"Jiefang, you're the deputy county chief, the people's official, so you have to stand up for us villagers and stop Ximen Jinlong from carrying out his crazy scheme," Hong said. "Your father was going to come and petition on our behalf, but your mother fell ill, so he couldn't come."

"Uncle Hong, Jinlong and I may have been born to the same mother, but we've never gotten along, not even as children. You know that as well as I." I wiped my bloody nose. "I'm as opposed to his plan as you are, so let me go."

"Did you all hear that?" Hong waved his ox bone. "Deputy County Chief Lan is on our side!"

"I'll forward your complaints up the line. But for now, you have to leave." I pushed aside the people in front of me and, as sternly as I could manage, said, "You're breaking the law!"

"Don't let him go until he signs a pledge!"

That made me so mad I reached out and snatched the ox bone out of Hong's hand and brandished it over my head like a sword, driving the crowd back, all but one person who got hit on the shoulder and another who took it on the head. "The deputy county chief is assaulting people!" That was fine with me, right or wrong. Right or wrong, county chief or not, you people had better get out of my way — I opened a path with the ox bone, broke through the crowd, and made my way into the building, where I took the stairs three steps at a time all the way up to my office. I looked out the window at all those shiny heads beyond the gate, then heard some dull thuds and saw a cloud of pink smoke rise into the air, and I knew that the police had finally resorted to tear gas. Bedlam broke out. I threw down the ox bone and shut the window, ending for the moment my dealings with the world outside. I was not a very good government cadre, because I was more concerned about my problems than the people's suffering. In fact, I was glad to see those poor people petitioning the government, since it would be up to Pang Kangmei and her ilk to clean up the mess. I picked up the phone and dialed the bookstore number. No answer. I phoned home. My son answered, which took the edge off my anger.

"Kaifang," I said as calmly as I could, "let me talk to your mother."

"What's going on with you and Mom?" he asked unhappily.

"Nothing," I said. "Let me talk to her."

"She's not here, and the dog didn't come to school to pick me up," he said. "She didn't make lunch for me, and all she left was a note."

"What's the note say?"

"I'll read it to you," he said. " 'Kaifang, make yourself something to eat. If Dad calls, tell him I'm at the Chili Sauce Shop on People's Avenue.' What does that mean?"

I didn't explain it to him. "Son, I can't tell you, not now." I hung up and looked around the office. The ox bone lay on my desk, and I had the vague notion that I ought to take something with me, but I couldn't for the life of me think what that was. I rushed downstairs. The area around the gate was chaotic, with the people crowding together to get away from the nose-pricking, eye-burning smoke. Coughing, cursing, screaming, the sounds all merged in the air. The clamor seemed to be coming to an end near the building, but only beginning out by the gate. Holding my nose, I ran around the building and slipped out through the rear gate, immediately heading east. I ran past the movie theater into Leatherwork Lane, then turned south and headed for People's Avenue. The distracted shoe repairmen in shops lining both sides of the lane obviously linked the fleeing deputy county chief to the commotion at the county office building. County residents might not recognize Pang Kangmei if they saw her out on the street, but every one of them recognized me.

I spotted her on People's Avenue, her and the dog beside her, the son of a bitch. Crowds were running all over the place, disregarding traffic laws, as cars and people came together; horns blared. I crossed the street like a kid playing hopscotch. Some people noticed me, most didn't. I ran up to her, breathless; she just stared at the tree. But you, you son of a bitch, you stared at me, a look of desolation in your eyes.

"What have you done with her?" I demanded.

Her cheeks twitched, and her mouth twisted into something close to a sneer. But her gaze stayed fixed on the tree.

At first all I saw were some black, oily smudges on the trunk, but a closer look revealed clusters of disgusting bluebottle flies. So I looked even harder, and now I saw the two words and three exclamation signs. I smelled blood. My eyes glazed over and I nearly blacked out. What I'd feared more than anything, it seemed, had occurred. She'd killed her and written on the tree with her blood. Still, I forced myself to ask:

"What did you do to her?"

"I didn't do anything to her." She kicked the tree, which sent the flies flitting away with a gut-wrenching buzz. She showed me her plaster-wrapped finger. "It's my blood. I wrote those words with my blood to get her to leave you."

Like a man who has been relieved of a crushing burden, I was overcome by exhaustion. I sank into a crouch, and though my fingers were cramped, twisted like claws, I managed to fish a pack of cigarettes out of my pocket, lit one, and took a deep drag. The smoke seemed to snake its way up into my brain, where it swirled amid all the valleys and canals to create a sense of well-being. When the flies were flitting away from the tree, the filthy words had leaped tragically into my eyes. But the flies quickly swarmed back and covered them up, making them virtually invisible.

"I told her," my wife said in a monotone, without looking at me, "that if she leaves you, I won't say a word. She can go fall in love, get married, have a child, and enjoy a decent life. But if she won't leave you, then she and I will go down together!" She turned abruptly and pointed her injured, wrapped index finger at me. Her eyes were blazing as, in a shrill voice that reminded me of a cornered dog, she said, "I'll bite this finger again and expose this scandal of yours by writing it in blood on the gates of the county office building, the Party Committee building, the Political Consultative Conference building, the local People's Congress building, the police station, the courthouse, the procurator office, the theater, the movie house, the hospital, and every tree and wall I can . . . until I run out of blood!"

47

Posing as a Hero, a Spoiled Son
Smashes a Famous Watch
Saving the Situation, a Jilted Wife Returns
to Her Hometown

Your wife, in a floor-length magenta dress, was sitting in the passenger seat of a VW Santana, smelling of mothballs. The neckline, front and back, were decorated with shiny sequins. My thoughts at that moment? If tossed into a river, she'd turn into a scaly fish. She had mousse in her hair and makeup that turned her face so white it looked like limestone and contrasted starkly with her dark neck; it was as if she was wearing a mask. She had on a gold necklace and a pair of gold rings, intended to give her a regal appearance. Your driver pulled a long face until your wife gave him a carton of cigarettes, which turned his face back to oval.

Your son and I were in the backseat, which was stacked high with packages: liquor, tea, pastries, and fabrics. This was my first trip back to Ximen Village since I'd ridden to the county town in Ximen Jinlong's Jeep. I'd been a three-month-old puppy then; now I was an adult dog with a full range of experiences. Emotionally, I watched the scenery go by on both sides of the broad, tree-lined highway. There were few cars on the highway, so my driver drove at speeds that seemed close to flying.

My excitement was not shared by your son, who sat quietly, absorbed in the Tetris game he was playing on his electronic toy. His intensity was visible in the way he was biting his lower lip, his thumbs dancing on the buttons. He stomped his foot and puffed angrily each time he missed.

This was the first time your wife, who in the past always took the bus or rode her bicycle back to the village, had ridden in the official car in your name. And it was the first time she'd returned looking like the wife of an official instead of wearing her stained work clothes and not bothering about her hair or face. It was the first time she'd brought expensive gifts with her instead of homemade oil fritters. And it was the first time she'd brought me along rather than locking me in the yard to keep an eye on the house. Her attitude toward me had taken a positive turn after I'd snooped out your lover, Pang Chunmiao; more accurately, I suppose, my importance had, in her eyes, increased considerably. She often talked to me about what was on her mind, like a garbage pail for her throwaway comments and complaints. And I was not just her confessor figure, I was, it seemed, a sort of adviser:

"What do you think I ought to do, Dog?"

"Do you think she'll leave him, Dog?"

"Do you think she'll go see him at his conference in Jinan, Dog, or will he take her someplace else for a little tryst?"

"Do you think there really are women who can't get by without a man, Dog?"

I dealt with these interminable questions the only way I could: with silence. I gazed up at her, my thoughts leaping up and down in concert with her questions; sometimes flying to heaven, sometimes plummeting to hell.

"Tell me honestly, Dog, who's right, him or me?" She was sitting on a kitchen stool, leaning up against the butcher block as she sharpened a rusty knife, the edge of the spatula, and a pair of scissors. Apparently, she'd decided to utilize our chat time to put a shiny edge on all the sharp objects in the house. "She's younger than me, and prettier, but I was young and pretty once. Isn't that right? Besides, I may not be young and good looking now, but neither is he. He never was good looking, not with that blue birthmark across half his face. Sometimes I wake up in the middle of the night, and the sight of his face makes me shudder. Dog, if Ximen Jinlong hadn't ruined my reputation as a girl, do you think I'd have stooped to marrying this one? Dog, my life was ruined, all thanks to those two brothers. . . ." When her complaints reached this stage, tears would moisten the front of her clothes. "Now I'm an ugly old woman, while he's a prominent official, so it's time to get rid of the old lady, like throwing away a pair of worn socks. Does that make sense to you, Dog? Is that a sign of conscience?" She sharpened the knife with determination. "I have to stand up for myself. I'm going to hone my body till it shines like this knife." She touched the edge of the blade to her finger. It left a white mark; sharp enough. "We're going back to the village tomorrow, Dog, and you're coming along. We'll go in his car. In all these years I've never once sat in his car, keeping public and private separate to protect his good name. I can take credit for half of the prestige he enjoys with the public. Dog, people take advantage of good people, just like people ride good horses. But no more. Now we're going to be like those other wives of officials, doing whatever we have to do to show people that Lan Jiefang has a wife, and that she is to be reckoned with. . . ."

The car drove across the newly built Bridge of Wealth and into Ximen Village. The squat old stone bridge stood unused nearby, except for a bunch of bare-assed boys taking turns diving into the river below and sending water splashing skyward. Your son put down his game and gazed out the window, a look of envy crossing his face.

"Kaifang," your wife said, "your cousin Huanhuan is one of those boys."

I tried to recall what Huanhuan and Gaige looked like. Huanhuan's face had always been sort of gaunt, and clean, Gaige's was pale and pudgy, and always decorated with a line of snot down to his lips. I still recalled their unique smells, and that triggered an upsurge, like a raging river, of all the thousands of odors associated with the Ximen Village of eight years before.

"Wow, standing there naked at his age," he muttered. I couldn't tell if that was a scornful or an envious comment.

"Don't forget, when we get home, say sweet things, be polite," your wife reminded him. "We want your grandparents to be happy and our relatives to admire you."

"Then smear some honey on my lips!"

"You love to upset me, don't you?" your wife said. "But those jars of honey are for your grandparents. Say you bought them."

"Where was I supposed to have gotten the money?" he said with a pout. "They won't believe me."

By now the car was driving down the village's main street, lined with rows of 1980s barracks-style houses, all with the word *Demolish* on the brick walls. A pair of cranes with their enormous orange arms stood ready to begin rebuilding Ximen Village.

The car pulled up to the gate of the old-fashioned Ximen family compound. The driver honked the horn, bringing a swarm of people out of the yard. I detected their individual odors at the same time that I saw their faces. Signs of age appeared in both their odors and their looks. All the faces were older, looser, and furrowed: Lan Lian's blue face, Yingchun's swarthy face, Huang Tong's yellow face, Qiuxiang's pale face, and Huzhu's red face.

Your wife wouldn't step out of the car until your driver opened the door for her. Then she scooped up the hem of her dress, climbed out, and, because she wasn't used to wearing heels, nearly fell. I watched as she struggled to keep her balance and not call attention to her gimpy hip.

"Ah, my darling daughter!" Qiuxiang cried out happily as she ran up to Hezuo and seemed about to throw her arms around her. She didn't, stopping just before she reached her daughter. The once willowy woman whose cheeks were now slack, her belly quite pronounced, had a loving and fawning look in her eyes as she reached out to touch the sequins on your wife's dress. "My goodness," she said in a tone that suited her perfectly, "can this really be my own daughter? I thought for a moment a fairy had come down from the heavens!"

Your mother, Yingchun, walked up, aided by a cane, since one side of her body was not functioning. She raised her arm weakly and said to your wife:

"Where's my darling grandson, Kaifang?"

Your driver opened the other door to bring out the gifts. I jumped out.

"Is that Puppy Four?" Yingchun gasped. "My heavens, he's big as an ox!"

Your son emerged, I think, reluctantly.

"Kaifang," Yingchun cried out. "Let Grandma look at you. You're a head taller, and it's only been a few months."

"Hi, Grandma," he said. Then he said, "Hi, Grandpa," to your father, who had come up and patted him on the head. Two faces with blue birthmarks, one coarse and old, the other fresh and supple, presented an interesting contrast. Your son said hello to all his grandparents. Then your father turned to your wife. "Where's his father? Why didn't he come with you?"

"He's at a conference in the provincial capital," she replied.

"Come inside," your mother said, thumping the ground with her cane, "come inside, all of you." She spoke with the authority of the head of the household.

Your wife said to your driver, "You can go back now, but be here at three to pick us up. Don't be late."

The people swept your wife and son into the yard, all carrying colorful packages in their arms. You assume I was left out of all the merriment, right? Well, you're wrong. While the people were enjoying themselves, a black-and-white dog came out of the house. The smell of a sibling filled my nostrils, a surge of memories filled my mind. "Dog One! Elder brother!" I greeted him excitedly. "Dog Four, little brother!" he replied, as excited as I was. Our loud vocalizations startled Yingchun, who turned to look at us.

"You two brothers, how many years has it been? Let's see . . ." She counted on her fingers. "One, two, three years . . . my goodness, it's been eight years. For a dog that's half a lifetime!"

We touched noses and licked each other's face. We were very happy.

Just then my second brother came toward me from the west, along with his mistress, Baofeng. A skinny boy was right behind Baofeng, and the smell told me it was Gaige. I was amazed by how tall he'd gotten.

"Number Two, look who's here!" Our elder brother cried out. "Dog Two!" I shouted as I ran over to greet him. He was a black dog who'd gotten our father's genes. We looked a lot alike, but I was much bigger. We three brothers kept nudging and rubbing up against one another, happy to be together again after so long. After a while they asked me about our sister, and I told them she was doing well, that she'd had a litter of three pups, all of whom had been sold, earning a lot of money for her family. But when I asked after our mother, I was met by gloomy looks. With tears in their eyes they told me she'd died, though no one knew she was sick. Fortunately, Lan Lian had made a coffin and buried her in that plot of land that meant so much to him. For a dog it was a fine tribute.

While we three brothers were getting the most out of our reunion, Baofeng looked over at us and seemed shocked when she saw me. "Is that really Dog Four? How'd you get so big? You were the runt of the litter."

I looked her over while she was looking me over. After three reincarnations, Ximen Nao's memories still hung on, although buried under a host of incidents over a period of many years.

On a page of history in the distant past, I was her father, she was my daughter. But now I was just a dog, whereas she was my dog-brother's mistress and the half sister of my master. She had little color in her face, and her hair, though it hadn't turned gray, looked dry and brittle, like grass growing atop a wall after a frost. She was dressed all in black, except for patches of white on her cloth slippers. She was mourning the loss of her husband, Ma Liangcai. The gloomy smell of death clung to her. But, thinking back, she'd always had a gloomy, melancholy smell. She seldom smiled, and when she did, it was like reflected light on snow — dreary and cold, a look that was hard to forget. The boy behind her, Ma Gaige, was as skinny as his father. A one-time pudgy-faced little boy had grown into a gaunt teenager with ears that stuck out prominently; surprisingly, he had several gray hairs. He was wearing blue shorts, a short-sleeved white shirt — the Ximen Elementary School uniform — and a pair of white sneakers. He was carrying a plastic bowl filled with cherries in both hands.

As for me, I followed my two dog brothers in a look around Ximen Village. I'd left home as a puppy and had virtually no impressions of the place outside of the Ximen family home, but this was the village where I was born; in the words of Mo Yan in one of his essays, "hometowns are tied to a person by blood." So as we strolled down the streets and scoped out the village in general, I was deeply moved. I saw some familiar faces and detected many unfamiliar smells. There were also a lot of familiar smells that were somehow absent — no trace at all of the strongest smells of the village back then, of oxen and donkeys. Many of the new smells were of rusted metal emanating from yards we passed, and I knew that the mechanization dream of the People's Communes had not been realized until land reform and independent farming were once again the backbone of agricultural policy. My nose told me that the village was awash in feelings of excitement and anxiety on the eve of major changes. People all wore peculiar expressions, as if they thought that something very big was about to happen.

We returned to the Ximen house, followed by Ximen Jinlong's son, Ximen Huan, who was one of the last to arrive. I had no trouble spotting him by his smell, even though he reeked of fish and mud. He was naked but for a pair of nylon bathing trunks and a brand-name T-shirt thrown over his shoulder. He was carrying a line of silver-scaled little fish. An expensive watch glittered on his wrist. He spotted me first, dropped what he was carrying, and ran up to me. Obviously, he saw me as a ride, but no self-respecting dog was about to let something like that happen. I moved out of the way.

His mother, Huzhu, came running out of the house.

"Huanhuan!" she shouted. "Where have you been? And why are you so late? I told you your aunt and cousin Kaifang were coming."

"I was fishing." He picked up the line of fish to show her. "How could I not greet such honored guest without fish?" he said in a tone of voice that belied his young years.

Huzhu scooped up the shirt he'd tossed to the ground and said, "Who do you think you're greeting with guppies like this?" She reached up and brushed the mud and scales out of her son's hair. "Huanhuan," she blurted out, "where are your shoes?"

He smiled. "I won't lie to you, dear mother, I traded them for these fish."

"What? You're going to be the ruination of this family if you keep this up! Your father had someone bring those shoes from Shanghai. They were Nikes, a thousand yuan a pair. And these few guppies are what you got for them?"

"There are more than a few, Mama," Ximen Huan said earnestly, counting the fish for all to see. "There are nine here. How can you say there are only a few?"

"See, everybody, what a foolish son I'm raising?" Huzhu took the line of fish from her son and held them high. "He went down to the river early this morning," she said to the people crowding into the main house, "saying he was going to catch some fish for our guests. This is what he brought back after all that time. And he had to swap a pair of brand-new Nike sneakers to get them. Wouldn't you say foolish is a good description?" In a blustery move, Huzhu smacked his shoulder with the line of fish and said, "Who'd you give the shoes to? I want you to go get them back."

"Mama," he said, looking at her out of the corner of his slightly crossed eye, "you don't expect anyone worthy of respect to go back on his word, do you? It's just a pair of sneakers. Why not just buy another pair? Dad's got plenty of money!"

"Shut up, you little imp!" she said. "Who says your father has plenty of money?"

"If he doesn't, then no one does," he said with a sideward glance. "My father is a rich man, one of the richest anywhere!"

"Now you're showing off, and showing how foolish you are," his mother said. "I hope your father raises welts on your bottom when he gets home!"

"What's going on?" Ximen Jinlong asked as he stepped out of his Cadillac. The car glided ahead silently. He was dressed for leisure. His head was shaved as clean as his cheeks, and he had a bit of a potbelly. Cell phone in hand, he was the prototypical big-time businessman. After hearing what Huzhu had to say, he patted his son on the head and said, "In economic terms, trading a pair of thousand-yuan Nikes for nine little guppies makes no sense. But from a moral perspective, willingly sacrificing a thousand-yuan pair of sneakers for some fish to greet visitors is unquestionably the right thing to do. So, based solely on this incident, I'll neither praise nor punish you. But what I will praise you for"—at this point, Jinlong thumped his son on the shoulder—"is your adherence to the principle of 'my word, once spoken, even a team of four horses cannot bring it back.' Once the trade was made, you could not go back on your word."

"What do you think of that?" Ximen Huan said to his mother, pleased with himself. He picked up the fish. "Grandma," he said loudly, "take these and make some fish broth for our honored guests!"

"The way you're spoiling him," Huzhu said to Jinlong under her breath, "I hate to think how he'll turn out." She spun around and grabbed her son by the arm. "Go inside, little ancestor, and change your clothes. How can you think of greeting guests looking like this?"

"What a fine animal!" Ximen Jinlong remarked with a thumbs-up as soon as he saw me. Then he said hello to all the people who had walked outside to greet him. He sang your son's praises: "Worthy nephew Kaifang, I can see you've got talent. You're no ordinary young man. Your father is a deputy county chief, but you'll be a provincial governor when you grow up!" Then he consoled Ma Gaige: "Stand up straight and proud, young man, there's nothing for you to fear or worry about. You'll never go hungry as long as your uncle has food on his table." Then he turned to Baofeng. "Don't be too hard on yourself. Don't forget, no one can bring back the dead. You're sad, well, so am

I. Losing him was like losing my right arm." He turned and nodded to the two elderly couples. Finally, he said to your wife, "I'd like to drink to my sister-in-law. At noon the other day, when I gave a celebratory banquet for the passage of our reconstruction plans, Jiefang was the one who suffered. That old scalawag Hong Taiyue may be stubborn, but you have to love him, and I hope a little jail time will teach him a lesson."

At supper that afternoon your wife maintained the proper attitude — not too cold and not too hot — of a deputy county chief's wife. As enthusiastic host, Jinlong made it clear who was the head of this family. But Ximen Huan was the liveliest person at the table, and the way he dealt with banquet etiquette showed what a sharp-witted boy he was. Since disciplining his son was not a concern of Jinlong's, Ximen Huan remained out of control. He poured himself a glass of the liquor and then another for Kaifang. "Here, Cousin Kaifang," he said with a stiff tongue, "drink this. I want to talk to you about something—"

Your son looked over at your wife.

"Don't look at her — we boys make up our own minds at times like this. Here, to you, a toast!"

"That's enough, Huanhuan," Huzhu said.

"Go ahead and touch it with your lips," your wife said to your son.

So the two boys clinked glasses. Huanhuan tipped his head back and drained his glass, then held the empty glass out to Kaifang, and said:

"Drink out of . . . out of respect."

So Kaifang touched his lips to the liquor and set down his glass.

"You . . . that's not how a pal does things—"

"That's enough," Jinlong announced as he tapped his son on the head. "Stop there. Don't try to force people to do something they don't want to do. Trying to get somebody to drink doesn't make you a man!"

"Okay, Papa . . . I'll do as you say." Huanhuan set down his glass, took off his wristwatch, and set it down in front of Kaifang. "This is Swiss-made, a Longines," he said. "I swapped my slingshot to a Korean businessman for it, now I'd like to trade it for that dog of yours."

"No way!" your son said staunchly.

Huanhuan was unhappy, of course, but he didn't make a scene.

"I'm willing to bet," he said just as staunchly, "that you'll make the trade one day."

"No more of that, son," Huzhu said. "You'll be going to town in a few months to start middle school, and you can see the dog when you visit your aunt."

And so the topic of conversation around the table turned to me. "I find it hard to believe," your mother said, "that a litter of puppies could all be so different."

"My son and I are lucky to have this dog," your wife said. "His dad is wrapped up in his work day and night, and I have my job, so it's up to the dog to watch the house. He also takes Kaifang to school and picks him up in the afternoon."

"He really is an awesome animal," Jinlong said as he picked up a braised pig's foot and threw it to me. "Dog Four," he said, "don't be a stranger just because you're part of a well-to-do family."

The smell of that pig's foot was enticing, and I heard my stomach rumble. But then I looked over at my brother dogs and let it lie there.

"They really are different," Jinlong said emotionally. "Huanhuan, you can learn some things from that dog." He picked up two more pig's feet with his chopsticks and tossed them to Dog One and Dog Two. "To be a real man you have to behave like a great one."

My brothers tore into the meat they'd been given, gobbling it up so fast their throats made funny sounds. But I let mine lie there as I fixed my eyes on your wife. When she gestured it was all right to eat, I took a tentative bite and chewed it, slowly and noiselessly. Someone had to preserve a dog's dignity.

"You're right, Papa," Huanhuan said as he retrieved his wristwatch. "I want to act like someone from a great family." He got up and went into his room. He came out again with a hunting rifle.

"Huanhuan," Huzhu shouted in alarm, "what are you doing?" She stood up.

Ximen Jinlong just sat there unflappably, a smile on his face. "I'd like to see what my son's made of. Is he going to shoot his uncle's dog? That's no way to be a virtuous man. Or will he shoot our and his aunt's dogs? That'd be even worse!"

"You underestimate me, Papa," Huanhuan said angrily. He shouldered the rifle, and though he could barely support it, the move showed he'd had practice, was a bit of a prodigy. Then he hung his expensive watch on the apricot tree, backed off ten paces, and expertly slammed a cartridge into the chamber. An adult sneer settled on his face. The wristwatch glittered in the bright noonday sun. I heard Huzhu's fearful screams retreat into the distance, while the sound of the watch had a profoundly affecting quality. Time and space seemed to freeze into a blinding beam of light, as the ticking sound created the image of an enormous pair of black scissors cutting the beam of light into sections. Huanhuan's first shot went wide of the mark, leaving a white scar in the tree trunk. His second shot hit the target. As the bullet smashed the watch into a thousand pieces —

The numbers crumbled. Time was shattered.

48

Public Anger Brings on a Group Trial
Personal Feelings Turn Brothers into Enemies

Jinlong phoned to tell me that our mother was desperately ill. But the minute I stepped in the door, I realized he'd tricked me.

Mother was ill, all right, but not seriously. Aided by her prickly-ash cane, she made it over to a bench in the western corner of the living room. Her head, now totally gray, quaked continuously, and murky tears slid down her cheeks. Father was sitting to her right, but far enough away that a third person could sit between them. When he saw me walk in the door, he took off one of his shoes, jumped to his feet, and, with a muffled roar, slapped me across the face with its sole. My ears rang, I saw stars, and my cheek stung like crazy. I couldn't help but notice that when he jumped to his feet, his end of the bench flew up and Mother fell first to the floor and then backward. Her cane swung out straight, like a rifle aimed at my chest. I remember calling out "Mother!" and wanting to run over and help her up, but I stumbled backward instead, all the way to the door, where I sat down on the lintel. Just when I felt a pain shoot up from my tailbone, I fell backward, and just when it felt like my head was cracked on the concrete step, I wound up lying on my back, head down, feet up, half in and half out of the room.

No one offered to help, so I got up on my own. My ears were still ringing and there was a metallic taste in my mouth. I could see that Father had put so much into the slap he was reeling. But once he'd regained his balance, he charged me again with the shoe. Half his face was blue, half was purple; green sparks seemed to shoot from his eyes. He'd experienced plenty of anger over a lifetime of hardships, and I was very familiar with how he looked when he was angry. But there were lots of new emotions mixed into his anger this time: extreme sadness and immense shame, to mention just two. He hadn't slapped me with his shoe just for show. No, he'd put everything he had into it. If I hadn't been in the prime of my life, with good, hard bones, that slap could have changed the shape of my face. As it was, it rattled my brain, and when I got to my feet, I was not only dizzy, I even forgot for a moment where I was. The figures in front of me seemed weightless, like will-o'-the-wisps, ghostly floating images.

I think it was Jinlong who stopped the blue-faced old man from hitting me a second time. But even with a pair of arms around him, my father kept jumping up and down and squirming like a fish yanked out of the water. Then he threw the heavy black shoe at me. I didn't try to get out of the way; my brain had fallen asleep on the job and forgot to tell my body what to do. I could only watch as the ugly thing flew at me like monster, but as if it were actually flying toward some other body. It hit me in the chest and stayed there for a split second before falling clumsily to the floor. I probably thought of looking down at that strange, shoelike object, but the cobwebs in my head and the veil over my eyes kept me from doing such an inappropriate, meaningless thing. My left nostril felt hot and wet for a moment before a worm began wriggling above my upper lip. I reached up and touched it, and when I pulled my hand away, though I was still in a fog, I saw some green, oily stuff that gave off a dull glow on my finger. I heard a soft voice — was it Pang Chunmiao?—whisper in my ear: Your nose is bleeding. As the blood flowed, a crack opened up through the fog in my brain, letting in a cool breeze that spread its coolness throughout, until I was finally able to emerge from my idiocy. My brain went back to work, my nervous system returned to normal. This was my second bloody nose within two weeks. The first was when I'd been tripped by one of Hong Taiyue's volunteer activists in front of the county government office building, and I'd sprawled on the hard ground like a hungry dog going after a pile of shit. Ah, now I remember. I saw Baofeng help Mother to her feet. Slobber was running down her chin on the twisted half of her face.

"My son," she said in a barely intelligible voice. "Don't you dare hit my son—"

Mother's prickly-ash cane lay on the floor like a dead snake. She was struggling with such astonishing strength that Baofeng couldn't hold her without help. By the look of it, she wanted to go pick up her dead-snake cane, and when that became clear to Baofeng, she reached out her foot, without letting go of Mother, and dragged the cane closer, then quickly bent down, picked it up, and put it in Mother's hand. The first thing she did was point the cane at Father, who was still wrapped up in Jinlong's arms, but her arm lacked the strength to control it, and it fell to the floor again. So she abandoned violence and railed at Father, her words muffled but understandable:

"Don't you dare hit my son, you mean . . ."

The unpleasantness continued for a while longer before peace was reestablished. The cobwebs disappeared. Father was crouching against the wall, holding his head in his hands. I couldn't see his face, just his quill-like hair. Someone had put the bench back the way it was, and Baofeng was sitting on it, her arms still around Mother. Jinlong picked up the shoe and laid it on the floor in front of Father.

"At first I didn't want to get involved in a scandal like this," he said to me icily. "But when they asked me to, as a son I had no choice." His arm described an arc from one parent to the other, and I saw that they'd done whatever they'd been moved to do, that now they were consumed with sadness and helplessness. That was when I spotted Pang Hu and Wang Leyun, who were sitting behind a table near the center of the room. The sight of them brought me crippling shame. Then I turned and saw Huang Tong and Wu Qiuxiang, sitting side by side on a bench against the eastern wall, and Huang Huzhu, who was standing behind her mother and drying her tears with her sleeve. Even in the midst of all that tension, I couldn't help notice her captivatingly glossy, lush, thick, and mysterious hair.

"Everyone knows you want a divorce from Hezuo," Jinlong said. "We also know all about you and Chunmiao."

"You little blue face, you have no conscience," Wu Qiuxiang said sobbingly as she made an attempt to come at me; Jinlong blocked her way, and Huzhu helped her sit back down. "What did my daughter ever do to you?" she asked. "And what makes you think she's unworthy of you? Lan Jiefang, aren't you afraid the heavens will strike you dead if you go through with this?"

"You think you can get married when you want and divorced when you want, is that it?" Huang Tong said angrily. "You were nothing when Hezuo married you, and now that you've had a bit of success, you want nothing more to do with us. Well, you're not getting off that easy. We'll take this up with the local Party Committee or the

Provincial Party Committee, all the way up to the Central Committee if necessary!"

"Young brother, divorce or not, that's your business. By law not even your own parents have the last word in that. But this whole affair touches many lives, and if word got out, there'd be hell to pay. I want you to hear what Uncle and Aunty Pang have to say."

I tell you from the bottom of my heart that I did not put much stock in what my parents or the Huangs had to say, but in the face of the Pangs, I felt like finding a hole and crawling into it.

"I shouldn't be calling you Jiefang anymore, I ought to be calling you Deputy Chief Lan," Pang Hu said sarcastically. He coughed a couple of times and then turned to his wife, who had grown quite heavy. "Which year was it they came into the cotton processing plant?" Without waiting for his wife to answer, he said, "It was 1976, when you, Lan Jiefang, were just a crazy, know-nothing kid. But I took you in and taught you how to evaluate cotton, a light but highly respectable job. Lots of youngsters who were smarter, better looking, and had a better background than you carried bundles of cotton weighing a couple of hundred *jin* apiece eight hours a day, sometimes nine. They were on their feet the whole time. You should know what kind of job that was. You were a seasonal worker who should have gone back to your village home after three months, but when I thought about how good your parents had been to us, I kept you on. Then, later on, when the county commune was looking for people, I argued your case until they agreed to take you. Know what the county commune leaders said to me at the time? They said, 'Old Pang, how come you want to send a blue-faced demonic-looking youngster to us?' Know what I said to them? I said, 'He's an ugly kid, I'll give you that, but he's honest and trustworthy, and he can write.' Granted, you did a good job for them and kept getting promotions, which made me happy and proud. But you have to know that without my recommendation to the county commune and Kangmei's behind-the-scene support, you wouldn't be where you are today. You're well off, so you want to exchange one wife for another. That's nothing new, and if putting your conscience aside and subjecting yourself to the taunts and curses of everyone around you don't mean a thing to you, then go ahead, get your divorce. What difference can that make to the Pang family? But, goddamn it, you've gone and taken our Chunmiao . . . do you know how old she is, Lan Jiefang? She's exactly twenty years younger than you, still a child. If you go ahead with this, then you're lower than a beast! How will you be able to face your parents if you do this? Or your in-laws? Or your wife and son? Or us?"

By this time both Pang and his wife were crying. She reached over to dry his tears; he pushed her hand away and said with a mixture of sorrow and anger, "You can destroy yourself, Deputy Chief, there's nothing I can do about that. But you cannot take my daughter with you!"

I did not apologize to any of them. Their words, especially those of Pang Hu, had bored powerfully into my heart, and even though I had a thousand reasons to tell them all I was sorry, I didn't. I had ten thousand excuses, and I knew that I ought to break it off with Pang Chunmiao and go back to my wife, but I also knew that was something I could never do.

When Hezuo had written that message in blood, I actually considered ending the affair then, but as time passed, my longing for Chunmiao increased, until I felt as if my soul had left me. I couldn't eat, I couldn't sleep, and I couldn't get a thing done at the office. Hell, I didn't *feel* like getting anything done. The first thing I did after returning from the provincial capital was go to the bookstore to see Chunmiao, only to find an unfamiliar ruddy-faced woman standing where she usually stood. In a tone of cold indifference she told me that Pang Chunmiao had requested sick leave. The other two clerks were sneaking looks at me. Go ahead, look! Say bad things about me! I don't care. Next I went to the bookstore's singles dormitory. Her door was locked. From there I managed to find the home of Pang Hu and Wang Leyun, fronted by a village-style yard. The gate was padlocked. I shouted, but only managed to get neighborhood dogs barking. Despite knowing that Chunmiao would not run to the home of her sister, Kangmei, I nonetheless summoned up the courage to knock at her door. She lived in top-of-the-line County Committee housing, a two-story building protected by a high wall to keep visitors out. My deputy county chief ID card got me past the gate guard, and, as I said, I knocked at her door. Dogs in the compound set up a chorus of barking. I could see there was a camera above the door, so if anyone was home, they'd see it was me. No one came to the door. The gate guard came running up when he heard the noise, a look of panic on his face. He didn't tell me to leave, he begged me to leave. I left and walked out to the busy street, barely able to keep from shouting:

Where are you, Chunmiao? I can't live another day without you! I'd rather die than lose you! I don't give a damn about my reputation, my position, my family, riches . . . I just want you. At least let me see you one more time. If you say you want to leave me, then I'll die, and you can. . . .

I didn't apologize to them and I didn't say what I was going to do. I got down on my knees in front of my father and mother and kowtowed. Then I turned and did the same to the Huangs, who were, after all, my in-laws. Then I faced north and, with all the respect and solemnity I could manage, kowtowed to Pang Hu and his wife. I was grateful for their support and even more grateful for bringing Chunmiao into this world. Then I stood up and backed over to the door, where I bowed deeply, straightened up, turned around, and, without a word, walked out of the house and down the road, heading west.

I could tell by my driver's attitude that my days as an official had come to an end. I'd no sooner returned from the provincial capital than he complained to me that my wife had made him drive her and my son somewhere, and not on official business. He hadn't come to pick me up, claiming that the car was experiencing electrical problems. I'd had to hitch a ride with the Agricultural Bureau bus home. Now I was walking toward the county town. But did I really want to go back there? To do what? I should be going to wherever Chunmiao was. But where was she?

Jinlong drove up in his Cadillac and stopped alongside me. He opened the door.

"Get in."

"That's okay."

"I said get in!" Clearly he would brook no disobedience. "I want to talk to you."

I climbed into his luxurious car.

Next I was in his luxurious office.

He sat slouched in a burgundy leather armchair, leisurely smoking a cigarette and staring up at the chandelier.

"Would you say that life is like a dream?" he asked light-heartedly.

I silently waited for him to go on.

"Do you remember how we used to tend our ox on the riverbank?" he said. "In order to get you to join the commune I slugged you once every day. At the time, who could have imagined that twenty years later the People's Commune would be like a house built on sand, washed away in front of our eyes? I'd never have believed back then that one day you would rise to the position of deputy county chief and I'd be the CEO of a corporation. So many of the sacred things we'd have lost our heads over aren't worth a dog's fart today."

I held my tongue, knowing that this wasn't what he wanted to talk about.

He sat up straight, stubbed out the cigarette he'd just lit, and gazed intently at me.

"There are plenty of pretty girls in town, so why jeopardize everything to chase after that skinny monkey? Why didn't you come to me if you wanted some fun? Black, white, fat, skinny, I could easily get you what you wanted. You want to try a change of diet? Those Russian girls only charge a thousand a night!"

"If this is what you dragged me over here to talk about," I said as I got to my feet, "I'm not sticking around."

"Stay where you are!" he shouted angrily, slamming his fist on the desk and sending the ashes in his ashtray flying. "You're a bastard, through and through. A rabbit doesn't eat the grass around its burrow, and in this case, it's not even very good grass." He lit another cigarette, took a deep drag, and coughed. "What do you know about my relationship with Pang Kangmei?" he asked as he stubbed out the cigarette. "She's my mistress! The planned Ximen Village resort, if you want to know, is our venture, our bright future, a future you're screwing up with your dick!"

"I'm not interested in what you're doing," I said. "My only interest is Chunmiao."

"I take it that means you're not giving up," he said. "Do you really want to marry the girl?"

I nodded forcefully.

"Well, it's not going to happen, no way!" He stood up and paced the floor of his spacious office before walking up and thumping me in the chest. "Break this off at once," he said unambiguously. "Anything else you want to do, just leave it to me. After a while you'll realize that women are what they are, and nothing more."

"You'll excuse me," I said, "but that's disgusting. You have no right to interfere in my life, and I certainly don't need you to help me arrange it."

I turned to leave, but he grabbed my arm and said in a milder tone:

"Okay, maybe there is such a thing as love, damn it. So what do you say we work out a compromise? Get your emotions under control and knock off this talk about divorce. Stop seeing Chunmiao for a while, and I'll arrange a transfer to another county, maybe even farther, one of the metropolitan areas or a provincial capital, at the same level you are now. You put in a little time, and I'll see that you get a promotion. Then if you still want to divorce Hezuo, leave everything to me. All it'll take is money, three hundred thousand, half a million, a million, whatever it takes. There isn't a goddamn woman alive who'd pass up money like that. Then you send for Pang Chunmiao, and the two of you live like a couple of lovebirds. Truth is,"—he paused—"this isn't the way we wanted to do it, since it's a lot of trouble. But I am your brother, and she is her sister."

"Thank you," I said, "for your wise counsel. But I don't need it, I really don't." I walked to the door, took a few steps back toward him, and said, "Like you say, you are my brother, and they are sisters, so I advise you not to let your appetites grow too big. The gods have long arms. I, Lan Jiefang, am having an affair, but, after all, that's a problem of morality. But one day, if you two aren't careful . . ."

"Who are you to be lecturing me?" He sneered. "Don't blame me for what happens! Now get the hell out of here!"

"What have you done with Chunmiao?" I asked him dispassionately.

"Get out!" His angry shout was absorbed by the leather padding on the door.

I was back on Ximen Village streets, this time with tears in my eyes.

I didn't even turn my head when I walked past the Ximen family home. I knew I was an unfilial son, that both my parents would be gone before long, but I didn't flinch.

Hong Taiyue stopped me at the bridgehead. He was drunk. He grabbed my lapel and said loudly:

"Lan Jiefang, you son of a bitch, you locked me up, an old revolutionary! One of Chairman Mao's loyal warriors! A fighter against corruption! Well, you can lock me up, but you can't lock up the truth! A true materialist fears nothing! And I'm sure not afraid of you people!"

Some men came out of the public house from which Hong had been ejected to pull him away from me. The tears in my eyes kept me from seeing who they were.

I crossed the bridge. The bright, golden sunlight made the river look like a great highway. Hong Taiyue's shouts followed me:

"Give me back my ox bone, you son of a bitch!"

49

Hezuo Cleans a Toilet in a Rainstorm
Jiefang Makes a Decision After a Beating

A category-nine typhoon brought an almost unprecedented rainfall at night. I was always listless during spells of wet weather, wanting nothing more than to lie down and sleep. But that night, sleep was the furthest thing from my mind; both my hearing and smell were at their peak of sensitivity; my eyesight, owing to the constant streaks of powerful blue-white light, was dimmed, though not enough to affect my ability to discern each blade of grass and drop of water in every corner of the yard. Nor did it affect my ability to spot the cowering cicadas among the leaves of the parasol tree.

The rain fell nonstop from seven until nine o'clock that night. Streaks of lightning made it possible for me to see rain flying down from the eaves of the main building like a wide cataract. The rain came out of the plastic tubing on the side rooms like watery pillars that arced downward onto the cement ground. The ditch beside the path was stopped up by all sorts of things, forcing the water up over the sides, where it swamped the path and the steps in front of the gate. A family of hedgehogs living in a woodpile by the wall was driven out by the rising water; their lives were clearly in danger.

I was about to sound a warning to your wife, but before the bark emerged, a lantern was lit beneath the eaves, lighting up the entire yard. Out she stepped, shielded from the rain by a conical straw hat and a plastic rain cape. Her thin calves were exposed below her shorts; she was wearing plastic sandals with broken straps. Water cascading off the eaves knocked her rain hat to one side, where the wind blew it off her head altogether. Her hair was drenched in seconds. She ran to the west-side room, picked up a shovel from the pile of coal behind me, and ran back into the rain. Pooling rainwater swallowed up her calves as she ran; a bolt of lightning smothered the light from the lamp and turned her face, to which strands of wet hair clung, ghostly white. It was a frightening sight.

She carried the shovel into the alley through the south gate. Crashing sounds came from inside almost at once. It was the dirtiest and messiest part of the yard, with decaying leaves, plastic bags blown in on the wind, and cat droppings. The sound of splashing water emerged; the level of standing water in the yard was lowering, and the drainage ditches were spiriting water away. But your wife remained inside, where the sounds of a shovel on bricks and tiles, as well as on the surface of water, came on the air. Her smell permeated the area; she was a hardworking, resilient woman.

Finally, she came out through the drainage ditch. The plastic rain cape was still tied around her neck, but she was soaked to the skin. Streaks of lightning made her face show up whiter than ever, her calves thinner. She was dragging the shovel behind her and walking hunched over, looking a bit like the way female demons are described in stories. She wore a contented look. She picked up her straw hat and shook it several times, but instead of putting it on her head, she hung it from a nail on the side room wall. Then she propped up a Chinese rosebush, apparently pricking her finger in the process. She stuck her finger in her mouth, and as the rain lessened a bit, she looked up into the sky and let the rain hit her squarely in the face. Harder, harder, come down harder! She untied the rain cape to expose her rail-thin body to the rain and stumbled toward the toilet in the southeast corner of the yard, where she removed a cement cover.

Your son came running out with an umbrella and held it over her head.

"Come inside, Mama, you're wet from head to toe." He was crying.

"What are you so worried about? You should be happy it's raining hard." She pushed the umbrella over your son's head. "We haven't had rain like this for a long time, not once since we moved into town. It's wonderful. Our yard has never been this clean. And not just ours, but every family's. If not for this rain, the town would stink."

I barked twice to approve her attitude.

"Hear that?" she said. "I'm not the only one who's happy with this rain. So is he."

But eventually she did go inside, where, my nose told me, she dried her hair and body. Then I heard her open her wardrobe, and I got a strong whiff of dry, mothballed clothes. I breathed a sigh of relief. "Crawl into bed, Mistress. Get a good night's sleep."

Not long after the clock struck midnight, a familiar smell came on the air from Limin Avenue, followed by the smell of a Jeep that was losing oil, accompanied by the roar of the engine. Both the smell and the sound were coming my way. It pulled to a stop in front of your gate. My gate, too, of course.

I started barking ferociously before whoever it was even knocked at the gate, and raced over there, my paws barely touching the ground, sending the dozen or so bats living in the gateway arch flying into the blackness of night. Yours was the only one of the several odors I knew. The pounding at the gate created hollow, scary sounds.

The light beneath the eaves came on, and your wife, a coat over her shoulders, walked out into the yard. "Who is it?" she shouted. The response was more pounding. Resting my front paws on the gate, I stood up and barked at the people on the other side. Your smell was strong, but what made me bark anxiously were the evil smells that surrounded you, like a pack of wolves with a captive sheep. Your wife buttoned up her coat and stepped into the gateway, where she switched on the electric light. A bunch of fat geckos were resting on the gateway wall; bats that hadn't flown away were hanging from the overhead. "Who is it?" she asked a second time. "Open the door," came a muffled voice from the other side. "You'll know who it is when you open up." "How am I supposed to know who comes knocking at my door in the middle of the night?" Speaking softly, the person on the other side said, "Deputy County Chief has been beaten up. We've brought him home." After a moment's hesitation, your wife unlocked the gate and opened it a crack. Your face, hideously disfigured, and matted hair appeared in front of her. With a scream, your wife opened the gate wide. Two men flung you like a dead pig into the yard, where you knocked her to the ground and wound up crushing her beneath you. They jumped down off the steps, and I ran, lightning quick, after one of them. I dug my claws into his back. All three men were wearing black rubber raincoats and dark glasses. The two made for a waiting Jeep, where the third man was sitting in the driver's seat. Since he'd left it idling, the smells of gasoline and oil came crashing at me through the rain. The raincoat was so slick the man slipped out of my grasp as he jumped into the middle of the street and ran up to the Jeep, leaving me in the rain, a predator without his prey. The water, which was up to my belly, slowed me down, but I pushed myself to go after the other man, who was climbing into the car. Since his raincoat protected his rear end, I sank my teeth into his calf. He screeched as he shut the door, catching the hem of his raincoat; my nose banged into the shut door. Meanwhile, the first man jumped in on the other side and the Jeep lurched forward, spraying water behind it. I took out after it, but was stopped by all the filthy water splashing in my face.

When I made it back through the dirty water, I saw your wife with her head under your left armpit, your left arm draped loosely over her chest like an old gourd. Her right arm was around your waist, and your head was leaning against hers. She struggled to move you forward. You were wobbly, but you could still move, which not only told her you were alive but that your mind was relatively clear.

After helping her close the gate I walked around the yard to get my emotions under control. Your son came running outside dressed only in his underwear. "Papa!" he shouted, starting to sob. He ran up to your other side to help your mother support you, and the three of you walked the remaining thirty or so paces from the yard to your wife's bed. The tortuous trek seemed to take an eternity.

I forgot that I was a mud-streaked dog and felt that my fate was tied up with yours. I followed behind you, whining sadly, all the way up to your wife's bed. You were covered with mud and blood and your clothes were ripped; you looked like a man who'd been whipped. The smell of urine in your pants was strong; obviously you'd peed your pants when they were beating you. Even though your wife valued cleanliness above almost everything, she didn't hesitate to lay you down on her bed, a sign of affection.

Not only didn't she care how dirty you were when she laid you down on the bed, she even let me, dirty as I was, stay in the room with you. Your son knelt by the bed, crying.

"What happened, Papa? Who did this to you?"

You opened your eyes, reached out, and rubbed his head. There were tears in your eyes.

Your wife brought in a basin of hot water and laid it on the bed-side table. My nose told me she'd added some salt. After tossing a towel into the water, she began taking off your clothes. You fought to sit up. "No," you sputtered, but she pushed your arms back, knelt beside the bed, and unbuttoned your shirt. It was obvious you didn't want your wife's help, but you were too weak to resist. Your son helped her take off your shirt, and so you lay there, naked from the waist up, on your wife's bed as she wiped your body down with the salty water, some of her tears, also salty, dripping onto your chest. Your son's eyes were wet, and so were yours, tears slipping out and down the sides of your face.

Your wife didn't ask a single question during all this time, and you didn't say a word to her. But every few minutes, your son asked you:

"Who did this to you, Papa? I'll go avenge you!"

You did not answer, and your wife said nothing, as if by secret agreement. Seeing no alternative, your son turned to me.

"Who beat my father, Little Four? Take me to find them so I can avenge him!"

I barked softly, apologetically, since the typhoon winds had scattered the smells.

With the help of your son, your wife managed to get you into dry clothes, a pair of white silk pajamas, very loose and very comfortable; but the contrast made your face appear darker, the birthmark bluer. After tossing your dirty clothes into the basin and mopping the floor dry, she said to your son:

"Go to bed, Kaifang, it'll soon be light outside. You have school tomorrow."

She picked up the basin, took your son's hand, and left the room. I followed.

After washing the dirty clothes, she went over to the east-side room, where she turned on the light and sat on the stool, her back to the chopping board; with her hands on her knees, she rested her head on her hands and stared straight ahead, apparently absorbed in her thoughts.

She was in the light, I was in the dark, so I saw her face clearly, her purple lips and glassy eyes. What was she thinking? No way I could know. But she sat there until dawn broke.

It was time to cook breakfast. It looked to me like she was making noodles. Yes, that's what she was doing. The smell of flour overwhelmed all the putrid smells around me. I heard snores coming from the bedroom. Well, you'd finally managed to get some sleep. Your son woke up, his eyes heavy with sleep, and ran to the toilet; as I listened to the sound of him relieving himself, the smell of Pang Chunmiao penetrated all the sticky, murky odors in the air and rapidly drew near, straight to our gate, without a moment's hesitation. I barked once and then lowered my head, overcome by weighty emotions, a mixture of sadness and dejection, as if a giant hand were clamped around my throat.

Chunmiao rapped at the gate, a loud, determined, almost angry sound. Your wife ran out to open the gate, and the two women stood there staring at each other. You'd have thought there was no end to what they wanted to say, but not a word was uttered. Chunmiao stepped — dashed is more like it — into the yard. Your wife limped behind her and reached out as if to grab her from behind. Your son dashed out onto the walkway and ran around in circles, his face taut, looking like a boy who simply didn't know what to do. In the end, he ran over and shut the gate.

By looking through the window I was able to watch Chunmiao rush down the hallway and into your wife's bedroom. Loud wails emerged almost at once. Your wife was next into the room, where her wails supplanted Chunmiao's with their intensity. Your son was crouching alongside the well, crying and splashing water on his face.

Once the women's crying stopped, difficult negotiations began. I couldn't make out everything that was said, owing to the sobs and sniveling, but picked up most of it.

"How could you be so cruel as to beat him that badly?" Chunmiao said that.

"Chunmiao, there's no reason for you and me to be enemies. With all the eligible bachelors out there, why are you dead set on destroying this family?"

"I know how unfair this is to you, and I wish I could leave him, but I can't. Like it or not, this is my fate. . . ."

"You choose, Jiefang," your wife said.

After a moment of silence, I heard you say:

"I'm sorry, Hezuo, but I want to be with her."

I saw Chunmiao help you to your feet and watched as you two walked down the hall, out the door, and into the yard, where your son was holding a basin of water. He emptied it on the ground at your feet, fell to his knees, and said tearfully:

"Don't leave my mother, Papa . . . Aunty Chunmiao, you can stay . . . your grandmothers were both married to my grandfather, weren't they?"

"That was the old society, son," you said sorrowfully. "Take good care of your mother, Kaifang. She's done nothing wrong, it's my doing, and though I'm leaving, I'll do everything in my power to see you're both taken care of."

"Lan Jiefang, you can leave if you want," your wife said from the doorway. "But don't you forget that the only way you'll get a divorce is over my dead body." There was a sneer on her face, but tears in her eyes. She fell as she tried to walk down the steps, but she scrambled to her feet, made a wide sweep around you two, and pulled your son to his feet. "Get up!" she growled. "No boy gets down on his knees, not even if there's gold at his feet!" Then she and the boy stood on the rain-washed concrete beside the walkway to make way for you to leave.

In much the same way that your wife had helped you walk from the gateway to her bedroom, Chunmiao tucked her left arm under yours, which hung loosely in front of her chest, and put her right arm around your waist, so the two of you could hobble out the gate. Given her slight figure, she seemed in constant danger of being knocked off balance by the sheer weight of your body. But she held herself straight and exerted strength that even I, a dog, found remarkable.

A strange, inexplicable emotion led me up to the gate after you'd left. I stood on the steps and watched you go. You stepped in one mud puddle after another on Tianhua Avenue, and your white silk pajamas were mud-spattered in no time; so were Chunmiao's clothes, a red skirt that was especially eye-catching in the haze. A light rain fell at a slant; some of the people out on the street were wearing raincoats, others were holding umbrellas, and all of them cast curious glances as you passed.

Filled with emotion, I went back into the yard and straight to my kennel, where I sprawled on the ground and looked over at the east-side room. Your son was sitting on a stool, weeping; your wife placed a bowl of steaming hot noodles on the table in front of him.

"Eat!" she said.

50

Lan Kaifang Flings Mud at His Father
Pang Fenghuang Hurls Paint at Her Aunt

Finally, Chunmiao and I were together. A healthy man could make the walk from my house to the New China Bookstore in fifteen minutes. It took us nearly two hours. In the words of Mo Yan: It was a romantic stroll and it was a tortuous trek; it was a shameful passage and it was a noble action; it was a retreat and an attack; it was surrender and resistance; it was weakness and strength; it was a challenge and a compromise. He wrote more contradictory stuff like that, some of it on target, some just trying to be mystifying. What I think is, leaving home, supported by Chunmiao, was neither noble nor glorious; it just showed we had courage and honesty.

When I think back on that day, I see all those colorful umbrellas and raincoats, all the mud puddles on the street, and the dying fish and croaking frogs in some of the standing water. That torrential rainfall of the early 1990s exposed much of the corruption masked by the false prosperity of the age.

Chunmiao's dormitory room behind the New China Bookstore served as our temporary love nest. I'd fallen so low I no longer had anything to hide, I said to Big-head, who could see almost everything. Our relationship was not built solely on sex, but that's the first thing we did after moving into her dormitory, even though I was weak and badly hurt. We swallowed one another's tears, our bodies trembled, and our souls intertwined. I didn't ask how she'd gotten through the days, and she didn't ask who had beaten me. We just held each other, kissed, and stroked each other's body. We put everything else out of our minds.

* * *

Forced by your wife, your son ate half a bowl of noodles, mixed with his tears. She, on the other hand, had a huge appetite. She finished her bowl, along with three large garlic cloves, then peeled a couple more cloves and finished off your son's noodles. The peppery garlic turned her face red and dotted her forehead and nose with beads of sweat. She wiped her son's face with a towel.

"Sit up straight, son," she said firmly. "Eat well, study well, and grow up to be a man I can be proud of. They'd like nothing better than to see us die. They want us to make fools of ourselves, well, they can dream on!"

It was time for me to take your son to school, so your wife saw us to the door, where he turned and wrapped his arms around his mother. She patted him on the back and said:

"Look, you're almost as tall as me, big boy."

"Mama, don't you dare—"

"That's a laugh," she said with a smile. "Do you really think I'd hang myself or jump down a well or take poison over scum like them? You go on, and don't worry. I'll be going to work in a little while. The people need their oil fritters, which means the people need your mama."

We took the short route, as always, and when some bright red dragonflies swooped by, your son jumped up and neatly caught one in his hand. Then he jumped even higher and caught another one. He held his hand out.

"Hungry, Dog? Want these?"

I shook my head.

So he pinched off their tails, plucked a straw, and strung them together. Then he flung them high in the air. "Fly," he said, but they just tumbled in the air and landed in a mud puddle.

The storm had knocked down the Fenghuang Elementary School buildings, and children were already jumping and climbing on broken bricks and shattered tiles. They weren't unhappy; they were delighted. A dozen mud-spattered luxury sedans were parked at the school entrance. Pang Kangmei, in knee-length pink rain boots, had rolled her pant legs up to her knees. Her white calves were spattered with mud. Wearing blue denim work clothes and dark sunglasses, she was speaking through a battery-powered bullhorn.

"Teachers, students," she said hoarsely, "the category nine typhoon has brought terrible destruction to the county and to our school. I know how bad you all must feel, but I bring sympathy and good wishes from the County Committee and the county government. Over the next three days there will be no classes while we clean up the mess and restore the classrooms. In sum, even if I, Pang Kangmei, Party secretary of the County Committee, have to work while sitting in a mud puddle, you children will have bright, airy, safe classrooms to learn in."

Pang Kangmei's comments were met with enthusiastic applause; some of the teachers had tears in their eyes. Pang Kangmei continued:

"At this critical moment, in the midst of our emergency, all county cadres will be here, demonstrating their loyalty and enthusiasm, performing great service. If any of them dare shirk their duty or slack off, they will be severely punished."

In the midst of this emergency, even though I was the deputy county chief in charge of education and hygiene, I was hiding in our little room, my body entwined with my lover's. Without question, this was unimaginably shameful behavior. Even though I was badly beaten and had no idea what had happened to the school and was a man in love, I could put none of these on the table as an acceptable reason. So, a few days later, when I sent in my letters of resignation and withdrawal from the Party to the County Committee's Organization Department, Deputy Director Lü said with a sneer:

"Old man, you no longer have the right to resign your position or withdraw from the Party. What you can look forward to is being fired from your job and kicked out of the Party, plus a ban on all public employment."

We stayed in bed into the afternoon, alternating between exhaustion and passion. The room was hot and muggy, and our sheets were soaked from sweat that also saturated our hair. I was captivated by the smell of her body and the lights in her eyes.

"I could die today, Chunmiao, with no regrets. . . ."

As I lay there making love and loving her, I was no longer in the grip of the hate I'd felt toward the goons who had blindfolded me, dragged me into a dark room, and beaten me bloody. Except for a badly bruised bone in one leg, they had left me with only flesh wounds. They knew their business. I also no longer harbored any hatred toward the people who had ordered the beating. I deserved the beating. It was the price I had to pay for the abiding love I received.

＊　　＊　　＊

The students whooped with delight when a three-day holiday was announced. The natural disaster, which exposed so many serious problems, meant a strange good time for the children. A thousand Fenghuang Elementary School students hit the road and spread out, wreaking havoc on the already chaotic traffic.

Without knowing where we were going, I followed your son to the doorway of the New China Bookstore. A whole group of kids went inside, but not your son. His blue birthmark showed up cold and hard, like a piece of tile. Pang Kangmei's daughter, Fenghuang, was there, in an orange raincoat and rubber galoshes, looking like a brilliant flame. A young, muscular woman stayed close behind her — obviously, her bodyguard. Coming up behind her was my third sister, her coat neat and clean. She tried her best to avoid the mud puddles, but inescapably dirtied her paws. When your son and Fenghuang spotted each other, she spat on the ground at your son's feet. "Hooligan!" she cursed. His head drooped to his chest as if he'd taken a sword swipe against the nape of his neck. Dog Three snarled at me. She wore the most mysterious expression.

I bit down on your son's sleeve and showed him it was time to go home. But he took no more than a dozen steps before stopping, his birthmark the color of jasper and tears in his eyes.

"Dog," he said emotionally, "we're not going home. Take me where they are."

Taking a break in our lovemaking, we fell into a half sleep, brought on by exhaustion. While she slept she muttered things like: "It's your blue face that I love. I fell for you the first time I saw you. I wanted to make love with you that first time Mo Yan took me to your office." For us to be doing what we were doing and saying things like that was shamefully inappropriate when all the county's cadres were dealing with the results of a devastating natural disaster. But I won't hold anything back from you, Big-head.

We heard our door and window rattle, then we heard you bark. We'd promised not to open the door even if God came knocking. But your barks were like an order that must be obeyed. I jumped out of bed, knowing full well that my son would be with you. Lovemaking had helped heal my injuries, so I dressed quickly and easily, though my legs were rubbery and I was still lightheaded. At least I didn't fall.

Then I helped Chunmiao, whose body seemed to have no bones to support her, get dressed; I straightened her hair a little.

I opened the door and was blinded by wet, hot rays of sunlight. Almost immediately a handful of loose black mud came hurtling toward my face, like a slimy toad. I didn't try to get out of the way; my subconscious wouldn't let me. It smacked me square in the face.

I wiped the mud from my face. Some had gotten into my left eye, which stung badly, but I could still see out of my right eye. It was my son, seething with anger, and his dog, which looked at me with indifference. The door and window were spattered with mud, scooped out of a mud hole in front of the steps. My son stood there with his schoolbag over his back. His hands were coated with mud, and there was plenty more on his face and his clothes. What I should have seen was a look of rage, but what I did see were the tears spilling from his eyes. My tears quickly followed. There was so much I wanted to say to him, but all that came out was a pain-filled:

"Go ahead, son, throw it. . . ."

I took a step outside, grabbing the door frame to keep from falling, and shut my eyes to await the next handful of mud. I could hear him breathing hard as handful after handful of hot, stinking mud sailed through the air toward me. Some of it hit me in the nose, some on the forehead, and some on my chest and belly. One handful was harder than the others; clearly doctored with a piece of brick or tile, it hit me right in the crotch; I groaned as I bent over in pain, fell into a crouch, and finally sat down.

I opened my eyes, washed by tears; I could now see out of both of them. My son's face was twisted like a shoe sole in a fiery oven. The mud in his hand fell to the ground as he burst out crying, covered his face with his hands, and ran away. After a few parting barks, the dog turned and followed him.

All the time I was standing there letting my son vent his anger by flinging mud in my face, Pang Chunmiao, my lover, was standing beside me. I was the object of the attacks, but unavoidably, she received some of the wayward hits. After helping me to my feet, she said softly:

"We have to accept this, elder brother. . . . I'm happy . . . it feels to me like our sins have been lessened. . . ."

Dozens of people were standing in the second-story hallway of the New China Bookstore building. I could see they were bookstore cadres and clerks. One of them, a young fellow named Yu, who had once asked Mo Yan to see if I'd help him get a promotion to assistant manager, was chronicling my troubles from a variety of angles and distances with a heavy, expensive camera. Mo Yan later showed me a bunch of the pictures the man had taken, and I was shocked by how good they were.

Two of the observers came downstairs and walked timidly up to us. We knew who they were at once: one was the bookstore's Party secretary, the other was the chief of security. They spoke without looking at us.

"Old Lan," the Party secretary said awkwardly, "I'm sorry, but our hands are tied . . . we're going to have to ask you to move out. . . . I want you to know we're just carrying a Party Committee decision—"

"You don't have to explain," I said. "I understand. We'll move out right away."

"There's . . . more." The security chief hemmed and hawed. "Pang Chunmiao, you have been suspended pending an investigation, and you're to move into the second-story security section office. A bed has been placed there for you."

"You can suspend me," Chunmiao said, "but you can forget about an investigation. The only way you'll get me to leave his side is to kill me!"

"As long as we understand each other," the security chief said. "We've said what we were supposed to say."

Arm in arm — to hold each other up — we walked over to a water faucet in the middle of the yard.

"I'm sorry," I said to the Party secretary and security chief, "but we need to use a little of your water to wash the mud off our faces. If you have any objections—"

"How can you say that, Old Lan?" the Party secretary blurted out. "What do you take us for?" He cast a guarded look around him. "Whether or not you move out is none of our business, if you want the truth, but my advice would be to leave as soon as possible. The person in charge is boiling mad."

We washed the mud off our face and bodies and then, under the watchful gaze of the people at the windows, went back into Chunmiao's cramped, muggy, moldy dorm room, where we embraced and kissed.

"Chunmiao . . ."

"Don't say anything." She stopped me. "I don't care if it's climbing a mountain of knives or swimming a sea of fire," she said calmly, "I'll be there with you."

On the morning of the first day back to school, your son and Pang Fenghuang met at the school entrance. He looked away, but she strode up and tapped him on the shoulder, indicating she wanted him to follow her. When they reached a French parasol tree east of the school gate, she stopped and said excitedly, her eyes shining:

"You did great, Lan Kaifang!"

"What did I do?" he muttered. "I didn't do anything."

"Don't be so modest," Fenghuang said. "I was listening when they reported to my mother. She ground her teeth when she said, 'Those two have no shame, and it's time they got what they deserved!' "

Your son turned to walk away, but she grabbed his shirt and kicked him in the calf.

"Where do you think you're going?" she spat out angrily. "I've got more to say to you."

She was a delicate little witch, pretty as a perfectly sculpted statue. With tiny breasts like budding flowers, she had a young maiden's beauty that was impossible to resist. Your son's face said anger, but in his heart he'd already completely surrendered. I could only sigh. While the father's romantic drama was playing out, the son's romantic history was just beginning.

"You hate your father, I hate my aunt," Fenghuang said. "She must have been adopted by my maternal grandparents, because she wasn't close to us at all. My mother and her parents locked her in a room and took turns trying to talk sense into her and get her to leave your father. My grandmother even got down on her knees and begged, but she wouldn't listen. Then she jumped the wall and ran off to her depraved life with your father." Fenghuang clenched her teeth. "You punished your father, and I want to punish my aunt!"

"I don't want anything more to do with them," your son said. "They're a couple of horny dogs."

"Right, that's what they are!" Fenghuang said. "They're a couple of horny dogs. That's exactly what my mother called them."

"I don't like your mother," your son said.

"How dare you not like my mother!" She punched him. "My mother is the County Committee Party secretary," she grumbled. "She sat in our schoolyard and directed the rescue operations there with an IV bottle hanging from her arm! Don't you have a TV set? You didn't see her cough up blood on TV?"

"Our TV is broken, but I don't like the way she does things. What are you going to do about it?"

"You're just jealous, you and your blue face, you ugly shit!"

He grabbed her schoolbag strap and jerked her toward him. Then he pushed her back so hard she bumped into the tree behind her.

"You hurt me," she said. "All right, I won't call you Blue Face again. I'll call you Lan Kaifang. We spent our childhood together, which means we're old friends, doesn't it? So you have to help me carry out my plan to punish my aunt."

He walked away, but she ran up and blocked his way. She glared at him.

"Did you hear what I said?"

The idea of moving somewhere far away never crossed our minds. All we wanted was to find a quiet spot somewhere to stay out of the lime-light and resolve my marital status through legal means.

Lüdian Township's new Party secretary Du Luwen, who had once succeeded me as political director of the Supply and Marketing Cooperative, was an old friend, so I phoned him from a bus station and asked him to help me find a quiet place somewhere. He hesitated at first, but in the end he agreed. Instead of taking the bus, we sneaked over to a little place by the Grain Transport River called Yutong Village, southeast of the county town, where we hired a boat at the pier to take us downriver. The owner was a middle-aged woman with a gaunt face and large, deerlike eyes. She had a year-old child in the cabin, tied to her leg by a length of red cloth to keep him falling into the water.

Du Luwen met us at the Lüdian Township pier in his car and drove us to the cooperative, where we moved into a three-room apartment in the rear compound. After taking a pounding by independent entrepreneurs, the cooperative was on the verge of closing for good. Most of the employees had moved on to new ventures, leaving behind only a few old-timers to keep watch over the buildings. A former cooperative Party secretary who had once lived in our apartment had subsequently retired and moved into the county capital. Completely furnished, the place came equipped with a bag of flour, another of rice, some cooking oil, sausage, and canned goods.

"You can hide out here. Give me a call if you need anything, and don't go outside unless you absolutely have to. This is Party Secretary Pang territory, and she often makes unannounced inspections."

And so we began our dizzying days of happiness. We cooked, we ate, and we made love.

Your son could not resist Pang Fenghuang's charm, and so, in order to help her carry out her plan to punish her aunt, he told your wife a lie.

I pursued the fused smells, like a braided rope, of you and Pang Chunmiao, with them right behind me; I unerringly followed your trail to the pier at Yutong Village, where we boarded the same boat.

"Where are you two young students going?" the friendly boat owner asked from the rear of the boat, her hand on the rudder.

"Where are we going, Dog?" Pang Fenghuang asked me.

I turned to look downriver and barked.

"Downriver," your son said.

"Where downriver?"

"Just take us downriver. The dog will let us know when we get to where we're going," he said confidently.

The woman laughed as she pushed out into the middle of the river and headed downriver like a flying fish. Fenghuang took off her shoes and socks and sat on the boat's edge to dip her feet in the water.

Before we went ashore at Ldian Township, Fenghuang generously gave the woman more than she expected, which made her nervous.

We had no trouble finding where you were living, and when we knocked at your door, we were greeted by looks of shame and shock. You glared angrily at me; I barked twice out of embarrassment. What I wanted to convey was: Please forgive me, Lan Jiefang, but since you left home, you're no longer my master. That role has been taken over by your son, and it's my duty to do as he says.

Fenghuang took the lid off a little metal bucket and splashed the contents — paint — all over Chunmiao.

"You're a whore, Aunty," Fenghuang said to Chunmiao, who stood there dumbstruck. Then she turned to your son and, like a commanding officer, waved her hand in the air and said: "Let's go!"

I accompanied Fenghuang and your son over to the township Party office, where she located Du Luwen and said — ordered is more like it:

"I am Pang Kangmei's daughter. I want you to call for a car to take us back to the county town."

— Du Luwen came over to our paint-spattered Eden and stammered:

"In my humble opinion, I think you two should get as far away from here as possible."

He gave us some clean clothes and an envelope containing a thousand yuan.

"This is a loan, so don't say no."

Chunmiao just looked at me, wide-eyed and helpless.

"Give me ten minutes to think this over," I said to Du as I offered him a cigarette. We sat down to smoke, but my cigarette had barely burned down halfway when I stood up and said, "I'd appreciate it if you'd pick us up at seven o'clock tonight and drive us to the Jiao County train station."

That night we boarded the Qingdao-Xi'an train. It was 9:30 when we reached the Gaomi station. Pressing our faces up against the grimy windows, we gazed out at all the waiting passengers, most carrying their heavy belongings on their backs, and a smattering of station personnel with blank expressions on their faces. Lights in the distant city sparkled, while in the square in front of the station, drivers waited by their illegal taxis amid the shouts of food vendors. Gaomi, will we ever be able to return as proper citizens?

In Xi'an we went to see Mo Yan, who had taken a job as a journalist for a local newspaper after graduating from a special writer's workshop. He set us up in the run-down room he rented in the Henan Villa, saying he could bed down in his office. With a wicked grin, he handed us a box of Japanese extra-thin condoms and said:

"I'm afraid this is all I have, but it's a gift from the heart. Please take it."

Over the summer holidays your son and Fenghuang again ordered me to follow you, so I led them to the train station and barked in the direction of a train heading west: the scent, like those railroad tracks, stretched far off in the distance, too far for my nose to be of any use.

51

Ximen Huan Tyrannizes the County Town
Lan Kaifang Cuts His Finger to Test Hair

By the summer of 1996, you'd been on the run for five years. During that time, Mo Yan, who had risen to the position of editorial director of the local newspaper, gave you a job as an editor and found work for Pang Chunmiao in the dining hall. Your wife and son were aware of these developments, but had, it seemed, forgotten all about you. She was still frying oil fritters, her taste for which was as strong as ever; your son was a studious first-year student in the local high school. Pang Fenghuang and Ximen Huan were in the same grade as he. Neither of them had grades that could compare with your son's, but one of them was the daughter of the highest-ranking official in the county, the other the son of the man who created the Jinlong Scholarship Fund with half a million yuan of his own money; the school gate would have been open to them if they had scored zero on their exams.

Ximen Huan had been sent to the county seat for his first year in middle school, and his mother, Huzhu, came along to look after him. They lived with you, instilling some life into a cheerless, long-deserted house — a little too much life, some would say.

Ximen Huan was not student material; he'd caused more trouble and created more mischief during those five years than anyone could count. The first year he was relatively well behaved, but then he took up with three young hooligans, and in time they became known by the police as the "Four Little Hoods." Beyond being involved in all the antisocial behaviors one normally associated with his age, he was guilty of a good many adult crimes. But to look at him you'd never believe he was a bad boy. His clothes — name brands only — were neat and clean, and there was always a good smell about him. He kept his hair cut short and his face clean; he sported a thin, dark mustache to show he was past childhood, and even his boyhood cross-eyed look had vanished. He was friendly to people and kind to animals, his speech was replete with fine words and honeyed phrases, and he was especially polite in his dealings with your wife, as if she were his favorite relative. So when your son said, "Ma, send Huanhuan away, he's a bad kid," she spoke up for him:

"He seems like a good boy to me. He has a way of taking care of things and dealing with people, and he's well-spoken. I admit he doesn't do well in school, but he's just not gifted that way. In the future he'll probably do better than you. You're just like your father, always moping around as if the world owes you something."

"You don't know him, Ma. What you see is all an act."

"Kaifang," she said, "even if he is a bad kid, as you say, if he gets into trouble, his dad can bail him out. Besides, his mother and I are sisters, twins in fact, so how could I tell him to leave? You'll just have to put up with him for a few more years. Once you're out of high school, you'll go your own ways, and even if we wanted him to stay with us then, he probably wouldn't want to. Your uncle is so rich he can build a mansion for him in town without missing the money at all. The only reason he's staying with us is so we can all look after one another. That's how your grandparents want it."

Nothing your son could say could win out over your wife's practical arguments.

Huanhuan may have been able to get away with his shenanigans with your wife and his mother, but my nose knew better. By then I was a thirteen-year-old dog, and though my sense of smell was feeling the effects of age, I had no trouble differentiating the smells of people around me and the traces they left elsewhere. I might as well tell you that I'd already given up my chairmanship of the County Dog Association. My successor was a German shepherd named Blackie, owing to the color of fur on his back. In the county canine realm, German shepherds enjoyed undisputed leadership roles. After stepping down, I seldom attended the gatherings in Tianhua Square, since the few times I did go they had little to offer. My generation had celebrated the gatherings with singing, dancing, drinking, eating, and mating. But the new breed of youngsters were engaged in unusual and, to me, inexplicable behaviors. Here, I'll give you an example:

Blackie once urged me to go so I could be part of, according to him, the most exciting, most mysterious, most romantic event imaginable. So I showed up in time to see hundreds of dogs converge from all directions. No shouts or greetings, no flirting or teasing, almost as if they were all strangers. After crowding around the newly replaced statue of Venus de Milo, they raised their heads and barked together, three times. Then they spun around and ran off, including their chairman, Blackie. They'd appeared like lightning and immediately disappeared as if swept away on the wind. There I was, alone in the moonwashed square. I gazed up at Venus, whose sculpted body gave off a soft blue glow, and wondered if I was dreaming. Later on, I learned that they'd been playing a game of Flash, which was all the rage, very cool, at the time. They called themselves a "Flash mob." I was told they did all sorts of other goofy things, but I refused to join in. I couldn't help feeling that Dog Four's party days were over, just as a new age dawned, one characterized by unfettered excitement and wild imagination. That's how it was with dogs, and for the most part, with humans as well. Pang Kangmei still held her county position, and word had it that she would soon be appointed to a high position in the provincial government. But before that happened, she'd be accused by the Disciplinary Committee of the Party of "double offenses," and would subsequently be tried by the Procuratorate and condemned to death, with a two-year reprieve.

After your son tested into high school, I stopped accompanying him. I could have stayed home and slept or occupied myself with thoughts of the past, but that had no appeal to me. It could only speed up the aging process, body and mind, and your son wouldn't have needed me anymore. So I began tagging along behind your wife when she went to work in the square. While I was there watching her fry and sell oil fritters, I picked up the scent of Ximen Huan in notorious hair salons, backstreet inns, and bars. In the mornings he'd walk out of the house with his schoolbag on his back, but as soon as he was out of sight, he'd jump on the back of a motor scooter taxi waiting for him at the intersection and head for the train station square. His "driver," a big, strapping fellow with a full beard, was happy to chauffeur a high school boy around town, especially Huanhuan, who always made it worth his while. The square was Four Little Hoods territory, a place for them to eat, drink, whore, and gamble. The relationship among them was like June weather, always changing. Some of the time they were like four loving brothers, drinking and gambling together in bars, dallying with wild "chicks" in hair salons, and playing mah-jongg and smoking, arms around each other, in the public square, like four crabs strung together. But then at other times they'd split into two hostile groups and fight like gamecocks. There were also times when three of them ganged up on the fourth. Eventually they each formed their own gangs, which sometimes hung out together and sometimes fought. The one constant was that they fouled the atmosphere of the public square.

Your wife and I witnessed one of their armed battles, though she wasn't aware that Ximen Huan, the good kid, was the instigator. It happened on a sunny day around noon, in broad daylight, as they say. It started with an argument in a bar called Come Back Inn on the southern edge of the square, but before long, four boys with bloody heads were chased out the door by seven other boys with clubs, one of them dragging a mop behind him. The injured boys ran around the square, showing no fear or any effects of the beating they'd sustained. And there was no anger on the faces of the boys chasing them. Several of them, in fact, were laughing. At first the battle looked more like a staged play than the real thing. The four boys being chased stopped suddenly and launched a counterattack, with one of them taking out a knife to show he was that the leader of that gang. The other three whipped off their belts and twirled them over their heads. With loud shouts they took out after their pursuers, and in no time clubs were hitting heads, belts were lashing cheeks, and the square was thrown into an uproar with shouts and agonizing screams. Bystanders were by then fleeing the square; the police were on their way. I saw the gang leader plunge his knife into the belly of the kid with the mop, who screamed as he fell to the ground. When they saw what had happened to their buddy, the other pursuers turned and ran. The gang leader wiped the blood from his knife on the injured boy's clothes and, with a loud whoop, led his gang down the western edge of the square; they ran off to the south.

While the fight was going on outside, I spotted Ximen Huan, in dark sunglasses, sitting at a window inside the Immortal, a bar next to Come Back Inn, casually smoking a cigarette. Your wife, who watched the fight with her heart in her mouth, never did see him, but even if she had, she'd never have believed that her fair-skinned boy could have been the instigator. He reached into his pocket and took out one of the latest cell phones, flipped it open, punched in some numbers, and raised it to his mouth. A few words were all he spoke before sitting back and continuing to enjoy his cigarette, with grace and expertise, like the gangster bosses in movies from Hong Kong and Taiwan.

Now let me relate another incident involving Ximen Huan, this one occurring in your yard after he'd spent three days in the local police station over a fight he was involved in.

Huang Huzhu was so enraged she tore at his clothes and shook him.

"Huanhuan," she said through tears of anguish, "my Huanhuan, you don't know how you disappoint me. I've done everything I could and sacrificed so much to be here and take care of you. Your father has spared no expense to give you everything you need to go to school, but you pay us back by . . ."

As his mother stood there crying, Ximen Huan coolly patted her on the shoulder and said nonchalantly:

"Don't cry, Mother, dry your eyes. It's not what you think. I didn't do anything wrong. I wasn't to blame, no matter what they said. Look at me, do I look like a bad kid? I'm not, Mother, I'm a good kid."

Well, this good kid went out and danced and sang like a paragon of innocence. And it worked. Huzhu's tears were quickly replaced by smiles. Me? I was disgusted.

When Ximen Jinlong heard the news, he came running, fit to be tied. But his son's honeyed words quickly had him smiling too. I hadn't seen Ximen Jinlong in a long time. Time had not been kind to him — rich or poor, everyone ages. His hair was much thinner, his eyesight much dimmer, his paunch much bigger.

"Don't worry about me, Father. You have more important things to worry about," Ximen Huan said with a fetching smile. "No one knows a son better than his father, as they say. You know me well. I have my faults: I'm a little too much of a smooth talker, I like to eat, I'm sort of lazy, and pretty girls drive me crazy. But how does that make me any different from you?"

"You might be able to fool your mother, son, but not me. If I couldn't see though this little act of yours, I wouldn't be able to get anything done in this society. Over the past few years, you've done all the bad things you're capable of. Doing something bad is easy. What's hard is spending your life doing only bad things. So I think it's time for you to start doing good things."

"What a great way to put it, Father. From now on I'll turn bad things into good ones." He nestled up to Jinlong and adroitly slipped his father's expensive watch off his wrist. "This is a knockoff, Father. I can't have my dad wearing something like that. So I'll wear it and suffer the loss of face for you."

"Don't give me that. It's a genuine Rolex."

Several days later, the local TV station broadcast the following newsworthy item: "Local high-school student Ximen Huan found a large sum of money, but instead of pocketing the ten thousand yuan, he turned it over to his school." The shiny, genuine Rolex watch never again adorned his wrist.

One day Ximen Huan, the good kid, brought another good kid, Pang Fenghuang, over to the house. By then she'd become a fashionable young woman with a nice figure, a languid look in her eyes, and a wet look to her hair. We all thought she was a mess. Huzhu and Hezuo, definitely of the old school, could not stand the way she looked, but Ximen Huan whispered to them:

"Mama, Aunty, you're behind the times. That's the fashionable look these days."

Now I know it's not Ximen Huan or Pang Fenghuang you're concerned about. It's your son, Lan Kaifang. Well, he's about to make an appearance.

It was a splendid autumn afternoon when your wife and Huzhu were both out. The youngsters had asked them to leave so they could hold a meeting. They sat at a table stacked with fresh fruit, including a sliced watermelon, which had been set up under the parasol tree in the northeast corner of the yard. Ximen Huan and Pang Fenghuang were dressed in the latest fashions, and their faces glowed. Your son was wearing passé clothes, and his face was, as always, ugly.

There wasn't a boy alive who could fail to be attracted to a pretty, sexy girl like Pang Fenghuang; your son was no exception. Think back to that day when he flung mud in your face, and then think back to the day I followed your scent to Lüdian Township. Now you see what I mean. Even at that early age, he was Fenghuang's little slave, someone to do her bidding. The seeds of the tragedy that would occur later were planted way back then.

"No one else is coming, are they?" Fenghuang asked lazily as she leaned back in her chair.

"Today the yard belongs to us three," Ximen Huan said.

"Don't forget him!" She pointed her delicate finger at the sleeping figure at the base of the wall — me. "That old dog." She sat up straight. "Our dog is his sister."

"He also has a couple of brothers," your son said, obviously in low spirits. "They're in Ximen Village, one at his house"—he pointed at Ximen Huan—"and one at my aunt's house."

"Our dog died," Fenghuang said. "She died having pups. All I remember about her is that she was constantly having pups, one litter after another." She raised her voice. "The world is unfair. After the male dog finishes his business, he takes off and leaves her behind to suffer."

"That's why we all sing our mothers' praises," your son said in a fit of pique.

"Did you hear that, Ximen Huan?" Fenghuang said with a laugh. "Neither you nor I could ever say something that profound. Only Old Lan here could."

"There's no need to mock me," your son said, embarrassed.

"Nobody's mocking you," she said. "That was intended as a compliment!" She reached into her white handbag and took out a pack of Marlboros and a solid gold lighter with diamond chips. "With the old stick-in-the-muds out of the way, we can take it easy and enjoy ourselves."

A single cigarette popped up when she tapped the pack with a dainty finger tipped with a painted nail and wound up between painted lips. She flicked the lighter, which sent a blue flame into the air, then tossed it and the pack onto the table and took a deep drag on her cigarette. Leaning back until her neck was resting on the back of the chair, faceup, lips puckered, she gazed into the deep blue sky and blew the smoke out like an actress in a TV soap who doesn't know how to smoke.

Ximen Huan took a cigarette from the pack and tossed it to your son, who shook his head. A good boy, no doubt about it. But Fenghuang snorted and said derisively:

"Don't put on that good-little-boy act. Go ahead, smoke it! The younger you are when you start, the easier it is for your body to adapt to the nicotine. England's prime minister Churchill started smoking his granddad's pipe when he was eight, and he died in his nineties. So you see, starting late is worse than starting early."

Your son picked up the cigarette and hesitated; but in the end he put it in his mouth, and Ximen Huan lit it. His first cigarette. He couldn't stop coughing, and his face turned black. But he'd become a chain smoker in no time.

Ximen Huan turned Fenghuang's gold cigarette lighter over in his hand.

"Damn, this is top-of-the-line stuff!" he said.

"Like it?" Fenghuang asked with disdainful indifference. "Keep it. It was a gift from one of those assholes who want to get an official position or a building contract."

"But your mother—"

"My mother's an asshole too!" she said, holding her cigarette daintily with three fingers. With her other hand she pointed to Ximen Huan. "Your dad's an even bigger asshole! And your dad"—the finger was now pointed at your son—"is an asshole too!" She laughed. "Those assholes are all a bunch of phonies, always putting on an act, giving us so-called guidance and telling us not to do one thing or another. But what about them? They're always doing one thing *and* another!"

"So that's what we'll do!" Ximen Huan said enthusiastically.

"Right," Fenghuang agreed. "They want us to be good little boys and girls, not bad ones. Well, what makes someone a good kid and what makes someone a bad one? We're good kids. The best, better than anyone!" She flipped her cigarette butt toward the parasol tree, but it landed on one of the eave tiles, where it smoldered.

"Call my dad an asshole if you want," your son said, "but he's no phony and he doesn't put on an act. He wouldn't be in so much trouble if he had."

"Still protecting him, are you?" Fenghuang said. "He abandoned you and your mother and ran off to play around with another woman — oh, right, I forgot, that aunt of mine is an asshole too!"

"I admire my second uncle," Ximen Huan said. "It took guts to give up his job as deputy county chief, leave his wife and son, and go off with his lover on a romantic adventure. How cool!"

"In the words of our county's crafty writer Mo Yan, your dad is the world's bravest guy, biggest asshole, hardest drinker, and best lover! Plug up your ears, both of you. I don't want you to hear what I say next." They did as she said. "Dog Four, have you heard that Lan Jiefang and my aunt make love ten times a day for an hour each time?"

Ximen Huan snorted and giggled. Fenghuang kicked him in the leg.

"You were listening, you punk," she complained.

Your son didn't say a word, but his face had darkened.

"The next time you two go back to Ximen Village, take me along. I hear your father has turned the place into a capitalist paradise."

"Nonsense," Ximen Huan replied. "You can't have a capitalist paradise in a socialist country. My dad's a reformer, a hero of his time."

"Bullshit!" Fenghuang said. "He's a bastard. The real heroes of their time are your uncle and my aunt."

"Don't talk about my dad," your son said.

"When he stole off with my aunt, he nearly killed my grandma and made my grandpa sick, so why can't I talk about him? One day I'll get really mad and drag them back from Xi'an so they can be paraded in the street."

"Hey, why don't we go pay them a visit?" Ximen Huan suggested.

"Good idea," Fenghuang said. "I'll take another bucket of paint with me, and when I see my aunt, I'll say, 'Here, Aunty, I've come to paint you.' "

That made Ximen Huan laugh. Your son lowered his head and said nothing.

Fenghuang kicked him in the leg.

"Lighten up, Old Lan. We'll go together, what do you say?"

"Not me."

"You're no fun," she said. "I've had enough of you two. I'm getting out of here."

"Don't go yet," Ximen Huan said. "The program hasn't started."

"What program?"

"Miraculous hair, my mother's miraculous hair."

"Hell, I forgot all about that," Fenghuang said. "What was it you said? You could cut off a dog's head and sew it back on with a strand of your mom's hair, and that dog could still eat and drink, is that it?"

"We don't need that complicated an experiment," Ximen Huan said. "You can cut yourself, and then burn a strand of her hair and sprinkle the ashes on the cut. You'll be good as new in ten minutes and no scar."

"They say you can't cut her hair or it'll bleed."

"That's right."

"Everybody says she has such a kind heart that if one of the villagers is injured, she'll pull out a strand of her hair for them."

"That's right."

"Then how come she's not bald?"

"It keeps growing back."

"Then you'll never go hungry," Fenghuang said admiringly. "If your father loses his job one day and turns into a useless pauper, your mother can keep the family fed and housed just by selling her hair."

"I'd go out begging before I'd let her do that," Ximen Huan said emphatically. "Although she's not my real mother."

"What do you mean?" Fenghuang asked. "If she's not your real mother, who is?"

"They tell me it was a high school student."

"The bastard son of a high school student," Pang said. "How cool is that!"

"Then why don't you go have a baby?" Ximen Huan said.

"Because I'm a good girl."

"Does having a baby make you a bad kid?"

"Good kid, bad kid. We're all good kids!" she said. "Let's perform the experiment. Shall we cut off Dog Four's head?"

I barked angrily. My meaning? Try it, you little bastard, and I'll bite your head off!

"Nobody touches my dog," your son said.

"So then what?" Fenghuang said. "You're wasting my time with your phony tricks. I'm leaving."

"Wait," your son said. "Don't go."

He stood up and went into the kitchen.

"What are you doing, Old Lan?" Fenghuang shouted after him.

He walked out of the kitchen holding the middle finger of his left hand in his right hand. Blood seeped through his fingers.

"Are you crazy, Old Lan?" Fenghuang cried out.

"He's my uncle's son, all right," Ximen Huan said. "You can count on him when the chips are down."

"Quit spouting nonsense, bastard son," Fenghuang said anxiously. "Go inside and get some of your mom's miraculous hair, and hurry!"

Ximen Huan ran inside and quickly emerged with seven strands of thick hair. He laid them on the table and let them burn, quickly turning them to ashes.

"Let's see that finger, Old Lan," Fenghuang said as she grabbed the hand with the bleeding finger.

It was a deep cut. I saw Fenghuang go pale. Her mouth was open, her brow creased, as if she was the one in pain.

Ximen Huan scooped up the ashes with a crisp new bill and sprinkled them over your son's injured finger.

"Does it hurt?" Fenghuang asked.

"No."

"Let go of his wrist," Ximen Huan said.

"The blood will wash the ashes away," Fenghuang said.

"No problem, don't worry."

"If that doesn't stop the bleeding," she said threateningly, "I'll chop those dog paws of yours off!"

"I said don't worry."

Slowly Fenghuang loosened her grip on your son's wrist.

"Well?" Ximen Huan said proudly.

"It worked!"

52

Jiefang and Chunmiao Turn the Fake into the Real
Taiyue and Jinlong Depart this World Together

Lan Jiefang, you gave up your future and your reputation all for love; abandoning your family was something upright people would not countenance, yet writers like Mo Yan sang your praises. But not returning for your mother's funeral was such an unfilial act I'm afraid even Mo Yan, who has a reputation for twisting logic, would find it hard to come to your defense.

I never received word of my mother's death. I was living anonymously in Xi'an like a criminal in hiding. I knew that no court would grant me a divorce as long as Pang Kangmei was in a position of power. Denied a divorce but living with Chunmiao, my only option was to reside quietly far from home.

At first we both worked in a factory established through foreign investment. They manufactured fuzzy dolls. The manager was a so-called overseas Chinese, a bald man with a big belly and yellow teeth, a lover of poetry who was friendly with Mo Yan. He was sympathetic to our plight, actually got a kick out of our experience, and was willing to find office work for me and take Chunmiao on as a bookkeeper in the workshop. The air there was pretty foul, and her nose was constantly being tickled by loose fuzz. Most of the factory workers were girls brought in from the countryside, some as young as thirteen or fourteen, by all appearances. Then one day the factory burned down, claiming many lives and leaving most of the survivors with horrible disfigurements. Chunmiao was spared only because she happened to be home sick that day. For the longest time after that, the tragic fate of those factory girls kept us awake at night. Eventually, Mo Yan found openings for us at his local newspaper.

On many occasions I spotted familiar faces out on the streets of Xi'an and was tempted to call out to whoever it was. But instead I lowered my head and hid my face. Sometimes, when we were in our little apartment, thoughts of home and family had us both weeping miserably. Our love was why we'd left our homes, and that love made it impossible to return. Time and again we picked up the telephone, only to put it right back down, and time and again we dropped letters into the mailbox, only to find an excuse to ask for them back when the postman came to collect outgoing mail. Whatever news of home we received came from Mo Yan, who passed on good news and withheld the bad. His greatest fear was not having something to talk about, and we figured he saw us as valuable material for his novels. And so, the crueler our fate, the more convoluted our story became, and the more dramatically our circumstances developed, the more it interested him. Although I was kept from going home for my mother's funeral, during those days I actually played the role of filial son due to a combination of strange circumstances.

One of Mo Yan's classmates from his writers workshop days was directing a TV drama about the bandit annihilation campaign by the People's Liberation Army. One of the characters was nicknamed Lan Lian, or Blue Face, a bandit who cut down humans as if they were blades of grass but was a devoted, filial son to his mother. Mo Yan introduced me to his friend as a means for me to earn a bit of extra money. The director had a full beard, a pate as bald as Shakespeare's, and a nose as crooked as Dante's. As soon as he saw me, he slapped his thigh and said, I'll be damned! We won't have to worry about makeup!

We were picked up by Ximen Jinlong's Cadillac to be driven back to Ximen Village. The red-faced driver refused to let me get in, so your son scowled at him and said:

"You think this is a dog, is that it? Well, he's an apostle who loved my grandmother more than any member of the family!"

We'd barely left the county town when snow began to fall, tiny flakes like salt crystals. The ground was blanketed with white by the time we reached the village, and we heard a distant relative who'd come to mourn Grandma's passing shout tearfully:

"Heaven and earth are weeping for you, Great-Aunt. Your goodness has moved the world!"

Like a soloist in a choir, his wails were contagious; I could hear Ximen Baofeng's hoarse crying, Ximen Jinlong's majestic wailing, and Wu Qiuxiang's melodic weeping.

As soon as they stepped out of the car, Huzhu and Hezuo buried their faces in their hands and began to cry. Your son and Ximen Huan held their mothers up by their arms. In anguish I walked along behind them. My eldest dog brother had died by then, but doddering old Dog Two, who was lying at the base of the wall, greeted me with a low whimper; I was too upset to return the greeting. Streams of cold air seemed to crawl up my legs and into my body, where they turned my innards into ice. I was trembling, my limbs were stiff as boards, and my reactions were hopelessly dulled. I knew I'd gotten very old.

Your mother was already in her coffin; the lid lay off to the side. Her purple funeral clothes were made of satin with dark gold longevity characters sewn in. Jinlong and Baofeng were kneeling at opposite ends of the coffin. Her hair was uncombed. His eyes were red and puffy; the front of his shirt was tear-stained. Huzhu and Hezuo threw themselves onto the coffin, pounded the sides, and cried bitterly.

"Mother, oh, Mother, why did you have to leave before we came home? Mother, it was you who held us up, now we have nothing! How can any of us go on living?" Your wife's lament.

"Mother, oh, Mother, you suffered all your life, how could you leave just when you could finally enjoy life?" Huzhu's lament.

Their tears wetted your mother's funeral clothes and the yellow paper covering her face. It almost seemed as if the paper had been wetted by tears from the dead.

Your son and Ximen Huan knelt by their mothers' sides; one's face was dark as iron, the other's white as snow.

Xu Xuerong and his wife were in charge of the funeral arrangements. With a shriek of alarm, Mrs. Xu pulled Huzhu and Hezuo's faces away from the coffin.

"Oh, no, all you mourners, you mustn't shed tears on her body. If she carries tears from the living, she may be stuck in a life and death cycle. . . ."

Master Xu took a look around.

"Are all the close relatives here?"

No response.

"I ask you, are all the close relatives here?"

The distant relatives exchanged glances, but no one responded.

A distant cousin pointed to the west-side room and said softly: "Go ask the old gentleman."

I followed Master Xu over to the west-side room, where your father was sitting against the wall weaving a pot cover with dry sorghum stalks and hemp. A kerosene lamp hanging from the wall lit up that little section of the room. His face was a blur, except for his eyes, from which two bright lights shone. He was sitting on a stool, holding a nearly completed pot lid between his knees. A rustling sound emerged as he wove the hemp around the sorghum stalks.

"Sir," Master Xu said, "did you send a letter to Jiefang? If he can get here in the next little while, I think—"

"Close the coffin!" your father said. "Raising a dog is better than raising a son!"

When she heard I was going to be in a TV show, Chunmiao said she wanted to be in it too. So we went to Mo Yan, who went to the director, who, when he saw Chunmiao, said she could play the part of Blue Face's younger sister. The series was planned for thirty episodes, with ten stand-alone stories, each dealing with a bandit annihilation campaign. The director gave us a summary of what we'd be doing: After the gang led by the bandit Blue Face has been dispersed, he flees into the mountains alone. Knowing his reputation as a filial son, the PLA convinces his sister and mother to fake the mother's death and sends his sister into the mountains to pass on the news. Blue Face comes down from the mountains in his mourning garments and goes straight to his mother's bier, where PLA soldiers, who are staked out among the mourners, rush up and pin him to the floor. At that moment, his mother sits up in her coffin and says, Son, the PLA always treats its prisoners humanely, so please surrender to them. . . . "Got it?" the director asked us. "Got it," we said.

Before sealing the coffin, Mistress Xu lifted the yellow paper covering your mother's face and said:

"Filial mourners, take one last look. But please control yourselves and do not let tears fall on her face."

Your mother's face was puffy and jaundiced-looking, almost as if a thin layer of gold powder had been applied. Her eyes were open a crack, enough to release a pair of cold gleams, as if to scold everyone who looked upon her dead face.

"Mother, why have you left me to live as an orphan? . . ." Ximen Jinlong was wailing so bitterly a pair of cousins had to come up and pull him back from the coffin.

"Mother, my dear mother, take me with you. . . ." Baofeng banged her head against the side of the coffin, producing dull thuds. People dragged her away. Ma Gaige, his hair prematurely gray, wrapped his arm around his mother to keep her from throwing herself on the coffin.

Your wife gripped the edge of the coffin and wept, open-mouthed, until her eyes rolled back in her head and she fell backward. Several of the mourners rushed up and dragged her off to the side, where some of them rubbed the skin between her thumb and forefinger and others pinched the spot beneath her nose to revive her. Slowly she regained consciousness.

Master Xu signaled for the carpenters to come inside with their tools. They carefully picked up the lid and placed it over the body of a woman who had died with her eyes still slightly open. As the nails were pounded in, the chorus of wails reached another crescendo.

Over the next two days, Jinlong, Baofeng, Huzhu, and Hezuo sat on grass mats watching over the coffin from opposite ends, day and night. Lan Kaifang and Ximen Huan sat on stools at the head of the coffin facing each other and burning spirit money in an earthenware platter; at the other end, two thick red candles burned in front of your mother's spirit tablet, the smoke merging solemnly with paper ash floating in the air.

A steady stream of mourners passed by Master Xu, who meticulously recorded every gift of spirit money, which quickly piled up beneath the apricot tree. It was such a cold day that he had to blow on the tip of his pen to keep the ink flowing. A layer of frost covered his beard; ice formed on the branches of the tree, turning it silver.

Under the director's guidance, we assumed the moods of our characters. I had to keep reminding myself that I was not Lan Jiefang, but the ruthless bandit Blue Face, a man who had planted a bomb in his stove to explode in his wife's face when she lit the stove to cook breakfast, and who had cut the tongue out of a boy who had called him by my nickname, Blue Face. I was grief-stricken over the death of my mother, but had to control my tears and bury my sorrow in my heart. My tears were too precious to let them flow like water from a tap. But at the sight of Chunmiao in mourning attire, her face dirtied, my personal grief overwhelmed the part I was playing; my emotions supplanted his. So I tried again, but the director still was not satisfied. Mo Yan was on the set that day, and the director went over and said something to him. I heard Mo Yan reply, "You're taking this too seriously, Baldy He. If you don't help me here, you and I are no longer friends." Then Mo Yan took us aside and said, "What's wrong with you? Do you have overactive tear glands or what? Chunmiao can cry if she wants, but all you need to do is shed a few tears. It's not your mother who's died, it's the bandit's. Three episodes, at three thousand RMB apiece for you and two thousand for Chunmiao. That's enough for you two to live on nicely. Here's the trick: do not mix this woman in the coffin up with your own mother, who's back home wearing silks and satins and eating fine food. All you have to do is imagine the coffin filled with fifteen thousand RMB!"

Forty sedans drove into Ximen Village on the day of the interment, even though the road was covered with snow, which their exhaust pipes turned black. They parked across from the Ximen family compound, where the third son of the Sun family, a red armband over his sleeve, directed traffic. The drivers stayed in their cars and kept their engines running, creating a blanket of white mist.

All the late-arriving mourners were people of means and power, most of them officials in the county; a few were Ximen Jinlong's friends from other counties. Villagers braved the cold to stand outside the gate waiting for the clamor that would accompany the emergence of the coffin. Over those several days everyone seemed to forget about me, so I just hung around with Dog Two, strolling here and there. Your son fed me twice: once he tossed me a steamed bun, the other time he tossed me some frozen chicken wings. I ate the bun, but not the wings. Sad events from the past as Ximen Nao kept rising up from deep in my memory. Forgetting sometimes that I was in my fourth reincarnation, I felt myself to be the head of this household, a man whose wife had just died; at other times I understood that the yin and the yang were different worlds, and that the affairs of the human world were unrelated to me, a dog.

Most of the people out to watch the procession were elderly, or were snot-nosed little children; the younger men and women were working in town. The oldsters told the children all about how Ximen Nao had seen his own mother off in a four-inch-thick cypress coffin carried by twenty-four strong men. The funeral streamers and wreaths had stood in an unbroken line on both sides of the street, and every fifty paces a tent had been thrown up to accommodate roadside sacrifices of whole pigs, watermelons, oversize steamed buns . . . I didn't stick around to hear any more. Those were memories too painful to recall. I was now a dog only, one who did not have many more years in him. The officials who had decided to attend the interment were all wearing black overcoats with black scarves. Some — the bald or balding — were sporting black marten caps. Those without caps had full heads of hair. The snow covering their heads beautifully matched the white paper flowers in their lapels.

At noon a Red Flag sedan, followed by a black Audi, drove up to the Ximen compound. Ximen Jinlong, in mourning attire, rushed out to greet the new arrival. The driver opened the door, and out stepped Pang Kangmei in a black wool overcoat. Her face looked even fairer than usual, owing to the contrast with her coat. Deep wrinkles at the corners of her mouth and eyes were new since the last time I'd seen her. A man, probably her secretary, pinned a white funeral flower to her coat. Though she cut an imposing figure, a look of deep sadness filled her eyes, undetectable by most people. She held out her hand, encased in a black glove, and greeted Jinlong, who took her hand in his. Her comment was pregnant with hidden meaning:

"Keep your grief under control, be calm, don't lose your cool!"

Jinlong, looking equally solemn, nodded.

The good girl Pang Fenghuang followed Kangmei out of the car. Already taller than her mother, she was not only beautiful but fashionable, with a white down jacket over blue jeans and a pair of white lambskin loafers. She wore a white wool-knit cap on her head and no makeup — she didn't need to.

"This is your uncle Ximen," Kangmei said to her daughter.

"How do you do, Uncle?" Fenghuang said reluctantly.

"I want you to go up to Grandma's coffin and kowtow," Kangmei said with deep emotion. "She helped raise you."

I imagined that there were fifteen thousand RMB in the coffin, spread all around, not tied in bundles, ready to fly out when the lid was removed. It worked. I strode into the yard, holding Chunmiao by the arm; I could feel her stumbling along behind me, like a child being dragged along against her will. I burst into the room, where I was immediately confronted by a mahogany coffin whose lid was standing against the wall, waiting to be placed on top — after my arrival. A dozen or so people were standing around the coffin, some in mourning attire, some in street clothes. I knew that most of them were PLA in disguise, and that in a moment they were going to pin me to the floor. I saw Blue Face's mother lying in the coffin, her face covered by a sheet of yellow paper. Her purple funeral clothes were made of satin with dark gold longevity characters sewn in. I fell to my knees in front of the coffin.

"Mother," I wailed, "your unfilial son has come too late . . ."

Your mother's coffin finally emerged through the gateway, accompanied by the mournful wails of those who survived her and funeral music provided by a renowned peasant musician's troupe. Excitement spread among the bystanders, who had waited a long time for this moment. The musicians were preceded by two men carrying long bamboo poles to clear the way ahead. White mourning cloth hung from the ends of the poles, like antisparrow poles. They were followed by ten or fifteen boys carrying funeral banners, for which they would be richly rewarded, reason enough for them to beam happily. Behind this youthful honor guard came two men who covered the procession route with spirit money. Next came a four-man purple canopy protecting your mother's spirit tablet, on which, in ancient script, was written: "Wife of Ximen Nao, Surnamed Bai, called Yingchun." Everyone who saw this tablet knew that Ximen Jinlong had established his mother's lineage as the deceased spouse not of Lan Lian but of his biological father, Ximen Nao, and not as concubine but as legal wife. This, of course, was highly unconventional, for a remarried woman was normally not entitled to interment near her original husband's family graves. But Jinlong broke with this tradition. Then came your mother's mahogany casket, followed by the direct descendants of the deceased, all walking with willow lamentation canes. Your son, Ximen Huan, and Ma Gaige had simply thrown a white funeral sackcloth over their street clothes and wrapped their heads in white fabric. Each supported his grieving mother, all shedding silent tears. Jinlong trailed his lamentation cane behind him, stopping frequently to go down on his knees and wail, shedding red tears. Baofeng's voice was raspy, all but inaudible. Her eyes were glassy and her mouth hung open, but there were no tears or sounds. Your son, with his lean frame, had to support the entire weight of your wife, requiring the assistance of some of the other mourners. She wasn't walking to the cemetery, she was being carried along. Huzhu's loose black hair caught everyone's attention. Normally worn in a braid and encased in a black net, now, in accordance with funeral protocol, she let it fall loosely around her shoulders, like a black cataract spreading out on the ground, muddying the tips. A distant niece of the deceased, who had her wits about her, trotted ahead, scooped up Huzhu's hair, and laid it across her bent elbow. Many of the bystanders were whispering comments regarding Huzhu's miraculous hair. Someone said, Ximen Jinlong lives amid a cloud of beautiful women, but he won't ask his wife for a divorce. Why? Because the life he lives has been bestowed upon him by his wife. It is her miraculous hair that has brought him wealth and prosperity.

Pang Kangmei walked hand in hand with Pang Fenghuang with the group of dignitaries, behind the direct descendants. She was but three months away from being tried for a double offense. Her term of office had ended, but she had not yet been reassigned, which was a sure sign that trouble was brewing for her. Why, then, had she chosen to participate in a funeral that would later become a major exposé by the news media? Now, I was a dog who had experienced many of life's vicissitudes, but this was too complicated a problem for me to figure out. Nonetheless, I think the answer lay not in anything involving Kangmei herself, but must have been tied to Pang Fenghuang, a charming but rebellious girl who was, after all your mother's granddaughter.

"Mother, your unfilial son has come too late . . ." After I shouted my line, all of Mo Yan's instructions disappeared without a trace, as did my awareness that I was acting the part of Blue Face in a TV series. I had a hallucination — no, it wasn't a hallucination, it was a real-life feeling that the person lying in the coffin in funeral clothes with a sheet of yellow paper covering her face was, in fact, my mother. Images of the last time I'd seen her, six years earlier, flashed before my eyes, and one side of my face swelled up and felt hot. There'd been a ringing in my ears after my father had slapped me with the sole of his shoe. What my eyes took in here — my mother's white hair; her face, awash in murky tears; her sunken, toothless mouth; her age-spotted, veiny, nearly useless hands; her prickly-ash cane, which lay on the floor; her anguished cry as she tried to protect me — all this appeared before me, and tears gushed from my eyes. Mother, I've come too late. Mother, how did you manage to get through the days with an unfilial son who was cursed and spat on for what he did? And yet your son's filial feelings toward you have never wavered. Now I've brought Chunmiao to see you, Mother, so please accept her as your daughter-in-law. . . .

Your mother's grave was located at the southern end of Lan Lian's notorious plot of land. Ximen Jinlong was not daring enough to open the tomb in which Ximen Nao and Ximen Bai were buried together, and that served to save a bit of face for his adoptive father and mother-in-law. Instead he built a splendid tomb to the left of his biological parents' tomb. The stone doors seemed to open onto a deep, dark passage. The tomb was surrounded by an impenetrable wall of excited bystanders. I looked at the donkey's grave, and at the ox's grave, and the pig's grave, and at a dog's grave, and I looked at the ground, trampled into a rock-hard surface. A succession of thoughts crowded my mind. I could smell the sizzling spray of urine on Ximen Nao and Ximen Bai's markers from years back, and my heart was struck by apocalyptic feelings of doom. I walked slowly over to the pig's burial site and sprayed it. Then I lay down beside it, and as my eyes swelled with tears, I reflected: descendants of the Ximen family and those associated closely with it, I hope you will be able to discern my wishes and bury the dog-body of this incarnation in the spot I have chosen.

I nearly swooned from crying. I could hear someone shouting behind me, but could not tell what they were saying. Oh, Mother, let me see you one more time. . . . I reached over and removed the paper covering Mother's face; a woman who looked nothing like my mother sat up and said with extraordinary seriousness: Son, the PLA always treats its prisoners humanely, so please turn in your weapons and surrender to them! I sat down hard, my mind a blank, as the people standing around the bier swarmed up and pinned me to the ground. Cold hands reached down and pulled a pair of pistols from my waistband.

Just as your mother's coffin was being placed in the tomb, a man in a heavy padded coat stepped out from the surrounding crowd. He staggered a bit and reeked of alcohol. As he trotted unsteadily ahead, he peeled off his padded coat and flung it behind him; it hit the ground like a dead lamb. Using both hands and feet, he climbed up onto your mother's tomb, where he started tipping to one side and seemed in danger of slipping off altogether. But he didn't. He stood up. Hong Taiyue! It was Hong Taiyue! He was standing, steadily now, on top of your mother's tomb, dressed in rags: a brownish yellow army uniform, with a red detonating cap hanging from his belt. He raised a hand high in the air and shouted:

"Comrades, proletarian brothers, foot soldiers for Vladimir Ilyich Lenin and Mao Zedong, the time to declare war on the descendant of the landlord class, the enemy of the worldwide proletarian movement, and a despoiler of the earth, Ximen Jinlong, has arrived!"

The crowd was stunned. For a moment everything stood still before some of the people turned and ran, others hit the ground, flat on their bellies, and some simply didn't know what to do. Pang Kangmei pulled her daughter around behind her, looking frantic, but quickly regained her composure. She took several steps forward and said, looking unusually harsh, "Hong Taiyue, I am Pang Kangmei, secretary of the Gaomi County Communist Party Committee, and I order you to stop this idiotic behavior at once!"

"Pang Kangmei, don't put on those stinking airs with me! Communist Party secretary, like hell! You and Ximen Jinlong are links in the same chain, in cahoots with one another in your attempt to bring capitalism back to Northeast Gaomi Township, turning a red township into a black one. You are traitors to the proletariat, enemies of the people!"

Ximen Jinlong stood up and pushed his funeral cap back on his head; it fell to the ground. As if trying to calm an angry bull, he slowly approached the tomb.

"Don't come any closer!" Hong Taiyue shouted as he reached for the detonator fuse.

"Uncle, good uncle," Jinlong said with a kindly smile. "You nurtured me like a son. I remember every lesson you gave me. Our society has developed along with the changing times, and everything I've done has befitted those changes. Tell me the truth, Uncle, over the past decade have the people's lives gotten better or haven't they? . . ."

"I don't want to hear any more fine words from you!"

"Come down, Uncle," Jinlong said. "If you say I've made a mess of things, I'll resign and let someone more capable take over. Or, if you prefer, you can be the one holding the Ximen Village official seal."

While this exchange between Jinlong and Hong Taiyue was playing out, the policemen who had driven Pang Kangmei and others to the funeral were crawling toward the tomb. Just as they jumped to their feet, Hong Taiyue leaped off of the tomb and wrapped his arms around Jinlong.

A muffled explosion sent smoke and the stench of blood flying into the air.

After what seemed like an eternity, the stunned crowd quickly converged on the spot and pulled the two mangled bodies apart. Jinlong had been killed instantly, but Hong was still breathing, and no one knew what to do with the mortally wounded old man. They just stood there gawping at him. His face was waxen.

"This is," he stammered in a soft, barely audible voice as blood oozed from his mouth, "the last battle . . . unite for tomorrow . . . Internationale . . . has to . . ."

Blood spurted from his mouth, a foot-high red fountain, and splattered on the ground around him. His eyes lit up, like burning chicken feathers, once, twice, and then darkened, the fires extinguished for all time.

53

As Death Nears, Charity and Enmity Vanish
A Dog Dies, but the Wheel of Life Rolls on

I was carrying an old floor-model electric fan given to us by a colleague at the newspaper who had been promoted and was moving into new quarters. Chunmiao was carrying an old microwave oven, also a gift from that colleague. We'd just alighted from a crowded bus and were sweating profusely. It was hot and we were tired, but delighted to have these new — to us — items without having to spend a cent. It was a three-*li* walk from the bus stop to where we lived, but we weren't willing to part with our limited funds to hire a pedicab, so we hoofed it, stopping frequently to rest.

Dusk was deepening when we reached our kennel-like apartment, where our fat landlady was cursing at two other tenants for using tap water to cool the street in front of the building. Those two young tenants, our next-door neighbors, were gleefully throwing curses right back at her. A tall, thin man was standing in our doorway, the blue birthmark that covered half his face looking bronzed in the twilight. I set the fan down on the ground, hard, as I was racked by a chill throughout my body.

"What is it?" Chunmiao asked.

"It's Kaifang," I said. "Maybe you should make yourself scarce."

"What for? It's time to deal with the situation."

We made ourselves as presentable as possible and, trying hard to look relaxed, walked up to my son carrying our new possessions.

He was quite thin, but taller than me, and slightly stooped. Despite the heat, he was wearing a black long-sleeved shirt-jacket, black trousers, and a pair of sneakers of an indefinable color. His body gave off a sour smell; his clothes were sweat-stained. His luggage consisted solely of a transparent plastic bag. Saddened by the sight of a son who looked so much older than his years, I was on the verge of tears. I ran up to him, but the off-putting look on his face kept me from embracing him. I let my arms drop heavily to my sides.

"Kaifang . . ."

He looked me over without a trace of warmth, disgusted even by the tears that were now washing my face. He frowned, imprinting creases on his forehead above a nearly unbroken line of eyebrows, like his mother's. He sneered.

"Not bad, you two, making it to a place like this."

I was too tongue-tied to say anything.

Chunmiao opened the door and carried in our fan and microwave. Turning on the twenty-five-watt overhead light, she said:

"Since you're here, Kaifang, you'd better come in. We can talk in here."

"I have nothing to say to you," he said with a quick glance inside, "and I'm not going inside your house!"

"No matter what, Kaifang, I'm still your father," I said. "You've come a long way, and Aunt Chunmiao and I would like to take you to dinner."

"You two go, I'll stay here," Chunmiao said. "Treat him to something good."

"I'm not going to eat anything you give me," he said as he swung the bag in his hand. "I brought my own food."

"Kaifang . . ." More tears. "Can't you give your father a little face?"

"Okay, that's enough," he said with obvious repulsion. "Don't think I hate you two, because I don't, not a bit. It was my mother's idea to come looking for you, not mine."

"She . . . how is she?" I said hesitantly.

"She has cancer." His voice was low. There was silence for a moment before he continued. "She doesn't have long to live, and would like to see you both. She says she has many things she wants to say to you."

"How could she have cancer?" said Chunmiao, now crying openly.

My son looked at Chunmiao and just shook his head noncommittally.

"Well, I've delivered the message," he said. "Whether you go back or not is up to you."

He turned and walked off.

"Kaifang . . ." I grabbed his arm. "We can go together. We'll leave tomorrow."

He wrested his arm from my grip.

"I'm not traveling with you. I have a return ticket for tonight."

"Then we'll go with you."

"I said I'm not traveling with you."

"Then we'll walk you to the station," Chunmiao said.

"No," my son said with steely determination. "There's no need."

After your wife learned she had cancer, she insisted on going back to Ximen Village. Your son, who hadn't graduated from high school, was bent on quitting school and becoming a policeman. His application was accepted by your old friend Du Luwen, once the Lüdian Township Party secretary, and now county police commissioner, either as a result of your relationship or of your son's excellent qualifications. He was assigned to the criminal division.

Following the death of your mother, your father moved back into the southern end of the little room in the western addition, where he resumed the solitary, eccentric lifestyle of his independent farming days. No one ever saw him out in the compound during the day, nor did they often see smoke from his chimney, though he prepared his own meals. He wouldn't eat the food Huzhu or Baofeng brought to him, preferring to let it go bad on the counter by the stove or on his table. Late at night he'd get down off his sleeping platform, the *kang*, and come back to life. He'd boil a pot of water on the stove and make some soupy rice, which he'd eat before it was fully cooked. Either that or he'd simply eat raw, crunchy grain and wash it down with cold water. Then he'd be right back on the *kang*.

When your wife returned to the village, she moved into the northern end of the western addition, previously occupied by your mother. Her twin sister, Huzhu, took care of her. Sick as she was, I never heard a single moan from her. She just lay quietly in bed, eyes closed as she tried to get some sleep, or open as she stared at the ceiling. Huzhu and Baofeng tried all sorts of home remedies, such as cooking a toad in soupy rice or preparing pig's lung with a special grass or snakeskin with stir-fried eggs or gecko in liquor. She refused to try any of these remedies. Her room was separated by your father's only by a thin wall of sorghum stalks and mud, so they could hear each other's coughs and sighs; but they never exchanged a word.

In your father's room there were a vat of raw wheat, another of mung beans, and two strings of corn ears hanging from the rafters. After Dog Two died, I found myself with nothing to do and no mood to try anything new, so I either slept the day away in my kennel or wandered through the compound. After the death of Jinlong, Ximen Huan hung out with a bad crowd in town, returning infrequently, and only to get money from his mother. After Pang Kangmei was arrested, Jinlong's company was taken over by county officials, as was the Ximen Village Party secretary position. By then his company existed on paper only, and all the millions in bank loans were gone. He left nothing for Huzhu or Ximen Huan. So after her son used up all of Huzhu's personal savings, he stopped showing up altogether.

Huzhu was living in the main house; every time I entered the house she was seated at her square table, cutting paper figures. Everything she made — plants and flowers, insects and fish, birds and beasts — was remarkably lifelike. She mounted the figures between sheets of white paper and, when she'd finished a hundred of them, took them into town to sell next to shops that carried all sorts of mementos; from that she maintained a simple life. I occasionally saw her comb her hair, standing on a bench to let it fall all the way to the floor. Watching the way she had to bend her neck to run the comb through it made me very sad.

Someone else I made sure to see each day was your father-in-law. Huang Tong was laid up with liver disease and probably didn't have long to live either. Your mother-in-law, Wu Qiuxiang, looked to be in good health, though her hair had turned white and her eyesight had dimmed. No trace of her youthful flirtatiousness remained.

But most of all I went to your father's room, where I sprawled on the floor next to the *kang*, and the old man and I would just look at each other, communicating with our eyes and not our mouths. There were times when I assumed he knew exactly who I was; he'd start jabbering, as if talking in his sleep:

"Old Master, you shouldn't have died the way you did, but the world has changed over the last ten years or more, and lots of people died who shouldn't have. . . ."

I whined softly, which earned an immediate response from him:

"What are you whining about, old dog? Did I say something wrong?"

Rats shamelessly nibbled the corn hanging from the rafters. It was seed corn, something a farmer values almost as much as life itself. But not your father. He was unmoved. "Go ahead, eat up. There's more food in the vats. Come help me finish it off so I can leave. . . ."

On nights when there was a bright moon he would walk out with a hoe over his shoulder and work in the moonlight, the same as he'd done for years, as everyone in Northeast Gaomi Township knew.

And every time he did that, I tagged along, no matter how tired I was. He never wound up anywhere but on his one-point-six-acre sliver of land, a plot that, over a period of fifty years, had nearly evolved into a graveyard. Ximen Nao and Ximen Bai were there, your mother was buried there, as were the donkey, the ox, the pig, my dog-mother, and Ximen Jinlong. Weeds covered the spots where there were no graves, the first time that had ever happened there.

One night, by jogging my deteriorating memory, I located the spot I'd chosen. I lay down and whimpered pathetically.

"No need to cry, old dog," your father said. "I know what you're thinking. If you die before me, I'll bury you right there. If I go first, I'll tell them to bury you there, if I have to do it with my last breath."

Your father dug up some dirt behind your mother's grave.

"This spot is for Hezuo."

The moon was a melancholy object in the sky, its beams translucent and chilled. I followed your father as he prowled the area. He startled a pair of partridges, which flew off to someone else's land. The rends they made in the moonlight were quickly swallowed up. Your father stood about ten yards north of the Ximen family graveyard and looked all around. He stamped his foot on the ground.

"This is my place," he said.

He then started to dig, and didn't stop until he'd carved out a hole roughly three feet by six and two feet deep. He lay down in it and stared up at the moon for about half an hour.

"Old dog," he said after climbing out, "you and the moon are my witnesses that I've slept in this spot. It's mine, and no one can take it from me."

Then he went over to where I had lain down, measured my body, and dug a hole for me. I knew what he had in mind, so I jumped in. After lying there for a while, I got out.

"That's your spot, old dog. The moon and I are your witnesses."

In the company of the melancholy moon, we headed home along the riverbank, reaching the Ximen compound just before the roosters crowed. Dozens of dogs, having been influenced by dogs in town, were holding a meeting in the square across from the Ximen family gate. They were sitting in a circle around a female with a red silk kerchief around her neck; she was singing to the moon. Needless to say, to humans her song sounded like a bunch of crazed barks. But to me it was clear and musical, with a wonderfully moving melody and poetic lyrics. Here is the gist of what she was singing:

"Moon, ah, moon, you make me so sad . . . girl, ah, girl, you make me go mad . . ."

That night your father and your wife spoke through the wall for the first time. He rapped on the thin wall and said:

"Kaifang's mother."

"I can hear you, Father, go ahead."

"I've selected your spot. It's ten paces behind your mother's grave."

"Then I can be at peace, Father. I was born a Lan and will be a Lan ghost after I die."

We knew she wouldn't eat anything we brought, but we bought as much nutritious food as we could. Kaifang, in his oversize policeman's uniform, rode us over to Ximen Village in an official sidecar motorcycle. Chunmiao was in the sidecar, with all the cans and bags we'd brought in her arms and packed around her. I sat behind my son, gripping a steel bar with both hands. He wore a somber look; the glare in his eyes was chilling. He looked impressive in his uniform, even if it was too big for him. His blue birthmark beautifully matched his blue uniform. Son, you've chosen the right profession. These blue birthmarks of ours are perfect symbols for the incorruptible face of the law.

Gingko trees lining the road were as big around as an average bowl. The stems of wisteria planted in the center divider were bent low by the profusion of white and dark red flowers. The village had undergone dramatic changes in the years I'd been away. And I was thinking, anyone who says that Ximen Jinlong and Pang Kangmei were responsible for nothing good did not see the whole picture.

My son pulled up in front of the family compound gate and led us inside.

"Are you going to see Grandpa first or my mother?" he asked frigidly.

I wavered for a moment.

"Tradition demands that I see Grandpa first."

Father's door was shut tight. Kaifang stepped up and knocked. No sound emerged from inside, so he walked over to the tiny window and rapped on it.

"It's Kaifang, Grandpa. Your son is here."

A sad, heavy sigh eventually broke the silence.

"Dad, your unfilial son has come home." I fell to my knees in front of the window. Chunmiao knelt beside me. Weeping and sniveling, I said, "Please open the door, Dad, and let me see you. . . ."

"I don't have the face to see you," he said, "but there are some things I want to say to you. Are you listening?"

"I'm listening, Dad. . . ."

"Kaifang's mother's gravesite is ten paces behind your mother's. I've piled up some dirt to mark the site. The old dog's grave is just west of the pig's; I've already framed it out. Mine is thirty paces north of your mother's; I've framed it too. When I die I don't want a coffin, and no musicians. Don't notify any friends or relatives. Just get a rush mat, roll me up in it, and quietly put me in. Then take the grain from the vat in my room and dump it in the hole to cover my face and body. It all came from my plot of land, so that's where it should return to. No one is to cry over my death; there's nothing to cry about. As for Kaifang's mother, you make whatever arrangements for her you want, I don't care. If there's still a filial bone in your body, you'll do exactly as I ask."

"I will, Dad, I won't forget. But please open the door and let me see you."

"Go see your wife, she only has a few days left. I should have another year or so. I won't die anytime soon."

So Chunmiao and I stood beside Hezuo's *kang*. Kaifang called to her and then stepped outside. Knowing we'd come, Hezuo was ready for us. She was wearing a blue jacket with side openings that had belonged to my mother — her hair was neatly combed and her face washed. She was sitting up on the *kang*. But she was almost inhumanly thin; her face was bones covered by a layer of yellow skin. With tears in her eyes, Chunmiao called out Big Sister and laid the cans and bags on the *kang*.

"You've thrown your money away on all that," Hezuo said. "Take it back with you and get your money back."

"Hezuo . . ." Tears were streaming down my face. "I treated you terribly."

"At this point, talk like that is meaningless," she said. "You two have suffered over the years too." She turned to Chunmiao. "You've gotten old yourself." Then she turned to me. "Not many black hairs on your head anymore . . ." She coughed, turning her face red. I could smell blood. But then the jaundiced look returned.

"Why don't you lie back, Big Sister?" Chunmiao said. "I won't leave, I'll stay here and take care of you."

"I can't ask that of you," Hezuo said with a wave of her hand. "I had Kaifang ask you to come so I could tell you I only have a few days left, and there's no reason for you to hide yourselves far away. I was foolish. I don't know why I didn't agree to what you wanted back then. . . ."

"Big Sister . . ." Chunmiao was weeping bitterly. "It's all my fault."

"It's nobody's fault," Hezuo said. "Everything is determined by fate, and there's no way anyone can escape it."

"Don't give up, Hezuo," I said. "We'll get you to a hospital and find a good doctor."

She managed a sad smile.

"Jiefang, you and I were husband and wife, and after I die, I want you to take good care of her . . . she's a good person. Women who stay with you are not blessed with good fortune . . . all I ask is that you look after Kaifang. He's suffered a lot because of us. . . ."

I heard Kaifang blow his nose out in the yard.

Hezuo died three days later.

After the funeral my son wrapped his arms around the old dog's neck and sat in front of his mother's grave from noon to sunset, without crying and without moving.

Like my father, Huang Tong and his wife refused to see me. I got down on my knees at their door and kowtowed three times, banging my head loudly enough for them to hear.

Two months later Huang Tong was dead.

On the night of his death, Wu Qiuxiang hanged herself from a dead branch on the apricot tree in the middle of the yard.

Once the funerals for my father-in-law and mother-in-law were over, Chunmiao and I moved into the Ximen family compound. The two rooms Mother and Hezuo had occupied now became our living quarters, separated from Father only by that thin wall. As before, he never went out in the daytime, but if we looked out our window at night we sometimes saw his crooked back along with the old dog, who never left his side.

In accordance with Qiuxiang's wishes, we buried her to the right of Ximen Nao and Ximen Bai. Ximen Nao and his women were now all united in the ground. Huang Tong? We buried him in the Ximen Village public cemetery, no more than two yards from where Hong Taiyue lay.

On October 5, 1998, the fifteenth day of the eight month by the lunar calendar, the Mid-Autumn Festival, there was a reunion of all who had lived in the Ximen family compound. Kaifang returned on his motor-cycle from the county town, his sidecar filled with two boxes of moon cakes and a watermelon. Baofeng and Ma Gaige were there. Gaige, who had worked for a private cottonseed-processing factory, had lost his left arm in a cutting machine; his sleeve hung empty at his side. You wanted to express your condolences to this nephew of yours, it seemed, but no words emerged when your lips moved. That was also the day that you, Lan Jiefang, and Pang Chunmiao received formal permission to marry. After years of hardship, your lover finally became your wife, and even an old dog like me was happy for you. You kneeled outside your father's window. In a supplicating tone, you said:

"Dad . . . we're married, we are a legally married couple, and will no longer bring you shame. . . . Dad . . . open your door and let your son and your daughter-in-law pay their respects to you. . . ."

Finally your father's dilapidated door swung open, and you went up to it on your knees; there you held the marriage certificate high over your head. "Father," you said.

"Father . . . ," Chunmiao greeted him.

He rested his hand on the door frame. His blue face twitched, his blue beard quivered, blue tears fell from his blue eyes. The Mid-Autumn moon sent down blue rays of light.

"Get up," your father said in a voice that trembled. "At last you've put yourselves in the proper roles . . . my heart is free of concerns."

The Mid-Autumn banquet was held under the apricot tree, with moon cakes, watermelon, and a variety of fine dishes arrayed on the table. Your father sat at the north end, with me crouched beside him. You and Chunmiao sat to the east, opposite Baofeng and Gaige. Kaifang and Huzhu sat to the south. The moon, perfectly round, sent its rays down on the Ximen family compound. The old tree had all but died years earlier, but in lunar August, a few new leaves appeared on some of the branches. Your father flung a glassful of liquor up toward the moon, which shuddered; the beams suddenly darkened, as if a layer of mist had shrouded the face of the moon. But only for a moment; the new light was brighter, warmer, and cleaner than before. Everything in the compound — the buildings, the trees, the people, and the dog — seemed to be steeped in a bath of light blue ink.

Your father splashed the second glassful on the ground. He poured the third glassful down my mouth. It was a dry red wine that Mo Yan had asked a German master winemaker friend to make. Deep red in color, with a wonderful bouquet and a slightly bitter taste, when it touched my throat it brought a host of memories.

It was Chunmiao's and my first night as husband and wife, and our hearts were so full of emotions sleep would not come. We were bathed by moonlight streaming in through the cracks. We lay naked on the *kang* my mother and Hezuo had both slept on, staring at each other's face and body as if for the first time. "Mother, Hezuo," I said in silent benediction, "I know you are watching us. You sacrificed yourselves to bring happiness to us.

"Chunmiao," I called out softly, "let's make love. When Mother and Hezuo see that we are in perfect harmony, they will be able to move on, knowing all is well. . . ."

We wrapped our arms around each other and began to move in the moonlight like fish tumbling in the water. We made love with tears of gratitude in our eyes. Our bodies seemed to float up and out the window, all the way to the moon, with countless lamps and the purple ground far below. There we saw: Mother, Hezuo, Huang Tong, Qiuxiang, Chunmiao's mother, Ximen Jinlong, Hong Taiyue, Ximen Bai . . . They were all sitting astride white birds, flying into a void we could not see. Even Ma Gaige's lost arm, dark as an eel, was following in their wake.

*   *   *

Late that night your father led me out of the compound. By this time there was no doubt that he knew who I was. On our way out we stood in the gateway and, feeling intense nostalgia, yet seemingly with no wistfulness at all, took a long look inside. Then we headed out to the plot of land, where the moon hung low waiting for us.

When we reached the one-point-six-acre plot of land, which seemed to us to have been carved out of gold, the moon began to change color, first to a light eggplant purple, and then, slowly, into an azure hue. At that moment, everything around us took on an ocean blue that merged perfectly with the vast sky; we were two tiny creatures at the bottom of that ocean.

Your father lay down in the hole he had dug. Softly, he said:

"You can go, too, Master."

I walked over to my plot and jumped in. I fell, down and down, all the way to the hall where blue lights flashed. The underworld attendants were whispering back and forth. The face of Lord Yama, seated in the main hall, was unfamiliar to me. But before I could open my mouth, he said:

"Ximen Nao, I know everything about you. Does hatred still reside in your heart?"

I hesitated momentarily before shaking my head.

"There are too many, far too many, people in the world in whose hearts hatred resides," Lord Yama said sorrowfully. "We are unwilling to allow spirits who harbor hatred to be reborn as humans. Unavoidably, some do slip through the net."

"My hatred is all gone, Great Lord!"

"No, I can see in your eyes that traces of it remain," Lord Yama said, "so I will send you back once more as a member of the animal kingdom. This time, however, you will be reborn as a higher species, one closer to man, a monkey, if you must know, and only for a short time — two years. I hope that during those two years you will be able to purge your heart of hatred. When you do that, you will have earned the right to return to the realm of humans."

In accordance with Father's wishes, we spread the wheat and beans in his room, as well as the corn hanging from the rafters, into his grave, covering his face and body with those precious grains. We spread some of it into the dog's grave as well, though that was not spelled out in Father's last wishes. We wrestled with one item for a while, but ultimately decided to part with Father's wishes by erecting a marker over his grave. The words were written by Mo Yan and cut into stone by the stone mason from my donkey era, Han Shan:

Everything that comes from the earth shall return to it.

Book Five

An End and a Beginning

54

The Face of the Sun

Dear reader, this would seem to be the logical place to wrap up this novel, but there are characters whose fates have not yet been revealed, something most readers want to see. So let's give our narrators, Lan Jiefang and Big-head, a rest and let me — their friend Mo Yan — pick up the threads and pin a tail on this lumbering animal of a story.

After Lan Jiefang and Pang Chunmiao buried his father and the dog, they entertained the thought of living out their days working Father's plot of land in Ximen Village; unfortunately, a highly respected guest arrived at the Ximen family compound. It was a man named Sha Wujing, who had attended the provincial Party school with Jiefang and was now Party secretary of the Gaomi County Party Committee. Deeply moved by Jiefang's life experience and the decrepit condition of the once illustrious Ximen family compound, he said generously to Jiefang:

"You'll never regain your position as deputy county chief, my friend, and restoring your membership in the Party is unlikely. But I think we can find you a government job to keep you going."

"I'm grateful for the thoughtful consideration of our leaders, but there's no need for that," Jiefang replied. "I'm the son of a Ximen Village peasant, and this is where I want to live out my days."

"Remember the old Party secretary Jin Bian?" Sha asked. "Well, here's what he had in mind. He and your father-in-law Pang Hu are good friends, and if you two were to move into town, you could look after your father-in-law. The Standing Committee has approved your assignment as assistant director of the Cultural Exhibition Center. As for Comrade Chunmiao, she can return to the New China Bookstore if she's willing. If not, we can find something else for her."

Dear reader, returning to town was not something Jiefang and Chunmiao ought to have considered; but the opportunity to be working for the government and to look after her aging father was too good to pass up. Keep in mind that those two friends of mine were ordinary people not blessed with the ability to look into the future. They returned to town without delay. Since it was ordained by Fate, they could not have done otherwise.

At first they moved into Pang Hu's house. Although he had once publicly, even heroically, disowned Chunmiao, he was, after all, a loving father, an old and ailing man, like a candle guttering in the wind, so he grew teary and his heart softened, especially after learning how difficult life had been for his daughter and the man who was now her legal husband. He put the ill will of the past aside, threw open his door, and welcomed them into his house.

Early each morning Jiefang rode his bicycle to the Cultural Exhibition Center. Given the cheerless, shabby layout of the center, assistant director was a title, not a job. There was nothing for him to "direct," and all he did all day long was sit at his three-drawer desk, drinking weak tea, smoking cheap cigarettes, and reading the newspaper.

Chunmiao decided to return to the children's section of the New China Bookstore, where she dealt with a new generation of boys and girls. By then the clerks she'd worked with before had retired, their places taken by young women in their twenties. Chunmiao also rode a bicycle to work; in the afternoon she'd swing by Theater Street to buy chicken gizzards or sheep's head meat to take home for her father to enjoy with the little bit of liquor he and Jiefang, neither of whom could handle much alcohol, drank before dinner. They'd talk about little things, like brothers.

Chunmiao discovered she was pregnant around lunar New Year's. Jiefang, who was in his fifties, was overjoyed. The news also brought tears to the eyes of Pang Hu, who was approaching eighty. Both men envisioned the joy of life with three generations living under one roof. But that image would quickly fade in the face of a looming disaster.

Chunmiao had bought some stewed donkey meat on Theater Street and was on her way home, singing happily to herself as she turned into Liquan Boulevard, where a Red Flag sedan coming from the opposite direction ran into her. The bicycle was turned into junk, the meat splattered on the ground, and she flew over to the side of the road, where she hit her head on the curb. She died before Jiefang arrived on the scene. The car that had hit her belonged to Du Luwen, onetime secretary of the Lüdian Township Party Committee, now deputy head of the county People's Congress; it was driven by the son of one of Ximen Jinlong's youthful pals, Young Tiger Sun.

I simply do not know how to describe what Jiefang felt when he saw her lying there; great novelists have set too high a standard in dealing with such traumatic moments.

Jiefang buried Chunmiao's ashes in his father's notorious plot of land, near Hezuo's grave site; no marker was placed at the head of either grave. After weeds grew around Chunmiao's grave, you could not tell them apart. Pang Hu died not long after his daughter was buried. Jiefang took the urns containing both his and Wang Leyun's ashes back to Ximen Village and buried them next to his father, Lan Lian.

A few days later, Pang Kangmei, who was serving a prison term, went slightly mad and stabbed herself in the heart with a sharpened toothbrush. Chang Tianhong retrieved her ashes and went to see Lan Jiefang. "She was, after all, a member of your family," he said, and Jiefang understood what he was trying to say. He took the ashes back to Ximen Village and buried them behind the graves of her parents.

55

Lovemaking Positions

Lan Kaifang rode his father, my friend Jiefang, over to the house on Tianhua Lane on his motorcycle. The sidecar was filled with his daily necessities. This time, instead of holding on to the metal bar, Jiefang wrapped his arms around his son's waist. Kaifang was still very thin, but straight and strong as an unbending tree branch. My friend wept all the way from the Pang house to 1 Tianhua Lane; his tears wetted the back of his son's police uniform.

He was understandably emotional as he stepped in through the gate for the first time since the day he'd left it supported by Chunmiao. The limbs of the parasol tree in the yard had reached the wall, with branches reaching over to the other side. As the old saying goes, "If trees can change, why can't people?" But my friend had no time to ponder such thoughts, for he'd no sooner stepped into the yard than he saw through the gauzy covering of an open window in the east-side room, which had once been his study, a familiar figure. It was Huzhu, sitting there making paper cutouts, oblivious to all around her.

No question about it, this had been Kaifang's doing, and my friend realized how lucky he was to have such a kind and considerate son. Not only did he bring his aunt and his father together, he also took Chang Tianhong, who had fallen into a depression, back to Ximen Village on his motorcycle to meet Baofeng, who'd been a widow for many years. He had once, long ago, been the man of her dreams, and he'd always had feelings for her. Her son, Gaige, was not a man with great ambitions; rather he was an honest, upright, hardworking peasant. He was happy to approve the marriage of his mother to Chang Tianhong, so they could live out their lives as a contented couple.

My friend Jiefang's first love had been Huang Huzhu — to be fair, it was her hair he'd fallen in love with, and now, after lives marked by sadness and pain, the two of them were able to walk through life together. Kaifang spent most of his nights in a dormitory room and seldom came home to the house on Tianhua Lane, not even on weekends, owing to the demands of his job. That left only Jiefang and Huzhu in the house; they slept in their own rooms but ate their meals together. Huzhu, who'd never had much to say, spoke even less now, and when Jiefang asked her something, she replied only with a weak smile. For six months or so that is how things went, and then everything changed.

After dinner one spring evening, as a light rain fell outside, their hands touched while they were clearing the table. Something happened to their mood; their eyes met. Huzhu sighed. My friend did too. In a soft voice, Huzhu said:

"Why don't you come in and comb my hair. . . ."

He followed her into her room, where she handed him her comb and carefully removed her heavy hairnet. Her miraculous hair fell like waves all the way to the floor. For the first time in his life my friend was able to touch hair that he had admired from afar since his youth. A delicate citronella fragrance filled his nostrils and reached deep down into his soul.

Huzhu took several steps forward in order to let her hair out all the way, and when her knees touched the bed, my friend scooped up her hair in one arm and with great care and great tenderness began to comb. In fact, her hair did not need to be combed; thick and heavy and slippery, it never had split ends; it would be accurate to say that he was stroking it, fondling it, sensing it. His tears fell on her hair like drops of water splashing on the feathers of Mandarin ducks, and rolled off onto the floor.

With an emotional sigh, Huzhu began taking off her clothes, while my friend stood back several feet, holding her hair like a child carrying the train of a bride as she enters the church and staring wide-eyed at the scene before him.

"I guess we ought to give your son what he wants, don't you think. . . ."

As his tears flowed freely, he parted the hair he was holding, like a man walking through the hanging branches of a weeping willow, not stopping until he'd reached his destination. Huzhu knelt on the bed to await his arrival.

The scene was replayed several dozen times, until my friend said he would like to make love facing her. She replied in a voice devoid of feeling:

"No, this is how dogs do it."

56

Monkey Show in the Square

Shortly after the first day of 2000, two humans and one monkey appeared in the square in front of the Gaomi train station. I'm sure, dear reader, that you have already guessed that the monkey was the latest reincarnation of Ximen Nao, following the donkey, the ox, the pig, and the dog. Naturally, it was a male monkey, and not one of those cute little things we're so used to seeing. It was a large rhesus monkey, whose coat was a dull green-gray, sort of like dry moss. His eyes, far apart and sunk deep into their sockets, gave off a frightful glare. His ears lay flat against his head like fungi, his nostrils flared upward, and his open mouth, seemingly without an upper lip, showed nothing but teeth; that alone was enough to frighten anyone off. He was dressed in a red sleeveless jacket, turning a savage monkey into a comical one. Truth is, there's no reason to call him either savage or comical, since a monkey in human clothes is just that and nothing more.

A chain around the monkey's neck was attached to the wrist of a young woman. I don't need to tell you, dear reader, that the young woman in question is our long-lost Pang Fenghuang, and that the young man with her was the long-lost Ximen Huan. Both were wearing filthy down coats over tattered blue jeans and dirty knockoff sneakers. Fenghuang had dyed her hair a golden yellow and plucked her eyebrows, leaving only thin arcs. She wore a gold ring in her right nostril. Ximen Huan had dyed his hair red and had a silver ring above his right eye.

Gaomi had come a long way by then, though it still didn't compare favorably with the big cities. There's a saying that goes: "The bigger the woods, the more diverse the bird population; the smaller the woods, the fewer the birds." These two strange birds and their ferocious monkey attracted an immediate crowd of curious gawkers, as well as at least one busybody who ran to the local police station to report what was going on.

The crowd instinctively formed a circle around Ximen Huan and Pang Fenghuang, which is what they wanted. He pulled a bronze gong out of his backpack and struck it — *bong bong* — which attracted even more people and tightened the circle. One sharp-eyed person in the crowd recognized the youngsters, but all the others were staring wide-eyed at the monkey and couldn't have cared less who his handlers were.

While Ximen Huan rhythmically beat the gong, Fenghuang took the chain off her wrist to give the monkey more room to maneuver, and then removed a straw hat, a tiny carrying pole, two tiny baskets, and a tobacco pipe from her backpack, laying them on the ground beside her. Then, to the rhythm of Ximen Huan's gong, she began to sing in a raspy but melodious voice. The monkey took that as his cue to stroll around the square. It was a stumbling gait, since his legs were bowed; his tail dragged on the ground behind him as he glanced all around.

> The bronze gong rings out *bong bong bong*
> I tell monkey to do nothing wrong
> He received the Tao on Mount Emei
> And returned home as king of his trade, truly strong
> He'll perform for our countrymen
> Who will pay for my song

"Move back! Clear the way!" Newly assigned deputy station chief Lan Kaifang elbowed his way through the crowd. He was born to be a cop. In two years on the force he had acquitted himself so well that at the unprecedented young age of twenty he'd been picked as deputy chief of the train station police substation, one of the most crime-ridden areas in town. It was a ringing affirmation of his talent and dedication.

> Be an old man with a straw hat and pipe
> Stroll round the square, hands in back, walking along

As she sang, Fenghuang tossed the straw hat to the monkey, who nimbly put it on his head. Next she tossed him the pipe; he jumped up and put it in his mouth. That done, he clasped his hands behind his back, bent at the waist, and bowed his legs; with his head rocking from side to side and his eyes darting, he looked like an old man out for a stroll, and was rewarded with laughter and applause.

"Move back! Clear the way!" Lan Kaifang squeezed up to the front. His heart had begun to sink when he received the busybody's report, for rumors had reached his ears that Ximen Huan and Pang Fenghuang had been kidnapped and sent to Southeast Asia, where one was forced to perform manual labor, the other was sold into life as a prostitute; another version had it that they had both died of drug overdoses somewhere in the south. But deep down, he believed they were alive and well, especially Fenghuang. You, dear reader, would not have forgotten how he cut his own finger so Ximen Huan could test the restorative powers of Huang Huzhu's hair. Well, that cut showed how he felt. So when he received the report, he knew who they were and knew they were back. He dropped what he was doing and ran to the square, the image of Fenghuang floating before his eyes the whole way. He hadn't seen her since his grandmother's funeral, when she'd been wearing a white down jacket and a white knit cap; her tiny face, red from the biting cold, had made her seem to be a pure and chaste fairy-tale princess. When he heard her raspy singing, Kaifang, who treated criminals with the callousness they deserved, felt his eyes glaze over.

> Let's see Erlang carry a mountain and chase the moon
> Then a phoenix spreading her wings to pursue the sun

Pang Fenghuang picked up the little carrying pole and its two tiny baskets with her foot and flipped it into the air with such skill that it landed on the monkey's back. First he rested it on his right shoulder, with one basket in front, the other in back; Erlang carrying a mountain and chasing the moon. Then he rested it on his back, with one basket to the left, the other to his right; a phoenix spreading her wings to pursue the sun.

> I perform all my tricks at least once
> So please pay up for my song

The monkey threw down the carrying pole, picked up a red plastic platter Fenghuang had thrown down for him, and began passing it around.

Good uncle, good aunt
Grandpa and Grandma
Brothers, sisters, fellow countrymen
I'll take even a dime if that's all you have
But give a hundred, and you're the Guanyin Bodhisattva come to earth

While Fenghuang sang, the people tossed money into the platter held high over the monkey's head. One-jiao, two-jiao, and three-jiao coins, plus one- , five- , and ten-yuan bills, fell into his pan with hardly a sound.

When the monkey was face-to-face with Lan Kaifang, the policeman put in a thick envelope containing a month's wages and overtime pay. With a screech, the monkey fell to all fours and, with the platter in his mouth, scampered over to Pang Fenghuang.

Bong bong bong — Ximen Huan struck his gong three times and bowed deeply to Kaifang, like a circus clown. Then he straightened up and said:

"Many thanks, Uncle Policeman!"

Fenghuang took the money out of the envelope and, holding it in her right hand, slapped it rhythmically against the palm of her left hand to show off to the audience as she imitated a pop song:

All of us, we're Gaomi folk
Every one of us a living Lei Feng
You gave us a wad of RMB
A good deed without even leaving your name

Kaifang pulled the brim of his hat down low, turned on his heel, and pushed his way through the crowd without saying a word.

57

A Painful Cut

Dear reader, as a policeman, Lan Kaifang had the authority to drive Ximen Huan, Pang Fenghuang, and their monkey out of the train station square, but he didn't.

Since his father, Jiefang, and I were like brothers, he might be considered my nephew, while in truth I barely knew him; he and I had exchanged no more than a few words. I suspected that he was prejudiced against me, since I'd been the one who'd introduced his father to Pang Chunmiao, and that had led to a number of disastrous consequences. I tell you, Nephew Kaifang, if not Pang Chunmiao, some other woman would have come into your father's life. That was something I'd wanted to say to you for the longest time, but the opportunity never presented itself, and now never would.

Since I lacked any real contact with Kaifang, anything I say about what was on his mind is pure conjecture.

I imagine that when he pulled the brim of his hat down and pushed his way through the crowd, he was beset by powerful mixed emotions. Not long before that, Pang Fenghuang had been Gaomi County's supreme princess and Ximen Huan the supreme prince. The mother of one had been the most powerful official in the county, the father of the other the richest. They were carefree and willful, spending money as if they had it to burn, and enjoying a large circle of acquaintances. The golden boy and jade girl were the envy of a great many people, but it did not take long for both powerful figures to pass from the scene, their glory and riches turned to foul dirt, and their favored offspring were reduced to making a living through the antics of a trained monkey.

I imagine that Lan Kaifang's love for Fenghuang had not faded.

Given the disparity between a onetime princess who had fallen to the role of street entertainer and the deputy commander of a police substation, he could not suppress his feelings of inadequacy. And even though he'd charitably placed a month's salary plus overtime in the monkey's platter, the sarcasm with which they had accepted the gift showed that they still felt superior, that this ugly policeman was beneath their dignity. It also served to erase any thoughts he may have had of stealing Fenghuang away from Ximen Huan and removed what remained of the belief and courage that he could rescue her from her demeaned circumstances. He lowered his brim to cover his face as he fled the scene; it was all he could do.

Word that the daughter of Pang Kangmei and the son of Ximen Jinlong were working with a trained monkey in front of the train station quickly spread throughout the city and into neighboring villages. People converged on the square for reasons that would have been clear if they'd been able to identify them. Neither of the local darlings, Fenghuang and Ximen Huan, felt the least bit of shame; they seemed to have cut themselves off from their past. For them the train station square might as well have been a foreign country, where they were among crowds of strangers. They worked hard and collected their rewards earnestly. Some of the people watching the monkey's antics shouted out the couple's names, and others screamed epithets at their parents, all of which they ignored and none of which had any effect on their radiant smiles. But, should anyone speak immodestly or act inappropriately toward Fenghuang, the monkey would be all over the offender, biting and scratching.

One of the notorious Four Little Hoods waved a pair of two-hundred-yuan notes in Fenghuang's direction and shouted, "Hey, girl, I see you've got a ring in your nose. What about down below? Drop your pants and let me see for myself, and these are yours." His buddies whooped and hollered, but she ignored the raunchy comment and, chain in one hand and whip in the other, sent the monkey out for donations.

> All you kind people
> It doesn't matter if you have money or you don't
> If you've got it, part with a little
> If you haven't a few shouts will help
> *Bong bong bong!*

Ximen Huan was smiling too as he beat a rhythmic tattoo on his gong. "Ximen Huan, you little bastard, what happened to the intimidating fellow we used to know? Go on, tell your girlfriend to drop her pants. If you don't—" The monkey hobbled up to the man and — some people said they saw Fenghuang tug on the chain, others said she did nothing of the sort — tossed his platter behind him, leaped up onto the man's shoulder, and began biting and scratching wildly. The monkey's screeches and the man's screams merged as the crowd fled, with the little hood's buddies out in front. Fenghuang pulled the monkey back and continued her little song:

> Riches are not ordained by heaven
> People all get their comeuppance sooner or later —

The bully, his face a mass of blood, was rolling on the ground and screaming in pain, which attracted a squad of policemen, who wanted to arrest Ximen Huan and Fenghuang. When the monkey bared his fangs and screeched, one of them drew his gun; Fenghuang cradled him in her arms like a mother with a baby boy. The crowd formed around them again to voice their support for Fenghuang, Ximen Huan, and their monkey. They pointed to the screaming man on the ground. "He's the one you should arrest!" Dear reader, mob psychology is mind-numbingly strange! When Pang Kangmei and Ximen Jinlong held sway in the county, Fenghuang and Ximen Huan were objects of the people's loathing, and their downfall was both predicted and longed for. But when that actually happened, they became underdogs, and everyone was now in their corner. The police knew all about these two and were aware of the special relationship they had with their deputy commander. So in the face of the crowd's militancy they simply shrugged their shoulders and said nothing. One of them grabbed the bully by the neck. "Let's go," he said angrily. "You can knock off the phony victim act!"

The incident alarmed members of the county Party Committee. Out of kindness, Party Secretary Sha Wujing sent his office manager and a clerk to the basement of the train station hotel to talk to Fenghuang and Ximen Huan. The monkey bared his teeth at the two men when they passed on the Party secretary's request, which was to send the monkey over to the new Phoenix Zoo in the western suburbs, after which he would find jobs for the two of them. For most of us, that would have been exciting news. But Fenghuang held the monkey in her arms and said with an angry glare, "Anyone who so much as touches my monkey will have to answer to me!" Ximen Huan merely smiled mischievously and said, "Thank Secretary Sha for his thoughtfulness, but we're doing fine, and his time would be better spent taking care of government workers who have lost their jobs."

From here my story takes a cruel and unhappy turn. Don't think I'm happy about that, dear reader. The characters' fates have made it inevitable.

The story continues that Pang Fenghuang, Ximen Huan, and their monkey were sitting at a food stall on the southern edge of the train station square eating dinner when the bully they'd dealt with that day, his face covered with gauze, crept up. The monkey screeched and sprang at him, but wound up doing a somersault, thanks to the chain around his neck. Ximen Huan jumped to his feet, turned around, and was immediately face-to-face with the sinister bully. Before he could say a word, the man stabbed him in the chest. Quite possibly, the killer may have wanted to kill Fenghuang while he was at it, but the screeching, jumping monkey frightened him off before he could even pull the knife out of Ximen Huan's chest. Fenghuang threw herself on Ximen Huan and wailed. The monkey stayed put, glowering at anyone who tried to come close. When Kaifang and several of his men ran up, they were stopped by the monkey's fearful screeches and threatening gestures. One of them drew his gun and pointed it at the monkey; Kaifang grabbed him by the wrist.

"Fenghuang, grab your monkey so we can send Ximen Huan to the hospital." He spun around. "Get an ambulance!" he shouted.

Fenghuang wrapped one arm around the monkey and covered his eyes with the other hand. He lay docilely in her embrace.

Lan Kaifang removed the knife from Ximen Huan's chest and pressed his hand over the wound to stop the bleeding. "Huanhuan!" he shouted. "Huanhuan!" Ximen Huan's eyes opened slowly. "Kaifang," he said as blood seeped from his mouth. "You're my brother . . . I've . . . gone as far as I can go. . . ."

"Hold on, Huanhuan, the ambulance will be here in a minute!" Kaifang put his arm under Huanhuan's neck; blood flowed between his fingers.

"Fenghuang . . . Fenghuang . . ." Ximen Huan was beginning to slur his words.

Siren whining, the ambulance drove up and the EMTs jumped out with their medical equipment and a gurney. But Ximen Huan lay in Kaifang's arms, eyes closed.

Twenty minutes later Lan Kaifang had his hands, covered in the blood of Ximen Huan, clamped around the killer's throat.

Dear reader, the death of Ximen Huan hurts me deeply, but in purely objective terms, it swept away the barriers keeping Lan Kaifang from pursuing Pang Fenghuang. That said, the curtain was raised on another, even greater, tragedy.

All kinds of mysterious phenomena exist in this world, but answers to most of them have come with advances in scientific knowledge. Love is the sole holdout — nothing can explain it. A Chinese writer by the name of Ah Cheng wrote that love is just a chemical reaction, an unconventional point of view that seemed quite fresh at the time. But if love can be initiated and controlled by means of chemistry, then novelists would be out of a job. So while he may have had his finger on the truth, I'll remain a member of the loyal opposition.

But enough about that. We need to look at Lan Kaifang. He took charge of Ximen Huan's funeral arrangements and, after gaining approval from his father and his aunt, buried Huanhuan's ashes behind Ximen Jinlong's grave. Now, instead of dwelling on the older folks' mood, we return to Lan Kaifang, who showed up every night in the train station hotel basement room rented by Pang Fenghuang. And whenever he wasn't tied up during the day he went to the square and fell in behind Fenghuang and her monkey, wordlessly following them like a bodyguard. When grumbling among his men at the station reached the ear of the old commander, he sent for Kaifang.

"Kaifang, my young friend, there's no lack of nice girls in town, but a girl with a trained monkey . . . the way she is . . . how do you think it looks."

"You can remove me from my post, Commander, and if you think I'm not even qualified to be an ordinary policeman, then I'll quit."

This stopped the talk immediately, and as time passed, the grumbling members at the station changed the way they viewed him. Sure, Pang Fenghuang smoked and drank, dyed her hair blond, had a nose ring, and spent her time roaming the square, the antithesis of a good girl. But how bad could she be? Eventually, the cops started making friends with her, and liked to tease when they ran into her on their beats:

"Say, Golden Hair, take it easy on our deputy commander. He's wasting away to nothing."

"That's right, you're going to have to ease up sooner or later."

Fenghuang never paid any attention to their well-intentioned taunts. The monkey snarled at them.

At first, Kaifang tried to get her to move to 1 Tianhua Lane or into the family compound, but after receiving one refusal after another, even he began to realize that if she stopped spending her nights in the train station hotel basement and roaming the square, he'd probably lose interest in working at that substation. It did not take long for the town's hooligans and troublemakers to realize that the pretty "golden-haired, nose-pierced, monkey-trainer girl" was the favorite of the blue-faced, hard-nosed deputy commander of the train station, and they abandoned any thoughts of moving in on her. Who'd be foolish enough to try to take a drumstick out of a tiger's mouth?

Let's try to imagine the scene of Kaifang's nightly visits to Fenghuang in her basement room. Originally a guesthouse, the place had been bought and turned into a hotel, and if regulations had been strictly enforced, it would have been a prime candidate for being shut down. That was why the fat face of the proprietress crinkled into an oily smile, honey dripping from her reddened lips, when Kaifang showed up

Fenghuang refused to open the door the first few nights, no matter how hard he pounded. So he'd stand there like a post and listen to her weep — sometimes laugh hysterically — inside. He also heard the monkey screech and, sometimes, scratch at the door. Sometimes he smelled cigarette smoke, sometimes liquor. But he never smelled anything illegal, at which he was secretly overjoyed. If she'd taken up drugs, she'd have been a lost cause. Would he still have loved her if that were the case? The answer was yes. Nothing could have changed that, not even if her insides had rotted away.

He never failed to bring a bouquet of flowers or a basket of fruit, and when she refused to open the door, he stood there until he had to go, leaving the flowers or fruit outside her door. With a decided absence of tact, the proprietress once said to him:

"Young man, I can get you a handful of girls. All you have to do is choose the one you want . . ."

The icy glower in his eyes and the cracking of knuckles as he clenched his fist nearly made her wet herself. She never said anything like that again.

Then one day Fenghuang opened the door. The room was dark and dank. The paint on the walls was peeling and blistery; a naked lightbulb hanging from the ceiling provided little light in a room heavy with the smell of mold. It was furnished with a pair of twin beds and a couple of chairs that looked as if they'd been scavenged from the local dump. Being in one was like sitting on cement. That was when he first tried to get her to move. One of the beds was for her, the other was for the monkey, who slept among some of Ximen Huan's old clothes. There were, in addition, two vacuum bottles for hot water and a fourteen-inch black-and-white TV set, also picked up at the local dump. In those shabby, uninviting surroundings, Kaifang finally said what he'd kept bottled up for more than ten years:

"I love you," he said. "I've loved you from the first time I saw you."

"You don't know what you're saying," she sneered. "The first time you saw me was on your granny's *kang* in Ximen Village. That was before you could even crawl!"

"I fell in love with you before I knew how to crawl!"

"No more of that, please." She lit a cigarette. "For you to fall for a woman like me is like tossing a pearl down a latrine, don't you think?"

"Don't run yourself down," he said. "I understand you."

"You understand shit!" she sneered again. "I've been a whore, I've slept with thousands of men! I've even slept with the monkey! You, in love with me? Get out of my sight, Kaifang. Go find yourself a good woman and stay clear of the foul airs I give off."

"Liar!" Kaifang said, covering his face with his hands and starting to sob. "You're lying. Tell me you haven't done any of those things."

"What if I have? And what if I haven't? What business is it of yours?" She sneered. "Am I your wife? Your lover? My folks have washed their hands of me, so what makes you different?"

"I love you, that's what!" he was screaming.

"Don't use that disgusting word with me! Get out of here, poor little Kaifang." She waved the monkey over and said, "Dear little monkey, let's you and me go to bed."

The monkey sprang onto her bed.

Kaifang drew his pistol and pointed it at the monkey.

Fenghuang wrapped her arms around her monkey and said angrily:

"Shoot me first, Lan Kaifang!"

Kaifang's passions were running high by then. He'd heard rumors that she'd been a prostitute, and he wasn't sure if he believed them or not. But when she maliciously told him to his face that she'd slept not only with thousands of men but with her monkey, it was as if a volley of arrows had pierced his heart.

Shocked and hurt, he stumbled out of the room and ran up the stairs, out of the hotel, and onto the square, his churning mind and heart erasing all threads of thought. As he passed a bar lit up by neon signs, two heavily made-up women dragged him inside. Seated on a high bar stool, he slugged down three shots of brandy and then laid his head down on the bar as a woman with blond hair, dark circles under her eyes, bright red lips, and lots of skin, front and back, drifted up to him — he never went to see Fenghuang in uniform — to reach out and touch his blue birthmark. As a recently arrived butterfly from the countryside, she didn't realize that he was a policeman. Almost as a conditioned reflex, he grabbed her by the wrist, drawing a shriek from her. He smiled apologetically and let go. She rubbed up against him and said flirtatiously, "Elder Brother has quite a grip!"

Kaifang waved her away, but she pressed her hot bosom up to him and sent blasts of air reeking of cigarette smoke and liquor into his face.

"Why are you so sad, Elder Brother? Did some little vixen break your heart? Women are all the same. But your little sister here can make you feel better. . . ."

As pangs of loathing swept through his heart, Kaifang was thinking: I'll get even with you, you whore!

He tumbled off the bar stool, and "little sister" led him by the hand down a dark corridor and into a will-o'-the-wisp room, where, without a word, she stripped and lay out on the bed. She still had a nice figure, with full breasts, a flat tummy, and long legs. Since this was the first time our good Kaifang had laid eyes on a naked woman's

body, it had its desired effect, although he was more nervous than anything. She, on the other hand, quickly tired of his faltering. Time,
after all, is money in her profession. She sat up.

"Come on," she said, "what are you waiting for? You can knock
off the little-boy act!"

Unfortunately for her, as she sat up her blond wig slipped off and
revealed a flattened head with sparse hair, which bowled Kaifang over.
Pang Fenghuang's lovely face beneath a full head of blond hair floated
before his eyes. He took a hundred-yuan note out of his pocket, tossed
it to the woman, and turned to leave, but not before she jumped to her
feet and wrapped herself around him like an octopus.

"You no-account prick!" she cursed. "You're not getting away
that easy, not for a measly hundred yuan!"

She reached down and felt around in his pants while she was cursing, looking for money, of course, but what her hand bumped into was
a hard, cold handgun. Knowing he couldn't let her pull her hand back,
he grabbed her wrist for the second time. The beginnings of a scream
leaked out of her mouth before she could swallow the rest of it as
Kaifang gave her a shove and sent her stumbling back onto the bed.

Kaifang emerged onto the square, where he was hit by a blast of
cold air. The alcohol he'd consumed came rushing up into his throat
and out onto the ground. The emptying of his stomach served to clear
his head, but did nothing to ease the pain in his heart. His mood
swung between teeth-clenching anger and heartwarming affection.
He hated Fenghuang, and he loved her. When the hatred rose in him,
it was swamped by love; when the love ascended, it was beaten back
by hatred. During the two days and nights he struggled with these
competing feelings, he turned his pistol on himself and contemplated
pulling the trigger more than once. Don't do it, boy! It's not worth it!
Finally, reason won out over emotion.

"She may be a whore," he said softly to himself, "but I still want
her."

Having made up his mind, once and for all, he returned to the
hotel, where he knocked on her door.

"What, you back again?" she said, sounding thoroughly fed up.
But he had obviously changed over the past two days. His birthmark
was darker, his face thinner, and his brows looked like a pair of cater-
pillars squirming above his eyes, which were blacker and brighter
than before; his glare, so intense it felt as if it were scorching her,

and not just her, but her monkey as well, drove the monkey into a corner, where he cowered. "Well, since you're here," she said, her tone softer, "you might as well sit down. We can be friends if you'd like, but don't let me hear any more talk about love."

"I not only want to talk about love, I want you to be my wife." With a hard edge to his voice, he continued, "I don't care if you've slept with ten thousand men, or with a monkey, or, for that matter, a tiger or an alligator, I want to marry you."

That was met with silence. Then, with a laugh, she said:

"Calm down, little Blue Face. You can't throw a word like love around, and that goes double for marriage."

"I'm not throwing them around," he said. "Over the past two days I've thought things out carefully. I'm going to give it up, deputy chief, my career as a policeman, everything. I'll be your gong-beater and become a street performer with you."

"Enough of that crazy talk. You can't throw away your future over a woman like me." Feeling a need to dampen his enthusiasm and lighten the atmosphere, she said, "Tell you what, I'll marry you if you can turn your blue face white."

As they say, "Casual words have powerful effects." Making jokes to a man as deeply in love as he was dangerous business.

Lan Kaifang took sick leave, not caring if his superiors approved or not, and went to Qingdao, where he underwent painful skin graft surgery. When he next showed up at the hotel basement, his face swathed in bandages, Fenghuang was stunned. So was her monkey, possibly recalling the swathed face of Ximen Huan's killer. He snarled and attacked Kaifang, who knocked him out with a single punch. Then he turned to Fenghuang and, like a man possessed, said:

"I've had a skin graft."

She stood there looking at him as tears welled up in her eyes. He got down on his knees, wrapped his arms around her legs, and laid his head against her belly. She stroked his hair.

"How foolish you are," she said, nearly sobbing. "How can you be so foolish?"

They embraced, and she gently kissed the side of his face where there was no pain. He picked her up and carried her over to the bed, where they made love.

Blood covered the sheet.

"You're a virgin!" he said in surprised delight, his tears soaking the bandages covering half his face. "You're a virgin, my Fenghuang, my love. Why did you say all those things?"

"Who says I'm a virgin?" she said with a pout. "Eight hundred yuan is all it costs to repair a maidenhead."

"You're lying again, you little whore, my Fenghuang. . . ." Mindless of the pain, he planted kisses on the body of the prettiest girl in Gaomi County — the whole world, in his eyes.

Fenghuang stroked his body, hard yet pliable, as if put together with branches of a tree, and said, sounding utterly forlorn:

"My god, there's no way I can get away from you. . . ."

Dear reader, I'd rather not continue with my story, but since I've given you a beginning, I need to give you an ending. So here it comes in all its cruelty.

Kaifang returned to 1 Tianhua Lane, his face still swathed in bandages, which threw a scare into Lan Jiefang and Huang Huzhu, who had had all the surprises they could take. Kaifang ignored their questions about his face and said passionately, in obvious high spirits:

"Papa, Aunty, I'm going to marry Fenghuang!"

With a pained furrowing of his brow, my friend Jiefang said decisively:

"No, you're not!"

"Why?"

"Because I say so!"

"You don't believe all those scurrilous rumors, do you? You have my word, she's absolutely chaste . . . a virgin. . . ."

"My god!" my friend exclaimed plaintively. "You can't do it, son. . . ."

"Where love and marriage are concerned, Papa," Kaifang said, his anger rising, "it's my life and you have nothing to say about it."

"Maybe I don't, son, but listen to what your aunt has to say." Jiefang went into his room and shut the door.

"Kaifang, poor Kaifang," Huang Huzhu said to him tearfully. "Fenghuang is your uncle's daughter. You and she have the same grandmother."

At that point Kaifang reached up and ripped the bandages off of his face, taking the new skin off with it and leaving a bloody wound. He ran out of the house and jumped on his motorcycle, speeding away in such a hurry that his wheel banged against the door of a beauty salon, scaring the wits out of the people inside. He lifted the front wheel and sped like a crazed horse straight to the train station square. He never heard the words of the beautician whose shop was next door to the house:

"Everyone in that family is mad!"

Kaifang staggered down the steps of the hotel and crashed through the door. Fenghuang was in bed waiting for him. The monkey attacked him, but this time he forgot all about police procedures, forgot just about everything. He drew his pistol and shot the monkey dead, bringing an end to the reincarnation cycle for a soul that had spun on the wheel of life for half a century.

Fenghuang was struck dumb by what he'd done. He raised his pistol and pointed it at her. Don't do it, my young friend — he gazed at Fenghuang's beautiful face, like a precious jade carving — the prettiest face in the world — the pistol drooped of its own weight. He raised it again and ran out the door to the steps leading upstairs — like a ladder leading from hell up to heaven — our young friend's legs turned rubbery and he fell to his knees. Then he pressed the muzzle of his pistol up against a heart that was already broken — Don't do it, don't be foolish — he pulled the trigger. A muffled explosion sent our Kaifang sprawling on the steps, dead.

58

Millennium Boy

Dear reader, our tale is drawing to a close. Bear with me a while longer, that's all, just a while longer.

Lan Jiefang and Huang Huzhu took Kaifang's ashes back to the plot of land that was now dotted with graves and buried them alongside Huang Hezuo. While they were cremating and burying their son, Fenghuang followed them, carrying the body of her monkey and weeping uncontrollably. She was so haggard everyone who saw her took pity on her. As sensible people, now that Kaifang was dead, Jiefang and Huzhu spoke no more of what had brought them to that point. Since the monkey was beginning to smell, Fenghuang took their advice to let him go, but asked that he be buried along with the people there. My friend unhesitatingly said yes. And so, now there was a monkey lying alongside a donkey, an ox, a pig, and a dog. Stuck for how to console Fenghuang, my friend brought together the surviving members of the two families. Chang Tianhong had nothing to offer, nor did Huang Huzhu. In the end it was Baofeng:

"Gaige, ask her to come here and we'll see what she plans to do. She started life here on our *kang*, and we have a duty to give her what she wants, whatever it takes."

Gaige returned with news that she was gone.

Like a river, time flows on and on. We are now in the waning days of the year 2000. Gaomi County was celebrating the dawning of the new millennium with lights and streamers in front of every house in the city. Towering count-down clocks had been erected in the train station square and Tianhua Square, where pyrotechnic specialists waited to have their fireworks light up the sky at the stroke of midnight.

As evening settled in, snow began to fall, with flakes dancing amid the bright lights and turning the night into a thing of beauty. Just about everyone in the city walked outside, some heading toward Tianhua Square, others for the train station square, and some just strolling up and down People's Avenue.

My friend and Huang Huzhu were among the few people who stayed inside. Here permit me to add a comment: They never did register as husband and wife. It didn't seem to make any difference to either of them. Well, after making some pork-filled dumplings they hung a pair of red lanterns outside their door and stuck some of Huzhu's paper cutouts in the window. The dead cannot be brought back to life, and everyone else has to keep on living, whether they do so by crying or laughing. That is what my friend often said to his partner. They ate the dumplings that night, watched a bit of TV, and, as was their habit, memorialized the dead by making love. But only after brushing Huzhu's hair, as we've already seen. What I want to say here is, in the midst of their mixed sorrow and joy, Huzhu abruptly rolled over in bed, wrapped her arms around my friend, and said:

"Starting tonight, we can be human again. . . ."

Their tears wetted one another's face.

At eleven o'clock they were jolted out of their sleep by the ringing of their telephone. It was the train station hotel. A woman on the other end told them that their daughter-in-law, who was in Room 101, had gone into labor, news that first puzzled them. Finally, it dawned on them that the woman about to give birth was Pang Fenghuang, who had been missing all these months.

Knowing there was no one they could call for assistance, and not really wanting to call anyone in the first place, they made their way to the square as fast as their frail legs would take them. Breathlessly, they ran and walked, walked and ran, making their way through crowded streets. There were people everywhere, on wide avenues and in narrow lanes. At first the crowds were heading south, but once my friend and his woman crossed People's Avenue, the crowds were heading north. Their anxieties quickened, their pace did not, as snow fell on their heads and blew into their faces. The swirling snowflakes were like falling apricot petals. The old apricot tree in the Ximen family compound had shed its flowers, so had the apricot trees at the Ximen Village pig farm, and all of them were being blown into town; all the falling apricot petals in China were blowing into Gaomi County, into the city.

Like a pair of lost children, they elbowed their way into the square, where young men and women were dancing and singing atop a tower that had been thrown up on the eastern edge. Apricot petals were dancing in the air. A thousand heads were bobbing on the square. The people, in new clothes, were singing and jumping and clapping and stomping their feet along with the music coming from the tower. Apricot petals were swirling among the dancers, who were dancing amid the swirling apricot petals. The digital clock was counting down, second by second. The climactic moment was approaching. The music and the singing stopped; the square was silent. My friend and his woman took the stairs down to the hotel basement. She hadn't had time to put her hair up; it trailed behind her like a tail. They opened the door of Room 101 and saw the face of Fenghuang, as pure as an apricot blossom. They also saw that the lower half of her body was covered in blood, in the center of which lay a chubby little baby boy. At that moment, fireworks lit up the sky of Gaomi County's new century, the first of a new millennium. The baby was a millennium boy; he'd come into the world via a normal birth. Two other babies had arrived as millennium babies in Gaomi's hospital, but they'd been delivered by caesarean section.

My friend and his woman picked up the baby, their grandchild, who bawled in Huzhu's arms. As his tears fell, Jiefang draped a dirty sheet over Fenghuang. She was virtually transparent, since all the blood had flowed out of her body. Her ashes, of course, were buried in the now famous family cemetery, next to Lan Kaifang.

My friend and his woman raised the big-headed baby with great care. He'd been born with a strange bleeding disease that the doctors called hemophilia, for which there was no cure. He would die, sooner rather than later. But when he bled, Huang Huzhu pulled a hair from her head, turned it to ashes under a flame, and put some of it in his milk and sprinkled the rest over the injury. While this was not a cure, it worked as an emergency treatment when needed. And so this child's life was tied inextricably to the hair of my friend's woman. As long as the hair held out, the boy would live; when it was gone, he would die. In this case, the heavens took pity, for the more hair she pulled out, the more hair grew in. So we needn't worry that the boy will die young.

He differed from other children right from birth. Small in body, he had a remarkably big head, in which near total recall and a extraordinary gift for language existed. Although his grandparents could not help thinking about his unusual entrance into the world, after talking it over, they decided he deserved to be given the family name Lan. And since he'd been born as the clock rang in the new millennium, they called him Qiansui, or "Thousand-Year." On the day of his fifth birthday, he summoned my friend, his grandfather, spread his arms like a storyteller, and embarked upon the narration of a long tale:

"My story begins on January 1, 1950. . . ."